"You would have another sire my child?" Nefertiry asked.

Seshena the magic worker laid her hand on Nefertiry's and said, "Your marriage contract holds no specific promise of fidelity. If you are to have a child, I recommend for the child's well-being that Ramessa not father him."

As much as Nefertiry loved Ramessa, she could not argue. What Seshena said was true.

"Remember, too, Ramessa has many wives. There will come times, Nefertiry, you'll ache for love and he'll be with someone else. I speak of legality and practicality. The decision is yours."

"You speak plainly, priestess," Nefertiry said bitterly.

Seshena stood. "Tomorrow I will bring you the names of those suitable to be your lover...."

SUNRISE OF SPLENDOR

by

Joyce Verrette

FAWCETT GOLD MEDAL • NEW YORK

SUNRISE OF SPLENDOR

© 1978 Joyce Verrette

Published by Fawcett Gold Medal Books, a unit of CBS Publications, the Consumer Publishing Division of CBS Inc.

ISBN 0-449-14041-5

Printed in the United States of America

10 9 8 7 6 5 4 3 2 1

SUNRISE OF SPLENDOR

1

Smoke from the Tameran army's campfires rose in gray curls toward the sky, where the setting sun spread its final light like a scarlet feathered fan. To the scouts from Khatti, the distant winking fires of the camp looked like reflections of the conflagration in the western sky, but they knew well enough what the small fires were, and it was their hope to approach the enemy closely enough to estimate his numbers and possibly learn something of his plans.

Within the camp where a ring of shields planted in the soil was used as a makeshift stockade, soldiers moved briskly about their evening tasks. It was early autumn, and the Tamerans, unused to the Qadesh climate, wrapped themselves in woolen cloaks against the damp chill of the air. A cloaked figure moved toward the camp's center, to a large tent which had the gold emblem of the royal hawk planted before its entrance. Pushing aside the tent flap, he entered, and paused until he could gain his king's attention.

Ramessa was unaware of his aide's presence. He was discussing battle strategies with Captain Khakamir. Finally, Ramessa's head lifted, and he turned toward the entrance impatiently muttering, "Before those servants come with my bathwater, my body will be stiff with cold." As he noticed the youth quietly waiting, Ramessa's expression softened. "Menna, you have seen to Nurit and Pehtee?" he asked.

Menna bowed and replied, "Yes, majesty. I have attended your horses and put your equipment in order."

Ramessa stood up. "Then you may do whatever you wish with the remainder of this night," he directed. "I doubt I'll need you before morning." Menna dipped his head in acknowledgment and turned toward the tent flap. "Menna!"

The aide turned to face his king. "Yes, majesty?"

"If you see a couple of worthless servants gossiping by the fire with a large container of water, remind them of their king, who is slowly turning blue with cold."

"Yes, majesty," Menna replied and left hurriedly.

Ramessa threw a woolen cloak over his short cotton tunic and began to pace. "My heart is yet uneasy about what those Shasu told us," he said.

"And mine," Khakamir agreed. "If, as the Shasu claim, Mutallu is near Tunip and afraid to move south lest he meet us marching north, why have our sentinals reported seeing a great number of birds rising from the distant marshes? I suspect it's our enemy that disturbed them."

Ramessa sighed. "The Shasu seemed anxious enough to join us, but I cannot help questioning the intentions of any defectors."

Khakamir shook his head, his dark eyes catching glimmers of light from the lamp. "I don't like having the regiment of Sutekh so far to our rear even if they are hurrying to gain lost ground."

"Nor I," Ramessa replied in a grim tone. At the sound from the tent flap, he turned to see two servants struggling

8

through the opening, carrying a great water container. "You've found your way back at last," he observed.

One servant began, "Majesty, we—"

"I don't care to hear your explanation," Ramessa interrupted coldly. "Pour the water without further delay." As he watched the servants hurry to their task, he wondered why the sound of their shuffling feet so irritated him. Finally deciding that he disliked these particular servants whatever they did, he asked, "Where's Nehri?"

"I'm here," Nehri's voice came from the tent flap. "I've brought clean linens," he added.

Ramessa glanced up at Nehri, whose arms were laden with folded cloth. Even the sight of his favorite attendant didn't lift his dark mood. He stepped forward to gaze suspiciously down at his bathwater. "I wonder if this river's water is wholesome or if I'll emerge from my bath with some disquieting rash," he muttered, handing his cloak to Nehri. "I'll have to chance it. My skin creeps with grit." Ramessa raised his arms and one of the servants began to pull his tunic up; this was an effort, because the servant was short and Ramessa tall in stature. When the tunic was in a tangled roll around Ramessa's armpits, and progress seemed hopeless, he snapped, "Are you an assassin sent to strangle me?"

Before the frightened servant could answer, a commotion outside the tent caught Ramessa's attention. He pulled down the twisted tunic and turned toward the sounds. A soldier entered the tent and bowed hastily.

"Majesty, we've captured two men who were sneaking around near the ring of shield's," the soldier announced. "Their features hint of Khatti."

Ramessa's eyebrows lifted. He ran a hand through his gold-brown hair and signaled to Nehri, who replaced the cloak on his shoulders. Then he smiled. "Perhaps we can learn the truth after all, Khakamir."

Khakamir lifted the tent flap and let his king pass. He too was smiling faintly, and his eyes gleamed with anticipation.

9

Outside, several soldiers were holding two men at spearpoint. One glance confirmed the men's features as those of Khatti. Ramessa's smile widened, but held no warmth.

"We came to the river for water, lord," one of the men said apologetically. "Why do you treat us like prisoners?"

"You are prisoners," Ramessa replied.

"Lord, if you object to our getting water here, gladly will we go to another place downriver," the other man said hurriedly.

Ramessa's smile faded. "A hot bath awaits me, which I don't intend to let cool too much while I hear your lies," he said, studying the men. Deciding that, of the two, the taller looked the more frightened, he turned to Khakamir. "Have Captain Paneb choose a sturdy stick and apply it vigorously to this spy's body. Then I'll learn the truth with a minimum of delay."

Khakamir gestured to the soldiers, who threw the unlucky scout to the ground. Captain Paneb disappeared around the tent corner, and, after a moment, returned, carrying a formidable-looking stick.

Ramessa watched the man on the ground, who was measuring the stick with fearful eyes. Ramessa gave him a moment longer to consider his peril, then approached him. "Captain Paneb is most experienced in such matters," he advised.

The scout stared up at Ramessa, his face stiff with the fear he tried to conceal.

"This stick will slowly turn your bones to jelly," Ramessa said softly, "and you will eventually scream the truth in the delirium of your pain." He rested one foot lightly on the spy's forehead and the man breathed a sigh of despair. The spy had no doubt that Ramessa would have him beaten to a mass of splintered bones.

Ramessa addressed the spy once more, "Consider the inevitable moment when pain drives the truth from your mouth. Perhaps your hands will be forever crippled, your fingers beyond repair. Surely your legs will be smashed,
10

your feet useless." Ramessa bent slightly to look solemnly at the spy. "Then to kill you would be merciful, for how would you live? As a beggar propped against a mud hut pleading for coins?" Ramessa's green-flecked eyes lifted to gaze at the horizon a moment, as if he were sympathetically considering the man's fate. "What woman will look at you? If you already have a woman, what will you do with her?" Ramessa looked again at the spy, smiled and asked pleasantly, "Will you be wise and speak now, while your body is whole?"

The man was silent.

Ramessa shook his head, as if genuinely grieved at the prisoner's decision. Then he removed his foot and gestured to Captain Paneb. "Allow a small space between each blow, so he may have the breath to speak, should pain add to his wisdom," Ramessa instructed.

At his king's nod, the captain raised the stick, then brought it sharply down. The spy choked back a cry.

Ramessa turned to the servants, who were standing by the tent watching the scene. "Go inside and cover my bathwater," he ordered. "I have no wish to wait again while it's heated."

Ramessa listened to the blows being delivered behind him, until the Khatti scout's cries of pain came as regularly as breathing. Finally, the king turned and again approached the spy. "Does not your common sense tell you this is useless? Speak now, and you will be treated by one of our physicians and held as a prisoner." Ramessa bent to peer carefully at the sweating spy. "Your arms are broken, you realize. I suspect one knee is also shattered. Still, my physicians can mend them, I think." He straightened and looked at Captain Paneb. "I grow impatient as my bathwater cools. Begin on his feet."

The spy saw a vision of himself as a beggar, unable to walk. He thought of a woman he'd been making fair progress with when he'd left Khatti. "No! No!" he cried. "I'll tell you all I know!"

Ramessa waved Paneb away. "Excellent," he said. "Proceed now."

"Majesty, the physician—" the spy panted.

"After you've told me what I wish to know, it will be best to speak the truth so this beating won't have to be resumed."

The scout shivered and whispered, "Son of Ra, I'll tell the truth. Send your captain away."

Ramessa smiled faintly. "Paneb will remain here to inspire you."

The scout moaned, but began. "King Mutallu has spared no expense to assure his victory."

Ramessa's smile grew larger. "How disappointed Mutallu will be."

The scout's eyes widened and he exclaimed, "He has in his ranks Dardanians, some mercenaries from Troy, some from Kashkash, Lycians, Mycenaeans, even some Shasu! I saw them myself. So great are their numbers they spread over the hills and valleys!"

Ramessa's smile faded. "What interests me more than their numbers is which hills and valleys they're in now. Speak! What is their location?"

"They're so near, my companion and I walked to your camp from our own," the scout replied.

"So, the birds rising from the marshes did mark their camp," Khakamir said softly, his eyes narrowing.

Ramessa lifted his head to gaze a moment in that direction and said quietly, "Paneb, find those two lying Shasu and kill them."

"At once, majesty," Paneb replied and, laying down his stick, turned away.

The scout closed his eyes in relief that Paneb would beat him no more and said, "My companion and I were to tell Commander Khatusaru how many you are and how equipped. If possible, we were to learn which way you would next move. From this information the final plans were to be made."

12

Ramessa turned to face Khakamir. "Khatusaru will know, when these men don't return, that we've captured or killed them. If fortune is with us, he'll think they died without speaking. But Khatusaru is an excellent soldier, and I doubt he'll count on that. He'll probably make his plan, keeping in mind the possibility that we know what this scout told us."

"What will we do, sire?" Khakamir asked.

Ramessa glanced at the Khatti scouts and signaled a physician, who had been standing nearby watching, to attend the man. "We'll discuss our plans as I bathe," Ramessa answered Khakamir. "I have no wish to reveal my mind to these spies. Although I intend them not to escape, I'll take no chances." Through the deepening shadows came a sharp scream of pain, then another. "The souls of the lying Shasu have flown to Asar—with Paneb's assistance," Ramessa commented, and suddenly anger lit his eyes. "I'll delay my bath for a small time more while I speak to our own spies about their lack of information!"

"But it's too dangerous!" Khakamir exclaimed.

Ramessa took a deep breath, knowing his friend would protest at length. He stepped out of his tub, saying nothing while Khakamir continued listing all the reasons the plans were dangerous. When Khakamir finally was silent, Ramessa said, "I wish one of my wives were here to share this night with me."

"You think of love at a time like this?" Khakamir was incredulous.

"The night before a battle arouses me," Ramessa replied. "Maybe it's because danger is near."

"If you ford that river tomorrow with only your personal guards close to you, death will be near!" Khakamir persisted.

"But Khatusaru will then be convinced I know nothing of their movements. If we dawdle breaking camp, and don't begin to march until midmorning, he'll think we're

13

weary and weakened. He'll be relieved and possibly be-come careless. Then he'll learn we're neither weary nor weak."

"But, sire, if only the regiment of Amen follows you—and since the regiment of Sutekh still hasn't caught up with us—"

"Enough," Ramessa interrupted. "I've laid my plans. In light of our situation I know nothing else to do."

"We could withdraw a little, beyond that narrow canyon we passed yesterday—and wait for Sutekh's regiment to join us, then attack Khatusaru's army with full force," Khakamir begged.

Ramessa threw down the towel Nehri had wrapped around him and turned to face Khakamir, with flashing eyes. "In all the years my father fought Khatti, never did he flee from them! How his soul would cringe to witness me running from Khatusaru's soldiers! I will not with-draw," he said coldly. He was silent a moment and Khakamir decided he'd better say no more. Finally Ramessa said, "Now, Khakamir, since I have none of my wives to pass this night more pleasantly, I think I should sleep."

"Yes, sire," Khakamir replied. "Fair dreams, sire," he added, as he left the tent.

Sunlight glanced brightly off the river's surface and the glare made Ramessa narrow his eyes as he drove his chariot into the water. He studied the opposite bank for any sign of King Mutallu's army, but saw nothing. He felt the webbing of the chariot's floor move and knew Menna too was uneasy. Alongside and behind Ramessa's chariot rode his personal guards. The sound of their horses' hooves close by reassured Ramessa, although Sutekh's regiment had not yet joined them and the regiment of Ptah was still assembling their equipment while they waited their turn to ford the river.

It would have been difficult for a chance passer-by to

14

imagine that battle was imminent. Although there were eighteen thousand Tameran soldiers on the riverbank, they appeared relaxed and unconcerned. Another thousand men entering the river seemed intent upon safely moving their equipment, and the officers' orders did not have the sharp tone of those given in the stress of anticipated combat. The soldiers on shore moved unhurriedly about their tasks, and occasional laughter rose from the hum of mingled conversations. The sun bathed the scene with warmth and light and the trees rustled peacefully in the soft wind.

Ramessa reflected upon the serenity of these things and felt the tension in his temples gradually begin to fade. He breathed deeply of the air, which was tinged with the sweetness of autumn, and watched a bird circling against the bright blue sky.

Ramessa was almost to the opposite riverbank when he saw the wave of riders burst from the forest and race toward the water. At the same moment, he heard a terrific uproar from the riverbank he'd left; glancing over his shoulder, he saw that a swarm of chariots rushed toward his army on that shore.

For a moment Ramessa didn't know whether to turn back or race forward. Then, confident of at least his personal guards and the regiment of Ra following him across the river, he decided to continue. Menna gripped the chariot's sides more tightly; Pehtee and Nurit sprang forward. Menna wasn't particularly alarmed at the forces sweeping toward the riverbank ahead, but he began preparing himself to pass Ramessa weapons as they were needed or to take the reins so Ramessa could fight.

Then Menna glanced back to see how the soldiers behind him were faring, and he paled. The regiment of Ra had turned back. Only the handful of Ramessa's personal guards was following. He turned to warn his king, only in time to feel the jolt of solid, dry ground under the chariot's wheels.

15

"Majesty!" Menna screamed. "The others have fallen back." Menna felt the king's body stiffen in shock as Ramessa turned to glance over his shoulder.

"They're gone!" Ramessa whispered. He was silent a moment until, recovering himself, he muttered, "May Montu lend me his skill and strength. We are alone."

"Sire, you can't fight them alone!" Menna cried.

"During the night Mutallu must have sent half his men across a ford," Ramessa muttered as if thinking aloud. To Menna, he raised his voice to reply, "What can I do but fight? Die? May Amen-Ra help us!" Ramessa pushed the reins into Menna's hands, which were stiff with terror. "Give me my bow and place my arrow case in my reach. You have my permission to throw a few of my lances." Ramessa glanced around to see that only five of his personal guards remained, and they had formed a fragile semicircle around him, its open end toward the river should he decide to retreat. He nodded grim approval at them and fitted an arrow to his long bow. Feeling Menna's body trembling with fear, Ramessa said encouragingly, "Try to calm your heart, Menna. What ten Khatti can match one of my guards? Even their chariots are inferior to ours. They build them like oxcarts, square. They must push the wind aside, while mine slips between the breezes."

Menna was silent as he watched his king's first arrow soar into the sunlight. He wasn't interested in chariots slipping through the breezes; he was thinking of a spear slipping between his ribs. The arrow struck its target cleanly, and one Khatti fell. Menna lifted Ramessa's shield to afford his king some protection.

"Put aside my shield," Ramessa said brusquely. "Use that hand for throwing spears."

Menna reluctantly put down the shield, then shakily pulled a long, gleaming shaft from the case beside him.

As Ramessa had anticipated, the Khatti horsemen weren't bothering to return his arrows. They wanted to get close enough to use swords, and by their sheer num-

16

bers overwhelm him and his few guards. Ramessa took another arrow, intending to bring down as many Khatti as possible from a distance. From the corners of his eyes he noted that his guards were following his example.

Menna, holding the reins with one hand and aiming a spear with the other, felt Ramessa lay down his bow and snatch the reins from him. Menna looked up at his king, his mouth open in surprise.

"Hold on," Ramessa warned, and snapped the reins over the horses' backs. Nurit and Pehtee were well-trained and they responded instantly, charging ahead with all their strength; and the light chariot leaped forward.

When they saw the chariot flying toward them, the astonished Khatti separated and watched as the chariot shot past them, its golden sides making a bright blur in the sun. Stunned, they turned their horses to gaze wonderingly as the chariot and its guards raced on. It took a moment before they recovered their wits and gave chase.

Ramessa drove toward a cliff rising from the rough ground, in order to have his back protected by its stone wall while he fought. Though a fallen tree lay ahead he drove on, encouraging his horses with his call, until they leaped over the tree. The chariot bounded high and landed with a jolt on the other side, careening from right to left for the moment it took to stabilize.

Ramessa's guards flew after him, in their headlong race toward the cliff wall. Then Ramessa swerved the chariot around in a swirl of dust and faced the Khatti. He'd been angered that he'd been virtually left alone by his entire army with only five guards loyally following him. But when he saw one of the guards, a man he personally liked, fall silently from his horse with a spear through his chest, its great jagged point protruding from his back, Ramessa's anger became a scalding fury that swept through his veins.

Eyes aflame with rage, Ramessa again raised his bow and in his fury he managed to release five arrows in deadly succession before the Khatti approached within range of his lances. One Khatti, swifter than the others, came screaming toward Ramessa, drawing back his arm to launch a spear. He swerved so close to one of Ramessa's guards, the surprised guard was struck off-balance by the Khatti's shield. The horse leaped in fright and the guard fell to the ground, to be crushed by his own horse's hooves. For this, the Khatti earned one of Ramessa's lances; *his* horse continued, riderless, toward the forest.

The other Khattis closed in, their curved swords flashing brightly in the sun; Ramessa and his remaining guards drew their own straight blades. Though the loyal guards did their utmost to protect their king, they were only three. In moments the Tamerans were embroiled by flashing swords from all sides except the rear, which was protected by the cliffs.

Menna thrust Ramessa's shield into his hands. This time he accepted it without protest. Even in practice bouts, Ramessa was a formidable opponent. But with his present rage driving him, he slashed at the Khatti with an agility that astounded them. One Khatti, seeing the fury blazing in Ramessa's eyes, withdrew a little. He was wise. The man beside him remained in the saddle for only a moment after his severed head bounced among the rocks on the ground. A dreadful power seemed to have invaded Ramessa's body. Its terrible force looked out from Ramessa's fiery eyes, having no pity on the enemy, but striking savagely again and again, slashing faces, chests, and backs alike. Taking cold notation that two more of the loyal guards had fallen in the fray, he continued to chop and slash and impale his enemies.

When the remaining guard turned to Ramessa and shouted that more Tamerans were racing toward them at last, Ramessa glanced up at him in time to see his face smashed by a Khatti mace.

Ramessa and Menna were suddenly surrounded by Tamerans. Ramessa was able to pause. He took that moment to brush away the sweat running into his eyes and

18

turn to Menna for a cloth so he could wipe the blood from his sword. Then he again lifted his arm and called savagely for another charge.

The turmoil of the fighting gradually swept the combatants toward the river. Finally, where the ground had been soaked with blood and strewn with mutilated bodies, now the water was spread with crimson pools.

Hoping to join their forces on the other riverbank, the Khatti fell back across the river. The Tamerans rushed after them like a fearful tide, Ramessa's golden chariot flashing ominously among them.

As the sun began to set, the distant sound of a trumpeting horn announced the arrival of the regiment of Sutekh bringing a thousand more men to Ramessa's forces, veteran fighters with fresh mounts. Khatti Commander Khatusaru signaled to his horn-bearer to blow the retreat, leaving an entire squad of his men, surrounded by his enemy, to be captured; for he was helpless to save them.

Ramessa directed Captain Khakamir to gather his men to the south bank of the river and there to establish camp. Khakamir hastily moved away. He recognized Ramessa's anger and quickly instructed the other captains to follow his example.

When his men were in the designated area, the king leaped off his horse and stalked toward a large stone, which he climbed with the nimbleness of a cat. There he stood for a moment, his tattered garments smeared with blood, looking at them with eyes like summer lightning. The whole army became so silent his words were heard even to its outer fringes.

"Truly, I cannot believe it!" Ramessa exploded. "Not one of you was there! Not one man among you was with me! Not one of you to lift his hand and help me in my fight!" Ramessa's eyes moved accusingly over the crowd while he paused for breath. "I call my father's spirit to witness that no man among you came!" he cried.

Ramessa's officers, who were standing at the foot of the stone, shifted their feet nervously. Some of them had their

19

eyes guiltily downcast; others stared at their king as if unable to look away.

Captain Arek had been in charge of the soldiers that should have followed Ramessa across the river, and he felt as if his king's rebuke was aimed directly at him. Feeling, too, as if Ramessa's eyes were drilling two holes in his feverish forehead, Arek lifted his gaze to look up at his king. "May I speak, majesty?"

"I would have an explanation from someone!" Ramessa declared.

Although Arek's insides felt empty, he took a deep breath and said, "When they attacked from both directions at once, I assumed we would rejoin our troops on the south bank and I turned."

"Did you hear such an order?" Ramessa asked.

Arek flushed under his deep tan. "No, majesty," he said softly, head bowed. For a long moment the silence rolled over him like a suffocating blanket. He lifted his gaze to Ramessa and added, "Sire, I could hear but the uproar of the fighting."

"And later, when you noticed I wasn't among you?" Ramessa asked.

"Majesty, we were attacked immediately!" Arek cried. "I couldn't know where you were in that confusion!"

Ramessa stared at Arek a moment, then slowly ran his gaze over the other officers. "Where would I have been?" he asked derisively. "Would I have run away like you? Would Seti's son flee?"

Another officer came forward and pleaded, "Sire, we didn't mean to leave you alone!"

Ramessa looked at the officer's flushed and sweating face, then at the blood seeping through the bandage he wore. "That may be. Yet, alone I was!"

A group of officers came forward together in one voice begging his forgiveness and excusing themselves.

Ramessa continued glaring at them until he grew impatient with their clamor. He lifted his hands and they were immediately silenced. He considered his problem.

He needed his officers; he couldn't punish his whole army. Yet he was no less angry with them. Abandoning him was the most serious of offenses. Finally he said, "Since the beginning of time men have earned respect for their deeds in battle, but I'll award no man among you, for you weren't with me when I was in the midst of my enemies." He paused and saw relief mixing gradually with the fear in their faces. "Only five of my guards were with me, and they're dead," he resumed. "Only my loyal Menna stood with me and survived—only my horses Pehtee and Nurit. Amen-Ra saved me."

Ramessa turned and made his way down the rock and stalked off to where his servants had already prepared his tent. They were silent when he entered and they wasted no time cooking his food and readying his bath.

Later, when the fire of his anger had diminished, Ramessa stepped out of his tent to walk among the wounded, giving them some comfort with his presence. He spoke to his own physician regarding the number of dead they'd sustained and gave directions for their bodies to be returned to their families in Tamera. After this grim chore was accomplished, he paused to gaze at the moonlight on the river while he considered tomorrow's battle strategy.

"King Mutallu's forces were greatly reduced today," said a quiet voice.

Ramessa turned to face Khakamir. "So were we diminished," he replied.

"It was worse for them, and we now have Sutekh's regiment," Khakamir persisted.

Ramessa sighed. "This is true," he conceded.

"I think we'll taste triumph tomorrow," Khakamir said.

Ramessa smiled slightly. He knew Khakamir wished to cheer him. "You needn't worry. My temper has calmed," he said. He noted the relief on Khakamir's face. "I, too, think tomorrow's battle will end this long struggle," Ramessa agreed. "I've been considering our strategy and have decided to keep our plans simple. We'll attack them immediately and continue attacking as vigorously as

21

we can until we drive them back to Hattusas—to the palace doors if necessary."

"I predict, after tomorrow's battle, you'll walk through those palace doors amid many deep bows," Khakamir said. "And you'll have your choice of Khatti's women."

"Their people are somewhat squat and generally unattractive to my eyes. I prefer Tameran figures, like Mimut of the long legs," Ramessa said. "Yet, a woman is a woman. . . . ."

"Ask for one of Mutallu's daughters," Khakamir suggested.

"He has no children."

Khakamir was surprised. "That's odd for a man with so extensive a harem."

Ramessa's eyebrows lifted. "Also embarrassing, I suspect."

Khakamir laughed softly. After a moment he said, "Then ask for his brother Hattusil's oldest daughter. I've heard she's beautiful."

"Beautiful among Khatti's women is yet squat and flat-browed," Ramessa said. "I'll probably be awarded her anyway." He shook his head and smiled. "Most treaty-signings these days seem to give me a new wife, and most wives acquired in this fashion aren't to my taste." He sighed. "I would, no doubt, spend an hour with her to seal the treaty, then retire her to the harem and look at her not again."

Khakamir laughed softly. "What a nuisance it must be to be king!"

Ramessa smiled wryly. "Do you recall what some of those wives in the recent past looked like? If not, look closely at the one they give me this time. You'll understand what I mean." Ramessa stretched and yawned, saying, "I think I'll go to bed."

"Fair dreams, sire," Khakamir said, glad Ramessa had gotten over his previous anger. He was gladder still that Ramessa hadn't asked him which side of the river he'd been on that afternoon.

Every man in Ramessa's army—and particularly his officers—that night gave silent thanks his king had been merciful and hadn't punished them for abandoning him in battle. Each of them also made silent promises to Montu, god of battle, to do their utmost in the next day's combat, so the king might look again with favor on them.

The Tameran camp was a scene of great activity several hours before any hint of light softened the sky's blackness. By the time the thinnest glow of orange had appeared on the eastern horizon, the army was ready to march. Having anticipated Ramessa's eagerness, King Mutallu had also marshalled his forces and he wasn't surprised that, as soon as the sun broke free of the earth's edge, Ramessa's army was on the move.

The intense rain of arrows that suddenly fell on Khatti's forces was followed by waves of racing charioteers with their deadly spears. During this attack, Mutallu's general of the charioteers was felled. Before the dust from the chariots had settled, Ramessa sent in his cavalry with their long, straight, slashing swords. Then came Ramessa's infantry with their deadly axes and maces, and Mutallu's general of the infantry fell amid many of his men. Ramessa's forces kept moving relentlessly against Mutallu's army. No matter how many of them were killed, the Tameran army kept coming anew, as if their dead bodies arose and continued the fight. Ramessa in his golden chariot flashed among them, a conspicuous presence, his hair catching gold lights in the sun, his arm upraised with sword or lance. He seemed tireless—and everywhere, firing his soldiers to greater efforts.

When the Tamerans charged for the eighth time, Mutallu's officers had been decimated; during that charge, Mutallu himself crumbled to his chariot's floor like a rag doll. In that moment Commander Khatusaru sustained a serious wound. Clinging to his horse's neck with declining strength, he ordered a retreat. What was left of the Khatti army was desperate to escape and, as they rolled their chariots into the river's currents, many of the vehicles

23

overturned and some of their occupants were washed away into deeper pools and drowned.

On the south riverbank, Ramessa paused to look across the water at the havoc, and beside him Khakamir said, "It's victory, my king." Then Khakamir asked, "Shall we pursue them to their palace doors, majesty?"

Ramessa took a deep breath and replied, "When the new king Hattusil hears of this slaughter, he'll send us an offer of peace soon enough. Until then, we can gather up our dead, attend to our wounded and rest."

When Mazraima walked into the garden, Hattusil took one look at his son's face and knew the news was grave. But when Mazraima knelt at his feet, Hattusil leaped up from his bench in alarm.

"Son, why do you approach me so?" he cried, already knowing but refusing to acknowledge it even to himself.

Mazraima lifted his eyes and said softly, "Because your brother, King Mutallu, is dead, and you are now my king."

Hattusil stepped back and sank again onto the bench. His mind was numb, with grief for his brother and by his own sudden elevation. "I should have realized it was possible for him to die in battle. But I never did."

Mazraima waited a moment for his father's grief to soften until he asked, "May I sit down, sire? I wouldn't dare ask this of my king, but I ask my father, for I'm weary from the battle."

Hattusil lifted sad eyes. For his answer, he took his son's hand and drew him to his side.

"I have more terrible news, Father," Mazraima said quietly. "I would wait with this news, but the kingdom is now in your hands."

Hattusil aroused himself with an effort. His head turned, and his eyes focused on Mazraima. "What news, my son?" he asked, again already knowing.

Mazraima said in a choked voice, "I'm afraid we've lost everything." Hattusil stared at his son and Mazraima con-
24

tinued, "Not only was King Mutallu killed, but Commander Khatusaru was grievously wounded."

"Will he live?" Hattusil cried.

"I think so. But it will be long before he stands up, much less fights," Mazraima replied. He shook his head, as if still incredulous at the day's results, and continued in a hushed tone, "Our generals commanding the chariotry and infantry were killed. Most of our officers are wounded. We had to flee across the river so fast, many of our men drowned."

"Tamera's losses?" Hattusil asked anxiously.

Mazraima looked away. "They were high, but not like ours. I wish I could have killed their King Ramessa," he said vehemently. "I had a chance as good as any. He somehow got separated from his men yesterday. I thought we had him for sure, but he fought like a demon, not a man. He held us off until his soldiers came."

"Are you sure it was Ramessa?" Hattusil asked.

"It was Ramessa. Who could mistake that gold chariot or that pair of white horses? Never have I seen a mortal man fight as he did!" Mazraima fell silent for a moment, remembering. "A new regiment arrived last evening to aid the Tamerans. A fresh regiment. Veterans! Sire, our men and animals were exhausted. Commander Khatusaru called a retreat, having to abandon a squad of our soldiers surrounded by the enemy." When Mazraima lifted his eyes to Hattusil's face, he stared at his father through his tears. "At dawn's arrival we again clashed. The whole Tameran army fought like Ramessa had fought yesterday. It was hopeless."

Hattusil sighed. "King Seti fought only when he thought it necessary, but when he did, he also was like a demon. Fighting him in one such battle was what gave me this twisted arm." Hattusil stared into the distance, thinking of the past. "Every time I went to the temple, I asked why Seti was so favored in war. When he finally died, I hoped his son was less so, but Seti evidently taught Ramessa well. So we have come to this."

25

"Sire, say the word and I'll gather together what remains of our army. We'll defend our city until we're all dead!" Mazraima said passionately.

Hattusil jerked his head erect and turned to stare at his son. He was horrified. Could he let his only son sacrifice himself for a lost cause? Could he allow the whole army of Khatti to be destroyed? Cold sweat trickled down his back to think of it. Mazraima now was in line for the crown—a thing Hattusil never had thought possible for his son, though he had dreamed of it. Only Sharula was an obstacle to Mazraima's new inheritance. Hattusil paled. Sharula was older than Mazraima, and strong-willed. She didn't believe women were inferior to men. She would surely defy Mazraima's right to the crown.

"What's wrong, Father? Are you ill?" Mazraima cried in alarm. When Hattusil shook his head, Mazraima said, "But you're so pale."

"What man wouldn't become pale on such a day?" Hattusil muttered hastily. "Let me remain alone in my garden a short time, my son," he said, more gently. "I must contemplate these astounding events before I can decide what to do."

"Yes, sire," Mazraima said softly and stood up. He began to bow, but Hattusil stopped him.

"You're my son, Mazraima, and the next king. You needn't bow to me again, except on high state occasions," Hattusil said gently.

"Yes, Father," Mazraima replied. He left Hattusil to his contemplation.

Hattusil sat silently staring at the shadows growing toward each other, mingling, until they formed the night's darkness. He knew he must offer the Tamerans a proposal for peace. Although he'd never expected to rule Khatti, he'd carefully followed the turnings of political matters. He knew he could easily take over for his dead brother where state matters were concerned. Khatti could be a friend to Tamera, a buffer between Tamera and the

26

northern peoples. If Ramessa was intelligent—and Hattusil had heard that he was—he would see the wisdom of friendship with Khatti; he'd recognize the difficulties he'd have keeping Khatti as a slave state. Yes, Hattusil was quite sure he could now end these eternal wars between Khatti and Tamera with a peace treaty.

But there was Sharula. When Hattusil had married Khataka, he had given her, as one of her wedding gifts, the promise that her unborn child would be as his own. When he had looked into the infant's face, at the almond-shaped eyes with the Tameran slant, at the rounded forehead and the high cheekbones of Tamera, he had seen Khataka's infant face, and he had loved the child Khataka had created. As Sharula had grown, Hattusil had forgotten she wasn't of his own blood. When Khataka had given him a son, Hattusil had never told either child that Sharula was not his real daughter. Hattusil had kept his promise well, so well he faced a new problem: Sharula, he knew, could be troublesome.

"What, Khataka, shall I do?" Hattusil cried into the night. "Answer me with your spirit's voice, I beg you!" Hattusil pleaded. "I love my stepdaughter, willful as she is, but I want my own son to take the throne unchallenged!"

Then, Hattusil remembered what he'd heard about Ramessa. The Tameran king had a harem, mostly populated by wives given him in treaties. Would it be wrong to give Sharula to Ramessa? Sharula was beautiful enough to please Ramessa, Hattusil had no doubt. Perhaps returning to Tamera, to the homeland she'd never known or seen, was Sharula's destiny. Hattusil wondered. If he told Sharula of her true blood, if he told her she wasn't heir to Khatti's throne, but in truth to Tamera's, if he made her believe her destiny was revealed to him by her mother's ghost—would she accept this? Would it be too cruel to her? Hattusil shivered. Sharula would have to accept it, although he knew acceptance wouldn't come

27

without protest—and Sharula's protests could be the equal to yesterday's battle with Ramessa's army. Hattusil sighed and slowly stood up. He was king now. He must wage this battle with Sharula. To protect his only son. He hoped Khataka's spirit understood.

2

Hattusil watched Sharula cross the room, and his heart again constricted with distaste for what he intended to do. She looked so much like Khataka, he felt almost as if he were giving his wife to Ramessa. When Sharula paused to bow gracefully at Hattusil's feet, he ached with his inner pain. When her clear green eyes lifted to regard him, he swallowed before he could speak.

"King Ramessa has agreed to our peace proposal," he said softly.

"I just met Mazraima in the corridor, and he told me," she replied, controlling her voice.

"Did Mazraima also tell you that you're to be given to Ramessa as wife?"

Sharula's face flooded with anger. "We fought his father for many years until he finally died. We have shed our blood and endured suffering at Ramessa's hands. Now you would have me marry him, lie with him!"

"It's necessary," Hattusil said in a choked voice.

Sharula recognized the pain in his face, and looked

29

away. She wondered why this unwanted marriage was necessary. When she finally raised her eyes, they were calmly lethal. "I know why you would have me marry him," she said quietly. "When he's weary after his passion has been appeased and he sleeps, you would have me accomplish what your army couldn't. You would have me kill him. That's the only way such a plan makes sense."

Hattusil shook his head and sighed. "Ferocity is not becoming to a female." He was silent a moment before continuing, "No, little Sharula, there's another reason. I regret it falls on me to tell you of your coming to Khatti."

She felt a chill run through her and suddenly she was afraid. "I was born in Khatti," she said suspiciously.

"You were born in this palace, true. But, little one, you were already in your mother's body when she came here from Tamera—even before I laid eyes on her and loved her so greatly."

Sharula's eyes widened in shock. "I'm not your child?"

"I married your mother though she was carrying a child not my own," Hattusil replied clearly. Looking at Sharula's expression he plunged on grimly, "After I had learned of Khatti's defeat, your mother's spirit came to me and advised that I arrange the treaty. It's your destiny to return to your own people."

Sharula stared at him. "My people?"

"You serve Khatti best by preventing more bloodshed, by being part of this treaty, which will give us peace," Hattusil said. He took a deep breath. "What I'll tell you, I must ask you to solemnly vow you won't reveal to Ramessa, because this is a matter that could destroy the treaty and Khatti."

Sharula nodded numbly. "I won't speak," she promised, not knowing what else to say.

"Sit down, child, while you listen," Hattusil urged gently.

Sharula sank into a chair, a look of pain flashing over her features when he called her his child. She waited staring into her lap.

"Your mother told me this long ago, before we were married. It was a thing I've told no one else," Hattusil said. "Those who knew—my own parents—were silent until they died." He took a deep breath and released it in a long, soft sigh. "Your mother's name wasn't Khataka, which is the name I gave her. Her true name was Memnet.

"Memnet was the daughter of a nobleman in a northern province of Tamera. She was very beautiful and she was also very young when King Seti first saw her." Again Hattusil sighed. "There was a great physical attraction between them. He desired her and pressed his case, using charm and wit as well as his good looks to win her. As I said, she was young and much impressed that her king wanted her. The inevitable happened. Memnet didn't know she was carrying a child when the Hyskos attacked her father's house. Her family was slaughtered and she was abducted. They were already in Akkad when her pregnancy began to make her ill. The commander of the Hyskos realized what she still didn't know. He didn't want to be bothered and slowed down by a pregnant young slave. So when they met a caravan, he sold her to a merchant traveling to Khatti. Memnet was one of many slaves this merchant was assigned to bring to my father's palace."

At Sharula's soft intake of breath, Hattusil turned to look at her. She was quietly staring at her lap. This was so unlike what he'd expected of her, so unlike her previous behavior, he felt his eyes fill with tears. Hastily he wiped them away and sat beside her.

"When I saw Memnet, I loved her immediately. I was the king's son, but unlikely to inherit the crown. My father was vigorous and would live long. My older brother was healthy and in line for the throne. When my father saw how I loved Memnet, he agreed after many discussions and arguments that I could marry her despite her condition. There was little chance my heirs would ever wear the crown."

"And now they're all dead," Sharula murmured. "Now

31

you want your son to take the crown uncontested when you die."

"This is true," Hattusil admitted. "Would you not feel the same?"

Sharula nodded, then lifted her eyes and said bitterly, "But I needn't worry about a crown. I don't even have a father."

"Haven't I been a father to you?" Hattusil asked anxiously.

"In all ways except that one, which now turns my life into a desert," she murmured.

"Sharula, Sharula," Hattusil groaned, "what else can I do?" She was silent as he declared, "Your father, little one, was King Seti himself! King Ramessa is your half-brother! Your blood is as royal as his!"

"Nevertheless, no one can know it. I cannot wear his crown."

"Who can know to what position you might rise if you properly apply yourself?" Hattusil asked. "You're beautiful and intelligent and you have spirit. The Tamerans believe their crown is mystically inherited through the royal blood. You possess that same blood. If you let Tamera's gods guide you, you might gain the power of a queen. You might at least be the mother of Tamera's next king."

"How can I conceive a child with my own brother?" Sharula spat. "I would bear a cripple, or a child weakened by our mingled blood."

Hattusil took her shoulders in his hands and asked, "Are you weak or crippled? Have you heard of any such malady bothering Ramessa?"

"If he had such an affliction, we might have won our war," Sharula said sarcastically. "Yet such things don't always reveal themselves each generation."

"Then what of a lover?" Hattusil suggested. "Perhaps you could choose someone more suitable, more to your personal liking to sire this child—if you were in a position to have that much freedom, if you had enough power to move freely among the lords in the royal court." When

32

Sharula said nothing to this idea, Hattusil declared, "What woman wouldn't leap at such opportunity? What woman wouldn't be happy to become the wife of the king of any land? You could look forward to a life of power and luxury. You might even return to visit Khatti, if you grow lonely."

Sharula's eyes lifted and again were filled with fire. "I am not like those other women!" she declared. "I'm not content with memories of the past or dreams of the future. I want now!" she cried. Then she lowered her voice and added, "I want the now of my own choosing."

"That isn't always possible even for kings," Hattusil said grimly.

"The alternative is that you denounce me as illegitimate and disclaim me as your daughter before the court so I will have no right to any place in Khatti," she said quietly.

"I wouldn't like to do that. I don't want to hurt you, little one," he replied.

"You merely wish to give me to Ramessa," she said bitterly. She stood up. "When will he come to sign the treaty?"

"Tomorrow," Hattusil answered. "You'll meet each other then."

"I will not meet him tomorrow!" Sharula said sharply. "I'll meet him soon enough in Tamera. I won't leave my quarters until I begin the journey to Tamera."

"What will I tell him? He'll think there's something wrong with you, that I hide you from his sight!" Hattusil cried.

"I don't care what you tell him!" she flashed.

When Sharula's face took on the implacable expression it now held, Hattusil knew further discussion was useless. "I suppose I can say you're preparing for the journey," he said lamely. "You'll have to leave quickly, before winter comes."

Sharula gave Hattusil a black look and, saying no more, turned away. He watched her stalk from the room, and he flinched at the crash of the slammed door.

"She'll bend the situation to her own liking, I think," he sighed. "When she decides what she wants in Tamera, she'll have it. Even as a child, her will was formidable." He reflected upon her temperament for a moment then declared, "Ah, Ramessa, you'll have a job with her!"

When the Tameran army entered the city, Sharula resisted the impulse to watch from her balcony. She lay across her bed, with a cold heart, listening to the marching feet, stamping hooves and creaking wheels, as she again wondered why destiny had chosen so unhappy a path for her.

"My princess, King Ramessa is a fine figure," one of the servingwomen said from her post by the window opening.

Sharula heard the procession come to a halt before the palace doors and knew, from the sudden silence, Ramessa was about to enter her home. Not her home, she corrected herself. Not any more.

"Royal Daughter, he appears not ugly," another servant remarked comfortingly.

"Be silent," Sharula commanded. "I wish to hear no flattering descriptions of this man who has defeated us." Sitting up, she regarded her attendants with fire in her eyes. "Close the shutters against this disgraceful event and leave me."

While the serving women closed the shutters to the balcony, Sharula fixed them with a stony stare; the purpose of her piercing look was to prevent her angry tears from falling. But once they had left the room, Sharula was mildly surprised to find her tears had suddenly vanished.

There's no purpose in repeatedly asking the gods why I've been placed in this disgusting situation, she decided. It's where I am and I must somehow deal with it.

She stared at the ceiling while she reflected on her dilemma. Again humiliation swept through her, and she decided this must be the first thing she dealt with. She couldn't endure living with so degrading a feeling as humiliation. Though I'll be handed to Ramessa like a newly purchased sheep, it doesn't mean I must behave like a sheep, she resolved. I must never forget that my blood is as royal as his even if it's unofficially so. She smiled faintly, as she decided she could endure bowing to Ramessa—if she always remembered that the gesture was respect for the crown he wore. She would not allow herself to appear intimidated by the situation, even if her heart was frozen with fear. She must never let him think she was afraid of him or his power. She must behave with dignity always.

Hattusil was right; she was intelligent and beautiful. Perhaps he was also right to predict her rise to power in Ramessa's court. She had handled some intrigues that had developed in Khatti's court deftly enough. She would demonstrate to Ramessa how valuable she could be to him.

Sharula further resolved she would please Ramessa in bed, as unpleasant as the task might be, more than his other wives. Surely he would be even more favorably disposed toward her if he found that much pleasure in her body. She wondered how she could accomplish it. She'd never been to bed with any man, while Ramessa was a man of experience and no doubt sophistication. She sighed. Her virginity would be no novelty to him. All his wives came to him untouched, and he must be bored with the necessity of teaching them his preferences. Innocence wasn't an advantage.

But there are many women right here in this palace who know the subtle aspects of love that I need to learn, she thought. One of her own attendants had a reputation for having many lovers and certainly would know what pleased men. I'll order her to come explain all this to me tonight when the other servants have been dismissed, she decided. I'll go to Ramessa physically untouched. But

35

because I'll know as much as if I were experienced, I'll surprise and please him with how quickly I respond—which he will, no doubt, attribute to his own skill.

Sharula's eyes narrowed as she considered what other talents her servants might have that she could use to favorably influence Ramessa. Chenmet is a slave from Tamera and well-educated, Sharula mused. She could help me improve my knowledge of the language and teach me the customs of the land. Sharula suddenly smiled and sat up. "O you gods of Tamera who have placed me on this path, Chenmet will also teach me about your habits. By the time my royal half-brother lays his accursed eyes on me, I will be so much like a daughter born and raised in the shadows of your temples, I will amaze him with my cleverness."

Sharula sat on the edge of her bed, thinking about other possible ways she could find to so please Ramessa that he would eventually elevate her to First Royal Wife. Then her son would have that much better a chance to claim the throne. What irony it would be if she gave Tamera its next king—a king not Ramessa's son, but a true king of Tamera through her own royal blood.

For a fleeting instant she thought of Ramessa simply as a man, possibly even an attractive or likeable man. A pang of guilt went through her for what she was planning to do. She pushed the guilt from her mind and decided one more matter. If by some remote chance she found it possible to love Ramessa, she wouldn't allow herself to surrender to this emotion. She would not love him or any other man, because love muddled the brain, and she was certain her very survival might depend on clarity of mind.

She looked upon this decision with some satisfaction for a moment before getting to her feet. Slowly she walked across the room and threw open the shutters, allowing the sun to stream over her face.

"My revenge, Ramessa, will be that my son, not yours, will rule Tamera," she said softly. "My child will have the place I can never claim."

36

3

Since early dawn, Lord Hesyra, Governor of Kharu, had watched the speck on the horizon move across the desert until it had multiplied to a cluster of dots, then a swarm of them. Now they were close enough so Hesyra could easily discern the figures of men riding horses and he knew an entire regiment of the royal army, led by King Ramessa, would converge upon his small city within the hour.

Hesyra sighed. The city was relatively small and unimportant and not on the major caravan routes. All work would be stopped while the townspeople watched the procession.

Hesyra had been surprised that the king would travel to Kharu. To Hesyra's knowledge, Ramessa had never set foot in the province before unless he'd crossed its corner on the way to fight those already legendary battles at Qadesh. Now Hesyra was to meet his king face to face, welcome him and present to him, Hattusil's daughter.

Only a few days ago Hesyra had welcomed another

caravan to his city and every activity had stopped while the city's occupants had watched that event. Hesyra could hardly blame the populace. The caravan that had brought the Princess Sharula from Khatti had been well worth watching. How the people had stared at the lines of richly fringed and tasseled camels, at the regiment of soldiers who protected the caravan. How the townspeople had gaped when the royal princess of Khatti had emerged from the caravan. Hesyra admitted to himself that he'd also gaped.

When Princess Sharula's sundry attendants had lifted the perfumed veils that had protected the princess' skin from the sand and sun, Hesyra had been amazed at her appearance. How could this beautiful creature have been born of Khatti? he'd wondered. For her features were not at all Khattian. In response to Hesyra's message asking what he should do with this royal surprise, the king had promised to come himself with soldiers and escort Sharula to the palace at Wast.

Hesyra had little time to worry about the handling of this momentous event, because Ramessa and his regiment were soon at the city gates, entering without pause—the king's awesome presence sufficient announcement—and marching straight toward Hesyra's house. Ramessa, riding one of his magnificient white horses, entered Hesyra's courtyard and shrugged off the cloak that had protected his white and gold tunic. A line of officers threw off their own saffron capes to reveal spotless scarlet uniforms. Lines and lines of foot-soldiers, their uniforms the color of dusty blood, soon crowded the enclosure. Copper spearpoints lifted like a forest toward the bright blue sky. Multicolored banners, unfolded by the light breeze, floated against the ivory background of the courtyard walls. Before the dust from the horses' hooves had settled, King Ramessa slipped from his saddle and stood for a moment to gaze at the scene, a frown creasing his forehead. Hesyra wondered with a sinking heart why the king looked so grim.

Ramessa was, in truth, less than happy to have undertaken this journey and had come only at his mother's persistent urgings, begrudging each step of the way across the dusty land. Tuiah, Ramessa's mother, had insisted it would please King Hattusil if Ramessa showed Sharula the honor of coming to meet her personally. Ramessa was less interested in meeting Sharula than in keeping Hattusil happy. Also, he had wished to silence Tuiah. He loved his mother well enough, but he sometimes wished she would harass him less.

Ramessa cast a disdainful eye on the group standing before Hesyra's house. He knew immediately who Hesyra was, by the look of awe on his sweating face. Ramessa was certain Sharula was among the group of women who stood a short distance behind Hesyra and his officials. He sighed and began to walk forward. When he stood above Hesyra and his assistants, who had prostrated themselves, he looked down at them and said impatiently, "You may rise. Rise!"

Hesyra's startled face looked up. Then Hesyra scrambled hastily to his feet, his officials hurrying up after him. "Magnificent sun, before whom I prostrate myself daily—" Hesyra began. At the expression on his king's face, he wisely decided to shorten his address and found he could only remember the formal greetings anyway.

When Hesyra fell silent, Ramessa thanked the governor for his welcome, then lifted his eyes to look beyond the governor's shoulder at the women standing by the doorway.

Not realizing that Ramessa had never seen Sharula, Hesyra stepped aside.

Ramessa, who had been regarding the whole event as one more chore before he could retire to his chamber and have a cool cup of wine, glanced at Hesyra with surprise. Then he shrugged faintly and walked toward the women.

Sharula took a deep breath to compose herself as her serving women parted, clearing the way for Ramessa's approach. The King was tall, broad-shouldered, tightly though not heavily muscled, and looked as trim as his soldiers, as if he trained as rigorously for battle as they did. His thick hair was light brown, ear-length and wavy, not long and curled like that of Khatti's men. Touched with gold streaks in the sun, it was an unusual color for a Tameran, Sharula knew. When he came nearer, she found herself watching his long-lidded eyes, trying to decide what color they were. They seemed composed of flecks light brown, golden green, grayish blue. She was pleased with his lithe, sun-bronzed body, but the arrogance of his bearing reminded her of her own place, a princess being given as though she were a horse handed to its new owner after the bargain had been struck. When he stopped walking and faced her, she knew she was expected to prostrate herself at his feet, as Governor Hesyra and his officials had, and she felt the old anger fill her inner being with cold fire. She would not bow, she decided. She was aware of the watching crowd's indrawn breath; all were shocked by her effrontery.

If Ramessa had been surprised at Sharula's unexpected beauty, he was amused by her display of defiance, which was a novel thing to him and refreshing in this crowd of groveling officials. Above all things, Ramessa loved a challenge, and he recognized the look in Sharula's eyes as certain challenge. He smiled faintly and inclined his head very slightly, even that small degree being the most profound compliment the Tameran king might bestow upon introduction to a foreign princess. Sharula knew very well what honor this gesture held, and the bystanders were stunned again that she still didn't bow. Instead, she stood defiantly erect, head high, staring at Ramessa with cool green eyes.

Speaking in almost perfect Tameran, Sharula gave only the formal flowery greetings she'd previously been ordered by Hattusil to memorize. Her low, husky voice mocked the words even as she spoke them.

Ramessa's eyes narrowed in momentary surprise and

all hint of his smile vanished. Never before had a woman behaved so with him. But he said nothing.

As the silence grew tight with tension, Sharula's calm mask of a face effectively hid her true feelings. In her brain, a voice that seemed like the voice of her own doom warned, "You've gone too far, Sharula. When you're in his house and he has you at his mercy, you'll pay for this." Yet her pride concealed her inner terror and she lifted her head even a bit higher.

Ramessa was all the more intrigued, and for the fleetest instant, the corners of his mouth lifted slightly, as if he was amused by her display. While Lord Hesyra hastily gave Sharula Ramessa's formal response, Ramessa regarded her with a look of annoyance for her disrespectful attitude—a look he considered the minimum official necessity. Then he turned from her and walked away without personally having spoken a word.

Watching his receding figure, Sharula remembered something Chenmet had taught her about Tameran customs—it sent a chill through her. Did not the Tameran king's silence convey that he may not acknowledge her existence? And did not this act, according to Tamera's law, mean she might as well not exist? It was as good as a death sentence, should he choose to carry it out. Sharula restrained her shudder, so it wouldn't be observed by those standing nearby. She wondered if, when she was behind the walls of Ramessa's palace, she was truly doomed.

Sharula had no way of knowing that, when Ramessa's back was to her, his eyes flared with his answer to her challenge, that his pulses accelerated to think of how he would later effect her surrender. But I must plan my strategy most carefully, he was thinking. She's beautiful; but she's also proud and intelligent, perhaps too intelligent.

Menna, glancing up for a moment at his master, was startled to see that the king was smiling faintly, as he sometimes smiled before a battle he felt confident of winning.

When all the officials and their endless documents had been disposed of and Ramessa was alone in the chamber Hesyra had given him for the night, he considered inviting Sharula to have the evening meal with him. His curiosity had been greatly aroused by her behavior that afternoon and he wanted to explore her peculiar attitude. Too, he was mildly surprised when he realized that for the first time in a very long time, he was physically aroused merely by having met a woman; not a man used to waiting for what he wanted, he wished to call her to him this very night. He sipped his wine and reflected on these matters for some time before he decided it would be unwise.

This princess obviously came unwillingly to him. Instinct told him that she'd be far more exciting if she were willing, and that he must convince her to become so himself. He put down his goblet and laughed aloud. He had never courted a woman and he found the idea intriguing. Having never failed in anything he'd attempted, the possibility of failure never entered his mind. As he picked up his goblet again, he thought about his strategy for Sharula's surrender.

The princess was not docile. Perhaps maintaining his aloofness tonight and tomorrow morning as they prepared to go on to Wast—even throughout the first couple of days of the journey—might worry her and cause her to soften toward him. Then, if he gave her some small sign of attention, she might welcome it more.

Ramessa leaned back in his chair, and thought about her. She was tall and put together much like a Tameran woman, he guessed. It was difficult to tell with the loose garments she wore, but he thought he'd seen the hint of a slender yet well-proportioned body. He felt his pulse quicken at the speculation and he turned his thoughts to her face. High cheekbones supported eyes of an almond shape like those of a Tameran—He had wondered about that earlier—a mouth, pursed in defiance, soft and full, which was a most inviting place to rest his own lips. Ramessa sighed and returned his attention to her eyes.

42

Green liquid, like the Nile where a tree shadowed the water, sometimes shifting emerald lights as when the sun struck shimmering paths through the currents beneath the river's surface.

When Sharula was at last in his bed at Wast, he anticipated a very interesting night. At the thought of possessing her, a very real and vigorous fire washed through him, and he wished one of his other wives were with him now so he could seek relief. Then he realized none of them would satisfy him at the moment. He wanted Sharula and only Sharula this night.

He frowned. For the first time in his life he felt the sharp stab of physical frustration, and he didn't like it.

After a night that was anything but restful, Ramessa arose when the stars were yet bright pinpoints in the black sky. Before the sun had begun to shine on the eastern hills, he had joined the crowd in Hesyra's courtyard to watch the preparations for the caravan's journey to Wast. The jumble of activities helped distract him from the persistent ache he distinctly felt in the lower region of his body. The ache became sharper when he saw Sharula step from Hesyra's door.

Ramessa hadn't expected Sharula to come outside until the last moment before the caravan left, and he was surprised at her appearance. He was also surprised at the garments she wore. Gone were the silken veils of yesterday, which had enveloped her body in their layers. She was wearing a robe styled like a Shasu woman's garment. A cord tied around her waist defined its smallness as well as the curving of her hips. The same cord held the material of the garment snugly against her breasts and Ramessa forgot even his ache as he stared at her.

Sharula didn't see Ramessa standing beside his horse. She was intent on finding the commander of the Khatti guards who had accompanied her to Kharu. Catching sight of the commander, she turned and walked quickly toward him, never realizing that Ramessa was carefully watching the way the robe moved against her legs, the motion of her walk.

When Sharula finished giving the commander his orders to return to Khatti, her eyes fell on Ramessa watching her. A cold finger traced an icy path across her heart, but she lifted her head, smiled and approached him.

"It appears we'll have a fair day for traveling, my lord," Sharula said easily.

Ramessa was disconcerted by her words. She seemed to speak to him as an equal, using only the one informal title to address him. When she smiled up at him, his previous plans to ignore her flew from his mind. "You will learn that almost all days are like this in Tamera," he replied.

"Forgive me, my lord, for my impudence," Sharula said anxiously. "I'm also a peculiarity in Khatti, for I speak without the usual reticence of my sex. My father and brother got used to me long ago. The court finally decided to accept my outspokenness. Now I hope you'll understand it's only my manner and not meant to offend you." Her voice was lowered with concern, but her eyes held another quality.

"It will certainly be a new thing for me, but I think I may not mind," Ramessa said slowly. A touch of sternness came into his voice as he added, "I may not mind as long as you remember with whom you are speaking."

Sharula's smile didn't falter, though her knees were shaking. "My lord, I will never forget who you are."

Ramessa looked at her for a moment, studying her expression, wondering what really was behind those eyes. Then he said, "I suggest you gather up your servants and assign them their places, then prepare to get into your litter. We will leave soon."

Sharula knew this was her dismissal courteously given, but she took a deep breath and said, "Although I'm most grateful you're so considerate of my comfort, my lord, may I ask a favor?" When Ramessa said nothing but merely nodded, she continued, "I would like to ride my horse on this journey."

44

Ramessa's eyes widened slightly. "You want to ride all that distance?"

Sharula wished she could see his eyes, but they were shadowed in the semi-darkness. She looked down at her feet and said demurely, "I rode almost all the way to Kharu in that fashion, which is why I wear this garment today."

Ramessa said nothing for a moment. He was again looking at her robe, at the soft curves and intriguing hollows it revealed. "We intend to travel fast," he said. "It will require skill and endurance, more I think than you may have."

Sharula lifted her eyes to his face. "We traveled fast from Khatti because winter followed on our heels. We of Khatti are known for our horsemanship. I'm very skilled in riding, having learned when I was a small child." Sharula smiled almost tremulously, as if pleading with him. "My lord, if possible, I would ride at your side," she murmured. "We could use some of the many long hours of this tedious journey to advantage by getting better acquainted."

Ramessa's eyebrows shot up in amazement. He'd never really held a serious conversation with any woman other than Tuiah. But he decided the idea was interesting. If after an hour or two he found Sharula's conversation boring or disagreeable, he could order her back to the litter. "That may be worth trying," he said. "For a while anyway."

"Thank you, my lord," Sharula said quickly. "I'll be ready in a moment."

Ramessa watched as Sharula approached her serving women to give them orders. One of the attendants held up the black coil of Sharula's hair, which was bound at the nape of her neck, while another arranged a cloak around her shoulders and drew its hood over her head. When he noticed that Khakamir was watching him with a faint smile, Ramessa turned away and mounted his horse.

Though Sharula reined her horse at Ramessa's side,

he didn't glance at her, but looked at Khakamir in signal for the march to begin.

As they moved across the desert, Ramessa said not one word to Sharula. He hadn't the faintest idea of what to talk about with this strange female. He wasn't sure he even wanted to begin a conversation. But with every moment's passing, he was sharply aware of her silent presence beside him. After a while, he began to glance at her from the corner of his eye, wondering if she was tired of riding.

"My lord?" Sharula finally said.

Ramessa turned his head to look at her and observed that her back was as straight as his.

"In Hattusil's palace I raised as a princess, given my freedom and thoroughly educated, my lord," Sharula said quietly. "My mind is of an independent turn, as I'm sure you've already noticed. I'm sure you've also perceived that my part in this treaty wasn't my choice." Ramessa looked at her sharply for her boldness, but she was determined, and continued. "I'm certain such an arrangement is customary upon the signing of a treaty and you also probably have no great enthusiasm for me." Ramessa said nothing, so Sharula went on. "Perhaps the gods are wiser than we know and we might yet make something of this situation."

Ramessa felt annoyance rise in him. Was she saying he was distasteful to her? he wondered. He frowned and said, "I've done this many times before. It's of little importance to my mind."

At this Sharula lost her control and flashed, "It means my life to me! Do you think I'm happy to hand my life to a stranger? Or do you assume that I don't have thoughts of my own?"

Ramessa stared at her. "I can easily tell that you have thoughts!" he snapped. "I'm not sure it's a quality I'll favor in you. I find I'm not sure I'll favor you in any way at all!"

"How do you think I feel?" Sharula asked. The intensity in her lowered voice made Ramessa turn to look at her again. He noticed that her eyes were bright with tears.

"To be told I must give up my place in Khatti and go to Tamera—a land I'd cursed each time you won a victory against Khatti—to be told I must give myself in marriage to a man who had until that moment been my country's greatest enemy! I admit, I don't find you physically repulsive. But how do you think I must feel about what will come?"

Ramessa smiled wryly. "I'm happy I'm at least not repulsive." His smile faded and he shook his head in amazement at her courage. "We must be what we are," he finally said. "I am king and must do certain things. You also must do certain things. I have no intention of arguing about it and certainly no intention of arguing about anything with you. You will quickly learn, Sharula, you don't argue with a king. At least not with this king." Ramessa turned his head to note her reaction. Although her lips were set in a grim line, her head finally was lowered. He smiled. "I would add that neither are you physically repulsive to me."

Startled by the expression in his voice, she looked up at him. His hazel eyes were filled with green lights, but his lips were unsmiling. "Thank you, my lord," she murmured.

Ramessa said nothing, but he knew very well the humility in her tone was false. He would have to set very firm limits for Sharula, he could see. She was a person who would take advantage of every cubit of freedom he allowed her. It certainly was interesting to have a woman behave this way. He wondered if she would be that spirited and aggressive in his bed. His mind dwelt on that fascinating prospect for the remainder of the afternoon.

After the cooking fires had dwindled to coals which glowed dully in the night, and everyone in the camp but the sentries had settled into their sleeping places, Ramessa found himself unable as well as unwilling to sleep. What Sharula had said that afternoon about her feelings lingered in his mind and he seriously reflected on it. He wondered if any of the women now in his harem felt that way. He decided it wasn't likely. He was sure they were unused to independent thoughts on any subject.

Motioning to his servant, Nehri, to remain in place, Ramessa stepped out of his tent. The camp had been established in an oasis so small most of the tents were pitched on the desert, with the space nearest the water under the trees reserved for the royal travelers. Ramessa walked to the pond and leaned his back against the curve of a palm tree's trunk to gaze at the water and listen to the palm fronds whispering in the breeze. Suddenly aware of someone standing behind him, he turned to see Sharula a short distance away.

"I'm sorry, my lord, if my noise disturbed your thoughts," she whispered.

Ramessa shrugged. "I heard no sound."

"How did you know I was here?" she asked curiously, hesitant to come closer.

Ramessa smiled. "I'm a soldier as well as a king. I sense many things in the darkness. Why do you walk when you should be resting from a day of riding?" he asked companionably.

"I enjoy the coolness of the night."

Realizing she wouldn't approach him unless invited, he waved a hand to her. When she'd moved a few steps closer, he said quietly, "Tamera's nights are always cool, partly because of the wind."

"It is most refreshing, this wind," she agreed. "Does it always blow from the north?"

"More or less," he replied. "It also relieves the heat of the days."

"You have no winter in Tamera?" she asked.

"We have a cooler season, but no winter like Khatti's," he answered, and he turned his head to look at her. "You wear only a nightdress? Are you not chilled?"

Sharula shook her head. "I was without sleep. I expected to meet no one at this hour."

Ramessa's eyes traveled over the outline of her body, which he could see in the moonlight. He turned his
48

thoughts from this and said slowly, "Regarding what you mentioned this afternoon, I have considered your feelings. I think, truly, you won't be too unhappy with life in Tamera. My palace is as comfortable as Hattusil's. As one of my wives, you'll have every consideration. You won't live like a slave, I assure you." He looked away and continued, "I confess I'd never worried about what my wives thought. I still doubt the others think much beyond what bracelets they'll put on or how they'll arrange their hair. But I can see you'll be different."

Sharula was surprised at his statement. She knew it was a great concession for him to have considered her viewpoint.

"I doubt you'll find my attentions too much of a chore," he said softly. "I admit I am most pleased by your beauty and look forward to our lovemaking. Yet, I'm not a savage to force myself on a woman, and if you're that unenthusiastic, I won't bother you too often or perhaps not at all after the first night that seals the treaty."

Sharula stared at Ramessa. The tone of his voice and the expression in his gleaming eyes made a tingle run down her spine. She felt an urge to move closer to him and, when he reached out to touch her cheek, the soft brushing of his fingers on her skin sent a strange snap through her nerves that made her catch her breath.

Ramessa felt as if the earth had moved under his feet. He suddenly stepped away from the tree and clasped her tightly in his arms. He brought his lips to hers before she could move or speak, he kissed her long and hungrily. His frustration of the previous night welled over him. He was aware that her body was melting willingly, eagerly against his, and this knowledge sharpened his desire.

Taken by surprise, Sharula had responded to a degree that momentarily stunned her. But when her spinning mind began to function, her body stiffened.

Ramessa moved his head back a moment to look at her, but his thoughts were too filled with desire to wonder at her reaction. He brought his mouth again to hers, trying to part her lips. He could not. He moved his head back and looked at her with eyes that slowly focused. Finally recognizing her adamance, he said, "Please try to subdue your passionate cries." He stared at her a moment and asked, "You responded fully at first and I was pleased and much aroused by your response. Why would you stop what you were so obviously enjoying?"

"My body responded. My mind, however, refuses," she said stubbornly.

He released her and stepped away. "Then return to your bed and discover if your mind so easily rejects the memory of that kiss," he said.

"It will," she replied too quickly.

He smiled at the obvious lie. "While you're busy refusing your mind the memory of that kiss, perhaps you should consider something else, Sharula. Our marriage must be consummated. If this can be as pleasurable as I think, why shouldn't you enjoy it?"

Sharula walked slowly back to her tent with the firm resolution not to think of that kiss. But when she lay down, she felt a strange aching in her limbs; her body felt heavy and exceedingly warm.

The next morning, Sharula found that the others were wasting no time breaking camp. She hurriedly ate the morning meal, hardly tasting it, while she wondered whether she dared ride next to Ramessa this day.

She kept her horse near her servants, afraid to speak to Ramessa or move closer, until, with a wave of his hand, he signaled her to approach. When she reined her horse at his side, she found herself without words, and hesitating even to look up at him.

"Did you sleep well?" Ramessa inquired.

Sharula felt her face grow hot and she hastily nodded.

"Then you didn't think about the wisdom of enjoying what is ahead as long as it's inevitable?" he asked softly.

She stared at her horse's mane. She didn't know what to say.

"Turn your face toward me when you answer, Sharula.

I would see what those eyes hold this morning." His command was a caress.

She lifted her head reluctantly and very slowly looked up at him. The aching of the night was renewed, and she found her eyes focused on his smiling mouth.

"You thought about it," he observed, "and you think about it yet. Good." When he waved for the caravan to begin moving, he laughed softly.

Through the days that followed, Ramessa signaled each morning for Sharula to ride beside him, and each evening he sent Nehri to escort her to his tent to share his evening meal. Sharula wondered all through these evenings if he would try again to kiss her. He did not.

Ramessa engaged Sharula in conversation, explaining to her the customs of Tamera and what was officially expected of the king's wives. Often he complimented her on her appearance, with a grace that surprised her. From time to time he even acknowledged admiration for her intelligence. When one of his officers entered the tent to make a report or discuss a state matter, Ramessa kept Sharula at his side. She listened to all of it and quickly concluded that Ramessa disliked being bothered by many details but had a very sharp mind.

One evening when it was time for Sharula to return to her tent, Ramessa walked with her to its entrance. As she faced him, he looked at her for so long a moment she wondered if he intended to kiss her. But, finally he bid her pleasant slumber and turned away, leaving her feeling a disappointment she wouldn't admit to herself.

4

The great bronze gates of Wast swung open to admit the royal caravan. The street was filled with people. When Ramessa and Sharula rode in side by side, a great noise went up from the crowd.

Sharula wondered at the sound; instead of the cheers she would have expected, Ramessa's greeting from his people seemed more like a chant. She listened carefully to the words for a moment and realized that Tamera's language made the cries of welcome seem like a spoken song. She examined the faces she passed and wondered at these people, who were her own and didn't know it.

Ramessa smiled in acknowledgment of his subjects' welcome, but he wasn't listening to their words. He was distracted by his own thoughts, because he was planning a surprise for Sharula designed to effect her total surrender, although he knew it would shock Tuiah, the court and the whole land.

Tuiah waited on the palace steps, trying to catch a glimpse of the woman who, she expected, would soon step from the sumptuous litter. She was astounded when Ramessa took the hand of the Shasu, who had ridden into the courtyard at his side, and led the creature to face her. Tuiah looked up at her son, her face a reflection of her confusion, and Ramessa smiled with a look of mischief in his eyes Tuiah hadn't seen since before he'd inherited his father's crown.

"Mother, I present Princess Sharula of Khatti," Ramessa said, suppressing a smile at Tuiah's expression. He looked down at the hooded Shasu, grinned and swept off her cape.

Tuiah felt as if lightning had struck her. How was it possible that the dead came back to haunt the living clothed in the same flesh? Why should Memnet return to Wast, untouched by time, though Seti had years ago passed to the afterworld and Tuiah's face had become feathered with the procession of her years? Tuiah's eyes took in Sharula's travel-stained garments, the smudge on her cheek, and finally realized it wasn't her old rival that stood before her—but somehow Memnet's daughter.

Sharula wondered why Tuiah stared so strangely at her. Did the woman think to intimidate her with those un-wavering eyes? Sharula looked as boldly at Tuiah, calculating Tuiah's influence on Ramessa. When Tuiah found her tongue and gave Sharula the formal greeting, Sharula knew at once Tuiah's influence on her son would be something to contend with in the future. Tuiah was a small woman, but her voice commanded both attention and obedience. If she was to chastise a child, she wouldn't have to shout or even frown, because her voice would evoke sufficient terror. And Sharula was sure a son who had grown up under Tuiah's influence would, to a certain degree, continue to attend to her commands, though the son had become a man.

"I know you're amazed by Princess Sharula's garments, but please look beyond the dust and recognize her beauty," Ramessa said, wondering what unspoken message had passed between the two women.
54

Sharula lifted her head and said crisply, "I wished to ride beside my lord on this journey to become better acquainted. My lord graciously agreed."

"It was a most interesting experience," Ramessa said.

Tuiah realized then that her son loved this princess, who was the daughter of Seti and his paramour; Tuiah also knew she must not speak too soon against Sharula within Ramessa's hearing.

"I would think it had been an interesting journey," Tuiah said quietly, wondering what they might have discussed on the way and dreading to think of it. She could tell Sharula didn't resemble Ramessa's other, docile wives in the slightest and that Sharula could cause Ramessa to love her made Sharula a formidable opponent. Tuiah took a deep breath and said, "I hope you'll forgive my staring." She watched Sharula's face carefully while she added, "You greatly resemble someone I knew a very long time ago."

That small comment told Sharula what had caused Tuiah to look at her so intently. Sharula wondered if Tuiah would speak of it to Ramessa, but decided Tuiah wouldn't do it yet. The woman was unsure what to do. By the time Tuiah had made a decision, Sharula resolved she would have given Tuiah excellent reasons to remain silent.

Ramessa led the small procession into the palace, where a group of people awaited them. He introduced Sharula to Prime Minister Henhenet, a sharp-eyed little man who studied Sharula thoughtfully but gave his greetings courteously enough.

When Sharula was presented to Akeset, the high priest of Amen's temple, she felt a chill run over her and wondered why. The priest's thin lips were curved in a smile and he welcomed her warmly enough. But there was a coldness in his hooded eyes, she finally decided, that put the lie to his words.

"That's enough introductions for now," Ramessa said abruptly. "The princess has made a hard journey and needs

55

to rest for the remainder of this day, for she faces another strenuous day of ceremonies tomorrow and a wedding banquet that will run far into the night." He smiled at Sharula, then gestured impatiently to the waiting servants.

Sharula watched one of the palace servants, a dwarf, approach Ramessa closely. Ramessa spoke softly to the man. She wondered what additional orders this involved, but dismissed it as unimportant.

Ramessa straightened and looked at Sharula. "Please follow these servants to your room. You'll have, as I said, all this day and night to rest and prepare yourself for tomorrow's rituals," he directed. He turned to Tuiah. "Mother, I want you, Henhenet and Akeset to follow me. I must explain some changes in tomorrow's ceremonies."

Sharula and her attendants were led to a suite of richly appointed rooms. As she inspected the rooms one by one with the anxious dwarf following on her heels, she wondered where all of Ramessa's other wives were.

Seeing Sharula's frown, the servant quickly asked, "Is your highness displeased?"

"What is your position?" she asked.

"Hapu, Superintendent of the Royal Linens, and I attend to many related housekeeping functions, highness. Have I offended you that you'd have me punished?" he asked fearfully.

"No, Hapu," Sharula answered. "I wished to know your function. I would speak frankly with you because I'm confused."

A look of profound relief came over Hapu's face. "Anything, highness, anything you wish to know I'll tell you if I can."

Sharula went to a nearby chair and sat down. "Will I later be moved to the harem?" she asked.

Hapu's eyes widened. "No, highness. These rooms are yours if they satisfy you," he answered quickly.

"Does each of the king's wives live like this, isolated from the others?" she asked in surprise.

The dwarf smiled briefly. This was a fortunate day, he
56

thought, that he might give Sharula such happy news and thereby win her immediate good will. "No, highness," he replied solemnly. "The wives live in the harem."

Sharula stared at him. "But I am to become another of his majesty's wives tomorrow!"

"Not merely another wife, highness, but First Royal Wife." At Sharula's expression, Hapu rocked happily on his heels. She knew nothing at all, he realized, and he quickly added, "I haven't been told that for a certainty, but I usually understand the king's mind and he quietly told me to show you to these apartments and make sure my new mistress was pleased with everything. This, I'm sure, means he has decided to make you his favorite wife."

Sharula said nothing for a long moment. Finally she gathered her wits to ask, "Where is the king's suite?"

Hapu gestured toward a large door, crusted with gold leaf. "His majesty's chambers adjoin yours, of course."

Sharula stared at the door. Ramessa would make her first royal wife when they'd shared only one kiss, which she'd fought? Sharula was so stunned by this news she sat silently gazing at the door for a long time. When Hapu began to fidget and caught Sharula's eye, she thanked him in a whisper and waved him away. She sat in the same chair for a very long time, thinking about this astounding turn of events.

Although Ramessa had gone through the marriage ceremony so many times before that on the last occasion he'd participated with eyes half-closed in boredom, he now stood in the great temple of Amen in a state of acute alertness. He was waiting for Sharula to enter the temple, and anticipating her reaction when he proclaimed her new status.

Ramessa had taken great pains to charm, amuse and intrigue Sharula. In doing so, he had found himself charmed, amused and intrigued by her. But he still wasn't sure how she'd react when they retired for the night. He had never dreamed he'd be so anxious for a woman to desire him, and he was yet amazed at the efforts he had gone through. So disturbed was he to think of making love to her stiff and possibly struggling body, thus destroying forever the progress he'd made on the journey, he decided to use the one weapon in his arsenal of items sure to win her willing surrender. To make Sharula First Royal Wife and therefore his queen, to give her a Tameran name and proclaim her Tamera's own child, would bestow such honor on her that he couldn't imagine she'd be able to resist.

When a wave of tension ran through the crowd, Ramessa took a deep breath. The great doors swung open soundlessly and he fixed his eyes on the distant figure entering the temple. As Sharula walked slowly through the patches of slanting sunlight, Ramessa smiled with satisfaction. Sharula had worn the garment he'd sent her, which was a veil of pleated golden gossamer and of undeniably Tameran design. She'd had the wisdom to apply eyepaint in the complicated tradition of Tamera's queen-goddesses and even had her hair simply combed and hanging loose, rather than elaborate curls, in the style of Khatti. Ramessa was satisfied that no one would dare say behind their hands that she wasn't a Tameran but for royal proclamation. They would accept her as a child of the Nile, somehow born in Khatti, because no other woman had ever appeared more suitably the daughter of Ra.

Tuiah's eyes on Sharula held considerably less warmth than her son's. Tuiah had spent the night praying Sharula would somehow become ugly or clumsy or demonstrate a lack of judgment in her dressing, but Sharula had done the opposite. With a sinking heart Tuiah watched Sharula move gracefully through the ritual, the golden web enveloping her body, hiding nothing. Instead of Sharula, Tuiah kept seeing the hated figure of Memnet claiming her son's heart as Memnet herself had claimed Seti's. Tuiah stared at Ramessa, watching as he smiled engagingly at the golden figure, noticing the proud lift of his
58

head as he sealed the contract. Tuiah clenched her teeth to hear what was coming.

Ramessa nodded to Henhenet, who had been standing off to one side. Henhenet came forward to hand Ramessa the gold diadem of Sharula's new status, then backed away, bowing.

Ramessa turned to face the noblemen and their ladies filling the temple from wall to wall. He drew Sharula to his side. In a clear, firm tone Ramessa announced, "From this moment into eternity the name of Sharula will become but a name in the Book of Royal Records. From this moment and into eternity I, first son of Ra who speaks for the company of divine beings in Tuat, proclaim this woman Nefertiry, First Royal Wife, Daughter of Ra—and my queen."

Ramessa smiled down at Sharula's expression, which gave no hint of her previous knowledge, because she was yet that shocked to hear the pronouncement from his own lips. He placed the diadem over her brow. He took her hand—which, he noticed with some satisfaction, was trembling—and led her out of the temple.

Nefertiry, Nefertiry—Sharula silently pronounced her new name over and over in her mind, wondering at the sound of it, thinking about its meaning: "beautiful companion." She sat beside Ramessa at the banquet table, so absorbed in her thoughts she seemed isolated from the company—a golden goddess deigning to spend an hour on earth with mortals.

Ramessa reflected that this was the way he had imagined Sharula, as a goddess of his own making. But as the evening wore on and Sharula remained aloof, Ramessa began to worry. He had anticipated some expression of happiness from her at his elevating her to this position. But she'd merely looked a little dazed for a while, then had become a statue of golden ice. She ate almost nothing of the feast before her. When Ramessa encouraged her to at least taste the wine, she took only a few sips.

Remembering the way she'd responded to his humor during the journey, he made various comments designed to cause her to smile. The smile forthcoming was that of a painted figure. Ramessa complimented her lavishly upon her appearance and demeanor, all to no avail. Finally he began to flirt with her, hoping his remarks would lift her mood by the very light-hearted way he offered them, but her cool, obtuse answers made his heart sink in fear that all his efforts had failed.

Sharula was not unaware of Ramessa's struggle; she was so touched she didn't know how to respond. She also was terrified into a state of near paralysis by the thought of spending the night with him. It wasn't that she was afraid of him. She was in a turmoil of conflicting emotions. Although she had originally intended to give Ramessa as much pleasure as possible to make him favor her above all others, if her reaction to that one kiss had been any indication of her own response, she didn't know how she could avoid losing control of herself. She acknowledged now that she liked him very much as a person and that she felt a certain affection for him. How could she like him and desire him and enjoy their lovemaking without loving him? she wondered, because she was determined not to give herself over to that emotion. She was afraid to lift her eyes to look into his face; his green-flecked eyes were filled with a confusion that wounded her. She was afraid to reply to his comments, not that she might encourage him, but too easily encourage her own feelings.

Tuiah, watching her royal son trying so hard to please the unmoved Sharula, began to hate Sharula for herself instead of merely being Memnet's daughter.

After a reasonable number of hours had passed, in which Ramessa wondered if he wished the evening quickly over or if he should continue trying to gain some favorable reaction from Sharula, he finally decided to accept whatever the gods had planned and whispered to Sharula that it was time for her to leave the banquet.

Sharula's eyes were unreadable as she arose and turned, leaving a trail of perfume behind her.

Ramessa spent a few more silent moments at the table, wondering what else it was possible for him to do. Finally, angry at his own helplessness, he stood up. At this signal of his imminent departure, Akeset blessed him, Henhenet made the appropriate announcements, and Ramessa turned to leave the company.

Tuiah watched him stalk from the flower-garlanded banquet room, feeling as if her head had been circled by a bronze band which was tightening.

Ramessa went directly to Sharula's apartments. Waving aside Nehri, who had intended announcing his monarch's entrance, Ramessa marched through the door without warning.

Sharula, who had been seated before her dressing table while Chenmet removed her jewelry, stood up quickly, waving Chenmet away.

Ramessa remained motionlessly silent for a moment, looking at her, measuring her attitude, never guessing the coolness of her glance was a disguise meant to conceal her panic, that the emptiness on her face was a mask of serenity covering her confusion.

"How you must have terrified them in Khatti," Ramessa finally said. "You have so regal a look you have even intimidated Henhenet, who is a crusty old snake I'd thought fearless." Ramessa paused a moment, as if making a decision, then said softly, "I am pleased with your queenliness and I encourage your remaining untouchable to everyone—but me."

A new chill of fear went through Sharula. Fighting to conceal it, she lifted her head a little higher.

Ramessa noticed the gesture; so excellent was her acting, he deemed her defiant. Anger flashed behind his eyes but he said quietly, "I have tried to please you, to win you to me, which is a thing I've never troubled myself with before. I have waited for you to soften toward me, but this game continues until I feel like a peasant

61

boy trying to woo a farmgirl into giving up her virginity—without result."

Ramessa came closer to look into Sharula's face, but he carefully didn't touch her. "I am not a peasant and I am not a boy. I am king." He paused a moment, then continued, "You were princess in Khatti, but let me remind you that you will never again be called Sharula. You are now and forever Nefertiry and you will resign yourself to this. You're in Tamera, and in Tamera everything is mine, including you."

Sharula's eyes didn't falter. Still not realizing she was frozen in fear, thinking this a new challenge, Ramessa said, "I have made up my mind, Nefertiry. I have waited long enough. Tonight marks the end of this game. I will go now to my bath. When I enter my chamber you will be present, awaiting me. You will yield your body to my pleasure, willingly or not."

Sharula hid her panic and asked, "If I am so unwilling that I resist, what will you do?"

Ramessa seemed to consider this a moment, while in his heart he was wondering if the passion aroused in her by resistance would give some expression to his maddeningly blank eyes. He said softly, "The treaty must be sealed. Although I prefer not to take you by force, this will not stop me. Let me remind you again you are no longer in your father's house, but mine, no one will dare come through my door to save you."

Sharula was silent for a moment, as if weighing this warning. Then, she sighed as if she resigned herself. Yet her heart was pounding when she looked away and murmured, "I suppose, like all the others, I must subject myself to you at least to consummate the treaty and the marriage before you forget me."

The effrontery of her put sparks of anger in his eyes and he stared at her. Then, he collected himself to say in a voice that was heavy with meaning, "I think you may be so unlike the others it's possible I will want you again. So do not hope this night will be the last. If and when I decide I want you again and call for you, Nefertiry, when I snap my fingers, you will come."

Ramessa regarded her for a moment, looking calm and confident. But when he turned to leave, he was perplexed. He knew he would never snap his fingers for this one.

While Ramessa bathed, he thought about Nefertiry's strange attitude, but he couldn't think why he had failed. He was now convinced he would have to rape her merely to seal the treaty. Briefly he considered putting off the struggle to the next night, when she might be more receptive, but he discarded that idea. He couldn't negate what he just had told her. As Nehri dried his body, he decided, if he must rape her, he would have to be as gentle as possible in the hope that his carefulness with her this time might make her less resistant the next time. He was sure there would be a next time with this puzzling, alluring woman.

Trying to hide his grim expression, Ramessa turned to Nehri and said, "You may withdraw for the night. If I need you again, I'll call."

The servant had disappeared through the door leading to his own quarters, and Ramessa took one more glance at his dressing room, then opened the door to his bed-chamber. His eyes swept the room quickly, as he wondered what he would do if she wasn't there. His eyes stopped to gaze at the golden drapery surrounding his bed. Beyond the softly glowing folds, he saw Nefertiry sitting upon the linens of his bed as if the place was her throne; he breathed in relief that she was there despite her sullen expression.

"I have obeyed you, my lord." Nefertiry's low voice floated across the room.

Ramessa walked slowly toward the bed. He pulled aside the veil of the curtains and stood silently, looking at her eyes which were the same clear green as the filmy cloth of her garment. "It isn't obedience I seek from you," he said quietly.

Nefertiry wondered at his hesitance. "If you expect enthusiasm, I think I can't manage that," she said in a faint voice. She was silent for a moment, and in that small space of time, her panic began to quiet. She wondered if she could now, at least, function as a female and accept whatever resulted. She suddenly felt drained of energy. "I can offer but cooperation," she murmured.

Ramessa sat on the edge of the bed. "Perhaps I can change that. Before today I never would have questioned my ability, but maybe that's because it was never tested. The others, I realize now, may have been merely obedient and behaved as they'd been trained to behave. It will be interesting for me to learn my true effectiveness." At Nefertiry's flush and suddenly downcast eyes he said, "We both will learn much about ourselves tonight. I know I am a man. Let me do what I will do and let what happens to you happen."

At Ramessa's touch, Nefertiry felt nothing more than the warmth of his solid flesh. Because there wasn't the violent response of the night on the oasis, she felt safer, and she relaxed a little. When Ramessa bent to kiss her, she merely felt warm lips softly pressing her own. After a moment the lips moved against hers more solidly, parting slightly to nibble at her mouth, and she felt a fluttering at the back of her neck, as if a butterfly momentarily fanned its wings. She closed her eyes to concentrate on the feeling, hoping to evoke it again. But Ramessa moved away. She opened her eyes. He was regarding her with an enigmatic expression.

"Are you so modest that nakedness would embarrass you with all the lamps lit?"

Nefertiry decided her curiosity was greater than her shyness. "I think I won't mind the lamps," she whispered.

Ramessa's lips tipped up at their corners. Without taking his eyes from her face, he stood up, slowly unfastened the sash of his robe and let the garment drop from his shoulders. "Look all you wish," he invited. "Before Ra rises over the horizon, you'll know this body more thoroughly than your eyes can perceive."

At first Nefertiry felt her face must be turning to the color of a pomegranate. But as Ramessa seemed unconcerned with the extent of her scrutiny, she felt she'd appear foolish if she didn't look. And she was curious.

Ramessa's whole body was the same bronze as his face and as trimly muscled as he'd appeared when clothed. His long legs were straight and well-formed. Her eyes slowly lifted to his broad shoulders, then to his face. He was still watching her.

"Now will you mind my doing the same?" he asked. At her silence, his smile faded. "It is only just," he said softly, "and as I already explained, before morning we will explore each other's bodies more thoroughly than mere eyes can. Come, Nefertiry. Or shall I remove your garment?"

Nefertiry slid slowly to the edge of the bed and stood up. She found the edge of her robe and wordlessly handed it to him. Then she turned until the robe unwound and slipped from her body to the floor.

Ramessa's eyes widened slightly and he dropped the corner of the robe. Her skin was like peach-tinted cream. His eyes moved from her throat to the moist satin of her rounded breasts, to the circle of her waist and the hips that tapered into long, well-shaped legs, legs like those of an ivory statue.

Nefertiry had anxiously followed the path of Ramessa's eyes. When they again lifted to her face, she asked, "Are you pleased, my lord?"

Ramessa's smile returned to his eyes, but his lips answered solemnly. "I am most pleased with your body's appearance. It will be inspiring to me, I have no doubt."

Ramessa put his hands on Nefertiry's shoulders and felt her tremble slightly.

"Do you tremble from fear of me?" he asked. She looked surprised and shook her head. "Then your trembling has another reason," he said softly. "Let us learn if I can increase this trembling."

His hands slid down her sides to her waist, He drew her closer to him, not roughly as he had in the oasis when they'd first kissed, but with firm gentleness, and he pressed his lips to hers with the same firm gentleness, kissing her unhurriedly. Slowly he again nibbled at her lips and finally parting them, touched the tip of his tongue lightly along their soft perimeter. Nefertiry wondered how the warm tickling sensation on her lips suddenly traveled down her backbone and settled at its base. It wasn't until Ramessa stepped away that she realized her arms had circled him and their naked bodies had pressed tightly together.

"That was a very satisfactory beginning," he said quietly. "You respond very well and the most marvelous part of all this is that you do so naturally. Lie down," he directed.

Nefertiry obeyed quickly, then lying there again under his gaze, wondered what she should do next, the information she'd obtained from her servant having flown from her head. A breeze from the window opening touched her and she shivered.

Ramessa knelt on the bed to look down at her. "You'll soon be warmer," he murmured and bent to kiss her again. But this kiss was less gentle; its sensation rapidly grew to a forcefulness matching that of their first kiss, until Nefertiry felt the warm weight of his chest against her breast and her arms around his back tightened to lock him to her.

But Ramessa loosened her grasp and drew a little away. While she lay trembling, he kissed her shoulders and breasts, touched his tongue to the side of her waist, until she moaned softly from the intensity of the sensations pouring over her. He straightened to look at her and smile.

When he saw her eyes focus he asked, "Are these feelings pleasing to you?" He watched her with knowing eyes as she nodded breathlessly. "Then I will proceed to their inevitable conclusion," he said.

She watched him again lean toward her and she closed her eyes to lie there and do nothing more than respond to him—until her joyously shrieking senses seemed unable to endure it—until her body writhed with the intensity of her feelings—until the length of Ramessa's body weighed pleasurably on hers.

The sharp pain was a small price for the sensations that followed, which slowly, then more rapidly increased; until it was as if she ran down a hill, gathering speed from her momentum—until sure she could endure no more, her consciousness shot off the hill's slope, soaring, merged with his into the full explosion of their senses.

Finally, like mortals crowned by the divine beings and for but a moment held in eternity's grasp, they were returned panting to the earth.

When their bodies, covered with a sheath of moisture, were chilled by a breeze coming from the window opening, Ramessa slowly sat up and pulled at the linens to cover them. Softly he said, "I always thought a woman's experience dictated the degree of my satisfaction. But though you were untouched, you've given me more joy than any other."

Nefertiry sat up to lean her cheek against his shoulder and weakly whisper, "Had I known what it was like, I would have lured you to my tent the first night of our journey from Kharu."

"You enjoyed it, despite the pain?" he asked softly.

She smiled. "To enjoy it more, I think, would be my end."

Ramessa held Nefertiry closer. After a moment he murmured, "I had begun to think you hated me."

She paused to think of something she could say, then whispered, "I hated to be given to you—to anyone."

Ramessa considered this for a moment, laughed softly, then kissed her ear lobe and said, "I've never sealed a better treaty."

Nefertiry smiled and murmured, "There's one thing I must confess."

"What is that?"

"You did everything, which makes me feel guilty," she replied. "I merely lay there receiving the gifts you gave."

Ramassa pushed her shoulders back until she lay looking up at him and he gazed down at her. "We will sleep for a time, Nefertiry. When we awaken, it will be your turn." He smiled happily and added, "I'll teach you what pleases me." He stretched luxuriously, then put his arms around her. "Of course, if you discover something new that pleases me, I won't mind."

Nefertiry settled nearer to the warmth of his body and closed her eyes contentedly. She knew she loved Ramassa now. But even while this bright flame burned in her heart, she also knew she must never let him know it. Loving him was folly enough. But for him to become aware that his every passing expression brought her joy or sorrow would surely bring about her destruction, because she was convinced it was her aloofness that would continue to fascinate him.

5

Still more than half-asleep, Nefertiry wondered if Tamera was often plagued by earth tremors, because it seemed the bed was shaking. When her eyes opened, her sleep-dazed mind slowly began to realize someone was trying to awaken her. Expecting Ramessa, she rolled over with a smile on her lips and welcome in her eyes to find Chenmet standing beside the bed. Nefertiry's smile faded. "Where's the king?" she demanded.

Chenmet backed away a step. "His majesty arose earlier and went to meet with his ministers, my lady. He gave me instructions to awaken you in an hour, attend you, then bring you to him to share the morning meal."

As Nefertiry swung her legs from the bed, she sat a moment thinking of the night, smiling again.

"My lady is like a newly opened lotus this morning," Chenmet said softly.

Nefertiry glanced up at Chenmet, ready to rebuke the servant for her curiosity, but her smiling lips couldn't form the words, and she said, "I'd best not delay dressing."

"I think this king has pleased you," Chenmet observed. Nefertiry said nothing. "I see your happiness and am gladdened by it," Chenmet added.

"Discard all the garments I brought from Khatti," Nefertiry said quietly. "The king will see me dressed in Tameran fashion or nothing." Her face sobered as she added, "Let us not waste time. I would join him before he waits overlong."

Later, Chenmet guided her mistress to the door of the room where Ramessa was having breakfast. Nefertiry dismissed the servant and turned expectantly to the guard posted before the door. "Stand aside," she directed.

"I have orders to allow no one entry," he said, his eyes fixed at some point beyond Nefertiry's shoulder.

"I'm to share the morning meal with his majesty," she declared.

"I have my orders," the guard replied, extending the spear he held so it stood in her way.

Amazed, Nefertiry stared at him. Could it be that Ramessa had changed his mind? she wondered. "Your orders are probably to let no one disturb us after I'm in that room," she said coldly. The guard gave no response. "I'm your queen, you stupid creature! I have patience, but not unending. I command you to stand aside. If your small brain cannot comprehend the complications of royalty, I'll simplify my words," she said venomously. "I'm First Royal Wife now. His majesty shared the whole night with me and was greatly pleased. He won't be pleased that you shut me away from him now."

The guard extended his hand slightly, as if to turn her away. But he was paralyzed at the sound of another voice behind him.

"Anyone who touches Queen Nefertiry without her permission will be put to death."

Ramessa stood aside so Nefertiry could enter the room.

As she passed, he bent closer to whisper, "His majesty was greatly pleased."

Nefertiry smiled up at him. "I began to fear you'd changed your mind and wanted to lock me out."

Ramessa led her to a chair and replied, "I wouldn't lock you out. I would tell you."

He said it so matter-of-factly a chill ran down her spine, but she continued smiling and sat down. "I'll keep that in mind," she said drily.

Ramessa returned to his place and sat looking thoughtfully at Nefertiry a moment. He extended his hand across the table and touched her fingertips. As during the night, even this slight physical contact sent a pleasant shock through her.

"What you just felt I also felt," he said softly. "Do you know what that means?"

Nefertiry's eyes didn't falter as she replied, "It means our bodies are compatible."

Ramessa shook his head. "I seem to be reasonably compatible with all my wives, but none of the others affect me quite that way," he said.

Nefertiry dropped her eyes. "We must be unusually so."

"You're very stubborn, Nefertiry," he observed, withdrawing his hand.

As she turned to deny it, her eyes widened. An animal resembling a large leopard, but with very peculiar black markings in its tawny fur, had entered the room and was regarding her with great amber eyes.

Ramessa realized Nefertiry's gaze was fixed on something behind him and he turned, too. Seeing the cat, he called, "Botar!" The cat slowly walked closer, still watching Nefertiry while it brushed its side against Ramessa's leg. Ramessa rubbed its head affectionately for a moment. "Botar won't harm you," he said, glancing up at Nefertiry.

"I was startled, but I'm not afraid," she replied. She extended her hand, palm side up. "Come, Botar, let us get acquainted," she invited.

71

The cat's great amber eyes looked at Ramessa.

"Although she won't harm you unless I give her the order, she isn't friendly with strangers," Ramessa said slowly.

"Then she and I may get along well because neither am I very friendly with strangers," she replied tartly.

"That's the truth," he said.

"Come, Botar," Nefertiry coaxed. "Let us at least observe the courtesies, though we both reserve judgment for later." Nefertiry laughed as the hesitating cat seemed to consider this proposal, then slowly approached to sniff her fingers. After a moment Botar allowed Nefertiry to rub her chin, then even her ears. Nefertiry glanced triumphantly up at Ramessa.

Ramessa watched with raised brows. "Perhaps you will be friends, after all. If so, there are some things I must tell you about Botar." At his words, Botar turned to look at him. Ramessa pulled out a chair, and Botar leaped up soundlessly to sit on the chair. Ignoring the dishes of food on the table, she merely looked from Ramessa to Nefertiry as if she listened and understood their conversation. Ramessa said, "Botar is from the south. As you may have realized, her name isn't that of Tamera, but that of Kenset. She's part black leopard and part cheetah, which is why she's the size and shape of a leopard but has a cheetah's coloring." Ramessa smiled proudly at the cat. "She's an excellent friend and does exactly as I tell her, whether I speak to her, whistle, or gesture."

"Botar must be very intelligent," Nefertiry observed.

"She is that," Ramessa agreed. "She has accompanied me on hunts and even into combat to do battle with my enemies just like my soldiers. If she becomes friendly enough with you, perhaps she'll someday answer your commands, though I doubt it."

"Did she go with you to Khatti?" Nefertiry asked, eyeing Botar's long fangs as the cat yawned.

"No. She remained here with Tuiah," Ramessa replied.

"Perhaps she'll accompany you on your next war, now

that I'm here in the palace and can come to your mother's aid, if needed," Nefertiry suggested.

Ramessa's eyes narrowed slightly at this. He wondered if Nefertiry planned to rule Tamera should he have to go into battle. If so, he foresaw some struggle between Nefertiry and Tuiah, because Tuiah usually kept matters under control when he was absent, almost acting as co-regent. Yet was it not possible that Nefertiry's hands might more suitably hold the scepter and that his mother might well step backward, now that there was a queen? Ramessa considered this a moment, but he simply answered, "I foresee no foreign powers likely to threaten Tamera in the near future. Most countries are now too weak to oppose us. Those who might be strong enough are impressed by that last struggle and seem content to trade peacefully with us."

A knock sounded on the door to the main hall and Ramessa waved to a servant attending them to open the door. He looked at Nefertiry and explained, "That's Arek, one of my personal guards. I told him to come during the meal. I have some orders to give him."

When the soldier entered, Nefertiry's indifference turned to curiosity. His face was familiar to her, but she couldn't think where she'd seen him before. Although he was dressed as a palace guard, his features like his name weren't Tameran. He was not as tall as Tameran men usually were; his dark brown eyes were rounder and lacked the slant of Tamera's people.

As Arek gave Ramessa a report, Nefertiry listened carefully to his voice and continued to study his features, searching her memory; she realized she had seen Arek in Khatti. Her face registered nothing as she recalled the occasion. Unable to sleep, she had walked in the garden's shadows, and seeing Hattusil's open window flooded with lamplight, she had thought to talk with him. But when she drew closer, she had seen this man, dressed in the flowing robes of a Shasu, speaking with Hattusil, and she had turned away. Neither Arek nor Hattusil had seen her that

73

night, she remembered with relief. Arek wasn't aware that she knew him for a spy.

While Ramessa gave Arek orders to speak to the appropriate ministers about strengthening the fortifications of the arm of land north of the Narrow Sea, Nefertiry considered what she could do to stop Arek's spying without causing new trouble for Hattusil.

Ramessa instructed Arek to speak to Henhenet, the prime minister, regarding the enlarging of strongholds at some places most threatened by the nomadic tribes. Arek bowed and left. Nefertiry decided to say nothing to Ramessa about Arek's treachery, but to wait until she could think of another way to rid the palace of this spy.

"This Arek isn't of your people, yet you speak to him on important matters," Nefertiry observed.

"Arek is a Shardanan we captured in battle, but he's since proved to be my friend," Ramessa said. "I have several such captured mercenaries in my personal guards and others in the army. They are ferocious fighters."

"I think I wouldn't trust a captured Shardanan or any foreign mercenary in a place so close to me and, therefore, so potentially powerful," Nefertiry commented.

Ramessa shrugged. "I trust Arek," he said firmly.

Nefertiry said no more about Arek. The stony look in Ramessa's eyes made it clear that pursuing the subject would be useless. She realized it wouldn't be easy to influence Ramessa on any matter.

"You will attend court with me this morning," Ramessa suddenly said. "As my queen, it's necessary for you to be at my side. When we've finished this meal, you must change into appropriate garments—quickly—so you'll be ready when I come for you."

Nefertiry wasn't ready when Ramessa came for her. She explained she'd had some difficulty finding appropriate garments to wear to court, having little other than those she'd brought from Khatti. She'd finally settled for some last-minute alterations on one of those robes. "You wouldn't want me to sit on Tamera's throne looking like a princess from Khatti, would you?" she finished.

Ramessa sighed, admitted he would not, then sat in a chair looking bored while Chenmet hurriedly arranged Nefertiry's hair.

When Nefertiry was ready, she turned to Ramessa and said, "Please don't frown, my lord. After all, who's waiting for you but your subjects? Surely they can await their king's convenience."

Ramessa took Nefertiry's arm and propelled her into the corridor. "It isn't that they await me," he said shortly. "It's that I must wait for you."

Nefertiry looked up at him through her lashes. "I am sorry, my lord. I was unprepared to attend court so quickly," she said contritely.

Ramessa looked down at her and sighed. "You will have the seamstresses make you a new wardrobe without delay."

"Yes, my lord," she murmured. "Immediately, my lord."

Ramessa looked more steadily at Nefertiry, wondering if she was as sorry as she appeared or if she merely wished to pacify him. He shrugged and slowed his steps as they approached the doors to the throne room. He nodded to the guards escorting them to enter the chamber.

Tuiah had dressed for court in anticipation of sitting beside Ramessa as she usually did; but when Ramessa's servant informed her that Nefertiry was accompanying him, Tuiah changed her garments. Then she concealed herself behind a column to observe how they behaved together this morning. When Ramessa and Nefertiry passed Tuiah, she inspected Nefertiry's gold-bordered robe, the scepters she carried crossed at just the right angle, and grudingly approved Nefertiry's appearance. She noted Nefertiry's downcast eyes and hoped, for Ramessa's sake, the night's events had improved Nefertiry's attitude. But Tuiah returned to her quarters feeling a sharp stab of jealousy that her place beside her son had been usurped by Memnet's daughter.

When they stepped over the throne room's threshhold, Ramessa purposely paused to give the waiting crowd a look at Nefertiry. At the same time, Nefertiry took the opportunity to run her eyes over the chamber's expanse and familiarize herself with it. In spite of her resolution to appear aloof and unimpressed, she was amazed at its beauty.

The walls and ceiling were lined with gold alabaster. In the light coming from the window-openings high above, the alabaster glowed translucent, like milky amber. The double line of columns forming the aisle they must walk were of immense proportions; the columns' surfaces were covered with delicate carvings richly decorated with gold leaf that sparkled in the sun. At the front of the room was a wide dais and upon the dais were two seats. Nefertiry caught her breath; the thrones appeared to be solid gold.

She was startled by Henhenet's call: "King Ramessa, son of Ra, comes! Be silent!"

When Ramessa stepped forward, Nefertiry lifted her head and walked proudly down the aisle of towering columns, but she was trembling with excitement. She had heard many stories of Tamera's splendor and, at last, she truly realized the wealth this land possessed. To have actually gained the status that she had so coveted in this magnificent palace made her feel drunk. She fixed her eyes on the guards who paced directly in front of her, carefully ignoring the curious and respectful faces she passed. She couldn't believe how well her secret plans already were evolving. She moved her fingers slightly, to assure herself of the hard reality of the gold handles on the small scepters she carried, and she was newly awed.

Ramessa stepped upon the dais and, sitting on his golden throne, motioned for Nefertiry to sit beside him. A glance at her expression told him nothing of the emotions behind her eyes, and his lips tipped upward in a smile of satisfaction, because he deemed her the very image of a Tameran queen: her eyes surveying the crowd with impartial interest, her brow under the coronet serene, her mouth neither pursed nor smiling. Nothing of Khatti seemed left in her that would remind his subjects of her alien beginning.

Again Henhenet's voice rang through the room. "On your faces before your king!"

When the roomful of people sank to their knees in obeisance, Nefertiry's pulses pounded so violently she wondered if she would collapse. She kept her breath even and silent only by a great effort.

The prime minister approached the foot of the thrones to bow deeply, then rise and say, "Merciful Heru, I place the petition of Lord Paser, governor of Kenset, before you. His northern province adjoining our south border continues to suffer deeply from famine and he begs your majesty for relief." Seeing Ramessa's frown, Henhenet came a step closer and pleaded even more fervently for Paser, who was his brother-in-law: "Since a locust horde devastated that province, there's so little left to eat people avoid their neighbors out of fear they'll ask for help that can't be given. The shops, formerly filled with foodstuffs, are now empty of all but such things as cannot be eaten." Henhenet lifted his eyes to look directly into Ramessa's face as he finished, "They're on the edge of starvation."

Ramessa considered this crisis in the south, which he had long ago foreseen, having received sundry messages from Paser reporting each event that had led to this state. He said, "I'm sadly mindful of all their sufferings and my prayers have flown to the One Alone that their next harvest will find abundant crops."

"Your majesty's prayers are gratefully received," Henhenet said quickly, "but the next gathering is yet a season away. Majesty, will you spare some supplies to give them relief until the next crop is ready?" He smiled hopefully at Ramessa, as if sure the king would agree simply because it was he who had made the request.

Nefertiry knew Henhenet was trying to appear to the others as if he were on even more friendly terms with Ramessa than was the truth. She disliked such ploys. While

77

Ramessa was silent, considering the request, Nefertiry resolved to find some appropriate way to remind Henhenet of his proper place.

Finally Ramessa said, "I'm filled with sorrow for Paser's stricken province and I've had an accounting made of what is in the storehouses that can be spared for his people. A letter has already been dispatched to Lord Paser regarding my decision and following on the heels of the courier who delivers this letter is a caravan of food-stuffs."

"Merciful Son of Ra, I give you thanks for Lord Paser," Henhenet declared.

"I'm sure Lord Paser will discover some way in which to thank me himself," Ramessa said sarcastically. "What is the next matter to be decided?"

Henhenet gave the message from Paser to Ramessa's scribe, Amten, then took out another roll of papyrus. "Regarding the appointment of a Master of the Secret of All Royal Words—" he began.

"There will be none," Ramessa interrupted.

"But the priests said—" Henhenet persisted.

"The priests say many things," Ramessa stated, "yet I've told them I wish to have no one fill that office. A man in that position has among his other duties the right to banish my subjects without my explicit permission. If someone of my kingdom is to be forever cut off from it, no one but myself will do it." He leaned back in his throne and stared coldly at the group of priests standing to one side of the room. "There will be no Master of the Secret of All Royal Words."

"Where's the artist I sent for?" Ramessa asked. "I would hear his qualifications from his own lips."

Henhenet laid down the scroll he held and looked over the company of petitioners. "Senti!" he called.

A small, dark-faced man with thinning hair worked his way out of the throng and, approaching the thrones, knelt.

"Rise and tell me about your skill," Ramessa directed.

Although he'd already had the artist's background thoroughly investigated, he wanted to learn something of the man himself before he was assigned the task Ramessa had in mind.

Senti looked anxiously at his king, took a deep breath and began, "I'm an artist who excels in my art, a man above the common mass in knowledge. I know the proper attitude for the statue of a man, the way a man poises himself to strike with the spear, the way an archer curves his arm, the tilt of a runner's body."

"What of a woman?" Ramessa interrupted.

Senti glanced at Nefertiry, afraid to hope it might be the queen's features he would carve. He took a breath and said, "Majesty, I know how a woman holds herself, how to catch a fleeting look in her eye, the soft curve of a feminine mouth—"

"Yes, yes, yes," Ramessa again interrupted. "What of your technical knowledge of the materials you may use?"

"Majesty, I even know the secret of making inlays that fire cannot melt or water dissolve. There's no man more famous for this knowledge," Senti declared.

Ramessa's eyes narrowed and he said, "I have in mind to sculpt a statue of my queen. Can you do that?" He glanced at Nefertiry and, seeing she was pleased, again looked at Senti.

Senti was staring at Nefertiry, amazed that he might actually gain such a commission. He quickly gathered his wits and said, "If the son of Ra gives his order, I will set to work to achieve it. Consult, majesty, with the director of the works. He'll advise you of my handiwork in every kind of precious stone, from ivory to ebony, gold, silver, bronze."

"This statue will be granite," Ramessa stated. "It will be life-sized. Can you do that?" Noting Senti's enthusiastic nodding, Ramessa directed, "You will select an appropriate stone without delay. It must have a green tint."

"Thank you, majesty," Senti declared. "I'll do my best work."

"If it shows any hint of inferiority, you'll be removed from the task and another selected," Ramessa said drily.

Senti backed away, bowing and nodding until he disappeared into the crowd. When he knew he could no longer be seen from the thrones, he edged himself out the door and ran home to boast to his family of this marvelous commission.

Ramessa took one more glance at Nefertiry, who was now almost smiling, and knew she was very pleased. He turned to Henhenet for the next case to be decided.

Henhenet approached the throne. "Majesty, the next matter to place before you is a happy one," he said. "Manefera, your twenty-fourth wife, has given birth to a son and has brought the child for you to inspect. She waits in the corridor."

"Admit Manefera," Ramessa directed, a wide smile suddenly on his face.

Nefertiry composed herself and looked curiously toward the door at the young woman who entered the throne room. She already had heard of this wife from Chenmet, who had said the gossip among the servants of the harem was that Manefera had managed to obtain a lover. Nefertiry wondered how Manefera had devised a way to sneak out of the harem. She wondered, too, how Ramessa would react if he knew one of his wives had been unfaithful.

Manefera was a tiny woman, little more than Nefertiry's age, with long black hair and great dark brown eyes. When she approached the throne, she knelt exactly as Senti had knelt. She remained with her forehead pressed against the floor until Ramessa gave her permission to rise. She took the infant from her attendant and approached Ramessa, extending the child in her arms, so Ramessa could inspect the baby and claim it as his own by taking it from her.

Nefertiry looked at the infant, who had blue eyes and vivid red hair. She looked at Manefera's coloring, then very pointedly turned to look at Ramessa's golden-brown
80

hair and hazel eyes. Ramessa, who had been gazing at the child, felt Nefertiry's eyes on him and looked curiously at her. Again Nefertiry looked at the child, at Manefera, then at Ramessa.

In a voice as cool as water from a deep well, quietly but very audibly, Nefertiry remarked, "When did the royal lion grow a red mane?"

Ramessa's eyes widened and his smile faded. He looked at the child more closely. He lifted his gaze to Manefera and for a moment said nothing. Manefera's guilt was on her face. Ramessa sighed. Because Nefertiry had spoken aloud and in public it was impossible for him to ignore what was obviously the truth.

He said quietly, "Manefera, this child is not of my flesh."

Manefera stared at Ramessa, frozen with fear. She couldn't speak for a moment, not even to deny her guilt. Finally, horrified, she whispered, "My lord, would you believe this of me?"

Ramessa extended one of his scepters and lifted the infant's bright forelock with the scepter's crook. "Yes," he said quietly. "I cannot let this pass, but I'm in a merciful mood. Manefera, you will remove this child from my sight and you will gather your belongings and take this child and yourself to Tamera's border, then proceed to any other land you choose."

"I'm banished, then?" Manefera asked softly. She could hardly believe her good fortune, knowing Ramessa might well have had her and her son executed.

"Never return," Ramessa said coldly.

Manefera looked once at Nefertiry, hating her for exposing her crime in public, then left the throne room with her head hanging. But Manefera's flushed cheeks revealed less her shame than her anger at Nefertiry, and she resolved to speak of this within the harem's walls. Though there were many rivalries between Ramessa's wives, they presented a firmly united front to any outside danger, because what threatened one threatened them all. If Nefertiry could, on her third day in the palace, cause Ramessa to banish a wife who had spent many nights with him, she could get rid of any of them. It wouldn't make the other wives happy with Nefertiry, but they hadn't been happy since the marriage ceremony, when Ramessa had made this foreign princess his queen, a position the other wives all coveted.

"So you've eliminated one of them already," Ramessa said softly.

Nefertiry's eyes widened and she whispered anxiously, "Could I remain silent about a wife who betrayed my lord?"

Ramessa turned his head to look at Nefertiry. "No," he murmured. "Any of the others would, but not you."

"I look after your best interests, my lord," she whispered.

Ramessa's eyebrows raised. They both knew she had just made the other wives in the harem her enemies. "Yes, it seems you do," he murmured. He smiled faintly and added, "My other wives will be even less pleased with you if you again occupy my bed tonight."

Nefertiry turned bright green eyes on him. "Will you call me tonight?" she whispered.

Ramessa's smile widened. "I would call you now, but for these matters of the kingdom. Yes, come to me again tonight, Nefertiry," he murmured. "I'm encouraged that I need not make it a royal command this time."

Perfumed from head to toe, Nefertiry entered Ramessa's room wearing a garment of seafoam shaded pleats demurely ordered, and her hair was meticulously arranged. But her eyes held a gleam of mischievous humor, which was new to him. And he was surprised to discover she was in a teasingly playful mood that rapidly transferred itself to him.

After an hour of tousling like two lion cubs at play, her garment was a mass of wrinkles on the floor and her hair
82

a swirl of tangles as she lay looking up at him. "I'm at your disposal, my lord," she panted.

"Gone is every trace of the drooping little princess of last night," he observed. "Will you now struggle with me like this each night into eternity?" he asked.

"I have been every moment in your power," she said softly.

Ramessa smiled. "That's true, yet tonight you seem to like it better."

Nefertiry's eyes widened with false innocence. "My lord, at the moment I realized the royal lion didn't bite, I liked it very much. But if this bold mood of mine displeases you, speak."

Ramessa released his grip on her wrists and sprawled on his back beside her. "But this lion does occasionally bite, though gently," he replied. "Your new mood pleases me well enough. It's a refreshing change from those who pause for my instructions or lie docilely at my side awaiting what I may do."

"You like surprises, then, my lord?" Nefertiry asked in a low, purposely seductive tone.

Ramessa laughed softly. "As long as they're pleasant."

Suddenly Nefertiry sat up and moved to kneel over him, straddling his hips. She looked down into his face. "Now I have you in my power!" she declared.

"Willingly enough," he admitted, "though I strongly suspect what will shortly follow will make us equally bound."

"What if that which follows brings us a child?" she asked softly, knowing this was impossible, because she had taken careful precautions against it.

"A royal son to more honorably replace Manefera's?" he asked.

"Perhaps," Nefertiry replied. "Was Manefera's son to be heir to the throne?"

Ramessa shook his head, "No."

"Whose son will inherit the crown?" she asked lightly.

83

"I haven't decided," he replied, becoming suspicious. He had often verbally sparred with his other wives over this matter, although they had been very careful and timid of how they broached the subject. Nefertiry, he was sure, would be bolder.

"Why not my son?" she asked, holding her breath.

"It may be your son whom I will choose," Ramessa said slowly. "I would decide this matter in the future, when I've had the chance to study each son's qualities, to discern if he would be a proper ruler."

"What a child you and I would make!" Nefertiry whispered. "Think of what a superior son would come of our bodies—handsome, strong, healthy, bold as well as intelligent!"

Ramessa sighed. "That may be so," he conceded, "yet I will make no decision for many years."

Hoping to lighten the conversation, Nefertiry shook her head. "I cannot produce numerous princes and wait long years to see if my pain was worth it," she quipped, smiling widely. "I would have some answer now, before the thing has begun."

Ramessa shook his head slowly and closed his eyes. "Your warm bottom on my hips is exceedingly stimulating to me," he murmured. "Let us get on with this before it becomes painful."

Thinking of the previous night and how intensely aroused Ramessa could become, calculating the depth of his desire, Nefertiry shifted her weight in a way designed not to soothe him. His eyes flew open and, noting their expression, she whispered, "Will I conceive a king tonight, my lord?"

Ramessa's eyes hardened as he stared at her a moment. He grasped her shoulders firmly and moved her off him to sit at his side. Then he sat up, swung his legs from the bed and sat unspeaking for some time. When he finally turned to face her, he said quietly, "You wish to trade sex for a favor I cannot give. I cannot allow that. The favors I grant you must be freely given." Ramessa stood

84

up and turned to look down at her. "Nefertiry, you've made an error," he said softly. "I cannot continue with you tonight."

Ramessa walked quickly to the door that led to the outside corridor; and pushing the door open but a crack, said sharply to the guard posted in the hall, "Bring Mimut here."

Nefertiry stared at Ramessa, stunned. He closed the door and walked slowly back to the bed.

"I'll call you when I want you," he said quietly.

Nefertiry was too shocked to speak immediately. She slid from the bed and stood on shaking legs for a moment. When Ramessa held out her robe, she took it and slowly put it on with tense movements. She looked up at him and said in a small voice, "I was wrong for what I said, my lord. I meant it more as a joke than it sounded." She paused for a moment, trying to control her trembling. "I beg your forgiveness."

Ramessa replied, "I forgive you."

Hope flashed in Nefertiry's eyes and she quickly whispered, "Then I must ask a favor, my lord."

Ramessa looked at her suspiciously. "What favor?"

Nefertiry's face flushed and she dropped her eyes before answering, "I'm in the same painful state you earlier described," she whispered. "I beg you, my lord, send Mimut back to the harem and keep me this night."

The stern look on Ramessa's face faded into compassion. He sighed. "I cannot. I've already called for her. She, like the others, expected you to spend the night with me and has, no doubt, come so hurriedly she now waits outside that door. If I tell her go, she'll wonder why and perhaps guess. If you leave through the other door into your room, she won't know I sent you away. I spare you this humility, Nefertiry," he said. After a pause he added, "You can use this night perhaps more profitably, reflecting on the uselessness of sex as a weapon held against me."

Controlling her tears with an effort, Nefertiry cried, "But I need you!"

Ramessa shook his head and said softly, "Go."

She stared up at him a moment and, realizing finally he wouldn't relent, she turned to silently leave.

Feeling most unhappy at the turn this night had taken, Ramessa watched Nefertiry walk toward the golden door. Her head was held high, but only by a great effort. Her slow and faltering steps betrayed her humiliation. When the door had closed tightly behind her, Ramessa sighed. He knew he would keep Mimut only an hour, perhaps less than an hour, only enough time to remove his own pain. He wondered how he could now manage even that, his emotions were so confused. As he returned to his bed, he felt as if the echo of Nefertiry's soft laughter remained hovering over the bed, a mocking in his ears.

Nefertiry lay rigidly in her bed, frustrated beyond sleep, wanting sleep more than she had ever wanted it, so she wouldn't think of what was happening beyond that door. Humiliated by her stupidity, angry with herself, she recognized that Ramessa had every reason to act as he had. She should have realized she could never exact such a promise from him. He had never told her he'd forsake his harem on her account. Bitterly, she admitted she wished so intensely he'd forget the others that she had deceived herself. She shivered as a fresh wave of pain assailed her.

"You fool!" she hissed into the darkness of her empty room, "those other women will always be available to him." At this realization her heart constricted. "You're jealous," she said contemptuously.

Nefertiry grimly reminded herself that there would be many nights when Ramessa would lie in the next room with another of his wives. A chill went through her at the thought. Again she reminded herself that a woman in love became helplessly foolish—this jealousy was such foolishness—and she must guard herself against the weaknesses of love. She must not mind Mimut's being there with Ramessa. She must not care about what they were doing.

But even while Nefertiry struggled to focus her mind

on this resolution, her ears were listening for the smallest sound that might come from the adjoining room—her closed eyes were seeing Mimut in Ramessa's arms—and Nefertiry's very skin knew what Mimut was experiencing perhaps even at this moment.

For three days Nefertiry stayed in her suite, listlessly being measured for her new wardrobe by the royal seamstresses. For two nights she lay in her bed waiting for Ramessa's call, wishing he would walk through the door. He did not.

On the third night she got out of bed and tiptoed to the golden door separating their rooms to press her ear to it and listen. But, hearing no revealing sounds and hating herself for spying, she soon returned to her bed and lay without sleep until exhaustion closed her eyes.

The following morning Nefertiry wearily arose to dress and stare at her breakfast without appetite. When Chenmet told Nefertiry that Captain Khakamir had asked if she would go riding with him, he recalled that in Khatti a ride in the open air had always distracted her from troubles and improved her mood. She accepted the invitation.

As Nefertiry rode beside Khakamir, she glanced at him from time to time. He wasn't as tall as Ramessa, but he was as trim. His dark brown hair, usually very neatly in place, was being ruffled by the wind. It gave him a reckless look and she found it attractive. In fact, she decided he was a most attractive man in every way. She wondered why he'd invited her to ride with him. He'd given her the impression that he was always occupied with military matters. He had also seemed less than outgoing; it appeared today, as long as she remained silent, he wouldn't speak at all.

"I've been wondering why you asked me to ride with you this morning," Nefertiry finally said. "You're so silent you could as easily have ridden without company."

"I enjoy a quiet ride," Khakamir replied. "If you didn't wish to speak, I didn't want to intrude on your thoughts."

Nefertiry turned to look at him. His dark eyes were on

her and there was something hidden behind those eyes, she perceived, something deliberately withheld from her. "Are you interested in developing a friendship with me?" she asked. "If so, what kind of friendship?"

Khakamir smiled faintly. "I'm interested in being a friend to my king's favorite wife," he replied.

"I'm not familiar with the rules of this palace. I would know if riding alone with you is frowned upon," Nefertiry said staring straight ahead.

Khakamir shook his head, his smile growing. "You're my queen," he said softly, "and untouchable to me. Didn't you know that nobody can touch the king or his queen or royal children without permission?"

"I know," she said. She turned again to look at him. "Do you hope to gain such permission from me?"

"That wasn't my reason for asking you to ride with me," he answered.

"What was your reason?" she asked.

"For the last few days you've been shut in your quarters and I thought you might be hesitant to leave that area if you didn't know that you could," Khakamir said slowly.

There was something in his tone that aroused her suspicion. "That wasn't your only reason," she said. "Speak frankly with me, Khakamir. What are you hiding?"

Khakamir took a deep breath. "I hide nothing. I'm trying to be tactful and spare you pain. I have no wish to discuss with you what may so distress you that you remain in your quarters. I merely thought to distract you from it by this ride."

Nefertiry reined her horse to a stop and turned to look at Khakamir. She was horrified to think the whole palace might know Ramessa had turned her away, but she couldn't imagine how they'd know. "I've been occupied with seamstresses preparing my new wardrobe," she said tartly. "What is it you think distressed me?"

Khakamir's face turned crimson under his tan. "Divine lady, I apologize for what I have to answer," he whispered.

"I accept your advance apology and advise you to
88

answer me fully and now," Nefertiry said coolly. "Your good intentions speak for themselves, so don't think whatever you have to tell me will bring my anger upon you."

Khakamir's eyes lowered for a moment. When he lifted them, they were bright with anger. "It's degrading to me as well as to you that I should bring you gossip originating in the harem."

"What gossip?" Nefertiry's voice was carefully controlled.

"They resent you, that you're first royal wife and queen," Khakamir began. "They're full of jealousy, each hoping the king will choose a son of hers to inherit the crown. But they're always careful to protect each other from outside dangers."

"I know all that. Continue," Nefertiry urged. A heat, which was becoming diffiicult to conceal was growing in her.

"When you exposed Manefera, they declared you their enemy," Khakamir said slowly. He looked at Nefertiry's eyes, which were green ice, and hurried on, "They're saying you aren't able to satisfy him. They're spreading the story that one night with you was enough. Mimut, who was his favorite before you came, has declared that you'll never have his child, because you'll never again be with him."

"My deepest gratitude, not my anger, is your reward for telling me this, Khakamir," Nefertiry said tightly, emerald fires rising from the ice of her eyes. She turned her horse sharply, touched his flank with her riding crop, and raced off in a swirl of dust, leaving Khakamir staring after her for a moment. Then, he turned his horse and followed.

Nefertiry raced into the royal courtyard, reined her horse to such an abrupt halt the horse almost slid on his hindquarters, and leaped from the saddle. Still carrying her riding crop, her eyes blazing with fury, she marched into the palace. She called for Chenmet and told the girl to show her the way to the harem.

"My lady, what will you do?" Chenmet asked, white-faced.

"What I must," Nefertiry answered, not slowing her steps. "If I allow those harlots to laugh openly at me just this once, they'll degrade me at every step of the way," she muttered.

When Nefertiry entered the harem, eyebrows raised and some faces became paler. But most of the women licked their lips in anticipation of piling another humiliation on their queen's head.

Nefertiry's eyes slowly scanned the women and noted that they still sat and lay as they had before she'd entered. "Stand up when your queen enters your presence, you lazy sluts," she commanded. Slowly the women began to rise. Nefertiry walked a little further into the chamber and stopped. "What is this gossip I've heard reaching even onto the palace's outer walls?" she declared. "I will not have it. I will not allow it."

A soft chuckle sounded behind Nefertiry and she whirled around to see who had laughed. Only solemn faces were revealed. "I'm your queen whether it pleases you or not," she spat.

A soft voice behind her murmured, "Maybe not for long."

Again Nefertiry whirled and fixed her fiery eyes on an older woman. "What have you to say in this matter?" she demanded. "The last time the king called you to his bed was long before I arrived." The smile that spread Nefertiry's lips held no humor, as she added viciously, "The dye in your hair and the cosmetics on your face don't change the parts of your body that matter. Taking you would be like entering a house without furniture."

Another woman, with long coppery hair, giggled. Nefertiry marched up to face her. "You will shut your mouth," she instructed. "I saw what you were doing with that slave when I entered the room. You've been so long
90

without Ramessa you have became a woman-lover to ease your pain."

There was a slight movement off to Nefertiry's side and she saw from the corner of her eye that Mimut was approaching. "Come no closer, Mimut," she commanded, "for my temper is not good today and difficult to control." When the copper-haired woman facing Nefertiry snickered, Nefertiry lifted her riding crop and slashed the sneering face, leaving a welt from the corner of her eye to her chin. The woman gasped and stepped away, holding her face.

But Mimut hadn't the wisdom to heed that warning and there followed a turbulent hour in the harem. After Nefertiry left, those who had dared mock her sent their servants in search of healing unguents to place on their bruises, while Mimut lay very still waiting for the physician to come and examine her bleeding scalp.

That afternoon Nehri came to Nefertiry's suite and told her the king wished to speak with her. Nefertiry followed the servant, holding her head high and back stiff; and meeting Arek in the corridor gave him an impulsive greeting.

Encouraged by her greeting, Arek said in sudden hope of gaining her favor, "Divine lady, do not fear this interview."

Nefertiry gave him a coolly appraising look. "I don't," she replied. "I think I have more wit than those creatures in the harem and can answer his majesty better than they."

"Divine lady, since I first looked upon you I've had nothing but respect for your wit," he said, but his glittering eyes were not on her face.

"Why, then, do you stare at my breast?" she snapped.

"I admire all of you," Arek, surprised by her words, blurted. He added, "Your physical beauty is as compelling as your other qualities."

Nefertiry gave him a hard look and replied curtly, "You may admire what you wish—at a greater distance." She brushed past him and continued following Nehri, who was struggling not to smile.

When Nefertiry entered the room where Ramessa set his seal, he was seated by a table waiting for her. She walked halfway across the room, then stopped to stare defiantly at him.

"You stand as if you would have your head reach the arch of the heavens," Ramessa commented. "Are you proud of what you did this morning?"

Nefertiry's eyes fired with renewed anger. "I won't be shamed by the tongues of those harlots!"

"They aren't harlots, but my wives, and you're one of their company," Ramessa said quietly. He stood up.

"I'm not so by choice," Nefertiry snapped.

"Neither did most of them have a choice."

"They haven't the brains to make choices!" Nefertiry declared. She came closer and lowered her voice to ask, "Would you have me endure such stories as are flying around the palace? Did you think I'd endure this degradation without murmur? No, Ramessa. I will not. Before I would silently suffer this humiliation, I would risk your anger." Nefertiry stepped closer and glared up at him. "Cut off my head if you wish. But I would go back and break another vase over that female's skull!"

When she fell silent, Ramessa remarked, "Perhaps you should live in the harem for a time so you could appreciate their problems."

Nefertiry said coldly, "You already have some idea what would happen if you put me in the harem."

Ramessa frowned. "Yes, I can't afford another battle in the harem—much less the wars your killing the daughters of other kings would cause me."

"If I'm such bother, why not send me back to Khatti?" Nefertiry suggested.

"You're such a defiant thing!" Ramessa burst out in exasperation. "I cannot send you back, and you know it, because doing so would be to break the treaty." He looked down at her a moment, at her still lowered eyes, began to smile, and finally sighed. "Nefertiry, you have turned my palace into a place of havoc," he said. "Did you know two of my lesser concubines were so terrified of you, they've run away?"

Nefertiry shook her head. "I didn't know," she replied, sounding as if she didn't care.

"I'll have to send Khakamir after them," he said. "Khakamir has other tasks to do, but he's the only one I can trust to pursue runaway concubines."

She raised her eyes to regard Ramessa coolly and said, "Enough of this talk about concubines. What of me? Will you send me to the harem or cut off my head or continue to ignore me?"

Ramessa seemed to consider these possible solutions to his problem, then said, "I won't send you to the harem or cut off that beautiful head, which causes so much trouble to me." He turned away and looked out the window opening at the garden beyond. "I shall reflect upon the matter during the rest of the day. Tonight you'll come to my room and I'll tell you my decision."

"To your room?" she asked faintly, "Tonight?"

Without turning Ramessa said over his shoulder, "Yes. To my room. Tonight."

Nefertiry stared at his back for a moment, still incredulous, but with a joy rising in her she couldn't completely keep from her voice when she answered, "Yes, my lord. Your room. Tonight."

When Nefertiry hesitantly walked through the golden doorway, expecting to see Ramessa naked and waiting in his bed, she found him instead wearing a robe and standing at the far end of his chamber, his back to her, looking out the window opening. Hearing Chenmet close the door behind her, and confused at Ramessa's appearance, Nefertiry stood silently waiting for him to acknowledge her presence. After some time had passed, she wondered if he were so deep in thought he hadn't heard her come in. She knew she was supposed to wait for him to speak, but was so filled with tension, she took a few steps closer. Ramessa still didn't turn or speak. Finally Nefertiry walked across the room to stand directly behind him.

"My lord, I have come as you ordered," she said faintly.

"I know," Ramessa replied. "Your silent presence fills the room."

"I didn't think you were aware of me," she whispered.

Ramessa turned and looked down at her. "I'm aware of you every moment," he said tightly. "I was aware of each turn you made in your bed these last few nights. I'm aware, I suspect, of your every breath." He shook his head and added passionately, "Why must your first words be that you've obeyed my order in coming here?" Nefertiry stared at him in amazement. He grasped her shoulders tightly in his hands and added, "Why must each time we're together be like one more charge in a battle?"

"My lord, I dared not enter without your permission," she whispered unsteadily. "I begged every divine being I'd ever heard of to let you come to me if you wouldn't allow me to enter here. I lie awake each night until exhaustion closed my eyes only to dream of you. I told you that last time I was here I was sorry. My lord, who else after that could I tell but the gods? I say it again—I'm sorry for what I said. I didn't mean it as it sounded. Didn't you know how I wanted you? Don't you know you need only touch me and I couldn't refuse you for any hidden purpose? I couldn't use sex as a weapon for that reason!"

Ramessa looked down at Nefertiry for a moment a bit dazed by this confession. Slowly he released her shoulders and slid his arms around her waist to hold her close. "You're like a curse on my house, Nefertiry," he whispered. "You cause me pain as no other; you disorder my palace and my mind as well. I call you to me

94

to scold you and end holding you close and wanting only to be closer."

Nefertiry shivered at these words and Ramessa saw that her eyes were closed; crystal droplets clung to her lashes. "No other women have been here these last nights," he whispered. "I didn't want Mimut after you'd left. I think it was because I sent her away that she spread those stories—from revenge, from knowing I wanted you."

Nefertiry's eyes opened to stare up at Ramessa. "You sent her away?" she whispered. "If I had known, I would have endured any gossip."

"Would you have me return you to Khatti?" Ramessa asked softly.

"I have no place there," Nefertiry murmured. "Tamera is my home."

Ramessa took her hand. "Then, what you do this night with me won't be because I've ordered your coming here?" he asked quietly.

Nefertiry looked up at him and her smile was as guileless as a child's. "No," she replied. "Neither will it be—as you said—like another charge in a battle."

Slowly, he kissed her waiting lips.

6

Nefertiry, approaching the temple, wondered if the divine beings of Tamera would hear the prayer of its illegitimate daughter. As she pulled open the heavy door and a cloud of incense-perfumed air surrounded her, the doubts she had felt were dissipated. The rich scent was like a warmly welcoming hand.

Slowly she walked through the rooms leading toward the inner sanctuary, where only the distant tinkle of a single bell and the soft chanting of priestesses at prayer could be heard.

She knew she couldn't enter the inner sanctuary, but she wanted to be as near to it as possible, so she stepped into the chamber just preceding it. She stood for a time looking at the sanctuary door, feeling its secret power reach out to reassure her. A smile was on her lips as she turned toward the chapel where she would make her devotions.

Although Nefertiry's religious habits had been casual in Khatti, she felt differently in Aset's temple than she had in any temple in Khatti. She wondered if this was because her blood was Tameran and the gods and goddesses welcomed their wandering daughter. She had brought a small bouquet of lotuses; after she laid them on the offering table, she prostrated herself on the floor before the figure of Aset as she had learned was the custom in Tamera. When she lifted her head, a deep feeling of peace entered her being. She remained kneeling back on her heels, looking up at the face of the goddess of women and magic-doing, listening for a time to the whispering of the air currents and the soft hissing of the burning lamps.

Finally, a shaft of sunlight freed by the moving clouds slipped through one of the window slits high above and fell on her in a golden spray. Warmed and encouraged by it, deeming it her permission, she prayed, "Come to my aid, Aset, beloved of Asar and mistress of magic, come to me and give me counsel. For on my shoulders is a mighty task, divine lady. I think I cannot manage it without your help; because I have enemies here, I find. Come to me and give me skill in your secrets, which excel all others. I have heard that she who masters your magic becomes a queen."

"Is it magical power you seek from Aset?"

Nefertiry turned at the sound of the soft voice behind her. Her eyes widened in wonder. Did Aset answer in person? If not, who was this creature coming from the sanctuary's depths? Nefertiry turned to glance warily at the statue. It remained immobile stone. She turned again to look at the white-robed woman standing in the doorway, then realized the silvery haze surrounding her were clouds of smoke from newly lit incense. The woman's pale golden face was human, yet Nefertiry wondered if those eyes were human, for they glowed through the shadows like blue fires. When the woman smiled and stepped off the sanctuary's threshhold, Nefertiry decided the woman was human, her eyes merely having caught the light strangely.

"I'm Seshena, high priestess of Aset," the woman said in a soft but very clear voice. She came closer. "You're Nefertiry, my queen."

Nefertiry realized Seshena didn't bow, a thing required even from high priests and priestesses. But Nefertiry also felt that from Seshena a bow would be somehow not proper.

"Why do you frown, Nefertiry?" Seshena asked quietly. "You've obtained all you wanted."

Nefertiry looked up at Seshena, confused, yet hesitant to question the priestess in any way.

Seshena smiled in understanding. "Come, Nefertiry, let us sit on one of the benches, which will surely be more comfortable than kneeling on the stone floor," she invited.

Nefertiry accepted the hand Seshena extended, and stood up to follow the priestess.

When they were seated Seshena said, "That cool and haughty mask you wear doesn't demonstrate to me that you are unfeeling, but that you feel too much."

Nefertiry stared into the depths of those dark blue eyes, wondering at how far into her being they penetrated. "You're very clever," she said nervously.

"You've forgotten I'm high priestess," Seshena said softly. "Or perhaps you don't know what that truly means." When Nefertiry said nothing, Seshena smiled. "You don't know that I've undergone training for this since I was a small child and that I've passed the test in the pyramid and obtained Aset's wings? My mind travels at my direction. It isn't cleverness that gives me understanding of you, Nefertiry. I know your past, the whole of it. I have seen it."

Nefertiry stared at Seshena, afraid to breathe or speak or now even to think a revealing thought.

Seshena smiled again. "Be not disturbed, royal lady," she said quickly. "I knew even before you crossed Tamera's border that you were Seti's child. I believe

I'm Aset's answer to the difficult task that's been set before you. Through me you'll receive Aset's help."

"Have you spoken to anyone of my past?" Nefertiry asked softly, still unable to believe what Seshena knew, but unable to deny it.

Seshena shook her head once. "Nor will I," she replied.

"What do you want of me?" Nefertiry asked suspiciously.

"Nothing," Seshena answered.

"When someone asks nothing for so great a favor, I know they want my gratitude at a cost they have yet to decide."

Seshena sighed. "Are you so used to corrupt priests you cannot trust Aset's priestess? Truly, royal lady, I am for you and for the strength of Tamera's throne. I will keep silent for Tamera's sake."

"You have the knowledge and the power to do magic and would yet follow my commands?" Nefertiry asked, hardly able to believe her good fortune.

"That I'm a magic worker means I follow Aset's commands and Ptah's laws," Seshena replied. "If what you ask of me is in accordance with these, I'll help you."

Nefertiry was silent. She considered the plan she'd made for her possible future son and felt guilty that Seshena might even sense this secret.

As if in answer, Seshena laid her hand on Nefertiry's and said, "It isn't right that a woman knowingly produce her brother's child. It isn't safe for the child."

"You would have another sire my child?" Nefertiry asked.

"Your marriage contract holds no specific promise of fidelity. If you are to have a child, I recommend for the child's well-being that Ramessa not father him. If the child were to become Tamera's next king—and I cannot decide that—he would rightfully be king by your own royal blood. You should, of course, choose his father
100

with great care. The man must be from a noble family."

"And who among the nobles would be suitable?" Nefertiry whispered.

"I'm familiar with the noble families and their circumstances, which you are not. If you wish, I'll consider their possibilities tonight and come to the palace tomorrow to advise you as to which of those men would be best for your purpose."

Nefertiry looked down at the long, slender fingers holding hers. "I'm ashamed to ask such a thing."

"You have affection for Ramessa and don't want to betray him," Seshena observed. "Many have been the kings and queens of Tamera, who married for some legal purpose though they were close of kin, yet their sons were strong, healthy, and intelligent rulers. That was because the son who inherited the crown was either the king or the queen's child, but not theirs together. If it was possible to proclaim your relation in blood to Ramessa, it would be expected for you to have lovers, and not a word would be spoken against any child you produced," Seshena explained. "Remember, too, Ramessa has many wives. There will come times you'll ache for love and he'll be with someone else. I speak, Nefertiry, of legality and practicality. The decision is yours."

"You speak plainly, priestess," Nefertiry said bitterly.

Seshena released Nefertiry's hand and stood up to leave. "When one sees into the minds of others at will, it becomes a foolish conceit to lie."

"Wait!" Nefertiry cried leaping to her feet.

Seshena turned to smile at her and said, "When I bring you the names of those suitable to be your lover you can ask me all the questions you wish for I know curiosity about me burns you. Meanwhile, I think you would be wise to consider the possible paths your life can follow."

Still numb from this strange conversation, Nefertiry nodded.

Seshena turned and left the chamber as soundlessly as she'd entered it. The very air that had surrounded the priestess seemed to vibrate and Nefertiry was left wondering at her.

7

"Majesty, Lord Rasuah, First Royal Envoy, requests permission to enter and speak," the servant announced.

"Admit him <u>after</u> a discreet moment has passed," Ramessa replied, releasing Nefertiry. The servant bowed and slipped out of the door. Ramessa stood up and smiled down at Nefertiry. "Would you care to stay? Rasuah is a friend."

"What is the first royal envoy's function?" Nefertiry asked, smoothing the folds of her robe. She was sorry to be interrupted when Ramessa was being impulsively affectionate. It was something he never did with his other wives and, so, set her above them.

"He's my preeminent envoy and my right hand," Ramessa replied. "His position is similar to that of an ambassador, only with more power. Actually, he has more power than the governors of my provinces. He goes wherever I send him, with the authority to make many decisions a governor cannot."

"Does he have an army to enforce his decisions?" Nefertiry asked.

"He has my army," Ramessa answered. Noticing Nefertiry's surprised expression, Ramessa added, "Rasuah is my friend. I trust him absolutely."

As Rasuah stepped over the threshhold, Nefertiry inspected him curiously. His plain blue tunic was still covered with dust from his travels and his thick black hair had a fine coating of more white dust.

Ramessa didn't wait for Rasuah to approach. He walked quickly toward Rasuah and greeted him as if they were brothers, grasping his broad shoulders in welcoming hands. Rasuah was half a head taller than Ramessa; when Ramessa led Rasuah farther into the room, Nefertiry noticed Rasuah's walk was as light and silent as Botar's. She sensed that he had an almost animal-like awareness of his physical self, and his strong features held a certain sensuality that fascinated her.

As Ramessa presented Rasuah to Nefertiry, Rasuah's tawny eyes calmly regarded her with an expression of impersonal admiration. Nefertiry wondered petulantly if Rasuah had royal blood; the very way he held his head was more fitting to a king than an envoy.

"Our new queen is most beautiful. I wish her happiness and health," Rasuah said quietly.

Nefertiry nodded, but didn't reply. She wondered if this lord's name would be one of those on Seshena's list.

"I can see you've come directly to me," Ramessa said, motioning a servant to pour wine for them. "Sit down, Rasuah."

"I'm very dusty from my journey," Rasuah warned.

"Sit down anyway," Ramessa urged and sat on the couch where Nefertiry reclined. When Rasuah had seated himself in a chair facing them, Ramessa asked, "You met no thieves on the road?"

Rasuah smiled faintly. "I always meet some," he replied in a soft tone. His hand touched the sword he wore at his hip and he added, "They did me no damage."
104

Ramessa turned to Nefertiry. "Lord Rasuah travels many dangerous and lonely roads. Later, we'll hear more about his adventures on this trip. But what I wish to know immediately is what you learned of the mines at Akiti."

Rasuah accepted a goblet from the servant and smiled as he lifted it for persmission to drink. "My throat is so filled with dust I can hardly speak," he said. At Ramessa's nod, Rasuah took several swallows of wine. Then, he settled back in the chair and said, "The mines still contain rich gold deposits and surely are worth reopening, but there's structural damage that must be repaired before they'll be safe to work. Also, the entrances to the passages are choked with sand drifts and weeds." Rasuah took another sip of wine and continued, "The greatest problem is with the cisterns, which are mostly unusable. They must be repaired before anything else can be done or there will be no water for the workers. Even those who would be sent to work on the cisterns would have to have their water hauled by convoy for long distances."

Ramessa sipped his wine and considered the problem for a moment. "It will have to be done," he said slowly. "Describe the cistern damage to Hapu so he can plan what must be done."

"I'll speak to him tomorrow," Rashauh promised. He frowned, took a swallow of wine and said, "I have some unhappy news for you."

"What news."

"It would appear the Hyskos are preparing more trouble for you," Rasuah said. "Tarmo's spies were seen in Kharu and I was told by someone I trust that Zahi's army seems to be rebuilding."

Ramessa was silent a moment before he said tightly, "The accursed Hyskos can never be quiet. Their troops are always on the move. Since the beginning of time, it seems, they've fought us, and they always try to catch us by surprise, never issuing a challenge like honorable men, but sneaking up on our outposts and distant provinces in the night's darkness."

Nefertiry recalled Hattusil's description of the attack on her mother's family. She remembered how they had been murdered and the Hyskos had carried away her mother from Tamera. She turned to Ramessa. "My lord, can't these evil ones be stopped?" she asked. Ramessa looked at her, surprised by the intensity of her tone, as she added, "I've heard stories of how they murder whole families and carry off slaves."

"I'll stop them," Ramessa said, lifting his head a little higher. "There's a certain fortress on Zahi's border, through which Tarmo will no doubt funnel his troops. If that fortress is in Tameran hands, I suspect he'll be less warlike."

"If you take Zurim, you'll first have to fight half his army, because Zurim is where they're gathering," Rasuah warned.

"Excellent!" Ramessa exclaimed, "I will level Zurim and decimate our tormentors in one stroke."

Rasuah stood up. "To do so would make the area around the mines a safer place to send workers." He was silent for a moment, then said, "If you have nothing more to discuss immediately, I'd like to go home and get my house in order."

"Yes, you may go," Ramessa said quickly. "You've been away for months, and I'm sure your servants have grown less energetic in your absence."

Rasuah smiled and nodded. He turned to Nefertiry. "You'll forgive my swift departure, divine lady?" he apologized.

"You're forgiven," Nefertiry replied. "Perhaps, after you've attended to your personal affairs, you'll return to the palace for a longer interview."

Ramessa laughed softly and said, "You'll find Rasuah strolling in and out of the palace almost as casually as if it were his home." He took Rasuah's arm, intending to lead him to the door.

"I'll walk through the garden," Rasuah said. "It's a

shorter distance to the courtyard and certainly would be a welcome sight after all the dusty roads I've traveled."

Ramessa smiled and stepped away from his friend. "Enjoy the garden," he said, "If you can extricate yourself from whichever ladies have been awaiting your return, come back tonight and have the evening meal with us."

Shaking his head, Rasuah said, "I'd prefer returning tomorrow morning."

"Tomorrow then," Ramessa agreed and walked Rasuah toward the door into the garden. "There's no lady you might wish to impress by bringing her to the palace tonight?" he asked. Rasuah shook his head. "You would pass the whole evening in her company impressing her with yourself?" Ramessa persisted. He was curious about the lady he assumed was so holding Rasuah's attention. Rasuah merely nodded, stepped into the garden and, saying nothing more about his personal plans, left Ramessa standing in the doorway, still curious.

Once out of Ramessa's sight, Rasuah turned off the path. Finding a quiet place among the shrubbery, he sank to the grass under a tree and sighed. The soft chatter of a group of girls drifted from the other side of the garden, and he lay back in the grass to look up through the leafy branches at the sky.

Although Rasuah wanted to think of nothing at all, Ramessa's curiosity about his personal life had reminded him that, at this particular moment, he had no woman, and no inclination to search for one. His last venture into love had been solely physical, and ended with his sudden journey to Akiti. At that point, he'd been glad to go. He had begun to wonder about his recent attitude toward women. He found he was less willing to expend any effort to find female companions. It wasn't that his body didn't crave a woman, but that he didn't seem to find any of the women he met interesting enough to bother pursuing them. He closed his eyes. He knew he simply was tired of women who wanted to use him as a male—of

107

women who wanted to be seen on the arm of the first Royal Envoy—of women who tried to manipulate him until he felt as if he negotiated a bargain in the marketplace. He sighed to think of how Ramessa had assumed he'd spend his evening, when actually all he wanted was to go home and bathe, then walk in his own garden. He wanted to eat his evening meal alone and negotiate nothing, not even lovemaking.

Rasuah opened his eyes, stretched and yawned, then slowly got to his feet. More than anything, he needed to wash the grit from his skin and hair and have Zehzee massage his aching body with soothing oils. He started walking toward the entrance to the courtyard.

When Rasuah reached the courtyard, he paused. A woman had entered the courtyard and was hurrying across the path.

Although the woman walked so rapidly she was almost running, her movements had the gliding grace of a dancer. Her hair fell loose to her waist and its black lengths shifted with her steps, gleaming in the sun like polished onyx. As she came toward the garden's entrance, Rasuah's unswerving attention was on her.

He stepped farther back into the garden, all thoughts of a solitary evening having slipped from his mind as he observed the curves of the woman's slender figure, revealed by the movements of her robe as she walked. After Nefertiry's richly embroidered garments, the simple white pleated shift this woman wore was as refreshing as a breeze from the sea. By the time she had entered the garden, he had resolved to make her acquaintance. He stepped onto the path and waited for her.

Surprised to find a man standing solidly in her way, Seshena stopped and looked up at his face. The golden eyes meeting hers sent a peculiar shock flashing along her nerves and for a moment she said nothing. She had the odd feeling she was in the presence of an irresistible force, of dormant power that could instantly be stirred. She
108

realized she should speak, but she found herself staring wordlessly up at him.

As Rasuah looked down into the golden oval of the face uplifted to his, his mind was emptied of all the things he might ordinarily have said to charm a woman. He simply asked, "Who are you?"

"My name is Seshena," she whispered. "Who are you?"

"Rasuah," he replied. "Why haven't I seen you here before?"

Seshena stared at Rasuah, wondering at this strange question. But she found herself answering, "I'm high priestess of Aset's temple and rarely have business in the palace." She tilted her head slightly to one side and asked, "Are you a guard, that a visitor's comings and goings concern you?"

"No. I'm the king's first envoy," he said quickly as if it were unimportant. "Let us sit down for a moment and talk." Without waiting for her answer, he took her hand firmly in his and led her to a bench away from the path.

"What do you wish to talk about?" Seshena asked as she sat down.

Rasuah sat beside her, "You're a priestess?"

"The high priestess of Aset," Seshena replied.

"Then, we'll speak of Aset's temple and her high priestess to begin with."

"Why?" Seshena whispered.

"Because I know very little about high priestesses," Rasuah answered. She seemed so open and guileless, he was beginning to feel more at ease with her and was rapidly regaining his composure. He moved a little closer and his eyes gleamed as he added, "I'm always interested to learn something new."

"You're flirting with me," Seshena concluded.

"You seem not displeased by my manner," Rasuah observed and, having no inclination to move away, didn't. "But what makes you think my flirting with you is a trifling matter?"

Seshena's eyes widened at his audacity, but suddenly realizing she thought him anything but trifling, she looked down at her lap.

Slowly, almost hesitantly, Rasuah said, "I think no man could look into your eyes and merely flirt with you."

Seshena watched his sun-bronzed hand slowly reach out, then cover hers. She raised her eyes to meet his again. His wasn't an easy face to read nor were the thoughts that moved behind his eyes readily discovered. She felt there was a great deal beneath his surface, and she was tempted to let her mind enter his thoughts, but she quickly rejected the idea. The powers she possessed were not to be used to satisfy personal curiosity, she reminded herself. Again she looked down at her lap, at the strong fingers covering her own.

"What are you thinking?" Rasuah inquired, fascinated by her changing expressions.

Seshena's eyes focused on Rasuah as she realized what he'd asked. Unwilling to describe such intimate thoughts, she impulsively said, "Have you ever seen the workers in gold at their art?" Confused by this question, Rasuah frowned slightly and nodded. "Then, you've seen when the molten gold lies freshly poured in the forms?" Mystified, Rasuah nodded again. Seshena said in a low tone, "It's the color of your eyes, this liquid gold. That's part of what I was thinking. The rest of my thoughts I cannot tell you now."

Rasuah stared at her, not knowing what to say. Her gaze was level and steady, as if she were beyond all deceit. "Is that in my favor?" he asked. "Have you decided anything at all in my favor?"

Seshena shook her head. "I know nothing about you. How could I make any decisions?"

"It's my wish that you learn more about me," Rasuah said softly. "I want to learn about you." His eyes left her face and traveled slowly from her throat to the swell of her breasts, where they briefly lingered, then shifted to the smooth curve of her hips, unhurriedly moving along the line of her legs. When his eyes again lifted to her face, they were shot with golden sparks.

"It would appear you wish to know a great deal about me," she noted drily.

Undisturbed, Rasuah smiled and answered, "Yes."

At an age when other young women had been learning how to conduct such conversations with grace, Seshena had been studying in the temple; now, she didn't know what to say.

Rasuah touched the coil of hair that lay on her shoulder and asked, "Is your errand in the palace very urgent?"

Reminded of her mission, Seshena made a move to stand up; but Rasuah's firm hands on her shoulders stopped her. "I have business with the queen," she said.

"After your business with the queen, will you stop at my house for even a short time?" Rasuah asked. "You will pass it on your way to the temple and the afternoon is very hot. Some cooling wine will refresh you."

"I don't know," Seshena said quickly.

"Perhaps I may visit your house," he suggested. When she remained silent, he persisted, "Would you like to accompany me to the palace to have the evening meal with the king and queen?"

Seshena felt a stab of alarm at this suggestion. Rasuah's name had been one of those she'd intended to give Nefertiry. But during these last moments, she'd decided to delete him from that list. "Do you visit the palace often?" she asked cautiously.

"I'm very close to the king," he replied. "I've just declined his invitation for tonight. But if you will come with me, I'll send him a message that I've changed my mind."

Seshena hastily shook her head. She preferred that Rasuah be in Nefertiry's sight as seldom as possible.

Rasuah's eyes narrowed. "Do you fear sitting with the king?"

"No." Seshena looked down at her lap.

"Do you dislike the queen?" Rasuah questioned, con-

111

fused by Seshena's declining an invitation any other woman would envy.

"No," she answered quickly. His fingers under her chin tilted her face so she must look up at him.

"Why do you want to avoid accompanying me to the palace? Do you prefer not to be seen with me at all?" He suddenly had a sinking feeling and said slowly, "Perhaps I haven't understood your hesitance. Are you married?"

"I'm not married," she replied. Having those golden eyes so intently fixed on her, she didn't know what more to say. Finally she whispered, "I'll stop by your house after I've left the palace. Where is it?"

Rasuah released her chin, but continued studying her expression. "It's the house standing alone, the large one with gold-colored walls," he replied. He was silent a moment, then said, "You seem reasonably interested in me, but you hesitate for some reason I don't understand. Perhaps you'll explain later."

"Are you very persistent?" she asked.

"The degree of my persistence depends upon the importance of my goal. I must confess I'm very curious about why you wish to avoid being with me at the king's table, but I don't want to anger you with my questions. I can be more persistent regarding other matters."

Seshena's eyebrows lifted. "We will see about that," she commented, then turned to follow the path to the palace.

Rasuah stood a moment longer, inhaling Seshena's perfume, which lingered in the air, until he reminded himself he'd be wise to go home and bathe before Seshena was at his gates.

As Nefertiry entered the room where Seshena was waiting, she seemed oddly distracted. But by the time preliminary greetings had been exchanged, Nefertiry's concentration was sharply focused on Seshena.

"I don't understand how you knew about my background," Nefertiry said. "Can you explain this?"

112

"To do so means to explain about temple training," Seshena replied. "If you wish to learn something of this, I'll try to simplify it and make it brief." Nefertiry nodded, so Seshena continued, "At a very early age I revealed an inclination toward using my mind in ways most people never do, and my parents took me to the temple to be examined by the priestesses. I was enrolled as a novice in Aset's temple. Under the temple training I learned how to develop my mind to so focus my will that I could enter the minds of others to discern the truth and enable me to help them. I learned how to set aside my own interfering thoughts and open my mind to sometimes foretell future events. But, as it turned out for me, I was better at probing the memories of Time. I can concentrate my thoughts to the point where they become real things, forces though intangible, and set them loose to accomplish things that cannot otherwise be accomplished. I was meditating one night and saw, with the eyes of my spirit, Hattusil as he told you of your mother and your true heritage. I heard your conversation with him."

"Are no private conversations closed to you?" Nefertiry asked. "Can you do these things whenever you wish, know everything others think and feel?"

"I can, but I won't," Seshena answered softly. "Part of the training I received engraved in my being the strict rules of the necessary ethics regarding what I do and why I do it. I'm not allowed to read another's thoughts at my whim."

"Yet, you've just said you heard and watched my conversation with Hattusil without your deciding to direct your mind to me," Nefertiry said cautiously.

"I knew nothing about you at the time," Seshena said. "I was led to you by a decision of the divine beings, not my own will. It was necessary I become aware of you so I could later assist you."

Nefertiry shook her head in wonder. "How difficult it must be for you to sort out all the decisions you have to make," she remarked.

Seshena smiled. "It isn't so difficult," she advised. "Either my purpose is a temple matter or the gods themselves decide. In my ordinary dealings and personal life, I behave as everyone else."

Nefertiry's eyebrows lifted. "I can't imagine your having ordinary dealings. How do you avoid using these special abilities in your personal life?"

"My training forbids it," Seshena answered. "In my personal affairs, I'm merely a trifle more perceptive than most people, but not abnormally so."

Nefertiry was silent for a time, trying to understand how Seshena could forego using so tremendous an advantage in her daily life. Finally, unable to imagine anyone having such self-control, she shook her head and turned her thoughts to other matters. "I don't know if that list you promised is necessary."

"You're torn by your emotions and loyalties," Seshena observed. "If you've decided not to bear a child, the matter is ended."

"I've wondered if Seti's blood actually carries any weakness," Nefertiry admitted. "There seems to be no problem with either my health or the king's."

Seshena sighed. "There are several children of other wives who have problems which may or may not have been inherited from the king. Other children died as infants. Such things happened to King Seti's children— your and Ramessa's half-brothers and sisters. There's no way we can know the answer, Nefertiry. Even if it could be proved that Seti's blood had nothing to do with these problems, you can't be sure your blood combined—if you wish to have a child with Ramessa—would be fortunate."

Nefertiry sighed in resignation. "If I bear a son, it mustn't be Ramessa's child."

"It would be wrong for you to knowingly do otherwise. It would be unfair to the child," Seshena warned.

"Which are the noblemen you recommend?" Nefertiry whispered.

Seshena recited the names of a dozen men, who were

114

unmarried, healthy, intelligent, and reasonably attractive, and added, "All these noblemen have easy access to the palace."

Nefertiry stared across the room into space, wondering why Rasuah's name was absent from the list. Gloomily, she decided he was omitted for a good reason; and she wasn't sure she even wanted to know the reason. "There's no one else?"

"Oh yes, I almost forgot!" Seshena exclaimed. "You see, it is possible for a priestess to be a normal person and even to forget things."

"Whom did you forget?" she asked without enthusiasm.

"Captain Khakamir," Seshena replied.

"Khakamir's very close to the king," Nefertiry noted.

"Because Ramessa trusts Khakamir, Khakamir will be that much more accessible to you," Seshena reasoned. "And since you already know him it will be easier to develop a friendship with him, if he were your choice," she added.

Nefertiry thought of Khakamir riding beside her, his hair blowing in the wind, his warm and sympathetic manner when he told her about the harem gossip. She stood up abruptly and said, "Thank you, Seshena, for your trouble, I'll consider these possibilities carefully."

Seshena got to her feet. "You have no further questions?"

Nefertiry shook her head. "I already have too many things to think about," she looked at Seshena and asked quietly, "You'll come again if I need you?"

"I promised I would," Shensha answered. "One other thing you'll quickly learn about me is that I never break promises or lie."

Nefertiry smiled faintly in return. "Considering what you've told me about the other rules you follow, I do believe that," she said.

Rasuah had entered his house and barely finished greeting his happy servants when he'd begun to give them

115

orders. "Zehzee, get the pomegranate wine that's stored in the cellar and put it deep in the well so it cools as quickly as possible!" Rasuah directed, sending Zehzee running from the room, his robe flapping around his legs. "Djanah, tell the cook to prepare a special meal for tonight—tell her to find a plump bird," Djanah, herself rather plump, hurried panting to the kitchen. "Taka, tell the housekeeper to pass a broom over these floors; I feel sand under my feet!" Rasuah snapped, and Taka rushed down a corridor, nodding to acknowledge Rasuah's shouted order to make sure the lamps had fresh, perfumed oil. When Zehzee returned from the well, Rasuah was in his bedchamber tearing off his soiled tunic and muttering to himself. As soon as Zehzee entered the room, Rasuah sent him rushing to prepare a bath and lay out fresh garments.

Rasuah spent little time bathing, fearing Seshena's momentary arrival. While Zehzee dressed him, he plagued the servant with continuous urgings to hurry—to attend to every detail assuring perfection. When Rasuah was finally clothed in a clean white tunic and his hair was smoothed, he took a breath, muttered with impatience about Seshena's delay and threw himself into a chair to stare out the window opening at the garden.

"Zehzee!" he called, leaping up from his chair to face the anxious servant. "Tell the guards at the gate to admit Seshena, the high priestess of Aset's temple when she arrives. Go, go! Tell them now so they don't turn her away!"

Zehzee ran from the house and down the long sun-drenched path to the gates, perspiring heavily and wondering at this high priestess who turned the house into such turmoil with only her promised visit.

At the thought of seeing Rasuah again, Seshena felt inexplicably nervous. She dawdled in the royal garden for some time before she left the grounds. By the time she began walking slowly through the dusty streets, the sun

116

was at the halfway point in its slide to the earth, and the heat and lack of a breeze added to her discomfort.

Seshena, seeing the distant walls she recognized from Rasuah's description, slowed her steps even more. She was surprised at the extent of the property the walls marked. Tilting her head to look beyond the wall's height, she noted the size of the house's roof at the center of the enclosure, and she began to understand just how elite a position the king's first envoy was. Her nervousness increased to almost a state of panic as she approached the gates, which were hammered copper richly trimmed with gold. Seshena recognized the uniforms of the two sentries as those of palace guards, and she wondered if the golden-eyed man in the plain, soiled tunic had been an impostor. She was tempted to turn away. But her promise to visit this house—whoever lived in it—held her. She stood before the gates for so long a time, one of the guards finally approached her.

"Are you ill, lady?" he asked courteously. Startled by his voice, Seshena stared wordlessly at him. "It's very hot in the sun," he noted.

Her promise demanded fulfillment, so, in a soft, but steady voice, she asked, "Is this Lord Rasuah's house?"

"Yes, lady," the guard answered.

"The Lord Rasuah expects me," she announced. "I'm the high priestess, Seshena."

"You're welcome," the sentry said and, stepping back, directed the other guard to open the gates. Then he requested that Seshena follow him.

Seshena looked at the gates opening before her, feeling oddly as if this one move marked an irrevocable change in her life. She took a deep breath and followed the guard. Inside the walls, she stopped again. A large, stone-paved area turned to the right, where she could see in the distance storage bins and stables. To the left of the house Seshena could see a private chapel and behind that the glimmer of a lotus pool and the trees marking an

117

extensive garden. Finally she became aware of the fact that the guard had paused to wait for her.

"If I'd known we had so far to walk from the gates to the house, I might have declined this invitation. Proceed," she directed, and continued following him toward the house, which she noted was constructed of large limestone blocks, not the more common mud bricks. Again, she questioned the identity of the man in the soiled blue tunic. She wondered if he had been a gardener or a worker in the stable, because his appearance could well have made him such, and had meant to play a joke on her. But it was too late to turn back.

The guard led Seshena along a corridor lined with white alabaster, and she began preparing apologies for the genuine Lord Rasuah. She followed the guard into a spacious sitting room, where a man wearing a short white tunic bordered with gold stood looking through a window at the lush garden. At her entrance, he turned, and she faced the golden-eyed man she'd met on the palace grounds.

Rasuah smiled and approached Seshena, saying, "I had begun to fear you'd changed your mind."

"I promised I'd come," she answered in a faint voice.

"I'm glad you did." Noticing the pallor of her skin and the moisture on her forehead, he quickly said, "Please sit down, Seshena. I've been thoughtless. I should have sent a litter for you. It's some distance from the palace and Ra's heat is fierce today."

Seshena gathered her confused thoughts, adjusted them and sat on the couch Rasuah had indicated.

As a plump woman with bright, curious eyes entered the room, Rasuah said, "Djanah, bring us something cool to drink." Rasuah sat beside Seshena, looking steadily at her, saying nothing, until Djanah returned with a covered jar and two goblets.

Djanah poured crimson liquid into the goblets, then stood back, looking at Seshena with curiosity.

118

"I'll call you if we need something more, Djanah," he said firmly. The servant left on silent, bare feet, and Rasuah handed Seshena a goblet. "Forgive Djanah's staring. She's been with my family a long time and appointed herself my guardian when my father died," he explained. "She yet watches over me."

"How long ago was that?" she asked.

"I was twelve," he answered with a grin. Seshena smiled, and Rasuah added, "I'm glad you can relax enough with me to smile. I really am not dangerous."

"I smile at Djanah's concern for you as if you're yet twelve," she declared. In a lower tone she added, "But I don't think you're entirely harmless."

Rasuah's voice had a touch of humor in it as he remarked, "I think the perfume you wear holds more danger than anything I could devise." He held up his goblet, inviting her to taste the drink.

Expecting wine, Seshena was surprised when she put her lips to the metal goblet's cool surface and tasted. Wine was there, but so was pomegranate juice and spices or herbs she couldn't identify. It was so refreshing she drank half the contents without stopping and, noting Rasuah's look of approval, felt not at all disconcerted when he lifted the jar and poured more of the mixture into her cup.

"I wouldn't think you discourteous if you wished to put your feet up and recline," Rasuah said. "You were so pale when you came in I was afraid the sun had made you ill."

"Forgive me for saying this, my lord, but I saw the richness of your house, recalled your appearance in the king's garden, and had begun to suspect a joke had been played on me," she confessed.

Rasuah thought about it and laughed softly. "I had just returned from a long journey and had gone immediately to give my report to the king. I can understand your doubting my identity; I looked more like a beggar."

119

Seshena smiled with him for a moment. Then, wondering again at his purpose, she asked, "Why did you wish to speak with me, my lord?"

Rasuah's smile faded. "Address me as Rasuah not 'my lord.' " He stood up and walked away a few paces. "It was as I told you in the garden. I would like to know you, to have you learn about me. Must an acquaintance between a man and woman have more reason than that?"

"An acquaintance," she repeated slowly as if she tasted the word in her mouth.

"Is an acquaintance with me not to your liking?" he asked softly. Seshena shook her head. "Why, then, are you so hesitant with me?" he inquired. She looked up at him and he added quietly, "I would have you explain this, truly, so I could understand."

When Seshena's eyes met his, she felt again the odd sensation she'd experienced in the royal garden; she wondered at the effect his mere gaze caused in her. She took a deep breath and noted his eyes remained on her face, not traveling over her body as they had before. Finally she confessed, "My attitude, which seems so peculiar to you, is simply a lack of sophistication. I don't know how to gracefully flirt. I spent too much of my girlhood at my studies and since have occupied myself with temple matters."

"You have no special friends among men?" Rasuah asked. She shook her head. "The temple must surely be kept dark these days that no man sees you and approaches." When Seshena was silent, he took her hand and said softly, "How pleased Djanah will be with you in these days of forward women."

Seshena's eyes flashed and she said, "Don't think I'll be foolish with you because of my lack of experience."

Rasuah sipped his wine thoughtfully, then put down his goblet. "I would never think you foolish about anything," he said softly. He leaned back against the couch and sighed. "You certainly will be a new experience for me also." Perhaps you're just what I've been searching for,"

120

he added. When Seshena seemed confused by this remark, he leaned forward and took her hand in his. "That statement should give you no alarm," he said. "In fact, it should be I who's alarmed by it." He pressed her hand and sighed. He was silent for a time, as if he were making an important decision. Finally he said, "The time is growing late and we've said little to each other. I have a need to learn about you, Seshena. Will you stay to share the evening meal with me?"

Seshena nodded agreement, and Rasuah got up. "Djanah!" he called. The woman instantly stood at the room's threshold. "The lady will remain for the meal," he said. Djanah nodded and disappeared. Rasuah turned to regard Seshena silently.

"You didn't think I'd stay," she observed. Rasuah shook his head. "You think I'll flee in panic at your every move."

Rasuah smiled and nodded. "You remind me of a gazelle, curious enough to step from its hiding place, but always ready to leap back into it," he said.

"Never having been in a situation like this, I am curious," she admitted. She smiled faintly. "I cannot promise what direction I may leap in, if I leap at all."

Rasuah sat beside her and again took her hand in his. "I will promise one thing, little priestess," he said. "I promise only that I'll try not to offend you; however, I'll definitely have to kiss you very soon if I continue to sit so near." Seshena didn't move. Rasuah looked at her speculatively. "A kiss wouldn't offend you?"

"How can I know until you've done it?" she inquired.

"In that case, I'll gladly satisfy your curiosity," he said. He put his hands on her shoulders and leaned forward to brush his lips lightly against hers. He drew away to look at her. She was smiling faintly.

"That was pleasant enough, though brief," she noted.

"Then I'll give you a longer kiss to judge," he whispered. His hands slipped from her shoulders and around her back, drawing her closer to him until he felt her breasts softly pressing him. Looking steadily into her eyes, he brought his lips to hers, kissing her slowly, lingeringly, as if he tasted the kiss, as if it was the first kiss he'd experienced. He savored its flavor, absorbing each tingling sensation it sent through him, until the sensations merged, becoming one sweet aching. He held her tighter, realizing, from the soft gasp that escaped her, that the desire growing in her matched his. Firmly, but gently, he held her away, so his heart might slow its pounding—before the blood coursing like fire through his veins demanded more than she was yet willing to give.

Her wide eyes were like dark blue smoke. Her lips were still softly pursed, waiting. He offered her a goblet and she took it distractedly. He lifted his own goblet and sipped the liquid that cooled his throat, but not his blood.

"Did you find it agreeable?" he asked cautiously, and was surprised when she raised her hands offering to embrace him.

"I would do it again," she whispered.

"I cannot endure too many kisses like those," he warned her. "I'd certainly frighten this little gazelle with what would too quickly follow."

Seshena's face flushed and she hastily sipped her wine. "I'm not sure I'd be frightened at all, But I liked it, perhaps too well," she added.

"Not too well, Seshena," he said. "Perhaps a little too soon, but certainly not too well." Not trusting himself, he stood up, and said, "Later, little one, when you're ready, I think we'll explore all of it." He lifted his goblet and looked at her over its rim, wondering if she might not be ready before the night ended. But he realized it must not be done tonight, not because of her, but because of himself. He sighed. This little priestess meant nothing less than love, and he was suddenly awed at the prospect of love. He needed time to think about it.

8

Ramessa's army was assembled at the palace and ready to march to Zurim within two decans. On the evening before they left, Ramessa was unusually weary and, lying down early with the intention of merely napping, had slept well into the early part of the night. When he awoke, he found himself no longer drowsy, but suffused with a strange loneliness that stole all possibilities of sleep from his being. He sighed and sat on the edge of the bed, wishing there were someone he could call to keep him company until the unpleasant feeling passed. He could call one of his wives, but he knew they'd never understand his mood and would think it was sex he sought of them.

From the next room came a soft sound, as if a door had been opened. Ramessa stood up, wondering if Nefertiry was still awake. He considered her possibilities for a moment and decided, if any of his wives might give him companionship, Nefertiry was more likely than the others. He walked silently to the golden door and listened. There were no further sounds. He opened the door and stepped into the darkened room.

Nefertiry's shadowy figure stood by the door that was opened onto the terrace; and at Ramessa's entrance, she turned.

"Why are you awake?" Ramessa asked softly.

Nefertiry glided soundlessly toward him. "On the night before you leave for battle, how would I sleep?" she murmured. "I had hoped you would call me this night before you left."

"Why could you not sleep before I leave?" Ramessa asked.

"You might die at Zurim," she whispered.

"You're worried?" He was amazed. None of his wives had ever expressed concern about his dying in battle. A glimmer in the moonlight on her face caused him to touch her cheek, and he found it damp. "You even weep?" he asked.

"Yes, my lord," she replied. "I even weep for you."

Ramessa put his arm around her waist and discovered she was naked. Then, he knew for a certainty she'd been in bed and unable to sleep. He was deeply touched. "I won't be killed in battle," he said, putting both arms around her, holding her close.

"Other kings are killed. Mutallu was killed," she said softly against his shoulder. "Kings are made of bones and blood."

Ramessa smiled. "Did not Amen-Ra once say to me: 'Rejoice, my son, who has honored me. I give thee the earth in length and breadth. With a joyful heart pass through it as a conqueror'?"

"Such words impress me not," she murmured. "You have flesh that bleeds, the same as I." She looked up at him. "I am foolish, I shouldn't doubt a divine promise. Perhaps I am so because I have never watched someone go into battle. Hattusil never did because of his arm."

"Mazraima, your brother, fought," Ramessa reminded.

"Yes. Mazraima, my brother," she whispered, thinking

124

that her true brother stood before her. She shook her head. "It wasn't the same."

Ramessa drew her close to him while he considered this strange attitude of hers. If others thought at all about his dying, they were more concerned about who would succeed him, he knew. It pleased him to have someone saddened that he might be taken by death. He smiled without knowing it. When he felt Nefertiry shiver, he held her away from him.

"The north wind blows directly through that door and you're cold."

"What does a chill from a wind matter tonight, my lord? There are many nights and days ahead of me when you'll be gone and I more deeply chilled?" she murmured.

Ramessa felt a chill run down his own back at her words. "You'll miss me in my absence?"

"Long will be those days and even longer the nights," she whispered. "Is this so strange a thing to you, that a wife should miss you? Other women worry about their men. How can it be that because a man is a king no one should worry when he leaves for battle?"

"I don't know," Ramessa whispered into her hair. He was silent for a time until he moved his arm from around her waist and said, "If my little Khatti princess is so different from my other wives, I must admit her difference pleases me. Let us go to your bed, where I'll protect you from this wind and warm your being as your words and tears have warmed my heart."

When Nefertiry lay on the bed looking up at Ramessa, he asked again, "You will truly miss me?", still incredulous that such a thing might be.

Nefertiry nodded. "I think, though, that you'll be happy to escape me and all the trouble I cause you."

"I think not," he replied. He got into bed and propped himself up on his elbows so he could look at her a moment. "I think not," he whispered again, then brought his lips to hers.

The salty taste of tears among the kisses he took was

another new thing to him and added piquance to their flavor. When he touched her breast and thought of the concern that heart within held for him, he knew another emotion he had never associated with his wives: tenderness, a need to protect this fragile body that responded so willingly to the caresses he was giving it. He pressed his face to the warm satin of her skin and inhaled its perfume while he kissed her. He would carry the scent of her all the way to Zurim, he knew. This would be a moment in his life nothing would ever erase from his memory. Her hands sliding down his sides brought him a sharp pleasure, just that light touch, and when he felt her hips moving under his, he was aware of his own sudden response.

"I don't want this to be over too fast," he whispered.

"It won't be, my lord," she murmured, feeling him shiver from her breath in his ear. "With your permission, I won't allow it for a very long time. I would have you remember this night for all eternity."

"I think that may be possible," Ramessa whispered and happily resigned himself to whatever magic she intended to work on him.

"Then you must lie back. As you instructed me on the first night I came to your bed, I ask that you allow me to do what I will and let what will happen to you happen."

Ramessa gazed down at Nefertiry a moment in speculation before he obeyed her. This time Ramessa was to return the kisses Nefertiry gave; Ramessa was to accept the impulses she directed through his nerves, until mere tremblings grew into the magnitude of inner earthquakes she brought to a shuddering stop that left him like a man hanging from a cliff edge, who needed to shakily regain a more secure hold before it all began again.

He reached out for her to end this thing, believing he could endure no more. But she eluded him, teaching him he could endure more, and he did.

Finally, when the intensity of his feelings had turned his flesh into a quivering mass, when he felt that he reached toward her through a long tunnel made of his own delightfully shattered nerves, she no longer refused him. She gave him release, which was like a prolonged flash of blinding light after the darkness of death.

When he could breathe, and his heart beat normally again, and his mind finally began to function, he wondered how he'd even survived. He couldn't move; no muscle in his body would obey his orders. He wondered that his body had the strength left to send out the moisture bathing him. He couldn't even shiver from the cool air on his back.

Somehow, as she had controlled his body all through the moments or hours—he had no way of knowing how long it had been—of ecstasy she'd given him, Nefertiry now realized that he was cold and helpless, and she pulled up the linens to cover him with them.

"I cannot move, but I'm heavy on you," he managed to whisper, as if he were dazed.

Nefertiry put her hands one on each side of Ramessa's face, kissed his lips very softly, then turned his head to rest on her shoulder. "Your weight keeps me on earth, when I think I could fly to the pillars of heaven."

"I thought I had flown to the afterlife," he murmured against her breast.

"Sleep, my lord," she whispered. "You have surely earned it."

Chenmet, who came in the morning to awaken her mistress, was stunned to find the king asleep in Nefertiry's bed. Noting the way they still were lying, she backed out of the room on silent feet. After several hours had passed and Chenmet could be reasonably certain the noises of the army in the courtyard had awakened the king and queen, she returned to Nefertiry's suite and found them innocently bathing.

When Ramessa and Nefertiry were dressed and on their way to the courtyard, Chenmet followed them with a smug expression on her face. The other servants would speak of Ramessa's sleeping all night in Nefertiry's bed. That news would pass like fire through the palace and to the harem

127

wives and concubines, because Ramessa never went to any of the others; they waited in hope until they were called to him.

Nefertiry stood beside Ramessa, looking up into his face, wishing with every fiber of her being that he would kiss her just once before he left. Her wish was in her eyes.

"You would have my entire army, thousands of men, wait while I kiss you?" Ramessa asked softly. Nefertiry nodded. "You would have me kiss and embrace you before all those watching eyes?"

"You'll be gone a very long time, my lord," she said softly.

Ramessa looked at her thoughtfully for a time, then suddenly said, "I don't want to leave."

Nefertiry said, "I hope my fears haven't contaminated you."

Ramessa smiled without humor. "I'm not afraid of battle. I've gone into it too many times before. I don't want to leave you," he confessed. He shook his head. "Why is it, Nefertiry, after I've had all the pleasure any man could want and should be content with for several days at least, only a few hours later I'm hungry for you again?"

Nefertiry continued looking steadily up at him and said quietly, "Between other men and women this is sometimes called love."

Ramessa bent a little closer and asked, "It isn't called love for us?"

Nefertiry smiled, but her eyes held a sadness he didn't understand as she answered slowly, "If it isn't allowed a queen to worry about her king going into battle, is love allowed them?"

Ramessa put his arms loosely around Nefertiry's waist. "Yet you do worry."

"Yes."

Ramessa suddenly drew Nefertiry close to him, and he bent to kiss her lingeringly before his officers and soldiers, who maintained expressionless faces only by the exercise of their wills—before his ministers and servants, who stared with wide eyes—before Chenmet, who smiled—before Tuiah, who frowned.

Ramessa released Nefertiry and turned quickly from her, walking toward Captain Paneb, who held Botar's leash. Ramessa took the leash and returned to Nefertiry to put it in her hands. Without looking again at her, he bent to ruffle Botar's ears and said softly, "Help keep your mistress company, Botar. Watch over her while I'm gone." Then, he turned reluctantly to mount his horse.

Nefertiry watched Ramessa lift his arm and give the signal for the march to begin. When he turned to look at her briefly, she wanted to smile at him—she willed herself to smile at him—but her mouth would not smile. Her eyes spoke eloquently enough for her as she watched him ride away.

Nefertiry hadn't lied when she'd told Ramessa she'd miss him. She hadn't exaggerated how long the nights would be for her. She hadn't even realized herself then how her body would react to prolonged frustration because she'd never experienced it before. She wanted Ramessa again; once she recognized her physical need, it bloomed into a hunger that gnawed at her without ceasing, that kept her sleepless in the night, recalling against her will each detail of the splendor they'd shared before he'd left. By the time he had been gone two decans, she was in a torment she hadn't known her body capable of causing her.

Nefertiry became easier to anger and her servants walked softly in her presence. To all others she was mirthless, silent.

Tuiah understood Nefertiry's suffering; having been one of Seti's several wives, she'd endured many nights of loneliness. Those nights had made Tuiah weak with a feeling of yearning and languidness, which was what she assumed must be Nefertiry's inner condition. Thinking now to take advantage of Nefertiry's situation and to recoup some of her authority, she dressed in her court robes and went to Nefertiry's suite.

"My dear Nefertiry," Tuiah began in her sweetest tone, "I know you have a great deal on your mind and I thought I might make your way easier by sitting for the audience this morning."

Chenmet had just finished arranging Nefertiry's own court robes and was about to place the coronet on her head, but hesitated to see what her mistress would decide.

Nefertiry turned to face Tuiah with a look in her eyes that reminded Tuiah of Botar, when the cat had once been cornered by a pair of foolish tiger dogs. Nefertiry silently motioned to Chenmet to place the coronet on her head. After the servant had handed Nefertiry her scepters, Nefertiry turned and walked to the door, still not having spoken to Tuiah.

"Nefertiry, will you say nothing at all to me?" Tuiah asked in a condescending tone as if she rebuked a child.

Nefertiry paused at the door and turned eyes of emerald ice on Tuiah. "I know you acted as regent in Ramessa's place when he fought in foreign lands, but that time is over. Ramessa now has a queen," she advised. "With all respect, divine mother, you must loosen your grasp on his scepter. You must step back into your rightful place." Tuiah was stunned beyond answering, as Nefertiry continued, "There can be only one king and one queen in the land." Then Nefertiry turned away and left for the throne room.

Tuiah stood silently staring at the empty doorway for several minutes before she was composed enough to return to her quarters. When she was in her room, she tore off her court robes and threw her jewelry into its place, resolving all the while to somehow, someday make Memnet's daughter sorry for this humiliation. But she knew she would have to be very careful how she did it. Nefertiry not only had Botar's expression in her eyes—she seemed to have Botar's claws as well.

Later that same morning, Khakamir returned to the palace to request an audience with Nefertiry, which she granted. When he entered the room where she awaited him, he saw shadows around her eyes and the stamp of tension on her mouth.

"Are you unwell?" Khakamir asked after greetings had been exchanged.

Nefertiry frowned, but answered, "I'm well enough."

"I would have given my report to the king, but in his absence I think I must speak to my queen," Khakamir said hesitantly.

"At least you know who the queen is," Nefertiry muttered sarcastically. She saw the confusion on Khakamir's face and smiled briefly in spite of her gloom. "Sit down, Khakamir, and tell me whatever it is."

Khakamir seated himself and, giving Nefertiry another uneasy glance said, "The king sent me in pursuit of two women who had run away."

"Yes, I know,' Nefertiry said shortly. "Have you managed to drag them back?" Khakamir shook his head.

"I pursued them all the way to Kenset," he apologized.

Nefertiry waved a hand, as if it was of no consequence. "They were only concubines," she said, and then added bitterly, "There are many others."

Khakamir was silent for a time, wondering at her unhappy mood. He wished he could leave, but she hadn't dismissed him. Finally he asked, "My lady, is there something else you wish of me?"

Nefertiry had been staring blankly at the colors and patterns of the cushions at the foot of the couch on which she reclined. At Khakamir's words, she raised her eyes to look appraisingly at him. His mouth was slightly pursed in a frown of concern. His slanted eyes were anxious. Her gaze passed over the trim lines of his uniform and she said softly, "Perhaps there is something you can do for me."

Suddenly, Khakamir noticed the expression in Nefer-

131

tiry's eyes; and when he realized its meaning, he was alarmed and at the same time aroused. He had wanted her from the moment he'd seen her dressed like a Shasu in Kharu.

"Do you remember, Khakamir, the time you invited me to ride with you, so you could distract me from the harem gossip?" she asked quietly. Khakamir nodded. "I need distraction from something else now," she said. "Will you ride with me this afternoon?" Still speechless, Khakamir merely nodded again. "Be ready after the noon meal," she said quietly.

"During the resting time?" he finally whispered.

"I don't rest these days or even during the nights," she answered. "Yes, Khakamir, we will go riding while everyone else sleeps."

Khakamir was very quiet while they rode and Nefertiry wondered if he realized what she had in mind. Of course he knew, she decided. He just didn't know what to do about it. She sighed. She would have to make her intentions very clear to him before anything would happen. "Is there a quiet place where we can walk?" she asked.

"Walk?" he echoed, looking as if he'd been startled from deep thoughts. "Yes, of course, my lady." He turned his horse down an unused path.

Nefertiry sighed again. During the time she'd waited for Khakamir, she had considered everything Seshena had told her and decided the priestess was right. It was impractical to think she could contain her frustration and there would be many times in the future she would feel this way. It was unfair to the child—if there would be one—to chance his carrying both Ramessa's and her own blood. Nefertiry wanted her son to be strong and healthy in every way because she saw a difficult path before him if he would be king. She also had decided it would be wise for her to begin a child as quickly as possible, thus further assuring her position with Ramessa. She was certain, Ramessa would be very happy if he thought she bore a son begun that ecstatic night before he'd left.

Nefertiry glanced at Khakamir. Although she thought his calm and reserved exterior concealed a passionate nature, she also was sure it wouldn't be easy to make him cast aside his loyalty to Ramessa.

When they reached a wood-enclosed glade, where sunlight sprinkled through the trees in narrow, slanting stripes, Nefertiry stopped her horse and waited for Khakamir to help her down. As Khakamir came to her side, she deliberately slid down into his arms. His eyes widened and he stepped away quickly.

"I've decided I would like to sit down for a time in this beautiful place," Nefertiry said softly. "Will you spread out your cape for me, Khakamir?"

Khakamir turned slowly to look at her, nodded, then obeyed her. When the scarlet cape was spread out on the grass, he stood over it, staring down at it, saying nothing.

"How long do you think the king will be on this expedition?" Nefertiry asked as she came nearer.

Khakamir's eyes rose from the cape and met hers. "Two months more, I'd guess," he answered.

Nefertiry sat down on the cape and looked up at him. "Sit beside me, Khakamir," she invited. He obeyed, but he stared straight ahead at the trees, reluctant to even glance at her. "It has been twenty days since he left," Nefertiry said. "Two more months is a long time." Khakamir nodded, but still didn't look at her. She took a deep breath. "You know why I wanted you to ride with me?" He was silent. She quickly added, "I am a human being, though I'm queen."

Khakamir turned his head to regard her solemnly. "The king is my friend," he said.

"Which throws you into my path often," she replied calmly. "Even after he returns, he has many other wives. What, then, am I to do? Shall I helplessly endure this pain I suffer? I had thought I could do it. But now that I've experienced its torment, I know I cannot."

Khakamir looked away. "I have no wish to be used by a woman, not even my queen."

133

Nefertiry sighed. "Neither would I wish to use a man," she said. "Khakamir, I'm in a peculiar position. I could, you realize, choose from a number of noblemen who would probably suit my purpose—if all I wanted was a man to satisfy my body. That isn't all I want or all I need. I want and need a man who can also be a friend to me in ways the king cannot. I couldn't be with someone I felt nothing for—I need someone I trust and respect."

"My lady—" Khakamir began, then fell silent. He didn't know what to say.

"I find you very appealing physically. I like you personally. People have married for less than that," Nefertiry said solemnly. "Do you find me so undesirable that loving me would be an unpleasant task for you?"

Khakamir turned to look at her, and his eyes held a strange glow. "Do you think I came only because my queen asked me to come?"

Nefertiry smiled. "It would have been awkward for you to say no, but I would have accepted your refusal."

Khakamir continued, looking steadily at her, "To have a woman such as you, whatever your title or place, call me to you with desire in your eyes renders me helpless."

"Not too helpless, Khakamir, I hope."

"Still, it's difficult to forget my king," he said.

"You do want me."

"I've wanted you since Kharu," he whispered.

"There are factors involved here you cannot know," Nefertiry said slowly. "There are matters I cannot disclose. But if you knew them, you wouldn't blame me, I think. If you knew them, you would feel less guilty." She was silent a moment, looking down at her lap, knowing he was staring curiously at her. She lifted her eyes to regard him. "You can know this, Khakamir. My marriage contract allows me lovers and even Aset's high priestess approves of my taking one."

Khakamir took a deep breath. "The king wouldn't approve," he insisted.

134

"He might, if he could know all that's involved," she said clearly. "But even he cannot know." Placing her hands on the sides of Khakamir's face, she felt him shiver. "Will you at least kiss me, Khakamir? If there's no magic in it for either of us, we'll return to the palace and say no more of this." She moved closer to him and her arms slid around his shoulders.

Khakamir suddenly put his arms around her. He felt her body move tensely against him. She was trembling as much as he. The softness of her lips became firmer under his own and poured fire into him, her perfume drowning him, the nearness of her banishing all his guilt, loosening the bounds of his sanity. Almost roughly, he pushed her down until her shoulders met the cape, until her trembling body was covered by his own. And he was aware of nothing but her seeking mouth and her eager body and the fire of his own need.

9

The stone corridors of the temple were deserted, and the oil lamps were empty shadows on the walls, but moonlight spilled through the window slits just under the high ceilings, and the alabaster floors shimmered like reflections in a lotus pond.

Seshena glided soundlessly past the curve of columns half-lit to soft radiance by the moonlight, and her troubled heart was soothed by the temple's peace. When she reached the door to the sanctuary, she paused for a moment to listen to the breeze murmuring through the dark corridors. Satisfied that no other steps followed her own, she pulled open the heavy silver door and stepped into the sacred chamber.

At the center of the room the offering table, sparkling with the moon's cool fire, awaited its gift from the priestess. Seshena paused, forgetting to close the door behind her as her eyes traveled up the white form of Aset's statue to rest on the goddess's serene face, for Seshena's mind was emptied of all thoughts but one: the

137

single request she had been making for the last seven months.

The crystal held in Aset's hands caught the moonlight and sent radiating streaks and wavering circles of light across the stone floor, as if it marked how near a human foot might approach. But Seshena walked soundlessly through the circles of light until she stood at the statue's base.

Laying her bouquet of lotuses and jasmine on the silver table, Seshena knelt and brushed her forehead to the stone floor, where she remained for a time as she again prayed to be given the gift of prophecy. For some time, Seshena had been aware of imminent trouble in the kingdom. Someone or some group sought to steal the power from Heru's crown and weaken the power of the throne, draining the very life from the country. Although Seshena had not yet learned the source of the threat or even what form it would take, she was sharply aware of its ominous presence hanging over Tamera. She knew she must play a part in the crown's defense. Thus, each month when the moon grew into a silver disc and the pupils in the eyes of cats enlarged, she went alone to the empty temple and begged for knowledge about those events still to come.

Seshena sighed, wondering if this would be yet another futile visit. Then, scolding herself for mortal impatience and reminding herself that what she needed would be given to her at its proper moment, she got to her feet and lit fresh incense in a censer at the statue's base. Raising her hands shoulder-level in supplication, she lifted her eyes to Aset's face and again took a moment to gather her thoughts.

"O Bast, who is the soul of Aset, she who is the eye of the One Alone, hear the plea of thy devoted priestess!" Seshena cried. Her voice glanced off the stone walls, echoing through the darkness until a legion of priestesses seemed to whisper the chant. As she concentrated on her prayer, she was unaware that beyond the sanctuary's

138

open doorway, a figure stood motionless in the temple's corridor, watching her and listening to her words.

"O Bast, hidden one, thou who walks in eternity's darkness as cats walk silently through the night, take thou my hand and lead me through the veils of time; as cats have eyes to pierce the earth's shadows, lend me your eyes that I may see beyond my ignorance, that I may know the secrets of what comes before the events are upon me."

When the echoes of Seshena's plea had faded, she stood staring up at Aset's face, waiting. After a time, she sank to her knees as before, repeated her request and again waited. She closed her eyes and once more begged that the hidden knowledge be revealed. But no images appeared on her eyelids and no words came into her consciousness; and when her knees had become stiff from waiting, she sighed and got to her feet, concluding that her visit once again was without result.

Instead of going back through the long temple's many chambers, Seshena left by a small side exit and turned into the garden.

After the penetrating fragrance of the temple incense, the light perfume of the garden's shifting breezes was like the stringing of a lyre after pulsing drums. All of the paths winding between the flowers and shrubs met at the temple's lotus pond. Seshena paused beside the pond and stared absently at the water. Its cool, dark surface was broken with ripples that glimmered with the north wind's kiss, while scattered among the silvery lotus petals, the reflections of the stars, like lovers, drew close to combine, then part in shimmers of moonlight.

The glowing pond gradually lulled Seshena's busy mind into submission and slowly her eyes unfocused, at last allowing Bast's message to enter her awareness. Like a soundless whisper, the words were placed within her brain.

'As many as are the directions whence evil may come, this evil was born within the land's heart. Look to the
139

priesthood of Amen's temple for treachery. All but Khenti are corrupt. You, my daughter, will be as Bast foretelling the evil, while Nefertiry will be as Wadjet, the cobra guarding Heru's crown."

"What are you doing here in the middle of the night?" The quiet voice came from behind Seshena. Startled, she turned quickly to stare at Lord Rasuah. As he drew closer, the moonlight caught gold sparks in his eyes. "The night is for sleeping—or loving."

Seshena smiled and pointedly ran her eyes over his rich garments. "Or for going to parties?" she remarked.

The corners of Rasuah's mouth lifted slightly. "Yes, sometimes. I was passing the temple on my way home and saw the open door. I entered and heard your prayer." He put his hands on her shoulders. "What's troubling you?" he asked softly.

"Priestesses sometimes go to the temple at night," Seshena whispered.

"I think it must be very important that you walk through the night to beg divine help."

"It is most important to the entire kingdom," Seshena said. "But I have just now learned my answer and am ready to go home."

"May I walk with you?" Rasuah asked.

Seshena wanted Rasuah's company, but at the same time, she was deeply troubled by what she had learned about Amen's priests.

"Is my company unwelcome?" Rasuah asked when she didn't reply. "If so, I'll go my own way and not trouble you."

Seshena looked up at him, alarmed. "Your company is very welcome. I just have unhappy matters to reflect upon. Walk with me, my lord. For I think I must speak to someone."

"Address me by my name," Rasuah reminded her. Taking her hand, he led her from the temple garden. He did not speak again until they were walking through the
140

deserted streets. "What problem is it that weighs so on you?"

Seshena was silent for a moment studying him. Finally, knowing there was no treachery in him she answered, "I've been aware of a darkness hanging over the throne. For seven months have I begged Bast to tell me about it. Tonight she answered that the priesthood of Amen is corrupt and seeking power which, if won, would eventually weaken the throne."

Shocked, Rasuah stopped walking and said, "Such a thing is insurrection!"

"They're clever and will do it in ways difficult to oppose," Seshena replied. "I'm to act as Bast and foretell their plans so they can be stopped."

"Who—" Rasuah began, then fell silent.

"Queen Nefertiry is to be guardian of the crown," Seshena answered. Rasuah began to turn as if to continue walking, but Seshena's hand on his arm stopped him. "This is my gate," she said. "Will you enter with me and share a glass of wine while we discuss this?"

Rasuah nodded and followed Seshena through the shadows of her garden and into her house.

They met a serving woman in the hall, and Seshena paused to say, "Bring us some wine, Nehara, please." Then Seshena guided Rasuah into a room and invited him to sit on one of the couches. When the woman came with the wine, Seshena said, "Go to bed now, Nehara. I won't need you later."

Rasuah stared at his goblet without tasting it. "The priesthood of Amen is powerful. If it's become evil, you must be very careful about how you oppose their plans."

"If Bast says they're evil, it is so," Seshena said.

"I'm filled with sorrow to hear this," Rasuah announced. "I now feel I cannot enter the temple with this darkness hanging over it."

"Although the priesthood may have become corrupt with greed, Amen-Ra is not," Seshena said firmly. "Honor

141

the divine being in his brilliance as always. But go to none of his priests except one called Khenti. The others are looking for themselves, and Khenti is the only true priest left among them."

"If one of them is untouched by evil that gives me some comfort," Rasuah said softly. He sipped his wine once, thoughtfully, then stood up. "I'll keep you from your rest no longer."

"I think I'll not rest," Seshena said anxiously.

"I thought a high priestess had absolute control of her mind's turnings," Rasuah said. "Yet it seems you worry the same as others do."

"Emotions sometimes interfere with the discipline we learn."

Rasuah looked at her steadily, wishing he could wipe the concern from her brow. "You have a friend and I'll help you however I can." He cupped her chin lightly in his fingers and bent to kiss her. Intending to kiss her as he would a sister merely to bid her good night, he found that, as before, when his lips met hers a brilliant fire leaped through him, and he lingered, despite his previous intentions. His arms circled her tightly, until he could feel her soft body melting against him and the thin fabric of their garments seemed to disappear.

Seshena withdrew from his arms and stared up at him with wide, glowing eyes. "Why do you make me feel like this? I become like a wild creature!"

"Perhaps it's because our minds are open to each other that so great a reaction comes from a kiss meant to be lightly given."

"I want you to stay with me," she said softly. "I want to explore this further."

"If we explore any further than a single kiss, I know I won't stop," Rasuah said. "You must think about this for a time, because it isn't a matter you'd take lightly, and I wouldn't want you to regret it once it was done."

"And can you take these matters so lightly, Rasuah?" she asked.

Rasuah looked intently down into Seshena's eyes, and admitted, "Not with you. I think it would be more likely the beginning of something having no end." Abruptly he turned away and walked toward the door.

"Will you come back?" she asked anxiously.

Rasuah regarded Seshena silently for a moment before answering. "I'll come back whenever you ask me to. The next time you invite me to your house at night I think it's possible I won't stop at any of your doors, so you should carefully consider if you wish to take this chance." Then, he turned and left.

The plain outside Zurim was strewn with bodies; here and there chariots, whose horses were now without masters, stood motionless against the crimson sky. Ramessa lowered his sword and scanned the fortress walls. Beyond a ragged hole that once held a massive door, he saw a large building being gutted by fire. He watched the small figures of men darting past until the roof of the building collapsed with a roar, sending a shower of golden sparks into the sunset. Dark smoke spewing from a myriad of places seemed to replace the stone towers the Tameran catapults had tumbled.

Arek drew his chariot alongside Ramessa's and said, "That city is like a maiden who has fought long and hard against a rapist, until she must surrender from exhaustion." When Ramessa glanced at him, Arek smiled confidently. "Zurim will soon relax her thighs. Most of their officers are dead. I don't know about Yafob, though. I haven't seen him lately."

"I've already killed him," Ramessa replied. "The next attack will carry us into the city. You lead it, Arek. I'm not of a mood to bother."

When Ramessa moved to turn the chariot away, Arek hastily asked, "Will you not later enter the city to negotiate with the governor?"

"What will he have to negotiate about? My orders were clear to you. I expect you to level the city to the ground.

143

I have no desire to negotiate with Zahi. Tarmo will understand my sentiments when he learns Zurim has been erased from the earth."

"What of prisoners?" Arek asked.

"Take none."

"And the women and children?"

"Someone must survive to carry this news to Avaris," Ramessa said softly. "Women make eloquent couriers, especially when they have vengeance in their hearts."

Cautiously, Arek asked, "When should I release them?"

"Tomorrow morning will be soon enough," Ramessa said quietly.

"A night with our mercenaries will give those women more cause for revenge," Arek said.

"Yes," Ramessa agreed. "I expect them to recount many unpleasant stories in Tarmo's ears to warn him against bothering us too soon."

Ramessa turned his chariot and rode away, leaving Arek wondering. He had never known Ramessa to give such commands before. Finally, he shrugged and prepared to lead the charge, concluding that Ramessa must truly wish to strike terror in the hearts of these Hyskos. Such orders would make the mercenaries happy, and he had no personal objections to them, either.

When Ramessa drew up his chariot, he directed his waiting servants to establish his tent among a grove at the edge of the plain. As he waited for the tent's preparation, he deliberately kept his back to the city that was methodically being reduced to rubble.

By the time darkness had fallen, the destruction was complete. But Ramessa had no curiosity about what was happening in the fallen city. He drank several goblets of wine and then, impatiently, directed his servants to extinguish the lamps. Lying in bed staring at the darkness, he wondered how long it would take for the goddess of sleep to carry him into oblivion so he wouldn't hear or think about the sounds still drifting from Zurim.

Ramessa was fully aware of the true reason for his

144

agitation. Nefertiry was what he wanted. That last night with her had been a marvel to remember and he had relived each detail of it many times since he'd left her. Yet remembering was a thing he constantly fought against, because he knew well enough how many nights would pass before he could return. Still, in idle moments during the journey to Zahi, Nefertiry had been like a ghost accompanying him. However he tried to turn his mind to other matters, she crept into his awareness as if she'd cast a spell on him.

The texture of her creamy skin was so vivid in his memory he seemed to experience its sensation against his own skin. The silk of her hair seemed to slide between his fingers. He could close his eyes, and his mouth felt her warm breath as her lips moved nearer and he became as aroused as if she actually kissed him.

Ramessa wondered what special qualities Nefertiry possessed that so aroused him. Their response to one another was beyond any degree he'd previously experienced. Her skill at love was not only greater than that of his other wives, who came to him well-trained, but Nefertiry coupled her knowledge with a delicate sensuality that maddened him.

Nefertiry behaved with him as no other woman dared, sometimes humbly calling him her lord and at other times defying him. Her mind was so clear it astounded him and he admitted only to himself that her remarks often brought him new insights on complicated problems.

But Nefertiry had more than an alluring body and agile mind. The unexpected wealth of emotions she directed at him surprised and pleased. He remembered how she'd genuinely worried about his going into battle, and he was freshly touched by her concern.

Ramessa turned to lie on his back and closed his eyes. He was never sure what she might do next and he realized this was part of her fascination. She was an endless puzzle, endlessly tantalizing. He owned her as surely as he owned his slaves; still she escaped his grasp. . . .

When the sounds coming from Zurim had finally ceased, Ramessa had long ago stopped hearing them. Sometime while he had been thinking about Nefertiry, he had fallen asleep to dream of her.

"I'm not sleeping," Nefertiry said, opening her eyes. "I can never really sleep in the daytime." She swung her legs off the couch and looked up at Chenmet. "What is it, Chenmet?"

"Captain Khakamir is here with a message," Chenmet replied.

Nefertiry's face brightened and she stood up, smoothing her gown. "Send him in immediately."

As Khakamir entered the room, Nefertiry waved Chenmet away. After the door had closed, Nefertiry walked quickly across the room to slide her arms around Khakamir's shoulders. He put his hands on her waist for a moment, then pushed her a little away.

"This time the message is genuine," he said quietly.

Noticing the grave look on his face, she asked, "What is it?"

"The royal army is but a few hours' march away. The king will arrive by sunset." Khakamir looked down at his feet. "This means, I suppose, we will now end what has been between us."

"No!" Nefertiry exclaimed, putting her hands on his arms. "Or do you wish it so?"

Khakamir's slanted eyes lifted in surprise. "You'll want to go on with this?" he asked.

"What some women have in one man I must seek from two. My choice, Khakamir, would be to have what we've shared during these last months go on and on. But if you wish to end it now, I'll only say you have given me joy and bid you go."

Khakamir's arms lifted and tightened around her. "Never. I never want to end it, although it may someday cost my head. I would chance that and even the loss of my honor, but I could never tell you no."

Nefertiry closed her eyes in relief for a moment. "For a time, Khakamir, we won't be able to meet. When it's again possible, I'll find a way to let you know."

Khakamir sighed in resignation. "It will be difficult for me to keep from my eyes the light that enters them when I see you, to guard against revealing words and deny myself such impulsive gestures as other lovers are free to make. I'm not a man given to deceits," he explained.

Nefertiry released him reluctantly and stepped away. "Khakamir, if ever you meet a woman who can offer you love you can accept in the full light of Ra, you must go from me and forget this."

Khakamir came to her, and, gripping her shoulders tightly, declared, "What woman after you could catch my attention, much less my heart? No such female exists upon this earth!"

"You must not think that way," Nefertiry said softly. "There can be nothing for us but momentary pleasure and unending friendship." She glanced at his hands on her shoulders and he released her. "I know this secret weighs heavily on you." She turned to look sadly at him. "And I care not to think of the day when you turn to another, but that day must come."

"It cannot come," he said, and turning away, left her.

Nefertiry sat quietly thinking about Khakamir for some time, until, remembering that Ramessa would be home before sunset, she called her attendants to prepare her for his arrival. Once the servants had finished bathing and dressing her, Nefertiry walked out onto her balcony.

In the shadow of the mimosa tree that shaded the balcony, Nefertiry sat on a chair and tapped her foot softly in impatience, not noticing the delicate flowers and sweet perfume the tree showered on her each time the wind fluttered the branches. Her heart was pounding in anticipation of Ramessa's return, and she was doing her uttermost to control her happiness. She had no intention of welcoming him with too much eagerness, lest Ramessa

147

become as confident of her reactions as he was of the rest of his wives.

The sun was low in the western sky, casting a rich gold tint over Wast. Nefertiry smiled because it seemed as if the gods so favored Ramessa's triumph they had arranged to gild the city in celebration of his return.

Nefertiry heard a distant roar rise from the crowds waiting at the city's gates and she knew Ramessa had finally entered Wast. Standing up, she stared at the city beyond the palace walls. Although she couldn't yet see the army, she could sense their progress through the streets. Her heart lifted in pride at the welcoming cheers of the people, the lavish trumpeting from the top of the palace walls.

The army turned onto the long avenue leading to the palace gates coming at last into Nefertiry's view, and she could see the countless flower petals the joyous people showered on their king, who was once again their conquering god on earth. Ramessa was riding at the front of the column in his gold-chased chariot, which in the peculiar light appeared as if it glowed with inner orange fire, and Nefertiry was reminded of another triumphal march. She was surprised at how long ago that lifetime seemed. Although less than half a year had passed, Princess Sharula of Khatti seemed like a stranger to her now.

As the King approached the palace gates and the crowds lining the avenue quieted, the steady confident rhythm of the soldiers' marching feet became a reassuring sound to her. Suddenly Nefertiry understood how it felt to be the king of a triumphant land, to be the directing force behind the power of such an army. Exhileration swept over her as she too learned that victory was more intoxicating than strong wine.

Ramessa's head was high held in triumph, but his eyes were lifted to Nefertiry's balcony. Recognizing her slender form, their myriad colors shifted and settled to a soft green haze. To have Nefertiry waiting and watching for him made his victory at Zurim seem like the most shining

148

accomplishment of his career. He felt almost as proud as when his father had made him coregent and placed the double crown on his head for the first time. Nefertiry didn't wave or make any gesture of welcome to him, but instead turned and disappeared through her doorway, and Ramessa's eyebrows lifted momentarily. He shrugged imperceptibly as he speculated on her attitude. Perhaps, to disguise her eagerness, she would behave with exaggerated dignity when she faced him. She did have a strong sense of pride. He might have to peel off her aloofness layer by layer even as he stripped her of all those jewels and garments.

Ramessa stepped from his chariot to greet Henhenet, his prime minister, with triumph shining from his eyes. Then Ramessa embraced Tuiah and walked into the palace with his arm still around his mother's waist, trying with affectionate indulgence to answer her many questions. But in Ramessa's innermost thoughts, some doubts about Nefertiry were beginning; he wondered if she was merely disguising her gladness at his homecoming or if she actually didn't care.

Ramessa loosed his arm around Tuiah, explaining that he was dusty from the road and eager to bathe.

Tuiah was aware of her son's unspoken eagerness to see Nefertiry. "Bathe yourself and take some time to rest as well," she suggested. "I'll dine alone tonight, so you need not come down for the meal, but you can send for a tray whenever you desire it."

"You won't be too lonely?" Ramessa asked doubtfully.

"I'm getting used to having my meals without company," Tuiah said drily, thinking of how seldom Nefertiry cared to share the table with her, but her meaning seemed to have been lost on Ramessa.

The lure of a cool, refreshing bath hastened Ramessa's steps. But when he entered his apartment and saw the golden doorway to Nefertiry's chamber, he decided to look in on her and perhaps gauge her temperament.

As Ramessa opened the door, Nefertiry turned quickly,

149

and with her motion, a drift of her perfume came to him, washing away the past lonely months as if they had never been. She stood in the center of the room, measuring him with her cool, green eyes. Clothed in silence as well as her snowy garments, she appeared as aloof as Aset. Why, he wondered, did she so often make him feel as awkward as a peasant boy? Annoyed with himself, he brushed aside his doubts to approach her smiling with more confidence than he felt.

Nefertiry stepped away from Ramessa's outstretched hands and, in her low-pitched voice remarked, "You smell like a blacksmith."

Ramessa blinked and his hands dropped to hang limply at his sides. He regarded her silently for a moment before saying, "You will prepare yourself and await me in my chamber."

Nefertiry's eyes widened. "Yes, my lord!" she exclaimed. Then she wrinkled her nose and asked, "Does it please my lord to bathe?"

"You'll accept me, whatever my condition," Ramessa replied, then turned and went back into his room.

Nefertiry stood in the same place, staring at the door for some time after it had closed. She was baffled by her own behavior. Only moments before Ramessa had entered, her heart had been racing with eagerness to see him; and she had been struggling to restrain herself, lest she run headlong into his arms. She shook her head. It seemed that in trying to subdue herself, she had been overly successful. Yet her first words to him, greeting him so, were incomprehensible to her. Even thinking of what she'd said made her blush in shame. She recalled the wounded look in his eyes and how the hurt had been replaced with a certain hardness, the edge to his voice, and she stamped her foot in anger at herself. How could she make him forget the terrible way she'd greeted him, she wondered. How could she make him smile again without humbling herself too much?

Ramessa too was wondering how to approach the

situation. In his preoccupation, he bathed hurriedly and, when Nehri was ready to give him his massage, Ramessa waved him aside. As Ramessa put on a robe, another servant approached him, intending to tie the robe's sash, but Ramessa stalked past without a word. Nehri barely managed to open the door to the bedchamber before Ramessa marched through the opening. Grasping the door's edge as he passed, with a snap of his wrist, he slammed it shut after him.

Expecting to find Nefertiry sitting sullenly on the bed as she had on their first night, Ramessa was surprised that she stood near the door wordlessly offering him a goblet of wine. He regarded her silently, not accepting the goblet.

"Surely you have a thirst after that long journey," she said softly.

"Put aside that goblet for later, when my thirst requires wine," he directed.

Nefertiry promptly placed the goblet on a table within reach of the bed. Then she removed her robe, dropped it on the floor and sat on the edge of the bed.

Ramessa stood motionless for a long moment staring at her nakedness, remembering how many times he'd thought of that body.

A fierce light was gathering in Ramessa's eyes, and Nefertiry wondered at it. After a long moment passed, she grew apprehensive. Her eyes widened and became like emeralds glowing. Her face paled and the smile that had been almost ready to appear vanished as her lips parted in dismay.

Seeing that look of alarm on her face, he forgot he was a king for whom physical desire was merely an appetite easily appeased by a willing harem. Ramessa reverted to a male creature long starved for a female, a conqueror facing a captive woman who was helpless. Nefertiry, acting frightened, detonated his primitive instincts; with one swift motion, he swept off his robe and walked toward her menacingly.

He put his hands on her side. Grasping her tightly, he lifted her and placed her on her back in the middle of the bed. So startled was she by his unexpected strength, she lay staring silently up at him. But when he roughly pushed his knee between her legs, as though he would take her by violence, she cried, "Am I an enemy woman you must rape?"

Ramessa glared down at Nefertiry and gradually the wildness left his eyes. Then, he moved over to her side and lay on his back. For a long time he said nothing while he tried to cool his temper. Finally, he turned his head to look at her profile and ask quietly, "Do you remember how it was on our last night together?"

Nefertiry nodded.

Ramessa recalled how he'd thought of little else, and said, "You will do it again that way."

Brushing back her disheveled hair, she promptly sat up. Without a word she knelt and leaned toward him.

"Suddenly you're obedient," Ramessa observed.

Nefertiry smiled cautiously and said, "Your order pleases me."

The tone of her words and the expression in her eyes finally told him all he needed to know. He realized he no longer cared about an apology and wouldn't demand one. He cared only that he was with her, that her soft lips held their old magical promise. He murmured, "Make it last as long as that other night." At his words, her eyes flashed green fire. Knowing, at last that her hunger matched his, he whispered, "Kiss me, Nefertiry."

She bent to press her lips to his, and her kiss was a spark igniting his being with sweet fire, flashing intense sensations through him; his arms lifted and circled her, pulling her to him. Her breasts crushed against his chest, her hips, the whole length of her warm body firmly fitting to his. Her arms crept around his shoulders, then grasped him with a strength he hadn't known she possessed. Her lips kissed and caressed his mouth, driving away his judgment and he forgot his previous request.

Again the primeval in him triumphed. But this time

152

his instincts recognized she was with him. Her kisses had become as fiery as his. He felt her nails pressing into his back, but this small pain only served to lash him to even greater arousal. He twined his legs with hers, locking her to him. With a sudden powerful twist of his body he rolled them over, so he rose and looked down at her face. In that moment, he recovered just enough of his reason to wonder at his violence and fear that he might hurt her.

But Nefertiry's eyes opened to blaze at him and she licked her dry lips and moaned softly, "Why do you stop?"

He was suddenly engulfed by a fire that took his reason, replacing it with pleasure so great it was almost pain; and he was lost in its intensity.

Later, when Ramessa awoke, darkness had crept over the world. The palace was silent. No servants had dared enter to light lamps and the room was only lit by the moon and the stars he could see beyond the window. Slowly he sat up. Then he got off the bed and walked soundlessly to the terrace door and gazed at the heavens. He wondered how it was possible to be so aroused by one woman; it was like a madness that took him. He turned, expecting to see her pale form still on the bed. But she too had risen and stood behind him.

Inhaling deeply, she whispered, "The night air is sweet with the scent of myrrh."

Ramessa took a breath, but said, "I smell no myrrh."

"It must be my lord's return that has put a charm on my senses," she replied solemnly.

"I was wondering just now if it was you that so charmed me," he murmured. He smiled and added, "I forgot my original request."

"The night has barely begun," she whispered. "See how the moon has only started its ascent."

"I'm aware of the hour. My empty stomach reminds me," Ramessa said drily.

"We did miss the evening meal," Nefertiry reminded.

"In my rush to return home, I also disregarded the noon meal," Ramessa said.

Nefertiry looked up at him in mock dismay. "After all

153

that energy you expended, you must feel greatly weakened! I'll have Chenmet bring us a tray."

Ramessa and Nefertiry finished the meal Chenmet had served them in bed, and after the servant had carried away the trays, they threw off the linens and sat looking speculatively at each other.

Finally Ramessa said, "Although I'm too awake to sleep, I find myself temporarily uninterested in love. I think you did too well last time."

"I'm of the same mind, my lord," Nefertiry confessed. "Tell me about the battle you fought, if you will."

Ramessa remembered the razing of Zurim and frowned. "I don't care to speak of that now. I'm not in a mood to remember blood and battle."

Nefertiry hadn't missed the look of pain that momentarily clouded his eyes and she decided to quickly change the subject. "Would you like to play a game of senit?" she suggested.

Ramessa tilted his head slightly to one side and asked, "You can play senit?"

Nefertiry smiled. "I had heard you were fond of the game so I asked Khakamir to teach me. Would you like a game now?" she coaxed.

When he smiled, she got out of bed and crossed the room to set up the game board and pieces. He also got out of bed and went to sit beside the small table where she was arranging the pieces.

Nefertiry glanced up at Ramessa. "Khakamir said I'm quite good at the game."

"The game calls for a mind capable of planning strategies in advance, a crafty mind. I don't doubt you'll be good at it."

Nefertiry looked at him and exclaimed in mock dismay, "Do you think I'm crafty?"

"Yes, as well as being a master of the element of surprise. I suspect you'll be a challenge."

Nefertiry made her first move, then raised her eyes to look expectantly at Ramessa.

154

"What would my other wives think if they knew I was sitting here naked in the middle of the night playing senit with you?" He shook his head and laughed.

"What would they think if they knew I am carrying a child?" she asked quietly.

Ramessa's startled eyes lifted and stared at her. "You are?"

"The night before you left for Zurim seems to have borne fruit," she said.

Ramessa thought of the tenderness as well as the passion they'd shared that night, and finally, he said, "It was an appropriate time to conceive a prince."

"It will be a prince, my lord. Seshena has predicted a male child."

Ramessa had been mildly happy when other wives had conceived, but the thought of Nefertiry's having his child was like a wave of joy washing over him, and he was filled with wonder at how much it affected him. Trying to appear calmer than he felt, he said, "My other wives will be greatly disturbed by this news."

"Shall I weep for them?" Nefertiry asked. She wore a look of triumph she didn't bother to conceal.

Ramessa put his arms around her and held her close for a time. "Seshena predicted a male child?" he asked softly. "I confess, Nefertiry, this news as no other gives joy to my heart."

"I'm one of many wives and this child will be one prince among many," she whispered.

He looked at her thoughtfully for a moment before saying solemnly, "I know it rankles in your heart that I have so many wives, yet you're unlike all of the others. You're my companion, not merely a body for my pleasure. You protect my interests though you make enemies for yourself by doing so. You're concerned for my well-being when no one else thinks of it. No, Nefertiry, you're not like the others. This I'll prove to you and the whole kingdom as well."

155

"Your words are proof enough for me," she whispered, genuinely surprised at his statement.

"There is something more I'll do," he insisted, a plan forming in his mind. "I'll have it proclaimed in stone, so there'll be no question in all the land.

"There's a certain turning in the Nile to the south where a piece of land reaches into the river like a welcoming hand. On this land rises a cliff like a guardian facing the east. I have intended a temple to be carved into that cliff's face for some time, because it would be at just the angle where Ra's first light could reach into the sanctuary at the solstice." Ramessa got up and turned to face Nefertiry. "I'll order this temple begun immediately and I'll have another temple carved beside it. The second temple will be consecrated to Hat-Hor—and you."

Nefertiry stood up. Her lips were parted and her eyes were great green orbs of light. She was stunned, but she gathered her wits enough to whisper, "An entire temple dedicated to me?"

"You and Hat-Hor," Ramessa said solemnly.

"Your other wives—" she began.

"They'll envy you as they have from the first moment they looked upon your beauty," he said.

"My lord," Nefertiry whispered, too awed to say more.

Ramessa smiled and said, "Do you realize this is the first time I've made you speechless? I think you must lie down and regain your composure. We can play senit another time."

156

10

"What do you think of the squabble between the Lords Amamu and Mesemneter?" Ramessa asked Rasuah.

Rasuah had come to greet his king and exclaim over his victory. He found Ramessa in the seal room sitting at the game board with Nefertiry playing senit, and he joined them for a cup of wine.

Rasuah sipped his wine before replying, "It's a healthy example of their jealousies. The arguments between the governors of the cities and the governors of the provinces keep them from growing too intimate with each other, and from thinking of ways to give you trouble."

"Is that why you never appoint a governor of a major city the governor of that province?" Nefertiry asked, moving her game piece to a particularly crucial place on the board.

"Yes," Ramessa said thoughtfully. He studied the move she had made. After a moment, he looked up at Rasuah and said in exasperation, "Come here, Rasuah, and see what she's done to me. I don't know how to move."

Rasuah stood up and walked over to look at the senit board. He suppressed his smile. Nefertiry had certainly trapped Ramessa's pieces. "I think you've lost."

"I've won my first game with you?" Nefertiry asked.

Ramessa rubbed his chin and stared at the board. "Khakamir taught you well. Yes, you've won the game as you know perfectly well."

Ramessa was still studying the trap Nefertiry had arranged, when a servant entered the room to announce, "The high priest of Amen-Ra Akeset and his assistants Nehemu and Befen beg a moment with you, majesty."

"I wonder what they want now," Ramessa said shortly. "Admit them. Maybe they'll distract me from the sorrow of my defeat at the hands of the queen. They come, no doubt, to remark on the new temples."

Rasuah saw Nefertiry's eyes narrow and knew she was preparing to do verbal battle with the priests, for Seshena had already warned her about Akeset. He strolled to a couch discreetly away from the others, hoping to remain unnoticed while he observed what followed.

Akeset, flanked by the two other priests, entered the room at a brisk pace, his bright eyes respectfully lowered. But as he approached Ramessa, he cast a distinctly cold glance at Nefertiry. He stopped before Ramessa and raised his eyes to regard his king.

"Is your mind so immersed in the problem you bring that you forget to bow?" Ramessa coolly reminded. The priests promptly lowered themselves to their knees. Ramessa let them remain there a moment while he lifted his goblet and took a swallow of wine before he said, "You may rise."

The priests obeyed quickly. Then Akeset began, "Divine son of Ra—"

"Enough," Ramessa interrupted. "I know when you address me by that particular title you've come to ask a favor. State it quickly, so I may return to what I was doing, which is of singular importance."

Akeset's eyes went to the senit board, and anger stirred in him. "Majesty, I've heard of your plans to build a new temple."

"Two temples, side by side," Ramessa corrected.

"They're to be dedicated to Hat-Hor?" Nehemu asked.

"The principal temple will be dedicated to Ptah and myself, the other to Hat-Hor and the queen," Ramessa said coolly.

"Majesty, long have I begged for certain repairs to be made on the temple of Amen," Akeset reminded.

"The needed repairs were made; the others were unnecessary," Ramessa said curtly. "Such repairs are costly, and I must set limits somewhere."

"But, majesty, did not Amen come to your aid in those recent battles and give you victory?" Befen asked.

Ramessa sighed. "Those victories came immediately after the temple was repaired and I deemed my triumphs as rewards from Amen-Ra for fixing his temple in the first place. The priests from Montu's temple aren't here asking favors. Montu rules over battles."

"Maybe I'm bold in my request, but the needs of Amen's temple force me to ask how Hat-Hor and Ptah have lately favored you, that you build such costly temples in their honor while you ignore Amen?" Akeset insisted on asking.

"I haven't ignored Amen," Ramessa said, "but I cannot each day issue new orders that add to your wealth."

"You won't grant our request?" Befen whispered.

"I'm considering it," Ramessa replied. "I cannot ignore Ptah, because he makes manifest many requests. I honor Hat-Hor for giving me my queen and the son she carries."

Akeset saw the smug look on Nefertiry's face before she turned away, and fresh anger rose in him. "This child—half Khatti blood, half enemy blood—deserves more honor than those of your sons who are pure Tameran?"

159

"This child knows nothing of battles and is, in any case, a positive result of the peace treaty," Ramessa said coldly. "And I wish to honor the love of my queen."

"This princess from Khatti is already more honored than any woman of Tamera by your having pronounced her First Royal Wife," Akeset said heatedly. "Now you would compare this foreign woman to Hat-Hor, set up her statue beside Hat-Hor's holy figures?"

"You say 'Khatti' as if it's a thing to spit upon," Nefertiry said softly. She turned slowly and lifted her head to stare at Akeset. "You will soon learn I'm not a thing to spit upon."

Although Akeset pretended to ignore Nefertiry's words, a great hatred for her was irrevocably congealing in his heart. He said, "Perhaps Amen-Ra will be angered by this decision, majesty. Perhaps he'll bring some evil on the land or to this unborn child you honor above Amen's own temple. I, however, will pray mightily that such sorrows will not come."

"I can see you're full of mighty prayers," Nefertiry said softly.

"It would be well for you to remember that Nefertiry does wear Hat-Hor's crown," Ramessa said. "And you might also remember that it isn't for the priesthood to question my decisions."

"Will you grant any part of our request?" Nehemu cautiously asked.

Ramessa turned to Nefertiry and asked, "What would you sacrifice from Hat-Hor's temple to further enrich Amen-Ra's?"

"Not one pillar, my lord," Nefertiry replied, staring through Akeset as if he didn't exist.

"Such is my decision," Ramessa declared. He turned to the priests and said, "You may go."

Akeset bowed to Ramessa and began to walk backwards, still bowing, toward the door. But his eyes, looking at Nefertiry from beneath his eyebrows, burned with fury.

When the priests had left, Rasuah got up from the

couch and, approaching Ramessa and Nefertiry, remarked, "You've made an enemy of him, divine lady."

Nefertiry sighed. "Every time I breathe I seem to cause new emnity."

"Enough of such dreary subjects," Ramessa said, beckoning to a servant, who refilled their wine goblets.

"Do you wish another game of senit?" Nefertiry asked.

Ramessa shook his head. "I haven't enough time before I must meet with my surveyors and architects," he said. "But stay a little longer, Rasuah. I would converse with you for a moment to lighten my mood after those accursed priests."

Rasuah's lips tilted with humor. "But, majesty, they're praying so mightily for your sake."

"They pray mightily for gold," Ramessa said, dropping into a couch. He patted the space beside him, inviting Rasuah to sit there. Tell us something of your latest lady and return to me my better mood."

"There's little to say on that account," Rasuah replied cautiously.

"Don't lie to your king, even if he is your friend," Ramessa cheerfully scolded. "I don't believe my first envoy cannot find a woman in all of Tamera who pleases him."

"There is one who may please me," Rasuah said slowly, "but I don't care to speak lightly of her."

"This sounds most serious," Ramessa observed, raising his eyebrows. "Then speak of her not at all, but bring her to the palace to share the evening meal with us." Rasuah opened his mouth as if to protest, but Ramessa added, "Have you forgotten the party tonight honoring the anniversary of the queen's birth? You will attend it, won't you?"

"Of course," Rasuah said.

"Tell me the name of the lady in question and I'll dispatch a messenger to give her a personal invitation," Ramessa urged.

161

Rasuah smiled at his king's curiosity and said, "I have in mind the high priestess of Aset's temple, Seshena."

Nefertiry lifted her eyes from the game board to say, "I already invited Seshena and she has accepted."

"Then the matter is settled," Ramessa declared, and got to his feet. Rasuah also stood up. "I'll walk with you through the garden. The perfume of the trees and flowers will clear from my nostrils the smell of those priests."

When Rasuah had bid Nefertiry a pleasant afternoon, she watched him walk with Ramessa to the door with a speculative look in her eyes. At last she understood why Seshena had omitted Rasuah's name from the list of Nefertiry's prospective lovers.

Although Nefertiry didn't expect to see Khakamir alone for some time—very likely not until after she'd borne the child—a vision of him rose in her memory that gave her a pang. His slanted eyes lit with the fire of when they had loved. The softness of his voice when he'd murmured love words to her. The touch of his hands on her flesh. The hard muscles of his soldier's body. The feel of his lips on hers. She cared nothing for Rasuah or for any of the other noblemen now, she knew. Khakamir would be the only man she'd require when Ramessa didn't call. Khakamir gave her his trust, his love and respect as generously as any man in love. Nefertiry wondered how it was possible to care so much for two men at the same time.

Seshena had never attended a party in the palace. Although she'd anticipated the occasion being lavishly elegant, she was surprised at the scene in the banquet room. The combined perfumes of the ladies and the flowers garlanding the room were like a solid presence in the air, strong enough to make Aset's temple's penetrating incense seem pallid by comparison. The chatter and laughter of the room's occupants practically drowned out the musicians' best efforts. Taking a deep breath, Seshena

162

moved to the side of the doorway, where she could accustom her senses to the scene before truly joining it.

One look at the other female guests told the priestess she was clothed more like a servant than guest. Although Seshena's garment was of the finest, silkiest linen, all that distinguished the simple shift from those of the servants was the gold-embroidered border circling her hem, her garment's fine pleats were not nearly so sheer as the servants', which were transparent enough to show the rosy nipples of their breasts through the cloth. Seshena sighed. At least her lapis lazuli necklace and gold bracelets were the match of the other guests' jewelry, although they wore it in more impressive quantities. But the other women's garments were a rainbow of colors and some were cut so precariously low they had to be held up with narrow beaded straps or were gathered up on one shoulder with the other side dipping so far a sneeze would mean disaster. Seshena smiled at the idea, but her smile slowly faded as she noticed the other women's hair, which was elaborately curled or braided with jewels, while hers was straight and unbound, adorned only by the golden cord drawn around her forehead, its loose ends hanging down in the back. Even the men wore long and colorful robes gathered at their waists with elaborately embroidered sashes, the fringed ends falling to their knees. Only the army officers wore simple, short white tunics, which were adorned by nothing but the swords that lay against their hips.

Ramessa had noted Seshena's entrance and had watched her carefully. Recognizing her confusion, he leaned closer to Rasuah and said, "Your little priestess has arrived. Bring her to our table."

Rasuah, who had been absorbed in a conversation with two ministers, immediately ended his part in the discussion and stood up. He walked with long strides toward the priestess.

Ramessa watched curiously to see how Rasuah and

163

Seshena would greet each other, and he wasn't entirely disappointed. Although they passed a moment in what he was sure was merely exchanging the ordinary courteous greetings, his sharp eyes observed a certain softening in Rasuah's expression. Rasuah moved to stand as if protecting her from the scurryings of the servants. Although Seshena's smile revealed little beyond friendliness, Ramessa noticed that she stood looking up at Rasuah with the attitude of a lotus reaching toward the sun. When Rasuah led Seshena to the royal table, Ramessa stood up.

"Majesty, this is too great an honor that I sit with you," Seshena murmured, beginning to gather her robe in preparation to bow.

"Don't bow, Seshena," Ramessa said warmly and extended his hand to her. He was aware that he caused a stir among the watching crowd by offering her his hand. He also noticed the fire momentarily flashing through Rasuah's eyes at his gesture. He smiled at both reactions. He didn't mind causing a raised eyebrow or two among the smug noblemen and their ladies, but Rasuah's quickly controlled possessiveness was especially interesting to him.

"Divine lady," Seshena said, beginning to bow before Nefertiry, half-expecting the queen to stop her from bowing as Ramessa had.

Nefertiry didn't. She, too, had raised an eyebrow at Ramessa's unconcealed warmth to Seshena. And when Seshena extended to her a small, exquisitely carved box trimmed with gold, offering Nefertiry congratulations on the anniversary of her birth, Nefertiry thanked the priestess coolly and handed the gift to Chenmet for later examination.

Thus dismissed by the queen, Seshena turned to Rasuah who helped her to a seat beside him.

"Don't feel unhappy that Nefertiry didn't look at your gift now. She's put aside all of them," Rasuah whispered, hoping to smooth over the deliberate snub.

Seshena smiled at him. "I understand the queen better
164

than she understands herself and what she did raises no pangs in my heart," she whispered. "Besides, my gift is far too humble and better left unexhibited to this elegant crowd."

Rasuah sighed. "I would think your gift was given with purer intentions than the others, who bring elaborate and useless presents hoping to gain favors." He paused while a servant poured wine into their goblets; then he lifted the goblet and murmured, "I give tribute to the most beautiful lady here."

Seshena lifted her goblet and, looking at Nefertiry, whispered, "She is beautiful, isn't she?"

"I mean you, Seshena," Rasuah said softly.

Startled, Seshena looked at Rasuah. But before she could reply, a servant had reached between them to place a basket of fruit on the table. He was followed by a line of servants who brought a bowl of herb-garnished vegetables, a platter of steaming fish and another of roast lamb.

As the guests were being served, the musicians began to play so vigorously that intimate conversation was impossible, so Seshena spoke little to Rasuah. But she was acutely aware of his eyes on her often.

A dancer, wearing nothing but a narrow beaded girdle around her hips and long, floating white feathers in her hair, slid onto the center floor like a snake. So sinuously and suggestively did the dancer perform, Seshena wasn't sure where to look. It wasn't that Seshena was ordinarily alarmed at nakedness or even suggestiveness, but with Rasuah sitting beside her, she found the thoughts that were going through her own mind distracted her. After dropping several small morsels of food, she began to feel as if she had no grasp to her fingers and became afraid to lift the food to her mouth, lest she drop something noticeable and embarrass herself in this elite company.

She brushed aside her confused thoughts and carefully lifted her goblet. The wine was the only thing she seemed able to taste, she decided. Maybe it was merely that the wine was cool, while the room had begun to seem stifling to her. It was especially warm when Rasuah occasionally touched her hand or, turning, brushed her arm. But by the time the main part of the meal was over and the servants came to carry away the used plates and platters of food that had been left, Seshena found herself feeling dizzy.

"You've been so quiet, I wonder if something troubles you," Rasuah asked.

Seshena turned to look at him and found it difficult to focus her eyes. "I'm not troubled," she managed to murmur. She remained staring at Rasuah, hoping that if she fixed her eyes on him his image would clear.

"It's very warm in this room," Rasuah observed tactfully. "Would you like to step into the garden and refresh yourself?"

"The warmth of the room has inspired my thirst, and I think I've drunk too much wine," she admitted.

"Perhaps the air will clear your head."

"I'm really quite dizzy," Seshena confessed, looking down in embarrassment at the table. "I'm not sure I should walk anywhere."

"Walking is the best answer," Rasuah replied and stood up. He bent toward her. "Others are also beginning to move around again so we'll go unnoticed. I'll put my arm around your waist and guide you, if you're unsteady."

Seshena stared at her lap for a moment, wondering if she should have Rasuah so close to her in her present untrustworthy state. She looked up at him while she was trying to decide. He took her hands in his, and, without waiting for her answer, gently but firmly, pulled her to her feet. Seshena was vaguely aware of a servant brushing past her, although she paid no attention to the man who was carrying one of the little golden urns. But he bumped Seshena in his passing and a bit of the liquid from the overfilled urn splashed on the hem of her robe.

As she glanced down at her robe, she was amazed to see a small black hole eating through the cloth. She stared at it for several seconds while Rasuah, not noticing the spill, thought she was trying to steady her balance.

"My lord—" Seshena began.

"How often must I ask you to call me by my name?" Rasuah reminded her.

"But Rasuah—" She began again.

Seshena was interrupted by a crash as a chair fell backwards and slid along the floor. Turning quickly, though her head spun with her movement, she saw that Nefertiry had leaped to her feet and was staring, horrified, at the floor.

"Take out that man and beat him!" Ramessa commanded a nearby guard.

"Is my life held in so little regard that the man who saved me—if only by his clumsiness—is punished?" Nefertiry asked in a peculiarly tight tone. Ramessa turned to look at her with a confused expression. Nefertiry pointed to the floor, where dark liquid was spreading along the stone, making a faint sizzling sound. "What do you think that wine would have done to me?" she demanded. "That wine is my favorite and was meant for me alone."

"Assassin!" Ramessa shouted. "Why did you do it?"

"I didn't!" the man cried. "I took the wine from the queen's private jar. I put nothing in it. Ask anyone! I drew the wine before them all, hiding nothing."

"You lie! What did you put into that wine?" Ramessa demanded.

"Nothing, majesty," the man gasped. "Call the guards, divine one, and let them whip the flesh from my spine, the skin from my feet! Have them split my tongue and force out my eyes, but I can tell you no more!"

Ramessa continued to glare at the shivering servant as he considered the possible penalties he might bestow, when he felt Nefertiry's hand tugging at his arm. He turned to face her.

Nefertiry's eyes had narrowed. "The priestess is here," she hissed. "Let her penetrate the minds of those present and tell us who's guilty."

Seshena stepped forward shakily. "Majesty, divine lady, I cannot tell you what you seek," she whispered. "My mind has been befuddled with wine, I'm shamed to admit."

Nefertiry looked at Seshena, surprised. "I don't believe it," she snapped. She came closer and stared into Seshena's eyes. "You've been drugged," she said softly. "The pupils of your eyes are abnormally enlarged. It was done so you'd be incapable of naming the assassin, who obviously knew you'd be here and what you can do."

"Yet I cannot help you, whatever the reason for the state I'm in," Seshena said sadly.

Nefertiry turned to Ramessa. "Have this servant released. He knows nothing," she said sharply. Taking a deep breath, she added more quietly, "Let me have Khakamir as my personal guard. I trust him alone among your soldiers."

"He's yours!" Ramessa agreed instantly. "But what of the one who so carefully planned your death?"

Nefertiry was silent a long moment as she considered who among her enemies would dare her assassination. The face of the high priest of Amen came to her mind. Akeset had good reason to want her out of his way, she realized. Akeset also knew what powers Seshena possessed. It would have been a small matter for him to learn that Seshena would attend this banquet. Her eyes narrowed. She would later give Akeset her own kind of warning, she decided. She looked up at Ramessa. "The assassin will eventually reveal himself," she said in a calmer tone. "In the meanwhile, I'll have tasters for my food, not slaves assigned to that task, my lord, but anyone I choose from those standing with me in such a company."

Ramessa nodded his head. "You're very wise," he

said. "As you've asked, so will it be. But I'll yet have an investigation made."

"It's gratifying that my lord places so high a value on my life," Nefertiry murmured. "I thank you."

"Although I surely value my queen, I also value the prince she carries," Ramessa whispered.

Nefertiry looked at Ramessa a little sharply, wondering how to accept this, but she quickly recovered herself and turned to Rasuah. "Lord Rasuah, will you see Seshena home safely?"

"I'll gladly escort her," Rasuah said with feeling. He turned to Seshena. "Perhaps we should go now."

Seshena nodded dazedly. "I am sorry, divine lady," she whispered.

"You cannot be faulted for a drug slipped into your wine by another's hand," Nefertiry said. "Return to the palace tomorrow, late in the day, for I know your recovery might be time-consuming."

Rasuah took Seshena's arm and led her carefully toward the door, his arm around her waist to steady her. "I think I'd best carry you," he murmured.

"Oh no!" Seshena protested. "I can walk."

Rasuah only smiled and picked her up in his arms.

The ride home in her litter was at first a confusion of lights and movements to Seshena, for her sight was yet blurred. But she applied her will to ridding her body of the drug's effects, and gradually her eyes focused. By the time Rasuah helped her from the litter, she was only mildly dizzy.

"I'll walk you into the house," Rasuah said sternly. He turned to the servants who had carried the litter. "Go to your beds," he directed. "I'll care for the lady and find my own way home." When the servants had disappeared into the courtyard's darkness, Rasuah said, "Now, I think you'd best walk to work off that drug's effect."

"It's mostly gone, I think," she said cautiously.

"Whatever your condition, I'm here," Rasuah replied, again sliding his arm around her waist.

"Don't you realize that drug could as easily have been poison?" Rasuah said anxiously.

"Who would poison me?" Seshena asked.

"Whoever tried to poison the queen."

"If the assassin understood my abilities—which I know he must—he also realizes it's a different thing to kill Aset's high priestess than the king's favorite wife," she declared. "If they value their soul's immortality or even their happiness in this life, they'd never poison me, for Aset herself would be my avenger."

"Tell me nothing of Aset's revenge," Rasuah said gruffly. "I don't want to think of your murder."

"Why does it make you angry to speak of it?" she asked.

"Let your thoughts explore mine, priestess, and you'll know," Rasuah whispered.

"I cannot. It's against my training." she said. "You must tell me."

Rasuah's golden eyes looked down at her for a moment. Then he bent closer; sliding both arms around her, he kissed her softly. His mouth lingered on hers, softly caressing her lips while he kissed unhurriedly, thoughtfully, as if he had made a decision.

Seshena's legs felt strangely weakened, and there was a pleasant, soft throbbing in her temples; it spread through her being. Finally, she drew away and stared at him.

"Is this how you behave when you promise to bring me home?" she asked, trying to disguise her feelings with the teasing accusation.

"I helped you home as I promised. I try to be on my best behavior at all times. At the moment, I'm doing the best I can for the situation I'm in." Then, he bent forward slightly; and his lips again took possession of hers.

Her arms lifted and encircled him. She wondered if it was yet the drug loosening her restraints. Then, she remembered that on the other two occasions he'd kissed
170

her her normal reticence had fled at the touch of his mouth on hers; the drug had long since left her brain. It was the texture of his hair brushing her cheek as his lips moved to her ear, the warm, slightly musky scent of his skin as he buried his face in her hair and the taste of his mouth that sent new spirals of fire down her spine. And she knew, if she would stop, it must be soon.

"Someone might come looking for me," Seshena whispered against his mouth.

"I'll kill anyone who touches that door," Rasuah murmured.

His lips again claimed hers, momentarily stopping further words as her senses were swept forward on the wave of desire he'd created in her. When she again was on the edge of moaning from the impact of the sweet aching he gave her, his mouth released hers and moved down her neck to the hollow of her throat, slowly and lingeringly traveling downward.

"Rasuah!" she gasped.

"What's wrong?" His whisper came from against her chest.

"I'm not sure I should do this," she said hastily, wishing her voice wasn't so breathless.

Instantly, Rasuah rose to kneel over Seshena and look down at her. "Have you taken a vow of some kind?" he asked. Hastily, she shook her head. "Is what I'm doing offensive to you?" he asked more softly, a knowing look coming into his eyes. Seshena stared up at him speechlessly and he smiled. "You know, Seshena, how I want you." She nodded weakly in answer. "Do you want me less than that?"

She was unable to lie and unwilling to admit how wild was her own desire when he touched her—and at that moment he was very lightly and with one finger stroking the side of her breast. "How can I think to answer when you're doing that?" she whispered helplessly.

"That is your answer," he murmured. "If I didn't affect you, I would get up immediately and go. What I'm

171

doing is really not so much. There is so much more to love."

His hands slipped lower, moving over her body, arousing her even through her garment. When her blood was like fire racing through her veins and she shuddered under his touch, he drew away and asked, "Does the lamp bother you?"

She stared at him as her mind struggled to focus on his question. "No," she managed to whisper.

"Excellent," he said clearly. "I want to see you while we make love. You can also see in my face how you're pleasing me."

Seshena shivered at Rasuah's words and at the glowing in his tawny eyes when the flickering lamp cast lights in them. He looked at her intently for a moment, then sat up.

With deliberately slow movements, he untied the golden cord at her waist, and she knew he was allowing her time to make any serious protests. The words died in her throat under his golden gaze. Slowly, purposefully, he untied his own sash and let it slide to the floor. When he again leaned over her, his robe fell apart. When his body pressed against her, his warmth penetrated the fragile fabric of her garment until it was almost as if she too were naked.

This time, when Rasuah kissed Seshena, her response rose unchecked. With the opening of her own floodgates, the full measure of her desire poured into her. Her mouth was as hungry as his and her body was as eager as his and the sensations streaking through her became a solid fire.

When Rasuah's lips again descended to Seshena's throat, she flung back her head. When his mouth moved lower, she trembled in anticipation. But his fingers could not further move the stubborn neckline of her robe, and he stopped. He reached toward her feet to tug at the hem of her shift with only small success. He looked at her meaningfully.

Seshena abruptly sat up and tore at her robe so fiercely

she heard the dainty pleats rip, but she pulled the garment up over her head and defiantly threw it on the floor. Rasuah shrugged off his robe, then leaned toward her.

He kissed her tenderly, many times, before his tenderness began to diminish in the face of his passion, and his lips grew harder, his mouth more demanding. Seshena's instincts, now loosed, guided her own response. She found her hands exploring his body as he had hers, and she felt his muscles tense and him catch his breath. This knowledge, that what she did so aroused him, was a new flare lighting in her. She pressed herself even closer; feeling his shudder, her arms locked around his back as if destiny had long ago decreed this moment. It was hers only to obey her fate. His body moved to cover hers, and the long, firm length of his legs twined with her legs.

Very carefully did destiny join them, so carefully it was but one more step on this path which stretched limitlessly before them.

Seshena opened her eyes to find Rasuah also acknowledged the significance of this moment—beyond the physical urges shrieking in their senses, this stepping into infinity together—for he had also opened his golden eyes and his look was filled with wonder. Finally, she heard his gasp—and their separate flares combined into the brilliance of one exploding sun.

11

The sun streaming through the windows finally penetrated the dark layers of Seshena's slumber. Her consciousness, catching onto one of the golden shafts, ascended slowly into daylight. She opened her eyes and turned her head to see Rasuah standing before the open doorway, looking out onto her garden.

"You're still with me," she murmured.

"Yes, I'm still here," he replied. "Did you think I would lie with you until you slept, then creep away in the night like a thief who carries away his loot after having accomplished his purpose?"

"Not after what we experienced," Seshena whispered. "It's only that the morning has already passed, I can see from the lack of shadows. Surely you have many things to do."

Rasuah's face relaxed and he approached her smiling. "I've sent Nehara away three times," he said softly, sitting down on the bed. "The many other things I have

175

to do can wait. I know what's important. Do you want me to leave you?"

Seshena's fingers slowly slid up his arms to his shoulders. "No," she said clearly.

Rasuah looked down into Seshena's eyes, whose blue had become a darkened, smoky color, and he whispered, "You know what we experienced last night went beyond the pleasures of our bodies." Seshena nodded. "It has begun as I predicted, a thing without limits, without end," he said. When she was silent he asked, "Do you fear such a thing?"

"A priestess learns not to fear the unknowns of infinity," she whispered. "A woman doesn't willingly turn from love."

Rasuah silently regarded her for a moment, the same look of wonder on his face as when they'd loved last night. He leaned down and gathered her in his arms, burying his face in her hair. Finally he drew away and looked down at her. "Can you wait a little longer for food?"

"I would gladly wait until I have no strength left and am capable of nothing else," she whispered staring into his tawny eyes.

"Nehara will be shocked, perhaps, with how long we stay together," he observed.

"If you already sent Nehara away three times, she's as shocked as she can become. Did she seem so to you when she came?"

"The first time I unfastened the door, she looked as if it weren't a common thing to find a man in your bedroom in the morning—a thing which gladdened, but didn't surprise me." Rasuah smiled. "She bid me good morning, asked if we wanted the morning meal, and left when I told her no. When she came the next time, she discreetly knocked before entering and went away with an expressionless face. The third time she went away unsuccessfully trying to conceal her smile." Rasuah leaned closer,

176

propping himself up on his elbows. "I heard the outer door close awhile ago, and I think she went to the market-place, so she must not disapprove of me too much because she trusts you alone with me."

Seshena considered this a moment, then observed, "She plans a special meal for us when we're ready, because my kitchen is not without food. She must approve of you to go through all that trouble." She put her hands at the sides of his face. "She'll be some time cooking whatever she has planned and we'll have considerable time before she'll come to us again. How would you like to use this time?"

"To our mutual benefit," he whispered. Her hands on his temples pulled his face to hers.

Nefertiry tilted her head to one side and raised her eyebrows in mock surprise. "It's twilight and almost time for the evening meal. Did the drug take so long to disperse?" she inquired. At Seshena's silence, Nefertiry smiled knowingly. "Answer nothing, for I know as well as you what needed dispersing. Lord Rasuah is an excellent choice."

Seshena watched Nefertiry walk to a couch and sit down. "I had no chance to meditate on last night's events and, so, yet have no answer for you," she admitted.

Nefertiry looked up at the priestess. "I don't doubt you had no time. Meditate if you must, Seshena, but I'm already certain who was behind the poisoning."

"Who do you think it was?" she asked cautiously.

"You already warned me of the priests' plots," Nefertiry said. "A few days ago Akeset came with two others and criticized the king's decision to build a temple in honor of me. Akeset wanted gold for his own temple. The discussion warmed when Akeset spoke about me as if I weren't in the room—making derogatory remarks about my being a princess from Khatti and being honored as Ramessa has honored none of his Tameran wives. I had

177

stayed my temper, but at this point, I answered him sharply." She paused for a moment, then declared, "I could do no less."

"More was at stake than a temple," Seshena murmured.

"Much more," Nefertiry agreed. "The priest pressed even further. The king's temper was rising, but my own was far beyond his. The priests accused me of having too much influence on the king's decisions. They did this carefully, without actually saying it, but their meaning wasn't lost to me."

"Did the king understand their purpose?" Seshena asked cautiously.

"Not entirely," Nefertiry replied. "It was necessary for him to then defend his own decisions, which he did, saying it wasn't for the priesthood to question him." Nefertiry raised her eyes to look at Seshena and anger blazed in their dark green depths. "The king asked me what I would give up from my temple so Amen's temple could have it. He put the decision in my hands out of defiance to them. Although I saw my own danger in Akeset's eyes, I was furious, and I answered that I would give up not one pillar. Akeset left giving me a look of hatred so thick it could have been measured and spooned into my wine as a potent enough poison."

"It probably was Akeset's scheme to poison your wine and get you out of his way forever," Seshena agreed. "He would certainly have grave misgivings about my presence at the banquet, because he'd know what I could do. He could leave nothing to chance and I have no doubt he would think of drugging me." She sighed. "He has enough knowledge of drugs—and poisons."

"So I thought," Nefertiry said. "Now I must decide what I'll do about him."

"You cannot denounce a high priest publicly unless you have evidence no one dares question," Seshena said quickly. "What you do must be most carefully planned. He's a formidable opponent."

"I can wait until the right moment. The pattern that wine ate into the stone of the floor will remind me every day of Akeset's capacity for evil," Nefertiry replied.

"A statue of Mut, our earth-mother, will be prominently placed in your temple. Her likeness will be modeled after your own," Ramessa said enthusiastically. He glanced up from the architect's drawing spread out on the table and smiled brightly at Nefertiry. "It will be most appropriate, don't you think, to have it carved while you're pregnant?"

"Yes," Nefertiry sighed, "as long as the statue can be done near where I may conveniently retire suddenly if this miserable nausea continues."

"It's too trying, this sickness?" Ramessa asked anxiously.

Nefertiry sighed again. "It comes and goes. Tonight it's most disgustingly present."

"Has the physician heard of this?" Ramessa asked.

Nefertiry nodded. "He has already made me drink some evil-smelling potion that made me worse, it seems." She took a deep breath, then looked at him and smiled wryly. "Continue to tell me about your plans. My ears aren't sick and discussion of this temple distracts me as pleasantly as any other way might."

"There will be two statues of me on each side of the doorway and between each of these pairs, there will be a statue of you—as tall in proportion to my statues as you are in proportion to me," he said.

Nefertiry knew the great honor Ramessa was conferring on her by not making her figures mere miniatures standing at his feet. "The priests will be further irked at the honor you're showing me," she murmured.

"Honoring you is this temple's whole purpose," he replied, looking very pleased at her recognition of his gesture. "The pillars inside will be statues of Hat-Hor, their faces carved after your likeness."

Ramessa looked so much like a young boy in his enthusiasm, Nefertiry smiled. "And the walls?"

"They will tell of how I obtained my Khatti princess," he said, excitedly.

"They will depict the downfall of Khatti?" Nefertiry asked. At his nod she shrugged, then lowered herself to a pillow on the floor and began to caress Botar, who had been drowsing.

"In keeping with the story of our meeting, I must have the battles recorded," Ramessa said.

Nefertiry reflected on the many factors involved that would never be recorded on stone or even papyrus. "Will the temple walls be covered with carvings of your face and name?" she asked thoughtfully.

Ramessa looked carefully at her expression. Her face, as she stroked the big cat, held no resentment. "I'm king and the temple is mine, though I dedicate it to you," he explained. "It's just as my lips must kiss every inch of you. You're mine, though I dedicate these kisses to love."

Nefertiry didn't wish to be drawn into another discussion regarding love, so she said nothing. In order to not dwell on love and the inward nausea that prevented love's expression, she turned her thoughts to Akeset and how she might stop him. She put her face closer to Botar's and stared into the cat's amber eyes, thinking how conveient it would be if Botar could devour Akeset.

Watching Nefertiry, Ramessa had the eerie feeling she was making an unspoken agreement with the cat. He shook off the feeling and said lightly, "When you get that calculating look in your eyes, someone is in trouble."

"I was merely thinking of Botar's unquestioning loyalty," she replied quickly, turning to face him.

He looked at her a moment. The glitter in her eyes put the lie to her innocent tone of voice. "Hah!" he said and turned to look again at his drawings. But Ramessa found it impossible now to concentrate on the temple's plans because his mind kept remembering the look in Nefertiry's eyes. He wondered why she was most provocative to him when she looked most deceptive. Finally, he rolled up the scroll and turned to face her. "The hour is late, I'm weary and would go to bed. Will you lie with me?"

Nefertiry glanced up at Ramessa. If he had been asking her for love, she would now have begged his pardon, because the physician's mixture hadn't lessened her nausea to the slightest degree. But as Ramessa had clearly mentioned his weariness, she decided he wanted only her warm body close to him. She stood up. "The son of Ra has only to speak and I obey," she said.

He took her hand and led her to his bed. "You will remove this garment?" he asked.

Nefertiry pulled the loose robe over her head. Noting how he looked at the beginning roundness of her stomach she said, "Soon I'll be so distorted you won't wish to look upon my nakedness."

Ramessa smiled and put his hands on her arms. "This isn't the first child I've sired and not the first pregnancy I've witnessed," he said. He put his arms around her. "I've made love to wives far more advanced than you are now. I expect to continue with you until it becomes unsafe." He felt her body stiffen against him, and instantly knew he shouldn't have mentioned his other wives. He was irritated. How could he forever avoid all reference to them, when Nefertiry had known from the beginning they had been in his harem long before he'd laid eyes on her? "Let us get into bed," he murmured.

As Ramessa dropped his robe and approached the bed, Nefertiry's perfume drifted to him on an air current, beckoning. As he put one knee on the bed, he smiled at her without realizing it. When she smiled in return, he mistook her smile for invitation. He got into bed and moved closer to her side, sliding one hand down to her thigh and stroking the satin skin, his intentions now unmistakable.

Nefertiry lay like a stone. She wondered what she might say without offending him. Noting that his caresses were becoming more insistent and he increasingly aroused, she decided she must remind him of her problem. "My lord," she whispered, "I would welcome your attention tonight, but, truly, the physician's medicine has taken no effect on me."

"You're yet unsettled?" he asked in a disgusted tone.

"In a tumult is a better description," she said regretfully.

He was silent for a long moment, very disappointed, but loathe to admit it. "Why didn't you say it before you got into bed?"

"But, my lord, I just did as we were discussing the temple!" she declared. "When you spoke of your weariness, I thought you wanted my company as you slept."

"When I intend to sleep, I lie down alone," Ramessa said sharply, his pride irked by her rebuff. He moved his hand and inadvertently rested his arm across her stomach.

At the pressure of Ramessa's arm on this now acutely sensitive area, Nefertiry felt a new wave of nausea roll over her. "My lord, I must arise quickly!" she gasped.

Ramessa's eyes widened at the panic in her tone and he instantly leaped out of bed. Nefertiry followed him, her face glistening with moisture and as pale as the linens. Hastily, she picked up her robe, but she yet ran naked through the golden doorway into her own chambers without a backward glance.

Ramessa stood silently a moment considering the situation. He was resentful without knowing why, because he realized Nefertiry's illness was no pretense. Yet he needed a woman with a sudden hunger that surprised him. He sighed, then walked toward the open doorway to her suite and stepped inside.

Chenmet emerged from an adjoining chamber and hurried toward another doorway. When she saw Ramessa, she stopped. "Yes, majesty?" she asked.

He frowned. "Tell the queen I bid her as good a night as is possible to her," he said. Then, he turned and went back into his room, closing the golden door behind him.

Ramessa sat on the edge of his bed staring into space

for a time, before he arose and went to the door that led to the outside corridor. He opened the door and snapped, "Bring Nofret to me."

When Nefertiry finally felt more settled, Chenmet put her arm around her waist and led her trembling queen toward the bed.

"The king—" Nefertiry began.

"His majesty stepped in to bid you as good a night as possible," Chenmet whispered. "You may rest without further explanations to him, I think."

"Did he seem angry?" she asked.

"I'd judge his majesty's mood to be more of disappointment," Chenmet replied.

Nefertiry got into her bed, suspicious of the clouds gathering in Chenmet's eyes. "He said nothing, then, to indicate he was angry?" she questioned. Chenmet looked at the floor and shook her head. "Then what is it that so disturbs you?" Nefertiry asked. When the maid remained silent, she demanded, "What is it, Chenmet? Look at me and answer!"

Chenmet dragged her eyes up to meet the queen's. "When his majesty returned to his room, I heard him ask for Nofret to be brought to him," she murmured.

Nefertiry stared at Chenmet for a long moment, a wounded look in her eyes. Finally she whispered, "Go to bed, Chenmet. I'll call if I need you."

She kept her face away from Chenmet until she heard the door close behind the servant. Then, Nefertiry turned to look accusingly at the golden door. As great, scalding tears ran down her cheeks, she whispered angrily, "And I cannot even blame him for giving me this child."

Finally Nefertiry blew out her lamp and lay back to stare through the darkness at the gold door gleaming softly in the moonlight, wondering that Ramessa could make love to Nofret while she lay ill in the next room. By the time dawn had begun to light the terrace outside

183

Nefertiry's window openings, she had decided she hated Ramessa, and she had cursed Nofret and every other occupant of Ramessa's harem many times.

With dawn's full blossoming, Nefertiry's nausea returned, and she remained in bed. By the time Nehri arrived to remind Nefertiry this was the day of audiences, her appearance was such that Nehri returned to report to his master with alarm. Ramessa at once marched through the golden doorway into Nefertiry's room.

Longing to scream at him, to leap up and rake his face with her nails, Nefertiry instead covered her head with the bed linens to hide the fury in her eyes as well as her tears of frustration.

Thinking Nefertiry didn't want to affront him with the sight of her wretchedness, Ramessa sat on the edge of the bed and consolingly patted her shoulder through the covers. "The physician will soon be here," he said. She shuddered with renewed anger, but he thought she wept from her misery. "Tuiah will sit with me today. Have no fear. Worry about nothing. Just rest yourself."

After a moment more—which seemed to Nefertiry like six eternities—Ramessa got to his feet and left the room. With fury, Nefertiry flung the covers off her head and sat up stiffly while Chenmet crept to Ramessa's door to listen.

"His majesty has gone to the audience," Chenmet finally said.

At this news Nefertiry leaped from the bed, her eyes blazing. "His majesty! His majesty and his mother at his side!" She screamed in the language of Khatti so the guards in the hall wouldn't understand her words. "The mother will be very happy to sit for the audience! One wife from his assortment took my place last night—his mother replaces me today!" She stamped her foot. "When that accursed physician comes—" She stopped.

The physician had just opened the door and stepped into her room. Her eyes narrowed like an attacking leopard's. The physician stared at her expression and
184

was afraid to move closer. She picked up a small alabaster lamp.

"Useless one! Your remedies put a sandstorm in my throat and a demon in my belly!" She threw the lamp like a javelin and the physician ducked. The lamp smashed against the wall. "Get out! Out! Out!" she screamed. "If you touch me again, I'll tear your skin from your body in small shreds with my own hands!" She fired a cosmetic jar at the terrified physician, who leaped backwards into the hall and slammed the door after him.

Nefertiry turned to Chenmet. "Get Seshena," she panted. "Ask if the healers from Aset's temple can help me. Ask her to cure me by magic—anything! I must be rid of this illness by nightfall."

As Tuiah came to meet him in the corridor, Ramessa merely nodded in answer to her greetings, paused so she might come to his side, then resumed walking toward the throne room, saying nothing to his mother. His thoughts were on Nefertiry.

He had never been aware of any of his other wives suffering so intensely from a pregnancy, and he had begun to fear that something was wrong with Nefertiry. It was a possibility he didn't like to face. Although he tried to push away his growing alarm, it receded only for short periods of time.

Ramessa marched through the throne room amid noblemen and ministers, who prostrated themselves as he approached and passed, but he didn't see them. He was still worrying about Nefertiry's health. He sat on his throne, waved Henhenet aside, and beckoned to the Royal Master of the Secrets of the Heavens, then quietly asked the astrologer to study the stars concerning the queen and the child to come. As the astrologer hurried away, Nehemu asked permission to approach the throne.

Ramessa granted the request, but looked suspiciously

at the priest of Amen. "Have you come about the matter of the temple?"

"No, majesty," Nehemu said, rising from his bow. "I've heard the queen is unwell, and I would visit her to offer help."

Ramessa recognized the sly gleam in Nehemu's eyes and knew this offer was made only to impress him, not help Nefertiry. He reflected for a moment, and decided that Nefertiry was capable of handling Nehemu. Further, she would no doubt turn away the priest in a fashion that would later be fascinating to hear about and which would also discourage Nehemu from bothering either of them for a long time. "Yes, you may visit her," Ramessa said, and watched Nehemu hurry from the throne room.

Henhenet approached the dais carrying a sizeable box. "Majesty, Lord Kemsiyet has sent a gift to you."

Lord Kemsiyet was always sending gifts in the hope that Ramessa would, out of courtesy, repay them with more valuable items. "Open it," he said coolly, then leaned forward to look at the gift. Inside the box lay a gold circlet to which was attached various jagged shafts of gold that stood upright from the circlet. "What is that?" he demanded.

"Lord Kemsiyet described it as a new design for a crown he had one of the workers fashion to his order," Henhenet replied quietly.

Ramessa looked baffled. "Lift it up," he muttered. As Henhenet obeyed, Ramessa's eyes widened. "Surely this is a joke. To put that object on my head would be to appear formed like an ibex!" he exclaimed.

"What Kemsiyet's gift lacks in taste, it compensates for in imagination," Tuiah commented, looking critically at the crown.

"Kemsiyet sends me a trinket so I might send him a treasure," Ramessa muttered. "If this continues, my treasury will be emptied for his sake." He fell silent for a moment as he considered the problem, still staring at the crown. Finally, his lips curled in a sneer. "Transfer Lord
186

Kemsiyet to Bakhau. Finding himself in that mountainous region governing goats and Shasu, he'll be less inclined to send gifts," Ramessa directed. He took one more glance at the crown before disdainfully waving it away. "What matter is next?" he muttered.

The minister of construction came forward; and after obtaining Ramessa's permission to speak, began to read a long report about temples ordered by King Seti that were yet unfinished. Ramessa listened with half an ear to descriptions of sanctuaries partly-roofed, columns half-erected, blocked-out statues, unfinished porticos, and walls where some figures hadn't even been sketched, much less carved. In Wast itself, there was a great temple balanced precariously over the Nile since the last flood, which had carried away much of the earth supporting the foundation, the minister reminded him.

Ramessa sighed wearily and said, "When the twin temples to the south have been finished, begin the repairs on the temple here in Wast."

"Majesty, the cities in the eastern part of the delta are yet in a shambles from the Hyskos," the minister reminded.

"It's disgraceful that these cities are so neglected, I agree," Ramessa said, sitting up more alertly. "I've thought at length on those broken places, which are of no use to their citizens now established elsewhere and bring no taxes to my treasury." He paused a moment, then continued, "I also have a large quantity of people descended from the prisoners of those wars, as well as prisoners from our last battle with Khatti, who serve little purpose. I don't need an army of slaves and I don't want to loose them only to have them form more bandit gangs to plague travelers. I've decided to send all those people to that northern area and set them to work rebuilding the very towns they and their ancestors devastated."

Henhenet stepped closer and listened with great interest to the king's words. When Ramessa finished speaking, the prime minister asked, "Majesty, who will live in these towns when they're rebuilt? For as you've already said, their previous inhabitants live in other places and probably won't want to move back."

"These repaired towns will be populated by the freed prisoners themselves," Ramessa replied. "They can establish new lives there and take up the industries proper to the area. The taxes we can again collect from their resourcefulness will contribute to the completion of these temples."

"As aways, the son of Ra is wiser than mere mortals," the minister of construction said and, bowing, backed away.

At this tribute, Ramessa gestured imperiously for the next case to be brought before him.

Several guards led in a long line of prisoners bound neck to neck by a single rope. When the prisoners stood crowded before the dais, the guards roughly pushed several of the men to their knees. The others had to fall as quickly or the ropes would strangle them.

"What have these men done?" Ramessa asked, amazed at the crowd. He stood up to better see the ones at the rear of the kneeling group.

At Ramessa's words, Arek entered from a side door, leading three more prisoners. When he had forced them to kneel before the throne, he bowed briefly and said, "There are a few more of them, who are injured and cannot attend the audience."

"Who are they?" Ramessa demanded. "Are those three the leaders?"

"The short one is the leader, the other two are lesser partners, I think," Arek said.

Ramessa wrinkled his nose. "He smells like a camel tethered too long in the same place," he remarked. "Of what are they accused? Also, who accuses them?"

"I've brought them to judgment on your own behalf, majesty," Arek replied. "This one was a merchant commissioned by your own ministers on your order to deliver a caravan of goods to King Hattusil in Khatti."

Ramessa's eyes widened. "The goods were gifts to

188

Hattusil accompanying the announcement of the child to be born!" he exclaimed. "What happened?"

"The caravan failed to turn east," Arek answered. "I received a message that the caravan continued north toward the coast, so I took soldiers and set out to investigate. I found this one trying to obtain passage for himself and his men on a ship ready to sail for Troy."

"Majesty—" the caravan leader began.

While Arek spoke, Ramessa's anger rose steadily. He snapped at the leader who addressed him without permission. "Silence!" He turned to Arek and directed, quietly, "Continue, Arek."

"There's nothing more to tell. We've dragged them back," Arek replied.

"Majesty—" the leader again said.

Ramessa glared at him. "What are you called?"

"Suti," the man answered, then hastily said, "I thought to save time and lessen the cost of the journey by traveling along the Great Green Sea instead of over land."

Ramessa smiled without humor. "Sea travel is more pleasant than the desert, is it not?"

Suti hung his head. "Yes," he said softly, hoping the king would believe he'd meant only to take an easier route instead of stealing the goods.

"That particular ship would have headed out to open sea, not along the coast. You chose most unwisely," Ramessa said. He lowered his eyes to inspect the bound men who huddled in a terror-stricken knot at his feet. "Bring that one forward," he said, indicating one of them with his scepter.

Arek turned to cut the man loose with one slash of his sword. Before the prisoner had a chance to get to his feet, Arek took hold of his garment and dragged him, still on his knees, to throw him at Ramessa's feet.

"I have it in mind to give all of you a most disagreeable sentence," Ramessa said softly, looking down at the cowering man. "If you tell me the truth of your leader's plans, I'll give you a lesser penalty."

The man looked at Suti, then up at Ramessa. He cleared

189

his throat noisily, and in a voice hoarse with terror said, "Suti meant to go to Troy and within that city's walls escape your hands. I'm Suti's slave, so what choice did I have? I thought only that Troy was as good a place as any to be a slave."

"Where I have it in mind to put Suti is considerably less pleasant than Troy," Ramessa commented. He looked at one of the guards. "Upon the soles of his feet so he walks not again for many days," he said quietly.

"And the others?" Arek asked.

"Since the others have so great an interest in gold, they'll be transported to Akiti to clear and repair and re-open the mines there. Once that has been accomplished, they will continue to work the mines until they're either too old or too disabled to lift their axes," Ramessa said.

A groan came from the throats of the sentenced men. Working in that arid region made young men old in only a few years and the chance of flight was infinitesimal. The only real possibility of escape was on the spearpoints of the marauding Shasu.

"And these three, the leaders?" Arek questioned.

"Behead them," answered Ramessa. "Do it mid-morning tomorrow when the marketplace is crowded. I would have the populace reminded of the penalty paid by any who would dare steal from their king."

When Chenmet returned to Nefertiry's apartment, she was accompanied by Seshena and another priestess. All three wore respectful expressions, but Chenmet was the only one who bowed. After Seshena had introduced the other priestess, Makhara, a healer, Seshena instructed Nefertiry to recline on her couch and listen carefully to Makhara's instructions. Then, Seshena lit a small container of incense she'd brought from the temple and, placing it on a nearby table, withdrew to the terrace.

Nefertiry glanced over her shoulder as Seshena disappeared. She was a little apprehensive at what this unknown priestess would do. Makhara had seated herself
190

on a chair close to Nefertiry's couch and was watching Nefertiry with a look of patient amusement in her eyes, as if she waited for a restless child to settle down.

Presently Makhara began to speak quietly to Nefertiry, directing her to relax, to close her eyes and allow the tension to run out of her, like liquid drained from an overfilled goblet. The priestess' soft but compelling voice was pleasant and seemed to draw Nefertiry's fears from her. Nefertiry obediently closed her eyes. The rich perfume of the incense crept over Nefertiry's senses even as the soothing voice seemed to lull her into so deep a calm she wondered if she would fall asleep. The drowsiness was so pleasant she was sorry when, after only a few moments, the priestess directed her to open her eyes.

"So soon?" Nefertiry asked in surprise. "Will you do nothing more?"

"Your distress has ended, hasn't it, divine lady?" Makhara asked.

Nefertiry realized then her nausea had vanished. "Yes," she said slowly. "But it was so pleasant just to lie here with nothing troubling me, not even my own disturbed thoughts."

"The feeling will remain with you for a time," Makhara said, getting to her feet. "If the discomfort returns, call me at any hour. I'll come and banish it again." She smiled wisely. "I think it won't return, though."

"But you did nothing!" Nefertiry exclaimed. "You didn't even touch me!"

"I did what was needed," Makhara answered. "Only far more serious problems would require my touching you." She nodded to Seshena, who had come in from the terrace. The two priestesses bid Nefertiry a pleasant day and turned to leave.

"Wait!" Nefertiry exclaimed. "What do you want in payment for your services? Although I don't understand what you did, my misery has left me. I would give you something." Nefertiry laid one hand on Makhara's arm and her other hand on Seshena's arm. A strangely pleasant
191

tingling sensation seemed to run through Nefertiry, as if a vibrant power came from one priestess and flowed to the other with her own self forming the connection. Surprised, she removed her hands.

"The generosity of the royal treasury supports the temple of Aset," Seshena replied. "We need nothing more from you, divine lady."

"But I've never seen you come to court asking for support, Seshena," Nefertiry said, "not like those of other temples."

"The gifts the king has given to Aset have been sufficient for our needs," Seshena replied. She walked slowly to the door with Nefertiry still following.

"Is there nothing I can do?" Nefertiry asked. "I wouldn't appear ungrateful."

Seshena opened the door and let Makhara pass, then turned to Nefertiry. In a lowered voice she said, "All I ask of you, and I ask as a messenger from Aset, is that you do as we already discussed." She raised her voice, again bid Nefertiry happiness in her day, turned and left.

Nefertiry felt as if the priestesses had brought a change to the very atmosphere in her suite, as if a refreshing breeze from the Great Green Sea had blown through the rooms and cleansed them. She returned to her couch and sank into it, closing her eyes to reflect on the puzzling, but effective visit from the priestesses.

When Chenmet touched her queen's shoulder, Nefertiry started so violently Chenmet regretted having to disturb her. "My lady, I'm sorry to awaken you," the servant whispered.

"What is it?" Nefertiry asked.

"The priest from Amen's temple, Nehemu, has come," Chenmet explained.

Nefertiry briefly considered sending the priest away; but assuming that Nehemu had received permission from Ramessa to approach her private quarters, she was curious about Nehemu's purpose. "I'll see him," she said.

Chenmet led Nehemu into the room, and the priest paused to bow before approaching too close to Nefertiry's couch. Nefertiry purposely let him remain bent at his waist while she turned to Chenmet. "Prepare a bath for me," she said, then unhurriedly told the attendant which scents and oils to use. After Chenmet left, Nefertiry looked at Nehemu. "You may rise," she directed. Nehemu straightened slowly, wincing from the cramp he'd acquired, and Nefertiry observed, "You're a young man, Nehemu, to have such pains. I think you exercise your body too little."

"It's your pains that concern me. I would banish them, if you let me," Nehemu said.

"How thoughtful of you. You're too late. Two priestesses from Aset's temple have just removed the problem."

"I don't wish to criticize their methods," Nehemu said, "but the purpose behind your illness isn't in Aset's domain. The relief they gave you will pass and the pain will return."

"They thought it wouldn't, but instructed me to call them if it did," Nefertiry replied.

"Aset's priestesses are as children compared to the skills of Amen's priests," Nehemu said derisively. "Akeset bid me to lay hands on you and drive out your pains."

At the thought of Nehemu touching her, Nefertiry shuddered. "The priestess didn't touch me, yet my pain is gone. You need do nothing."

'Forgive me, royal lady, but there's more to this pain than the physical factor," Nehemu said in a condescending tone. "I must speak to you about this unpleasantness."

"Which is?" Nefertiry asked, raising an eyebrow.

Nehemu drew himself taller to look at her sternly. "You must beg Amen's forgiveness for interfering with his temple's repairs." Nehemu lifted his hand and pointed at Nefertiry, who stared at his finger with anger rising in her heart. "You must beg forgiveness and undo the damage you've already caused. If you don't, even worse pains will be given you."

"Do you threaten me with a spell?" Nefertiry demanded.

"Amen makes his own spells," the priest said solemnly.

"What do you know about Amen or his spells?" Nefertiry retorted. "What do you know about anything but what Akeset places before you?"

"Speak not so to a priest of Amen and use the high priest's name with care or worse punishment may fall on you!" Nehemu warned.

Nefertiry's eyes glittered with angry, dark green lights. "I think you judge me wrongly, Nehemu. You think I'll be as easily intimidated as would be the king's lesser wives. That's one reason they are lesser wives and will remain so," she snapped. "I think you know nothing that would frighten me."

"To speak so will seal your punishment," Nehemu declared. "Seek forgiveness immediately!"

Nefertiry's lips curved in a smile of derision. "You're a fool," she said. "I always thought you were a fool. At a time when I yet knew little of the priesthood I judged you as a fool."

"Surely for speaking so disrespectfully to a priest of Amen will you bring down a multitude of evils on your head," Nehemu said angrily.

"And will you make a spell to call those evils down on me, foolish one?" Nefertiry asked in a softly dangerous tone. "Will the next so-called spell put new poison in my cup? I have no doubt Akeset was behind the last plot."

Nehemu came a step closer. "If you're so sure of that, you must accuse him. What evidence to you have?"

"Many were the times in Khatti when I knew someone had done a thing, yet couldn't prove it. Such is the case here," Nefertiry said quietly. "My mind has given me the knowledge, but not the evidence I can hold in my hand and place before the king." Her eyes narrowed, but retained their glitter. Nehemu was reminded of a cobra's slitted stare as she added softly, "I can't accuse Akeset yet, but I have no doubts he'll make another attempt to kill me, especially after you relate this conversation to him. Perhaps, though, I can think of some way to warn him off," she said speculatively. "Perhaps I could accuse a lesser priest of the attempted poisoning, a lesser priest like you."

Nehemu stared at her, horrified. "It couldn't be done!" he exclaimed. "You have nothing to connect me with that!"

"For a high priest I would need more proof, but not for a lesser priest. Proof of a lesser nature could be found—or contrived. Remember, Nehemu, I am queen. I have the resources at my command to accomplish many things."

Fear rose in Nehemu's eyes. "You wouldn't do so evil a thing!"

"It's an evil thing to poison your queen," Nefertiry replied. "I think Akeset should be warned off, and I think punishing you for his crime would be an excellent way to warn him."

Terror crept like a myriad of small, stinging insects on Nehemu's skin. He began to sweat. "I can't let you do such a thing," he whispered, taking a step toward her menacingly.

Nefertiry paled and moved back. "There's nothing you can do."

"I can only think of one thing," Nehemu said softly. "To do it means I would flee Tamera, but such exile would be preferable to having my head parted from my neck." He came another step closer.

Recognizing his intentions, Nefertiry again moved backwards, saying "You couldn't escape."

"I would try," Nehemu replied. "It will be some time before even your maid returns, perhaps enough time."

Nefertiry grew cold with fear. Nehemu had gone too far. Even if he was afraid of killing her, he had already said he would. This was enough for his own instant execution. She thought rapidly. The hall guards had gone for their

195

midday meal. She had sent Khakamir on an errand. She could be strangled in a moment and no one could come quickly enough to save her. Then, she remembered that Botar was in the next room. Would the cat obey her, she wondered.

"Botar," she called.

Botar came from around the doorway, stretching lazily from her interrupted nap.

"You can't fool me," Nehemu said. "It's well known that creature obeys the king only." He put his hands on Nefertiry's neck.

Nefertiry prayed for the leopard's obedience and commanded, "Botar, kill him!"

To Botar, the fact that Nefertiry's voice held terror, that this man threatened her, and that Ramessa and this woman were almost as one being in the cat's comprehension was enough. Nefertiry's voice was an extension of Ramessa's voice in Botar's mind.

Nefertiry felt the leopard's whiskers brush her cheek as Botar leaped with the speed of a striking cobra, dashing the priest to the floor. Nefertiry stared at the tawny blur of the cat's body as Botar sprang again, landing on Nehemu's chest.

Nehemu screamed once before the leopard's fangs tore the scream from his throat and the sound died in a liquid gurgle as his blood spouted from his shredded flesh. At the same moment, Botar's hind legs were working furiously at Nehemu's abdomen, her long claws disemboweling him. Blood ran in streams over the white floor, splashing on Nefertiry's dress. She was too stunned by the cat's speed even to move.

Botar's attacking snarl warned a servant passing in the hall; and the terrified man, fearing it was his queen the cat had turned on, screamed for guards. Khakamir had paused to speak to several soldiers downstairs, and, at the sound of Botar's roar, he paled and raced up the stairs, the guards at his heels.

Ramessa, too, heard the sound, and he ran barefoot

through the corridor toward the clot of terrified servants standing outside Nefertiry's door. Khakamir and the soldiers bounded from the last step and raced toward their king. Ramessa didn't wait for them, but threw open Nefertiry's door, then paused to stare in horror at the scene.

Nefertiry, pale and stunned, stood gazing at the torn body by her feet. Blood stained her robe and spattered her face. Botar lay nearby, peacefully licking her paws.

"Nefertiry," Ramessa whispered.

Nefertiry didn't want to tell Ramessa what had truly passed between her and the priest. To have Ramessa know Akeset was behind the attempted poisoning might cause him to impulsively execute the high priest, and unless real evidence was provided, the people might turn from their king at what would seem like the murder of a holy man. The whole priesthood, perhaps from every temple, might turn against Ramessa; they were too politically powerful to make enemies of. She shuddered also at the curses they might level on herself if they knew she'd ordered the leopard to kill a priest. She decided she must speak to Seshena before she spoke at all.

Nefertiry didn't have to pretend the horror in her voice or put on a mask of shock. One more glance at the shredded body was enough. She lifted her head and looked at Ramessa with wide green eyes. "Nehemu put his hands on me and Botar thought he meant me harm," she whispered. "It was over before I could call Botar back." She glanced at her robe and shivered. "So much blood— so much! I've never seen so much blood," she mumbled.

Ramessa opened his arms to her. "Come, Nefertiry," he said softly. She remained in the same place, as if she were afraid to walk over the blood-slippery floor. He shook his head and swiftly went to her. "There's nothing to fear," he soothed her as he put his arms around her. "Come out of this room with me. Come into my chamber and remove these garments. We will bathe together and cleanse ourselves of these stains."

Nefertiry stared up at him. "And Botar?" she asked fearfully.

Ramessa shook his head. "She thought she was protecting you, as I'd instructed her to do before I left for Zahi. She can't be punished for that." He gestured to Khakamir. "Take Botar outside and have someone clean her, as is done after a battle she's participated in."

"I'll see to it," Khakamir said shortly and turned away so Ramessa wouldn't read anything in his eyes.

Ramessa held Nefertiry a little tighter and looked down at her uplifted face. "Come out of this room now," he urged. "You can stay with me while this place is cleaned. During the night the breezes will wipe all traces of horror from here," he soothed, leading her toward the golden door. But Nefertiry still trembled, so he added, "Nehemu wasn't so close to me that I'll weep over him."

After a smiling Nehara admitted Rasuah, she led him through Seshena's house to a room facing the garden. The far side of the room wasn't limited by a wall. Only a series of slim, widely spaced columns—carved to resemble bundles of lotus stems, with their flowers forming the column's capitals—marked the room's extent. Beyond the columns lay the garden, bathed in the gentle lavender tints of early evening.

"My lady is enjoying the twilight," Nehara said. "She invites you to join her." Nehara stepped aside and motioned for him to pass.

Seshena was gazing into the dark purple waters of her pond when Rasuah stopped before her. The palm fronds whispered in the breeze, and a bird gave soft reply, but Seshena was silent. She only looked up at Rasuah while the starlight seemed to pass behind her eyes instead of reflect upon them.

"You say not even a greeting," Rasuah remarked quietly, reaching down to take her hand.

Although Seshena's smile barely touched her lips, it lit her eyes to sapphire iridescence. "I like to look at you with

198

your head lifted proudly against the sky. I always wanted a man who wasn't afraid to stand straight."

"I've been afraid of many things, but the truth was never one of them," he answered solemnly.

Seshena reached up to take his other hand and drew him toward her. "Sit beside me for a time," she invited. "Share with me this moment."

"Why?" he asked, knowing her reason as easily as his heart kept its rhythmic beat.

"I wish to share one of life's beauties with you," she replied.

Rasuah sat beside her. "Life's greatest beauty would be the sharing of its every moment."

"That isn't possible now," she said regretfully.

Rasuah sighed and his gaze moved from her face to the garden's distant shadows. "I love you, Seshena. I want you for my wife. I think you feel the same emotion as I, but I would hear you say it." He looked at her for a long time, waiting for her answer. She remained silent. "If you don't feel as I do, tell me this."

Seshena looked at Rasuah, at those golden eyes clouded with pain. "We have met in the body of eternity and our meeting will reverberate through the endless corridors of time," she whispered.

Rasuah took a deep breath and asked, "You don't love me?"

Seshena lifted his hands to her lips, kissing one, then the other, before she said, "Only one thing do I love as I love you—Tamera. And I have a purpose appointed me since the beginning of time. My purpose prevents my obeying my heart just now. You, too, have a destiny. At the moment, we must both be as undistracted as possible to accomplish our necessary tasks. In a time not very far from our grasp, our separate destinies will become one."

Rasuah's hands tightened on hers. "Does this destiny of yours involve your close relationship with the queen?" he asked. Seshena nodded. "You're her adviser in one respect," he said softly, as if uttering his thoughts aloud

199

while he tried to understand. "I'm a close friend of the king's and have his ear. Is there some reason in regard to this that prevents our marriage?"

Seshena stared with peculiar intensity at him. "You're correct in what you've said," she admitted. "It involves what I told you about the priesthood of Amen and their plans. It means the strength of the throne and the very life of Tamera. More I cannot tell you at this time."

Rasuah stared at her for a moment. Then his hand released hers and lifted to her chin to tilt her face toward his. "We spend almost every night together. Your house is as open to me as my own. My house is as much yours as mine and we're as bound as if we are married. Ramessa knows it. Nefertiry knows it. Our love is secret to no one. How could it matter if we were married?"

"It isn't a question of keeping it a secret from others," she whispered. "A heart filled with love is too content with its own world. If I married you, I'd care less for my work. I'd avoid thinking about priestly plots and prefer to think about what favorite dish of yours I'll have the cook prepare for the evening meal. Never would I arise from our bed in the night to go to the temple and meditate. I would be less a priestess at the very time I should be the most dedicated priestess I'm capable of being. And your mind must be as clear as mine, because your purpose is as important."

Rasuah looked away, his face reflecting his disappointment. "How long will it take?" he asked.

"A year or two, perhaps more," she answered.

"Our lives must wait meanwhile. Even our unborn children must wait," he sighed.

She put her hands on his shoulders. "Beloved, I cannot suckle a child while I invoke Bast to share her secrets with me."

Rasuah shook his head slowly. "Are you sure we won't have to wait too long to have children?"

Seshena smiled. "Yes," she said softly. "Our commitment will have been fulfilled long before that."

200

Rasuah put his arms around Seshena and she laid her head against his chest. They sat silently comforting each other with this hope, while fate delayed for a time before once again catching them in its net of duty. But the gods wouldn't give them peace for long and soon sent two messengers to remind them of their unavoidable path. The messengers came in the forms of Nehara and another servant.

Neither Rasuah nor Seshena were aware of Nehara and the other girl's presence until Nehara said, "My lady, Senta has brought news from the palace!"

"What is it, Senta?" Seshena asked.

"Lady, the king's leopard attacked Nehemu this afternoon!" Senta exclaimed.

Seshena's eyes widened. "Nehemu, the priest?"

Senta nodded rapidly. "It killed him."

Rasuah leaped to his feet. "How did it happen?" he asked tensely.

Recognizing the royal envoy at last, Senta fell silent and stared at him in awe.

Nehara said, "The priest came to speak to the queen, to offer his help for her illness." She glanced at Seshena and, noting her narrowed eyes, hurriedly explained, "He mustn't have known you'd already been there, my lady. The queen later said Nehemu put his hands on her and Botar thought the priest's gesture threatened the queen. When the king and his guards came, the queen was standing over Nehemu's body."

"Queen Nefertiry was alone with the priest?" Seshena asked, stunned.

"Where were her servants, her guards, Captain Khakamir?" Rasuah demanded.

Nehara stepped backwards, intimidated by his rising anger. "I don't know, my lord," she whispered.

Seshena looked up at Rasuah. His face had hardened and his lips had drawn into a tight line. "I thought Khakamir was to be with her at all times."

"The queen had sent Captain Khakamir on an errand,"

Senta ventured. Her courage drained, she felt silent again.

"Thank you, Senta, for telling us," Seshena said. When Nehara and Senta had left, still casting anxious glances over their shoulders, Seshena turned to Rasuah and whispered, "What will you do?"

Rasuah turned away. "I can do nothing until Ramessa asks me to," he answered grimly. Again he turned to face her. "But you, perhaps—"

Seshena nodded. "I'll go to the palace in the morning. Nefertiry will tell me the truth, I think."

Rasuah's fierce anger had slowly decreased its heat, and when his eyes met Seshena's, she recognized the sadness rising in them. "I don't feel like waiting until Tamera's problems are solved, but I understand why we should."

Seshena slid her arm around his waist. "Let us return to the house and share what we can."

Rasuah nodded and put his arm around her waist, then silently led her up the path.

12

Nefertiry sat in the garden until the sun disappeared behind the western hills, leaving in its stead purple clouds trailing golden streamers. She wasn't interested in the glories of the sky, but sat reflecting bitterly on her loneliness during the six weeks since the priest was killed by Botar.

On the day of Nehemu's death, Ramessa had spent time comforting her and trying to calm her, and she had expected him to stay to make love. He had not, even though she had assured him that her nausea had vanished under Makara's ministrations. He had been visibly relieved to hear that her health had improved, but still he'd sent her to her own room to sleep, saying that she needed rest.

Since then, Ramessa was courteous and attentive during the days and evenings, but at night he called another wife or concubine to his bed. The women, the wives especially, made a great deal of noise as they passed Nefertiry's door each night, letting her know that Ramessa preferred one of them to her—their enemy.

The time was rapidly approaching for the child's birth, when lovemaking would be unsafe. Nefertiry feared the king would never want her again, and her fear and jealousy were sharpened by her physical frustration. Ramessa had assigned Arek as an extra guard after Nehemu's death, and he thus prevented her from arranging any interludes with Khakamir.

From their first meeting, Nefertiry had recognized the warmth in Arek's eyes as more than loyalty to his queen and now with him guarding her, they were in almost daily contact, and the warmth seemed to have grown to banked fires.

Nefertiry lifted her head to look at Arek, who stood a discreet distance from her, his eyes constantly sweeping over the garden's shadows, alert to possible danger. But when, at her gaze, his eyes moved to meet hers for a moment, she saw clearly the desire smoldering in their dark depths. She quickly lowered her head, reflecting on the irony of Ramessa having such faith in Arek, a man who not only spied against him but lusted after his queen. Idly, she wondered what Ramessa would do if he became aware of Arek's desire for her, or if Ramessa thought that she had betrayed him with Arek. She frowned. Ramessa would probably send her back to Khatti in disgrace, banish her the way he had Manefera. But her frown faded as she realized Arek's penalty would more than likely be execution.

The vanished sun sent one last flash of golden light into the garden, slanting down on Nefertiry's lowered head. As if Amen-Ra's fire carried inspiration, Nefertiry suddenly saw a possible way to rid Tamera of this spy without causing new trouble between Ramessa and Hattusil. All would depend on whether Arek's desire for her outweighed his fear of Ramessa. She realized she'd have to appear innocent of any wrong-doing and she didn't know how she would accomplish it. But she decided that during the next few months, while she awaited the child's birth, she would measure the degree of Arek's lust. Having made this decision, she took a deep breath and stood up, slowly turning to fix her newly purposeful gaze on Arek.

"I'll return to my quarters now, Arek," Nefertiry said in a deliberately husky tone.

"Yes, divine lady," Arek replied, stepping expectantly to the side of the path.

Nefertiry allowed the corners of her lips to tilt up in a smile as she approached him, and as she began to pass him, he placed himself at her side instead of walking respectfully behind her. Surprised at his boldness, she drew back to look at him, but at her glance, his eyes slowly moved to the path before them. The line of his lips had tightened with tension and she was sharply aware of a heavier warmth emanating from his body.

At a bend in the path, Arek's hand touched Nefertiry's waist in order to guide her, deliberately lingering until she moved away. She was amazed at his effrontery since she had given him so little encouragement.

Remembering her purpose was to eventually trap him, she said nothing in rebuke. But neither did she look at him again, for though her physical need for a man was great, she had no desire for this Shardana spy walking so smoothly beside her.

The afternoon heat lay on Seshena's head like a heavy hand, and the pavement under her sandals radiated new streams of heat that seemed to smolder when they touched her skin.

Having heard nothing more of Nefertiry during the weeks since Nehemu's death and having received no summons to go to the palace, Seshena had finally decided to consult with Khenti, the only priest of Amen's temple she trusted. She was certain Akeset would shortly demand something from Ramessa as payment for the dead priest and she hoped Khenti might have some idea what form the demand would take, since Bast yet seemed reluctant to reveal it to her.

Seshena hurried her steps as she approached the temple's entrance and walked swiftly through the courtyard, which felt as if she had stepped into a baker's oven. When she passed the threshold and entered the building's shade, the semi-darkness was like a cooling balm applied to her skin. She stepped out of her sandals and the cold stone of the floor felt like the benediction of a sympathetic spirit.

Her bare feet were soundless on the stone. Not hearing even the faint noises that usually drifted through a temple, she began to wonder if anyone was there. Although she had no desire to pass even courteous greetings with any of the priests but Khenti, she felt an uneasiness that the temple seemed deserted. It was an hour when no services were held, and with this oppressive heat assaulting Wast, it was unlikely that visitors would come. Yet Seshena couldn't brush aside the feeling of foreboding she had at the utter silence of the place.

Aset's temple had been built using white—the color most favored by the goddess who in many guises was symbolized by the moon—but in Amen's temple, gold was the dominant color and the stone lining the interior was yellow jasper. On a day when Tamera's sun had become a torturer rather than a benevolent spirit, the gold of the temple might have appeared an extension of the searing heat outside, but the color here was broken by the long shadows cast from the soaring columns. Its majesty was a lofty reflection of Amen's authority.

Seshena found a small bench at the back of an obscure niche, and sank down to consider what she might next do. While she was anxious to speak to Khenti, she couldn't ignore the uneasiness she felt. Loneliness was a thing a priestess accustomed herself to, which eventually bothered her not at all, and silence was a friend encouraging her daily meditation. Why should the stillness of an empty temple so disturb her, she wondered. She was startled from her contemplation by the sound of a closing door in the next chamber. She lifted her head and waited, her instincts at last confirming that her uneasiness had been a warning.

Even before Seshena's eyes saw the priests, she knew Akeset and Befen had entered the room. She silently apologized to Amen for feeling so discomfited in his temple, then squeezed farther into the shadows, hoping the high priest's mind was too occupied with his own thoughts to become aware of her presence.

Although Seshena's hearing wasn't so acute she could understand the priests' conversation, she was elated to discover her mind perceived their very thoughts.

As they walked through the enormous room, Akeset spoke bluntly of his plans to turn Nehemu's death into another way to squeeze more gold and, therefore, more power from the throne. The priests paced the length of the massive chamber so slowly, Seshena wondered if they'd ever get out of the place so she could leave and warn Nefertiry that Akeset intended to shortly go to Ramessa and present his demand.

The priests' saffron robes finally disappeared from Seshena's view, but still fearful Akeset might discover her presence, she waited, using that precious time to offer Amen her own silent thanks; entering Akeset's thoughts was a far greater accomplishment than exploring the mind of an ordinary person. The high priest's abilities had always before been equal to her own and Akeset's will, working as an invisible shield, was able to effectively camouflage his thoughts from intruders even while he spoke to someone he wanted to understand him. Although Seshena had the same ability and had tried to use it to conceal her presence, it took great strength to pierce Akeset's shield while maintaining her own; she'd been doubtful she could accomplish it. But when her perception followed Akeset and Befen all the way out of the temple, she realized she had apparently acquired a new level of strength.

Seshena emerged from the shadowy niche with a surer step. She was confident Akeset could eventually be defeated, if the divine beings continued to give her their assistance and her goals remained the same as theirs. Walking swiftly away from the temple, she hurried to the palace.

Nefertiry's night had been a fretful one, as she thought about Arek's standing outside her doorway inadvertently preventing Khakamir from coming to her; her sleeplessness hadn't improved her disposition.

Seshena stepped into the room to find her queen pacing back and forth, wearing a morose expression. At Seshena's entrance, Nefertiry dismissed Chenmet, and catching Seshena's hands in her own, almost dragged her to the couch.

"You come when I need you without my even calling," Nefertiry said quickly.

Alarmed by Nefertiry's agitation, Seshena asked, "What is it that so distresses you?"

"Fear treads constantly on my heels. Since Nehemu's death, Ramessa has behaved toward me much as he would with Tuiah. I'm not his mother, Seshena! I cannot endure this frustration. Ramessa recently assigned an additional soldier to guard me, which prevents any plans I might contemplate making with Khakamir." She paused, then added, "I have been alone until I ache with pain."

"Do you think Ramessa suspects you and Khakamir?" Seshena asked.

"No, no," Nefertiry answered irritably. "I feared I was no longer alluring in his sight until I remembered his previous remark that others of his wives in this state had offended his eyes not at all. My fear now is that Ramessa doesn't want me, whatever my condition, and so won't want me after I'm rid of this burden I carry. The fear is like a creature stalking me. Seshena, is it possible to use your magic to learn Ramessa's purpose? If you discover he no longer wants me, is it possible to make him want me again?" Seeing Seshena's frown, Nefertiry hastily added, "If I lose all influence on him, who will help you save the throne?"

208

"I'll learn what Ramessa's mind holds; and if it's necessary, I can influence him," Seshena said. Noting that Nefertiry seemed little soothed by this promise, she added, "I think he avoids your bed for some reason we have yet to discover. Would Aset decree you must help her if she knew you'd fall from favor and be useless to her cause? Remember, Aset's eyes are those of Bast, who sees the future as easily as today's events."

"Maybe you're right," Nefertiry whispered. "Are you certain Aset has named me her instrument?"

"How else would I have known your heritage while you were yet in Khatti?"

Nefertiry considered this a moment, then nodded. "No one could have told you but the goddess," she agreed. She was silent a moment, then asked, "Did you come because you knew I needed your counsel or did you have another purpose?"

"I had another purpose!" Seshena exclaimed. "I know what Akeset intends to demand from the king in payment for Nehemu's death."

"Payment? How can he demand payment for another priest?" Nefertiry looked confused.

Seshena's head lifted as if she were listening: "I can't tell you everything; I have no time," she whispered, looking at Nefertiry. "Akeset has just now arrived at the palace and he will momentarily speak to Ramessa. You must be present when Akeset presents his demands."

"That priest possesses the brains of a fish!" Nefertiry declared. "How dare he demand anything from the king?"

"Akeset dares," Seshena replied, then quickly added, "He wants more land, more gold, more influence. He wants Botar slain, and he'll complain about you again."

Nefertiry's eyes widened in fear. Did Akeset somehow know she'd loosed Botar on Nehemu? She leaped to her feet. "You have my gratitude, Seshena," she said. "Wait here until I return so that we can discuss the results of this audience." Then, with tightened lips and narrowed eyes, she departed.

The footsteps of Khakamir and Arek, who fell in behind Nefertiry when she left her suite, gave her added confidence. She lifted her head a little higher as she walked swiftly to the stairway. No one watching her would have guessed her heart pounded in a mixture of anger and fear. She was affronted by Akeset's unending nerve. But at the same time, she dreaded what he might say about her.

Nefertiry stared at the door for a moment, trying to ignore her trembling knees. She turned to her guards and said crisply, "Remain with me, both of you." Then she entered the room.

Akeset and Befen were in the midst of a deep bow before Ramessa, who was sitting on a couch looking mildly annoyed. Botar was sprawled at his feet. When Nefertiry took a step toward them, Botar's head came up alertly. Ramessa motioned for her to sit beside him and she obeyed. Botar promptly got to her feet and began rubbing the side of her face against Nefertiry's legs.

"You may rise," Ramessa directed the priests.

As Akeset straightened, his eyes fell on Nefertiry's fingers absently caressing Botar's head. He took a breath and said coolly, "I thought this was to be a private audience, majesty."

"It is," Ramessa replied.

Akeset's eyes moved to the two guards standing alertly behind the couch, and asked, "Does his majesty fear attack from two priests?"

Ramessa's annoyance faded to a look of boredom. "The soldiers have been assigned to guard the queen since that attempt to poison her."

"You haven't learned who did that, majesty?" Befen ventured.

Nefertiry turned toward the priest. "My chemist analyzed the poison and found it a common enough mixture—though costly to prepare—which narrows the suspects to the wealthy," she said softly, her green eyes moving to Akeset. "I've given considerable thought to those who might wish to poison me, but I cannot accuse anyone—yet."

Akeset allowed his mind to enter Nefertiry's, and he was surprised to learn he was her only suspect. Suddenly, he realized Nehemu's death wasn't an accident, but a warning to himself.

"Perhaps you'll find new evidence to catch the poisoner," Befen offered cautiously.

Nefertiry's eyes remained on Akeset. "Perhaps."

Ramessa sensed the undercurrents, but his expression didn't change, and he asked the priests, "Why have you come?"

"I've come to beg your majesty to have that dangerous creature destroyed," Akeset said.

"What dangerous creature?"

"Majesty, the cat lying at your feet killed my priest!" Akeset exclaimed indignantly.

"Botar is only dangerous on my orders," Ramessa said coolly. "If Nehemu hadn't put his hands on the queen, Botar wouldn't have attacked him. Botar did have my order to protect the queen."

"But Nehemu wanted to heal the queen!" Befen declared.

Ramessa looked at Nefertiry. "Did Nehemu ask permission to touch you?" Nefertiry shook her head and Ramessa turned to face the priests. "By touching the queen without her permission, Nehemu broke the law. Botar merely acted as Wadjet, the divine cobra who guards the crown, would have." Ramessa shrugged. "Of course, Botar can't spit heavenly fire, can you?" He leaned forward slightly to ask the cat, who looked up at him with wide orange eyes.

"Perhaps the divine lady will tell us what happened," Akeset suggested, turning to Nefertiry. "As you were the only witness, we have until now heard only second-hand reports."

Nefertiry lifted her eyes from Botar and fixed them on Akeset. "Because I am from Khatti, I had no idea what a priest of Amen might do to heal me, so I was naturally apprehensive. Botar, as you can see, is fond of me and must have sensed my feelings and, thus, acted on the

211

king's previous orders. It all happened so quickly, I could do nothing."

Befen hadn't missed the flash of green fire in the queen's eyes as she spoke, and he inadvertently stepped back a pace. Akeset, however, stood looking at his feet and silently rubbing his chin as if he considered this explanation reasonable.

Finally Akeset lifted his gaze to Ramessa. "If that creature, then, is to remain in this mortal world, I must ask, majesty, what I think is small compensation for the temple's loss of a priest, who has been trained for many years at great expense to the temple."

Ramessa knew this was the real reason Akeset had come to the palace. "What compensation?"

"A tract of land to the east of Wast surrounded by barley fields. The land lies unused and apparently deserted. It's where the river turns sharply. There's a grove of sycamore trees at its center," Akeset answered promptly.

Nefertiry asked guilelessly, "My lord, who claims this land and does nothing with it? Would it not be to your benefit that someone uses it?"

Ramessa considered her questions for a moment. Nefertiry had sat at court yesterday when this very piece of land had been discussed. Why did she ask such a question? he wondered. Had she already forgotten? He said, "I've already promised that land to Tehuti's temple."

Nefertiry leaned closer to Ramessa and whispered, "It's appropriate that Akeset wants land promised to the god of intelligence." She was thinking that Tehuti would be the first divine being Akeset must silence to succeed in his ambitions, but she said no more.

"I cannot break a promise to one temple by giving the land to another," Ramessa said. He was silent a moment, then declared, "I don't know why you need payment for Nehemu's loss. You have a host of other priests."

"Majesty, though you think so little of a priest's loss, let me remind you that Amen holds his servants in higher

212

regard," Akeset retorted. "It would be wise to regain Amen's favor after the killing of one of his servants."

"I'm sure Amen could see that particular priest of his was breaking a divine law by touching the queen without permission," Ramessa snapped. He was losing his patience at Akeset's constant conniving.

"Of course, the queen shouldn't be touched without permission—if she is truly the queen," Befen commented.

Ramessa's anger reached new heights, but he commented coolly, "You know Nefertiry is the queen because you saw my own hands crown her."

Akeset took one look at Ramessa's narrowed eyes and quickly replied, "Of course, my queen is my queen! Befen meant nothing, majesty!"

"He'd better mean nothing," Ramessa said.

Nefertiry smiled benignly. "My lord, don't you think Amen's temple deserves something for Nehemu's loss?"

Ramessa was surprised at her taking Akeset's side and he asked, "What do you think they should have?"

Nefertiry shook her head. "I have no idea, my lord. Who am I to speak of such matters or make such decisions? It's just that I heard the legend of how Aset assigned one-third of Tamera to the king, one-third of Tamera to the soldiers and one-third to the priests."

"The priesthood doesn't have its third." Befen quickly fell into her trap.

Ramessa turned to look at Befen, aghast at the idea. He said, "The soldiers are meant to keep physical order. The priests are meant to keep moral order. The king is meant to keep all order." He turned to Nefertiry. "That's what is meant by the legend."

"Thank you, my lord, for explaining it to me," Nefertiry murmured humbly.

"Majesty, don't the priests have some influence on the king—by guiding the morality of his decisions?" Akeset asked.

From the stiffness of Ramessa's neck when he turned to regard the priest, Nefertiry could see her ruse had worked perfectly. The conversation had followed the direction she'd wished. She knew Ramessa was trying to control his inner fury. When he spoke, anger colored his words despite his efforts.

"The gods themselves guide the morality of the king's decisions. When it comes to administering the land, the king's authority has no limits. I don't intend to take a vote when a decision is to be made. My voice will always be over that of the high priest and the military commander!" Ramessa took a deep breath, glaring at them a moment more, before he added, "I'll consider what compensation you'll receive, if any. I'll send you my decision when I've made it." He waved impatiently in dismissal.

Akeset bowed deeply and turned to leave, finally realizing that Nefertiry had cleverly steered the conversation precisely to the conclusion she'd desired, and the priest quickly revised his previous estimation of her intelligence. She was a far more formidable enemy than he'd ever guessed.

Nefertiry returned to her quarters to find Seshena standing on the terrace looking out over the garden. At Nefertiry's entrance Seshena immediately came back into the room.

"Seshena, I'm afraid of that priest—" Nefertiry began.

Seshena raised her hand and said, "You needn't tell me what happened. I followed the conversation in my head. You have better reason than you even know for fearing Akeset. He crept into your mind and learned of your conviction that he tried to poison you. He also knows what truly happened to Nehemu."

Nefertiry realized that Seshena too must know her secret. "Nehemu tried to strangle me!" she exclaimed.

Seshena nodded. "I learned the truth of it from your own thoughts. It's Akeset you should worry about, not me." She came closer to Nefertiry and took the queen's hands in hers. "I know the remembrance of it yet haunts you."

Nefertiry shivered. "I try not to think of that bloody scene and try never to dwell on it, for it evokes horrors in my spirit's nightly wanderings." She was silent a moment, before she asked, "Akeset entered my mind?"

"It is a thing I won't have happen again," Seshena said firmly. "I will this very night make a spell to Seker to blacken and silence your thoughts from Akeset's prying will."

"Is nothing impossible to you?" Nefertiry asked.

"My powers have some limits, although lately they've expanded," Seshena replied.

"To think of Akeset peering into my mind when he chooses is a horror," Nefertiry sighed. "Your powers increase while mine must be hidden."

"It still angers you that though you're Seti's daughter you cannot take your rightful place?"

Nefertiry nodded. "Ramessa merely has to give an order to have his way. But I must work my will through hidden paths in all but insignificant matters."

Seshena released Nefertiry's hands. "Although I'm not the daughter of a king, I also work my will through secret ways, but my results are no less effective."

"No one is trying to kill *you*. I'm terrified, Seshena, that Akeset will somehow harm my child. I've thought that a woman cannot be more helpless than at the time she is giving birth and I'm afraid he'll find a way to do it then—perhaps through bribes or threats to someone of those attending me."

"Although I haven't read this in his thoughts, I can make a protection for the child once it's born," Seshena said. Nefertiry lifted her head to look at the priestess and the expression in her face was so piteous that Seshena moved to comfort the queen, wondering if Ramessa ever saw this side of Nefertiry. "If you wish, I can be present at the birth," she offered. "All you need do is insist on having me there. Makhara can come too, and with her methods ease your pain."

The tension on Nefertiry's face slid off like a wax

215

mask that had melted. "Your presence would comfort me greatly."

"Then, we'll be there," Seshena promised. "When the pains begin, send a messenger to me. Makhara and I will be at your side through all of it."

"You must safeguard yourselves," Nefertiry said anxiously. "You must be sure not to eat or drink something that could blur your mind or make you ill."

"I'll have Makhara live with me when your time approaches. In my house there's no fear of such dangers, for my servant, Nehara, loves me," Seshena assured the queen.

Nefertiry leaned back on the couch, shut her eyes and sighed. "Ah, to live in a house without danger. No danger can touch you wherever you live." She opened her eyes and looked at the priestess. "Come to the palace to live, Seshena. With your presence in my house, perhaps the evils dwelling here will depart. I'll find a way to add to your titles. I'll arrange for your marriage to someone in a high place—one of the ministers or perhaps the governor of a rich province."

"Don't be offended by my answer, divine lady, but I love my own house and I'll protect you anyway. I'm high priestess of Aset's temple and wish no higher rank than that. As for marriage, I'm already loved by a man who is all I want."

"And when he steps out of your sight, he finds another," Nefertiry said bitterly.

"No. I don't have to enter his mind to know he is not like that," Seshena replied. "His time is filled with his work, and since we met he has never been seen with another woman. I may come to his house unexpectedly at any hour or go to places he frequents without warning and he greets me with undisguised joy. We love often and each time he's as hungry for my body as I am for his."

Nefertiry said nothing for some time. Finally she spoke. "I speak from my own frustration. Don't let my unhappiness spoil your joy." And again Seshena reached out to comfort the queen.

The king gave little thought to Akeset and his motives or demands. Ramessa had known for a very long time that Akeset was driven by greed and a hunger for power. In fact, Ramessa lived each day with the knowledge that most of his ministers, counselors, and magistrates were as avaricious as Akeset to some degree. But Ramessa spent no sleepless nights worrying about it. They could only gain as much power as he allowed them and he was confident he could keep them within safe limits. He endured Akeset as he endured all priests. Ramessa had been taught from childhood that he was himself divine and that canceled out much of the awe he might have developed for the priesthood. He also expected little from them because he'd known few uncorrupted priests—those few dreamers who seemed to accomplish nothing or previously corrupt priests who, when their ages advanced, tried to make peace with the divine beings.

Ramessa thought briefly about Akeset's interview, but only in relation to how Nefertiry had guided its direction. He smiled in admiration of her cleverness and wondered at her reason, but his mind soon moved to what the astrologer had told him about a darkness connected with the birth of the child. The fear of Nefertiry's dying in childbirth crept over him again, and his heart began to constrict in worry. He decided he must distract himself, because he wasn't inclined to favor prolonged periods of worrying.

Ramessa arose from the couch and walked out of the room. Botar followed at his heels. After wandering through the corridors for a few minutes, Ramessa decided to visit his stables, a favorite place of his, for an inspection of his horses.

Ramessa was happily stroking Pehtee's snowy head as the stableboy brushed the animal, when Rasuah came to find him.

217

"I dislike having to take that smile from your face, but I have a problem to lay in your hands," Rasuah said softly.

Ramessa slowly turned from the horse. "What problem?"

"I've received a report from a reliable source that Lord Tefen has neglected a section of his irrigation system, which connects with that of Lord Wenamon's," Rasuah explained. "The report says some of the canals are clogged with mud and some of the banks have crumbled. When the next flood comes, Lord Wenamon's outlying fields won't receive water, while on one area of Tefen's land the flood will spread too quickly and the water will remain too long to plant seeds. My source said Tefen won't care about that particular field because it will lie resting next season anyway. However, Wenamon's loss could mean catastrophe for him."

"Tefen has no love for Wenamon?" Ramessa asked. Rasuah shook his head.

"It's a serious offense," Rasuah reminded him.

"I know, I know," Ramessa said irritably. "I'll send Tefen a warning."

"Will he listen to a warning?" Rasuah pressed.

"He'll listen to the kind of warning I have in mind," Ramessa snapped.

Rasuah stared at Ramessa, surprised at his shortness of temper. "What else is troubling you?" Rasuah asked softly. "Is there anything I can do about it?"

Ramessa looked up into his friend's eyes and saw the concern they held. "You will speak of it to no one." At Rasuah's solemn nod he said, "There's nothing you can do but listen to my sorrow, and, perhaps, in the telling of it, I'll be somewhat relieved."

"What sorrow is this?" Rasuah asked quickly.

"The master of the secrets of the heavens has told me an unhappy thing," Ramessa said slowly. "There's a darkness surrounding the birth of the next prince."

"You're afraid for the queen?" Rasuah asked quietly.

"Yes," Ramessa confessed. He took Rasuah's arm and began to walk away from the stables and out of the hearing of those who worked there. When he was far enough away he said softly, "Nefertiry is unlike the others of my harem and affects me more than all the rest of them put together. I don't want to give her over to Asar, but neither do I wish to surrender the child to the Lord of Eternity."

Rasuah asked, "How is the queen so different?"

"Though she often angers me, she warms my heart even more than she warms my bed. She's wise in the ways of the court and sees aspects in the various intrigues of the government that I sometimes miss. If she passed to the next life, it would be not only a personal sorrow for me, but a loss to the land as well."

"You love her?"

"If a king is allowed to love, then I love her," he replied. "But in this time of fear, I've not called her to my bed. This angers her, I know, because she doesn't understand. But I cannot tell her I fear causing whatever may go wrong at the birth. I have a hunger for her also, which shortens my temper during the day."

Rasuah said, "I cannot imagine how love can harm her at this point, but I'm not a physician."

"I don't wish to confer with the royal physician on this matter," Ramessa said quickly. "He is excellent in his craft, but he's as celibate as if he'd taken a vow. He would have each of my subjects sleeping in a separate bed."

Rasuah smiled faintly. "I wouldn't care to speak with him, either, in that case," he murmured. He was silent, thinking of possible solutions. Finally he said, "Perhaps, if you behaved with restraint with the queen——"

Ramessa shook his head. "Restraint is difficult, if not impossible, with her," he replied. He sighed and moved to return to the palace. "There's nothing for it, my friend, but to wait and hope Nefertiry survives," he added, beginning to walk slowly up the path. Abruptly he burst out, "I'm tired of the priests' plots, the nobles' deceits,

219

the intrigues of the court! I'm weary of the complaints pouring from the provinces!" He stopped walking and turned to face Rasuah. "I need to escape these things for a while. I would go on a hunt before Nefertiry's time is upon us," he said impulsively. "Accompany me, Rasuah. Help me forget my troubles for a few days."

"What do you wish to hunt?" Rasuah asked.

"This heat makes it a good time to hunt lions," Ramessa suggested.

"I dislike killing lions unless they're attacking people," Rasuah replied. "What of bringing back a wild bull?"

"A bull it will be," Ramessa agreed. "I'll give orders so we may leave tomorrow."

"Not too early tomorrow, I hope," Rasuah said.

Ramessa raised his eyebrows. "You wish not to tear yourself too soon from the priestess?" he asked. "Seshena is beautiful and it seems a cut above the other priests and priestesses I've known."

"Seshena is so different from those you have in mind, she's like a ghost come from the past," Rasuah whispered.

13

Ramessa was there—just a few steps beyond that door—making love to Mimut.

Hoping to turn away such thoughts as well as ease the ache at the small of her back, Nefertiry lay gazing at the dark ceiling of her bedroom; but her thoughts remained on Ramessa and her back ached even more. Finally, she turned awkwardly to her side and glared angrily at the door glimmering in the moonlight, a golden barrier between them, one of so many barriers. She sighed and turned awkwardly to lie on her stomach, her face away from the door, not wanting to see it. But the ache at the base of her spine increased, so she turned again to her side and closed her eyes, curling up as much as her bulk allowed.

When it came, Nefertiry didn't recognize the first pain or what it struggled to announce. She thought it was a muscle spasm brought on by her tension. She lay very still, trying valiantly to relax; until, the pain subsided. A breeze from the garden bathed her in cool perfume and she felt a little refreshed. Finally she closed her eyes to the golden door and her mind to Mimut and gradually felt her body growing lighter until she drowsed.

The sharpness of the next pain snatched her from the hands of sleep and her eyes snapped open. She was bewildered at the length of the pain and wondered about its cause until she realized that she was beginning her labor.

Slowly, she stood up and went into the adjoining room to call Chenmet.

The servant arose immediately and lit a lamp. Seeing Nefertiry's pale face shining with moisture, Chenmet quickly began to dress. "Is there anything I can do before I go to the house of the priestess?" she asked.

"Call Khakamir."

When Khakamir came, he was startled by Nefertiry's appearance and asked anxiously, "What's wrong, divine lady?"

Nefertiry smiled wanly. "My time has come," she murmured, adding "No one will be told until Seshena arrives." She paused and studied his eyes, which were dark with concern. "You will remain with me while I wait," she directed. Khakamir nodded; and she turned to Chenmet, signaling the servant to go.

As previously instructed, Chenmet slipped out the terrace door so she could make her way through the garden and into the street unseen. Nefertiry watched by the door until Chenmet had disappeared in the shadows, then turned to Khakamir. "Sit down," she invited. "I've been unable to speak alone with you for a long time and I must use this moment of privacy to tell you many things."

Khakamir said, "First you must sit down."

Nefertiry shook her head. "I'm more comfortable standing and walking," she replied. She waited until Khakamir sat on a chair looking uneasy. "I wish I had told you this sooner," she said and turned away.

Khakamir saw her hands at her sides clenching and unclenching. "Is it another pain?" he asked.

"No." Nefertiry turned to him. "It's a different kind of pain," she whispered. She took a deep breath and said softly, "Khakamir, I made sure that this child would be yours." Khakamir's mouth dropped open; he stared at her, speechless. "No one will ever know this prince isn't the king's son," she added.

Khakamir swallowed once and recovered himself enough to say, "But Ramessa might choose this child to be king if it's a boy! It cannot be king! I have no royal blood!"

"But I do," Nefertiry announced as she approached him and took his hands in hers. "I am Seti's daughter, Ramessa's half-sister."

Khakamir stared incredulously at her. "But how? You're Hattusil's child!"

"So I'd thought all my life," she said in a tight voice. "It was only when I was to be given to Ramessa that Hattusil told me the truth. I have no time, Khakamir, to relate the story now; I will tell you later."

Khakamir shook his head. He took a deep breath and whispered, "My lips are stones."

Nefertiry squeezed his hands. "I know. I wouldn't have told you otherwise. I debated telling you at all, but I thought you had a right to know my child is yours," she murmured. "And our son, this prince who soon will struggle into the world, will be the next king if I have my way."

Khakamir stood up, walked to the door opening into the terrace and inhaled deeply of the night air. He remained standing with his back to her, staring at the darkness outside, as he said, "This news gives me joy, but adds to my guilt."

Nefertiry approached him silently. She put her arms around his waist and leaned her cheek against his back. "Why do you feel so guilty?"

"Because I betray the king by loving his wife, by siring a son who might take the crown with Ramessa thinking the prince is his," Khakamir whispered.

Nefertiry moved around Khakamir to face him. "Seti's blood runs in this child as purely as in Ramessa's other sons. Maybe more purely because you're one of a long line of nobles, not a foreigner as are most of Ramessa's wives." Khakamir continued staring at the darkness beyond her shoulder. He said nothing. She put her hand on his cheek and turned his face to hers. "Do the women of his harem think they betray me, their queen, by seeking joy in his bed and bearing his children?" Nefertiry asked softly. "Where, Khakamir, is the difference?"

Khakamir dropped his eyes, unable to disagree. He had seen the women passing each night to Ramessa's room. He knew, when they spoke to him outside Nefertiry's door, it was to announce their success to Nefertiry.

"We sought a companionship, a happiness we could find nowhere else," Nefertiry said softly. "Call it love if you will. It is that, Khakamir, at least a kind of love. We may not possess the love that was Asar and Aset's, but love has many guises."

Wanting to believe he'd betrayed no one, Khakamir accepted her explanation. Finally, he asked, "What if, in your pain, you cry out something and reveal your secret!"

"I won't," she assured him. "I would die before I spoke of this. Only the priestess knows; she learned it from a vision. That's another reason I must have her with me. I trust her absolutely. She'll make sure I don't speak of the child's father."

Three months before, Akeset had learned from Nefertiry's thoughts that she feared for her child's safety as well as her own. At the same time, he'd also learned that she intended to have Seshena with her when the child was born. After that, abruptly, Nefertiry's mind had closed to his probing.

When Akeset found he could no longer penetrate Nefertiry's thoughts, he was appalled and amazed. He had never heard or seen any sign that she'd been trained
224

for the temple in Khatti. Trying to bypass the barrier protecting her thoughts from him, he found he couldn't; where before he had regarded Nefertiry as merely a clever woman hindering his plans, now he was afraid of her. She seemed to resist even the spell he'd cast, and he concluded she was very adept in the use of her will and, so, very powerful in her magic. He immediately decided he must find a way to destroy her.

Akeset had made a plan to have the child switched with a dead infant, so he might at least have no magically inclined prince to deal with later. He had also paid the royal physician to cause Nefertiry to bleed uncontrollably, thus removing her from his path. But if Seshena were at Nefertiry's side when the child was born, the physician would be unable to carry out his part of the plan. So Akeset had made a habit of entering Chenmet's mind to learn what was passing in the palace—and to learn when Nefertiry's time approached. Before Chenmet was dressed to go for Seshena, Akeset had sent for Shemal and his gang of Shardanans.

Akeset paced the floor restlessly while he waited for the men to come. The former prisoners of war had no loyalty to Ramessa and no great knowledge or even an interest in the inner workings of the kingdom. They took their pay and asked no questions. They accomplished their tasks efficiently. Tonight he would direct them to Seshena's house.

The Shardanans would follow the priestess; when they came upon a conveniently dark place, they'd attack her. Akeset stopped pacing and smiled. Such war-trained men could easily overpower Seshena and whatever servants accompanied her. Without Seshena watching the physician, the infants could be exchanged. Then, Nefertiry's blood would gush forth like a new spring until she was drained and dead.

Rasuah's senses had been finely tuned by many nights of sleeping on bandit-infested trails. So when his ears heard Nehara's soft footsteps rushing down the hall, though he still slept, he was alerted. He awakened and sat up. "What is it, Nehara?"

"The queen's child is coming!" Nehara answered, shaking Seshena.

Rasuah sighed, not anxious to leave the warm bed, but he got out and reached for a robe. "I'll get the horses ready."

"Hurry, beloved," Seshena urged, leaping out of bed.

In answer, Rasuah ran his hand through his tousled hair and left the room.

"I'll dress myself. Get Makara," Seshena said. Nehara ran off at once to obey.

Seshena dressed as quickly as Rasuah had. By the time she had gathered the articles she needed, Makara was standing outside her door. They huried down the hall and out the entranceway, where Rasuah awaited them in his chariot.

Chenmet stood nearby. "Captain Khakamir is waiting with the queen until you come."

"Excellent," Seshena said as she ran to the chariot.

"Are all three of you going?" Rasuah asked in dismay.

Seshena looked at Makara and Chenmet. "Yes, we must."

"It will be tight," he advised.

"Can you drive with all four of us squeezed in the chariot?" Seshena asked, looking doubtfully at the vehicle's size.

"One of you will have to stand in front of me and the others will have to hold the sides tightly," Rasuah replied.

Seshena got into the chariot and gripped the front. She felt the chariot spring slightly as Makara and Chenmet got into it. Then, Rasuah stood pressed against her back. "Are you sure we shouldn't have our own horses?" she asked.

"We don't have time," Rasuah replied. "Just none of you fall out!" He snapped the reins over the horses' backs.

The horses leaped forward and raced through the courtyard and into the street, their hooves clattering over the stones, the sound echoing off the walls, destroying

226

the night's silence. Since the streets were empty, Rasuah urged the horses into even more speed. But when the chariot careened around a corner at too close an angle to suit him, he pulled back on the reins and slowed the horses.

"Can we not go faster?" Seshena asked over her shoulder.

"You're too distracting, pressed against me like this," Rasuah replied lightly.

Seshena smiled at his words; but she knew from the rigidity of his body they were much too close, and it was difficult for him to maneuver down so narrow and winding a street. "Perhaps we should go another way," she suggested.

"This is the fastest," Rasuah answered. "Don't worry."

"If you say not to worry, I won't worry," she replied and lifted her head confidently.

As he turned the horses into a still darker street, Rasuah's senses from long habit became more alert; but even when he saw two shadows detach themselves from the blackness of the alleyway, he didn't realize what they were until they ran toward the chariot.

"Great Asar, Lord of Eternity!" he gasped as the shadows flung themselves at the horses' heads. He slapped the reins to speed the animals, but they were confused and frightened, and they screamed and reared up. The chariot bounced from wheel to wheel and jolted backwards and forwards.

"What is this?" Rasuah demanded, his sword making a rasping sound as he took it from its scabbard.

The men at the horses didn't answer, but two more men detached themselves from the cover of a building's shadows and walked swiftly toward Rasuah. He leaped from the chariot, and, noting the gleam of the swords they held, tore off his cloak.

"Have a care, thieves," Rasuah warned. "I may be more than you think." He watched the strangers carefully. They paused just outside the reach of his sword.

One of the men spoke quietly to the second, advising

caution. The other reminded the speaker they were four and this man was accompanied only by women.

Rasuah understood their language, and he exclaimed in surprise, "You're Shardanans!"

At Rasuah's words, the two men facing him moved menacingly. Rasuah took a purposeful step forward and raised his sword at one of them as if he had singled out that man for attack. But he merely threw his cloak over the alerted man's head, entangling him momentarily in its folds. Then he wheeled around toward the other man. His arm rose; the sword glittered in the moonlight, then fell. The man's severed head dropped in a shower of spurting blood.

Rasuah turned to face the other Shardanan. The man had thrown the cloak aside and was ready for him. Rasuah's eyes narrowed and ignited with new fire. "You would be wise to leave now," he said softly.

Suddenly Rasuah realized his horses were no longer stamping and snorting; he judged one of the men must be holding them. He decided that the extra man was probably creeping up behind him. In Rasuah's mind there suddenly appeared a picture of the scene and he saw the man's location. The picture came to him as if he'd seen it all through Seshena's eyes. He thanked Seshena silently for telling him.

Rasuah lowered his sword slightly and waited a moment longer for the man to come closer, while he seemed to focus his attention on the Shardanan facing him. When he judged the man behind him close enough, he grasped his sword in both hands and whirled. The blade became a shimmering circle in the moonlight that struck the man's side and nearly sliced through his waist. The only sound the man made was the heavy thud of his split body tumbling to the stones.

Rasuah spun around to face the other Shardanan, who stared at him from a pale face. Rasuah didn't wait for the man to recover his wits, but attacked him immediately. The man warded off Rasuah's first blows automatically.

228

Rasuah's blood ran hotly high now and he slashed and hacked at the Shardanan with a ferocious precision, giving the man no chance to strike a blow of his own. The night was torn with the ring of Rasuah's blows and the noise of clashing swords echoed from the walls until the air vibrated with the sound of Rasuah's fury.

The Shardanan began to tire under Rasuah's relentless attack. His arm grew imperceptibly slower, his movements just a little heavier. Rasuah felt the difference in his sword and pressed even harder. The man began to falter in his defense, but Rasuah's thrusts and slashes were pitiless. The Shardanan stepped backwards, his foot landing in a pool of blood and he crashed to his knees just as Rasuah's sword came down to decapitate him.

The Shardanan holding the horses released the reins and retreated into the shadows. When Rasuah looked around, he saw the man slinking into an alleyway.

Rasuah ran to the chariot. Putting the bloodied sword in Seshena's hand, he commanded, "Stay here."

Seshena stared wordlessly at Rasuah. His eyes contained a gold fire Seshena had never seen in them and she shivered. When Rasuah turned and raced after the fleeing thief, Seshena watched his smooth run and was reminded of a lion in open pursuit.

Rasuah ran into the black maw of the alleyway, and, seeing that it curved almost immediately, he flattened himself against the wall and crept softly to the turning. He heard the scrape of a horse's hoof and, calculating the distance of the sound, broke into a half-run toward the noise.

Rasuah ran around the corner in time to see the shadowy figure of a man furtively mounting a horse. Rasuah, body coiled like a cobra preparing to strike, launched himself at the man and, aiming accurately, gripped the man's shoulders with both hands, then flung himself sideways. Rasuah dragged the man from his saddle and both fell to the stones with a crash.

The Shardanan was momentarily dazed by the attack,

but Rasuah sprang to his feet like a cat. As the Shardanan lifted himself from his knees, Rasuah used his full force to kick the side of the man's head. The Shardanan fell on his face.

Rasuah stood panting for a moment before he pulled the unconscious man up and pushed him over the front of the saddle. Rasuah wiped his brow, leaving a red streak from the blood smeared on his hands, and still panting, swung up into the saddle.

When Seshena saw the horseman slowly approaching, she was afraid for a moment. But she recognized the set of Rasuah's shoulders and she breathed in relief.

Rasuah stopped beside the chariot and bent to take his sword from Seshena's cold hands. "I would bring this one back still able to talk," he said softly. "Can you drive the chariot?"

"I'm not sure," Seshena whispered, "We must hurry even faster now."

"Would you mind riding this horse then?" Rasuah asked. He glanced at the Shardanan stretched limply in front of him. "This one won't awaken until after we've reached the palace," he added, dismounting.

Seshena took a breath and stepped out of the chariot. "If he awakens too soon, I'll hit him with my censer."

Before Seshena got up on the horse, she turned and remarked, "If that fight was a typical demonstration of your skill, I'm surprised the king hasn't made you commander of the army."

From the chariot, Rasuah explained. "Ramessa wanted to do that once. I preferred being an envoy. I'm not fond of fighting."

Seshena's eyes registered surprise, but she said nothing. She raised her robe to swing upon the horse. Then, she reined the animal behind the chariot to let Rasuah set the pace.

When the little group entered the palace, Seshena pressed Rasuah's hand once before she joined Makara and Chenmet to hurry to Nefertiry's room.

Rasuah asked to see the king, and Nehri ran upstairs to tell his master. When Nehri returned to call him to the king's bedchamber, Rasuah ran lightly up the stairs, and marched swiftly to Ramessa's door, which had been left open.

Ramessa had gotten out of bed and was knotting the sash of his robe. He turned to stare at Rasuah. "What happened to you?" he asked.

"We were attacked by Shardanans on our way here," Rasuah explained. When Ramessa gestured toward a chair, Rasuah fell gratefully into it.

"Who was with you?" Ramessa asked, bewildered.

"Seshena, Makara and Chenmet," Rasuah replied, watching Nehri pour a goblet of wine. "There were four Shardanans. I think you'll want to send someone to carry away the three bodies that now lie in the street. They would be a grim sight for the populace to come upon in the morning."

"And the fourth?" Ramessa asked, accepting a goblet from Nehri.

"I gave him to the guards," Rasuah replied. "Perhaps you can get some answers from him, but I doubt it." Taking a goblet, he drank thirstily.

"Shardanans never give answers," Ramessa said thoughtfully. He looked at Rasuah questioningly. "What were you doing riding around at this hour with the priestesses?" he asked.

Rasuah realized Ramessa still knew nothing about Nefertiry. He lowered the goblet and grinned. "The queen's time has come. Nefertiry wanted Seshena with her at the birth. I escorted them to the palace—a good thing too."

Ramessa turned to Nehri. "Arouse the physician," he ordered.

"I'm sure Seshena has sent for him," Rasuah said. He finished his wine and stood up. "Perhaps you'd like to speak with the queen before she's too far along?" he suggested.

Ramessa looked a little dazed, but he said quickly, "Yes, right now!" Rasuah followed the King through the golden door into Nefertiry's apartment.

Nefertiry was pacing up and down before the window openings. Seshena was at a small table lighting incense. The physician stood helplessly in the hall, his admittance checked by Khakamir, who stood like a tree in the doorway.

"Sire, the captain won't allow me past!" the physician called.

"I'm under orders to admit no one to the queen's room," Khakamir said over his shoulder.

Ramessa was still a bit stunned by all of Rasuah's news. "Who gave that order?" he snapped.

Nefertiry, turning to look at Ramessa with a pale face, said "You did."

Ramessa ran a hand through his tousled hair. "It does sound like something I said," he sighed. "Allow the physician inside." He paused for a moment, then added, "Also allow admittance to any servants or assistants he needs."

Nefertiry marched across the room to stare up at Ramessa's face. "Do you think I want a crowd gaping at me?" she demanded. "I do not! I wish only those as are necessary, Seshena, Makara, Chenmet and the physician. In fact, you can dismiss the physician. Chenmet knows what must be done."

"Seshena, Makara, Chenmet—and the physician—will remain," Ramessa said firmly. He put his hands gently on Nefertiry's shoulders. "What else do you wish?"

Noticing Tuiah hovering in the hall, Nefertiry's eyes filled with anger. "Only that no one else be admitted and that Khakamir will remain outside my doorway assuring this." She opened her mouth to say more, but her breath was taken away by another pain. When it had passed, she whispered, "Leave me, my lord. I don't want you to see me so."

Ramessa didn't move. He wished he could say something to comfort Nefertiry, but he didn't know what to say.

232

Recalling what the astrologer had said, fear constricted his heart. He stared at Nefertiry, not wanting to let her see his fear and at the same time unwilling to leave her.

"Please go," she gasped.

Ramessa gazed wonderingly at Nefertiry. Was she always so small as she seemed now, her head bent as she endured her pain? When she lifted her head, Ramessa again went to her. He put his hands lightly on her shoulders and bent nearer to whisper in her ear, "You wondered once if between a king and queen such a thing as love can be." He squeezed her shoulders and added gently, "It can be, Nefertiry."

She turned to look at him, but he had walked away, and she gazed at his retreating back until the door closed between them. She took a deep breath and was gripped by another pain. It seemed to last a lifetime. Finally it passed and she turned to Chenmet. "How long will this go on?"

Chenmet came to put her arm around Nefertiry. "You must walk as long as you're able, until the last minute if you can, so Keb's force can help you, drawing the child toward the earth," she whispered. "Lean on me, my lady. I'll help you stay upright."

Nefertiry saw that the servant's eyes had filled with tears. Wordlessly she leaned on Chenmet, resigned to the pain that was slowly lowering her endurance. Cool fingers suddenly touched her temples and she looked up into Makara's sympathetic face.

"Close your eyes, my queen," Makara murmured. "I'll give you relief."

Nefertiry obeyed and squeezed her eyes shut. As Makara continued murmuring in her soothing voice, Nefertiry's eyelids gradually relaxed and lay lightly on her eyes. She felt renewed strength fill her body. When Makara withdrew her hands and ordered Nefertiry to open her eyes, the queen obeyed as meekly as a child.

"How are you now?" Makara asked.

"The pain is yet there, but I feel almost as if I don't

233

mind it," Nefertiry said wonderingly. "I feel almost as if it's a good thing." She stared at Makara, surprised at her own conclusion.

"Now that fear of the pain has left you, you can recognize the pain's usefulness," Makara said softly. As Nefertiry continued to stare wordlessly at her, she added, "Does it not announce the coming of your son and help you prepare the way for him?"

Nefertiry nodded but said nothing.

Unsure of what Makara had done, Chenmet gave her a look of bewilderment mixed with gratitude, then whispered, "My lady, she's right. Very soon the pains will be a signal you'll heed and use to help your child enter the world. Come. Let us continue walking."

Nefertiry nodded and turned in the direction Chenmet steered her, grateful that friends surrounded her.

Khakamir closed the door behind the king as he stepped into the corridor outside Nefertiry's door. Pausing, Ramessa stood next to him, deep in contemplation for a long time.

Having Ramessa stand so close for so long a time, while Nefertiry was just beyond the door preparing to bear his own child, unnerved Khakamir. He fidgeted, moving his weight from one foot to the other. He had a pain in his own back, as well as a headache. He thought of Ramessa's belief that the child was his and he tried not to focus his eyes on Ramessa's worried face. Khakamir's forehead was so stiff from tension that he felt if someone were to tap it in just the right place—the way sculptors did when they shaped statues—his whole face would drop off. The spear he held upright at his side seemed twenty times heavier than usual and he fervently hoped he wouldn't drop it. He tried to ignore the cramp in his arm and was relieved when Ramessa began speaking to Rasuah.

"Do you think those Shardanans were anything other than thieves?" Ramessa asked.

"They seemed no more than that, yet I have never before heard of bands of Shardanans carrying on their activities right in Wast's streets," Rasuah replied.

"I've had reason to question many Shardanans," Ramessa said quietly. "I've found none who would tell me more than their name, though they were beaten to jelly. I might as well give the order for that one you brought to be executed. He probably is just a thief, bolder than most."

"Yes," Rasuah sighed. "How could he and his companions have known what night we would be on that street, or even that particular street which I decided only on impulse to use?"

"Maybe it was this execution the astrologer meant," Ramessa murmured as if to himself. He raised his head and said firmly, "I'll have it done now. Then it will be the darkness the astrologer predicted."

"Do we have time before—" Rasuah looked at Nefertiry's door.

"You will send someone if the child comes while we're dealing with the Shardanan," Ramessa ordered Khakamir.

Khakamir nodded and was relieved that Ramessa turned away. When Ramessa and Rasuah disappeared down the stairs, Khakamir closed his eyes for a moment and took a deep breath.

The Shardanan was placed before Ramessa, who looked at him disdainfully. "On your face," he snapped.

The Shardanan remained stubbornly upright and Ramessa looked at the guard. The soldier put out his foot and pushed the prisoner forward, so he tripped and fell to his knees.

"I said—on his face," Ramessa reminded coldly.

The soldier gripped the man's thick, curling hair and pushed his face to the floor. When Ramessa nodded, the Shardanan lifted his head to stare implacably at the king. The Shardanan's eyes were like black stones in his face.

"You've decided not to speak. I can tell," Ramessa said

235

softly. "Although I might lighten your sentence and give you slavery instead of death, I can see you're determined to say nothing." He waited without much hope for the Shardanan to consider this possibility and reply. But the man remained silent. "You can speak, can't you?" Ramessa asked. The man nodded, but said nothing. Ramessa looked up at the soldier. "Take him," he said in disgust.

The soldier dragged the man to his feet and propelled him down the hall into another room.

Ramessa wordlessly turned away and left the room. Rasuah quickly followed him. They walked swiftly across the courtyard and reentered the palace. Ramessa ran lightly up the stairs, intending to resume his vigil in his room and drink a great quantity of wine. But when he reached the top step, he saw Khakamir standing before Nefertiry's open door speaking to the physician. Ramessa broke into a half-run.

Khakamir whirled at Ramessa's approach, a wide smile on his lips. "It's a boy, sire!" he called.

Ramessa ran past Khakamir without noticing the look of joy and relief lighting Khakamir's face. Nor did he see Seshena, who stood next to a table on the far side of the room holding a tiny necklace of dark reddish-purple stones over the smoking censer while she begged Aset's protection of the new prince. Ramessa didn't even notice Makara, who stood before Seshena holding a small bundle in her arms. He passed the birth chair without a glance and approached the bed. Gazing with relief into Nefertiry's green eyes he whispered, "The prophecy's meaning was of death, but a thief's death at the moment the child was being born. Not your death, not the child's."

Nefertiry understood nothing of his meaning except that he'd been concerned about her. She smiled weakly and whispered, "You worried I might die?"

"Why do you think I didn't call you to me all those nights?" he exclaimed. "I was terrified to do you harm!"

Nefertiry stared wordlessly up at him, wondering at the softened light in his eyes.

"Have you no curiosity about the child, sire?" Makara asked.

Nefertiry's smile slowly faded and she held her breath. Now approached the moment she'd feared most.

Ramessa turned to look at the small burden in Makara's arms. "Yes, of course," he said distractedly.

Makara unwrapped the infant and held him out in offering, so the king could inspect the child and claim or deny him as his son. Ramessa peered confidently into the infant's face, at the long, slanted dark green eyes, the yet-shapeless nose, the high round cheekbones, the tiny pursed lips, the thatch of straight black hair. Then, he slipped his hands under the baby and lifted the minute body, in official proclamation before witnesses that the child was in fact his son.

Ramessa glanced at the physician. "Let his name be recorded as Setnau." Then, Ramessa's eyes moved to Nefertiry and he smiled. "Setnau's coloring is yours, but his eyes are my father's eyes—and my own," he said happily.

Nefertiry's smile was serene as she whispered, "I like the look of your eyes."

The physician marched down the corridor with angry steps. If Akeset thought he wouldn't have to pay him because the stupid Shardanans hadn't managed to prevent Seshena's coming, the priest had a surprise coming. He would never return the gold the priest had given him. The risk he had taken was enough alone to earn that gold, and, he reminded himself, he'd had to pay that girl from the lower city for her baby. He dared not give the baby back now. He dared not keep it. He supposed he must kill it—smother it or something—and carry its body away. He would drop it in the river, perhaps. The river was close and the crocodiles would dispose of the body.

The physician paused by the door to the garden. Should he go now to speak to Akeset? he wondered.

Yes, he decided. He should see Akeset while his indignation at the priests' failure to anticipate Rasuah's interference would show clearly in his face as well as in his thoughts. He got into his waiting litter and leaned back among the cushions to relax and enjoy his ride to Askeset's house. He didn't realize that Akeset didn't need his report.

Akeset had remained awake through the whole night while he'd sent his mind out like a messenger to follow the results of the attack on Seshena. With its failure, he'd sent venomous thoughts to Nefertiry's chamber, intending to kill her himself in his fashion, if possible. Failing again, he tried mightily to stop the infant's breath with his own will. It didn't work. The healthy child had cried lustily upon entering the world. Now Akeset was even further convinced that Nefertiry was the most powerful worker-in-magic he'd ever encountered.

Akeset was aware of the physician's decision to come to him, but he didn't want the physician in his house. He didn't want to set eyes on him again. Akeset called Shemal, leader of the Shardanans and directed Shemal to send an arrow into the physician's body when the litter passed a certain place where an archer could aim from a rooftop and not be seen.

Akeset had watched the Shardanan carrying arrow case and bow leave the house from a rear door, then had turned away, smiling. Now he would never have to worry about the physician haggling with him over gold or speaking to anyone about the plan to kill Nefertiry and the prince.

14

Ramessa pulled at his new bow several times in experimentation, then turned to Rasuah. "You didn't come to practice merely to pass an idle hour."

Rasuah frowned and, fitting an arrow to his bow, said, "You read behind my eyes."

"If I could read behind anyone's eyes, I wouldn't need an army to keep order in the land and I could dismiss my personal guards," Ramessa observed, watching his friend's tilted eyes in profile as he took aim, remaining silent until Rasuah's long bow released the arrow. Ramessa narrowed his eyes against the glare of the sun and followed the arrow's flashing flight until it reached its target. "You don't seem to need to sharpen your skill," he remarked.

Rasuah lowered his bow and turned to Ramessa. "I've received a message you should know about from one of my acquaintances," he said softly.

"You do have a multitude of spies," Ramessa commented.

"There are a multitude of possible mischief-makers in the kingdom," Rasuah retorted.

"That's true," Ramessa admitted. "This time it must be someone in a high place, if you think you must disguise your report by appearing to need practice with the bow."

"It could," Rasuah said softly, dropping his eyes to his bow while he adjusted the string. "Lord Paser has been withholding some of the tax tribute due the throne and concealing the difference by keeping a second—secret—set of records."

Ramessa stared at Rasuah. "Your spy is Paser's scribe?" he asked.

"I would rather not name the friend who told me this, but he is in a position to know the truth."

"But Paser pleaded a crisis due to a drought and a horde of insects, and I just recently sent him a caravan of foodstuffs!" Ramessa exclaimed.

"It may be that his people starve, but I can assure you Paser lacks nothing," Rasuah said firmly.

"Why didn't Henhenet know of this?" Ramessa snapped. "It's part of his job to be informed of what goes on in the provinces as well as in Tamera."

"It may be that Henhenet, too, was deceived," Rasuah suggested, "but he's Paser's brother-in-law and it's also possible he wasn't anxious to look too closely into this matter."

Ramessa turned to face Rasuah, with eyes that flashed amber lights. "Part of Henhenet's oath of office was that he show partiality to no one."

Rasuah selected another arrow and fit it to his bow. "My informant isn't mistaken," he said bluntly. "I can give you a copy of part of Paser's accounting record and I think you will see it is not the one you saw at tax-gathering time. Maybe Henhenet thought he'd persuade Paser to obey your laws and make amends before you found out."

Ramessa did not comment, but fitted an arrow to his bow. When he released it, the missile made a peculiar

240

whirring sound, unlike Rasuah's arrows, which had been silent.

Ramessa dropped the bow on the grass. "I don't like this bow; it pulls too easily," he said shortly. "I'll send soldiers to persuade Paser to obey me."

"And what of Paser?" Rasuah asked.

"When he finds himself sitting in an empty house and still having to obey me, he'll realize the error of his ways."

"He surely will," Rasuah agreed. "Others, who see the results of Paser's double books, will be warned against trying similar methods. Whoever you send to do this thing you must trust to bring back what's due you. It would be a fine opportunity for a man in such a position to conceal many objects and make excuses about their disappearance, because you can't know for sure what is there and what is not."

"I would trust you to accomplish it," Ramessa said.

"You need a soldier for that work. I'm not such a man," Rasuah replied.

Ramessa smiled faintly. "If those dead Shardanans could talk, I'm sure they'd disagree."

"I'm not made for the work you have in mind," Rasuah insisted. "It's one thing to kill thieves, another thing to invade a man's house."

"You killed the thieves enthusiastically enough," Ramessa observed. "I heard a description of how those bodies looked."

"My anger was inspired by the need to defend Seshena," Rasuah answered firmly.

"And the need to defend my taxes doesn't so inspire you," Ramessa noted, smiling at Rasuah. "I can understand that. You needn't apologize."

"I wasn't going to apologize," Rasuah replied, without smiling. He bent to pick up his arrow case and bow. "Who else would you send?"

Ramessa turned to Menna, who had been standing several paces away. "Take my arrows, but discard that bow. Have another fashioned with a broader curve."

"Yes, majesty," Menna replied, kicking the bow aside and picking up the arrow case.

As Menna picked up Rasuah's equipment too, Rasuah turned to ask Ramessa, "Can you think of no one to send to Kenset beside me?"

"Perhaps Arek—or Khakamir," Ramessa answered and turned to walk back toward the palace. He considered it a moment, then said, "I think Arek. He'll have no qualms about what must be done there."

"No, Arek won't have qualms," Rasuah said softly.

"I have no sympathy for a governor who lets his people starve while he hoards supplies to conceal his own profit." Then Ramessa asked, "Do you know of a good man I could trust to replace the royal physician?"

Rasuah raised his eyebrows at Ramessa's sudden change of subject. Used to his friend's mercurial mind, he shrugged and replied, "I visited Seshena's physician recently regarding a small matter—and found him to my liking."

"He is skilled?" Ramessa inquired.

Rasuah smiled. "Although he isn't well-known among the wealthy, he is very skilled," he replied. "As for the pureness of his heart, Seshena wouldn't have him if he weren't trustworthy, and she can look inside his mind to determine his motives."

Ramessa smiled faintly and asked, "What is the man's name?"

"Resy," Rasuah answered. "I could ask Seshena to speak to you about him," he offered.

"I would have you do that," Ramessa replied. "Come and have some refreshment with me. After standing in that sun, I have the taste for a cup of beer."

Rasuah nodded and followed Ramessa into the palace.

For more than a month after Setnau's birth, Ramessa hadn't allowed Nefertiry to exert herself in any way—not even to sit in audience or attend meetings with any of his ministers. Quickly tiring of her unaccustomed idleness,

Nefertiry had asked Ramessa if she could resume sitting for the statue the sculptor had begun before her pregnancy, and Ramessa agreed. Aside from the time she spent with the baby, these sittings were her only real activity. At first, she'd looked forward to them, but now the sessions seemed tiresome.

Sitting quietly, her head turned at an uncomfortable angle to accommodate the artist, Nefertiry bore her discomfort with unusual patience only because she was reflecting on Ramessa's attitude since Setnau's birth. Although she would have preferred to resume her normal activities a week after the birth, she hadn't protested Ramessa's decision that she do nothing, because he had seemed solely concerned with her well-being. For a time it had been pleasant to forget the intrigues of the court and enjoy the simple pleasures of tending Setnau. Ramessa came often to her suite to visit. He brought foolish little gifts, lavished praise on her appearance and expressed satisfaction with the son she'd produced, which pleased her. But as time went by and he gave no indication of desiring her, she was reminded of her old problems with the harem and began to worry.

Suddenly the cramp in Nefertiry's neck became a sharp pain, and she announced, "If I must hold my head at this angle much longer, it will crack off."

"Divine lady, please excuse my slowness! Allow me to change your position!" the sculptor exclaimed. He hurried forward and carefully directed her into another pose.

Once the artist stepped away, Nefertiry found herself looking directly at Arek, who stood on guard near the door. She didn't miss the hard brightness that momentarily gleamed in Arek's eyes when he saw the direction of her gaze and she lowered her eyes to the floor so she need not stare at his face while the sculptor worked.

Nefertiry had gradually become so accustomed to Arek's constant presence that a certain amount of easiness had developed between them and the loneliness of her relative seclusion since Setnau's birth had prompted

243

her to talk with Arek from time to time. She'd carefully limited conversation to inconsequential matters or even to childhood reminiscences of Khatti; and when he'd sometimes ask questions, she'd answered as if she weren't aware of how familiar he was with her homeland. This restrained friendliness had gradually caused Arek to be less cautious of how he looked at her when they were alone and his eyes often held such desire she found it necessary to turn away. She was aware that, when he made solicitous gestures, his light touches were deliberate. Every time he brushed against her, she knew it was no accident, but she had never rebuked him. Although she had no actual plan, she knew his desiring her would eventually trap him and end his spying. She merely waited to see how the gods would reveal the details of the trap.

Still thinking of this and her ultimate triumph, she lifted eyes gleaming with anticipation and again found herself gazing at him. He continued to stare unblinkingly at her. Uneasily she shifted her gaze to the sculptor, who was polishing the area he'd just carved.

Nefertiry stood up and declared abruptly, "I would end today's sitting now."

The sculptor straightened in surprise, but quickly recovered himself and bowed, murmuring, "You are gracious, divine lady." Still bowing, he backed to the door.

Nefertiry stepped down from the small platform on which she'd been posing and, without looking again at Arek, began to cross the room. Instead of walking at her side or stepping behind to follow, Arek approached to stop in front of her. She raised her eyes to regard him questioningly. He was standing very close, but she decided not to step back.

"Divine lady, may I have a moment with you?" Arek asked. As Nefertiry nodded her assent, Arek said, "I have stood by that door watching you through all these sessions and wish to say, although that sculptor is the best in Tamera, it would take the skill of the gods to recreate your beauty."

244

Surprised, Nefertiry murmured, "Thank you, Arek." When Arek didn't move, Nefertiry asked, "You have something else to say?"

Arek nodded, but was silent for a moment. Then he took a deep breath and whispered, "Divine lady, I stand by your door night after night, knowing the king calls someone from his harem even while you are alone."

Nefertiry's eyes narrowed in warning, but Arek recklessly went on, "I may pay for this conversation with my life, yet I must say the truth. His majesty is blind to ignore such loveliness as yours. Such warmth and passion as you have is wasted in fruitless waiting."

"You have no right to speak so," Nefertiry reminded him, but her tone lacked conviction.

"You are my queen, but you're a woman as well," Arek whispered. "I've seen you wait these months for love, but his majesty comes to visit as if only on an errand. Can you deny your loneliness, my lady?"

Nefertiry stared up at Arek, for his words, whatever his motive, contained a truth that pained her. Ready to retort sharply, she stilled her reply while a voice inside her reminded her that she was the daughter of Seti—the queen of Tamera—and Arek was a spy.

"Are you not lonely, my lady?" Arek asked again.

Nefertiry dropped her eyes in mute answer. She felt Arek's hand cautiously touch her cheek and the warmth of his body as he moved closer. His hand caressed the curve of her jaw and moved to lift her chin so she looked up at him. His dark eyes smoldered with desire.

"Even a royal body has human needs, and one day your body will hold so great a hunger you will think of a lover," he whispered. "When that day comes, my lady, remember me."

Although Arek withdrew his hand, he remained standing so close his body brushed Nefertiry's. With her face yet tilted toward his as if his hand still held her chin, she murmured, "I have heard Shardanans are as passionate in love as they are fierce in battle."

"You will never know the truth of that rumor!"

Nefertiry paled at the sound of the voice and stepped quickly back to stare at Ramessa, who stood on the threshold. Behind him, Khakamir was frowning.

"Majesty, I was overcome by my queen's beauty, but she did nothing!" Arek cried.

Realizing that this was not the time to condemn Arek, Nefertiry said quickly, "Arek did nothing wrong. I spoke foolishly."

Ramessa came closer to glare at Arek. "You will prepare a regiment to march to Kenset and teach Lord Paser never again to withhold taxes," Ramessa directed. "During your long march through the heated plains and into the jungle to the south, you will reflect on the penalty you could pay for what you were thinking of a moment ago. Contemplate also the fact that you will be ending your military career if you even approach the queen that closely again."

"Yes, majesty," Arek said, his tone softened by fear and humiliation. ·

Ramessa turned to watch Arek leave hastily, then motioned for Khakamir to enter. "Khakamir, stay at her side for the day while I decide who I next dare name as her guard."

Khakamir nodded, for his lips were too stiff from anger to speak.

While Ramessa gave these orders, Nefertiry managed to compose herself, and asked, "You are so angered by that foolish comment I made to Arek?"

Ramessa's eyes narrowed to cold, gray-green slits. "Have you been so long without love that you've forgotten the look in a man's eyes when he's tempted, and so tempt him even more? Tonight you will occupy my bed. I'll teach you again about these things." Then, Ramessa turned and walked stiffly from the room, leaving Nefertiry staring after him.

She was quiet for a moment, wondering now what she could say to Khakamir, who remained coldly silent. Finally she said, "We will stay here a moment more. Later I will go to my quarters and remain there for the day,

246

freeing you of the task of guarding me." When Khakamir did not reply, Nefertiry urged, "Come closer. I have no wish to be overheard."

Khakamir obeyed, and she told him how she had seen Arek in Hattusil's palace, explaining that she wished to end his spying without causing more trouble between Khatti and Tamera. Khakamir said nothing, but his eyes remained filled with the orange light of anger. Resigned, Nefertiry told him the story of how her mother had been taken to Khatti and of her own birth. When she finished relating the events leading to her having been given to Ramessa, she added, "I have no wish to bring myself disgrace, or, through my actions, bring disgrace upon my son. I intend him to be the next king."

Frowning, Khakamir concluded, "You hunger to obtain through Setnau a throne you cannot claim. I hunger for a son who must remain a stranger to me."

"Setnau needn't be a stranger to you," she whispered. "You can have any part of his affection you wish."

"You mean I may have any part of his affection I can win as his friend," Khakamir said bitterly. "Just as I'll have only that part of your affection left over after Ramessa, and—if it suits your purpose—other men!"

"I have no interest in any other man but you," Nefertiry vowed.

"And Ramessa, of course," Khakamir added.

Nefertiry said quietly, "I told you before that you wouldn't be happy with this arrangement. I once begged you to consider other women who could give you what I cannot."

"That was before you gave me a son," Khakamir reminded her. "I hadn't counted on having a son I can watch only from a distance."

"Not a great distance," Nefertiry replied. "You can be closer to him than even Ramessa. The king has many children and must spread his attention among them."

"As he spreads his lovemaking thinly among his wives," Khakamir said sarcastically.

Thinking she knew what was behind Khakamir's tension, she took his hand in hers and promised, "As soon as possible I'll find a way for us to be together."

"I'm not yet convinced Arek hasn't been added to your list of lovers," Khakamir said.

"You're a fool if you believe that!" Nefertiry exclaimed.

"Haven't I had you to teach me how to be a fool?" he retorted.

Nefertiry stood up. "I already explained my purpose with Arek."

Khakamir stepped away. "I don't care to discuss your plans," he said looking at her from narrowed eyes. "I want to be no further involved with your scheming."

"Khakamir, I will—" she began.

"You wanted me to accompany you to your quarters, divine lady?" Khakamir asked coldly. "Then shall I find someone to guard your door?"

Nefertiry stared at him, for a moment, angry beyond speaking. Wanting to strike back at him, she spat, "Make sure you choose another Shardanan to guard me. I hear they are good lovers!"

Khakamir's eyes flashed with momentary fire. But he lifted his head, turned, and stalked out of the room leaving her to follow him or not. Blinking away angry tears, she straightened her shoulders and rearranged her features into a mask of haughty calm that would reveal nothing of her inner emotions.

Determined to settle the problem of Arek as quickly as possible, Nefertiry sent Chenmet to find him and bring him to her.

When Arek entered the suite, he glanced fearfully at the golden door to Ramessa's chamber, then walked lightly across the room, afraid his footsteps would be heard.

"He isn't there," Nefertiry said stiffly. "I would not call you to me if he were." Arek paused and stared at her. She smiled wanly and said, "I wish to thank you for attempting to take the blame."

248

"It was I who spoke first, my lady. You diverted his majesty's anger to yourself to save me," Arek protested.

"You would have paid a harsher penalty than I, Arek. Any punishment I receive will be no worse than more loneliness, a penalty I have paid many times already." She sank into a chair and gestured that he join her. Glancing again at the golden door, he sat in a chair discreetly distant.

While Chenmet poured wine into their goblets, Arek studied Nefertiry. Taking a sip of the wine to lend him courage, he remarked, "You find this palace less happy than Khatti's. Perhaps a crown weighs too heavily on that beautiful head." His eyes moved from her downcast eyes to the full lips he hungered to kiss, sliding to her creamy shoulders and the rounded softness of the breasts under the clinging robe, to the curving hips he could almost feel pressed against him. Slowly, he arose and came closer to look down at her. The cloud of her perfume engulfed him. He lifted his eyes to make sure Chenmet had left, he whispered, "Do you wish to escape this unhappy place?"

Although Nefertiry's heart pounded in anticipation, she kept her eyes downcast and murmured, "It is not possible."

Feeling as if a drum beat inside his temples, Arek stooped to sit on his heels before her. "It is possible," he said quietly.

"To escape to another land would require wealth I don't possess. I have only my jewelry, which is stamped with one or the other royal house's insignia. No one would dare touch them," she murmured.

Arek's hand trembled slightly as he reached out to raise her chin so she would look at him. "I can help you," he whispered.

Nefertiry's eyes widened, but she said nothing.

"I have some gold put aside no one knows about," Arek said slowly.

Nefertiry knew his gold came from spying for Hattusil.

Arek quickly added, "What I have now is not enough,

249

of course, for a goddess like you, but Kenset is filled with gold. You know what I'm expected to accomplish there. In the confusion, a good portion of Paser's unaccounted wealth could be diverted into my hands."

Arek's willingness to steal Ramessa's gold as well as his wife, made Nefertiry's eyes turn a darker green. But she still said nothing.

"I will take you from this place to another land where, although you won't be a queen, you will live well," Arek urged. At her continued silence he added, "If you later decided you didn't want me, you could take up another life without me, a life you chose, not one someone else decided for you."

"But I must give myself over to you," Nefertiry whispered.

"Your father handed you to Ramessa, but you can choose whether you want to go with me," Arek reminded her. "Would being with me be a chore? The stories you've heard about Shardanans are true, at least for me. I am as passionate in bed as in battle." He smiled and asked, "You do know my reputation as a soldier?"

Nefertiry nodded, shivering as she remembered the stories of Arek's exploits at Zurim. He mistook her shiver for withheld desire.

"I've dreamed of possessing you and have awakened from my dreams almost sick from wanting you. I am mad with desire for you. Is it not a sign of madness for me to even speak of such things as I have today?"

"And Setnau?" she whispered.

Hope flared like a torch in Arek's heart and he quickly answered, "To the king Setnau is one of many sons and, being half-Khatti, not likely to inherit the throne. He is your only son. I would not deprive you of him."

"You propose treason," Nefertiry whispered.

"Treason to whose king?" Arek asked. "You were born in Khatti and I'm a Shardanan." He stood up and, reaching down, took her hands in his to pull her to her feet. Then, he slid his arms around her and bent to press his lips to hers.

Arek's proposal of treason, his daring to embrace Nefertiry as if she were any woman, caused her to tremble with anger. Arek, thinking she trembled from his kiss, pressed his mouth more hungrily to hers, while he held her body tightly against him. A fresh flood of fury rose in her and she broke away.

"We can't be seen!" she gasped.

"The next time I kiss you we won't be seen because we'll be far from this place," he promised. Taking a deep breath to compose himself, he reached again for his wine goblet. He drank slowly, contemplatively, until finally he said, "I will need a place to hide the gold."

Nefertiry considered this a moment. Deciding she wanted the evidence of Arek's treachery nearby, she suggested, "There's a place near the outer wall in the garden under that great acacia tree where the paving stones are loose and the guards never pass. Who would suspect a place so near the palace?"

"I'll examine it tonight," Arek promised. He was silent a moment, in awe of the plans they'd just made. Then, he sighed and said regretfully, "I must go before anyone discovers us. I probably won't see you before I leave for Kenset."

"It would be safer for us not to meet again," Nefertiry replied, relieved she wouldn't have to endure his embrace again. She lead him to the door, saying, "I'll think about you often while you're in Kenset."

"I'll think of nothing else," Arek whispered, then opened the door a crack, looked cautiously up and down the hall, and quickly slipped out.

After Nefertiry had closed the door behind him, she waved to Chenmet, who had been watching from the next room.

"You have trapped a spy, my lady, and none will be the wiser."

"Arek is trapping himself," Nefertiry replied. She pressed her fingers to her temples and said, "My head feels like a bronze ring is tightening around it. Prepare a bath, Chenmet. I wish to cleanse myself of that Shardanan's touch."

Ramessa attended a meeting late in the afternoon, the angry fire still in his eyes. His ministers and servants shrank in fear from his gaze, carrying out his commands with even more speed than usual. By the time the meeting was over, Ramessa had no taste for the sumptuous evening meal that would be served if he went to the dining room. So he stalked into his own chambers, sending Nehri running for a tray. It wasn't until Ramessa had bathed and lay on a table, with Nehri massaging his tense muscles, that he dared think of Nefertiry's coming to him that night.

The desire that arose in him became subtly mixed with his anger; he soon found that he felt much as he had when he'd returned from Zurim. Disgusted with himself, he tried to put down the feeling. But he failed. Later, while he awaited Nefertiry, he paced back and forth beside his windows like a wild creature in a cage.

What was taking her so long? he wondered, not realizing that his earlier passions lay just under the surface of his consciousness, ready to rise up like a cobra from a basket. Finally, he marched to the golden door and, giving it a violent pull, threw it open.

Nefertiry stood in the center of the room with Chenmet adjusting the hem of her shimmering golden shift. At Ramessa's unexpected entrance, she turned in a whirl of gauzy veiling to stare at him.

Ramessa stood looking at Nefertiry silently a moment, observing her newly slender silhouette as the lamplight shone through the robe. Finally, he snapped, "The morning sun will warm my body before you're ready!"

Nefertiry glanced at Chenmet. "Leave us," she said quietly. She waited until the maid had gone, then looked up at Ramessa. "Do you wish to remain in my room?"

"I said you would occupy my bed," he replied curtly. Taking her wrist in a tight grasp, he turned and pulled her into his room, kicking the golden door shut after
252

them. Next, he picked her up in his arms, marched to the bed and dropped her on it.

Nefertiry took but an instant to recover herself. Pushing away her apprehension, she stretched luxuriously, aware that Ramessa's fiery eyes took in each sinuous motion. She smiled up at him and asked, "Do you behave so roughly with all your wives, my lord?"

Ramessa stepped back from the bed, gazing at her a moment longer before he turned and walked to a table to pour a goblet of wine. When he again faced her, the fires that had filled his eyes were carefully banked. "No," he finally answered, "only those who don't know when they are tempting a man."

Nefertiry rolled on her side to regard him with steady, green eyes. "I'm amazed you blame me for that incident and not Arek, who truly was the aggressor."

Ramessa lowered the goblet. "Arek knows better."

"And I don't?" she asked coolly. "If you think such a thing of me, who will you now trust to guard me?"

Ramessa's eyes narrowed and he said sarcastically, "Senti may be sufficiently ugly."

"Senti is a fine choice to guard your wives," she agreed.

"I have only one wife who presently needs guarding." Ramessa came closer until he gazed down at her. "I hadn't thought you'd look at another," he said softly.

"I'd never look at a Shardanan," Nefertiry said coldly, "not even after years without love." She lifted her eyes to Ramessa's face. "Did you drag me here to discuss that remark I foolishly made to Arek?"

At her effrontery, the colors in his eyes blurred, shifted, then settled into a myriad of amber-green flecks. "No," he replied. He bent closer to touch his lips to hers, intending to kiss her lightly, but exquisite fire immediately ran through him to light his soul like a flare. He hesitated.

"Is something wrong, my lord, that you pause?" Nefertiry whispered against his lips.

Again Ramessa tasted Nefertiry's lips, tentatively, as

253

if in experiment. A trembling deep inside him forced its way to the surface against his will. "We have been too long separated," he murmured.

"I've been without love longer than you," she whispered. "Why should it matter how sharply the fire comes upon you when I'm even more eager?"

Ramessa saw the naked hunger on her face and knew she didn't lie. He straightened to stare across the room at nothing.

Nefertiry raised her hand to run her fingers up his arm. "My lord, how much longer must I wait?"

Ramessa's eyes dropped to rest on her. "What is it you do to me, Nefertiry?" he asked softly. "I've called my choice from the harem every night these last months, but you touch me and—"

Nefertiry got up to kneel on the bed and look into his eyes. "And you tremble as if long deprived of love," she finished.

"Yes, I tremble," he whispered. He put his hands on the satin of her shoulders and a wisp of her hair brushed his arm. His body tensed like a bow drawn fully back. Although her glittering eyes remained fixed on his, he felt her hands slowly begin to untie the knot of his sash. When the robe was loosened, her hands eased the cloth from his shoulders and it slipped to the floor like a cool, silky pool at his feet. She was so close he could feel the tips of her breasts brushing his chest.

"Do you wish it to be over too soon?" he whispered.

Her eyes flashed dark fire, like lightning on a summer night. "I wish it to begin just this way now."

Nefertiry leaned closer, and Ramessa felt her warm, smooth skin against him. The deep inner trembling he'd known before burst through his wavering control like mountains burst when the earth tremors came. He pulled away the golden gauze she wore, casting it to the floor. He put his arms tightly around her, holding her crushed against him in the hope he would stop trembling. The trembling dissolved in the face of a new
254

turbulence that rocked him and he pushed her to the bed almost as he would have thrown down an enemy in battle.

Fear flashed through her at his violence; his lips claimed hers, more as if he wished to conquer than arouse her. His hands didn't caress, but vanquished her; when she squirmed, he gripped her tighter, throwing his leg over her, pinning her down as if he thought she might escape. The fury of his passion inflamed her until she was like a torch flaring against the darkness.

Nefertiry succumbed willingly to his violence. She plunged into it with an enthusiasm that lashed Ramessa's senses to an even higher pitch. Reason slid into the vacuum of their hunger and all thinking evaporated until their bodies were appeased.

15

The golden disc of the sun would soon be no more; its glowing face showed only a fiery arc over the dark line of the hills. The redness of the sky was rapidly becoming purple, and clouds were like dark foam on the horizon.

Along the riverbank, papyrus stalks made a soft hissing in the wind; and their golden pollen fell soundlessly to the Nile. Rasuah bent to pick up a small, flat stone from his terrace's pavement. Straightening, he drew back his arm and, with a snap of his wrist, sent the stone skimming along the tops of the stalks, making a soft whistling sound. A flock of small birds arose from the plants, adding the whirring rhythm of their wings to the evening's music.

Rasuah watched the wildly beating flashes of white against the sumptuous colors of the sky, then lowered his gaze to the little triangular sails of boats rounded by the wind and gilded by the sun's fading light, moving down the river.

He was about to sit down on the low stone wall that

bordered his terrace when he saw the silhouette of a woman walking quickly up the hill. Seshena. He watched for a moment as she moved with that peculiar, gliding half-run of hers up the slope toward his terrace. As she neared, he turned to pour a goblet of wine for her, knowing she would welcome a cool sip after her journey. When he turned to greet her, she was already entering his terrace. Smiling, he opened his arms to her.

The warmth of her firm little body pressing so happily to his was like the sun relit in his soul. He held her close for a long time without speaking.

"Would you like wine?" Rasuah murmured into her hair.

Seshena smiled. "I'm already intoxicated with you," she whispered. "Yet my tongue is dry from that climb and I suppose I must appease it."

Rasuah drew away and handed her the goblet. Seshena sipped the cool liquid slowly and turned to gaze beyond the wall at the river. In the distance she saw a large ship coming from the north, a merchant ship returning from the Great Green Sea and the lands beyond.

"I came to you like that ship on the horizon," she whispered, "with wings for sails, folding as I neared my home."

"You are weary from your day?" Rasuah asked quietly.

Seshena nodded. "Weary in the heart, but not the body," she replied. "It's difficult sometimes to be high priestess. There's a darkness over Wast like a coming sandstorm. The darkness spreads over all the land, for it hangs over the throne."

Rasuah sat beside Seshena. "What darkness do you mean?" he asked quietly.

"Sundry plots, plotters spinning sticky webs like the spider. The stickiness is the honey that lures so many to corruption and traps them there."

"You speak of Paser?" Rasuah asked.

"He's only one," Seshena replied. "There are many others."

258

Ramessa is sending Arek to stop Paser," Rasuah said softly. "Knowing Arek's methods, I think the other governors will be warned when they see what Arek does with Paser."

"Arek, too, is corrupt," Seshena whispered. "Only Arek will be dealt with sooner than he knows. Nefertiry has already laid a trap for him. But unless she looks to her own methods, she also will become corrupt."

Rasuah didn't know what to reply to this and he was silent for a moment. Finally he said, "At first Ramessa asked me to deal with Paser. I told him I wasn't made for what he had in mind. But the day will come, Seshena, when I must travel to another province or even another land. It's part of my job, this traveling."

"I'll be lonely when you're away," she said, gazing up at his tawny eyes.

"I would take you with me, if you'd come," he said slowly. "Will you think about it?"

"I need think of nothing," she whispered. "I would go gladly."

"You could lay aside your temple duties?" he asked. "You'd leave Nefertiry in her troubles?"

Seshena's smile faded slowly, and she turned to look toward the east, where the night had already spread its dark wings. The wind spread her hair against Rasuah's shoulder, allowing him a moment to enjoy its soft touch before it moved away.

"I cannot go," she whispered. "I must remain in Wast near Nefertiry until this thing is over. My heart is heavy to say this. It causes me great pain. Yet I must stay."

"I thought that," he said quietly. "But I couldn't deny myself the hope you might for a time withdraw from this struggle and come with me."

"There are those who strain against their soul's destiny, thinking they can cheat the divine beings, pretending they're wiser than the One Alone," Seshena said. "I'm not one of those rebels. I reach ever upward. When my task causes my spirit pain, I reach farther so I may grow beyond the unpleasantness. For that is sorrow's

259

purpose—to stimulate you to reach above it and thus escape its pain." She touched Rasuah's face and asked, "You will reach with me, beloved? The rewards will be greater than the present pain."

Rasuah sighed. "I also have no choice. Our paths are the same," he replied. He turned his head to look at the city beyond the slope. "Someone is playing a flute. It sounds like a soul lost in the circles of time."

"We aren't lost," Seshena murmured. "Our souls have known a better time, but we aren't lost. We bring from that better time a wisdom and strength. We offer it like a gift to Tamera."

Rasuah tilted his head to gaze at the growing darkness above. "You think that we've lived before, that we've known love in another life?" he asked quietly.

"The wheel of time makes countless circles," she whispered.

"Your arms seemed familiar to me from the first embrace," he admitted.

"We're like lotuses, which close during the night and await dawn to blossom again," she said.

"You speak of death," he observed.

"Each death is but another night of waiting for each other and love," she replied.

Rasuah again looked up at the sky, where the moon tossed its silvery veils to the blackness. "Now the dark things arise from their hidden places," he whispered, "like the dark things arise in our lives. The sabau come bringing sorrow."

"The sabau aren't all that occupy the night," Seshena said. "There are others, more difficult to perceive and understand. But they aren't evil like the sabau. They steal the fire from brows stricken with fever; they give refreshment from the sorrows of the day—for isn't it true a man sitting in his moonlit garden learns much he didn't know by day?" Seshena asked. "The night things creep softly past window openings to give pleasant dreams to sleepers, spreading fragrant pollen over lovers." Seshena lifted her hands to the night. "Feel the wind. It's like flower petals brushing the skin. The wind whispers secrets through the voices of the palm trees. The secrets are caught by the petals of the lotuses, who wisely close at the coming of darkness and hold the knowledge safely to their hearts until Ra signals his victory over darkness."

"Again you speak not of lotuses and night, but of souls and death," Rasuah observed. "I've often looked at the sky on nights like this, feeling as if my sight can pierce that infinity to each darkened pillar of heaven. I've felt a sense of waiting mixed with wonder, as if something might happen in those black depths, something only for my sight."

"And what have you seen, beloved?" Seshena asked.

Rasuah sighed. "Merely stars and the moon and occasionally passing clouds as there are tonight, from time to time a comet, but nothing more—only such things as other men can see. Yet I have a sense of waiting."

Seshena put her hands at his temples and turned his face to hers. "I give you something no other man can see against the sky," she whispered, "No man can ever see me bend near him in the night to kiss."

Her lips touched his softly, caressing his mouth sensitively, penetrating his sadness and driving it away, arousing a sweetly piquant aching in him that soon turned to exquisite fire. Their lips clung, savoring the tremulous flames that rose to exhilarate them, until the fire burned brightly.

Ramessa had decided it wouldn't be proper to rejoice openly at the degradation of Paser, one of Tamera's noblemen, at the hands of Arek, a Shardanan mercenary; thus, Ramessa hadn't formally announced that the banquet was a celebration of Arek's success in Kenset. But Ramessa had ordered the banquet room to be decorated in purple and gold, the royal colors of Arek's native land.

Ramessa scanned the banquet room slowly. The guests were unusally subdued, he noted with satisfaction.

261

Although wine flowed freely from the purple-garlanded jars and the girls in violet shifts played their instruments with merry industry, the lords and ladies had gathered into little groups. Ramessa knew their whispers were of Paser's downfall.

Paser's personal crops had been destroyed. His palm and olive trees had been cut down and his vineyards torn up. His flocks of sheep and goats, his herds of cattle had been seized. His house had been swept clean of all its valuables and most of the servants had been taken away. Ramessa had ordered Arek to do all these things to show the other noblemen that withholding taxes wasn't worth risking the penalty.

Ramessa should have been happy, if not at least smug, over the success of his latest manuever. But anyone able to read his look would have wondered what he brooded over and speculated on who had made him so unhappy.

Earlier in the afternoon when Ramessa was ready to take his bath, Chenmet had come to Nehri with the request that Nefertiry be given a private moment with Ramessa, which Nehri granted. The moment was less than private because Nefertiry kept Chenmet at her side while she told Ramessa that Arek had been steadily making advances to her and swore that Arek had offered her gifts of gold and jewels if she'd surrender to him, that Arek had promised to take her from Ramessa's palace and transport her to his own land there to be his honored and only wife.

Then Chenmet swore she'd seen Arek in the garden the very night he'd returned from Kenset. In the garden, he'd appeared to be lifting some of the paving stones in a secluded area and digging beneath them.

Shocked at his friend's betrayal, Ramessa had sent Arek on an errand to the far side of Wast and had ordered Khakamir to lift the paving stones. Ramessa was stunned by the cache of gold and gems deposited there. He and Khakamir carried away the loot and secretly deposited it in Ramessa's bed chamber until it could be openly brought to the treasury. Ramessa obtained Khakamir's promise of silence, and arranged to keep Arek busy, in the event he might think of returning to examine his loot and find it had vanished.

Despite the evidence, Ramessa had found it a bitter struggle to accept Arek's treachery. Now Ramessa sat silently surveying the banquet in honor of Arek, watching carefully each move Arek made. And Arek was finally condemned by his own black eyes, which had followed Nefertiry furtively from the moment she entered the banquet room.

Although Ramessa appeared to be as much at ease as Botar sprawled on the floor at his feet, his mind was searching for a way to solve this new problem. Before the evening was half-through, Ramessa was ready to plunge the skewer, on which pieces of lamb were served him, through Arek's heart. With every look Arek cast Nefertiry, Ramessa's temper rose higher. But to kill his most trusted guard before all the guests would have required some sort of explanation even from a king. So Ramessa had no intention of publicly accusing Arek of trying to seduce his queen. And it would be equally embarrassing if Ramessa were to condemn Arek for stealing Paser's gold, because it made Ramessa look the fool for having given Arek the assignment of punishing Paser in the first place.

Finally, Ramessa stood up and walked at a leisurely pace to Khakamir, who stood a few feet away near the doorway alternately frowning into his goblet and staring at Arek.

"This wine isn't to your taste, Khakamir?" Ramessa asked softly. Khakamir's eyes rose from his goblet and he shook his head. "I had thought to further honor Arek by having this wine served at the party, because it's favored by the Shardanan. Tonight I've grown to hate it."

"I never liked anything of Shardana," Khakamir murmured, looking at Arek's eyes staring hotly at Nefertiry. He wondered how much encouragement Nefertiry had secretly given Arek, and his temper rose at the thought. "What will you do about him?" he asked.

Ramessa sighed. "I don't know," he admitted. "To accuse him in court of pursuing the queen is as embarrassing as charging him with the theft."

"I know what I'd do if I were in your place," Khakamir murmured. His eyes took on the orange light Ramessa recognized from seeing Khakamir in battle.

"It would be most fortunate if he was attacked by thieves, as Rasuah was attacked the night Setnau was born," Ramessa observed. "That would eliminate the problem most discreetly."

Khakamir looked speculatively at Arek, who had noticed Ramessa talking to Khakamir and had taken the opportunity to venture a knowing smile at Nefertiry. "Arek knows too well the way thieves fight, and he'd surely best them if their numbers were less than three."

"I've seen you beat him when you practiced with the swords recently," Ramessa said.

"I don't fight like a Shardanan thief," Khakamir said contemptuously. "I fight like Rasuah, for we had the same teacher, a Tameran master."

"Although having Arek killed by thieves seems the only discreet way to rid myself of him, I cannot hire real thieves," Ramessa murmured.

Khakamir's slanted eyes turned to regard Ramessa questioningly. "Are you suggesting I act as the thief who eliminates Arek?"

"I would be grateful," he replied.

"How would we get him out of this party?" Khakamir murmured. "He won't leave as long as the queen is here to gape at."

"He might leave if he received a message to meet her in the garden," Ramessa suggested. "Chenmet could deliver such a message, if you'd be willing to act as executioner."

Khakamir's eyes narrowed as he considered the effects of this strange assignment. He could kill Arek even as he'd dreamed of doing many times since he'd seen Arek and Nefertiry whispering together. He could kill Arek not only with Ramessa's permission but with his gratitude.

"I'd gladly end this Shardanan's treachery," Khakamir whispered. "Have Chenmet deliver the message at once and let the message say the queen will meet Arek where we found the gold."

"It will be done, my friend," Ramessa said. He looked intently at Khakamir's angry eyes and added, "I wish I could be the one to do it."

When Ramessa returned to his place at the table, he looked up at the servant standing by his elbow and said, "Bring me a new goblet filled with the wine I favor. My mouth is dry."

Nefertiry glanced at him and commented, "I don't doubt it."

Ramessa lifted his eyebrows. "Why do you say that?" he asked innocently.

"Because of that long discussion you held with Khakamir," Nefertiry replied. "I wondered what you both found so fascinating."

"We discussed my problem," Ramessa murmured. "It seems that Khakamir will solve it for me."

Nefertiry's eyes widened. "How?" she asked.

"With his sword, I think," he replied. "Did you know he was taught by the same master as Rasuah?"

Nefertiry shivered. "Khakamir will kill him?"

"Execute is the proper word," he advised.

"Perhaps Khakamir will die!" she whispered, suddenly terrified for Khakamir.

Ramessa turned to look at her. "I doubt it," he murmured, "but if Khakamir does die, he'll do so happily, for he'll have done it in our service." Seeing her disbelieving look, Ramessa added, "He gladly defends your honor as well as mine."

Nefertiry nodded but she wondered, if between the four of them, Khakamir was not the only one who still knew what honor meant.

When Arek had passed from the view of the guards who stood at the palace doors, he quickened his pace. His heart beat with a peculiar rhythm when he thought of Chenmet's message that Nefertiry would leave the banquet to follow him into the shadowy garden. The trees and shrubs would form a black wall against prying eyes while the moonlight filtering down into the small clearing would light her face as he took her. Arek smiled widely, and the smile was still on his lips when he stepped into the clearing.

Suddenly an arm shot past his shoulder to lock around his throat. He was pulled back against a hard body and his right arm was gripped and twisted around behind him.

"You thought you'd have Nefertiry, but you will not."

Choking, Arek could only manage a whisper, "Khakamir! Why? How is it possible?"

"She betrayed you," Khakamir whispered.

"But she pursued me! I never—tonight was to be the first time—" Arek gasped.

"There will be no time for you," Khakamir said quietly. "You fell into a trap baited with green eyes."

Suddenly understanding the passion in Khakamir's words, Arek choked and whispered, "And you? You fell into the same trap."

"Perhaps so, Arek, but tonight you'll escape her," Khakamir murmured. "I cannot." Then, Khakamir released Arek's arm and drove his dagger into Arek's back. He withdrew the dagger and let Arek slip to the ground.

Khakamir, bending to wipe off his blade on Arek's tunic, whispered bitterly, "I would have given you a chance, but a sword fight would have made too much noise, and I must preserve Nefertiry's honor."

Sitting anxiously in the empty throne room, Nefertiry listened to Khakamir's soft footsteps as he paced through the room's expanse. She had sent Chenmet to direct him to her, but now that he'd come, she didn't know what to say. Part of her wanted to greet him with open arms, and part of her wanted to apologize. But for what? she wondered. She had neither betrayed him with Arek nor had she sent him to kill Arek.

"You wished to speak to me, divine lady?"

Hearing his voice, she immediately felt his old command over her. Suddenly, she realized she was afraid of Khakamir, because he was stronger than she. He had yielded to her crown, but not to herself. Then she knew she had never lied to him—she did love him. With this discovery, the old willfulness rose in her and, defiantly, she raised her head very slowly toward him. She sat on her throne and he knelt before her. Still, she said nothing, her eyes glittering with a strange mixture of emotions. When her folded hands ceased their traitorous trembling and her voice seemed more dependable, she asked softly, "Do your knees ache?"

Khakamir's dark eyes rose to meet Nefertiry's, and she felt shame wash through her.

"It isn't important, divine lady," he replied clearly.

Tears suddenly filled her eyes and she whispered, "Rise, Khakamir. I have no wish to see you kneel before me. It isn't fitting."

Khakamir stood up. "You're my queen."

"Queen, yes," she repeated bitterly. She looked down at her lap and murmured, "I didn't give my body to Arek. I didn't tell Ramessa to send you to kill him. I thought Ramessa would find another way, perhaps banish him." She lifted her eyes to gaze at Khakamir through a blur of tears.

"You needn't explain to me, divine lady," Khakamir said coolly.

"But I do!" she cried. "I have to explain to you, of all people!"

"Lower your voice or someone will hear," he whispered.

Nefertiry looked down at her hands. Again they were trembling. Perhaps it was best if he hated her, perhaps simpler, she thought. A pain shot through her, leaving emptiness in its wake. She couldn't let him hate her, after all. She raised her head. "You know I didn't trust Arek from the beginning," she murmured. "But I knew he wanted me. I let him reveal his desire while I tried to think

267

of a way to trap him. But I never so much as kissed him. Khakamir, I cannot let you think such a thing of me!"

"I believe you," he whispered, "but what does it matter? I'm only a captain in the royal guard."

"And the father of my child, and I love you," she said softly. She stood up. She was silent a moment. Then, she sighed and said, "If you would go from me, then go. I will remain true to my promise that I would end it when you wished, and you wished it a month ago."

Khakamir remained where he was, looking at Nefertiry, at her lowered eyes, at the hands that were trembling at her sides. "Nefertiry?" he whispered.

She raised her head slowly, with great effort, to look at him. "Yes, Khakamir," she said in a tone so low it was merely a release of her breath.

Khakamir moved a step closer and took her shaking hands in his. "I cannot do it," he whispered. "I cannot walk away."

Nefertiry stared at him in disbelief for a long moment, until slowly, very slowly, she began to realize the meaning of his words. "Are you certain, Khakamir?"

Khakamir drew her from the dais and put his arms around her. She laid her head on his chest and clung to him. "I'm sure," he whispered into her hair. "I am very sure."

16

Rasuah had warned Seshena that Ramessa would soon send him on a journey and his prediction was fulfilled all too quickly. On the day following the banquet Ramessa had commanded him to go to Nehren to arrange for the collection of Prince Pekharu's taxes. Ramessa deliberately chose Pekharu's far-distant province as the next from which he'd collect, because it was widely known that Pekharu's mother was a Shasu woman and a perfect example of her fierce and untameable people. But it wasn't widely known that the son she produced was a coward. Ramessa knew that Pekharu, intimidated by Paser's punishment, would eagerly surrender his tribute. The other governors, seeing that even a man half-Shasu cooperated with Rasuah, would quickly cooperate with the other tax collectors.

Until now, Rasuah hadn't realized how all-pervading was his need of Seshena. It had grown to the point where he couldn't sleep without the warmth of her body curled close to him.

Ra had risen and fallen twenty times since Rasuah had

left Wast. On the edge of this twenty-first dawning, Rasuah still turned restlessly, his unquiet heart forbidding peaceful slumber. Why did he struggle to sleep? he wondered. If he hadn't been able to rest even while his ship had rocked gently on the crystal waters of the Great Green Sea, why should he expect slumber to find him in the bed Pekharu's palace offered? Sighing, he struck aside the linens covering him, and sat up to reflect on his situation.

"You are already awake?"

Rasuah turned to see Zehzee entering the room. He nodded. "I'm as awake as when you left me all those hours ago."

"How delighted will Djanah be when she sees the circles of sleeplessness around your eyes!" Zehzee exclaimed. "Djanah will know that thoughts of the priestess have kept you from sleep, and she'll rejoice that your heart has finally found a home."

"That spying woman learned it long ago," Rasuah grumbled. "I cannot imagine how anyone would be happy to lay eyes on as weary a creature as I'll be when I return."

"Today marks the last of this work," Zehzee said encouragingly, holding out Rasuah's robe. "The messenger you will send speeding back to the king tonight will announce your complete success." He chuckled softly and added, "Even more success than his majesty anticipated, my lord."

"Don't call me your lord now, you meddlesome lizard," Rasuah said affectionately. "You've been placing your ear against the wall again, I can tell."

Zehzee finished arranging the robe and stepped back with a contrite expression. "All of Prince Pekharu's household know he readies his eldest daughter for the long journey to Wast."

"I have no doubt you knew before the rest of them," Rasuah retorted. "Come to the bath and wash my back, you with the nose of a ferret. Help cheer me up so I'll at least appear to Pekharu as if I'm alive."

Zehzee's face took on a sly look as he announced, "Your bathwater will enliven you."

Rasuah stopped and slowly turned to look at the servant. "The water is cold again?"

Zehzee gestured with his fingers. "Just a little."

"That no doubt means I'll have to break the ice on its surface before I get in," Rasuah said grimly.

"Oh no, my lord. I already did that," Zehzee replied. And Rasuah groaned.

"You dislike bathing in cool water in the morning?" Pekharu asked incredulously. "It's a particular treat to my mind. It awakens and refreshes me."

"It does awaken me," Rasuah agreed.

Rubbing his chin reflectively, Pekharu said, "Perhaps I've been so long in this place my body has changed to accommodate it. But the water running from the mountaintops is supposed to be very healthful."

"With joy do I drink that cold water, but when I bathe in it, my body remains implacably Tamera's," Rasuah said. Then he added, "It really doesn't matter because I'll be leaving tomorrow morning."

"But Lord Rasuah!" Pekharu sat up stiffly. "Will you not wait for my daughter? Or has King Ramessa declined my child?"

"The king would see her before he decided," Rasuah answered promptly. "Shala won't be ready to leave tomorrow morning?" Pekharu shook his head and visions of more frigid baths chilled Rasuah. "When will she be ready to go?" he asked quickly.

"Only a few more days, Lord Rasuah," Pekharu assured him. "To move a woman's belongings is like moving the contents of an entire city."

"Will her belongings fit into my ship?" Rasuah asked tartly, thinking of his delayed reunion with Seshena. Without his knowing it, his tawny eyes had darkened.

"Oh yes, Lord Rasuah, of course!" Pekharu replied,

271

uneasy at Rasuah's reaction. "Shala will be no trouble to you. She just has difficulties deciding what to take, what to discard. She wishes to please his majesty."

Rasuah sunk down a little in his chair, his expression like his temper, not improving.

"The king's taxes are already being loaded on the ship, so you may send your messenger to reassure his majesty that all is well," Pekharu tried to sooth the royal envoy. "Have no fear, Lord Rasuah. I'll see to it myself that tomorrow morning's bath is warmed."

"Calm yourself, Pekharu," Rasuah finally said, straightening up. He reached for his wine goblet and explained, "My unhappiness is due to personal reasons. I'm not displeased with what you've done."

Pekharu didn't trouble himself to hide his relief. "I was afraid you'd send an unfavorable message," he admitted, looking pale. "I didn't want the royal army at my walls."

Rasuah sipped his wine, smiling faintly. "I don't think the king will send them merely because I'm a few days delayed in returning."

Pekharu managed to smile stiffly. "I understand that Commander Arek was mysteriously killed," he said. "This new commander, Khakamir, do you know him?"

"Arek was never commander of the army," Rasuah corrected. "Arek was captain of the royal guards. There was no commander of the army other than the king. Khakamir was captain of the archers. When the king elevated him to captain of the royal guards, he gave him the additional title of commander of the army."

"I'm happier to see a Tameran nobleman commanding the royal guards than a Shardanan mercenary," Pekharu commented, secretly hoping Khakamir was more gently disposed than Arek had been. "What kind of man is Commander Khakamir?"

"Khakamir is more reserved in manner than Arek, and he's as loyal to the crown as it's possible for a man to be," Rasuah said. He took another sip of his wine and added

272

pointedly, "Khakamir was chosen for his excellence in battle as well as his loyalty."

"Certainly he must be skilled in military matters," Pekharu mumbled.

"Khakamir's an honorable man, but also a fierce and cunning fighter," Rasuah advised, thinking it best that Pekharu not be too soothed about Arek's successor.

"Yes, of course, of course," Pekharu muttered. He looked down into his goblet for a moment before lifting his eyes. "Have you heard anything regarding how or why the unfortunate Arek died?"

"It happened after I'd set sail," Rasuah replied. "I've only received a message that he was stabbed to death in the king's garden one night."

"In the king's garden!" Pekharu exclaimed. "Is it safe nowhere these days? In the king's garden! Is the royal family safe?"

"Commander Khakamir will see to the royal family's safety, I'm sure," Rasuah said firmly. "Probably Arek's murder was for some personal reason known only to Arek and his assassin. Arek was a man likely to have enemies."

Pekharu nodded gravely and was silent. Sensing Pekharu had something more to say, but was hesitant to speak, Rasuah waited patiently, trying to appear friendly, so Pekharu would speak. Moments passed without result. The atmosphere grew pregnantly oppressive. Finally, hoping to lighten the situation, Rasuah said, "I seem to have acquired a taste for your wine, Pekharu." Pekharu started and looked up. Rasuah smiled. "I would have my goblet refilled."

"Yes, of course." Pekharu watched the attendant pour the wine, then gestured for him to leave the room.

After the servant had gone, Rasuah again looked at Pekharu expectantly. When Pekharu remained nervously silent, Rasuah sighed and said, "You've been trying to decide whether or not to tell me something. I had thought your dismissal of the servant meant you'd decided to speak. But apparently I was wrong. Still, my curiosity forces me to put aside discretion and ask what you have on your mind."

"I do have some information of interest to you and your king," he said slowly.

"It must be alarming that you hesitate so long over the telling of it," Rasuah said, more lightly than he felt.

Pekharu shrugged. "My hesitance is because I know so little and must surmise so much from it. It's too early yet to decide anything definite."

Rasuah leaned forward and asked, "What do you know?"

Pekharu took a swallow of wine, not to taste it but merely to moisten his dry throat before he began. "Because many ships stop here to get fresh water and supplies, many strangers come to my city. Sometimes they drink too much at the inns and speak more freely than their masters would wish them. Many couriers have passed between Keftiu, Shekel and Isy these last few months, and some of them have gotten drink here—and careless. They boast to impress the girls and stories have come back to me. It seems possible that Keftiu, Shekel and Isy are building up their stores of weapons and that they've made secret agreements joining them in a warlike cause."

Rasuah considered this a moment before asking, "Even if this is true, why should you fear them? You're under Tamera's protection. All three of those lands together couldn't gather an army which would pose more than a moderate threat to Tamera."

"Perhaps, but what threat would they present if other lands joined them—like Shardana?" Pekharu asked, raising his eyebrows.

"Has Shardana done so?" Rasuah asked quietly.

"My spies haven't had the opportunity to look into the couriers' pouches, so I can't be sure, but I think Shardana is favorably disposed to the idea," Pekharu answered. Noticing how Rasuah's eyes took on a harder glint, Pekharu quickly added, "Teresh, Achaiwasha, and Ekwest have recently begun to participate in this flow of messengers. If war is planned, I suspect they also will throw their forces into it."

Rasuah stared into his goblet. "Isy has always been a peaceful and harmless island, and Achaiwasha never seemed interested in launching invasions of other lands. Shekel is an island of fishermen." He paused a moment, thinking about the people of those lands, knowing their tempers could be raised to a ferocity worth considering. Aloud he said, "Shardana has always been a warlike nation, but it's never been inclined toward allying itself with others." He lifted his eyes to Pekharu's. "Why would these lands suddenly unite their armies?"

"Shardana joined Khatti to fight Tamera before," Pekharu reminded him. "Khatti's pride yet stings over the humiliation of Tamera's defeating them. They've never been against the principle of joining many armies to accomplish what a single army cannot."

"We have a treaty with Hattusil!" Rasuah declared. "Would he dare break it?"

Pekharu shook his head and answered slowly, "I doubt he'd join them in an open fight, but I can see his hand in this. It's his style and he could be quietly encouraging them."

Rasuah's eyes slowly lit with golden flickers as he thought about that possibility. "If Khatti's wealth and genius for strategy was coupled with the island kingdoms' passionate temperament, they could present a formidable threat," he said softly, thinking aloud. "You have specific reasons for thinking Khatti is involved?"

Pekharu quickly replied, "I've heard that Hattusil has sent many couriers of his own to these countries. Lately the messengers have been followed by merchants who, upon arrival in these lands, shed their merchants' disguises as butterflies shed their cocoons."

"And become what?" Rasuah demanded.

"My spies have recognized the faces of many of Khatti's finest military men," Pekharu whispered.

Rasuah stared at Pekharu a moment, saying nothing. Then, abruptly putting down his goblet, he stood up. "I must dispatch a courier so King Ramessa will know when to expect my ship. If you receive any other news, advise me."

"I will," Pekharu promised.

As Rasuah left Pekharu, he wondered if these latest treacherous events were connected with the things Seshena feared. He was no longer merely lonely for her. Suddenly, he was afraid.

Nefertiry watched Ramessa's expression as he read Rasuah's message. Although he had frowned at some passage, she now noted a lightening of his expression, and she wondered what mixture of news the scroll held.

Finally Ramessa's eyes lifted from the papyrus to regard Henhenet, who stood at the base of the dais. "Lord Rasuah has been successful as usual," he announced. "In fact, he has been so successful we must prepare for the arrival of a lady. Lord Pekharu's daughter, Shala, will be presenting herself at court for my approval. Lord Pekharu is sending her to Wast as a gift—as a prospective royal wife."

Nefertiry forced herself to keep her eyes fastened on the crowd of people before her, while she made her face a mask of uninterested haughtiness, although her heart was beating wildly to think of having to contend with a new wife.

"I've heard of Lady Shala's beauty," Henhenet said solemnly. "If the stories aren't wildly exaggerated, she will grace your harem."

"It's been a long time since a new lady entered my palace," Ramessa replied softly, as he contemplated the pleasant prospect.

Nefertiry turned slightly toward Chenmet, who stood at her side, and Chenmet motioned to the slave behind Nefertiry to resume fanning the queen. Nefertiry turned her head to regard Ramessa with a carefully bored expression. "Another wife, my lord?" Ramessa's smile increased at her question, but her own expression remained unchanged. "When will you tire of these women's distant relatives sending you messages addressed to 'my dear cousin-in-law,' 'my honored uncle-in-law,' 'my illustrious son-in-law' begging you for favors and gifts?" she murmured, stifling a yawn.

"When will Lord Rasuah's ship reach Wast, majesty?" Henhenet asked. "I would prepare for his arrival—and the lady's."

"I anticipate their arrival in five days," Ramessa replied. "Prepare a banquet in celebration of Lord Rasuah's success two evenings after he arrives. That will coincide with the festival of the next year's birth."

"Yes, majesty," Henhenet replied. As he turned to look at the crowd, his eyes fell on the saffron robes of Akeset. He turned back to Ramessa. "Majesty, the first servant of Amen-Ra's temple begs audience."

Ramessa sighed in resignation. "Let Akeset come forward."

Akeset approached and bowed at the foot of the thrones.

"Rise, Akeset," Ramessa directed in a weary tone. "What matter have you to set before me?"

"Sire, as you are divine, and the god before whom I prostrate myself daily, surely you know the will of my temple's patron, Amen-Ra," Akeset said loudly.

"I've had little time lately to meditate and speak with Amen. I've been occupied with state matters," Ramessa said shortly. "What does Amen-Ra want now?"

"The most adept of the temple's oracles, Petet, has advised that Amen-Ra grows impatient with waiting for his temple's repairs," Akeset replied.

"That again," Ramessa muttered under his breath. Aloud he asked, "Why cannot Amen-Ra rest his divine eyes on the glories of the new temple in the south that's being constructed to his and Ptah's mutual honor? Surely Amen-Ra doesn't begrudge sharing the temple with Ptah and me."

"Amen-Ra rejoices to have you seated at his side in
277

any temple," Akeset replied tactfully. "But Petet says the god is less than satisfied with that temple because it's so near a temple to be dedicated to the honor of one foreign-born."

Akeset glanced at Nefertiry, but returned his gaze to Ramessa as he continued. "Majesty, I wish no offense to the queen. I merely repeat what Amen-Ra has revealed to Petet during his meditations."

"Continue," Ramessa directed.

Akeset took a breath. "I also have the unhappy task of telling you that Petet said Amen-Ra sent Sekhmet to strike down Captain Arek as a warning that more evil may come if his temple isn't repaired."

"Must the god use a dagger?" Nefertiry asked sarcastically. "Has Amen-Ra given up his time-honored weapons of droughts and floods?"

Henhenet looked aghast. "Don't mention such things!" he cried.

Nefertiry went on. "I wonder if he ran out of locusts."

"Please, divine lady! Don't tempt Amen!" Akeset exclaimed, horrified.

Nefertiry seemed to be too immersed in her thoughts to hear Akeset and she added, "Can he not find a spare pestilence to send?"

"That's enough," Ramessa whispered tolerantly. He looked at Akeset and Henhenet. "Do you really believe Amen-Ra would curse all Tamera merely because of a discussion?" he asked.

"Majesty, I believe the divine beings should not be spoken of lightly," Akeset replied sternly. "If Amen-Ra finds one temple's location so unfavorable that he sent Sekhmet to kill Arek, I think we must consider the gravity of the situation."

Ramessa regarded Akeset silently for a long moment. Did the priest actually believe all that, he wondered. He studied Akeset's expression, which seemed to be one of genuine concern. "Do you truly believe Sekhmet used a dagger to kill Arek?"

"Petet has never been mistaken," Akeset replied. "No dagger was found in Arek's body or near it. I believe Sekhmet's cold finger was the instrument of death."

Again Ramessa considered Akeset's motives and he began to wonder if Akeset were more the fool than he'd thought. He knew Akeset was greedy—and persistent. It appeared Akeset would never stop harassing him until he gave the temple something. Finally he said, "The workers in stone are employed in the construction of the temple in the south. Considering some other problems which I must deal with shortly, I cannot pay additional workers."

"Majesty?" Henhenet asked. At Ramessa's nod, he suggested, "If the temple of Amen-Ra was given a piece of land producing something of value, the priesthood could earn the cost of repairing their temple."

Nefertiry lifted an eyebrow. "What land?"

"What of a small quarry?" Henhenet asked. "Then they could even use their own stones for the repairs."

"There are no small quarries," Ramessa replied. "The only quarry close enough to interest the priests is one from which the stones for the construction of the temple in the south are being taken."

"Would my lord like to pay the priests for the stones needed in his own temple?" Nefertiry asked softly.

"No," Ramessa answered aloud.

"Perhaps the flax field to the north," Henhenet suggested.

"What do the priests know of growing flax?" Ramessa inquired with unconcealed disdain.

"Perhaps your majesty, in your generosity, would provide workers to tend the field," Henhenet persisted.

Nefertiry could no longer contain her irritation. "And workers to harvest the flax and workers to spin the flax, workers to weave the linen, workers to dye, workers to cut and make garments—until all of Wast is clothed by the priests—until our own garments come from Akeset!" She turned eyes of green ice on Ramessa and said tartly, "You may remember, my lord, that Henhenet also advised you to help Paser while Paser's storehouses were filled with valuables he kept secret from you."

Henhenet cast Nefertiry a black look, but said nothing. Akeset lowered his gaze to his sandals and wondered how Ramessa would decide this matter, which appeared to have become a contest between the queen and the prime minister.

Ramessa was silent as he considered his decision. He understood Nefertiry's reasoning, but her words also reminded him that he had been fooled by Paser. Humiliation stung him. "I'll give Amen-Ra's temple the flax field, and the workers who now tend the field for me will tend it for the temple," he said coldly. He paused for a moment to look pointedly at Nefertiry. "However, the agreement will clearly state that the priesthood will sell the raw flax and others will spin and weave it."

Henhenet gave Nefertiry another angry look before turning away to face the court and announce Ramessa's decision.

"His majesty's soul shines like Ra with wisdom," Akeset said fervently. He bowed from the waist and began to back away. Raising his arms as if in supplication to his god, he loudly cried, "His majesty is radiant with Amen-Ra's blessings, for his heart is generous to the temple of his god!" Noting that Ramessa's hand discreetly waved dismissal, Akeset lowered his arms and resumed backing away from the dais. But he observed that the king, pleased with the flowery praise, looked more warmly upon him.

When Akeset had rejoined the crowd, the priest looked speculatively at Nefertiry. Under the haughty mask she wore, Akeset thought he saw a hint of annoyance. He wondered if Nefertiry's star was beginning to fade, and if her slide from power had finally begun.

Seshena hurried through the street, her dark blue robe clinging to her legs at each step, impeding her progress. As she neared the shop where she usually purchased her fruits, she saw the proprietor step from his doorway. She knew from the expression on his face that he expected her to stop and chat. When she merely nodded but didn't pause, he looked disappointed. But she was in too much of a hurry to get to the dock to worry.

Why had she dawdled over bathing and dressing when she was so anxious to see Rasuah? she wondered. On many a lonely night she had imagined how she'd run into his open arms, but now she realized she didn't know if he'd want her to behave so in public or if he'd prefer her to greet him with more restraint. Suddenly, she felt shy.

When Seshena rounded the last corner, she came to a sharp stop. There was the great ship drawing next to the quay, its billowing white and gold sails being slowly furled, while sailors threw lines to the workers on the dock. Seshena's heart sank in dismay at the throngs of people who had gathered on the landing.

But, studying the faces of those lining the ship's rail, Seshena felt the old excitement rising in her. She was newly surprised at how elated she became, merely to anticipate meeting Rasuah—even before she saw him. She reflected on this for a moment, until she realized each corridor of life she turned with him was a new and surprising experience, because the whole experience of love was new and surprising—and delightful—to her. Would it always be a delight? she wondered, still scanning the faces on the deck. Perhaps it wasn't possible in daily mortal life. Yet she would gladly risk whatever undelightful events were in store for her.

Then, Seshena saw Rasuah's dark head lifted above the others. When he turned onto the causeway, her heart fluttered in her breast as if a bird was behind her ribs preparing to fly. She watched the smooth movement of his walk, and the bird fluttered more violently as his searching eyes found her. When his arms opened in welcome to her, the bird was set free, and she flew into his embrace.

Rasuah stood silently holding Seshena for a long mo-

moment, not wanting to release her, absorbing the scent of her, the feel of her body pressed to him, the silk of her hair against his cheek. Finally he whispered, "Long have I dreamed of this moment."

"I dreamed of it so much that when Ra lifted his face over the eastern horizon I couldn't believe this day had finally come," Seshena murmured, "But when I arrived here to actually see the ship you were on, I found myself unsure of how to greet you under the eyes of all these others."

Rasuah drew away to look down at her, a smile in his eyes. "You were shy?" he asked softly. When she nodded and looked down in embarrassment, his smile reached his lips. "I find your inexperience a constant delight," he commented. "What we are to each other is a thing of pride, and I would announce it to the entire royal court assembled in the throne room, if you need assurance of my feelings."

"That's unnecessary," she replied. "Your arms around me are enough."

As Rasuah lifted his eyes to gaze beyond Seshena's shoulder, he said, "Djanah's watching us, and I can see from her smug expression I need announce our intentions to no one. What we are to each other has been confirmed in her mind and this news will travel from Noph to Abtu before night falls."

"But she has been witness to the many nights I've spent at your house," Seshena declared.

"She witnessed your comings and goings, all right, but she was never certain of our plans. How we behave at this moment after so long a separation reveals we have longed for each other and supplies the last proof that our affection is no passing thing."

"She has seen her hopes fall many times in the past?" Seshena asked.

Rasuah considered an answer to that question, but decided it would be best not to discuss the past. He said, "Djanah will shortly begin to plan our wedding, as would I, if a wedding were possible to us now."

Seshena frowned. "It will probably seem even farther in the future than you'd thought after you hear what's been happening in the palace."

"I received a message about Arek's death," he replied slowly.

"What happened to Arek marks the beginning of the real struggle and merely brings the matter closer to its crisis and thus its resolution."

"More blood will flow?" Rasuah whispered and felt Seshena's answering nod. He was silent for a long moment before suddenly saying, "Let us discuss something more pleasant. Where's your litter?"

Seshena answered, "I walked, so my servants wouldn't watch us." She glanced meaningfully at the crowd and added, "That was foolish."

Rasuah laughed softly and turned to Zehzee. "I'll accompany Lady Seshena to her house, before I go to the king to make my report," he advised. "I'll return to Lady Seshena's house afterwards and remain there throughout the day. Later, you can bring what I'll require for the night."

"Yes, lord," Zehzee promptly replied. "I'll deliver what you wish after the noon resting time," he promised. Noticing Rasuah's arm slide around Seshena's waist, Zehzee lifted an eyebrow and asked, "Will that be convenient?"

"If not, you know what to do," Rasuah replied. "And lower that eyebrow." Then, he led Seshena away.

"The Lady Shala is quite beautiful," Nehri remarked as he helped Ramessa remove his court robe.

"Yes," Ramessa replied, remembering Nefertiry's cool silence when Shala had knelt before them. He wondered how difficult Nefertiry would be if he accepted this new wife and was irritated that he should even worry about it. He was the king, he reminded himself.

"It could be most pleasant to have a wife who understands so little of your language and speaks less," Nehri commented.

Ramessa smiled to think of Shala's necessary silence. At least Shala wouldn't argue with him as Nefertiry did. He remembered Shala's eyes, dark as the night, looking up at him, her full lips curved in a knowing smile. Shala would be the first new wife he'd accepted since his marriage to Nefertiry. Irritation at Nefertiry, and at his own hesitance because of her, was beginning to annoy him like an ill-fitting sandal.

"Sire, Lord Rasuah has arrived to make his report," Nehri said.

Startled from his thoughts, Ramessa glanced up at the doorway, where another servant stood with Nehri. Ramessa sighed. He hadn't even heard the servant's tapping. "Bring him to me here," he said shortly. The servant in the hall left, and Ramessa snapped, "Nehri, get me out of these things so I can relax with Rasuah."

Nehri had barely finished peeling off Ramessa's court beard when a tap on the door announced Rasuah's arrival. At Ramessa's impatient expression, Nehri hastily stuffed the beard into his sash and went to the door to admit Rasuah.

Ramessa extended his hands in greeting, and Rasuah walked swiftly into the room to grasp them.

"Welcome back."

"Thank you," Rasuah replied, wondering at the shadows in Ramessa's eyes. "If you have something else to do, I can return later."

"Your tone of voice tells me you have something to report that I should hear now," Ramessa said. He released Rasuah's hands and turned to recline on a couch. "Sit down and gather your thoughts while Nehri pours wine for us. Then you can tell me what you did, aside from collect tax."

Sitting in a nearby chair, Rasuah turned troubled eyes on his king. "You're right, Ramessa. There is something we should discuss as soon as possible." He accepted a goblet from the servant, then commented, "You seemed to have something on your mind, though; I dislike adding to your unhappiness if you wish to wait for my report."

"It's a small thing—a domestic problem—a difficulty that I think will be with me forever." Ramessa waved a hand as if to dismiss the subject, took a sip of wine and urged, "What do you have to tell me?"

"Pekharu gave me some information that could cause Tamera future problems. It seems the island kingdoms to the north are making an alliance for war."

"I already know about Keftiu, Shekel and Isy." Ramessa sounded as if he were already weary of the subject.

Rasuah's eyes widened in surprise. He was quiet a moment before asking, "Do you also know Shardana has joined the alliance?" Ramessa's lips set in a line and he nodded. Rasuah leaned forward tensely. "Just before I left Pekharu, I learned that Teresh, Ekwesh and parts of Achaiwasha have added their strength to this gathering force." When Ramessa looked unsurprised, Rasuah said, "Surely you don't know this next news. Pekharu's spies just discovered that ships from all these lands have already set sail and it appears that Kinanu is being threatened first."

"While you were at sea, I received a plea for help from Kinanu. The ships were in sight of their harbor and invasion seemed imminent. They've probably already fallen. Kinanu is a land of merchants, not soldiers."

Rasuah stared at Ramessa. "You refused to help them?"

Ramessa nodded. "Kinanu isn't the only place the island peoples will attack," he said. "If I send my army to help Kinanu, I'll have to send it to whichever land is invaded next, then the land threatened after that, and so and so and so." He took a sip of wine. "I won't decimate my own army for these other kingdoms. Tamera can trade with Kinanu no matter who occupies its throne."

Rasuah leaned back against the couch, staring at his wine, to think about the king's argument.

"You don't approve of my decision?" Ramessa asked.

"It isn't for me to approve or disapprove your decisions," Rasuah replied. "I understand your reasoning."

"But you don't agree with it, do you?" Ramessa asked.

When Rasuah didn't answer, Ramessa concluded, "You don't agree." He was silent for a moment, considering. Then he said in a bored tone, "If I send my army to protect other lands now, those kings will expect me to always settle their disputes for them. I don't wish to waste Tamera's soldiers on such disputes. I don't want to replace Tamera's men with foreign mercenaries. Such a thing is dangerous. I already have enough foreign mercenaries in my army."

"I had thought defeating the invaders at Kinanu might stop them completely," Rasuah said slowly.

"No doubt I would defeat them at Kinanu. But unless I pursued them all the way back to their separate islands and attacked their lands one by one to decimate their armies, they would only return to cause trouble in another place."

"They'll cause trouble in another place for a certainty if they aren't stopped by someone," Rasuah said drily.

Ramessa nodded.

"One day, encouraged by their victories, they'll look to our shore," Rasuah said.

"I expect them to do that," Ramessa agreed. "When they attack us, we'll drive them back into the sea."

"But by that time, the invaders will have grown in strength," Rasuah pointed out.

"Tamerans always fight better when they defend their own land."

Rasuah nodded, but said nothing for a moment. He still thought it preferable to meet the invaders before they grew stronger. Finally he said, "Pekharu thinks King Hattusil is encouraging the island kingdoms. His spies have recognized Hattusil's military officers disguised as merchants in the capitol cities of each of those lands."

Ramessa's eyebrows lifted. "That's interesting," he commented, and was silent for a time as if lost in thought.

Rasuah began to hope that Ramessa might reconsider; but when Ramessa lifted his eyes, all hint of solemnity had left them.

"Will your priestess accompany you to the banquet?" Ramessa asked.

Rasuah nodded in answer, knowing the door to further discussion of the island peoples had been tactfully and officially closed.

During the night, Rasuah awakened from disturbing dreams, which he immediately knew had been inspired by his visit with Ramessa. Recalling Ramessa's uncern when they'd discussed the impending wars, Rasuah was troubled anew. He turned restlessly many times before he chose to lie on his side and gaze at the moonlight pouring through the window, in the hope it would soothe him. But his mind remained on the alliance made between the island kingdoms in the north.

Although Rasuah could understand why Ramessa refused to do anything to stop the island people's aggressiveness immediately, he disagreed. He was convinced that the invaders were at their weakest and most disorganized now. Time would teach them new strategies and victories would give them encouragment and possibly more allies; by the time they turned toward Tamera they would be formidable.

Rasuah was torn between loyalty to his king and apprehension about Ramessa's judgment as a man. They had been friends for many years, and Rasuah knew Ramessa's personal shortcomings well enough. Ramessa sometimes brushed aside unpleasant matters simply because he had other things on his mind, and those other things were not necessarily more important to the kingdom's well-being. Rasuah felt sure that Ramessa's attention was being distracted by something else, and he was pretty sure that something else was Nefertiry and the harem. Rasuah wondered to what degree Ramessa's decision to wait for the island kingdom's army to invade Tamera had been inspired by his desire to remain comfortably in the palace with his harem.

Ashamed of such speculations, Rasuah tried to turn his

mind to something else; but his thoughts went 'round and 'round until he was so frustrated and impatient with himself, he realized sleep was impossible.

Rasuah got out of bed and walked to the window to stare accusingly at the night sky, as if the heavenly forces had caused the predicaments of men. But the ancient stars seemed unaware of the events on earth and the moon was serenely unconcerned. The north wind alone whispered of mankind's foolishness, and the moving black silhouettes of the trees bent in laughter, as if mocking his need to understand. Gaining no comfort from the night, Rasuah turned to gaze at Seshena's sleeping form.

The moonlight made a pale oval of her face, and he could see her clearly. The long eyelashes spread like small black fans resting lightly on her cheeks, the full lips faintly curved in a smile at a pleasant dream. His eyes traveled the length of her body, and he inhaled the perfume that rose from her like an invisable aura. Yes, he reflected, the mere sight and scent of her soothed him.

Rasuah leaned over the bed to gaze at Seshena, remembering how they had loved only a few hours before. Her eyes, then, had been wide open and glowing darkly into his. He could feel again how those soft lips had kissed him a hundred times, how her body had responded so eagerly to his love. Her hair had been like an onyx waterfall flowing over him and washing away all thoughts of the kingdom and its troubles. He reached out to gently touch a black strand and her eyes opened.

"Beloved, why are you awake?" Seshena whispered in concern. "Is something troubling you?"

Rasuah's fingers slipped from her hair to rest lightly on her shoulder. "I was too long in Nehren," he murmured. "I need to refill my eyes with the sight of you."

Seshena considered his answer and, realizing after a moment what truly troubled him, decided to distract him. She smiled and whispered, "While you were in Nehren, many times your thoughts of me were a silent command on the wind that called me to your side. When you looked
288

upon Ra's setting behind those purple mountains, I saw his golden reflection in your eyes, for I was with you."

Rasuah's finger traced small, invisible circles on her shoulder. "I know your spirit came often to me, for I felt your presence, but I wished your mortal body had accompanied it."

Seshena reached up to touch his face. "My mortal body is here now," she whispered. "Fill your eyes with the sight of it and, if you will, your senses with my love of you."

Rasuah gazed into her eyes for a long moment. Finally he stood up and looked down at her. "Will ever there come a time when you will not invite me?"

"Never," she answered. "To say no would be to will an end to my breath and my heart's beating."

Rasuah marveled at how easily she made him forget his anger. Finally he murmured, "I think you aren't high priestess of Aset's temple. I think you're Aset."

Seshena understood and whispered, "And you, beloved? Who would Aset love but Asar?" She reached up to place her hands one on each side of his face. "Does this Asar choose to merely look at Aset?"

Rasuah leaned closer to put his mouth to hers, caressing her lips gently for a moment, but the sweet fire ignited again as if the previous evening had never happened; and he moved back to look at her with glowing eyes. "Let us go slower," he whispered.

"It's difficult to do when you touch me and my blood turns to a river of fire," she murmured.

"We will see," he replied and slid his arm under her shoulders to cradle her. His kiss dwindled to a touch that was delicately tantalizing, his lips barely brushing hers as he explored the shape and texture of her mouth, making her want more, so that she lifted her head to reach for him. He withdrew slightly. She lifted her head again, and again he moved away. Finally, her hands cupped the back of his head to pull him closer.

"I had it in mind to linger," Rasuah murmured against

her mouth. "Such kissing as you plan will too soon arouse our fire."

"I planned to kiss your face most tenderly and with more affection than passion," she said slyly.

Rasuah's tilted eyes narrowed with suspicion, but he said nothing while she touched her lips to his eyelids, to his forehead, sliding to lightly brush his cheekbones, leaving little spots of fire where she'd kissed him. And as her lips moved to his ear, he withdrew.

"You're a crafty priestess," he remarked, moving away. He got up to kneel on the bed at her side. "I said I'm in no hurry."

"I'll try my uttermost to be less affected by you," she replied solemnly.

Rasuah gazed down at her a moment. Finally he said, "I'm not sure I like that idea."

Seshena ran her fingers up his forearms and began to lightly stroke his skin. His bare arm under her hand was firm with the strength of the finely tuned muscles beneath. She looked up at him and whispered, "My suggestion was born of a plot to win your confidence so I could trap you, but I cannot do it. I immediately reveal my true feelings."

"It wouldn't have worked for another reason," he whispered. "I'm already too confident of your response."

"Then, let us love as we will," she suggested. "We have the remainder of the night and all of tomorrow to quench our fires."

"Eternity has not enough time to do that," Rasuah whispered.

His mouth took hers again, caressing, nibbling, renewing its discovery of her, until the urgency in him commanded more. Then, his lips left hers to circle the outline of her face, moving lightly as the fluttering of a butterfly's wings. When they left her chin and traveled down her throat to the hollow by her shoulder, she trembled. His lips continued on the same descending path until her trembling became more violent and her hands on his sides

290

were like fire. Finally, he raised himself until his face was on a level with hers. The smile on his mouth was a foil for the gold lightning in his eyes.

"You see?" he said softly. "You can control yourself."

"But I'm not!" she replied in a shaking voice. "It's you who restrain yourself while I'm trembling like a leaf in a high wind."

"What would you do?" he asked quietly. He moved away to kneel beside her and look silently into her eyes.

She reached her arms up toward him in mute invitation, but he didn't move. "Would you have me beg?" she asked.

"No," he replied, still unmoving. "I would have you act."

She stared at him, surprised for a moment. Slowly she sat up. "What would you have me do?" she whispered.

Rasuah regarded her silently a moment longer, before lowering himself to the bed to lay on his back at her side. He said nothing, but turned his face toward her to gaze up at her. Finally he murmured, "You're a priestess. Enter my mind and explore its contents."

Seshena stared at him a moment before she whispered, "I think I need not do that."

"Enter my mind anyway and see if there's something you've missed," he invited, still looking steadily up at her.

Seshena closed her eyes and did as he asked and she was shaken by her discovery. How, she marveled, could he lie so quietly and speak so calmly when he contained so great a hunger it seared her mind to touch it? When she opened her eyes, they were filled with awe of him. "I feel like a moth that has flown into a lamp."

"Moth singe their wings, but they yet return to the flame," he murmured. "I won't burn your wings, beloved."

Needing a moment to compose herself, she turned to rest her cheek on his shoulder. His scent was that of the oils of his bath, clean and slightly sweet, warmed by the fire of his body. She marveled again at the depth of passion his body held. She felt his shoulder curve as he

291

turned his head to press the side of his face to hers, the soft texture of his hair against her cheek. She felt his fingers trace a narrow path along her side and she shivered like the river when its surface was blown by the wind. Then his fingers withdrew.

"I think enough time has passed for you to consider your decision," he said softly. "What will you do, beloved?"

"I tremble merely to see the look on your face," she murmured.

"But isn't it a pleasant trembling?" he whispered. He was silent a moment, continuing to look steadily at her in the same way. "I cannot change my expression, for I now burn for you beyond my controlling it."

"You will restrain yourself a little longer," she whispered leaning toward him.

"I'll try," he murmured as his lips received hers.

Rasuah did try to restrain himself while Seshena kissed and caressed and stroked his body until the sensations pouring through him became almost more than he could endure. The desire in him was becoming a frenzied demand for release and he began to fear he would soon lose all control and throw her down to take her like a lion took his mate.

But Seshena, who had again entered Rasuah's mind and blended her thoughts with his, knew what he felt as easily as she knew her own response; and she surrendered to him even as he wished, their bodies merging into one sweet explosion that consumed their fires with its impact.

Much later, when their hearts had slowed their pounding and their panting had dwindled to regular breaths, Rasuah loosened his arms around Seshena and smiled up at her.

"The whole world thinks it's wonderful to be king, but the world is sadly misled," he murmured. "Even if such a thing were possible, I wouldn't exchange my place with Ramessa. I would have to step down from you to do it."

292

Seshena, who had sat up to pull the linens over their moist bodies, turned to look thoughtfully at Rasuah. "Ramessa's blood gave him his crown, but the One Alone has given you yours," she said.

"My crown is the love you give me," Rasuah murmured.

Seshena shook her head. "Our love is the double crown handed us by the Maker," she said softly. "It's a higher award than all earthly titles, for it was created in eternity."

Rasuah opened his arms to her and folded her within their circle. After a moment he said slowly, "I was right before. You are Aset, not merely her priestess."

Seshena looked solemnly into his eyes to whisper, "And you are Asar, Lord of Eternity, wearing flesh as a disguise so you may mingle with mortals when you choose." She smiled faintly and added, "Your disguise isn't perfect, however, for Ra shines from your eyes."

Rasuah gazed at Seshena for a moment, unable to answer the beauty of her words. But as he studied her expression, he was even more surprised to realize this was no mere compliment. She was serious. "You really think that?" he asked.

"I know it. Remember? I entered your mind and explored its contents."

17

"Setnau soon will be walking," Khakamir observed, watching the boy, who stood between Nefertiry's knees.

"Why do you never touch your son?" Nefertiry asked, raising her gaze from Setnau to Khakamir.

Khakamir's eyes scanned the shrubs around them. "For the same reason I speak so softly of him," he said. "I'm never sure when someone may be nearby."

"Do you want to touch him?" Nefertiry asked quietly.

"Countless are the times I stopped my hands from reaching out to him," Khakamir whispered.

"No one can see us from the palace," she said. "Why do you think I always sit with you in this part of the garden? And if they did, what would they assume? That you find the child charming and that I trust you enough to let you touch him? Why should I not so trust you when Ramessa once appointed you to guard our lives?" she reasoned.

Khakamir hesitated, torn between his desire to hold his son at last and his fear that, if he touched the boy, it would be that much more painful to let him go. Setnau looked up at Khakamir. His green eyes crinkled with laughter, his bud of a mouth pursed as if in teasing, and Khakamir surrendered. He came forward to stoop before his son and very carefully touched the child's soft black hair. Setnau relinquished his grip on Nefertiry's thumb and his tiny hand reached out to his father. Khakamir touched the hand, which grasped his finger with surprising strength. He looked at Nefertiry, who smiled.

"He knows you instinctively," she said softly. "He doesn't go so easily to Ramessa, who is gentle and loving with him and pays him more attention than he gives the other children." She noted the aching in Khakamir's dark eyes and suggested, "Take his other hand also. Better still, lift him in your arms." When Khakamir's eyes dropped to rest longingly on Setnau, she added, "He wants you to, Khakamir."

Khakamir stared at Setnau. One small hand grasping his finger, the other small hand his mother's, as if he was caught between two worlds, this tiny innocent creature, this child of a happier hour. Khakamir wondered when he would again have an opportunity to hold his son. Abruptly, he reached out to take Setnau in his hands and lift him to rest against his heart. He gazed at the green eyes upraised to his face and marveled at the tenderness that flooded him. He stood up slowly, still looking wonderingly at the child's face.

"I wish Setnau went as easily to Ramessa," Nefertiry commented. "It's beginning to look as if Ramessa's interest in me has faded since he saw Shala. Perhaps if he were to love Setnau enough, he would choose him for the throne despite his indifference to me."

"Ramessa isn't indifferent to you," Khakamir whispered, wishing he were.

"He told Henhenet to prepare the marriage ceremony," she said quickly.

"That means nothing," Khakamir replied. "Many marriage ceremonies have taken place."

"He has decided to rename her Raneferu," Nefertiry said bitterly. "Perhaps he wishes not to be reminded of a similar name—Sharula."

"He finds foreign names difficult to pronounce," Khakamir mumbled, still staring into Setnau's face. "Do you really think Setnau looks like King Seti?" he asked.

Nefertiry looked up at Khakamir. "Ramessa thinks Setnau's eyes are his father's, but I think their shape is yours," she said quickly. She was silent a moment, then said softly, "I wish I could somehow get rid of Henhenet."

Khakamir took his eyes from Setnau's face and stared at her. "Why?" he asked, shocked. "You wish him dead?"

Nefertiry shook her head. "I wish he could be banished," she said quickly. "He hates me and it would be wise to rid myself of as much opposition as possible. Henhenet influences Ramessa lately even more than I do, it seems."

Khakamir shifted Setnau in his arms, merely to feel the weight of the child, and wanting to absorb another sensation associated with his son. "You fear Shala's marrying Ramessa because you haven't witnessed how he behaved with all the other women he's married. It's always the same," he sighed. "He pays great attention to the attractive ones for a short time, because they're a novelty. Then he sets them aside when their newness wears off or when some undesirable trait of theirs irritates him."

"Tuiah has hinted otherwise," Nefertiry said angrily.

"I don't know what Tuiah has against you, but she lies to spite you," Khakamir advised. "She knows well enough he has behaved toward no other wife as he has toward you. She knows also that Ramessa has never looked at any of them as he does each time his eyes fall on you."

"Do you really think so?" Nefertiry asked anxiously. "How does he look at me that's different?"

Khakamir brushed his cheek against Setnau's soft

297

hair with infinite gentleness, but when he looked at Nefertiry, his eyes were lit with anger. "How can you ask me such things?" he said quietly. "Have you no mercy that you ask me to describe the look of desire for you in another man's eyes? It's too much!" he declared. He held Setnau closer to his chest, almost as if shielding him from an enemy. "I must share the woman I love with another man. I must keep silent when I wish to shout to the world that this son is mine. I even must murder for you. But this is too much. I cannot calmly discuss Ramessa's desire for your body. What do you think I am?" he demanded.

Nefertiry's eyes widened at the fury on Khakamir's face. Quickly she said, "I'm sorry, Khakamir. You're right. It's just that I'm so close to you, I sometimes regard you more as a friend than my lover."

"You can forget so easily the stolen moments we've shared?" Khakamir exclaimed. "They mean that little to you?"

"I couldn't forget the love we've had and still look forward to so eagerly," Nefertiry whispered.

Khakamir continued to stare past Nefertiry. "I begin to wonder if I alone am eager for those moments. I begin to wonder if I'm only part of a game you play."

Nefertiry leaped to her feet. "Never!" she exclaimed. She came closer and whispered. "It's no game to me. Can't you tell that when we love? You know I'm not one of those women who can deceive the man in whose arms she lies. You know that, don't you?"

Affected by the anger he sensed in the air, Setnau began to whimper. Khakamir held the child more gently and began to soothe him. When Setnau's whimpers had ceased, Khakamir lifted his eyes to regard Nefertiry. Finally he nodded. "I do know that," he said. "Yet this confirms that you also look eagerly to Ramessa's attention."

Nefertiry had no answer. She knew Khakamir was watching her, waiting for her reply. But she couldn't deny Ramessa gave her pleasure. Finally, she whispered, "I said before, all this between us began that you would have to resign yourself to sharing me with him."

"I don't have to enjoy it," Khakamir snapped.

"Neither do I enjoy the deception," she murmured. "No more than I enjoy competing with a hundred other wives or having Setnau compete with other royal sons."

Khakamir looked down at Setnau, whose wide green eyes gazed innocently up at him. Again a great tenderness flooded him and his throat was stopped. Why should his son compete with other children for love from a man who wasn't even his father? Suddenly, he couldn't bear the idea. He took a breath and said brokenly, "Setnau doesn't have to risk an inferior status. He would never have a lesser place than first son if he grew up in my house."

"What do you mean?" Nefertiry asked softly.

Khakamir swallowed before speaking. "Do you love this child?" he asked quietly.

"Of course I love him!" she declared. "He's of my own body."

"He's of my body also," Khakamir reminded her. "I've loved this child all those months when I've restrained myself from even touching him. I didn't touch him because you had convinced me his inheritance was assured and I thought the throne the highest place a man could wish for his son. I loved him enough to silently hand him to another man so my son could have a brighter future than any in the land."

"What are you leading to?" Nefertiry asked slowly.

"It appears—and you said it yourself—that Setnau's chances of inheriting the throne are diminishing," Khakamir replied. "And even if he did win the throne, I think I don't want it for my son. The throne is a seat of pain, however elevated and honored."

"What do you mean?" Nefertiry demanded. "You can't declare Setnau yours. To do so would be to condemn us all!"

Khakamir lifted his eyes to Nefertiry's. "If you loved this child as much as I love you, you would look for his happiness."

"I do love him! I look only for his happiness!" Nefertiry cried.

"Lower your voice and listen to me," Khakamir commanded. "My wealth isn't stamped with Ramessa's insignia. It's my own, inherited from my father. I can do whatever I wish with it, even leave Tamera."

"You want to take Setnau from Tamera? From me?" Nefertiry whispered, stunned by this idea.

"I wish to take Setnau from Tamera, yes. I wish to raise him in my own house even as my son should be raised, though that house would be far from Tamera's valley," Khakamir said softly. "But I wish to take you with me. You're the mother of my son, the woman of my heart. Together we could start a new life, a life containing more happiness than this life can ever promise."

"You would give up your place here?" she asked incredulously. "You would leave your homeland forever and hide like a criminal? You would dishonor your family name in Tamera for all time?"

"What place have I here? I'm commander of the army —a glorified soldier at Ramessa's knee," Khakamir said bitterly. "I hide my heart like a criminal hides his crime! My wealth is enough for us to live like a noble family elsewhere. My name in Tamera would be in disgrace, that's true," he whispered. "But think of it, Nefertiry, does it matter if my name is honored on earth when it already has been dishonored in the records of eternity?"

Nefertiry stared at him. "What do you mean?" she snapped. "Your name isn't dishonored in eternity. I told you, my marriage contract doesn't forbid me a lover."

Khakamir's eyes narrowed. "My offense has been to betray a friend who trusts me. But it is in my mind an even greater offense to deny my own child, to sacrifice
300

his happiness to my conceit of having him possibly someday sit on the throne."

Nefertiry's eyes widened. "You speak as if Setnau doesn't deserve the crown, as if he's a thief who would steal it from its rightful owner. You forget the royal blood in his veins comes straight from King Seti through me."

Khakamir shook his head. "The royal nursery abounds with royal sons whose divine blood has come to them from Ramessa. Let one of them inherit the misery of the crown," he said. He looked down again at Setnau, who was engrossed with the trim of his uniform. "This child knows nothing of crowns or kingdoms. I beg you, Nefertiry, let us all go to another land where we may be happy together. I have a terrible feeling none of us will ever know happiness unless we escape this royal trap."

Nefertiry reached out for Setnau, but Khakamir held the child close. "Would you keep him from me?" she asked.

Khakamir shook his head sadly. "I give him reluctantly to his mother. A child needs its mother." He sighed. "If you fear I might steal him and leave you, I promise I will not." He held out Setnau. Relieved, Nefertiry took the child quickly. "Think well upon what I've offered you," Khakamir said. "Freedom from all these plots. You would never have to worry about Tuiah or Henhenet or Akeset or competing with other wives. I swear there would be no one else for me. You know that, don't you?"

"I know," Nefertiry whispered.

"Think also upon what I've offered this son of ours, a healthy, and likely a happier, life. I offer him a future without assassins' or ministers' plots to unwind, a future without having to sentence men to death, a life unfettered by any such royal chains. As my son, he would one day choose his wife out of love, not marry a succession of women to seal political alliances and remain without love for any of them." Khakamir put his hand on Nefertiry's arm. "Make your decision with love for Setnau in your heart, remembering that the touch of a father's loving hand holds more joy and security than grasping a golden object called a scepter."

At the sound of approaching voices, Khakamir quickly stepped away. When two gardeners came into sight and set down their tools to work at the shrubbery nearby, Khakamir turned from Nefertiry and walked over to the tree where he'd stood his spear. Taking the weapon in his hand, he said quietly, "Divine lady, the sun is hot today. Perhaps you'd prefer to take the child into the palace?"

Nefertiry looked down at Setnau in her arms. "Yes, I'll return to the palace now."

Khakamir waited for her to approach before he whispered urgently, "Think about what I've said."

Nefertiry nodded as she passed him.

18

Nefertiry stood on her terrace watching the activities in the city below. It was the last night of the old year, the night called the Festival of the Dead, when fires were kindled before the statues in the temple sanctuaries and in the chapels of the royal tombs to light the way for the gods and goddesses and for the returning souls of the dead. Every family placed on their doorstep a new lamp in which burned oil mixed with lotus essence and saturated with salt, so the spirits of their returning ancestors might easily and safely find their way among the streets of Wast. However poor the families were, they managed to obtain the lamps and oil, and lights burned as brightly before mud huts as before rich estates. All of Wast, like the cities of the entire land, was so ablaze with light even the stars seemed to fade.

"Tonight the city is silent, but tomorrow the people will be marching in processions chanting to the temple."

Startled by the voice, Nefertiry turned quickly to face Ramessa.

"Did I startle you?" he asked.

"It has been so long since you've entered my chamber at night that I had forgotten the sound of your step," she said tartly.

Ramessa's expression didn't change as he approached. "The city seems filled with stars," he remarked looking past her. "It's to honor the souls of the dead and the divine beings that the lights burn."

"I remember," she said. "Tomorrow they celebrate Asar's return to his temple, the next day Heru's, the third day Sutekh's, the fourth day Aset's, the fifth Net's. On the next morning Sept, Aset's star, rises with the dawn and the new year begins," she said woodenly. "You explained it to me last year."

Ramessa was silent for a time, watching the people gathering on the avenue leading to the palace. Finally he said, "I wasn't sure you'd remember the rituals of my religion."

"I had Chenmet explain much of it even before I left Khatti," she said bitterly. "Seshena has since told me more. I follow it now as faithfully as you."

"Why do you bother?" he asked quietly.

She glanced at him briefly before turning her eyes to the avenue. "I was told I must become a Tameran. I've done my best to do so," she replied in a cold tone.

"Do you ever miss Khatti?" he asked.

"My mind is too occupied with the activities of being First Royal Wife in Tamera," she said shortly. "Perhaps those activities will be decreased before very long and I'll have time to wonder what might have been if I'd stayed in Khatti."

Ramessa studied her profile thoughtfully for a moment, until the crowd on the avenue before the palace began to cheer, calling blessings for the return of King Seti's soul and wishing King Ramessa, his son, joy and health in this life. Even at that distance, the shouts of "Life, health, strength to King Ramessa!" could be clearly heard.

"They do love me," he whispered almost to himself.

"They're in a festive mood tonight," Nefertiry snapped.

"You obviously are not in a festive mood," Ramessa observed. "Why do you think your activities as First Royal Wife will decrease?"

Nefertiry who continued staring at the scene below, replied, "Since Raneferu entered the palace, I've not spent a night with you. You haven't called me to sit beside you in court." She fell silent, remembering what Khakamir had said. She was suddenly, unexpectedly weary of being queen.

"Tuiah has sat with me in court, not Raneferu," he said quietly. "Raneferu would waste her time sitting in court, she understands so little of our language."

"It would seem you need no language when she enters your chamber each night," Nefertiry said tartly.

"Some things need no words for a time, but it tires me to hear her speak so brokenly and with so heavy an accent. I don't understand half of the little she says."

"Caresses and kisses need no words."

"You and I speak to each other at such times," Ramessa said quietly. "There's why you're angered. I haven't called you to me lately."

Nefertiry turned to glare at him. "What do you think I am? A bow that you can pull once in a while? A horse that you ride every few months?" she flashed. "I'm a woman, Ramessa, with a body that aches."

"I know," Ramessa said. "That's why I've come to you tonight."

"Why not Mimut or Nofret? Have you gone through all of the others and finally decided it's time to bestow the honor on me?" she snapped.

Ramessa stared at her in amazement. But he said calmly, "I cannot speak with the others as I do with you. I crave your mind as well as your body."

Nefertiry turned her eyes again to the city, astounded by his contrite tone of voice. She didn't know what to say, but hope again fluttered in her heart like an awakening bird.

When Nefertiry remained silent, Ramessa explained, "Raneferu was only someone new. The others are distractions from time to time. You're the only one of them all who knows how to keep my interest."

Nefertiry's throat felt dry and she swallowed tightly. Her hopes pounded like drums in her temples and her hands were moist from agitation. She didn't know what more to say to him. She didn't wish just yet to fall into his arms. Her decision was delayed, for Chenmet entered the chamber and called that she'd brought Setnau before putting him to bed. Nefertiry took a breath and turned to walk swiftly into her room, leaving Ramessa on the terrace without a word.

Ramessa looked at Nefertiry's stiff back and understood. She wanted him, but her pride stood like a wall between them. Sensing that her attitude changed as soon as she took Setnau in her arms, he realized how he might mend the situation and followed her.

As Ramessa entered the room, the lamplight glanced off a gold medallion he was wearing and caught Setnau's eyes. The boy reached past Nefertiry toward the brightness and Ramessa smiled and approached them. He put out his arms and Setnau leaned toward him. "Give him to me," Ramessa said. Nefertiry obeyed and Ramessa took the child, who immediately began to play with the glowing medallion. "He recognizes me at last and comes to me," Ramessa said happily.

"He wants your medallion," Nefertiry muttered. Ramessa gave her a look that stopped her from saying more. Then he gazed down at the boy who was engrossed with the medallion.

"I wonder if Setnau is so advanced in his intelligence he knows the value of this," Ramessa quipped.

Nefertiry smiled in spite of herself. "He is trying to devour it."

Ramessa's eyes lit with warmth. "He appears to have a strong jaw even if he's yet without teeth."

Nefertiry took the medallion from the child's mouth and
306

began to untwine his fingers from it. But each time she got two fingers loose and began to work on a third, the first two resumed their grip. "He has strength in his hands also," she muttered.

Ramessa laughed softly. "A prince should have a firm grip so he may later hold heavier objects," he said pointedly. He didn't miss Nefertiry's brief but startled glance at him. He knew what she'd thought, and he decided to encourage that line of thinking for the time being. "A prince should also obey his father," Ramessa said happily. Then he commanded, "Setnau, release that medallion." Surprised by the tone of Ramessa's voice, Setnau dropped the medallion. Ramessa handed him to Nefertiry, commenting, "He obeys his king quickly, which is a good omen. A prince should learn to recognize the tone of authority so he may himself later effectively use it."

"I'm glad Setnau pleases you."

"I'm more than satisfied with this son."

"I rejoice in your praise of him," Nefertiry replied and gave the child to Chenmet to put to bed. She kept her back toward Ramessa, wondering what she should do now. She felt his hands on her shoulders.

"Shall I remain here or will you come to my room?" he asked softly.

He was standing so close she felt his breath in her hair and she shivered, but she said nothing. He moved a little closer and she could feel his body pressed against her back. Her heart seemed to be beating out of rhythm, but still she said nothing.

"Or would you rather I didn't share the night with you?" he asked.

"Choices are your domain, not mine," she murmured.

"I have always said I want you to come to me of your own will, not because I order it," he said quietly. When she did not reply, he turned her around to face him. "What's your decision, Nefertiry? I think I see the answer in your eyes, but your stubborn mouth won't utter the words. Perhaps I can convince that mouth to speak."

Ramessa bent, intending to kiss her softly as he had done on their wedding night, but the door was flung open suddenly, and he straightened to stare angrily at the intruder.

"Forgive me, majesty!" Henhenet exclaimed. "I thought you'd come here merely to see the child."

Ramessa glared at the prime minister and said nothing for a moment. He turned his attention to the soldier who stood behind Henhenet and wore a tense expression. "You're supposed to guard this door!" Ramessa said.

"Forgive me, sire. Henhenet said nothing, but walked right past me," the guard muttered.

Ramessa stepped away from Nefertiry and asked the man coldly, "Would you let an assassin past you as easily, just because he wears a familiar face?" He looked at Henhenet, who was pale with fear. "What was so important that you risked walking into the queen's chamber without permission or even announcement?"

"Majesty, forgive me," Henhenet whispered. Not sure what else he should do, he began to lower himself to his knees.

"Get up and speak, or your relatives in Tuat will see you within the hour," Ramessa warned.

Henhenet straightened hastily. "Majesty, a message just has come. The sea peoples have invaded Zahi."

Ramessa's eyes narrowed in fury. "Why do you come to tell me that? What do I care?"

"I'd thought if the sea peoples had the courage to attack so powerful a land as Zahi, you should know!" Henhenet exclaimed.

"I rejoice that Zahi has someone else to fight besides me for a change," Ramessa said curtly.

"Arvad has already fallen!" Henhenet cried. "Enenes was attacked, but the sea peoples were repelled!"

Only curiosity about Zahi's defense strategy made Ramessa ask, "How was that done?"

"The archers saved Enenes. They have a new captain, Tenes, who has proven exceptional," Henhenet replied.
308

"I'll remember that when we next do battle with Zahi." Ramessa said sarcastically.

"Majesty, there's more to the message," Henhenet whispered.

Ramessa glared at him. "Not much more, I hope, for your well-being."

Henhenet took a step backwards, his words suddenly tumbling from his mouth, "Avaris also was besieged. Peleset watched Avaris fall, then allied itself with the sea peoples, no doubt hoping to save itself."

"Thus demonstrating the loyalty typical of that whole treacherous country," Ramessa replied. When Henhenet still didn't turn to go, Ramessa asked, "There's yet more to this story?" But Henhenet shook his head, and Ramessa suggested in a deadly tone, "Then why don't you remove yourself from my presence?"

"You have no orders?" Henhenet asked incredulously. "There's nothing you wish to do about this news?"

"Shall I send congratulations and encouragement to the commander of the sea people's army for attacking my old enemies?" Ramessa snapped, taking a step toward him. Henhenet turned and fled. Ramessa was amused at the prime minister's lack of dignity; but his smile faded when he turned his attention to the guard who yet stood in the doorway. "You will improve your watchfulness, or you will lose your rank."

"Yes, sire," the soldier murmured.

"Get out," Ramessa directed.

The guard immediately stepped outside and closed the door carefully behind him.

Ramessa turned to Nefertiry, muttering, "Where was I?"

"At the beginning," she said drily.

He looked down at her thoughtfully a moment, then observed, "It would appear your stubbornness has faded."

"You have frightened it away, my lord."

"You don't seem frightened," he commented, then bent to press his lips to hers, caressing her mouth more than

309

kissing it, deliberately exploring its roundness, knowing from experience how that aroused her. Feeling her lips soften, he was sure she'd argue no more.

Nefertiry sat on her terrace under the mimosa tree, watching a white-robed procession, which was filing through the street in the distance, its members chanting and waving palm fronds. Her mind wasn't on the procession; it was on Ramessa and the night they'd spent together. Last night had been like the nights they'd shared after they'd first been married, and she was well-pleased with the results.

"My lady, Nehri is here with a message from the king," Chenmet called from the doorway.

Nefertiry brushed the mimosa's fallen flowers from her robe and stood up. "What is it, Nehri?" she asked, frowning slightly as she waited for her eyes to adjust to the room's shade.

"His majesty requests you to dress in your formal robes and attend court with him today," Nehri announced.

Nefertiry blinked. "He did?"

"I did," Ramessa said from the doorway. He stepped into the room, already dressed for court. "The hour grows near," he added.

Nefertiry turned to give her maid orders, but Chenmet already held the appropriate garments in her hands. Nefertiry took them from her and said, "I'll put these on myself. Get my eyepaint."

Chenmet turned and rushed out of the room.

Ramessa put down his scepters and approached Nefertiry. "I'll help fasten your robes," he offered. Nefertiry stared at him in amazement, but began to unfasten the gown she wore. Ramessa glanced at Nehri. "You may leave," he directed. Nehri obeyed swiftly.

"I would have already been dressed, had I known your plans," Nefertiry said, struggling out of her gown. "Tuiah isn't available?" Nefertiry asked as Ramessa helped fasten her court robe.

"I didn't ask her," Ramessa replied.

Nefertiry was surprised, but said nothing as she turned to Chenmet to have her eyelids painted. "My hair needs arranging," she observed. "Chenmet, what can you do with it in so little time?"

Before Chenmet could answer, Ramessa said, "Your hair won't show under the double crown."

Chenmet dropped the brush she was using and hurriedly bent to retrieve it.

Nefertiry turned slowly to look at Ramessa with wide eyes. "The double crown?" she whispered. "I've never worn the double crown."

"Today you will wear it," Ramessa said casually, knowing how pleased she was at this unheard-of honor. "It's a time of celebration."

"Yes, a celebration," she whispered. She turned again to Chenmet too stunned to utter another word.

Tuiah heard Ramessa's guards coming down the corridor and, expecting to join her son, she nodded to her servant to open the door. But when the door swung open, Tuiah saw that Ramessa already had Nefertiry at his side. Tuiah's mouth dropped open in amazement, for on Nefertiry's head gleamed the double crown.

Tuiah stood silently as they passed, then recovering herself, ordered the servant to shut the door. Once the door was closed, she tore off her own little coronet and threw it on the floor with such force it bounced.

"Pick it up or let it lie. I care not which," Tuiah snapped to the terrified maid, as she ripped off her court robes and let them drop to the floor, then deliberately stepped on them.

"He dares to put the double crown on her head, when my own head has never known its weight!" Tuiah cried, and stalked across the room to fling herself into a couch and stare at her coronet with smoldering eyes.

"Silence! Fall on your faces! King Ramessa, son of Ra, comes!"

Nefertiry watched the crowd of people drop to their

knees as wheat fell before the scythe; and her heart pounded. As she walked beside Ramessa, between the guards, her step was firm only because she willed it to be each time she brought a foot forward. Her head was high only because she had imagined her neck an iron rod, for she knew the whole roomful of people stared in astonishment at the crown she wore. Her moist hands gripped the scepters crossed over her breast as if they held the key to her life, and her pulses hammered so loudly in her temples she wondered if everyone in the silent room could hear them. Somehow she managed to step up on the dais, and somehow she managed to seat herself on the throne. No one—not even Ramessa—knew her inner excitement because her mask of aloof calm had again slipped over her face.

Ramessa nodded to Henhenet and the prime minister approached the thrones. "Rise," Ramessa directed. "What is the first business of the day."

Henhenet struggled up from his knees awkwardly, because his eyes were fixed on Nefertiry's crown, as he began, "Merciful Heru—"

"The last time you said that, Paser was finding a way to extract supplies from me," Ramessa said, his lips curled in a sneer. "What lord wants something now?"

"Majesty, Lord Bekhten begs audience with you," Henhenet croaked.

Neither Ramessa nor Nefertiry moved their heads to watch Lord Bekhten approach from the side of the room, and the nobleman was grateful because he felt as if his legs would surrender to his fear and he'd collapse. When he bent his knees to kneel at the foot of the dais, he was sure he'd never get up. But Ramessa commanded him to rise and his knees obeyed although his ears hadn't heard the words, so great was the thunder in them.

"Majesties," the nervous lord said. There was a great intake of breath from the crowd and the nobleman realized his mistake. The king was addressed as "majesty," the queen as "divine lady." Bekhten fell silent, frozen with fear, and the crowd held its breath, waiting to see if the king would correct him. When Ramessa merely urged Bekhten to speak, the throng was aghast. Did the king in this fashion proclaim Nefertiry co-regent? they wondered.

Bekhten took a deep breath, then said clearly, "Glory and praise be unto you, oh sun of the nations. Grant that we may live before you."

"Yes, yes," Ramessa said impatiently. "I grant it. What do you want?"

Bekhten thought he would faint, but he summoned the strength to go on, "I have come to you, my sovereign lord, on behalf of Reshet, my youngest daughter, for an evil disease has laid hold upon her body. I beseech your majesty's help or she'll surely die."

"What disease has she?" Ramessa anxiously asked, fearful that a plague may have visited the land.

"Majesty, I don't know. The physicians of my province have no idea," Bekhten answered. "Numbers of them have marched through my house to examine her and they go away shaking their heads."

Ramessa turned to Nefertiry. "Where is that priestess friend of yours?"

"Seshena's in the palace," Nefertiry whispered. "I have called her to me, but had to ask her to wait while I was in court."

"Commander Khakamir, send for the priestess Seshena, who is in the queen's chambers. Have her brought to us," Ramessa directed. He looked again at Bekhten. "If the physicians know nothing of your daughter's malady, perhaps it isn't a thing of the body, and this priestess can discern its cause."

"Thank you, majesty, thank you," Bekhten said in a shaking voice.

At Ramessa's command to bring Seshena, Rasuah's wandering attention had returned to the court, and he turned to watch Seshena enter.

Seshena stood on the threshold like a shining silver

goddess as the blazing light of the sun flashed on the embroidery of her robe. Rasuah caught his breath, wondering what she would do, because he knew she'd never been to court before. Seshena began walking through the long expanse of the room, moving with that peculiar gliding grace of hers, with head held as high as Nefertiry's had been, her face as serenely calm as the statue of Aset. He felt a strange, inner trembling at her demeanor. The goddess herself could be no more beautiful or would walk with no greater dignity through the throne room. When Seshena approached the royal dais and sank to her knees, Rasuah had the feeling it was not suitable for her to go on her knees to those who occupied the thrones.

"Seshena, high priestess of Aset's temple!" Henhenet announced loudly.

"Yes, we know," Ramessa said curtly. In a friendlier tone he said, "Get up, Seshena. Tell us what you can of this man's daughter, who is ill."

Seshena rose from her knees and turned to Bekhten.

"You're from the island province," Seshena said clearly.

Bekhten was surprised and wondered if the guard had told her on their way to the throne room.

"Come closer," she directed. Bekhten moved like a man whose feet had become paddles. He stared at Seshena's wide, clear eyes and wondered at the strange blue light flickering in their depths. She placed her hand on his forehead.

"My daughter—" Bekhten began.

"Be silent," Seshena said. "I'll learn of your daughter without words."

Bekhten wondered how he could be silent. His breath seemed to fill the room; his heartbeat echoed off its walls.

After a long moment, Seshena removed her hand from Bekhten's forehead and stepped back. She turned to look up at Ramessa. "The aura of his daughter's spirit should be clear, pale gold," she said. "It's murky yellow now. She has an illness of the spirit."

314

Ramessa stared at Seshena. "How do you know what color her aura is?" he asked.

"My eyes travel far," she replied. "If Reshet would be saved, you must send the healing priestess of my temple, Makara, to her."

"That's the priestess who stopped my nausea and gave me comfort when I bore Setnau," Nefertiry whispered.

"You think I should send her?" Ramessa murmured.

"If Seshena thinks Makara can save the girl, Makara will do it."

"Makara will travel to Bekhten's house and do what she can for Reshet," Ramessa announced.

Seshena bowed her head and backed away slowly.

"Wait, Seshena!" Nefertiry called. Seshena paused. Nefertiry had planned to tell Seshena about Khakamir's offer, but since Ramessa's treatment of her last night and this morning had changed, Nefertiry decided against it. "I won't need to see you today, after all," she said. And Seshena, who read every thought as it went through Nefertiry's mind, said nothing, but merely resumed backing away.

Next, the prime minister announced, "Lord Hera has returned from Kenset!"

Lord Hera approached the throne slowly and uncertainly, supported by an attendant, because his leg was in a splint.

"You needn't bow," Ramessa said quickly. "Tell me what has happened that you're in such condition."

Hera tilted his head back so his dark brown hair fell away from his eyes before saying, "I've come to report the results of my journey to Kenset."

"Yes, you did go to Kenset, I remember," Ramessa said.

Hera nodded, and his hair again fell in his eyes. His attendant hastily brushed it back. "My father died while traveling in Kenset. When you awarded me his title, you gave me permission to go to Kenset and bring back

315

his body for proper burial," Hera said. "No sooner had we crossed Kenset's border and entered the area of many treacherous rockpiles than my party was attacked. Most were slaughtered. The rest of us had to flee. None escaped without a wound." Hera looked down at the floor a moment, then lifted angry brown eyes to regard his king. "I cannot return to Kenset with this leg, but I would have my father's body buried in its rightful place!"

Ramessa's eyes narrowed. "A new party will be sent to Kenset for your father's body and they'll be accompanied by a regiment of my soldiers."

"I'm grateful, majesty," Hera replied with feeling.

"What did your attackers look like?" Ramessa asked.

"They weren't the people of Kenset," Hera answered slowly. "They were our own people."

Ramessa leaned forward tensely. "Our own people? You're sure?" he asked. Hera nodded. Ramessa stared at him a moment, then leaned back against the throne. "So Lord Paser's people have become thieves."

"We have no proof of that, sire," Henhenet said nervously.

Ramessa looked at Henhenet. "Who of our people are in Kenset but Lord Paser's workers?" he snapped. "Perhaps your brother-in-law has put himself outside my law," he suggested, his face tight with anger. "Why not? We know he's a thief."

Henhenet said nothing. His face was pale and stiff with fear.

Ramessa looked at Hera. "Thank you for this warning," he said. "As I've promised, soldiers will be sent to recover your father's body."

After Hera hobbled away, Ramessa nodded coldly at Henhenet, and Henhenet came forward to announce, "The priest, Petet, oracle to Amen-Ra's temple, begs audience."

"What does that fool want now?" Ramessa muttered under his breath. Impatient to get off the throne and organize the expedition to Kenset, he looked down at the

316

bowing oracle and snapped, "Get up, get up, get up. Tell me your problem without delay, for I have other things to do this afternoon."

Petet, who had been ordered by Akeset to go to Ramessa with his story, wished Akeset had come instead.

"Majesty, I've been sent by my high priest, Akeset," he began.

"Are Akeset's sandals worn out from coming to me to beg favors, so he's sent you?"

Petet recovered some of his poise and said apologetically, "My high priest thought it more fitting I speak to you and recount the vision I've experienced."

"That old snake saw a vision born of strong beer," Ramessa muttered under his breath to Nefertiry who struggled to control her smile. Ramessa said aloud, "Why should I know about this vision?"

"Amen-Ra came to me during my meditations, traveling from his realm of the heavens in his shining chariot . . . I beg your majesty's mercy, but I must relate exactly what the divine being said, must I not?" he asked.

"That means it's unpleasant," Ramessa surmised. "Yet why should I be optimistic when Akeset never brings me good news? Tell me quickly, Petet, and waste as little time as possible."

Petet wished fiercely that he were somewhere besides the throne room reciting Akeset's words and going through this farce for the high priest. He cleared his throat and said quickly, "Amen-Ra is greatly offended that a foreign woman sits on Tamera's throne." He glanced up nervously at Nefertiry's tense face under the double crown and rushed on, "Amen-Ra threatened disaster on the land if a child of Khatti inherits the throne."

"He has a face like a rabbit, but he spits venom like a serpent!" Nefertiry said in a voice cold with anger.

Ramessa sat up stiffly and looked at Khakamir. "Commander, have Prince Setnau brought to me," he directed.

Khakamir paled and dispatched another guard to the queen's chamber.

Ramessa and Nefertiry sat like statues on the thrones until the soldier returned, with Chenmet, carrying Setnau, on his heels.

Ramessa stood up and put down his scepters. His movements were stiff and quick from anger. Reaching down to take Setnau from Chenmet, he lifted the child high so the court could see him. "Can the divine blood of my fathers be doubted?" Ramessa demanded. "Look well at this prince's face. See my own eyes set into his. His hair is as black and as uncurled as the wings of an ibis. His bones are those of Heru. Who would deny the origin of this royal prince? Who dares call this Khatti's child?"

The room was as silent as if everyone occupying it had stopped breathing. All eyes were fixed on the uplifted child.

Nefertiry's heart had stopped and was trapped in her throat. Ramessa's public defense of Setnau was almost a declaration of his inheritance. She stared at Ramessa's eyes, which had narrowed and were ablaze with green fire. Was Ramessa at last so angry that he would punish Akeset?

An idea entered Nefertiry's mind and grew in size until it seemed to fill her entire being. Akeset must be warned to withdraw his fangs and, at last, he had done something to infuriate Ramessa. If this pesky oracle was to meet misfortune, it might serve as a second warning to Akeset. Ramessa wouldn't mourn Petet's loss, she was sure. But how could it be done? she wondered. Then she remembered a method she had once used on an enemy in Khatti, a potent poison that stopped the heart's beating so the victim appeared cut down by a natural malady. Everyone would be at the banquet the night of the new year, even Petet. Many times during dinner parties she had asked anyone standing nearby to act as her taster, thus discouraging possible poisoners. Whoever might cry poison could never point an accusing finger at her if the poison was in her own goblet.

Ramessa lowered the infant to rest in his arms against

318

his chest. "Return to your high priest," he said sternly to Petet. "Tell Akeset how false your vision was and instruct him that I want to hear no more of your distorted dreams. Amen-Ra wouldn't come to you to deny a son of his own."

Again the crowd gasped, because Ramessa had just called Setnau a son of Ra, and it appeared to the on-lookers that the crown might as well be placed on Setnau's small head now.

Ramessa didn't give the child back to Chenmet. He motioned for her to stand behind him. Then, he reseated himself on the throne, holding Setnau in his lap—as his father had so many years ago held him during audiences.

"There are so many flowers in this room I wonder that my perfume will survive them," Nefertiry remarked, eyeing the baskets of scarlet roses, jasmine sprays and blue cornflowers set at intervals on the banquet table.

Ramessa squeezed her hand. "Your perfume surpasses all these," he said softly, tilting his head to look up at the garlands of blue lotuses and white lilies festooning the ceiling. "I only hope those wires are strong enough to bear the weight of all those flowers all through the evening," he commented. "I wouldn't care to have them fall on our heads."

"Keep watching them," Nefertiry advised.

Ramessa lowered his eyes to look questioningly at her. Then, he followed the line of her vision and smiled. A dozen girls, barely covered with shimmering, almost transparent, dark blue and green veils, had just glided onto the center of the floor. "You're afraid I'll find the dancers too alluring?" he asked.

"Hapu knows how to choose entertainers for their physical attributes," Nefertiry said, appraising the girls' gold-dusted bodies.

"If they dance well, I'll watch them. If they're clumsy, I'll turn my eyes elsewhere," Ramessa promised with a grin.

Nefertiry turned to fix him with a look of mock reproach. "You know well enough they can dance or they'd never get within the palace walls."

"I hope so," Ramessa answered. "I'd hate to embarrass myself and bore my guests with dull entertainment."

"Have no fear of that," Nefertiry said, and reached for a honey-coated fig. A great burst of sound came from the musicians and she lifted her eyes to watch. The timbrels rose above the other instruments and the flutes began a melody that wound through the music like a serpent. Nefertiry's eyes moved to the dancers. They, too, moved like serpents, she decided—serpents with headdresses of peacock feathers. She glanced at Ramessa and, seeing his attention fixed on the dancers, began to look around the room, searching for Petet. He hadn't once come near the royal table and she assumed he was afraid to approach them after what Ramessa had said in court. She sighed, wondering how she could ask him to be her taster when he was so far away.

When the girls ended their dance in a swirl of veils and peacock feathers, Ramessa turned to look at Nefertiry, his eyes filled with green flecks. "They were very good dancers."

"They aroused your interest?" Nefertiry asked, lifting an eyebrow.

"Would you care to later reap the rewards of their efforts?" he inquired.

"I would prefer to make you forget them," she replied.

"You'll have the opportunity," Ramessa said softly. He lifted a hand to the servant standing behind him. When the servant bent closer he said, "Open a new jar of wine, one of those from the queen's favorite supply." The servant backed away and disappeared. Ramessa looked at Nefertiry. "I just sampled some of that wine this morning," he said. "It's especially good." He noticed Nefertiry's eyes were on something across the room. "Who are you looking for?" he asked.

"The priests of Amen-Ra's temple," she murmured.

"I don't care to see them," Ramessa declared in surprise. "Why do you search them out?"

Nefertiry continued to look over the room as she answered, "The priests and priestesses of every temple but Amen-Ra's have presented themselves to you this evening to give you blessings."

"That's true," Ramessa said slowly.

"They insult you by remaining at the opposite end of the room," she observed, "as if they withhold their blessings from you and wish you ill."

Ramessa thought about that and sat up a little straighter. He inclined his head to Henhenet, who leaned closer. "I've observed that Amen-Ra's priests ignore me and I'm not pleased by this."

Henhenet immediately began to make a circuitous path through the room, pausing at intervals to speak to groups of people, sometimes smiling or laughing, being careful to appear as if he were just casually mingling with the guests.

"Neither have I seen Lord Rasuah or Lady Seshena at the banquet," Ramessa said quietly.

"Seshena's servant came to me early in the evening to extend their apologies," Nefertiry explained. "Seshena seems yet too weary from her temple duties during the festival and Rasuah is remaining with her." Nefertiry looked at Ramessa from the corner of her eye.

"I wish them joy," Ramessa replied and shrugged his shoulders. "Rasuah also sent a message that, according to some reliable sources of his in Kenset, Lord Paser is at his wits' end worrying about the peasants he supervises having become criminals. It would seem Paser is innocent of the attack on Lord Hera."

"What will you do?" Nefertiry asked softly, her eyes on Akeset, Befen and Petet, who were making their way across the room. Her head pounded with tension she hid only with a great effort.

"I'll send soldiers, as I promised," Ramessa replied. He lifted his eyes and saw the priests. "So they come at the
321

same time as the servant brings our wine," he murmured.

"Perhaps we should offer some to them to lift the dark clouds I see hanging over them," she said lightly.

The priests bowed solemnly before the royal table, and Ramessa told them to rise, but Akeset straightened slowly. He hadn't been happy to hear that Ramessa had given Nefertiry the double crown to wear in court; he had been further angered by Ramessa having brushed aside the story about Petet's vision; but his full fury was aroused when he learned that Ramessa had all but declared Setnau royal heir. With all these things on his mind, he couldn't hide the flash of hatred in his eyes when he looked at Nefertiry, although he managed a cool smile at his king.

"Amen-Ra is a merciful divinity," Ramessa said, "but I had begun to think he was angered that I denied the vision of your oracle. I couldn't understand why Amen-Ra would feel that way when I had merely defended his child."

Akeset clenched his jaw at Ramessa's repeating the implication that Setnau would inherit the throne. "Amen-Ra, I'm sure, doesn't smile when one of his priests is accused of lying," he replied. "Yet Amen-Ra extends his blessings for the new year because he is, as your majesty said, merciful."

Nefertiry was surprised at the high priest's audacity, but she said nothing. She sensed how Ramessa's body had stiffened and knew he was angry. It would make her way easier, she decided.

"Watch your tongue, Akeset, or you may find it absent," Ramessa murmured. In a louder tone he said, "I'm grateful for Amen-Ra's benediction." He glanced at the servant standing by his side with the urn of wine. "Pour it," he snapped.

Nefertiry studied the look in Petet's eyes. "Have you prayed for Amen-Ra to look with compassion on your own offense, Petet?" she asked slyly.

Petet stared at Nefertiry. "How have I offended Amen-Ra?" he asked.

"By lying," Ramessa answered softly.

Petet leaned over the table. "I didn't lie!" he exclaimed.

Nefertiry shook her head in reproach and commented, "A double lie now."

Ramessa stared at Petet. "Your hands resting on my table affronts me."

Petet stepped back as if the table had burned him. "I cannot help it if you don't like the words of Amen-Ra! I only told you what he told me," he said hoarsely.

"Your lies stick in your throat," Ramessa said in a voice soft with menace.

Nefertiry saw her opportunity and picked up her goblet. "Be my taster for this new wine," she invited. "Perhaps it will soothe your throat."

Petet stared at the goblet she offered.

Ramessa looked at Nefertiry, saying, "I wouldn't want his lips to touch my cup."

"The rim will be wiped," she replied, then urged, "Taste it, Petet. I have a feeling if anyone in this room would wish me death, he isn't far away." She glanced at Akeset.

Knowing he dared not refuse to taste her wine, Petet took the goblet and sipped once.

"Is something wrong with its flavor?" Nefertiry asked quietly, knowing the poison had no taste. "Perhaps it's from a spoiled jar."

Petet took another swallow. "It isn't spoiled," he said quickly. "Its flavor is excellent."

"Good," Nefertiry said, timing the poison's results. "This wine is my favorite and is kept especially for me." She lifted the goblet, but paused before sipping from it to add, "My lord is generous to provide me with this particular wine, which must be imported." Petet appeared to be wavering on his feet. "Is something wrong, Petet?" she inquired. "Perhaps you've already drunk too much wine."

Petet opened his mouth to answer, but no sound came out. His hands grasped his chest for only an instant before he fell like a stone.

Ramessa leaped to his feet and leaned over the table

323

to peer at the fallen priest. Nefertiry stood up slowly, as if unsure what had happened. Akeset dropped to his knees to put his ear to Petet's chest.

"Is he dead?" Ramessa whispered, too surprised to say more.

Akeset lifted his head slowly and looked at his king with thoughtful eyes. "Yes, he's dead," he answered quietly.

"From what?" Ramessa asked.

"The blue tint of his skin would indicate his heart stopped," Akeset replied. He was silent a moment, then added, "I'm not a physician to say for a certainty."

Ramessa turned to Nefertiry, who still held the goblet in her hand. Fear flashed through him. "Put that down!" he exclaimed. "You didn't drink any of it, did you?"

Nefertiry stared at the goblet, as if shocked. She shook her head and quickly placed the goblet on the table.

Khakamir rushed to Ramessa's side, his face pale with fear for Nefertiry. "Shall I take that to the chemist, majesty?" he asked.

"Yes," Ramessa replied sharply, "and take the jar it came from. Arrange for Petet's body to be carried away— quickly." He sank into his chair and was silent for a time. Finally, he said softly, "If Seshena had been here, she might have warned you. It is interesting that she's indisposed tonight, as she was that night the servant spilled your wine before you drank it."

"You don't think! Oh no! Seshena is trustworthy!" Nefertiry said quickly.

"I don't suspect her," Ramessa replied. "I was only wondering if she might have been drugged again today."

Nefertiry's eyes widened. "But how? She said long ago her household servants were absolutely loyal."

"Perhaps it was in something that had been brought to her house," Ramessa murmured. He watched two soldiers pick up Petet's body, then begin to carry it away. He lifted his eyes to look at his guests. No one moved. No one spoke. They were all staring at the soldiers carrying Petet's body.
324

Ramessa got to his feet and snapped his fingers. The sound was like an explosion in the silent room.

Henhenet hurried to Ramessa's side. "Yes, majesty? What shall I do?" he breathed.

"Tell my guests the party is ended," Ramessa said brusquely. He took Nefertiry's arm and turned away to lead her from the stares of the crowd.

"You killed him!" Ramessa whispered.

"Why do you say that?" Nefertiry asked with false calm, glad that she'd sent Chenmet away.

"Seshena had been drugged," he replied, staring at Nefertiry as if still incredulous that she'd done it. "You sent a jar of your favorite wine to Seshena this afternoon, bidding her to enjoy it with Rasuah. She never suspected you'd drug them. They drank it. That was why neither of them came to the party. They were too drowsy and thought it was because of the festival." Ramessa took a deep breath and dropped his eyes to his feet before continuing. "The chemist analyzed the wine in your goblet. He said the poison was very rare, a kind not available in Tamera. Its essence had to be imported from Khatti." He raised his eyes to meet Nefertiry's. "You lied!" he said.

"I did not lie," Nefertiry replied quietly. "I didn't deny killing Petet. No one asked me."

"Why," Ramessa asked, chilled at her calm.

"If someone attacked you with a sword, you'd defend yourself, wouldn't you?" she asked. "Akeset tried to poison me once. He wants me dead and he won't stop until he's accomplished this, but you ignore it. He sent Petet to say those things about me and Setnau. Has Akeset ever said one good or even a moderate word about me?" Her hands had begun to tremble and she clasped them together tightly to conceal it. "Now his attention has turned to Setnau," she said, and her voice rose. "I cannot lift a sword, but I'll defend myself. I will defend Setnau!"

If Ramessa was aghast at the idea of one of his wives

325

actually plotting a murder, he was even more horrified that a high priest might think of murdering his son. He didn't want to consider such a possibility. "You're lying!"

"I am not lying!" she cried. "Akeset will kill me if he can. I have given him a warning. If you'll do nothing to stop him, I'll defend myself however I can!"

"A priest!" Ramessa whispered. "You could have killed any one of a thousand others and not a murmur would be heard—but a priest!"

"An evil priest who wants me dead," she reminded him.

As if he hadn't heard her, he said, "It has no defense."

Not realizing his mind refused to accept her accusation, she was horrified that he would defend a priest who wanted to murder her. She reached up to grasp his arms as if she would shake him. "Akeset wants me dead. Even Nehemu tried to kill me!" she cried, almost hysterical now. "When Nehemu's hands were on my throat, Botar defended me! But you won't help me. You don't believe me. Must I be dead before you'll believe it?"

Ramessa shrugged off her hands and backed away. His eyes were filled with an agony of confusion.

Nefertiry took a deep breath, and since Ramessa continued backing away, she followed him. Suddenly he turned and began to walk toward the door.

"Ramessa!" She spoke in the tone of cool authority. "Hear me, Ramessa, though you love me not this day. I speak the truth. I'm the only one who dares bring truth to you."

Ramessa resumed walking toward the door.

"There's your answer, as usual!" she flung after him. "Do you go to find another battle or to the harem to escape?"

Ramessa walked quickly through the door with Nefertiry still following on his heels. He began down the hall away from her.

Nefertiry took a breath, then begged, "Ramessa, have I ever lied to you—never!"

Ramessa had reached a corner and turned to give her one last confused and angry look as he passed from her sight.

Nefertiry stood in the empty hall a moment, staring at the corner he'd disappeared around. "But you like not the taste of truth, it seems."

Her gaze dropped to the floor and her shoulders sagged in disappointment and frustration. She stood for several minutes longer, staring at the floor.

Finally, she lifted her head and, with narrowed eyes, returned to her chamber. She was determined, if Ramessa wouldn't stop Akeset or even listen to her warnings, to find some way to stop him herself.

19

Ramessa reined in his horse as he reached level ground and turned in his saddle to watch the columns of soldiers carefully filing down the steep, boulder-strewn hill. Even from a short distance, the soldiers resembled a monstrous scarlet and white snake winding down the slope. A snake that had slithered down several similar hills as well as through canyons and over parched sands; one that had crept through tall, waving grasses and had slipped through shadowy forests while it stalked its prey—Paser's peasants turned criminal.

At first the expedition had seemed to Ramessa to be a good way to avoid conducting an investigation into Petet's poisoning. He hated the machinations of court diplomacy at any time, preferring the strategies of war. There were no lies or half-truths to guess about when a man held a sword in his hands. He hadn't the patience to conduct an inquiry that he must make sure reached no conclusion so the truth would remain a mystery. During his angriest moment, he'd never really considered charging Nefertiry with the poisoning.

Ramessa's shock at Nefertiry's being capable of murder had worn away during the attack he'd led on the first Kenset village. When he'd drawn his sword to face the first rebel, Nefertiry's words about defending herself in any way she could rang in his ears; by the time he'd killed the man, he'd begun to sympathize with what she'd done. By the time the first village had been vanquished and the Tameran criminals bound and handed over to Paser's captain, Ramessa had accepted the idea of one of his wives actually doing violence; he'd developed a certain grudging admiration for Nefertiry's courage. His other wives would have wept and wrung their hands helplessly, but not Nefertiry. Like him, she preferred action, and he wondered if Setnau had inherited a measure of this trait from both of them. What a king such a man would be, Ramessa mused.

"Sire, we're assembled," Khakamir said, drawing his horse beside Ramessa's.

"Beyond that next ridge is the village?" Ramessa asked, narrowing his eyes in the sun's glare.

Khakamir turned to regard the ragged villager riding at Paneb's side. Paneb questioned the man in the language of Kenset, and as the man answered, studied the expression on his bloodied face to be sure he spoke the truth. Then Paneb turned to Khakamir. "The village is just beyond the ridge among a grove of trees."

"Tell him again we aren't interested in gathering slaves from among his people. We wish only to capture our own people who are criminals," Ramessa said to Paneb.

Paneb obeyed, but he asked quietly, "What will we do if the villagers resist?"

"As before, we will do what's necessary to take the rebels," Ramessa answered. "When we get to the top of the ridge, we'll spread out. We'll form a circle and ride down on the village from all directions, so none will escape. We can sort out the rebels from the villagers later."

"That's been our most successful strategy so far," Khakamir remarked.

330

Ramessa smiled briefly and without humor. "I think this will be the last of it."

"I can understand why we must make a show of punishing someone for attacking Lord Hera's party, but is it really worth this trouble to drag all these ragged peasants back to Paser?" Khakamir asked.

"My laws must be obeyed," Ramessa replied. "If Punt were under my rule and the province disobedient, we would travel there to bring order."

"Yes, of course, majesty," Khakamir quickly agreed. "It's just that the people of Kenset are so different from ours, so ignorant—the land so poor, it seems we give them more than we get."

Ramessa sighed. "We give them food only and teach them how to be a little less ignorant, whether they like it or not," he replied. "Kenset is a valuable province for only one reason."

"Which is?" Khakamir asked.

"Gold," Ramessa said drily. "Great quantities of the metal lie in Kenset's rocky hills, and I can make good use of it." He raised his eyes to the ridge ahead. "Let us proceed, Commander."

The people of the village had heard about Ramessa's soldiers attacking other villages to capture the rebels they harbored, and had considered the real possibility of a similar attack on theirs. Wisely, the village chief had posted sentries who warned them of the approaching soldiers. The chief immediately directed the Tameran fugitives to leave his people.

As Ramessa's soldiers drew their ring around the village, they were surprised to meet no resistance. Still, they rode into the village cautiously, alert for a trick. Ramessa gave the order not to dismount until Paneb spoke with the village leader.

The chief was stooped with age and only a few tufts of frizzy white hair adorned his wrinkled head. But he lifted

331

eyes gleaming with dark fire to Ramessa. "I speak your language, majesty, though poorly," the chief said.

"Where are the rebels?" Ramessa asked quietly.

"They're gone," the chief answered.

"I can see that," Ramessa snapped. "Where have they gone?"

The chief shrugged. "They left in many directions."

Ramessa's eyes glittered with impatience. "I think you know where they went because you directed them to a safer place."

The chief's eyes shifted to the bloodied villager in bonds behind Paneb. "Even though you beat me as you did him, I could give you no other answer," he said calmly.

Ramessa thought about this for a moment, then said, "I can see you're too stubborn to speak so I won't waste my time having you beaten. It would only give the criminals a greater lead." He smiled coldly. "I'm sure there are others among you who might be persuaded."

The chief's eyes widened, and he asked, "Would you rape our women as your other captain and his men raped the women of Paser's peasants?"

"I think he means Captain Arek and his mercenaries," Khakamir whispered.

"It would seem Arek's loss was less than I'd thought," Ramessa commented. He continued staring down at the chief for a moment until he said, "We have no interest in your women, nor will we burn your huts if you tell us where the criminals went."

"I don't know where they went," the chief answered, deciding they could rebuild their thatched huts.

Suddenly Khakamir's gaze fell on a tall young man who stood in the doorway of the chief's hut watching anxiously as they questioned the old man. "I think that warrior cub is close to the chief," Khakamir whispered to Ramessa.

Ramessa's eyes moved to the youth and briefly appraised him. "He might even be the chief's grandson." He considered this possibility for a moment, then commanded, "Find a sturdy stick, Paneb."

332

Paneb shouted. "Ikhy! Meru! Put that man on the ground and bind him so he can be questioned!"

The youth, not understanding their language, merely looked curiously at the Tameran captain. But the chief turned pale. "Majesty, Suma knows nothing," he said anxiously. "He wasn't even here when the criminals fled."

"What is Suma to you?" Ramessa asked coolly.

The chief glanced away, so Ramessa couldn't read his eyes as he answered. "Just one of my people."

"In that case, it won't bother you too much to watch him being questioned," Ramessa said.

The chief turned at the sound of scuffling to see his grandson's feet kicked out from under him by one soldier while the other soldier threw himself across Suma's chest so his partner could get a good grip on the struggling youth's free arm.

"I don't like to see any of my people suffer," the chief declared.

"We need another for his feet!" Meru called.

Khakamir gestured to the nearest soldier and the man quickly dismounted to obey.

Ramessa sighed loudly and turned to the chief. "Then you'd better take a walk—a long walk, so you won't hear Suma's cries of pain."

The chief raised his eyes to stare across the clearing at Paneb, striding rapidly toward them, carrying a long, heavy stick. "I will remain," he said.

"I don't know why you'd let this handsome young man be beaten to jelly to hide the escape of criminals not even of your own people," Ramessa remarked, genuinely puzzled.

The chief's eyes widened as he watched Paneb raise the stick over Suma's prone body. The stick came down with a force he feared must have broken a rib. But although the youth's body quivered with the shock, Suma made no sound. "You would have him beaten to jelly?" the chief asked, incredulous.

Ramessa nodded solemnly. "I must learn the information," he said softly. "If my captain kills Suma, we will take another who would speak. I will learn where the rebels went!"

Again the stick came down and the chief flinched. "You would leave if you knew this information?" he asked.

"As I promised, I would not even have the village burned," Ramessa replied.

The chief looked steadily at Ramessa's eyes, which gleamed with hard green spots of light; he decided this king was capable of watching a man beaten to death. He sighed and said, "Tell your captain to stop beating Suma. I'll tell you where the criminals went."

"Pause in your work, Paneb!" Ramessa called. He continued looking at the chief. "Not only will you tell me where they are, you'll lead me to them," he advised. "We'll take Suma with us and Paneb will also bring the stick." He smiled coldly and added, "You can understand I don't want to waste time circling around this land while you lead us on a useless hunt and your people move their village."

The chief nodded numbly.

Tuiah stared at the incredibly beautiful girl who knelt before her. "Rise, Lady Reshet," she said softly. Reshet straightened, and Tuiah noted her grace of movement. When the girl lifted large, cinnamon-colored eyes to meet hers, Tuiah settled back on the throne to study her a moment longer.

"Divine mother, do you find something offensive about my appearance?" Reshet asked uncertainly, noticing Tuiah's unwavering stare.

"Quite the opposite," Tuiah answered. "I'm surprpised at your odd coloring," she remarked, running her eyes over Reshet's long hair, which flowed like a stream of sun-bright honey down her back.

"My father is Tameran and gave me my eyes," Reshet said. "My mother came to him from the valley of the two rivers and her hair is as mine."

334

"Akkad?" Tuiah asked. When the girl nodded, Tuiah was again silent for a moment before she inquired, "Why have you traveled to Wast?"

"Divine mother, I have journeyed here to beg audience with King Ramessa, so I could thank him for sending Makara to me. I would have certainly died if the priestess hadn't called upon the spirit of Khonsu to drive away that evil malady. The king himself came in Khonsu's place wearing the form of a hawk with golden feathers, which perched on my very window opening. When it left, flying in the direction of Wast, I knew it had been his majesty's spirit that saved me."

Tuiah marveled at the girl's simple faith. "The king has gone to the south on an errand," Tuiah said.

Reshet looked disappointed. "I wished to throw myself at his feet so he could see my renewed health with his own eyes. My father sent a chariot filled with gold as a small gesture of his gratitude. This I was to present to his majesty." She sighed. "It's sad I'll be unable to obey my father's wishes, but it's a great personal disappointment that I won't be able to gaze upon his majesty's radiant face."

Tuiah wondered how much more radiant Ramessa's face would become if his eyes fell upon this beauty. The thought struck her that Reshet might be just the woman to distract Ramessa from Nefertiry. Tuiah was especially glad Nefertiry hadn't wanted to attend court this morning. "Wasn't your father worried to send you on a journey carrying gold with only your maids and a few guards as companions?" she asked.

Reshet smiled, showing neat white teeth. "I hope the divine mother isn't offended by my immodesty to say this, but my father trusts me to act as his courier. He knows I'm sensible and would behave with intelligence."

"It would appear your father has educated you almost like a boy," Tuiah observed.

"He did that," Reshet confirmed. A look of uncertainty flashed over her face and she quickly added, "I hope I don't appear unfeminine in any way because of it."

"You don't," Tuiah said thoughtfully. Reshet was both astoundingly beautiful and well educated, but she didn't appear to have grown very sophisticated in the process. Having realized long ago that Ramessa seemed to find Nefertiry's intelligence an added attraction, Tuiah had no doubt he would find this a favorable quality in Reshet as well. She wondered again if Reshet might be the instrument by which she could lessen Nefertiry's influence over Ramessa. Reshet would make an excellent ally. Tuiah recalled how confident Nefertiry had appeared with the double crown on her head and made her decision.

"Lady Reshet," Tuiah said sweetly, "I think you should remain in the palace until my son returns. Then, you will be able to express your personal gratitude as well as accomplish your father's wishes. The king looks with favor upon so obedient and loving a daughter."

"I would be most honored to remain, divine mother," Reshet replied. "I will send a message immediately to my father."

Tuiah stood up, and, turning to Henhenet, said, "Adjourn this session now."

Henhenet looked startled. "Divine mother, we've hardly begun the audience. There are many who wait to be heard."

Tuiah stepped down from the dais. "I'm an old lady, Henhenet, and weary easily. They can all return tomorrow. Nefertiry has more energy than I." She put her hand lightly on Reshet's creamy shoulder. "Come with me, Reshet. While your quarters are being readied, we will wait in my sitting room and converse."

Surprised at this unexpected familiarity, Reshet said, "Divine mother, it's too great an honor."

"A pleasant conversation over a cup of wine will distract an old lady from her aches and pains," Tuiah said warmly.

Henhenet stared at Tuiah, but said nothing. He wondered what plot she was hatching now, pretending such

336

infirmity. One of Tuiah's greatest conceits was that the years had touched her lightly. As he watched Tuiah lead Reshet away, his eyes remained admiringly on the girl. Suddenly, he began to understand Tuiah's purpose. He smiled to think of Nefertiry's fury if Tuiah were to be successful.

Nefertiry was informed of Ramessa's nearing Wast well before his soldiers even appeared on the distant horizon, and she ordered the preparations to be made. Yet, while her attendants bathed and perfumed her body, she was peculiarly withdrawn and worried.

Ramessa had left for Kenset the morning after Nefertiry poisoned Petet, and she had waited for several days to see if he'd left orders to punish her in any way. When it appeared he hadn't, she had begun to hope he'd forgiven her. No one in the palace spoke about the poisoning or Chenmet would have heard the gossip—and Nefertiry began to believe Ramessa had kept her secret. Still, she couldn't help wondering why no investigation, not even an informal inquiry, was made into the incident. Her thoughts had been in a turmoil every minute during the three months Ramessa had been away and there had been no one she dared speak to about it.

A great blare of trumpets announced the king's homecoming. Doors slammed and servants ran through the halls. Tuiah's voice traveled all the way up the stairs as she greeted her son in the entrance hall. Nefertiry could not hear Ramessa's reply and she felt eerily as if Tuiah had spoken to a voiceless spirit. The guard standing before Ramessa's chamber nervously dropped his spear. Nefertiry started at the sound, glanced self-consciously at Chenmet, who sat tensely in a corner of the room, then turned to again stare at the door. Although Ramessa's steps were soundless, Nefertiry heard the footfalls of the guards accompanying him. Expecting them to march past her quarters on their way to his suite, she was paralyzed when they stopped at her door.

The door opened, and Ramessa stood with one hand on the door handle, as he dismissed his guards. Nefertiry silently stared at him, her heart pounding.

"No one will disturb me until I send word to the contrary," Ramessa directed the guards and closed the door firmly behind him. He said nothing, but stood motionless for some time, looking at her.

"Welcome back, my lord," Nefertiry whispered. She heard Chenmet sink to the floor in a bow and wondered if she should follow her maid's example. But something in Ramessa's eyes, as he moved toward her, held her upright.

"I brought this from Kenset for you," Ramessa said quietly, producing a gold necklace of beads shaped like lotuses. He placed it in Nefertiry's hand and the unexpected weight almost caused her to drop it.

Glancing nervously up at him, then down at the gleaming ornament she whispered, "It's very beautiful, my lord. I'm glad you thought of me while you were away."

"I thought of you," Ramessa said brusquely and put his arms around her to pull her to him in so tight an embrace she gasped. He bent to crush her mouth with his in a kiss as implacable as a royal command. His mouth grew no softer as he kissed her; his arms held her like a band of iron and she became a weak thing, pliant and surrendering, her lips clinging to him. She lifted trembling hands and eagerly clasped him even more tightly to her.

When his mouth withdrew, it was only far enough so he could murmur against her lips, "Though I smell like a blacksmith, it doesn't seem to bother you this time." Nefertiry shook her head slowly, so as not to move her lips too far from his. He smiled against her mouth and asked knowingly, "Shall I go to my chambers and bathe?" She again shook her head slowly. When her lips reached for his, he released her and stepped back. Her eyes flew open in alarm. But he smiled and turned to look at Chenmet, who was still on her knees. "You may rise," he said. "And prepare a bath."

Chenmet turned to go through the golden door to Ramessa's chambers, but he held up a hand.

"The bath will be taken in the queen's pool," he said. "After the water has been prepared, make available sufficient cloths to dry both myself and the queen, then leave us."

"Majesty, do you wish another to serve you?" Chenmet asked.

"I want no one to serve us," Ramessa replied. "Tell the others to keep away until I call them."

"Yes, majesty," Chenmet said and, bowing, backed away toward the bathing chamber.

Ramessa turned to Nefertiry to ask, "You've already bathed in preparation for my coming?"

"Just an hour ago," she whispered.

Ramessa smiled as he removed his sword and dropped it on the floor with a metallic clatter. "Shortly you will need to bathe again," he advised, slowly untying the sash of his tunic. When the sash slipped past his hips onto the white stone floor, he raised his eyes to look at her. "Remove that garment," he directed.

Nefertiry hurried to unclasp the ornament that was fastened at her waist. Just as she had managed this, Ramessa came closer to regard her with a critical expression.

"You're very slow," he said softly, then lifted his hands to grasp the top of her robe. As if the linen was no more than gauze, he tore the robe down the front, and let it fall to her feet.

Nefertiry stared up at him, too surprised to speak for a moment. Finally she whispered, "I didn't—"

"Be silent," Ramessa commanded and picked her up in his arms. "I grow impatient," and he carried her to the bed.

Ramessa put his hand on Nefertiry's bare shoulder before she was awake, and her arms reached out instinctively for him. But she realized his body wasn't stretched out beside her, and she opened her eyes quickly. He was fully dressed and sitting on the edge of the bed, looking down at her.

"It is yet early," he advised. "Though I have no wish to leave you, I must go downstairs to learn from Henhenet what has happened in my absence."

"Three months is a long time," she whispered. "I would have you stay three months here in this room with me."

"If I so neglected the kingdom, we would have a famine, thieves would infest the land, and your illustrious father might very well declare another war," he said.

"The wheat would continue to grow; Khakamir would chase the thieves; Hattusil will never make war on you while I'm in your palace," she replied.

"Nevertheless, I must go," he said with genuine regret. "There are countless reports to read and many documents to which I must set my seal." He bent over her to brush his lips to her forehead. When he straightened, he gazed at her for a moment, his fingers caressing her shoulder as if he loathed to take them from her. Finally, he stood up. "Go back to sleep," he said quietly. "Renew your strength for tonight."

Nefertiry rose to lean on her elbow. "You wish me to come to you tonight, my lord?" she asked.

Ramessa smiled briefly. "I do," he said, then turned to leave her.

"I have a pleasant surprise for you, my son," Tuiah said.

Ramessa raised his eyes from the reports he had been sealing. "Your surprise may be delightful, but unless it's of the greatest importance, it must be delayed while I catch up on these documents."

Tuiah stepped across the threshhold, eyeing the many scrolls piled on Ramessa's table. "Don't you wish to view the results of your healing?" When Ramessa's eyebrows lifted in question, she explained, "Surely you haven't forgotten how you sent Makara to save the Lady Reshet from a mysterious illness."

"Evidently, she's recovered. Good," Ramessa said shortly and looked down at the scrolls, hoping his mother would take the hint and leave.

"Lady Reshet journeyed to Wast to thank you in person," Tuiah advised. "She has waited two months for your return."

Ramessa sighed. "If she will come to the audience this afternoon, I'll meet her then."

A soft, low voice from the hall murmured, "Divine mother, I'll wait for the audience as his majesty wishes."

"If she's already here, let her in," Ramessa directed. "I'll spare a moment, but no more."

Ramessa watched closely as Tuiah drew a shapely arm into view, then a delicate shoulder and finally a woman. He sat back in his chair and stared at the woman.

A tall, slender form, whose grace was swathed in sheer, orchid folds. Pale golden shoulders of a perfection even Senti's artistry couldn't produce. A pair of lips, generously curved. Long waves of honey-gold hair touched with copper lights where the sun fell on it. But her wide eyes were what held his gaze like a magnet, depths of melted cinnamon, luminous and haunting.

"This is Lady Reshet," Tuiah announced and, noting the expression on Ramessa's face, smiled with satisfaction.

As Reshet bowed low, Ramessa stood up so he could see her over the table. "You may rise," he whispered wonderingly. "Surely some god, jealous of earth's possession of you, wanted to call you to him when Makara interfered."

"It was you, majesty, who saved me—not Makara," Reshet murmured.

Ramessa, watching her coral lips form the words she spoke, whispered, "I saved you?"

Tuiah moved as silently as a ghost out of the room, soundlessly closing the door behind her.

Reshet looked perplexed for a moment before her

smile reappeared. "Pehaps it was your spirit that came to me while your body slept, if you don't remember."

Wanting to continue watching that mouth move in speech Ramessa said, "Tell me what happened." As Reshet came a little closer to the table, Ramessa's eyes dropped to watch the smooth movement of her hips; when she stopped, they lifted again to her face.

Noting her king's expression Reshet blushed faintly and continued, "The priestess Makara came when I was in a deep sleep, but I couldn't be awakened. They told me she called upon Khonsu, the patron of our province, to help me. I only know during my slumber Heru came to my side. He took my hand and led me from the depths of my sleeping. When I opened my eyes, a hawk was perched on the edge of my window opening, a hawk with feathers of a golden tint. We regarded each other for a moment before he flew away. I'm convinced it was you who came. For isn't his majesty the god Heru, who sometimes wears the form of a hawk?"

Recovering from watching her lips move through so long a speech, Ramessa blinked then said, "Yes. Heru is often depicted as a hawk so humans can recognize him. I suppose it was my spirit wandering while my body slept. In any case, I rejoice that so lovely a woman has not yet gone to Tuat." He moved around the table and approached Reshet, wondering if a flame burned inside him to give him a sudden fever. "It's warm and airless in this room. Let us step out to the terrace."

"If you wish, majesty," Reshet replied.

Ramessa took her hand and felt at the contact as if a streak of lightning flashed in his brain. He said nothing, all thought having deserted him, while he held her hand and led her outside.

A cool breeze came from the north. Although it brushed his face and parted his hair, it gave him no refreshment. He felt no cooler in the garden.

"Majesty, my father is so grateful for your help he sent you a gift," Reshet said.

342

Ramessa turned to look again into her eyes and was as before caught by the cinnamon lights of them. "Gift?" he whispered absently.

"He sent a chariot filled with gold to thank you for saving me," Reshet said.

Ramessa focused his mind with some effort. "Where is this chariot?"

"I think the chariot is in the stable. The gold was taken away, for safekeeping." She looked down at Ramessa's hand, which still held hers. Then, she raised her eyes again to his. "The chariot, however, was specially made. It is trimmed all over with hammered gold."

Ramessa took a deep breath. "Perhaps I should examine this marvelous chariot," he said, ignoring the fact that he already had such a vehicle. "Would you come with me to look at it?"

"I'll go with you wherever you wish," Reshet murmured.

Again the lightning flashed in his brain and he asked, "If I wished to try this chariot, would you fear riding in it with me?"

"I would fear nothing with you at my side," Reshet whispered.

Ramessa smiled. "Then, let us go to try the chariot," he said and, gripping her hand more tightly, began walking toward the stable.

Reshet lay awake staring at the darkness of her ceiling, wondering at the afternoon she'd spent with her king, wondering if her memories of clinging to his waist while he drove his horses through the royal preserve were dreams. Was it really the king who had caused the chariot to speed through sun-dappled avenues of trees? She remembered the foliage only as so many shades of green, blurring as they raced past. The king had drawn the horses to a stop at a pond covered by blue lotuses, and he had turned to lift her from the chariot with a look in his eyes that made her tremble.

343

Reshet sighed to remember it. Never had a man's kiss so affected her, awakening sensations in her being she hadn't known existed. No man could have kissed her so. But then, she wondered, wasn't the king divine? Who else could give so enchanted a kiss but Heru? Only the kiss of a god could be magical. She turned restlessly to her side.

King or not, god or not, she must think of the afternoon as a wondrous experience never to be repeated, like a dream whose substance can't be recalled upon awakening. She closed her eyes, wishing he had done more than kiss her, so she could remember always how it had been to love him.

"Reshet?"

The whisper was that of the breeze that slipped through the open doorway from the garden. She sighed, not believing it was more than the wind.

"Reshet? Are you sleeping?"

"I'm dreaming of a god," she murmured, still half-asleep. She opened her eyes to see Ramessa standing beside the bed looking down at her. "I'm yet dreaming," she whispered, closing her eyes again.

"Is the dream welcome?" he asked softly.

"Yes," she murmured, "most welcome."

"I too am dreaming, I think," he whispered, longing to touch her, longing to look again into her eyes. "May I join your dream?"

Then Reshet began to question if she was dreaming. She felt the bed dip from a very solid weight that had been placed upon it and her eyes flew open. Ramessa sat by her side, gazing at her. She stared at him. "Who are you? Are you flesh or spirit?"

Ramessa's fingers lightly touched Reshet's cheek, as he murmured, "I am flesh. Only too painfully am I flesh."

"This cannot be!" she said incredulously.

Ramessa looked disappointed for a moment, then realizing she still didn't believe he was really there, he said softly, "It can be if you wish it so. It needs but one small word on your lips—yes."

"I am dreaming," she murmured and closed her eyes. "This can't be happening."

Ramessa looked at Reshet for a moment, wondering if she was using this as an excuse to reject him or if she truly didn't believe he was present. He decided to convince her of his reality in a way she couldn't question. If she pretended to continue sleeping, he would go without further effort, so she might later think of him as a dream. He bent toward her, toward that golden face, those soft full lips. He pressed his mouth very gently and carefully to those lips and felt their responding roundness, the small movements of the kiss returning to him. Two golden arms lifted to encircle him and welcome him closer.

"You are real," Reshet murmured. "I thank Hat-Hor you're real and not a dream, after all."

"You won't send me from you?" he whispered, moving back.

"It would have to be you who sent me away," she murmured.

"Will you go with me tomorrow to the temple of Khonsu?" Ramessa asked.

"Anywhere," she promised.

Ramessa said, "I'll think of other places to go and other things to do, but tomorrow I would lay your father's gold at Khonsu's feet in thanks."

"I will lay my soul at Khonsu's feet in thanks," she murmured and reached up toward him.

20

Nefertiry stared suspiciously at Mimut and Nofret. "Why have you come to me?" she demanded.

"We know you have no liking for us, nor do we like you," Nofret said quietly. "Yet there is a matter we think it mutually beneficial to discuss."

"Anything that benefits one seems always to be to the other's disadvantage," Nefertiry said.

Mimut shook her head. "The king called neither of us to him last night, nor did he call any other of his wives," she said solemnly. Nefertiry's efforts to conceal her shock weren't entirely successful.

"Even a king must sometimes spend a night sleeping," Nerfertiry snapped, remembering how she'd waited for Ramessa's call for hours, then had finally crept through the golden door to find his room empty, his bed unoccupied.

"He slept alone?" Nofret asked, feigning surprise.

Nefertiry cast a meaningful glance at the gilded door. "Would I not know?"

347

"Let us tell you, divine lady, what we have heard. For it's so unbelievable a thing you'll probably, then, be amused by it," Mimut said, a strange expression lighting her eyes.

Nefertiry sighed with impatience, but she didn't tell them to leave. She had a horrible feeling that some disaster hovered over her head. "How unlike you to wish to lighten my day with humor," she remarked. "This is, indeed, a rare opportunity. What is this amusing thing?"

Mimut looked at Nofret, urging her to speak; but Nofret stepped back, afraid to go too near Nefertiry.

"Tell me this tale, whatever it is, or go," Nefertiry said shortly. "I have other matters on my mind."

"It has run through the palace like fire through a grain bin," Mimut ventured. "A woman has been quartered just below the king's chambers the past two months, but she has never left the room. It is known the divine mother has visited that room frequently."

"Servants must bring this mysterious woman food. They must clean her room and change her linen," Nefertiry reasoned, leaning forward with interest. "Someone knows who she is."

Nofret's great, dark eyes regarded Nefertiry with a conspiratorial expression. "It's that woman from Bekhten's house, Lady Reshet, they say."

Nefertiry was surprised. "She's been here two months?" she asked. "How did she come without my knowing it?"

"She came one day when the divine mother sat in audience," Mimut replied. "The divine mother adjourned the audience early and led this woman to her own chambers while the downstairs quarters were being prepared. Once the woman moved into those quarters, she didn't leave them—on advice from the divine mother it's said."

Nefertiry leaned back in the chair. "Why would Tuiah hide this woman like a political prisoner?" she mused. She looked up at Mimut and asked, "What more of this story is there? So far, I'm not amused by it."

"Yesterday the divine mother took Lady Reshet to his majesty so the lady could thank him for sending Makara to heal her," Mimut said softly.

"And?" Nefertiry prompted.

"His majesty went with her to the stable, then took her in his chariot to the royal park," Mimut whispered.

Nefertiry, feeling as if the disaster were about to swoop down on her, asked, "What has this to do with any of us?"

"I know a king must have many wives and I've resigned myself to my fate in the harem," Nofret declared with sudden vehemence. "I have seen other wives added to his majesty's harem, and I accept them as creatures that must share his presence and steal yet another night from me. Even concubines I can endure, for they have so lowly a place they're hardly noticeable. But I'm not happy when a woman may enter the palace merely to visit the king and he creeps into her room to spend a night with her—a woman who has not even the status of a concubine!"

Nefertiry continued to look at her lap while she asked, "Then the gossip is that this woman lured the king into her room downstairs?"

"He also went out with her this very morning," Mimut said in a stiff voice.

"Where?" Nefertiry asked quietly.

"Divine lady, he went with her to the temple of Khonsu to lay gold at the god's feet!" Nofret declared. "Gold to thank Khonsu for bringing this thief to the palace."

"It's the gold her father sent his majesty in thanks for sending a priestess to heal this creature's body!" Mimut exploded.

"It would have been better had her body crumbled to dust," Nofret muttered.

Nefertiry stood up, her face a mask of unconcern. "You are upset over nothing. As I've already told you, the king slept in that very room." She gestured toward

349

the gold door. "It's fitting that his majesty brings Bekhten's gold to the temple of the patron of his province."

"If that's what the divine lady believes, further discussion is useless," Mimut said and began backing away to the door.

Nofret followed Mimut. But when they reached the door, she raised her head to stare defiantly at Nefertiry and say, "If my son were so near to having the crown placed on his head, I would consider this news carefully."

"I'll consider it with as much concern as I give all the other gossip I hear," Nefertiry said in a voice like ice.

"Divine lady, I would take a look at this woman if I were you. She's a formidable enemy," Mimut advised.

"You've seen her?" Nefertiry asked.

Mimut whispered, "I saw her from my window as she walked through the garden hand in hand with the king yesterday."

"Hand in hand?" Nefertiry repeated incredulously.

"She has hair like honey poured in the sun," Mimut advised. With a little sigh she added, "Yes, I did see them myself."

When Mimut and Nofret left, Nefertiry sank into a chair, her strength drained from her. How was it possible that Ramessa would invite her to his room and forget it? she wondered. Where could he have been all night?

"Hair like honey poured in the sun," she whispered. She shivered, feeling as if the earth had crumbled under her feet.

For the next few weeks Nefertiry pretended to have no inkling of what she slowly became convinced was truth. She held her head high under the gleaming double crown and marched at Ramessa's side to sit on her golden throne in aloof grandeur. Ramessa never saw her except in audience, and they didn't speak to each other about anything other than the business before them.

Nefertiry's seething emotions were effectively concealed
350

by her usual mask of haughty disdain. No one dared mention within her hearing the name of Reshet.

Although Ramessa had again taken up his official duties, there was an underlying excitement in all he did, which further eroded his always-tenuous attention span. He forgot or ignored many small details which Nefertiry had to remember and attend to. She couldn't bear to look into his eyes, for they held an eager light she'd never seen before; she knew he spent every spare moment in Reshet's company. Once, when Nefertiry passed Mimut in a corridor, Mimut nodded calmly enough in greeting. But her eyes on Nefertiry were filled with mute anger and pain at this insult Ramessa's affair with Reshet had dealt all his wives.

Nearly three months passed before Nefertiry actually saw the face of her enemy. One day as she was sitting in the garden playing with Setnau, Ramessa and Reshet strolled down a nearby path. Glancing up from her game with Setnau, Nefertiry saw the couple walking together gazing at one another as lovers will. The pleasure in her eyes faded and Nefertiry held Setnau closer, as if she were shielding him from the sight she beheld. She averted her eyes as they passed, but it was at that moment that the flower of Nefertiry's hatred for Reshet opened to full bloom. Her heart became a piece of granite in her breast—a cold, hard weight that was dead.

She recalled Khakamir saying again and again: *"My wife would never endure such agony. Even if my son were exiled in another land, he would never be exiled from me. His future would be secure because he would never have to fear me setting him aside for another woman's son."*

Nefertiry pushed the memory away and stood to go back to the palace. So great was her rage that she held Setnau too tightly, until his whimper reminded her, and she cradled him against her shoulder softly again.

Fortune placed Tuiah in the corridor at that moment

as Nefertiry walked slowly toward her apartments, and Tuiah was less than wise to smile smugly at Nefertiry's head bowed over Setnau.

"You appear pale, divine lady," Tuiah declared. "If you're unwell, perhaps you should visit the priestess who healed Lady Reshet."

Nefertiry lifted eyes burning with so intense a maelstrom of hatred, their fury seemed to spill out of them and cover her face. "Have a care I don't visit the temple's corner where Sekhmet resides," she said in a tone harsh with venom.

Tuiah stepped back from the shock of Nefertiry's quiet ferocity. "Divine lady, do you threaten me with a curse?" she whispered.

"If ever you are stricken with a curse, you won't suffer it alone," Nefertiry replied. She stood motionless, staring at Tuiah. Finally, unable to endure the dark menace in Nefertiry's eyes, Tuiah turned to walk away, resolving to ask Ramessa to be more discreet with Reshet. Because she was suddenly terrified, Nefertiry might find a way to get revenge on all three of them.

Tuiah hurried into the room where Ramessa set his seal. He was sitting at his table, a scroll spread before him. Amten, his chief scribe, sat on a cushion on the floor, writing rapidly to Ramessa's dictation.

"My son, I fear she has gone mad!" Tuiah exclaimed.

Ramessa looked up from the scroll he was studying. "Who has gone mad?" he asked distractedly. Then, he noticed the look of terror on his mother's face, and he said, "What's happened?"

"Nefertiry—" Tuiah began.

Ramessa held up a hand and told Amten to return later.

The scribe, who saw the possibility of witnessing a fascinating discussion slip from his grasp, sighed with disappointment, gathered up his materials, and got to his feet to leave.

When the door had closed behind the scribe, Ramessa

turned to his mother and asked, "What has Nefertiry done?"

"Her eyes were like those of the sabau—no, they contained the fires of Sutekh's violence."

"Mother, I've seen Nefertiry's eyes like that before, but she certainly hadn't lost her sanity," Ramessa said. "Calm yourself and tell me what took place."

"Just a moment ago in the hall," Tuiah said. Her face was pale, and it shone with moisture.

"Sit down, Mother," Ramessa directed. "You look unwell."

Tuiah sank weakly into a chair. "I look terrified, not unwell," she muttered over her shoulder to Ramessa, who had gone to pour a goblet of wine for her.

"What happened a moment ago?" he asked, handing her the goblet.

"I met Nefertiry and commented that she looked pale," Tuiah said. She sipped the wine, then put down the goblet and looked up at Ramessa. "I suggested she go to see Makara."

"Mother, it isn't wise to poke at a lion with too short a spear."

Tuiah gazed up at her son, trying to appear innocent of any ill intentions. "I only inquired after her health!"

"What did she say?" Ramessa asked.

"She said she might go to Sekhmet for help," Tuiah whispered. "She meant she would put a curse on all of us."

"A curse!" Ramessa sneered. "Do you believe she could do such a thing?"

"You didn't see the look on her face," Tuiah whispered. "If Nefertiry couldn't place a curse herself, isn't she a friend of that high priestess? Seshena could crumble the palace with the powers she has."

"If Seshena could do such a thing, she wouldn't," he said. "But Nefertiry saw me walking through the garden with Reshet a short while ago."

"What did she say? What did she do?" Tuiah asked.

353

"Nothing," Ramessa replied. "She turned away."

"She is contemplating the murders of us all!" Tuiah declared.

Ramessa thought of Petet and of Nehemu, torn by Botar's fangs and claws. "What can I do?" he whispered. "She's done nothing."

"Punish her for threatening you with a curse!" Tuiah cried.

Ramessa shook his head. "Were I to punish Nefertiry for her angry thoughts, I would have to do the same with every occupant of my harem. They're all angry that Reshet has neither been proclaimed a concubine nor married to me."

"Why don't you do one or the other?" Tuiah asked.

"To put her in the harem would be a death sentence," Ramessa said. "The others would tear her to pieces and find some way to call it an accident. To marry Reshet and put her in separate quarters would be to proclaim her First Royal Wife and move Nefertiry into the harem. If Nefertiry were to enter the harem and become an ally of the others. . . . " Ramessa's voice trailed off and he shuddered at the thought.

"What of Reshet?" Tuiah asked. "Is this situation fair to her? Doesn't she mind that she has no place?"

"Reshet asks for nothing," Ramessa said in a sudden harsh tone. "That's part of what I love about her."

"You love her?" Tuiah asked.

"I'm not sure. Nefertiry taught me what it was to love." He shook his head and added, "I cannot lock Nefertiry in the harem. Besides, she's too wise in the running of the kingdom. She helps me."

"My son, you ruled Tamera before she placed one foot over the border!" Tuiah exclaimed, shocked at this admittance.

"Perhaps, but not as well," he said. "I cannot deny Nefertiry often sees hidden factors in matters I miss, and her brain's calculations defy nobles, priests and ministers alike."

"What of Reshet's mind?" Tuiah whispered.

Ramessa shook his head. "Reshet is sweet, devoted, and loving, but she has no head for matters of state. She is, in her own way, too innocent."

"You must do something to get Reshet out of Nefertiry's sight." Tuiah declared. "If you don't, I fear not only for Reshet's life, but for yours and mine as well."

Ramessa remembered Nefertiry saying she would defend herself and her son however she could. He turned cold when he recalled her vehemence. "You are right, Mother. I must get Reshet out of the palace."

"Now Ramessa has moved Reshet into a house of her own, a house comparable in luxury to the palace," Nefertiry said bitterly. "She has more servants than I do." When Seshena said nothing to this, Nefertiry whispered, "I know you despise me for poisoning Petet, but I don't know where to turn. I'm besieged with enemies. Akeset waits to spit venom at me. He withheld his fangs only because he feared me for killing Petet—but now he laughs in derision at my plight. Henhenet twists everything I do in the hope of causing me disaster, and I must watch him every moment. Tuiah plots during her every waking moment how to get rid of me, as do others."

"I don't hate you," Seshena said quietly. "I don't approve of your killing Petet, but I don't hate you for it."

"How could you know how I feel, the pain I'm suffering! You have Rasuah in your arms every night!" Nefertiry said helplessly. "Mimut, Nofret, all the others of the harem know something of how I feel. To think that the harem is in sympathy with me!"

"You're better off than they are. You have Khakamir," Seshena reminded her.

"Yes, Khakamir—if I had the heart to call him to me. . . . Sometimes I wonder if I should leave Tamera with him as he asked."

"He's asked you to go into exile with him?"

Nefertiry lifted her eyes to Seshena's and nodded. "Yet

I would have the crown for Setnau. It was so close, only three months ago."

"Setnau's inheriting the crown was never my promise," Seshena said. "It was my promise to help you protect the kingdom."

"I cannot protect the kingdom. I seem unable to help myself," Nefertiry muttered. "I would win Ramessa back from that creature. I would make him want me again before I could go with Khakamir."

"As a woman, I would advise you to forget it all and go now. As high priestess, I think you cannot," Seshena said quietly.

"Who would stop me but the soldiers Khakamir commands?" Nefertiry flashed.

"Whether it pleases you or not, you have made a pact with the gods," Seshena reminded her.

"What have these gods done for me?" Nefertiry exploded. "I've done everything I could to keep Akeset from gaining power. I've watched every scheme the nobles have hatched and have found ways to stop them. Where is my reward?" she asked. "Are these gods so selfish they offer nothing in return for my struggles? How can I even do their bidding if my power is drained from me by that woman he lies with each night?"

"I've been too caught up in my own affairs," Seshena confessed.

"You're in love!" Nefertiry exclaimed. "You've been caught up in your own joy—a joy I envy you, a joy I think I'll never know." She threw herself again in the chair and muttered, "Perhaps I should go to Khakamir now and tell him to plan our escape. If Tamera is covered over by the desert the moment my feet step from its border, at least my son will be spared being cast aside."

Nefertiry took a breath and looked at Seshena with new fire in her eyes. "You were supposed to help me protect the kingdom! This Reshet is a new threat to Tamera, I think, beyond even Akeset, for she's draining the power from the throne with every kiss she gives

356

Ramessa. That little fool hasn't yet realized what power she has in her grasp. With the hold she has on him she could rule Tamera!" Nefertiry was silent a moment, then asked, "What if Reshet should acquire a taste for power? What if Reshet decides to influence the running of the kingdom?"

Seshena knew Reshet was still too distracted with Ramessa's love to get involved with matters of state. But if she changed, the results could be catastrophic. "I will try to protect you from Reshet," Seshena promised.

Nefertiry leaned forward, her eyes glittering. "Will you give him back to me?"

"I cannot do that by magic without also binding you to him," Seshena replied.

Nefertiry stared at Seshena. "What good are you if you cannot do a thing any priestess in Khatti can arrange?"

"The priestess anywhere who does that cares nothing for more far-reaching consequences," Seshena declared. "To make a love-slave of one partner is evil. The thing must be done to both."

"There must be some other way," Nefertiry whispered. "A way to dim his interest in her?"

"That would be temporary," Seshena said thoughtfully.

"Temporary is all I need!" Nefertiry exclaimed. "I'm not without my own allure! I held him once against all the others. Give me one night—just one night—to distract him. I would distract him until he has not the strength to lift his head from my pillow. I've done it before. Get Reshet out of his mind for only one night."

"Then would you leave Tamera?" Seshena asked doubtfully.

Nefertiry raised eyes as green as emeralds—and as cold. "Then I would go with Khakamir, and Ramessa could weep for love of me."

Seshena shook her head slowly. "I think you won't leave," she murmured. "I think you love him and will be as caught by him as he by you. Yet, I will arrange what you ask and I will continue protecting Tamera. Perhaps it's what the divine beings wish. Maybe all of this is in their design."

"Just lessen Reshet's influence on Ramessa. I'll do the rest."

Chenmet straightened from her bow and addressed Ramessa. "Majesty, my mistress requests you to come to her."

Ramessa looked suspiciously at the maid. "It's important?"

"My lady said it was most important," Chenmet whispered, keeping her eyes downcast.

Ramessa glanced at Reshet, then asked, "Your mistress sent you here—to Lady Reshet's house?"

"My lady said to find his majesty. She didn't say where I would find you," Chenmet whispered.

"But she had an idea, I should think," Ramessa said softly. He thought about Nefertiry's message, which was the first time in over a month that she'd tried to communicate with him about anything. "Nefertiry didn't say why?"

At the sound of the name Reshet feared most, she stepped behind Ramessa and took his arm. "Don't go, my lord," she begged.

"Nefertiry didn't say why she wanted to see me?" Ramessa asked again. Chenmet shook her head, still keeping her eyes on the floor. "Why won't you look at me, Chenmet?"

The servant lifted her dark eyes to stare fixedly at Ramessa. "I look at you, majesty," she said.

"But not at Lady Reshet," he observed. Chenmet dropped her eyes.

"Please stay with me, my lord," Reshet whispered again. "I have an oppressive feeling about this."

Ramessa took her hand from his arm. "Nefertiry wouldn't call me without good reason. It may be something about Setnau. Perhaps he's ill."

"I would give you a stronger son," Reshet said.

358

Ramessa frowned. "We'll discuss that at another time," he replied, an edge to his voice. "I won't turn my face from the children I already have. How did you come to this valley?" he asked Chenmet.

"I walked, majesty."

"All that way?"

"I hadn't known I must come so far to find you, majesty," she replied.

"You'll return with me in my chariot. Come Chenmet," he called over his shoulder as he disappeared around the corner.

"Yes, majesty," the maid replied hurrying after him.

When Ramessa stood outside Nefertiry's door, he turned again to Chenmet. "What mood was your mistress in when she gave you the message?" he asked cautiously.

"My lady was calm," Chenmet replied evasively.

Ramessa sighed, "You answer, but I'm no wiser," and he opened the door. The room was lit by only one lamp so that he could barely see Nefertiry standing by the door opened to her terrace. He bent toward Chenmet. "Why is it so dark?" he whispered, handing her his cloak.

"I suppose my lady wished it so," Chenmet replied, backing away.

Nefertiry turned in a swirl of whispering green veils. "You've come as I asked, my lord," she said in a low, soft voice, and walked slowly toward him. "You will enter my chamber a little farther?" she asked, touching his hand lightly. "Come, my lord," she said and turned away to lead him to the center of the room. "Chenmet, bring us wine."

"Why did you call me?" Ramessa asked.

"Sit down, my lord," she invited. When he didn't move, she raised her hand to run her fingers lightly up his bare arm. "Will you not be comfortable while you drink your wine? You appear tense."

Ramessa looked at the goblet Chenmet offered and didn't put out his hand.

Nefertiry's low laughter was like golden bubbles floating toward the moon. She picked up one goblet and took a sip, then the other goblet. "I didn't ask my lord here to poison him," she said softly.

Ramessa accepted one of the goblets and, taking a sip from it, recognized it as the wine he most favored. "Why did you call me?" he asked.

"You may go, Chenmet," Nefertiry directed. Then she looked up at Ramessa and slowly shook her head, while the gold beads falling over her black hair twinkled in the flickering light. "The cushions aren't poisoned," she said in a humorous tone. "There are no daggers pointing from them, my lord. I don't wish to harm you in any way."

Ramessa's curiosity was piqued. He sat on the couch. Nefertiry moved to stand behind the couch; he looked back to see what she was doing, then felt her hands on his shoulders, skillfully erasing the tension from his muscles. He sighed. "What do you want, Nefertiry?" he asked.

Her hands slid off his shoulders to his chest and she leaned forward to put her cheek against his. "Something that has been denied me."

"You've never been denied anything, Nefertiry, but that which would have reduced my authority," Ramessa replied. He felt her lips brush his cheek, while her hands slipped inside his tunic.

"You have denied me yourself," she murmured close to his ear, "and I intend to take you back tonight."

"You want to lure me from Reshet?" he asked hesitantly. He felt Nefertiry's breath in his ear and he shivered.

"Yes, my lord," she whispered, her lips against his temple. "You haven't called me for some time. You know I cannot endure neglect. I have need of you, my lord."

Ramessa turned his head to look at her, but she was so close he could see only the black blur of her hair.

"You're trying to trick me." Inhaling her perfume, he was reminded of other nights.

"I'm trying to seduce you," she murmured, moving her fingers over his chest. "Before very long I'll have so great a hunger, I'll rejoice at the arrival of any man in my chamber. This I wish not to do."

"You want to turn me from Reshet," Ramessa said accusingly.

"Yes," Nefertiry whispered in his ear. "You're surprised I admit it? Why should I not? I can do it, I'm sure." She withdrew her hands from his tunic and moved around the couch to sit close beside him. "I want you, my lord," she murmured, leaning her breasts against him. "I wish to ease my aching with your body."

Ramessa stared at Nefertiry. He knew she was weaving her old magic over him. He felt the warmth beginning to flow through his body, the need she was arousing.

Nefertiry's parted lips were only a breath from his mouth when she whispered, "What would be but an hour's pleasant passing to you means so much more to me. I will do for you what I did before you went to Zurim."

"That would take more than an hour," he said softly.

"It would take the night," she admitted. "I want you to stay all night. But I'll only do what you ask, my lord, only what you want. You have merely to say what you want."

"I can say nothing with your lips on mine," he whispered.

"You need say nothing now," she murmured. "You can think about your answer while I kiss you."

"I can't think while you kiss me," Ramessa declared.

Nefertiry's hands slid to his waist. "I would kiss you again," she whispered.

Without waiting for his reply, she leaned closer to press her lips again to his. But this kiss hadn't the delicate touch of the earlier ones. Her lips were firm on his, moving with an expertise that lit within the core of him a hot, sweet flame. It ignited his whole being like a flare. When she could feel his breath accelerating, she drew away.

"Have you decided what I will do?" she asked softly.

Ramessa focused his eyes with some effort, but he didn't speak.

She stood up and took his hands to guide him slowly toward the bed. He followed as if she'd hypnotized him, wondering at himself standing docilely while she untied his sash and it fell to the floor, obeying her when she asked him to lift his arms and she pulled his tunic over his head.

"Now, my lord, is the time to tell me," she whispered, running her fingers up his naked sides. Still, he said nothing. "Lie down," she murmured. "If I do something you wish me not to do, you must speak then."

Ramessa lay on her bed and waited to see what she would do. He watched her unwind her robe. The fluttering green veils floated to the floor. He watched her lean toward him and closed his eyes to lie there and do nothing more than respond to her, wondering where he would find the strength to tell her to stop—until he began to tremble and the voice of reason faded to nothing, until the tremors going through him seemed to shake the earth from its axis, until he writhed with the intensity of his sensations. And she stopped.

"You stop!" he panted.

"You wish me to go on?" she whispered, as if in apology, then again bent toward him to work her magic until his joyously shrieking senses seemed unable to endure it—and she stopped again.

He reached out to her, like a man groping in the dark. She started all over again, as if it were the beginning. Slowly she rebuilt his tension until he felt like a bowstring pulled too far, threatening to snap, and when he was sure it was the end and she would give him release—she stopped.

Then she bent to kiss his mouth, but her kiss sent new spirals of fire through him, searing the soul within his body; he moaned softly from ecstasy. She removed her lips and began at the beginning.

362

The impulses flashing through his body grew in intensity, and again he reached out to her; but she eluded him, enticing him further, luring him to madness. When he felt sparks flashing along his nerves and his blood turn to liquid fire, when his body seemed like a torch that would blaze in eternity, she freed him in a bursting of sensations that made of the sun's flaring but a shadow.

Though Nefertiry had the strength to remove herself from Ramessa, he didn't speak. She covered his exhausted body with the linens and leaned over him. His eyes stared up at her, incredulous.

"Ra rises soon," she said.

"It matters nothing," he whispered. He was silent, while she wiped his shining brow, then added softly, "You never would have stopped."

She smiled. "I would have, if you'd told me to." She lay beside him, not touching him now. "Sleep, my Ramessa," she murmured. "When you awaken, you can decide what you'll do."

"What I'll wish to do after I've awakened will guarantee me an early death," he whispered.

"No man dies from love," she murmured. "Only women die from lack of it."

Using his last bit of strength, Ramessa slowly turned to lie on his side and put his arm around Nefertiry. He shut his eyes, knowing he wouldn't leave her in the morning, but never dreaming he would stay in her bedchamber for a week.

Rasuah and Seshena lay on their backs in the leafy softness of the grasses that grew along the Nile's bank. The papyrus' tall stalks formed pale, green walls topped with gold, umbrella-shaped flower clusters that swayed in the wind, showering tiny weightless blossoms over them.

Rasuah's eyes were closed as he inhaled the warm fragrance of the sun on the flowers, the moist, green, earth-scent rising around them, and listened to the peaceful swishing of the wind in the plants.

"We lie like broken lotuses floating aimlessly with the river's currents, accomplishing nothing," Seshena murmured lazily.

Rasuah opened his eyes to gaze at the golden papyrus flowers swaying over their heads. "Yet would I remain here, sheltered from that world of turmoil beyond," he said softly.

"It's a time of sorrow," Seshena whispered.

"You speak of the situation in the palace," Rasuah observed. He was silent for a moment while his hand crept into hers. "They have brought their unhappiness upon themselves, yet the blame of it cannot be heaped solely on their jeweled heads."

"They are what they are and their crowns only contribute to their painful mistakes," Seshena whispered. "Nefertiry came to me begging for help, but the help she sought had vengeance at its core, and I couldn't give her that. I gave her a substitute to placate her instead."

Rasuah turned to look at Seshena and put his arm under his head. "Neither Nefertiry nor Ramessa knows what to do with love," he murmured. "Before they met they had never seen love's face. They always thought love was what a man and woman did when they lie together, not knowing love is what lifts them from pleasure into ecstasy."

Seshena closed her eyes. "Yet they need to learn this more than any two people I've met," she said. "The destiny of an entire kingdom could rest on whether they learn it."

"The kingdom's destiny never rests on one man's head, even though he wears the crown," Rasuah said softly. "But I need no temple training to foretell a great sadness. I can feel it in my blood, as I feel the nearness of Tamera's shores when I'm returning from a journey." He was silent a moment. Then, he sat up and leaned over her. "I sometimes feel like a jackal waiting for his victim to fall before I can claim what I want."

Seshena opened her eyes to look up at him. She lifted
364

a hand to touch the side of his face. "We're the opposite of that," she said softly. "We delay our happiness, so we may concentrate on helping them, but the gods ask too much of me. I cannot teach Ramessa and Nefertiry how to love with their spirits."

"How could we direct the king and queen to lie under the papyrus like this talking quietly while they fill their souls with each other's being as we do?" he whispered, turning his head to kiss her hand. "No, we cannot teach them this thing which must arise from their own hearts."

"It is too sad, their loneliness," she murmured, moving closer as he pulled her to him and put his arms securely around her.

Seshena gazed up at Rasuah's eyes, which were lit to streaks of bright gold by the sunlight falling through the swaying papyrus. "Will no one come here?" she asked.

"This is my land, inherited from my father," he replied. "No one comes here." Then, he bent closer, slowly bringing the warmth of his lips to hers.

21

The day Reshet had strolled through the royal garden on Ramessa's arm she had seen and recognized Nefertiry. Reshet was surprised that Nefertiry had paled and averted her eyes, like any woman of the harem, too timid to speak or do anything but clasp her son close to her breast. Reshet had decided then that Nefertiry's fierce reputation was exaggerated. But later, as she was about to tell the king she had begun his child, Nefertiry's servant came for him and he left at her call.

As the days crept by and Ramessa neither returned to her nor sent a message, Reshet began to fear that Nefertiry had somehow won him back. She shuddered at the thought of being brushed aside like an object, used and discarded. How could she return to her father's house with a child—even a royal child—growing within her? The child would be living evidence she had been the king's mistress, one not even well enough regarded to be given any official recognition. What man of any prominence would seriously consider her for marriage, now? As the daughter of an old and honored family, of the governor of a rich province, she couldn't marry beneath her station. What humiliation and what loneliness there would be in her future if she were to remain unmarried with an il-legitimate child. How foolish she had been to be so flattered by her king's attention that she'd allowed herself to surrender to him. He had given her the chance to refuse, yet she had been excited by his advances. Upon surrendering to him, she had found he'd awakened a physical need in her she'd never before known. Soon she discovered that she loved him.

But Nefertiry had waved a hand and Ramessa had left Reshet, and each day's passing seemed less likely to bring him back.

One of Reshet's servants returned from a trip to the marketplace one morning and announced she'd heard a proclamation that the king and the queen were to sit in open audience the next morning, Reshet decided to go to court and take another look at her rival.

After a night in which sleep was impossible, Reshet rose to dress. She donned a simple gown that would help her blend into the crowd. Covering her rich hair with a thick veil, she went to the palace to wait in the midst of the throng in the golden throne room until her rulers appeared.

"On your faces and be silent!" called Henhenet. "King Ramessa, son of Ra, and Queen Nefertiry approach!"

Reshet knelt and bent her face as low as the others, but her eyes were lifted to watch the doorway. Reshet's heart seemed to lose the rhythm of its beat when the doors opened and Ramessa stood tall and regal in his white and gold robes of state. Were those hands holding the scepters crossed over his chest the same hands that had caressed her? Were those imperial lips the same ones that had kissed her and whispered love words in her ear? He seemed like a different being in the throne room, a separate creature from the man who had laughed with her and
368

bathed with her and loved with her. Reshet took a deep breath and reminded herself she had never before seen him in his crown and court robes, and she tried to convince herself that was why he seemed like a stranger to her. But as she watched him walk down the row of guards toward the throne, she felt as if a stone had been placed on her heart.

Once Ramessa mounted the royal dais and stood for a moment, running his eyes over the crowd, Reshet turned her attention to Nefertiry. Reshet wondered if she was living a dream that was rapidly becoming a nightmare. This wasn't the woman she'd seen in the garden, not this regal creature standing so confidently at the king's side, not this woman whose head serenely wore the gleaming double crown. Those cool, green eyes never had been downcast; they weren't capable of it. Those full, red lips could never have shown fear or humiliation.

By the time Ramessa and Nefertiry had seated themselves on their thrones and the crowd was allowed to rise, Reshet felt like a ghost standing among mortals, able to see and hear, but invisible and silent. Ramessa and Nefertiry leaned closer to each other to whisper and smile, and a ripple of whispers went through the crowd, surprised murmurs that the rift had been mended—for many stories, concerning palace gossip, had flown through Wast's streets.

Reshet didn't hear the whispers. She wished she could leave now, but knew her lone departure would attract too many eyes. She was trapped in the nightmare.

"Lord Sebeko, governor of Khent-Abt Province! Mekmel, Prince of Akkad!"

Reshet automatically raised her head at the prime minister's commanding announcement and wondered distractedly if Henhenet's expression was always so austere. Then her eyes shifted to the two men bowing before the thrones, and she tried to imagine how it must feel to have princes and noblemen prostrate themselves at your feet.

"Rise," Ramessa ordered. "Why have you come, Prince Mekmel? Has your father appointed you ambassador?"

"Illustrious ruler, my father King Ninurta sends you his greetings and all good wishes. I've come to discuss a matter too complicated and personal to entrust to a mere ambassador," Mekmel answered with some difficulty. He took a breath and apologized, "My knowledge of your language is a struggle to my tongue, and Lord Sebeko has accompanied me to explain the problem in my stead. If he forgets something, I'll add to it. For although my mouth is awkward with your words, my ears understand them."

Ramessa nodded and looked at Sebeko. "Describe the problem," he said.

Sebeko decided, since his king and queen appeared amiable and whatever problems they'd had seemed at least temporarily resolved, he'd best include Nefertiry in his address. "Radiant majesties, who are the rudder of the kingdom—"

At Sebeko's words, Reshet couldn't help but shudder. Was Nefertiry queen in reality as the whole land had whispered. How could a foreign woman be queen. Was Ramessa, after all, that enamoured with Nefertiry? No. It was merely more of this evil dream she was experiencing.

"I'm involved as more than interpreter in this matter," Sebeko went on, "because my province is nearest of all Tamera's provinces to the valley of the two rivers. King Tukulti of Assur has charged that King Ninurta of Akkad has stolen one of his wives. King Tukulti has demanded the woman be returned, although King Ninurta has repeatedly denied having ever seen the woman. King Tukulti has threatened King Ninurta with an invasion, and the situation has become so acute a war seems imminent. Since your majesty's words carry weight with King Tukulti, King Ninurta begs you to send him a message advising him of his error."

Ramessa smiled faintly. His words certainly did carry weight both in Assur and Akkad, which though foreign

370

kingdoms were little more than provinces of Tamera, because their kings feared Ramessa's military might, and had practically become his own administrators. Ramessa looked at Mekmel. "Is this woman in your father's hands?" he asked bluntly.

"No, majesty," Mekmel replied.

Ramessa lifted his eyebrows at Mekmel's downcast eyes, which had remained on his feet even while he'd answered. Ramessa leaned closer to Nefertiry and whispered, "I think the prince lies for his father's sake."

"He has a look of guilt," she murmured.

In a louder tone Ramessa announced, "Women are plentiful enough in most lands. Is there a shortage of females in your valley kingdoms that you must wage war over one woman?"

Hearing Ramessa's words made Reshet's heart constrict in humiliation. Did he have such freedom with women that he could feel that way? she wondered. But she knew Ramessa held so much power that, if he'd stolen one of Tukulti's wives, Tukulti would dare not mention a word of it.

Mekmel's dark eyes lifted to Ramessa's face. "King Tukulti regards the matter as a personal insult," he said slowly.

"It seems to me if one of these kings stopped the river leading to the other's city, that would be a matter to fight over. But not the abduction or escape of one woman," Ramessa said drily.

Even Nefertiry was surprised at Ramessa's casual attitude on this matter. Would he be as tolerant if she were to leave him for Khakamir, she wondered.

"It's a matter of the pride between two very stubborn men," Mekmel admitted.

Ramessa sighed. "I don't care if Tukulti and Ninurta fight between themselves," he said impatiently. "If Tukulti captures Akkad or Ninurta takes Assur, what does it matter to Tamera? As long as they both obey me, I don't care about their fights among themselves. If one of them threatened me, then I would move to crush him."

"Majesty, they may possibly threaten Khent-Abt Province," Sebeko said hesitantly.

"Why?" Ramessa asked in surprise. "You're far enough to the west of their possible battleground."

Sebeko coughed self-consciously, then murmured, "The lady in question recently fled over Tamera's borders and is hiding in Tahalu—my own city."

"How foolish of you!" Ramessa declared. "Since the woman belongs to King Tukulti, she must be returned to him, and quickly."

Nefertiry leaned closer to Ramessa's shoulder and murmured in his ear, "If you send a few of your soldiers to escort the lady back to Assur, they'll represent your whole army in both Tukulti and Ninurta's eyes. I suspect, then, the matter would be spoken of not again."

Ramessa smiled at Nefertiry's suggestion and ordered, "A squad of soldiers from Khent-Abt regiment will be sent back with you to Tahalu. They will escort the lady in question to Assur and deliver her to King Tukulti."

Prince Mekmel's eyes had flared with anger at this decision. Sebeko quickly said, "Yes, majesty. You are wise." Then, he took Mekmel's arm in a tight grip and promptly drew him back into the crowd.

Ramessa looked expectantly at Henhenet, but the prime minister had stepped to the side of the room to consult with someone Ramessa recognized as a courier.

Henhenet sent the courier away, then approached the dais.

Henhenet announced, "Lord Metenu, governor of Sun-Amenti Province! Minister Rehi!"

"Rise," Ramessa directed the prostrated officials. He pointed his sceptor at Metenu and instructed, "You will speak first."

"Majesty, my province is on the western border and for over a year we've been receiving refugees from Djemeh until there are hordes of these alien people settling in Sun-Amenti."

"Why do they come?" Ramessa inquired.

"Majesty, they're improverished in their own land, they claim. They beg to begin new lives in Tamera, promising to be obedient to your divine laws," Metenu replied.

"Djemeh seems to be in a constant state of famine," Ramessa said drily. "Proceed."

"Once these people are established in my cities, they seek no work, but steal the goods Tamera's hands have fashioned and pull up the vegetables Tamera's soil has produced. They sneer at your laws and won't work unless forced, then in a grudging manner. Instead of gratitude we have to endure their jealousy and hatred, their greed and eternally empty bellies."

Again Nefertiry leaned close to Ramessa and murmured, "Whispers of this problem have already reached my ears. The attitude of these people from Djemeh has become a sore on Tameran backs. I have heard the people in Metenu's province fear to step out on the streets at night because there are many robberies and more than one son of Tamera has been murdered."

Ramessa looked at Metenu and asked, "Why don't you eject the troublemakers? How do these people continue to flood into Tamera?"

Metenu took a breath, looked at Rehi and said angrily, "Minister Rehi protects them."

Ramessa's eyes moved to Rehi as he asked, "What have you to answer?"

"How could I protect them? I'm only an official on the frontier, just one man!" Rehi said hotly. "Governor Metenu hopes to cover his own failings with that charge." Turning to glare at Henhenet, he asked, "Will you not speak for me?"

"What do you have to say about this matter, Henhenet?" Ramessa inquired.

"Minister Rehi speaks the truth," Henhenet said firmly. "Lord Metenu blames Rehi for his own failure to keep order. If he stirred himself to investigate whatever crimes have been committed and issued punishments, he wouldn't have this trouble."

"Every time I send my helpers on an investigation, the complaint vanishes like smoke in the wind!" Metenu cried. "My own people are terrified to come forward and give evidence, because those few that had the courage to do so were attacked, some completely disappeared!"

"No, no." Henhenet waved a discrediting hand. "Those people who disappeared no doubt merely moved to another location."

"The petty pilferings that have actually been traced to the Djemeh people are due to their hunger and need," Rehi declared. "If they were put to work, if they were properly clothed and fed, even these disturbances would be ended. But Lord Metenu privately applauds each time the Tam-eran peasants and merchants turn away one of these people seeking work."

"Majesties, there are too many of them!" Metenu declared. "Shall I remove my own people from their shops and farms and establish these others in their place?"

"There's work enough for all of them," Henhenet said quietly. "There are public projects needing workers—a new park being built, a road to be paved, a temple being erected."

Metenu's mouth dropped momentarily. Then his eyes relit with a warlike gleam. "He lies!" he exclaimed. "The park is a small one, only enough to occupy five workers. The road has already been paved by the crews your majesty himself assigned. This temple the prime minister speaks of is merely a chapel, a small and private place of worship to be constructed in my own garden. I planned to have it dedicated to the patron of my province. Shall I have these Djemeh thieves and murderers construct a holy place?" he cried, outraged.

"Metenu is the liar!" Rehi declared. "He tells you stories to cover his own——"

"Silence, Rehi," Nefertiry suddenly commanded. "Your

tongue is like a race horse. The less it carries the faster it runs." She turned to Ramessa, who was regarding her with an amused expression.

"What do you know of this that hasn't been said here?" he asked, smiling faintly.

"I know Rehi is paid by each refugee that enters Tamera," Nefertiry said clearly. "He collects a horde of followers, who will do whatever he asks of them, so they can remain in Tamera, living an easy life." She glanced pointedly at Henhenet. "I also recall that Rehi was highly recommended for this particular office by no other than Henhenet. I wonder how much gold from Djemeh Henhenet's accounting room contains."

"That's not true!" Henhenet declared, his face flushed and twisted with anger at Nefertiry. "I swore an oath upon taking office that I would show favor to no man!"

"Various cases of questionable turnings can be traced perilously close to the prime minister. But he, who should be aware of all important business in the land, has no knowledge of so many transactions which take place under his very nose," Nefertiry remarked. She looked at Ramessa and added, "Like Paser's double accounts."

Ramessa was thoughtful a moment before saying, "I will dispatch Lord Rasuah to Sun-Amenti Province to investigate this matter. Lord Metenu and Minister Rehi will remain in Wast until Lord Rasuah returns with his report."

Metenu backed away, looking relieved. He knew about Rasuah's reputation for honesty and thoroughness, and he was confident what that report would contain.

Rehi retreated, lowering his eyes to hide the terror in them. He wondered how he could flee Wast before Rasuah returned.

Henhenet had carefully removed the anger from his face and wore a mask revealing nothing of his thoughts as he stepped away to consult with the scribes, who were recording the audience. But even as he spoke to Amten, his mind was on whether it would be wiser to hire some of

Rehi's Djemeh thieves or pay a band of Shardanan to make sure Rasuah never reported back to the king. He recalled how Rasuah had disposed of the Shardanan who had attacked him the night Setnau was born, and he decided in favor of the Djemeh, whose crescent-shaped swords posed a different threat.

Reshet had paid little attention to the debate, but when Henhenet announced that the twin temples in the south would be finished in two decans, and that one would be consecrated to Ramessa and Amen-Ra and the other to Nefertiry and Hat-Hor, Reshet listened intently. Recalling the rumors she'd heard—that Ramessa would have the second temple dedicated to honor Setnau's birth, Reshet thought again of the arrival of her own child and contemplated his possible gloomy future if he were only the king's illegitimate child. How could Ramessa give anything to a child he didn't know existed? In that moment she resolved to send Ramessa a message, as Nefertiry had done. When he came, she would tell him about his coming heir. Maybe, Reshet speculated once she had Ramessa in her arms, she could find some way to keep him there.

Although it was the twilight hour when Seshena came to Rasuah's house, he still wasn't home. But Djanah admitted her and invited her to wait on the terrace where a cooling wind blew.

Perched on the wall where Rasuah usually sat while he waited for her, Seshena watched the river's lazily swirling currents pass. As she dropped her gaze to the slope below, where the wind parted the grass into dark green undulations like the waves of the sea, a man's figure appeared on the next hill silhouetted by the sky's glowing. The set of the man's shoulders and the smooth swinging of his walk marked him as Rasuah. The sun caught fire on the sword at his hip and remained there, rhythmically flashing with his stride. And she fancied that Ra, before passing from the land, had given Rasuah his divine light to carry in his stead. When Rasuah came closer and she could see the glint of his golden eyes, she decided he did carry Ra's fire, but in his soul. He leaped lightly over the wall and held out his arms.

Seshena went into them like a dove returning to her nest and remained within their warm circle for a long moment before murmuring, "I was watching you walk, and I forgot to pour wine for you as you've always done for me after I've climbed that slope."

"Your perfume is refreshment enough," Rasuah said, burying his face in her hair.

"You're troubled," she observed in a soft tone. "Why, beloved?"

"I don't want to travel north tomorrow," he said quietly and released her.

Turning to pour a goblet of wine, she said softly, "It's more than that."

Rasuah took the goblet from her and nodded. "Yes, Ramessa just told me he's thinking of sending two expeditions to Punt, a caravan across the eastern desert and a fleet of ships on the Narrow Sea, in case the caravan is attacked by Shasu and doesn't make it."

"Is the danger in crossing the desert that great?" Seshena asked.

"Even the gods must take steps to protect themselves from the Shasu." Rasuah sighed and sipped his wine. "I have no doubt, when he starts making the actual plans, the king will ask me to go on one of the ships. A journey like that would take almost a year."

Seshena was silent for a moment while she thought about the loneliness of such a year. Finally she said, "Maybe by that time the trouble here will be resolved and I'll be able to accompany you."

Rasuah took another sip of wine, then lowered his goblet to stare into it a long moment before he said, "I hope that will be the case. I don't want to leave you for two decans, much less a year. A year is a long time and you might be attracted by another man." When she opened her mouth to argue, he raised his hand to silence her.

"Wast is filled with men who would throw themselves at your feet, and I know better than you how the physical need for love can grow into a pain that can make you forget many things."

Shaking her head, she took a step closer and put her hands at his waist. "Your body taught me the delights of love, I admit. I know so long a separation would find me aching for it, but, beloved, no matter how my body might pain me, no one else could give me relief. During that first night we spent together, your seal was stamped on my soul for eternity." She paused, lowered her eyes for a moment, and whispered, "If such a separation should come, beloved, what of you? You're too passionate a man to remain unaffected."

Rasuah put his hands gently on each side of her face. "When I was in Nehren, often my need of you became so strong it was like a living thing; and I paced the floor restlessly at night, wondering if I could endure it, wishing for but a glimpse of you. I saw beautiful women every day in Pekharu's house. I looked at this one's grace and knew yours surpassed it. I looked at that one's eyes, and they were as nothing when I remembered yours. Some smiled warmly in my direction, but they didn't tempt me, because none of them were you. So if I must go to Punt alone, during such moments I will say your name aloud while I pace. Its sound is like fire to me. It will warm my cold flesh and give light to my darkness."

When Rasuah finished speaking, Seshena moved away a few steps and stared at him.

"You already know my soul," Rasuah said quietly. "I'm surprised that you back away as if my words amaze you."

"They're so beautiful I have no answer to them," she whispered.

"Our first kiss meant nothing less than love. I knew it and restrained myself out of awe for what I also knew would come. Now it's here, and I'm as caught by you as the music of those bells from the temple below are caught by the wind," he said. He was silent a moment before add-

378

ing softly, "I think, if I were dead, your message of love would come winging to me even through the heavy fabric of that veil. There will never exist another who can possess my heart as you have."

The wind caught his thick hair and lifted it from his brow. He closed his eyes, enjoying the night's fragrance. He felt Seshena touch his hand and her perfume spread around him like a cloud.

"Your hand on mine unquiets my heart," he murmured. "Perhaps it's your presence that weaves a spell on this night." He opened his eyes and looked down at her. "As unhappy as I was when I left Ramessa, my worries have dropped away like a cloak I've discarded."

She looked up at his tawny eyes and raised her hand to brush his cheek. Her hand trembled unashamedly. "How you affect me!" she breathed. "Just to touch you—look at how I am!"

"And once I compared you with a gazelle I feared would flee from me."

She moved a little closer, until her body was against his, and she could feel his strength. "You have kisses awaiting my lips?" she asked quietly.

Rasuah's hand reached up to catch a tendril of her hair. He was silent as he wound its black silk around his finger. "They are there. But another question needs answering first." She looked up at him expectantly. "You know, don't you, how long it will take before the trouble passes the land, and we can be bound together by our laws?"

"Bast has recently given me far-seeing eyes," she admitted quietly.

"How long?"

"Before this year has ended," she said quietly.

Rasuah slid his arms around her waist. "I plan to leave for the north before the sun rises. You will stay here with me and fill those hours with more than sleeping?" he asked, knowing her answer. When she nodded, he bent closer until his mouth was but a breath from hers, and said, "Those kisses I withheld now demand release."

He moved no nearer, but waited for her kiss, and she reached up to give it gladly.

"I wonder where the king has been these last few days," Nefertiry murmured, as Chenmet massaged her back.

"Perhaps his majesty is occupied with arrangements for the temple dedications," Chenmet suggested.

Nefertiry rolled over and looked up at the servant. "If he doesn't speak to me soon, I won't know what I'm expected to do during the ceremonies." Sitting up, she swung her legs from the table, where she sat dangling her feet for a moment, reflecting on the ritual's possibilities.

"I'm sure someone will describe what you must do, my lady," Chenmet said gently.

There was a peculiar huskiness in Chenmet's voice that aroused Nefertiry's suspicions. As she raised her head to study her maid, a shadow in Chenmet's dark eyes was instantly hidden. "Tell me what you've heard," Nefertiry said softly, taking the robe the servant offered her.

"My lady—" Chenmet stopped and nervously bit her lip.

Nefertiry slid down from the table and commanded, "Tell me, Chenmet."

The maid looked plaintively at Nefertiry. "My lady, I can tell you little."

"Tell me," Nefertiry insisted.

Chenmet hung her head and murmured, "Three days ago his majesty received a message. He left the palace immediately afterwards and hasn't since returned."

Nefertiry's hands took a firm grasp on the maid's shoulders. "Was it a sealed message?" The miserable servant shook her head. "Then whoever in the palace carried it to the king read it. What did it say?"

"Nehri took it, my lady," Chenmet whispered.

"Bring Nehri to me," Nefertiry directed, releasing the maid. "And send a guard to find Kakamir!"

Chenmet almost ran from the room. Nefertiry was sure she knew what the message contained, but she had to
380

have it confirmed. At the thought of it, she knotted the sash of her robe so tight that she almost tore it. Then, she began to pace back and forth until Chenmet returned, almost dragging the unhappy Nehri. Nefertiry whirled on her heel to face them.

"What did that message say?" she demanded. "Remember its wording accurately, or I'll assure you never again ride in the king's chariot."

Nehri's lips trembled with fear as he whispered, "The message said his majesty must come as quickly as possible to the Lady Reshet's house."

Nefertiry felt as if something exploded inside her. "That miserable creature called, and he went back to wallow with her!" she cried. "He's been with her these last three days, leaving the kingdom for me to rule while he ruts with her like a bull after a cow! I make myself a hundred enemies keeping the realm in order—enemies that imperil my very life—and the kingdom regards me as 'that foreign woman who usurps the throne.' And that slut rolls around with him in bed, or wherever they do their rolling!" Nefertiry struck a tray of cosmetics, dashing them to the floor, where they shattered. "What good are these to me." she screamed. "What good are all the skills at love I've shown him!"

At the sound of the crash, Khakamir, who was approaching her chamber, flung open the door and raced into the room to stare at Nefertiry. "Divine lady, what happened?" he asked in alarm.

"I'll kill her," Nefertiry said viciously. "I'll kill her! There's no other way to rid him of the spell she's cast on him."

Khakamir walked cautiously closer. "Divine lady, what are you talking about? Whom do you wish to kill?" But, suddenly he realized that Nefertiry had at last heard about Ramessa's going to Reshet, and he stopped.

"You knew about it," Nefertiry said in a menacingly quiet tone. "From the look on your face, I'll wager you know more even than the servants." She took a step toward Khakamir. "You will tell me everything!"

Khakamir glanced at the two servants. "What you wish to hear, I think, is better told in private," he said quietly.

Nefertiry turned to the servants. "Get out."

Chenmet and Nehri, exchanging frightened glances, turned to rush out of Nefertiry's chamber. Once in the corridor, Chenmet leaned against the wall and began to weep quietly. But Nehri put his ear to the door and listened, regretting he could only hear the queen's voice when she raised it to a scream.

"Reshet is pregnant," Khakamir said softly.

"How do you know?" Nefertiry cried.

"You've been shielded from this knowledge, but everyone else knows," Khakamir replied. "The king has made no secret of it."

Again Nefertiry began to pace furiously. "When will it come? How long do I have to think of a way to end it?"

"You mustn't think such things," Khakamir said softly.

"I will stop her!" Nefertiry declared. "She won't take my place—she cannot! Her child will not steal Setnau's crown from him!"

A look of inner pain flashed over Khakamir's face as he said, "There's more."

Nefertiry stopped pacing to stare at him. "More! What more can she do to me?" she cried, putting her fists against Khakamir's chest as if she wanted to beat him, but restrained herself. "Tell me!"

Khakamir took a breath. "Leave Tamera with me as I asked," he pleaded. "Put this misery behind us."

"What more?" Nefertiry cried.

"Perhaps knowing all of it will make you decide in my favor," he muttered. "Reshet has asked that a temple be built for her son, if she has one, and the king seems inclined to grant her wish."

Nefertiry stamped her foot and cried, "She'll have no temple! She won't have a crown! Sutekh will get her first!" Wanting to destroy something, anything, she
382

picked up a large alabaster urn and threw it on the floor, shattering it. "She'll have nothing—nothing but a mummy case!" she screamed.

"Nefertiry, the servants will hear you!" Khakamir warned. "Please try to calm yourself!"

Nefertiry lowered a vase she held poised. "You're right, Khakamir. I don't want my head separated from my neck when her corpse is found."

Khakamir took the vase from her and put it on a table. Then, placing his hands on her shoulders, he said urgently, but quietly, "Please, Nefertiry, come with me and put all this unhappiness behind us."

She shrugged off his hands. "Not yet, Khakamir. I will not leave Tamera defeated and humiliated." She turned away, took a deep, ragged breath, and brushed back her disheveled hair. Although Khakamir was relieved she seemed more composed, his relief faded when she lifted her eyes to meet his. They were hard and glittering like green glass.

"Someone must find the king and remind him that we must soon leave for the south to dedicate the temples," she said tightly. "Send someone to him, Khakamir, someone who won't know I'm the dispatcher of this message."

Khakamir looked at her uncertainly and asked, "Are you all right now?"

"I have recovered myself," she answered. "When you leave, send Chenmet back to me."

"You have put aside this idea," he hesitated, hating to say the words, "of killing Reshet?" When she gave no answer, a trickle of cold sweat ran between his shoulder-blades and his body stiffened. "If you do kill Reshet, Ramessa would be forced to punish you," he whispered. "Nefertiry, he's the king!"

"And I am the queen, whether he knows it or not," she said bitterly. "If Ramessa doesn't know I'm the queen, the gods know it." She fixed him with her stare and added coldly, "Wadjet, the royal cobra, knows what I am—and Reshet will know Wadjet's sting."

Seshena watched the double line of Amen-Ra's priests making their way up the hill toward Ramessa's new temple and felt revulsion coil around her soul as if it was a snake wrapping itself around her ankles. The bright saffron robes, supposed to remind the priests of their spiritual allegiance with the ruler of warmth and light was a mockery hanging from those shoulders, Seshena thought—except for Khenti. His was the only body housing a soul that deserved the honor. As if Amen agreed and had made the other priests as ugly in their bodies as they were in their souls, Khenti was the only one whose robe didn't make his skin sallow and dead-looking. The complexion of the other priests reminded Seshena of the color of duck fat. To hear these twisted and corrupt priests piously chanting the Litany of Ra's praises made Seshena's stomach rise. To see Ramessa and Nefertiry leading a trail of such creatures to a temple to sanctify it made Seshena shudder.

"Praise be to thee, O Ra, exalted power, destroyer of thy enemies; thou art he who decrees destruction for the wicked. . . ."

Seshena watched Ramessa and wondered what his thoughts were as he paced beside the wife he had ignored for more than a decan. He had come to Nefertiry from Reshet's bed. What could they speak of when they were alone, Seshena wondered. Perhaps nothing had been said, perhaps they never were alone, she thought. Nefertiry looked today like a statue incapable of speech. Her face seemed frozen in its dignity. Her eyes were without life.

"Praise be to thee, O Ra, exalted power, thou shining one who sends forth light upon the waters of heaven."

Akeset walked slowly toward where Seshena and her priestesses waited, his face set in a solemn expression, although his eyes glittered like beads of jet, and around his thin lips played the shadow of a smile. Seshena wondered what evil he was plotting even while he sang of the glories of the god he betrayed.

384

"Praise be to thee, O Ra, exalted power, who stands up, the First Soul who avenges his children."

Seshena glanced in signal at the priestess beside her; and Amset began to shake her sistrum softly as a warning to the other priestesses that they would soon enter the temple.

"I don't care to follow on the heels of such as they," Amset whispered.

"Indeed, it's as pleasant as following a herd of camels, but we must do it," Seshena muttered.

Amset smothered her smile at the high priestess' remark and nodded. "The king and queen lead them, so what can we do?"

"We can weigh each prayer that the disgusting one mouths and measure its meaning," Seshena mumbled.

Amset gave her a startled glance, but said nothing more, for Seshena had turned to fall in behind the priests entering Ramessa's temple.

"Praise be to thee, O Ra, exalted power, exalted of soul; thou destroyest thy enemies; thou sendest fire on the wicked."

The priests' chanting voices bounced off the ceilings and walls of the vast, colonnaded room as if they made the prayer a challenge to Ra to destroy them and, finding their challenge unanswered, went boldly into the temple, defying the divine being they were supposed to serve.

As Seshena's eyes scanned the carvings covering the temple walls, she observed that they depicted Ramessa's triumphs in battle almost solely. She sighed, wondering if Ramessa ever thought about anything other than war and love, wishing her ethics didn't forbid her entering his mind to discover what it contained. Did Nefertiry look at those scenes and bitterly remember the humiliation of being given to Ramessa? Was she comforted by the fact that the carvings of herself were as tall beside Ramessa as she was in reality, instead of being shown as a small figure dwarfed by the king as was usual?

At last the Praises of Ra were ended, as the company

stopped in the chamber just outside the open door to the sanctuary. Seshena shuddered again to see Akeset walk beside Ramessa into the holy place.

While Akeset began the prayer before the consecration, Seshena looked about the room in which she and her priestesses waited with Nefertiry. Mounds of yellow poppies banked the walls so high that the feet of the persons in the carvings were covered by the bright flowers and Ramessa's chariot wheels seemed to glide through a summer meadow. Garlands made of almond leaves, one leaf up, the next down, so the effect was of alternating dull and bright leafs, were twined around the columns while strings of mandrake leaves and its pale yellow fruit festooned the ceiling. Seshena wondered that all the torches attached to the wall—hooded so as not to stain the carvings with their smoke—would not too soon wilt the fragile flowers.

"Homage to thee, O thou greatest of all the divine beings, who art crowned king in Tuat."

Seshena sighed. Akeset would go through all the attributes of Amen and Ra separately. She wondered if he did this so as to deliberately pass the hour appointed for the dedication of Nefertiry's temple and thus shorten the tributes he anticipated Seshena would offer Nefertiry. Seshena shifted from one foot to the other, and wondered if Amset shared her restlessness. She glanced at Amset with lifted eyebrows, and the priestess nodded in agreement. Their own ritual would certainly be delayed.

"Hail to thee, Amen-Ra, maker of all things; thou art the protection of thy people of Tamera," Akeset prayed. "Thou art the lord of the throne of the Two Lands; thou shinest on the children of our true blood; thou brings fire to the pretenders; thou vanquishes the imposters; thou strikes down the usurpers of thy throne!"

Seshena's eyes widened at Akeset's effrontery. He dared, under the guise of making a prayer of protection, to denounce Nefertiry as a foreigner, her child as an imposter about to usurp the throne.

"Praises to thee, O Amen-Ra, lord of the horizon, mighty one of victory, whose name is sweet on the lips, who makes an end of the false ones, who protects Ramessa, Lord of the Two Lands, who protects the beloved of our king and awards divine Ramessa, the son of his heart, for the crown!"

How Nefertiry must be raging at this public denunciation of her royalty and Setnau's inheritance, Seshena thought.

"High one, how does he dare—" Amset's shocked whisper came to Seshena's ear like a hiss.

Seshena silenced Amset with a look, then sent the priestess the comforting thought that Akeset's prayer might well be amended in her own invocation yet to come.

Amset's fingers trembled so violently she had to struggle to concentrate on the rhythm of shaking her sistrum while she watched the king and queen lead the procession from the temple. The king's face was solemn, but serene, as if he'd not understood Akeset's full meaning. The queen's face was empty, her eyes wide and blank. Amset saw Akeset glance once at Seshena, then turn away, a smug expression on his face.

When the procession stepped into the sunlight and turned toward Nefertiry's temple, Akeset and his priests stepped aside so Seshena and her priestesses could walk behind Ramessa and Nefertiry. Amset glanced at Seshena to see what her face contained as she passed Akeset. She noted that Seshena's eyes had ignited with blue fire, her mouth curved neither up nor down, but she had raised her proud head yet a little higher, and her white-robed shoulders were set defiantly straighter.

"We won't chant as we'd planned," Seshena advised. "We'll sing about Aset's powers."

"But, high one, this is a temple to Hat-Hor," Amset whispered.

"Aset is Hat-Hor as well as Wadjet and also Sekhmet." Seshena began to sing in a clear, light voice, praising

387

Aset as the cobra that protected the crown and the lioness who guarded justice.

Amset smiled faintly and joined Seshena in the song about divine cobra stings and sacred claws—a stern reminder to Akeset to watch his place, she concluded. She glanced down at Seshena's hands, which were twining a length of blue cord into a series of protective magical knots as she walked.

When they entered Nefertiry's temple, Seshena stopped singing, and the other priestesses obeyed her unspoken orders to remain silent. As they paced soundlessly through the lotus-decked rooms of the temple, only the silvery voices of the sistrums and the soft snapping of the torches were heard.

At the door of the sanctuary, Seshena turned to face Nefertiry. "You will enter with me," she instructed. Nefertiry stared at Seshena in surprise and Seshena whispered, "Are you not queen?" Then Seshena took Nefertiry's elbow in a firm grasp and led her into the sacred chamber amid the hushed whispers of Akeset's priests, who thought Nefertiry of too low a status to enter a sanctuary, not knowing her claim to the throne was as firm as Ramessa's. Seshena drew the still hesitating queen to the offering table, then turned to her.

"You will lay your head and shoulders on the offering table," Seshena directed. "My queen's offering of her own self to the goddess is a far better gift than a bouquet of flowers," she said. Then she put her hands on Nefertiry's shoulders and firmly pushed her down to the table. "Remain bending there, however uncomfortable, until I'm finished," she whispered.

Hearing a new murmur rise from the ranks of Akeset's priests, Nefertiry knew what Seshena intended to do disturbed them, and she resolved that, no matter how uncomfortable she became, she would remain where Seshena placed her. Any distress she could cause Akeset was worth a few stiffened muscles.

Seshena stepped back a pace and lowered herself to

her knees, her robe making a white circle around her. She bent to touch her forehead to the floor at the base of the table, knowing Akeset never prostrated himself before the figure of Amen-Ra. She smiled and lifted her head to the statue of Hat-Hor.

"Hail, great mother of creation! Thy face is the second sun in heaven. Thy star is the light in Ra's crown which guides him. Hail, great divine one, thy veil has not been loosed. Unloose thy veil and reveal thy face for me!"

Seshena got up and turned to the censer at the foot of the statue. The scent of burning incense rose in gray curls of smoke that floated over the priests in a fragrant cloud.

Seshena lifted her arms to the goddess and declared, "My eyes are the eyes of Hat-Hor. My wings are the wings of Aset; my soul is the soul of Bast. My nails are the claws of Sekhmet; my teeth are the fangs of Wadjet."

At this, another murmur arose from the priests, and Seshena could hear their feet uneasily shifting around. They knew well enough that what Seshena was doing was far from merely consecrating the temple to Hat-Hor.

Seshena raised triumphant eyes to the statue of the goddess and spoke in a compelling tone, "Hat-Hor, mistress of Tuat, lady of the temple, I offer thee this daughter of Ra, Mut-Nefertiry. She is a daughter known to her mother; she lives in the house of Aset; behold, the goddess of united faces is with her!"

Seshena laid her hands on Nefertiry's head and declared, "Daughter of Hat-Hor, thou art made to triumph. Hat-Hor has made thy face perfect among the company of divine beings. She shall make thy place; every divine being will take the hand of Mut-Nefertiry. They conduct her to the Mistress of Light and Mut-Nefertiry's words shall be heard in Tuat!"

Seshena lifted her hands from Nefertiry's head and whispered, "You may now rise."

Nefertiry turned her head to the side and murmured, "If my priestess will discreetly help me, I think I can manage it."

389

Seshena took Nefertiry's arm and helped her to stand up, then turned toward the waiting priests and priestesses with a smug smile on her face. As she led Nefertiry from the sanctuary she chanted, "Hail, mother of mothers, great lady of the south, who gave birth to Ra, who made the seed of gods and men, who thus created that which exists, this temple is thy house! She who came from herself, who is everything which has been, lives now in this place and makes it holy! Mistress of light, who has loosed thy veil for our queen, Daughter of Ra—"

When Seshena walked past Akeset, her smile widened, though she didn't cast her glance toward him.

Nefertiry rejoined Ramessa with a springier step. She held his arm tightly as they led the procession from the temple. She didn't let loose of his arm until they stepped again into the sunlight. Then, she relinquished her hold on him to go to Seshena.

"For what you did, I haven't enough thanks," Nefertiry whispered.

"I merely obey Aset as always," Seshena murmured. From within the folds of her robe she produced the blue cord, now in a series of intricate loops knotted together. "Take this charm I have made for your protection," she said in an even softer tone. "Keep it with you always. Even though I consecrated your soul to divinity, your body is still mortal. I suspect Akeset now more than ever longs to rid himself of you."

"But what of you?" Nefertiry whispered, taking the cord. "He must hate you as much as me!"

"He doesn't know I'm anything more than loyal to my queen," Seshena replied. "In any case, Tuat's penalty for murdering Aset's high priestess would be terrible. Weak though Akeset's faith may be, he wouldn't want to kill me for being a nuisance."

Nefertiry considered this a moment, then asked, "Will you ride in my compartment on the royal ship back to Wast?"

"I must remain with my priestesses on our ship," she
390

answered. "There are things we must yet do together. Won't the king be with you?"

"Ramessa will be on the ship, but I won't share his company. He avoids me," Nefertiry replied. "Will you, then, sit at my side during the celebration banquet?"

"I'll be there," Seshena answered and, bowing her head to Nefertiry, backed away.

Beyond the mountains in the east the sun was just beginning to weave a faint orange thread into the blackness, giving earth the hope of approaching dawn, but not yet lifting its dark cloak. Rasuah yawned as he rode through the blackness still covering the deserted road, for he had arisen early so he might return even more speedily to Wast. He had a report to make that would shock Ramessa.

Rasuah was wearing a filthy, flea-infested robe to disguise himself as a man from Djemeh. Thus, he might mingle more safely with a particularly unsavory group to learn the information he sought. Lord Metenu hadn't exaggerated. Those of Djemeh who had entered Sun-Amenti as refugees weren't refugees at all, but bandits and murderers who, having heard of the state of affairs in Tamera's western province, had hurried to join the easy reaping of loot. Rasuah felt that soldiers would be necessary to patrol the cities and restore order. It might even take a minor war to drive the well-entrenched Djemeh out of Tamera. Again Rasuah yawned and lifted his head, intending to stretch his arms and shoulders in an effort to awaken further.

A strange shadow on the road ahead caught his attention, and he stared at it curiously for a moment until he came close enough to recognize that it was a rope stretched across the road level with his chest. He started to drop down to his horse's neck, but he was too late. The rope struck his forehead with a lash like a whip, sweeping him off his horse. He fell heavily to the hard-packed soil, where he lay still for a second trying to regain his senses.

But his body, well-trained by many skirmishes, didn't wait for his mind to clear its thoughts. Like an animal reacting instinctively to attack, Rasuah rolled and got dizzily to his feet, then ran, staggering, into the bushes. He ran back along the road for a short distance until his brain began to clear. Then he ran up a slight incline to hide among the rocks.

Aside from his shoulder aching from his fall and his forehead stinging from the rope, he decided he had escaped injury. But who had strung that rope to catch him? he wondered. Hastily, he sought his dagger. It was gone. His bow and arrows were bound to his saddle, and his horse was well down the road by then. Feeling foolish for not having seen the rope sooner, Rasuah got to his feet and, half-crouching, began to move silently among the rocks and shrubs. His sharp ears had picked up the sound of someone creeping stealthily through the foliage and he intended to learn who had set this trap for him.

He saw the faint outline of a dark shape, then the gleam of metal. Whoever was walking so softly through the foliage carried a sword or a dagger. Thieves, he finally decided. After what he'd learned in Sun-Amenti, he could summon from within his heart not one shred of mercy for bandits. His fingers felt for the soft knot of his sash and very carefully untied it. Then, grasping the sash in both hands, he gave the cloth several twists to give it a ropelike strength, before he crept closer to the dark figure.

When Rasuah stood immediately behind the man, whom he recognized from his garments as a Djemeh, he dropped the sash over the man's head and raised his knee to plant it in the small of the thief's back. The sash jerked tight. Although the man made a weak effort to twist free, he could not. The sash held the thief fast until Rasuah felt the man's body sag against him. Rasuah waited a moment more, then eased the Djemeh quietly to the ground.

Rasuah dropped to his knees beside the body, seeking the weapon he'd noticed before. He had no illusions that
392

the man was alone. Finding only a dagger, he sighed and got to his feet.

Hearing the hasty sounds of someone running clumsily through the bushes toward him, Rasuah immediately backed around the boulder. Another thief rushed out of the foliage toward his companion's body. As he stopped momentarily to look down at the corpse, Rasuah poised himself. Then, the coiled strength of his muscles lengthened as he leaped at the thief. But the man turned just as Rasuah struck; when he fell, Rasuah's momentum sent them rolling and struggling down the hill to land on the road below. They continued twisting and rolling back and forth, each trying to get on top of the other and gain the freedom to use his blade.

"Hanu!" Hanu!" came a shout from the bushes.

"Here! Here!" The man struggling with Rasuah cried out.

Realizing yet another thief was coming, Rasuah gathered his strength to wrench his hand free of the man's grasp and plunge the dagger into his throat. Rasuah felt blood spurt on his chest before he leaped to his feet and turned to face another Djemeh. Rasuah backed away warily. This one carried a heavy, crescent-shaped sword.

The man drew the sword back and whipped it forward. As Rasuah leaped away, the blade narrowly missing his waist. Again the sword flashed and again Rasuah leaped back. But this time he continued across the road to pick up a long, heavy branch that had fallen from a tree. Still grasping the dagger in one hand, Rasuah held the branch in the other, much as he would have held a sword. Then Rasuah faced the thief. The man's eyes gleamed as if he considered the potential threat of the branch to be negligible. He rushed forward to slash at Rasuah's chest. Rasuah stepped lightly back, at the same time lowering the branch and swinging it sharply to strike the man's legs. The thief almost tripped, but nimbly caught his balance before falling. Rasuah raised the branch and brought it

393

heavily down on the thief's head. The sharp crack, then a dull moist sound told Rasuah he had broken the man's skull. He stepped backwards slowly, looking suspiciously at the bushes overhanging the road, wondering if any other thieves were left.

From the hillside's darkness came the sound of a horse stamping nervously, as if it was being mounted by someone in a hurry. Rasuah began to walk cautiously toward the sound, but stopped when he heard a man call out in alarm.

"Don't go! What will we tell Henhenet?"

Rasuah's body stiffened at the name. He couldn't believe his ears.

"Henhenet will have to find me in Djemeh!" another voice cried.

Rasuah's jaw dropped. Henhenet had sent these men to kill him on the road? A sudden, hot flood of anger rushed through him. The prime minister really was the director of the crimes in Sun-Amenti! Rehi must only be Henhenet's agent!

Rasuah began to move swiftly in the direction of the calls he'd heard, but stopped when the sound of horse's hooves racing away reached him.

He threw down the branch in a burst of disappointment. Then he whirled and ran down the road to find his own horse. Catching the assassins had lost its importance. Racing back to Wast and giving Ramessa his report was what concerned him now.

Seshena sat at Nefertiry's side during the meal, but she watched the dancers and listened to the singers with only half her attention, because her thoughts were on Rasuah. She had no idea of what had occurred on the road. Her mind had been so saturated with loneliness it hadn't reached out to explore his adventures.

"Seshena, you haven't heard a word I said," Nefertiry declared in exasperation.

394

Seshena lifted startled eyes to her queen. "I'm sorry. My thoughts were elsewhere."

"You were thinking of Lord Rasuah," Nefertiry guessed. Seshena nodded. "After what you did yesterday afternoon for me, I could forgive your mind's wandering for any reason." Nefertiry then suggested, "Would you like to take a walk in the garden? I should think trying to appear interested in this banquet with Lord Rasuah on your mind is a strain."

Seshena smiled in embarrassment. "Maybe it would be a good idea for me to spend a few moments alone. Then I could return refreshed."

"Don't stay away too long," Nefertiry directed. "Akeset, Henhenet, Tuiah—all my enemies are at this banquet. If poison is put in my wine, I would have you here to warn me of it."

"Tonight I would know of poison added to anyone's wine," Seshena warned.

Nefertiry shook her head. "If such is done, it won't be by me." Her lips tightened and she added, "I couldn't promise that so easily if Reshet were here, though." She patted the blue cord, which she had added to the ribbon she wore at her waist. "In the meanwhile, your charm will have to protect me."

Seshena stood up, and, nodding respectfully at Ramessa, who glanced up at her, left the table to make her way across the room to the doorway that led to the garden.

Nefertiry turned her head to speak to Chenmet, who stood behind her.

"Bring Rehi to me," Nefertiry directed. "I would speak quietly to him—without Henhenet's long ears listening."

Chenmet nodded and slipped away. Moments later she brought Rehi to Nefertiry.

"Sit here in Seshena's chair," Nefertiry invited. "The priestess will be gone a few moments."

Rehi obeyed, feeling nervous. For over two decans he had tried to get out of Wast, but one of the palace guards seemed always to be nearby. Knowing that Lord Rasuah's return was imminent, Rehi had finally planned to escape tonight, while the banquet kept everyone else occupied. He forced himself to smile at Nefertiry and say cheerfully, "The banquet is very enjoyable, divine lady. The singers were superb."

"Yes, yes," Nefertiry agreed impatiently. "They were excellent."

"May I say, divine lady, you're more beautiful than ever I have seen you. I have no doubt Hat-Hor's spirit entered your being in the temple and gave you added beauty with her divinity."

"I didn't call you to my side to listen to flattery," Nefertiry said shortly.

Rehi dropped his eyes, not knowing what to say next.

"I have very reliable information, Rehi. I know you've made a profitable venture out of your ministry," Nefertiry said bluntly. Rehi's eyes lifted in alarm, but she added, "I want you to tell me in your own words about Henhenet's part in this. I want you to tell the king."

"Divine lady, the prime minister—" Rehi's voice trailed off.

"If you're afraid of the punishment for yourself, I can tell you frankly that you're a small fish in this river of deception. If you were to confess your own crimes and beg forgiveness, telling the king about Henhenet would go in your favor." Nefertiry said, "I don't make promises I can't keep. You would, of course, be stripped of your title. That would be necessary. Perhaps nothing more would be done to you. At the worst, I could promise mere banishment."

Rehi swallowed, then whispered, "If you're so sure about all this, why haven't you told the king?"

Nefertiry's eyes hardened and she said quietly, "You've heard the gossip. The king isn't inclined to listen to me these days." Nefertiry took a breath. "Measure my request and the weight of my promise against my frankness with you in this personal matter. It isn't you I want. It's
396

Henhenet. If you spoke the truth, a confession implicating yourself, the king couldn't ignore Henhenet's crimes." She was silent a moment, then added softly, "Lord Rasuah will soon return. You know what he'll report. Why take the blame alone? Tell the king now—before Rasuah comes back—about your activities and Henhenet's. Beg for mercy. I'll see that you get it."

"Excuse me for saying so, but if as you just admitted, the king pays little attention to your counsel, how can you be sure he'd show mercy to a criminal?"

"Once it's been proven to him I was right about Henhenet, he'll listen to me." She glanced up and saw Henhenet walking toward them. "Speak to me again about your enjoyment of this banquet—and smile while you do it. Henhenet is coming."

Fear clouded Rehi's eyes, but he forced himself to comment lightly, "Those dancers were beautiful and most graceful."

"They were particularly good," Nefertiry agreed calmly.

"Divine lady, you possess the beauty of Hat-Hor herself tonight," Henhenet said in an oily tone. He looked at Rehi and speculated on what they'd really been discussing. Was that sheep of a minister trying to ingratiate himself with Nefertiry? Henhenet wondered. He realized he'd never told Rehi that Rasuah wouldn't be able to make his report to Ramessa. He wondered if Rehi might, out of panic, consider making a full confession in the hopes of saving his own neck. His eyes traveled to Nefertiry's face. It was no use trying to read her expression. She was too good at hiding her thoughts.

"Why are you so silent, Henhenet?" Nefertiry asked softly.

"I'm sorry, divine lady," Henhenet said quickly. "I suddenly recalled something I wanted to do, but forgot. I must return to my quarters for a moment and take care of this matter. Will you excuse me for but a short interval?"

"You're excused," Nefertiry said coldly.

Henhenet bowed his head and walked swiftly away. Nefertiry again looked up at Rehi. "You realize he's worried that you'll speak?"

"It hasn't been established I have something to speak of," Rehi reminded her. He had almost decided he'd be wisest to simply escape during the banquet. He didn't care to throw himself on the king or the queen's mercy.

"You need a little time to think about my proposal," Nefertiry observed. "You'd best think quickly. With Lord Rasuah on his way and Henhenet already suspicious of your motives, I think you walk a dangerous path."

Rehi smiled uneasily. "That could be true, if I were guilty."

"I know you're guilty. I also know you're considering escape. Who wouldn't?" Nefertiry shifted her gaze to the guards posted at all the doors. "I've given them orders to make sure you remain in the palace until Rasuah returns. Haven't you noticed the presence of a royal guard wherever you've gone these last two decans?"

Rehi's face paled. How could he get away from this banquet now, he wondered. "Divine lady, Henhenet is coming back," he said suddenly.

"I'm glad you enjoyed the dinner," Nefertiry said graciously. "Have you ever tasted my special wine?"

Rehi shook his head. "No, divine lady," he replied. "I've never had the honor to be this close to you."

Nefertiry raised her hand and Chenmet stepped closer. "Refill my goblet," Nefertiry directed. "Pour some wine for Minister Rehi and Prime Minister Henhenet." She glanced up at Henhenet, who had again posted himself behind Rehi. "You would enjoy a cup of my favorite wine, wouldn't you, Henhenet?" she asked.

"Yes, divine lady, I would enjoy it very much," Henhenet replied, suddenly smiling. He glanced at Chenmet and asked, "Why does your personal servant attend to so menial a task as pouring wine?"

"Because I trust her," Nefertiry replied.

398

"Yet, you have someone taste it for you," Henhenet noted.

"Only sometimes," she answered. "But because possible assassins don't know when I'll have it tasted or even who will be called to do so, they must find another way to get me."

"What a grim conversation," Rehi commented, lifting his goblet to sample the wine. It had a flavor he didn't like. Although he tactfully tried to conceal his distaste, he was unsuccessful.

"How do you like it, Rehi?" Nefertiry asked. "You seem less than delighted."

"It's not sweet enough for me," Rehi said. "Forgive me, divine lady, but taste is very individual."

"There's nothing to forgive," Nefertiry said easily, and glancing meaningfully at Rehi added, "I always value the truth." She looked up at Henhenet to see him regarding Rehi with a very peculiar expression. "You haven't tasted your wine, Henhenet," she said, beginning to feel uneasy. "Taste it from my goblet."

Henhenet smiled and reached out for her cup. "Do you fear poison despite your precautions?"

"I never know," she said thoughtfully, watching Henhenet sip her wine without hesitation.

Rehi suddenly clasped his hands to his stomach. Sweat broke out on his forehead and his face twisted in pain. "I have a cramp," he gasped.

Nefertiry turned to stare at him in surprise. "Have you drunk too much already?"

Rehi doubled over and a moan escaped his lips. He began to rock from side to side in anguish.

Nefertiry stood up. "Chenmet, get the physician," she ordered sharply.

Ramessa came to her side. "Did you do it again?" he whispered in her ear.

Nefertiry turned to stare at him. "Don't be foolish," she snapped. Then, lowering her voice she added, "Why

399

should I poison him? Besides, did you see Petet suffer that way?"

"Perhaps Rehi's agony entertains you," Ramessa murmured.

Nefertiry opened her mouth to answer angrily, but didn't, because Rehi pitched face forward and lay on the floor at her feet, moaning and writhing pitifully. Nefertiry raised her head. "Where's the physician!" she demanded. Her eyes fell on Henhenet, whose smug expression was quickly covered by an anxious look. "You did it!" she declared. "You poisoned Rehi to keep him from telling me about your crimes!"

Henhenet raised his eyebrows. "I have no crimes to hide," he said calmly.

Nefertiry turned to look up at Ramessa. "Henhenet went to his room just a moment ago. He could have got the poison and returned to drop it in Rehi's cup. He could easily have done it. I wasn't watching his hands!"

Rehi's moans had been growing fainter and his writhings less violent. Suddenly he stopped moaning. They looked down to see him twitch twice, then lie still.

Nefertiry raised her eyes to search for Seshena, who had heard the commotion and now stood just inside the doorway to the garden staring at the scene before the royal table.

"Seshena can examine Henhenet's thoughts and confirm his guilt," Nefertiry said in a harsh voice. She looked at Henhenet. "I command you to answer your queen. Did you poison Rehi? Take time before you answer, Henhenet. Consider it well, for Seshena will know the truth."

Henhenet, who didn't believe Seshena could read minds, said calmly, "Time is needed to think of lies. I speak the truth."

"Seshena *can* read your thoughts," Nefertiry declared. "Consider also what Lord Rasuah will say about your enterprise in the north when he returns."

"Lord Rasuah won't report against me," Henhenet said coolly.

400

"Henhenet didn't expect me to report anything, because he thought I'd be dead!"

At the sound of Rasuah's voice from the doorway, everyone turned to stare at him. Rasuah stood with his head back, his eyes flashing gold fire. "Excuse my appearance, majesties, but I wish to make my report before the words I have to say devour my insides like that poison just devoured Rehi."

Eyeing Rasuah's blood-smeared tunic, his dust-caked hair, Ramessa called, "Come forward."

Everyone quickly stepped aside to make room for Rasuah, who marched across the large room to face Ramessa.

Ramessa stared for a moment at Rasuah's furious expression, then said quietly, "I have never seen you so angry."

"I have never been attacked by five paid assassins before!" Rasuah declared. He shifted his gaze to Henhenet; when his eyes regarded the prime minister, they became triangles of glittering gold ice. "Two of your assassins escaped me," Rasuah said in a softly menacing tone. "I heard them speak between themselves just before they fled. They mentioned your name."

"You mistook the name," Henhenet said, terror fading his voice to a whisper.

"That was what I'd thought the first time I heard it, but they convinced me when they said it a second time." Not taking his eyes from Henhenet, he said to Ramessa, "There's nothing wrong with my hearing. The place and time were well-chosen to do murder—a deserted road just before dawn."

Ramessa nodded to Khakamir, who was standing near him. Khakamir drew his sword and pressed its point to Henhenet's back.

"If there's anyone whose words I trust, it's Lord Rasuah," Ramessa declared. "Take Henhenet away, Khakamir," he directed. "I don't wish to lay eyes on this traitor until he's executed tomorrow morning." Ramessa

401

looked again at Rasuah. "You will sit with me a moment?" he asked.

Rasuah looked at the chair next to Nefertiry's, then at Rehi's body. "Can we speak tomorrow? I've seen enough of blood and corpses and I'm weary."

"Yes," Ramessa said slowly. "I would imagine you are weary. You killed three of them?"

"Three," Rasuah replied. Then he turned to walk through the banquet hall. Halfway across the room he was joined by Seshena and they left the palace together.

22

The morning air still held the coolness of the night's slight damp and the smell of the sweet green earth mingling with the sun's growing warmth to make a perfume that flowed like honey on the soft wind. The whispering trees seemed to form a background music for the birds' chorus and out of their harmony occasionally rose a soloist's trilling.

Rasuah held his horse to a slow walk while he kept his arms firmly around Setnau, who was perched on the saddle in front of him. Rasuah was careful not to relax his vigilance over the small, warm body he guarded. The little boy, who had never been in the royal forest before, often turned suddenly to peer excitedly at each new sight.

When the horse moved slowly between the shafts of sunlight falling through the trees like transparent golden columns, Setnau reached out to wonderingly pass his hand through them. As they went around clumps of orange lilies, Setnau turned quickly to watch them with longing in his eyes. He sat up and twisted to follow the flight of a low-flying bird that made a bright scarlet flash against the foliage and, feeling Rasuah's grasp automatically tighten, he looked up at Rasuah's face, his eyes wide with wonder, his small mouth curved in a delighted bow.

Feeling a sudden warmth flow through him as he looked down into the child's face, Rasuah smiled and said in a soft tone, "I saw the bird, Setnau," even though he wasn't sure the child understood his words.

Seshena, riding a little behind Rasuah, noticed Setnau's squirming and called, "Is he too much trouble?"

Glancing at her over his shoulder, Rasuah replied, "So small a boy is no problem to hold securely. Anyway, we're coming to a clearing where we can dismount and rest a while. Come closer and ride beside us, beloved. The trail has widened enough now." He reined in his horse and waited for Seshena. When she was at his side he commented, "Setnau seems unusually alert and curious for a child so small."

"He's very intelligent—and sensitive," Seshena replied. "Have a care about what you discuss in his hearing. He understands far more than he can say."

Rasuah smiled in good humor, then turned to guide his horse along the trail toward the little clearing he sought. He'd said nothing to Seshena about where he was taking her because it was a favorite place of his, and he'd wanted to keep it for a pleasant surprise. When the horses reached the end of the forest's shadows and entered the glade, Rasuah reined to a stop. He turned to see Seshena's reaction and noted her delight with satisfaction.

In the center of the clearing stood the ruins of a small, but ancient temple. Although only part of the entrance wall had remained standing and flowering vines had crept up the two cracked columns that were still upright, the temple had an ethereal kind of beauty that seemed to haunt the glade, an enduring majesty that denied its ruined condition—as if the divine being once worshipped here still lived within the shattered walls. One obelisk at the entrance had collapsed and fallen among the feathery ferns and the top of the other obelisk had broken off.

Seshena turned to ask Rasuah, "Whose temple was this? It's too small to have been intended for public use."

"All the writings on it have been worn beyond reading," Rasuah answered with a shrug.

She studied the ruins with a thoughtful expression for some time before finally saying, "It makes me feel as if it's waiting for something—or someone."

"When I first came here, I felt that same way," Rasuah agreed. "Despite the crumbled state of the temple and the growth of weeds, I always feel as if time has been suspended within this clearing, as if the wheel of heaven stops turning here." He was silent for a moment before adding softly, "Maybe this temple has been waiting for you."

Surprised, Seshena looked at Rasuah and said, "How fanciful you are."

"Why not you?" he asked quietly, keeping his golden eyes steadily on her. "Maybe it's been waiting for us to come here together. Let us discover if the atmosphere changes once we've entered it." His heels touched his horse's sides, and he rode toward the temple's entrance.

As they rode through the opening Seshena realized the front of the building was the only wall that had survived. The sides and back had long ago collapsed, and only the bases remained to outline the space the walls once had enclosed. Tall, silky grass speckled with small, white flowers sprouted among the scattered stones and tumbled, broken columns. At the far end of the ruin on a gentle rise marking where the sanctuary once had been, stood a cluster of low palm trees, whose fronds moved slowly with the wind, inviting the riders to come nearer.

Rasuah glanced back to look meaningfully at Seshena. "They call to you," he quipped.

They reached the cool shadows beneath the palms, and Rasuah stopped his horse to wait for Seshena to dismount so he could hand Setnau down to her. Seshena put Setnau on the ground, but she held his hand tightly while Rasuah dismounted and led the horses a little distance away to tie them.

Walking back toward Seshena, Rasuah saw that she and Setnau were still standing in the same place, holding hands and gazing around as if they had found themselves in a foreign land.

"I can see you both have a rather peculiar reaction to this place," Rasuah commented when he'd reached Seshena's side.

"This temple does have a strange effect on me," Seshena admitted. "Maybe it's because I've never seen a ruined and deserted temple before. Yet, instead of feeling sad, I have a sense of peacefulness, an impression of being safe."

"Why don't you sit down," Rasuah suggested. "There's something I'd like to talk about with you."

Setnau had begun to tug impatiently at Seshena's restraining hand, obviously wanting to explore the place. Seshena looked down at him with a solemn expression and advised, "I'll let you go, Setnau. But you must stay nearby." The child's large, green eyes glanced up at her in silent reproach, and Seshena struggled not to smile. "If you come upon a scorpion or a cobra, don't move. Call me," she directed before releasing his hand.

As Rasuah watched the child walk a few unsteady steps away he asked, "Don't you think he's a little young to understand that?"

Seshena kept her eyes on Setnau, who had stooped to study something on the ground. Then realizing he was watching the progress of a harmless caterpillar, she lowered herself to sit on the grass. "I wasn't joking when I said he understands far more than he speaks. Besides, I send my thoughts into his mind in the form of pictures. He knows what I mean as well as what scorpions and cobras look like."

Rasuah glanced again at Setnau, shook his head, then smiled faintly. "If Nefertiry gives Setnau to you often, he'll soon be sending you his own thoughts."

Seshena nodded in agreement. "He learns fast," she said. "Nefertiry wants me to teach him everything I can and she has recently had him brought almost daily to Aset's temple. She intends him to be the next king and she recognizes the advantages of a king's being aware of possible dangers before they have the chance to become more than an idea in a malicious mind."

"Possessing that ability would be helpful." Rasuah sighed and lowered himself to the grass beside Seshena.

"You seem able to deal with danger," she observed. Then she added, "Besides, when you have me at your side, I can always warn you."

Rasuah plucked a long blade of grass and began to turn it idily around his finger. "But I don't always have you at my side, which saddens me for better reasons than that of my protection."

"Our time swiftly appproaches," Seshena said, "which is another reason I asked Nefertiry if we could take Setnau with us to the royal forest. I want Setnau to become better acquainted with you. I want him to learn to trust you as he does me. There may came a time when he'll need us both."

Rasuah asked quietly, "Why should he need us? Have you learned something I should know?"

"I'm not sure why he might need us, but I think it's best for us to be prepared," she replied. She noticed that Setnau was slowly walking toward them, and she warned, "Don't speak of this in his hearing."

Rasuah turned to see Setnau pause, as if he were making a choice between them. Then he headed toward Rasuah, holding out his hand. Rasuah peered into the boy's palm to see a brightly colored caterpillar. Rasuah admired Setnau's prize and said softly, "Be careful not to squeeze it." Setnau turned away, returned to where he'd picked up the caterpillar and carefully replaced it in the grass. "He's very gentle," Rasuah remarked. "Perhaps too gentle to be a king. Yet there is a certain strength behind gentleness."

"Maybe Tamera will need a king who is gentle," Seshena murmured.

"Perhaps," Rasuah agreed. "Maybe a king less impulsive and more self-disciplined in some respects than our present ruler."

"You don't agree with Ramessa's way of ruling?" Seshena asked.

"In some ways I don't," he replied. "Ramessa is a good king and he has the best intentions, but there are some things that happen beneath the surface in his own court, as well as those of other lands, that Ramessa misses."

"Why do you think he misses them?" Seshena asked slowly.

"Out of impatience. He brushes aside details he should take note of, and he's too easily distracted by his own pleasures," Rasuah answered. "He leaves many important matters in the hands of others."

"Nefertiry compensates for a lot of this by following such details with the eye of a tax assessor," Seshena declared, "but lately she too has been distracted from state matters by this trouble with Reshet." She was silent a moment before asking, "What's happening in other lands that Ramessa should know about?"

Rasuah shook his head. "Neither of them are aware that this trouble between Akkad and Assur was carefully nurtured by Hattusil."

"Hattusil!" Seshena stared at Rasuah. "Why would he wish to cause trouble between Akkad and Assur?"

"He wants to cause trouble for Ramessa," Rasuah explained. "Hattusil's pride yet stings from Khatti's defeat at Ramessa's hands. Although he knows Khatti couldn't win an actual war against Tamera, I think he hopes to harrass Ramessa and weaken Tamera by promoting small disturbances that can't very easily be traced back to Khatti. Also, I'd wager he's heard about Ramessa's treatment of Nefertiry. He's probably humiliated by Ramessa's abrupt rejection of her. I suspect he has a certain affection for her and isn't happy at her plight, which he is responsible for, having given her to Ramessa."

"And if other countries thought Hattusil's grandchild would one day ascend Tamera's throne, Hattusil's power would rise a cubit or two," Seshena observed. She stared blankly at the grass while she considered this. Finally she raised her eyes to Rasuah's face and asked, "How do you know about Hattusil?"

Rasuah leaned his weight back on his hands, tilted his face toward the sun and closed his eyes. "I have sources of information in many places because of my travels. Like Nefertiry, I too keep a close watch over the schemes of others; that is one reason Ramessa has asked me to accept Henhenet's title."

"First minister?" Seshena exclaimed.

Rasuah opened his eyes and sat up. "This is what I wanted to discuss with you," he said. He watched her expression carefully as he continued, "Being first minister would make my authority second only to the members of the royal family and, in some circumstances, second only to the king's. Would you like to one day be the wife of the first minister? It isn't an easy place for a woman."

Seshena stared at him, obviously awed. "I would be, then, second only to the queen," she whispered. Rasuah nodded solemnly. She thought about it for a long moment, then remarked, "It would be an odd combination—the first minister married to the high priestess of Aset."

"Odd, yes," Rasuah agreed, "but also very powerful. If I accepted the title, you could, with your temple training, attend to many matters I wouldn't be able to touch. You could advise me about things I'd otherwise never be aware of. I suspect the two of us could be very effective in helping to straighten out all the tangled threads Ramessa brushes aside." Then Rasuah sighed wearily, and said, "But I'm not sure I'd really want to accept the title. I'd lose a portion of my personal freedom because I'd have to spend a lot more time in the palace than I do now." Although he kept his eyes downcast, a new gleam

409

entered their depths as he said, "Of course, I'd also travel less, so it wouldn't be likely I'd have to be away from you for decans at a time."

"For that reason alone, I'd urge you to accept the title," Seshena promptly muttered.

Rasuah laughed softly at her tone of voice. "That position would also give me ways to fill the hours when you're in the temple pleading with Bast to advise you about Nefertiry's difficulties with Akeset."

"I no longer have to beg Bast," Seshena said slowly. "I simply wait a few moments. If there's something I should know, it comes quickly and easily to me. Last night while I was bathing—certainly not thinking about Nefertiry, much less Akeset—"

"I should hope you weren't thinking about them while you were bathing with me!" Rasuah declared, hoping to lighten the growing darkness in her eyes.

But Seshena continued to be serious. "Without preparation of any kind, and I was certainly in a less than meditative mood, I received more information. When we return Setnau to Nefertiry, I have to warn her again about Akeset."

"Is he going to try to murder her, that you look so solemn?" Rasuah asked anxiously.

"Not now," Seshena replied softly. "Akeset wants to contact Reshet and offer to help her against Nefertiry with magic, but even he dares not approach her without Ramessa's permission, so he's going to ask Ramessa if he can visit her on the pretense of giving her blessings for the coming birth. Nefertiry must be told so she can think of some way to prevent Akeset's obtaining this permission."

"Are you afraid Nefertiry won't be able to devise a way?" Rasuah asked.

Seshena shook her head. "She's clever enough to think of something."

"Beloved, what are you afraid of?" he asked quietly.

410

"I see those shadows you've tried to hide from me—that look of dread," he whispered.

"It is dread you see—dread of what soon will come. I know the time approaches because it has grown so easy for me to learn what I need to know. I should be happy because the evil we've been fighting will soon be destroyed. But I am, instead, fearful of how Akeset and his corrupt priests will come to their end. I don't know how it will happen, but I have a feeling of horror about the culmination of events that will lead to it."

Rasuah slid his arms around her to draw her close. "Nothing will harm you, beloved. I'll stay near you until this is over," he promised. "When we return to the palace, I'll go to Ramessa and tell him I'll accept Henhenet's title. Then he won't send me to Punt or anywhere else for some time."

"I'm not afraid for myself," Seshena whispered against his shoulder.

"Nonetheless, I won't leave you. I want you to move into my house until this is finished."

"How the gossips would enjoy that," she murmured.

Wanting fiercely to change her mood, Rasuah asked, "Do you object to my becoming first minister?"

"Only if you don't want the title," she replied.

"Then I'll accept Ramessa's offer and be his first minister," he said quietly.

"You won't mind giving up the excitement of traveling to strange places, the adventures of being royal envoy?"

"Being attacked on lonely roads is the kind of adventure I can sacrifice," he answered. "What would you like to do to celebrate my elevated position?"

Rasuah felt Seshena's smile against his neck as she replied, "I think we'll celebrate tonight, after the servants have moved me into your house."

Rasuah looked down at Seshena with eyes like powdered gold. "I can assure you of that celebration," he said, "but what of a small kiss of congratulation now?"

Before Seshena could answer, a small voice beside them demanded, "I kiss too!"

Rasuah and Seshena turned to look into bright green eyes that were crinkled with mischief.

Rasuah glanced at Seshena to comment, "He does understand a lot more than I'd thought." Then, he turned again to Setnau. "Yes, you too," he said warmly and reached down to the boy.

As Ramessa walked between his guards on their way to Nefertiry's door, he wondered if she had learned that Reshet had given birth to a boy. Although no one but Reshet and the few who had attended her were supposed to know—and Ramessa had given strict orders for all their lips to remain sealed for a time—he was aware that Nefertiry's efficient spy system might have transmitted the news to her despite his orders.

The guards had barely arrived at Nefertiry's chamber when the door opened and she stood silently on the threshhold wearing her court robes and crown, holding her scepters crossed over her breasts, looking more like an exquisitely carved statue than a living woman. As she stepped into place at Ramessa's side, he studied her expression. But her face was as unreadable.

Ramessa nodded to the guards to continue toward the throne room, while he recalled the times he'd waited in Nefertiry's chamber as she finished dressing. All the while her eyes were gleaming with the knowledge that she'd deliberately delayed so he would watch her dress and possibly become aroused. He thought of the many audiences he'd sat through struggling to appear dignified while he burned with frustrated desire. When those sessions had been concluded, likely as not Nefertiry would hurry on to some other task, holding him off even longer. Yet whether she'd made him wait or her steps to his chamber had matched the speed of his own, their coming together had been a glorious thing, always varied in its mood, always different, like a jewel slowly turning its facets before an ever-changing light. Ramessa missed those times.

For more than a month Ramessa hadn't visited Reshet either, because she'd been so close to the birth. So he had begun to recall what he'd experienced with Nefertiry, unwittingly comparing the two women. Reshet had always been willing. All he'd had to do was enter her presence. There had never been a need to guess her mood or wonder about her motives. Only during the last few days he had realized that Reshet had never presented any sort of challenge to him; he wondered if this had been a great part of her attraction in the beginning—utter docility that was volunteered instead of the obedience he demanded of his harem, and a refreshing calm after Nefertiry's tempestuous nature. Now he found himself wishing Reshet had been less fertile and his dilemma with Nefertiry were not further complicated.

Ramessa wondered what he would do about this latest son of his. Although everyone in the land would know he'd fathered the boy, being king, he could ignore the child's existence and not a voice would be lifted in accusation. When he considered this solution, he was mildly surprised that the pangs he felt were less than the stabs of guilt he felt when he thought of his treatment of Nefertiry.

Or was that only because Nefertiry now walked beside him, her rich perfume rising seductively to his nostrils, conjuring memories of warm, moist skin and the silken tangle of her hair. He looked down at her from the corner of his eye and saw the roundness of her lower lip, the gleam of an emerald eye under sooty lashes, the ripe promise of her curves under the moving robe. He took a breath and tried to gather his wits, so his composure would not altogether desert him.

Nefertiry had never appeared more poised than during this last month, but then he saw her only when they attended court. She never spoke to him during those hours they sat on their thrones, except to give an occasional opinion about the matter before them if he asked for it.

Although, at first he had been relieved it wasn't necessary to conduct stilted conversations, later he began to wonder how Nefertiry managed to completely vanish between court appearances. She never sat in the garden as she had once loved to do. He never met her when he visited Setnau, though he came at times she ordinarily would have been with the boy. She didn't go downstairs to dine. He never even passed her in the corridor. He had begun to get the eerie feeling that she no longer lived in the palace, but only came when it was necessary to hold court or to attend formal ceremonies, such as Rasuah's installation as first minister a few days before.

Despite a voice loudly announcing that the king had arrived and ordering those present to prostrate themselves, Ramessa's mind was so submerged in his private thoughts he didn't realize he'd entered the throne room. Looking as impervious as Nefertiry, he marched past the rows of bowing officials without being aware of their presence, stepped onto the dais and automatically sat on his throne. He was considering the possibility of giving Reshet a large and soothing sum of gold and sending her away, when he was startled by Rasuah's quiet voice.

"Majesties, I hope you don't object to my having Zahti make the proclamations."

Ramessa blinked and stared uncomprehendingly at Rasuah, who stood at the base of the dais holding the gold cobra-entwined staff of his new office.

"My voice doesn't carry well unless I'm angry, majesties. I ask permission to have Zahti make the proclamations."

Finally aware of his surroundings, Ramessa leaned forward and told the scribes, "Let it be recorded that Zahti will call the proclamations." Ramessa suddenly realized this would be the first time Rasuah publicly functioned as first minister and he wanted to be ready to help his friend should he become confused by court rules. Then, Ramessa laughed at himself. He was the one, it seemed, who might require prompting if he didn't keep

414

his mind on the matters before him. "Who's the first petitioner?" he asked.

"Before we call the petitioners, I have news about the army of the peoples from the northern islands," Rasuah said in a lowered tone.

"What land have they conquered now?" Ramessa asked in an equally soft tone.

"Naharin has been invaded," Rasuah replied solemnly.

Ramessa's eyes widened briefly, then narrowed. "Naharin isn't as easy a prey as Retenu. King Kheta, I assume, is fighting?" When Rasuah nodded, Ramessa asked, "How does it go?"

"Not well for King Kheta," Rasuah answered. "Araina already has fallen."

"Governor Satirna surrendered?" Ramessa asked.

"He had no choice. He and his daughter, Kirgipa, were captured," Rasuah said. "The fighting in other parts of Naharin is fierce, but the chances are against King Kheta's small army driving out the invaders."

Ramessa looked down at his lap and was silent a moment, as he absorbed this grim news. When he lifted his eyes he said softly, "The sea peoples are working their way in our direction."

"Naharin is uncomfortably near," Rasuah agreed.

Ramessa nodded almost imperceptibly. Then, he lifted his voice to ask, "Who's the first petitioner?"

Rasuah, stepping back from the dais, said clearly, "As no doubt you're aware, sire, the royal assessors are now collecting taxes."

Ramessa sighed and leaned his back against the throne. "Then we have a few cases disputing the amounts. Who is the first of them?"

"Hakhnet of Ta-She Province," Rasuah replied and backed away to look expectantly at the farmer. When Hakhnet seemed uninclined to step forward, Rasuah made an impatient gesture with his staff; and Hakhnet moved out of the crowd to sink to his knees before the thrones.

"I hope Rasuah won't use his staff as a prod next,"

Ramessa said under his breath to Nefertiry, hoping to elicit a response. When he heard nothing, he glanced at her from the corner of his eye, but she had kept her gaze fixed on Hakhnet, who remained on his knees. Ramessa turned his attention to the farmer. "Rise, Hakhnet."

Hakhnet got to his feet slowly, but said nothing.

"Speak, Hakhnet!" Ramessa said impatiently. "Why don't you want to pay your taxes?"

"Majesties, I would gladly pay them if I but possessed the goods!"

"Why don't you possess them?" Ramessa asked suspiciously.

"Sire, during the last flood the river changed its course in passing through the fields you have so graciously assigned me. A portion of the fertile land has been left an unproductive marsh. In the adjacent fields worms have destroyed half the wheat and a rampaging hippopotamus trampled the rest. Now there are but swarms of rats along that bank of the river and in chasing some of them with my hoe, the throngs binding the tool broke; and so I have no hoe. My ox team died at the plow and the horse I would have used in their stead has gone lame, majesties!"

Despite her inner misery, Nefertiry was amused by this elaboration of catastrophes and remarked, "Truly, no other farmer in the whole land can have such woes as yourself."

Wondering if she were being sarcastic, Ramessa glanced at her and was amazed to see that a smile had lightened her features. Encouraged, Ramessa said, "I cannot tax what doesn't exist. What you owe will be accordingly lowered."

"Thank you, majesty," Hakhnet said, obviously relieved.

"Of course, the king will send an inspector to assess the new tax," Nefertiry advised.

"Of course," Ramessa echoed, realizing he'd forgotten about having someone confirm the truth of Hakhnet's story. Under his breath, he observed, "It's good you

remind me of such details or I'd give the kingdom away."
He glanced at Nefertiry from the corner of his eye and
was saddened that her smile had faded.

"Praise from my lord is gratifying," she murmured.

In the past such a remark from Nefertiry had usually
been meant in playful sarcasm. Ramessa turned his head
slightly to discern if there was any hint of humor in her
face. But finding there was not, he suddenly had a
poignant wish to hear the sound of her vanished laughter.
"Who's next?" he asked dully.

"Another farmer, Mahmu, from Sun-Amenti Province,"
Rasuah replied.

Hardly had Mahmu's knees brushed the floor when
Ramessa snapped, "Rise, Mahmu. What's your problem?"

Mahmu leaped to his feet and, hastily clearing his
throat, said, "Majesties, I have also come to beg a re-
duction in my assessment."

"Why?" Ramessa demanded.

At his king's harsh tone, Mahmu involuntarily took a
step backward. "My crops came up, sire. But they were
destroyed by a horde of grasshoppers. The little birds
too have pilfered. Whenever I turned away for an instant, quantities of what remained on the ground was
carried off by robbers."

Ramessa lifted his eyes. "Has every sheaf of wheat
been ruined? Am I to believe your barley is completely
destroyed? How fat those grasshoppers and little birds
must be!"

Nefertiry leaned closer to Ramessa and a cloud of her
perfume enveloped him, almost making him dizzy. "My
lord, the Djemeh bandits have caused terrible losses among
all the farmers in Sun-Amenti," she whispered.

Ramessa looked at Rasuah and asked, "How severe is
the loss from thieves in Sun-Amenti?"

Rasuah replied, "The farmers have set up watches
both night and day in an effort to guard their crops. They
take their hunting bows and arrow cases with them, I
heard."

Ramessa sighed. "The situation is not pleasant," he noted.

Again Nefertiry leaned closer to Ramessa and his heart increased the tempo of its beat as her shoulder brushed his arm. "My lord, perhaps a general adjustment might be made for all Sun-Amenti's farmers, thus sparing you from having to hear their individual petitions," she whispered.

Before Reshet had come, Ramessa would have regarded the suggestion as being prompted by a certain impatience for the audience to be quickly ended, so they could be alone. Although he doubted such was her intention today, he felt hope begin to flower among the ashes of his sorrow. "You wish to save me effort?"

"I would save my lord's energy for other tasks," she whispered.

Ramessa turned to look incredulously at her. "What tasks?"

"Surely my lord has other things to do besides sit in audience," she replied quietly.

The colors in Ramessa's eyes shifted, settling to a green haze. He raised his head to regard the farmer. "The tax collectors will suspend their operation in Sun-Amenti Province while inspectors investigate the situation. The taxes may then be adjusted," he declared.

"Thank you, majesty! Thank you, divine lady!" Mahmu exclaimed in relief and began to back away. But a sudden thought caused him to stop and his smile faded. "Majesties?" he whispered. At Ramessa's nod he asked, "What of the bandits, sire?"

Ramessa's eyes narrowed as he asked Rasuah, "What is Lord Metenu doing about the Djemeh?"

"Now that he has no interference, he's trying to control them. But their numbers make it a difficult task," Rasuah advised.

"If I receive an unfavorable report from Lord Metenu after the next decan, I'll dispatch soldiers to Sun-Amenti

418

Province. The law-breakers will be subdued or all the Djemeh will be driven from the land," Ramessa promised.

"Thank you, sire! Thank you!" Mahmu cried. "May the blessings of the whole company of divine beings shine on you! The son of Ra is good and mighty!"

"I'll have proclamations made in Sun-Amenti warning the wrongdoers to cease or depart before violence becomes necessary." Ramessa watched Mahmu merge with the crowd, then looked at Rasuah and said, "I trust that disposes of a number of other petitioners?"

Rasuah nodded, "Akeset, high priest of Amen-Ra, begs audience."

Ramessa sighed and again leaned his back against the throne. "Let him come forward."

Akeset didn't need Rasuah's signal to approach the royal dais. He had been listening carefully. At Ramessa's words, he immediately came forward and knelt at the foot of the thrones.

"Rise, Akeset," Ramessa said wearily. "What do you want now?"

Akeset straightened slowly, his eyes glittering with anticipated triumph. "Majesty, I have merely come to ask permission to give a blessing."

Ramessa's eyes narrowed suspiciously. This was too simple a request from Akeset. "A blessing for what?" he inquired sharply, aware of Nefertiry's sudden tension.

Akeset's eyes shifted to gaze at Nefertiry. "Divine lady, why do you glare so at me? Have I done something to offend you?"

Ramessa looked at Nefertiry from the corner of his eye. She was sitting as stiffly as if she faced a rearing serpent.

"That you breathe offends me," she whispered venomously. "You've done nothing to offend me today—that I know of yet. What blessing do you speak of?"

Akeset's eyes hesitated, then returned to Ramessa. "Sire, I've heard that a certain noble lady from the south, who is your guest in Wast, is nearing the time when she will bear a child." Akeset paused, wondering at the sudden, cold light that had entered the king's eyes, then realized Ramessa didn't want Reshet discussed in front of Nefertiry. He sighed. It was too late. He must continue. "Sire, I intend to go to the lady and give her Amen-Ra's blessings so the birth will proceed without problems and she will bear a healthy child. However, I don't know where she's staying in Wast. Sire, will you tell me in which house she resides?"

Ramessa glanced at Nefertiry. Her eyes flashed green fire and he knew she was seething with fury despite her calm exterior. He couldn't help but admire her control. He took a breath and said, "You're too late, Akeset. I have already received a report that Lady Reshet gave birth to a son early this morning." He heard Nefertiry's sharply indrawn breath and fervently hoped she'd remain silent before the court.

Akeset looked startled at this news, but recovering himself quickly, he ventured, "Sire, then I would go to the lady's house and bless her and the child."

Ramessa was silent for a moment as he considered this offer. He saw no harm in it and was just about to give Akeset permission when he was interrupted by Nefertiry.

"My lord, I think this is a good idea," she said clearly.

Ramessa turned to look incredulously at Nefertiry. Why would Nefertiry want Reshet and her son to be blessed by Akeset, when she herself hated them, he wondered.

"My lord, surely you wouldn't deny the lady and her newborn son every blessing the divine beings would give," she said eagerly.

Ramessa remained silent. Nefertiry wanted nothing good for Reshet, so she must anticipate Akeset's doing something harmful, he reasoned. He remembered how Nefertiry had claimed Nehemu had tried to strangle her, how she had accused Akeset of paying the previous royal physician to kill her or Setnau at his birth and had insisted Seshena attend her. He thought of the many times Nefertiry had warned him about Akeset's treachery and wondered if she knew Akeset meant similar harm to Reshet.

Ramessa said, "No, Akeset. Once the child has been born, I think it's more fitting that a priestess from the temple of Aset bless the infant." He raised his eyes and scanned the crowd. As he had anticipated, Seshena had come to attend Rasuah's first court session as first minister. "Call the priestess Seshena," he directed.

"Seshena!" Rasuah said.

Although Seshena's ears hadn't heard the conversation at the royal dais, she had been following it by projecting her mind into Nefertiry's; and she'd found it difficult not to smile at the way Nefertiry had managed to convince Ramessa to keep Akeset from Reshet. She composed her face, took a deep breath, and slipped through the onlookers to approach the thrones and kneel at Ramessa's feet.

"Rise, Seshena," Ramessa directed.

Seshena gracefully got to her feet and looked at the king with a blank expression, although her dark blue eyes glowed with silent congratulations to Nefertiry. "Yes, majesty?" she said softly.

"Akeset has proposed to go to Lady Reshet's house to give her and her newborn son Amen-Ra's blessing, but I think it's more fitting that Hat-Hor's favor be evoked for a new infant. Is this not proper?" Ramessa asked.

"Yes, majesty," Seshena replied. "Hat-Hor comes in seven forms to the side of a new mother and her child."

"Will you go to the lady Reshet's house and give her and her child the appropriate blessings?" Ramessa asked.

Seshena knew she couldn't in good faith visit Nefertiry's enemy and with a true heart bless her and the child. "I cannot go," Seshena said quietly. "Could Amset go instead?"

Ramessa remembered how Seshena had so peculiarly and loyally consecrated Nefertiry's temple and realized Seshena didn't want to bless Reshet. He asked, "Is that the same priestess who attended the queen at Prince Setnau's birth?"

"Makara accompanied me at the prince's birth," she said.

"Can Makara give this blessing?" Ramessa asked, wanting to be sure he knew the priestess who would visit Reshet.

"Yes, sire," Seshena answered.

"Then Makara will be sent to the Lady Reshet," he directed.

Seshena nodded in assent, "I will tell Makara where Lady Reshet resides."

"How do you know?" Ramessa demanded.

"I have just this moment learned where," she replied. At Ramessa's doubtful expression, she asked, "Shall I repeat them to make sure I'm correct?"

Ramessa glanced warily at Akeset, then hastily answered, "No, no. If Makara has any difficulty finding the house, she can come to me." He paused a moment, perplexed at how this priestess knew the secret he so carefully guarded. Finally he said, "That's all, Seshena. You may withdraw." When Seshena bowed her head and began to back away, he added, "Maybe some day you will tell me how you learned the directions."

Seshena paused, and not wanting to tell the king she could read his mind, she said quietly, "My goddess told me, as she tells me whenever I need to know something." Then, she resumed backing away from the dais until she melted into the crowd, leaving her king still looking perplexed.

Ramessa turned his eyes on Akeset, who had remained standing before him. "How is it Aset's high priestess knows such things and Amen-Ra's high priest does not?" he asked with more than a hint of sarcasm in his tone.

Anger flashed through Akeset's dark eyes before he had the chance to smother it and answer smoothly, "One of Aset's faces is that of Bast, the mistress of prophecy, she who knows all secrets."

Ramessa smiled without humor and said, "How convenient for Seshena to be on such intimate terms with her goddess. You may withdraw, Akeset."

The priest bowed his head and backed away as Seshena had, wondering at the scope of Seshena's powers, finally concluding Nefertiry must have known where Reshet's house was and had told the priestess.

Ramessa leaned closer to Nefertiry and whispered, "After this audience has ended, you will come to my chamber."

Nefertiry continued to stare directly ahead. Once, such an invitation would have meant love. Now, at the thought of being with Ramessa, a void seemed to open before her. What else could Ramessa want of her she wondered. "May I ask why, my lord?"

Ramessa murmured, "Although I'm king, you question me?"

Nefertiry turned her head to look at him. "I must know how to prepare myself," she whispered. At her words she saw Ramessa's eyes fill with glittering green flecks and she knew what he wanted. A peculiar chill crept up her spine and settled across her shoulders. A strange thumping began in her temples. "I know I cannot refuse you. So I ask, my lord, instead of me take Nofret or even Mimut to your bed."

Stunned, Ramessa stared at Nefertiry for a moment before whispering, "Must I now issue a command to my queen?"

Nefertiry's eyes didn't falter as she urged in a hushed tone, "My lord, I plead with you. Call any of the others rather than me."

Ramessa was shocked that Nefertiry begged him to take one of the wives she'd previously regarded as enemies. "I want you!" he insisted.

Nefertiry lowered her eyes and nodded helplessly, saying no more.

Ramessa lifted his gaze to Rasuah, who stood at the foot of the thrones, expecting to tell Ramessa the name of the next petitioner. "This audience is ended now," Ramessa directed. "Dismiss the court." Then, he stood up.

After waiting for the moment it took Nefertiry to get to her feet, Ramessa turned, and surrounded by his escort of guards, walked swiftly out of the throne room. At his side, Nefertiry rushed to keep up with his stride.

As they approached Nefertiry's door, Ramessa put both of his scepters in one hand and, with his free hand gripped her elbow, propelling her past her door to his.

Khakamir, who had walked ahead of Ramessa and Nefertiry, opened the door to the king's suite, then stood aside and watched them pass, wondering why they wore such peculiar expressions. He closed the door and assigned the door guards, nodding in dismissal to the other soldiers. As they marched away, Khakamir stood by the door for a moment, his dark eyes clouded with worry.

"Leave us, Nehri," Ramessa ordered, handing the servant his scepters. He watched as Nehri accepted Nefertiry's scepters, then left, carefully closing the door behind him. Nefertiry, who had stopped only a few feet from the doorway, stood staring at her feet. "Sit down," Ramessa said as he removed his ceremonial beard.

Nefertiry walked a little farther into the room and sat on a couch without once raising her eyes.

"Not there," Ramessa said.

She glanced up and saw that he gestured toward the bed. Again, she lowered her eyes, then got to her feet, walked to the bed and sat on its edge like a bird ready to fly from its perch.

Ramessa followed Nefertiry to the bed, bent closer to remove her crown, then merely stood in front of her, regarding her thoughtfully. "Have you been with another man, that you refuse me?"

Nefertiry slowly shook her head. "I cannot refuse you, my lord. You know that."

"I asked you as a man asks a woman, not as the king asks one of his subjects," Ramessa said, taking off his
424

crown and moving away to place both coronets on a nearby table. "Have you been with a lover?" When Nefertiry again shook her head, he concluded, "If you've been with no one else, your body must need love." Nefertiry nodded. Ramessa looked at her silently for a time before he observed, "But you don't want me."

"I have no choice in the matter," she whispered keeping her eyes downcast.

"You've always had a choice," Ramessa said. "For you there is no other way."

Nefertiry finally lifted her head and revealed eyes that flashed green fire. "You have used my body many times without regard to my desires. What is this one more time to you, that I must endure a discussion?" she said angrily.

Although Ramessa was startled by her sudden show of spirit, he said, "Wasn't it you, Nefertiry, who finally taught me to pay attention to your desires? Isn't it you, alone among my wives, who has personal feelings about me?"

"You acknowledge that I have feelings? I can hardly believe it!" Nefertiry snapped. She stared at him while she struggled to control herself, but failing, burst out, "You wish me to lie again with you, to share my body— my very soul—with you and after I've done it, you'll go again to that woman! You want me because you cannot have her now! When she's recovered from her childbirth, you will return to her like a stallion after a mare." Nefertiry paused only for breath, then added bitterly, "How much time do I have? A little more than a month until that female is again ready to perform?"

Ramessa had involuntarily stepped back in the face of her fury, but now moved forward to ask, "Why do you object to Reshet more than any of my harem?"

"She's an insult to all of us!" Nefertiry said recklessly. "Even Mimut and Nofret came to me to ask what we might do. They called her a thief who sneaks through the darkness to couple with you, thus depriving your legal wives of the rights to your body we so pitifully share."

425

"If I married Reshet, would you like her more?" he asked.

"I hate them all!" she said fiercely. "But this one—it's as if she's put a spell on you! This one is evil for all her unassuming ways!"

Ramessa stood silently gazing at Nefertiry, who had again fixed her eyes on the floor. "What would you say if I told you I have no intention of marrying Reshet?" he asked. Nefertiry continued to stare sullenly at the floor as if she hadn't heard him. "What if I told you I've decided not to acknowledge Reshet's son as my own?"

"You say that now to soften me toward you because you want to lie with me and you wish my cooperation," she muttered.

Ramessa stooped to sit on his heels. "Mimut would cooperate. Nofret would be happy to come to me, whatever I intend for Reshet," he observed. "Why would I bother going through this trouble with you if I only wanted a female?" Nefertiry said nothing, and he reached out to lift her chin so she had to look at him. "You have no answer? Or are you afraid of the answer?"

At Ramessa's touch Nefertiry felt the old lightning streak through her nerves, but she hardened herself against it and said tartly, "After what I've experienced since coming to your palace, I think I fear nothing."

"You are stubborn, Nefertiry," Ramessa murmured. "It's true that I want your body hot with passion for me," he said. "I admit I'm in need of love. I haven't had a woman for more than a month." He put his hands, one on each side of her head, and forced her to look at him. "I could call another of my wives and get relief from her, but I want none of them. I want you, Nefertiry." He held her head firmly and moved slowly closer until his lips possessed hers. He kissed her lingeringly, savoring the taste of her mouth at last, feeling her respond to him though she struggled fiercely with herself not to reveal it. Finally, he moved away.

"I admire your control," he remarked. He looked at her

intently for a long moment, then said, "Raise your eyes, Nefertiry. Let me see what they contain, for they tell the truth even though your lips are silent." When she kept her eyes lowered he said sharply, "I command you to look at me, Nefertiry!"

She obeyed. "I ask again why you make me endure this conversation. If you would take me, do so, and have it over."

Ramessa blinked in surprise at the quiet bitterness of her tone. "You're foolish to pretend you were unaffected by my kiss. I can see clearly in your eyes how you struggle to put down all traces of your passion. I know I can arouse you beyond your control. I've done it in the past—as you also have excited me beyond my ability to restrain anything or even think. Yet, Nefertiry, I want more from you than a mere physical joining. I want love, Nefertiry, from the one woman who gives it to me." His fingers threaded through her hair, loosening it, then moved to grip the back of her head. "I love you, Nefertiry," he whispered. "You're the one woman I'm able to love— and you know you love me as well."

Ramessa's hands pulled Nefertiry's head toward him and he leaned forward until his lips again joined hers. Nefertiry tried not to respond to that restlessly seeking mouth and the spirals of sensation he aroused in her. But a small moan escaped her lips without her knowing it. Hearing the sound, Ramessa felt a brilliant fire run along his nerves. He drew away.

"You will tell me how you love me," he whispered. "There can be no lies between our bodies, no half-truths or secrets."

"What of later?" Nefertiry asked. "What of Reshet?"

"However I would answer about Reshet, still you will love me," he insisted.

Her eyes raised and again flashed in anger. "What of Reshet?"

Ramessa regarded her silently a moment, then observed, "How awesome is your ability to hate. My father

427

once told me that a person's capacity for hatred equals his capacity for love. Do you love me as much as you hate her?"

"What of Reshet?" she demanded.

"When I entered the throne room this morning I had already decided to give her gold and send her away," Ramessa said quietly. "I won't recognize her son as a prince." He was silent while his hands slipped from the back of her head to her shoulders. "Today, Nefertiry, we will love—not merely take pleasure from our bodies."

Nefertiry's eyes deepened almost to black as she whispered, "We always have loved."

Ramessa's hands moved from her shoulders and slowly slid down her body, caressing her almost casually as they descended, until they rested warmly on the curve of her waist. "But today, Nefertiry, is the first time we've both admitted it," he murmured and brought his lips to hers.

For almost a decan Ramessa was as attentive to Nefertiry as if he were newly married to the one woman of his heart. They slept together every night; they ate their meals together; they walked in the garden and rode in the royal park. Only when Ramessa had business to attend to did he leave her side, but Nefertiry feared the day Ramessa would go to tell Reshet she must leave Wast. She was certain Ramessa would choose to do this personally, not having the heart to merely send a messenger. And once before Ramessa had spent a long interval with her only to return to Reshet's arms. This knowledge lay heavily on Nefertiry's mind. She thought of going to Reshet and threatening her so Reshet would be afraid to approach Ramessa, but she knew of no way to get past the king's guards, and instinct told her it would be wise never to let Ramessa become aware that she might contact Reshet for any purpose.

Then a chance remark from Chenmet told Nefertiry that one of Chenmet's lovers had recently been assigned to guard Reshet's gate. And this knowledge gave the breath of life to Nefertiry's plan, so she took Chenmet aside and confided her innermost heart to the loyal servant. Chenmet readily agreed to go to Reshet's house and distract the guard from his duties while Nefertiry slipped unseen through the gates.

Chenmet, dressed in the rich garments of a royal servant, rode in a comfortable litter carried by four slaves. But Nefertiry wore the rough-woven burnoose she had brought from Khatti. With the hood pulled over her head, she walked at an unobtrusive distance in the perfumed wake of Chenmet's litter.

It was some distance to Reshet's house and it didn't take long before Nefertiry looked as hot and dusty as the part she played. When she walked slowly along the wall that enclosed Reshet's garden, the guard ignored her approach as if she were invisible. True to her promise, Chenmet engaged her lover in a conversation that distracted him with so skillfully subtle a display of passion, that Nefertiry was able to sneak past the guard close enough to have touched him.

Nefertiry walked swiftly through the garden, aware that a chariot stood empty in the courtyard, although she paid no attention to it. When she entered the house by a side door, she was surprised to hear Ramessa's voice. She followed the sound and stopped beside an open doorway where she could listen to the conversation.

"Look, my lord, is he not a beautiful child?" Reshet coaxed. And Nefertiry's jaw tightened until her teeth ached from the pressure. "I've called him Meri-Amen, knowing you would wish him to be loved by Amen."

Nefertiry's pulses pounded in her temples, because Meri-Amen was one of Ramessa's several names.

Then Reshet asked, "Does the name meet with your approval, my lord?"

Nefertiry held her breath, waiting for Ramessa's answer, hoping he'd voice disapproval of the name, but she heard him mutter something that sounded politely admiring. Nefertiry's heart fell.

Ramessa sighed loudly as if he were resigned to the unpleasant chore. "You may name your child whatever you wish," he said.

A silence followed until Reshet hesitantly asked, "If his name displeases you, my lord, I can change it. I haven't yet had it recorded. I'd just thought my lord's son should have a name equal to his royal blood."

"Reshet, you make this difficult for me," Ramessa said quietly.

"What is difficult, my lord?" Reshet asked.

Ramessa said, "Reshet, I'm not going to claim this son." Nefertiry smiled to hear this, although her tension didn't fade. The crisis wasn't resolved yet and she couldn't be confident Ramessa wouldn't soften until Reshet had left Wast forever.

"My lord!" Reshet whispered, shocked. "What then am I to do?"

"I'll give you double the gold it will take to feed and clothe him like a nobleman's son, to educate him and see to his every need for the next twenty years. You'll return to your father or go wherever you desire to take up a new life. But I won't claim this child as my son," Ramessa said firmly.

Nefertiry heard the swish of Reshet's robe as the woman approached Ramessa more closely. Sweat broke out on Nefertiry's forehead.

"My lord, all I wished for out of life was never to leave your side," Reshet said in a tremulous voice. "That was before I had this child. Now I'm a mother and must think of my son before myself. I'll go away if you command this, but our son must have the dignity of his father's recognition." She paused, then said tearfully, "How will he feel when he is old enough to understand?"

"When he's old enough to understand, then, he will understand!" Ramessa exclaimed. "You'll have to explain it to him."

"My lord, marry me! Put me in your harem! Never

430

call me to you, if you've tired of me, but I beg you to recognize this child as your own!" she cried.

"My other wives wouldn't allow you to live," Ramessa said softly. "They're so angry with you that I'd be afraid to have you walk among them. I dare not have the child in the palace for fear he'd never live out the year."

"I can hardly believe such a thing!" Reshet said. "Who would kill a helpless child? He would be only one among the others. You have many other children, don't you?"

Ramessa sighed. "Yes, scores of them. All their mothers want their sons to take the throne or, failing that, some other high place," he said tensely. "Don't you realize how my wives and even my concubines hate you? Nefertiry told me that two of my wives actually spoke to her about what could be done with you. They're furious that I would yet go to a woman who has no honorable status in the palace, not even the recognition of a concubine. Your child is innocent of what we've done, but he's the end product of it. I cannot allow him in the palace."

"Nefertiry made up that story. She's jealous," Reshet said petulantly.

"Nefertiry is jealous to the point of obsession," Ramessa agreed, "but she didn't lie. She never lies to me."

Reshet was silent a moment, then asked in a faint voice, "Can't I live outside the palace as I am now? Can't you unofficially recognize your child by occasionally visiting us?"

The hairs on Nefertiry's head rose in fury as she heard this; she was amazed at the extent of Ramessa's patience when he quietly answered, "I came this one time without an escort, dressed like a merchant in an old chariot I borrowed from a courier, so no one would recognize me. Why do you think I've put a guard at your gate?" he asked wearily. "I have to protect you and the child."

"Protect us from women who are locked in your harem?" Reshet said derisively.

"Nefertiry isn't locked in the harem," Ramessa said quietly. "Neither are several others of them confined to

431

the harem. The servants who attend my other wives aren't locked in the harem. They have to be free enough to move about so they can accomplish their tasks. Many are loyal or ambitious enough to follow my wives' orders."

"Even orders to do murder?" Reshet asked, shocked by the idea.

"Certainly friends enough to arrange for someone else to do it," Ramessa said tensely. "How ignorant you are of the influence held by rank. The wife of a king—even if she's one of many wives and lives in a harem—holds a certain amount of power." He raised his voice to exclaim, "You aren't a peasant's daughter! You come from a noble's family! Have you learned nothing?"

Nefertiry's eyes narrowed as she observed that Reshet had learned far more than Ramessa thought. Reshet had learned how to appear innocent and even simple, while she used every method ever devised by women to accomplish her goals. Nefertiry clenched her fists as she heard Reshet suddenly begin to weep.

After a short time the sound of weeping subsided and Reshet said tearfully, "I must protect my child. If you won't recognize him, I'll return to my father's house. For my child's sake, I'll make it no secret that you're his father. I'll take occasional trips into Wast and pretend you've called for me. People won't know you've tired of me and don't even wish to see your son. They'll be afraid to speak harshly about his birth, if they're convinced your protecting eye watches him."

"Take the gold I'll give you and go home, Reshet. Many young women have had children before they've had husbands. If you pretend I still have an interest in you, a man who might be inclined to look upon you for marriage will be afraid to come near you," Ramessa's voice had a pleading note that caused Nefertiry to fear he was weakening.

"But I want no one else, my lord. I want only you!" Reshet cried.

Nefertiry lifted her hood over her head, as she imagined

432

the new stream of tears pouring down Reshet's cheeks. She turned away, disgusted. Mere pride should have prevented Reshet from behaving in such degrading fashion. As devious as she'd sometimes found it necessary to become, Nefertiry had never resorted to the pretense of helpless weeping and even doubted herself capable of calling up false tears.

Although Nefertiry crept soundlessly through the house, she steadily grew more angry as she reflected on Reshet's superior acting ability. By the time she stepped into the garden, she had forgotten to worry about discovery. So, it was Nefertiry's good fortune that Chenmet had wisely lured the guard into the little watch-house to seduce him, because Nefertiry, in her fury, marched openly through the gates and stalked down the street at a pace surpassing even that of a man's, which was certainly suspicious in a woman.

Although her temper fed her energy, her feet weren't accustomed to such extended excursions; they began to clamor for mercy in a way she couldn't ignore, forcing her to slow her pace and finally turn to limp down to the riverbank, where she tore off her sandals and sat among the weeds with her feet dangling in the Nile's cool water.

When the stabbing pains began to lessen, she turned her mind to possible solutions and could think of only one. She must get rid of Reshet. There was also only one way she could be certain she had eliminated her enemy forever: death. The thought of Reshet's death gave Nefertiry so deep a feeling of relief, she threw off her stifling hood and lay back in the weeds to reflect on the pleasure the contemplation gave her.

But once Nefertiry found a solution to a major problem, she was not one to merely dream about it. She began to consider plans.

If it appeared that Reshet had taken all her belongings, Ramessa would have to conclude Reshet had returned to the south, as she'd threatened. If inquiries were made and

Ramessa discovered she had never reached her father's house, he might assume that Reshet had been carried off by bandits or possibly had decided to leave Tamera for a new life in another land.

That would mean Meri-Amen also must be dealt with, a thought that chilled Nefertiry. The child was innocent and not to blame for his parents' behavior—but that same child would grow into the man who would threaten Setnau. Nefertiry decided she must think of Meri-Amen in that way, not as a child, but as a potential man to steal her own son's place. She thought of Setnau's bright little face, his green eyes that already were wise beyond his years. Fear for him suddenly streaked through her being. If Reshet stayed and gained a place in the palace and realized Setnau was an obstacle to her ambitions for her own child, would Reshet arrange an accident for Setnau?

Nefertiry reached for her sandals without knowing it. She put them on without feeling their presence on her feet. She was suddenly overwhelmed with the need to see Setnau, to confirm his safety.

23

Akeset stared up at Shemal, whose broad shoulders filled the doorway. Even when Akeset got to his feet, he had to look up at the Shardanan. "Why have you come?" he asked curtly.

Shemal smiled, showing brilliantly white teeth in his sun-bronzed face. "To tell you I've been given a job," he said, "by the queen."

Akeset stared at Shemal in disbelief. "Don't joke, Shemal," he snapped.

The Shardanan stepped into the room and closed the heavy door carefully behind him. "I possess little sense of humor," he replied and leaned his back against the wall next to the door. "Have you no interest in knowing why the queen paid me?"

Akeset dropped his eyes. He knew, if Nefertiry had paid Shemal and his men to do something, it would be an important and very dirty task. Akeset's suppressed smile made a jagged crack of his lips. His dark eyes had already begun to gleam with anticipation. "For what would our queen hire a Shardanan?"

Shemal's lips curled at Akeset's sarcastic tone, but he said coolly, "I came not out of love for you. What will you pay?" Akeset didn't immediately answer, and Shemal added, "I know you burn to interfere with all her plans and I promise this particular plan is of the greatest interest to you." Shemal grew impatient. "Come on, priest. You won't obtain for nothing what I can tell you." He threw the flap of his cloak over his shoulder and produced a small woolen sack. "Weigh what the queen already has paid me and let it make up your mind."

Akeset took the bag, which was very heavy for its size and, unfastening its cord, looked inside. "Gold?"

Shemal grinned and answered, "It isn't sand."

"I'll pay another bag of gold one-third this weight," Akeset quickly offered.

"This same weight," Shemal said calmly.

Akeset's mouth fell open. "Even a third is too much!"

"Not to know what I can tell you," Shemal said. "Yes or no, priest? I won't bargain this time."

Akeset considered the ultimatum. Shemal's prices were usually high, but he'd always given what he'd been paid for. To have him confidently insist on so large an amount of gold must mean he thought the information extremely valuable to Akeset. The priest shook his head and said glumly, "The same amount of gold, then."

Shemal nodded, still smiling. "After you've heard what I have to say, you'll agree it's a bargain." He took the sack, closed it and replaced it under his cloak.

"How did Nefertiry come to you?" Akeset asked suspiciously.

Shemal shook his head. "Not the queen, that slanty-eyed servant of hers. She never mentioned the queen's name, but I recognized her."

"Chenmet?" Akeset asked. When Shemal nodded Akeset muttered, "It's true Chenmet serves no one but
436

Nefertiry. Yet how would the queen know about contacting you?"

"There are ways to contact me and in some places I'm known for my efficiency," Shemal replied.

"You're also known for your willingness to do anything for enough gold," Akeset observed drily. "What's the task Nefertiry set for you?"

"My men and I are to go to the Lady Reshet's house, kill her and the infant, then dispose of their bodies and personal belongings, making it appear as if the lady decided to leave Wast forever."

Akeset hid his surprise, and after a moment, asked, "How are you to kill them? Did Nefertiry leave the method to you?"

Shemal's fingers slipped into his sash and came out with a small bottle carved from a piece of malachite. "She gave me this poison, which she said is painless and fast enough to cause no outcries if a mere undiluted drop is placed on their tongues," he replied. "She wished to produce no blood that would have to be washed away."

"Let me see that," Akeset said, eagerly reaching for the vial.

Shemal's fingers closed around the dully glowing bottle and a smile crept over his lips. "For any alterations you wish me to make in the queen's plans, you will pay an additional bag of gold the same weight as the first."

"Nefertiry wants it to appear as if Reshet left by choice," Akeset muttered.

"Because she fears the king's anger," Shemal observed. "Reshet is the king's favorite woman and the queen is jealous. I know her mind."

"No one knows Nefertiry's mind but Nefertiry," Akeset snapped. "Nefertiry is moved by more important reasons than jealousy, but you're too ignorant of the palace's inner workings to judge. No matter how many women the king takes, he always goes back to Nefertiry. She's his favorite."

Shemal blinked. "But the child? It is his son."

"Ramessa seems to have delayed for some time in

recognizing this particular son," Akeset said gruffly. "Maybe it isn't his son, but some other man's and an embarrassment to him. Maybe Nefertiry is acting as Ramessa's agent. I doubt she would otherwise be told the location of Reshet's house—unless that priestess told her."

"The king is powerful enough to have his killing done without being questioned," Shemal scoffed.

"Sometimes discretion is necessary even for a king," Akeset murmured.

"If you want me to do nothing about the matter in your behalf, get the gold you promised for my information, and I'll leave," Shemal said impatiently. "A woman is waiting for me."

Akeset raised his eyes. "She can wait a little longer."

Shemal sneered. "Just because you don't appreciate the value of a female doesn't mean I'll stand here all night while you think what to do about my information."

Akeset gave him a sharp look. "If you're implying I have other tastes, you're mistaken," he snapped.

"I know you have no interest in these matters at all," Shemal said sarcastically.

"Be silent!" Akeset snarled. He turned and walked across the room, then back. He wheeled around to walk away again.

"I have better things to do," Shemal muttered and put his hand on the door latch.

"Wait, you fool!" Akeset called.

"Bring my gold," Shemal said softly.

"Nefertiry is taking great care to make it seem as if Reshet has decided to disappear. If Nefertiry is working as Ramessa's agent, he must want Reshet removed quietly. But if these murders are Nefertiry's idea, she doesn't want him to know she ordered them," Akeset muttered.

"I don't care one way or the other," Shemal said, shifting his weight impatiently.

Akeset seemed not to hear. He came closer to grip Shemal's arm. "You will kill Reshet and the child and
438

there must be no outcries," he directed. "But there must be a great deal of blood that won't be washed away—blood that will testify to their torment and will thus infuriate Ramessa, whether he ordered the murders or not."

"I'm not interested in deliberately inflicting pain," Shemal said slowly.

"But you will inflict pain," Akeset insisted. "They must be tortured and left the way they died."

Shemal shook his head and shrugged off Akeset's hand. "Such deaths involve time and time involves extra risks. For that risk I would require still another bag of gold," he said. "I would require all the payment before anything is done. After it's finished, my men and I will have to leave this land. We can't risk waiting around for you to pay, in the event the job is somehow traced to us."

Akeset recognized the fear in Shemal's eyes and immediately assured him, "I don't want any of you to be caught and tortured, you might reveal my name. When are you to go to Reshet?"

"Two nights from now," Shemal answered.

"You'll have half the gold before you leave for Reshet's house—the other half on your way back," Akeset directed.

"I said I wanted all of it before," Shemal reminded him.

Akeset shook his head. "I don't want Reshet to die of old age."

Shemal grasped Akeset's shoulders with his great hands. "I never go back on an agreement, even one I don't like," he snarled. "I always keep my word."

Although Shemal's grip was like that of a vise, Akeset replied with a sneer, "Oh yes, we're both honorable men." He stared up at Shemal without flinching. "You'll get the other half of your gold immediately after you return from Reshet's house. As proof that you've done the job, you must bring me one of her eyes."

Shemal's hands released Akeset's shoulders as if he
439

held a venomous serpent. "And what do you want of the child?"

"I asked for one of Reshet's eyes because they're of a singular color and you can't kill some tavern maid and bring me the wrong eye," Akeset said coolly. He paused a moment before adding, "You will bring me the part of the child revealing that it's a male."

Shemal frowned. "My men won't want to torture a woman. But to torture a boy-child will be against them all the more, and to cut off pieces to bring back as prize—"

"Remind them how much gold those pieces are worth to you," Akeset advised. "That might make the task less disagreeable for them."

Shemal shook his head. "There's only one man—not a regular of mine—but a man who would do this." He raised his eyes to Akeset and added, "It happens that he's mad, made so during his years of priesthood in your temple."

"Oh? Who is that?" Akeset asked too casually.

"I won't tell you his name because I can see his reward from you would be the same one you gave the physician—an arrow in his back. He won't know who paid us, don't worry. If ever he is tortured, he won't be able to mention your name."

"If you even hint at who paid you, my curse will follow you to whatever land you choose," Akeset warned.

"I don't believe in curses. If I did, I wouldn't believe in yours," Shemal declared. "If you had the power to do such things, you wouldn't have to pay me." He took a step toward Akeset and said, "Bring me the gold you promised for my information. I've spent enough time in your presence."

Akeset smiled smugly. "First you'll give me the poison." When Shemal hesitated he added, "Poison isn't your method; you have no use for it. I may."

Shemal reached into his sash and produced the vial. "Don't think you'll use it on me after this job," he said.

"Nothing from your house will touch my lips or my men's."

Akeset took the poison and turned away, saying "So refined a death would be wasted on you!"

Shemal and a handful of his men soundlessly climbed the wall into Reshet's garden. The sentry at the entrance gate had no idea of anything happening, and continued his watch speculating on possible ways to remind a certain friend of the debt he owed.

When Shemal and his men entered Reshet's house, they systematically went all through it to assure that the servants would raise no alarm. They silenced their outcries before they could begin by slicing their vocal cords at the same time they severed the arteries of their throats. Then, soundlessly, they lowered their victims to the floor where their hearts would shortly stop pumping the blood that made large, dark pools around the bodies.

Shemal politely knocked at the door to Reshet's bedchamber. She, finding no servant answered her call, hurriedly put on a robe to open the door. Shemal explained they were couriers from the palace, and Reshet stepped aside so they could enter and give her Ramessa's message in private.

Shemal nodded to his companion. The man pretended to walk past Reshet, but instead, he suddenly whirled to clamp one hand over her mouth and, with his other hand, grip both her wrists so tightly behind her, she could neither move nor scream. Only her cinnamon-colored eyes stared at them in helpless terror.

"Where's the child?" Shemal asked quietly.

A new terror, worse than that for herself, froze Reshet's heart. She began to struggle against her captor's grip.

"Calm yourself, Lady," Shemal said in a soft tone. "We intend only to bring you and the child to the palace."

Reshet's heart leaped in hope, but just as quickly fell. Ramessa had been implacable about her coming to the palace. In any case, he never would have ordered such rough treatment of her. An idea came to her; slyly, she stopped struggling.

Shemal scanned the room and, not seeing the child, directed, "Yarsu, take your hand from the lady's mouth so she may tell me where the child is and instruct me how to wrap him for traveling."

When the sweaty hand left her mouth Reshet whispered, "If my lord calls me to his presence, gladly will I go without a struggle. Release me so I may prepare the baby with my own hands."

Shemal looked speculatively at her for a moment. There was a strangely regretful look in his eyes that only added to the fear Reshet was so desperately trying to conceal. "Yarsu, let her go to the child," he said.

Reshet turned slowly and walked into the adjoining room. Carefully, she picked up the infant, cradling him for a moment in her arms as if soothing him, then suddenly whirled around to race toward the door to the garden. But Yarsu was after her with the speed of a striking cobra. He threw one arm around her waist, the other hand over her mouth to stifle her screams, then lifted her off her feet and carried her squirming body to Shemal.

"What now?" Yarsu asked quietly.

Shemal's eyes darkened as the frightened infant, still clasped to Reshet's chest, began to wail. "Quiet him," he commanded.

Yarsu, not knowing what would quickly silence an infant, pressed his wrist against the child's mouth without realizing that he'd also covered its nose. Shemal could see how tightly Yarsu's wrist pressed the child and he considered telling Yarsu, but he changed his mind. It was merciful to smother the baby. Watching the infant's face pale, then begin to take on a blue tint, while Reshet struggled to free the child from the suffocating wrist, Shemal commented, "It's best he dies so painlessly."

Reshet managed to free her mouth to cry, "How can he order his own son to death?"

Hearing a dragging footstep behind him, Shemal turned slowly to face the mad priest who had entered the room with several of Shemal's men. Again Shemal turned to Reshet. "If it's any comfort to you, Lady, know the king didn't order this."

Reshet dropped her gaze to the now-dead baby in her arms. In that moment, it seemed as if all the spirit had drained out of her.

"Release her," Shemal ordered.

Yarsu obeyed and Reshet walked slowly toward a couch, still staring down at her dead son in disbelief. "Then this must be Nefertiry or some other wife's doing," she whispered.

"This particular thing is the doing of no one in the palace," Shemal replied.

"Who then?" she murmured dully.

"Akeset," Shemal answered.

She lifted eyes that contained no light. "But why?"

"Does it matter?" He turned to the mad priest with an almost imperceptible shudder. "You have your orders, Irai. Neither I nor my men will help you with this."

"But you must bind her for me," Irai whined. "I cannot restrain her by myself."

Shemal's eyes held disgust as he looked at the priest and asked, "Where?"

"If we could have done this in the daylight, I would have said bind her to the ground in the garden so I could pin her eyelids open and let the sun burn out her sight while I attended to other matters." Irai turned slowly to scan the room. Finally he said, "Under these circumstances the bed seems most suited for my purpose." He went to a small table and laid down a bundle he'd carried, then began to unwrap it, saying, "It's too bad your clumsy man smothered the child."

Shemal came closer to look at the contents of Irai's bundle and saw it held the surgical instruments used by Anpu's priests during the preparation of corpses for embalming. He shuddered and watched as his men bound Reshet to the bed.

"For once I congratulate Yarsu for his clumsiness," Shemal remarked. He glanced again at the gleaming instruments and watched Irai lovingly inspect a long, dainty probe. He turned to his men and ordered, "Cover her mouth securely." Seeing Reshet's cinnamon eyes widen in fresh terror, Shemal turned away. As he walked toward the door he said, "Remember, Irai, the souvenirs I must give him who pays us. Make sure he can recognize them."

Irai's chuckle was like a cold wind among the dried leaves of a dead tree. "He'll know the child's male part," he replied. At the sounds of Reshet's renewed struggle against her bonds, he added, "I'll be sure to save one eye."

Shemal heard Yarsu gag, and his own stomach rose. He was little comforted to hear the door close behind him. Yarsu, looking pale, sank to a bench in the corridor, and Shemal leaned his back against the wall, closing his eyes to shut out the horror of what he guessed Irai would soon do to Reshet.

"What of Nefertiry's hairclasp?" Yarsu asked softly.

Shemal opened his eyes. "I forgot it," he groaned, reaching into his tunic for the stolen ornament Akeset had instructed him to plant in Reshet's room. He looked at Yarsu, but saw in Yarsu's eyes the refusal to obey his unspoken order. Finally, Shemal said angrily, "Open the door."

Yarsu obeyed, and Shemal stepped into the room to find Irai sitting with his scrawny legs locked around Reshet's hips. Shemal realized with a shock that the mad priest was raping her. He marched to the bed and slapped the priest hard, across his face. Irai's motions stopped abruptly.

"Get off!" Shemal cried. "You need not do that!"

Irai's face twisted into a crooked smile. A trickle of

444

blood threaded down his chin from his gashed lip. "Why not before it's too late?"

"Get away, I said!" Shemal commanded, unable to look at Reshet who had turned her face toward him in mute appeal.

"If I do, I'll only resume after you've left—unless you want to watch everything I do," Irai insisted.

Shemal stared at him a moment, greatly tempted to end Reshet's suffering now and immediately afterward mingle the evil priest's blood with hers. Then, muttering an oath, he tossed Nefertiry's hairclasp on the floor and stalked out of the room, slamming the door after him.

Turning to his men, Shemal said hoarsely, "You will remain here." He looked at Yarsu and whispered, "Come with me to see if we can find some wine or beer. I need a few goblets to wash this taste from my mouth."

"And I," Yarsu agreed.

"What of us?" one of the other men asked.

"If we find some, we'll bring it to you," Shemal said over his shoulder and walked quickly away.

Ramessa turned his head to look at Nefertiry, who walked beside him. Her face wore a small smile and he could see, beneath the fringes of her long black lashes, the gleam of her eyes tinted golden-green by the early sun. "You seem in good spirits this morning," he remarked.

Nefertiry, who had been wondering if Reshet's disappearance would be announced during the audience, looked up at him. "That's because I no longer have to endure your moaning about your aching tooth," she said tartly.

Ramessa smiled sheepishly. "Was I that bad?"

Nefertiry's eyebrows lifted pointedly, but she continued to stare directly ahead down the sun-streaming corridor as she answered, "One day of suffering from your suffering wouldn't have been too bad, but three days and nights!"

"Think of my torment," Ramessa reminded her.

"Which could have been shortened to merely a few hours had you let me send immediately for Makara," she said. She was silent a moment before she added, "I don't suppose you will take her advice and have the tooth extracted before the pain returns?"

Ramessa winced at the thought of having his tooth torn from his jaw. He didn't want to admit how the idea horrified him and he had hoped Nefertiry hadn't heard the priestess agree with the physician. "The tooth will yet serve me for a time," he replied coolly.

Nefertiry's laughter floated through the hall. "You wish to forget about the tooth. While the pain is gone, you're content to think it won't return—but it will and again you'll have a temper like a serpent painfully shedding its skin."

"Maybe it won't come back," Ramessa said.

Nefertiry stopped walking and their escort of guards halted. "Both Resy and Makara said the ache will return. If you ignore both the physician and a priestess, you deserve the pain."

"How can you say such a thing? Have you no compassion?" Ramessa asked, his eyes gleaming with amber streaks of humor.

"The pain you experience is nothing to the torment everyone else in the palace must endure from your sharpened temper," Nefertiry advised him. "It will return," she said. "When it does, after I can no longer endure your misery, I'll find a way to end it."

Ramessa's eyes widened in mock terror. "What will you do?" he asked.

Nefertiry raised one of her scepters and gestured threateningly. "I'll ask to see the offending tooth and will rap it with my scepter, thus removing the source of all our torment. The tooth will be at your feet before you'll guess my purpose."

"I think you'd better stop waving your scepter around

and appear more dignified," Ramessa advised. "We're almost at the throne room door."

Nefertiry obediently recrossed her wrists against her breast and resumed walking toward the throne room, where the herald had begun to call the royal court to silence.

Although Ramessa faced forward, he observed from the corner of his eye how Nefertiry had raised her head a little higher under her gleaming double crown, how she stood a bit straighter. He smiled as he slowly paced through the expanse of the room among his bowing subjects.

When they had reached their golden thrones and seated themselves, he whispered, "Your new necklace lights your face and your eyes take on the color of the Nile when its green is lit by the sun."

"I thank you, my lord," she murmured. "You're especially generous to so compliment me after I've just threatened to strike out your tooth."

Ramessa's lips drew in a tight line as he struggled to control his smile, but then Rasuah rose from his bow and looked up at his king with careful solemnity. "Majesties, I have received a message from Lord Metenu about the Djemeh in Sun-Amenti Province."

Nefertiry had anticipated the Dejemehs wouldn't easily relinquish their hold on the place they'd gained in Tamera. It was too profitable and, so far, too easy to prey on the province. She had no doubt the army would have to be sent to drive them away. So she listened with only half an ear to Metenu's message, which merely confirmed her opinion. Instead, her mind was on how she should react when the news was brought that Reshet had apparently left Wast.

Nefertiry sat silent as a statue, her face from long habit not revealing her inner thoughts, but carefully wearing its usual mask of haughty indifference. By now Reshet and her son were dead, Nefertiry thought, and their threat to herself and Setnau had quietly and forever been

447

ended. Anticipating the news, her eyes scanned the crowd in the throne room as she wondered if any of Reshet's guards stood among them or if the list of the day's petitioners, which Rasuah held, contained the name of one of Reshet's attendants. She sighed softly and decided, if it wasn't announced during this audience, she would find it very difficult to calmly go about her normal, daily affairs.

"It's too bad Arek is no longer among the living or I'd send him to help Metenu. He'd know how to deal with the Djemeh," Ramessa said.

"What of Captain Paneb?" Rasuah suggested.

"Perhaps Paneb——" Ramessa said softly, then fell silent while he considered Paneb's qualities.

"But I must speak to the king! I must!"

Ramessa lifted his head at the shout from across the room. He turned to Rasuah. "What is that disturbance?"

Rasuah tried to peer over the heads of the crowd and shrugged. "I don't know," he said. "I cannot see."

"Clear the way for the intruder and we will learn of his purpose," Ramessa said, waving one of his scepters.

"Bring him forward!" Rasuah commanded. "Stop this foolish commotion!"

Nefertiry sat up, wondering if this was the message she awaited. Then she decided it couldn't be. It must be news of some emergency, a violence of some kind, to be so rudely announced.

A man came half-running toward the royal dais. When he threw himself prostrate at the foot of the thrones, Nefertiry saw the look of horror on his face. She wondered what new catastrophe had befallen the kingdom.

"Peheti!" Ramessa exclaimed in surprise. Then he lowered his tone and asked quietly, "Why are you not at Lady Reshet's gate?"

"Because there's nothing within that house to guard." Akeset stepped out of the crowd, as if he had followed the man, but at a little distance.

448

"What's happening here? Arise, Peheti. What's wrong?" Ramessa demanded, becoming alarmed.

"Majesty, I'm afraid to get up," Peheti gasped. "I'm afraid to tell you my news."

Ramessa leaned forward tensely. "Get off your knees and tell me!"

Peheti stood up slowly, trembling, his eyes round with terror. "Majesty, it didn't happen while I guarded the house." His voice trailed off at the look on Ramessa's face.

"Bring this man some wine or water," Nefertiry directed in a tense tone. "He appears ready to collapse."

Peheti's eyes turned to Nefertiry, then quickly looked away. He shook his head. "No wine, nothing. I'll control myself," he whispered.

"Tell them what you found," Akeset urged.

Ramessa looked curiously at the priest, wondering what Akeset had to do with Peheti who was really a palace guard, but he did not ask, because Peheti seemed about to speak.

"Majesty, they didn't get past me—" Peheti began.

"Make sense!" Nefertiry snapped. "Tell us what happened without making endless excuses for yourself."

Peheti's eyes went to his feet at Nefertiry's words. They remained there as he whispered, "My watch at the lady's gates began at dawn. I exchanged greetings with Susu, the guard I was relieving, and he left." Peheti paused to swallow and continued to whisper, "As was my habit, I went to the kitchen to have my morning meal—" Again, his voice faded.

"Go on, Peheti," Ramessa urged, a shadow beginning to move over his heart.

Peheti raised his eyes slowly, glanced at Nefertiry and wondered at the strange expression on her face. He shifted his gaze to Ramessa and whispered, "The cook was dead. Her throat had been cut." At Ramessa's soft gasp Peheti continued woodenly, "She, like all the servants in the house, lay in pools of congealed blood, as if

449

someone had gone through the house during the night slashing all their throats."

"What of Lady Reshet? Her child?" Ramessa asked hoarsely. "Tell me about them!"

Peheti glanced at Nefertiry, who looked stunned by this news. He wondered again at her expression, at how fine an actress she must be, even to grow pale when she wished. He dragged his gaze from her wide green eyes and looked at Ramessa. "I found them in her bed-chamber."

Ramessa stood up. "You found them! How did you find them? Tell me!" he commanded, his face graying.

"I'm afraid to tell you, majesty. I don't think I can describe—" Peheti's voice failed him.

"You will tell me exactly what you found," Ramessa and softly, raising his scepter as if he would strike the guard.

Again Peheti fell to his knees. "Majesty, I haven't the words!" he cried. "Strike my head from my shoulders if you will, but I don't know how to say it!" He raised his head to look up at Ramessa, his eyes brimming with horror. "Would you have me describe it here—in court —before them all?"

"Tell him," Akeset said softly.

"Be silent, priest," Ramessa snapped. He looked at Peheti. "Tell me," he said coldly.

Peheti swallowed again, then said, "The lady was bound to the bed. She had been tortured in so many ways I couldn't know all that had been done to her. Blood covered the linens and had splashed even upon the floor." Peheti paused and, as if in remembering the scene he became nauseated, he swallowed before he continued in a trembling voice, "Wounds had been inflicted upon her that I cannot describe. So much blood, from all over—" Once again Peheti paused, breathing great gulps of air as if he feared he would faint before he continued, "Some-one who knew the embalmer's art had opened her body
450

as if to remove her organs for burial, as if to prepare her mummy! The parts were cast aside on the floor."

"On the floor?" Ramessa repeated, incredulous, and sank weakly back into his throne.

"Yes, on the floor!" Akeset declared. "Lady Reshet's heart, her viscera, even her brain had been drawn out and tossed aside!"

"Akeset, enough!" Ramessa shouted. He looked at Peheti with fiery eyes. "What of the child?"

"The child was likewise mutilated. But I think he had died before, because little blood had run from him, as if his heart had stopped before the wounds were made," Peheti said. He had sunk from his kneeling position to that of sitting on one hip. He knew this posture was less than reverent before the thrones, but he was too weak with horror to move.

"Give your king what you found on the floor of the bedchamber," Akeset urged.

"What have you to do with all this?" Ramessa demanded. "Why do you prompt Peheti?"

Akeset lowered his head. "I was passing near the lady's house when Peheti came running out. Observing his disturbed state, I naturally inquired what was wrong. I accompanied him back into the house to see if anything could be done, if the spark of life remained in any of them. They all were long dead." Akeset raised his head and, glancing again at Nefertiry, urged, "Peheti, show his majesty what you found on the floor near the lady's bed of pain."

Peheti reached into his sash and with shaking fingers took out a small, glittering object.

"What is it? Bring it closer!" Ramessa said softly.

Peheti moved like a man sleepwalking, as he slowly got to his feet and took the two steps toward Ramessa, then dropped the object in his king's outstretched hand.

"A hair ornament?" Ramessa whispered, his face paling.

"Look closely at it," Akeset advised. He turned triumphant eyes on Nefertiry. "Examine it also, divine lady. Do you not recognize it?"

Nefertiry stared at Akeset a moment. Then, she turned her head to look down into Ramessa's open palm. The blood crusting the hairclasp didn't hide the royal insignia of Khatti. Her face grew even whiter. "How—" she whispered.

Ramessa raised terrible eyes to Nefertiry. "It's yours," he said clearly. "It carries your insignia." A dusky red now flooded his face under his tan.

Nefertiry's gaze remained fixed on the ornament. She couldn't speak. She felt as if she couldn't breathe.

"The queen must have watched her rival's anguished writhings, no doubt enjoying the torture inflicted on the body that had loved you," Akeset said viciously.

Ramessa turned his stare on the priest and warned, "You will silence your tongue or I'll have it removed!"

"My lord," Nefertiry finally whispered. "Surely you can't believe such a thing of me."

"You hated her." Ramessa's tone was as pitiless as his eyes. "No one hated her as you did."

Nefertiry lifted her gaze to Ramessa. "But, my lord, surely you don't believe—" she whispered, then stopped.

A great fury had risen through Ramessa's shock. It blasted a path through his horror. It overwhelmed him like an enormous red wave. He was visibly trembling with the urge to kill Nefertiry now—to stop her breath, to close those green eyes that stared at him. It took the greatest effort to clench his fists around his scepters instead of her throat, to stand up and look down at her a moment and ask clearly, "Who are you to end her existence?" Then he whirled, his court robe billowing in a crimson blur, and walked stiffly out of the throne room.

Nefertiry leaped to her feet and watched Ramessa disappear into the corridor. She stood silently a moment, staring at the faces of the shocked court. No one moved or made a sound. It seemed as if none of them breathed. They were like the figures of a tomb's painted mural.

452

Finally, Nefertiry turned to face Akeset, and when her eyes fell upon the priest, her being was filled with an anger equal to Ramessa's.

"You haven't won, Akeset," she whispered.

Akeset felt as if lightning had struck at him from her eyes and he moved back involuntarily. When she stepped down from the dais, he again retreated a pace. But she brushed past him, so near he felt as if the air around her crackled—and like a great emerald-eyed cat, she stalked from the throne room.

Although Nefertiry was trembling from head to foot, she walked rapidly through the corridor toward her room, her sandals clicking on the stone floor like a very fast beat on an instrument.

Chenmet ran after her mistress. When Nefertiry paused by the door to her bedchamber, Chenmet threw it open; Nefertiry entered her apartment, pausing only for the moment it took to tear off her crown and toss it and her scepters on a table. Then, she turned to stare at the great, golden door to Ramessa's chamber.

"My lady, you can't see him now!" Chenmet exclaimed, looking terrified.

"It is this moment, above all others, when I must speak to him," Nefertiry said clearly. Taking a firm hold on the door's handle, she threw her weight against it. The door swung open and she stepped into Ramessa's room.

He was standing by the window with his back toward her. He seemed not to have heard her enter. Waving Chenmet back, she closed the door and latched it, locking herself in with him.

"You know I would have killed you a moment ago," Ramessa said, still staring out the window.

"You may kill me now, but you'll first hear what I must tell you," she said quietly.

Ramessa turned to look at Nefertiry. His narrowed eyes were filled with amber points of color, like live sparks glowing. "Is there nothing you wouldn't dare?"

453

She took a step toward him, and he warned, "Stay a distance from me, Nefertiry. I don't trust myself."

Nefertiry walked quickly across the room to face him. "Kill me then," she said defiantly.

Ramessa stared at her, the same fury she'd seen in the throne room again lighting his eyes. But he turned away, his fists clenched at his sides.

"Can a brother kill his sister?" Nefertiry asked.

Thinking she meant the terms as endearments, Ramessa sank into a chair to regard her with an expression of revulsion.

Nefertiry followed him, but she stopped a few feet from the chair to lower herself to the floor and sit with her robes spread around her, staring up at him.

"You do not understand what I mean by the words I just used so I'll explain them to you. If you have me executed and begin a new war with Khatti as a result of what I'm going to tell you, I cannot help it," she said quietly. "I only hope Hattusil will forgive me for breaking the vow I made to remain silent."

As if Ramessa hadn't heard her, he said wearily, "Now you'll tell me you didn't kill Reshet and her son. Now you will lie."

"Do you think I stood by and watched her tortured as Akeset suggested?" She shook her head slowly from side to side. Nefertiry lifted her eyes to regard Ramessa steadily. "I didn't kill Reshet and her son, but I paid a Shardanan to do it. His name is Shemal."

Ramessa stared at her. "You admit it?" he whispered.

"I gave him a vial of poison, a liquid which would have brought both of them instant and painless death. I instructed him to carry off the bodies as well as their belongings and make it appear as if Reshet had decided to leave Wast," Nefertiry said.

"I told you I'd make her leave!" Ramessa exclaimed. "Why did you do it?"

"I was in her house the day you spoke to her," Nefertiry replied. "I realized that she would never leave; she
454

would find ways to cling to you until you finally fell again into her bed. Nevertheless, Ramessa, I didn't kill her. Shemal betrayed me. He was paid by someone else to do what was done. If you can catch him, you might force the truth from him. Never have I wanted the revenge Peheti described. If I'd so hated Reshet, I would have gone blind with rage to her house and with my own hand put a dagger through her heart."

Ramessa stood up, stared down at Nefertiry a moment longer, then turned away. "But the child!"

"That child I thought of as a potential man who would threaten Setnau's place, the place I made for him," Nefertiry said clearly. Ramessa turned again to look down at her, his disgust unconcealed. She got to her feet. "Don't hold your head so high, thinking yourself so far above me. I've had better reasons for what I've done than you imagine." As she took a step toward him, he recoiled. But she went on speaking. "I know it was Akeset who had Reshet and the child murdered that way. He made sure my hair ornament would be placed in her room so I would be blamed. He and his priests are after me with such determination now I know I must tell you the truth."

"What do you know of truth?" Ramessa sneered.

"Although I've concealed some things from you, I've never lied to you," Nefertiry replied. "Now I'll tell you those truths I'd kept hidden."

Nefertiry sank into a couch and leaned her head back, closing her eyes. "What I'll tell you is what Hattusil revealed to me only after Khatti had lost that final great battle with your army," she murmured. "He decided to rid himself of a child he'd officially recognized as his firstborn, which I wasn't, by giving me to you as part of the treaty."

"You weren't his firstborn?" Ramessa asked softly, coming closer.

Nefertiry shook her head wearily. "I wasn't his child at all, and he wanted Mazraima, who is his son, to inherit his throne without my causing him difficulties. That

night he told me why it was necessary to give me to you."
Nefertiry sighed before continuing, "My mother's true
name was Memnet. She was the daughter of a lord in a
northern province of Tamera. She was unmarried and
pregnant when her father's house was attacked by the
Hyskos, who carried her away. When they discovered she
was pregnant, they sold her to a slave-trader, who sold
her as part of a lot of slaves destined for Khatti's palace.
Hattusil saw her and loved her immediately. Mutallu, his
older brother, was heir to the crown, so Hattusil was able
to marry her. When I was born, out of love for Memnet
he proclaimed me his own child, and he cared for me as
if I were a child of his body. When Mutallu was killed
in the battle, Hattusil was surprised to find himself wearing Khatti's crown. Understandably, he wished to have
Mazraima inherit the throne. But as he already had
publicly proclaimed me his firstborn, he would have had
to deny me as his daughter. He was fond of me and
wished me no sorrow so he told me the truth."

Ramessa had walked to the window during this story.
He turned to face Nefertiry and ask, "What does all this
have to do with me or Reshet's murder?"

Nefertiry opened her eyes at last. "My mother's lover—
my father—was King Seti, your own father. I'm your
half-sister," she said clearly.

Ramessa took a step closer, his eyes wide with shock.
"My sister?"

"Hattusil told me to obtain my rightful place in Tamera
by my cleverness." She smiled ruefully. "My rightful
place. I could never have that place. I could have the
crown only if I remained your favorite wife."

"I can't believe this!" Ramessa walked to the chair
directly in front of Nefertiry and sat down to stare at her.

"The throne is mine as well as yours, mine by my
father's blood, but I could never claim it. In obedience to
Aset through Seshena's powers I have given guidance to
the land, I have destroyed our enemies, I have strength-
ened this throne." She sat up stiffly. "Tell me, Ramessa,

456

do I look like a Khatti woman? Have I behaved ever as a Khatti princess? Would a Khatti princess make herself deadly enemies for Tamera's sake? Would a Khatti princess embroil herself in intrigues to keep your land strong? Deny, Ramessa, that I've loved this land only as Ra's own daughter could love it! Deny even what Tuiah guessed from the beginning—that I'm the child of her old enemy and the daughter of your own father!"

Ramessa shook his head weakly, unable to argue. "I'm married to my sister," he finally whispered.

"You wonder how I could come to you when I knew this? I had no choice!" she declared. "You wonder how I could set aside this knowledge and love you as a woman? You know how strangely I behaved at our wedding banquet. You also know how it was between us from our first kiss." She stood up and began to pace the room as if she were a lion in a cage, an exhausted lion resigned to imprisonment. "Love is not denied by bonds of blood, I quickly learned, but by the laws of knowledge. My desire for you was never pretense. I have lived, therefore, as your wife though I'm your half-sister," she murmured.

"And had our child!" Ramessa whispered.

Nefertiry paused to look at him. "Not our child, Ramessa," she said. "I couldn't allow myself to bear your child, but I wished a son of mine to take the throne I couldn't have. Setnau is the child of another man's body. His father's blood is noble enough to sire a future king. I chose my lover carefully."

Ramessa was silent a moment before demanding, "Who is Setnau's father?"

"Not even your torturers would obtain that name," Nefertiry said, and she turned defiant eyes on Ramessa. "You have a whole harem! Our marriage contract didn't forbid me one lover!"

Ramessa sighed. "It was understood you wouldn't have a lover."

"The marriage contract didn't forbid me one," she insisted. "I broke no promise to you."

457

"No, I suppose you didn't," he said finally.

"All the things I've done that you haven't understood were for the purpose of keeping the throne strong, for giving the crown to my son. I wished Setnau to have every advantage so he could hold his place—so he could rule wisely. I have even been sending him to Seshena that he might learn more than I'd ever known."

"My mother knows who you are?" Ramessa asked quietly.

"Tuiah recognized me immediately because I look like my own mother. She knew of Seti's interlude with Memnet. Tuiah resented my being at your side, but what could she do? She couldn't come to you, who were so hungry for my body, with such a wild tale. She had no evidence." Nefertiry walked slowly to the window. She stared at the sunlit garden for a time. Finally, she turned to face him. "I've loved you, Ramessa, and not like a sister. But I admit my first purpose was to put Setnau on the throne. Now you can understand why I couldn't allow myself to become merely another concubine, why I had to be first royal wife and the queen."

Shaking his head, Ramessa asked, "What shall I do about this sister who is my wife—my heir who is another man's son—my wife who arranged for my lover and my son to be murdered?"

Nefertiry sighed again, a long, deep shuddering sound. "Do you think with shame of the nights we've lain in each other's arms? I've known the truth from the beginning and I have yet come to you gladly. Could you keep secret this knowledge as I have and keep me at your side as I've been all this time?"

"How do you know I won't have you executed?" Ramessa asked quietly.

"I think you haven't the heart for it," she answered slowly, hoping he didn't. "I think you also wouldn't wish to return me to Hattusil, because to save his own honor he would have to renew his war with Tamera. I think you'd like to avoid that. You might strip me of my titles

458

and power; if you do, the priests will at least cease their efforts to kill me, which might be a favor to me." She lifted her eyes to regard him steadily. "But to do that, you would have to turn me away forever. To do that you would have to renounce Setnau as your son, bringing disgrace upon him, and he is innocent of all this. He also is Seti's grandson and a royal child, despite his father." She walked closer, until she stood before him, looking directly into his eyes and said clearly, "For my own choice, I would continue to take my chances with the priests. I would risk staying with you, not only for Setnau's sake, but because I wish to remain at your side."

Nefertiry turned away and walked toward the golden door. Before opening it, she looked again at Ramessa. "Perhaps you're filled with shame that you have lain with your sister and enjoyed it so much. The thing was done so long ago I doubt the gods would be angry with you now."

Dazed by the shocks that had been dealt him one after another during this last hour, Ramessa stared numbly at Nefertiry until she opened the door, slipped outside and closed it quietly after her. He continued to stare at the door for a long while before his mind began to function, before the myriad pains once more assailed him. He stood up and paced the room for a time, exactly as Nefertiry had. Finally, recognizing how alike their impulses were, he went to his bed and threw himself among its tumbled cushions to stare at its draperies while he tried to collect his thoughts.

Although Nefertiry's story had stunned Ramessa, he was even more shocked at his delayed reaction to Reshet's death—and the death of the son he'd never claimed. How they had died horrified him as it would have horrified him to hear of anyone else he knew having died in that fashion—but his grief was no more than it would have been if some other of his household had been so murdered. He also realized that, had it been Nefertiry and Setnau who had been killed, his grief would have been overwhelming. His sense of justice hungered for reprisal, but against whom would he take revenge? He considered Nefertiry's paying the Shardanan to kill Reshet and found he could understand her reasons as perhaps no one but a king could understand. And although Ramessa didn't approve of murder, Nefertiry's wanting Reshet dead didn't shock him now. He knew, under the same circumstances, his own impulse would have been identical. In that moment, without consciously realizing it, he had dismissed any thought of executing Nefertiry. Instead, Ramessa found himself wondering if the reason for their peculiar compatibility was their mutual father.

Ramessa didn't doubt Nefertiry's claim to being his half-sister. But he found it was impossible for him to feel a brotherly impulse toward her. He realized that she was right—the bonds of blood didn't necessarily shut out love. It was the knowledge taught from childhood which put a sister beyond her brother's embraces. When he recalled Nefertiry's behavior on their wedding night, despite his consternation, he smiled faintly with new understanding. With remembrance of that night and so many others, he felt the same desire for her rise in him as always. He considered her suggestion of keeping their secret and going on as before. That they hadn't conceived a child and never would seemed to give them a kind of exoneration.

Again Ramessa remembered that Nefertiry had taken a lover, and he was fired by jealousy which shamed him for several reasons, but that jealousy he couldn't completely control. He reflected upon his own extensive harem and how Nefertiry had resented those women. He recalled the nights she had lain awake, knowing he was with another of his wives. Turning his eyes to the golden door between her quarters and his, he realized he had used that door more as a barrier than as a portal between them. He remembered the marriage contract, which left fidelity to their own discretion. He briefly recalled how passionate was her nature. But he quickly pushed aside
460

that thought, because despite what he now knew, it again had awakened in him desire for her.

Ramessa turned his thoughts to Setnau, the dancing green eyes beneath tousled black hair, the little arms that had lovingly reached toward him so many times. If he went this moment to Setnau, the boy would reach toward him in his innocence, trusting the man he thought was his father. Ramessa forced himself to concede Setnau was not only a charming child, but more intelligent and sensitive than any child he'd begotten by his other wives —a son any man would claim with pride. Setnau could, if properly guided, grow into a man who would be supremely deserving of a crown. If Nefertiry's plans had come to fruition, it would not have been the first time in Tamera's history that the king's nephew had inherited the throne. It would have been legal in the eyes of men, had they known of it. It would have been accepted by the company of divine beings, Ramessa realized. He turned over to lie on his stomach and bury his face in a pillow. He couldn't let another man's son take his throne, even if the boy did carry royal blood through Ramessa's own father.

Ramessa forced himself to turn his thoughts to another aspect of this peculiar situation—Nefertiry's latest accusation against Akeset. For some reason Ramessa didn't fully understand, Nefertiry had hated Akeset from the beginning. She had accused the priest of all manner of crimes, which she obviously believed him guilty of, but many of which Ramessa doubted because they had seemed so wild. Although Ramessa had merely endured most priests he'd had contact with, he firmly believed in his religion. He'd been sternly taught that the office of high priest deserved respect, even if the man who held it wasn't to his personal liking. Seti, he recalled, hadn't shown much camaraderie with any priest, but he had treated all of them with respect. It had been unthinkable until now for Ramessa to do otherwise. To consider seriously Amen-Ra's high priest capable of committing

461

such sacrilege as Nefertiry accused Akeset, was so stunning as to force Ramessa to reconsider concepts he'd accepted from his earliest childhood.

Recalling how, though pale and trembling visibly with fear of him, Nefertiry had entered his room and even defied him to kill her, Ramessa had to admire her courage. All through her confession she had been so quietly dignified, though she was helpless and resigned to her helplessness. Her attitude gave credence to her explanation, but he knew from past experience how cleverly she could influence him in her favor. He couldn't deny he admired the complicated workings of her brain. She had, as always, managed to anger, utterly confuse as well as frustrate him, and he still wanted her. He felt a fresh stab of guilt to think of it.

Ramessa sat up, his head spinning with his conflicting feelings. He rested his chin in his hands while he considered the situation.

If he excluded Nefertiry from his daily business, it would indicate he'd decided her guilt and only delayed considering her punishment. If she seemed to have fallen so far from royal favor and Akeset really was ruthlessly plotting against her, Ramessa shuddered to consider what the priest might think it possible to do to her. If Ramessa continued with Nefertiry at his side as before, it would appear he'd judged her blameless. To have her assume this would very likely open the way for an entirely new set of problems.

Another idea occurred to Ramessa. Were he to delay making any decision—if Nefertiry was forced to continue wondering for a time about her fate—he could finally tell her he intended to resume their old relation, with some restrictions on her part. Then she might be sufficiently grateful and relieved that he could command a new—although he would never expect a total—obedience from her. He thought again of how he must plot to extract from Nefertiry even a small portion of what his other subjects gave wholly and without question. He conceded she surely had royal blood in her veins to be so unbendingly rebellious. Suddenly, he stood up and called for Nehri.

When the servant, pale and fearful, hesitantly entered the room, he was amazed to hear his king calmly advise, "I've decided to personally lead the attack on the Djemeh. Begin the preparations immediately so I can leave for Sun-Amenti Province tonight."

24

"My lady, during the three days of his majesty's absence, the priesthood of Amen-Ra has constantly spoken against you," Chenmet said anxiously.

"I'm well aware of it," Nefertiry replied crisply, giving her attendant a warning glance not to say more about the subject while Setnau was playing in the room.

"Are you also aware that after the noon resting time, Akeset himself led a crowd to the palace's gates to make an inflammatory speech against you?" Khakamir said from the doorway.

Nefertiry turned to face him. "Why do you think my windows have been covered?" she said. "They'll leave when it's time for the evening meal and their bellies grow emptier than Akeset's lies."

"That time already approaches and they remain at the gates," Khakamir declared, his dark eyes narrowed with anger. He saw Nefertiry glance nervously at the windows and he walked swiftly across the room to throw open the shutters. An ugly, low buzzing assaulted the room's serenity. "Just because you couldn't hear or see them doesn't mean they're gone. Come here and listen to what that priest is saying about you."

Nefertiry felt the hairs on the nape of her neck rise, but she turned a calm face to Chenmet. "Take Setnau for his meal," she said quietly. Setnau's questioning eyes lifted from his game, and Nefertiry immediately stooped and opened her arms to him. Keeping a bright smile on her face, she watched as he toddled toward her. Scooping him into her arms, she said, "I won't be able to have the meal with you tonight, dear one, but I'll come in to see you later."

When Setnau stepped away, his green eyes looked intently at her a moment before he asked, "Khakamir stop man from saying bad things?"

Nefertiry glanced meaningfully at Khakamir, then nodded to Setnau and replied with forced calm, "Yes, dear one. The bad man will be stopped." She smiled brightly and added, "Now go with Chenmet. I'll come and help you bathe for bed."

Setnau turned away and raised his hand to grasp Chenmet's fingers and, giving Nefertiry one more glance, obediently went with the maid.

Nefertiry watched the door close behind them before turning to Khakamir. "He's the reason I kept the windows covered—and why I seemed so uninterested in Akeset's speech. Have a care, Khakamir, about how you speak in his hearing!" she snapped.

Khakamir nodded, but said no more. He watched Nefertiry march angrily toward the door to the terrace.

"I think Akeset may keep them at the gates until it's dark," she said coldly. "What a disgusting creature he is!"

The sound of Akeset's voice floated over the walls, across the garden and into the room, his words falling like rocks on Nefertiry's head, "If his majesty thought her to be innocent, why didn't he say so in court or make some proclamation before he left?"

"Yes, indeed, why didn't he?" Nefertiry muttered as she stepped onto the terrace.

"Surely Ramessa doesn't think you're guilty," Khakamir whispered as he followed her.

Nefertiry shrugged and lifted her head to listen to Akeset's continuing harangue.

"Our king left so suddenly out of grief for the woman he loved—out of horror for what was done to her and her child!"

"Ramessa left as usual, I think, to avoid the whole matter," Nefertiry mumbled.

"She's an alien from a barbaric land, this woman who sits on our throne!" Akeset cried. "Nothing is beyond her! She influences our king with evil magic! She has cast a wicked spell on him that blinds him to Amen-Ra's light!"

"He'll work them up to storming the gates yet!" Khakamir said angrily.

"Be silent," Nefertiry warned. "I want to hear what he's saying so I can accurately repeat it to Ramessa when he returns—if he'll listen to me."

"Because of her corruption, taxes have been diverted from the projects they were legitimately intended!" Akeset cried. "Didn't he build a great temple to her?"

"Because of your corruption, Akeset, our people are near rebellion," Nefertiry muttered.

"I would silence that priest with a squad of soldiers so you could answer his lies," Khakamir snarled. "Let me send the soldiers to carry him off."

Nefertiry shook her head. "There's a trace of truth in what he says," she whispered.

"What truth could come from his rotted heart?" Khakamir snapped.

"I paid a Shardanan to kill Reshet and her child," Nefertiry said slowly. "He did it in a different way than I'd ordered, though." She turned to look at Khakamir and saw the shock on his face. "I gave him a poison to use that would have stopped her heart without pain," she

467

added. She looked away, unable to endure the expression in Khakamir's eyes. "It was Akeset, I'm sure, who paid the Shardanan to torture Reshet. But I've killed others, Khakamir. I set the leopard on Nehemu. I poisoned Petet. It was because of me you killed Arek."

"You can't blame yourself for everything that's happened. Nehemu tried to strangle you! Arek had far overstepped his place with you!" Khakamir cried.

"What of Petet, Khakamir?" Nefertiry whispered.

Khakamir shook his head as if he would hear no more. "I beg you, leave Tamera with me—now, while Ramessa is gone!"

"You wish to take a murderess for a wife? A woman who has slain even a priest?" Nefertiry asked.

"I would go down to the gates right now and with my own sword kill the high priest!" Khakamir declared. "Kill a score of priests and I'll yet want you. Come with me to Punt, Nefertiry. It's a beautiful place and far enough away."

"I cannot go," Nefertiry whispered.

"You won't go because you do love Ramessa!" Khakamir gripped her shoulders and turned her to face him. "But what about Setnau? What about his future."

"It's because of Setnau's future that I stay," she said wearily. "At last Ramessa knows the truth about me. I had to tell him!" Seeing the look on Khakamir's face, she said quickly, "He knows Setnau isn't his son, but I didn't tell him you fathered him. I think it's very possible, from the way he behaved, he wants me enough to go on as before—that he loves me as no other and will forgive me my lover. I think he might even accept Setnau, whose blood is yet his own!"

Khakamir lifted his hands, as if he would touch her, then changed his mind and let them drop to hang at his sides. He looked down at his feet for a moment before raising his eyes to meet hers. "Still, Nefertiry, Setnau is my son. I love him and his mother. But if you won't
468

abandon this madness and come with me, I must defend you. You are my queen."

Nefertiry inhaled deeply as if she had been afraid to breathe these last minutes. Finally she asked, "What will we do about this mob outside the gates?"

Khakamir's eyes narrowed at a new surge of sound from beyond the walls. "In a short time I'll have no choice but to take my soldiers out there and crack some heads. I would start with Akeset's."

"Akeset will slip away before your soldiers open the gates. There's no way to get Akeset other than to present evidence that he paid the Shardanans to kill Reshet by torture."

"What evidence does a serpent leave that would show the path he slithered down?" Khakamir said angrily.

"He must have paid the Shardanans gold—a lot of gold—to do so evil a task," Nefertiry replied. "Akeset doesn't personally have that much gold. It had to come from the temple and somewhere in the temple there's a tally scroll that accounts for gold Akeset can't produce."

"Do you think he'd let someone walk into the temple and study his records? It would need Ramessa himself to do that!" Khakamir declared.

"The gold wouldn't have come from the temple in Wast. Akeset would be more careful than to take gold from a temple so near the palace." She paused a moment, waving to Khakamir to remain silent while she thought about it. "What place under Akeset's influence would be least suspect than the most holy of all temples? The temple Seti added to and Ramessa finished—the place where Asar's sacred mummy lies—Asar's special shrine!"

Khakamir groaned. "The temple at Ahbidew?"

"Yes!" she cried. "That has to be the temple from which Akeset took the gold. Who would think of it?"

"Only you," Khakamir admitted. "We can tell Ramessa when he returns and this whole thing will be cleared up."

"I don't want to give Akeset enough time to think of transferring gold from some other temple and escape his punishment," she declared, her eyes glittering like emeralds. "I must get the evidence myself—now, while Akeset thinks I'm afraid to leave the palace for any reason."

"You can't go!" Khakamir exclaimed. "You wouldn't know where to look! It could be anywhere in the temple! A regiment of soldiers would have to go through the temple's chambers one at a time, searching every corner for the tally scrolls."

Nefertiry shook her head and whispered, "I know exactly where to search. In the treasure room."

"But its door is concealed!" Khakamir cried. "I understand such doors have a bolt that can be thrown only by one who knows how!"

"But I do," Nefertiry replied calmly. "All those nights Ramessa was occupied with Reshet and I didn't call for you, do you think I spent my time helplessly grating my teeth? Oh, no. Each night I gathered up an armful of scrolls from Ramessa's private library and studied them, then replaced them before dawn." When Khakamir remained silent she added, "I doubt even Ramessa realizes I can read the hieroglyphs that well. And I'd wager Akeset is convinced I can do nothing more than recognize my name."

From beyond the palace walls came another wave of sound, which carried a menacing tone. Khakamir lifted his head to listen. "Now I must take my soldiers out there," he said. "Now I have no choice but to use violence."

"What kind of violence?" Nefertiry asked anxiously.

"Clubs, swords, and possibly arrows from the walls," he answered in a hard, tight tone. Seeing her alarmed expression, he added, "The king left me in charge. What else do you think I can do with your subjects, divine lady? Would you prefer letting them storm the palace and tear you to pieces?"

"I don't believe they'd go that far," she whispered.

"Normally, I don't think they would. Maybe Akeset

has hypnotized them. Whatever method he's used, he's turned them into a mob. You've never seen such a thing before, have you?"

"No," she murmured. "I have not."

"I'll make sure you don't today," Khakamir declared. He walked toward the door. But before he left, he asked, "When will we go to Ahbidew?"

"When darkness has fallen. I'd planned to leave the palace wearing simple garments. If we use a small boat and behave like commoners on a pilgrimage, we'll draw no attention. We should reach the temple late tomorrow, but we won't enter it until long after everyone else has left," she answered. "I'm grateful you'll come with me, Khakamir. Your company will be comforting."

"Did you think I'd let you go alone?" he snapped.

"No," Nefertiry said. "In case Ramessa still doesn't believe me, you'll be a witness he trusts."

Khakamir's eyes glowed with an anger, but he said nothing. Neither of them had noticed that the great, golden door to Ramessa's chamber was slightly ajar. When Khakamir stepped into the outside hall and shut that door after him, the golden door also closed with an almost imperceptible click.

Nefertiry turned to study her appearance in the sheet of polished gold that served as a mirror and smoothed her hair. Then, adjusting the ribbon she wore at her waist, she left her quarters to keep her promise to Setnau. Once Setnau was in bed, she planned to ask Chenmet to borrow the maid's plainest garments, but she would not reveal even to Chenmet what she planned to do.

Rasuah stopped his chariot at the base of the last hill before he reached his house and, as was his habit, he threw back his head to look for Seshena. He expected her to be sitting on his terrace wall waiting for him. But Seshena's figure wasn't silhouetted against the purple and red-streaked sky. She might have gone inside for a moment, he reasoned, but he urged his horses to ascend the slope at a swifter pace.

When he stopped the chariot in the courtyard, without waiting for a stableboy to take the reins, he leaped lightly from the vehicle, dropped the reins and walked swiftly into the house.

"Djanah! Zehzee! Where is everyone?"

Zehzee's thin brown face briefly peered around a corner before the servant hurried to greet Rasuah. Djanah, a worried look on her face, promptly followed Zehzee.

"I'm glad you're home, my lord!" Djanah said fervently. "Terrible things have been happening in the city!"

"What's happened? Where's Seshena?" Rasuah asked, handing Zehzee his dusty cloak.

Djanah clasped her hands together so tightly her knuckles whitened. "The little one hasn't come. There's a disturbance in the streets. She might be afraid of leaving her house!"

"What disturbance, Zehzee?" Rasuah gripped the servant's arms tightly.

Zehzee's words tumbled from his mouth, "My cousin, who lives near the marketplace, said that priest has been speaking every day against the queen since the king left for the north. This afternoon a great crowd went to the palace gates. We heard an uproar even from here just a short time ago and I think Commander Khakamir has led the royal guards against the people."

"You've received no message from Seshena?" Rasuah asked anxiously. When Zehzee and Djanah simultaneously shook their heads, Rasuah's eyes narrowed. "She knew I was returning today?"

"She knew," Zehzee said tensely.

"My lord, I'm afraid she tried to come and got caught in the rioting!" Djanah cried.

Rasuah paled and his hands left Zehzee's shoulders. "Have my horse prepared. I'm going to Seshena's house," he said. When Zehzee turned to obey, Rasuah looked at

Djanah. "Stop wringing your hands. I'll follow the route she would have taken." He managed to force himself to smile as he added, "We'll be back in an hour and we'll both be hungry."

"Can I help you with anything before you go, my lord?" Djanah asked.

Rasuah shook his head. "I'll just change my tunic," he said, not mentioning that he also planned to take his sword. When he turned to walk quickly toward the stairway he muttered, "I leave the city for only three days to investigate a report of Shasu secretly camping in my province and that accursed priest causes a riot."

As he entered the city, Rasuah slowed his horse to a walk and, following the route Seshena would most likely have taken, watched carefully for her. But his eyes took in scenes he had never before seen in Tamera. He was shocked.

People ran through the streets as if they were fleeing something, scattering as soon as they saw even a lone soldier, leaping for the shelter of doorways and shadowed corridors. The soldiers, usually in pairs and on foot, followed the people brandishing spears and clubs. Although they seemed to do no more now than wave the weapons and shout, Rasuah saw evidence that weapons had been used.

Some of these people who were running held bleeding wounds or favored arms that were obviously broken. Others hobbled close to walls, leaning their weight against the bricks and relieving the pain of injured legs. Rasuah saw a few people sitting on the pavement, their backs propped against walls, holding their bleeding heads or looking dizzily about. In one narrow lane, Rasuah hastily stopped his horse and dismounted with a pounding heart to go to a woman who lay on her face unconscious. When he turned her over, he was relieved it wasn't Seshena, but he lifted the woman in his arms and looked around to see if anyone passing recognized her.

Another small group of people with peculiarly blank-looking eyes ran past Rasuah. Several soldiers on horses followed the people, herding them almost as a shepherd would drive his flock, and Rasuah was horrified that the people seemed as senseless as sheep.

A large crowd of subdued people escorted by soldiers turned a corner and flooded the lane, crowding Rasuah aside. One of the soldiers marching at the crowd's edge, saw Rasuah and approached him.

"I'll find out who this woman is," the soldier said and carefully took her into his arms. He glanced at Rasuah's garments and said sternly, "You should get off the streets, my lord. Although the worst is over, further violence is possible."

"I'm looking for Aset's high priestess, who might have come this way," Rasuah advised. "Do you know what she looks like? Have you seen her?"

"I know who she is, but I haven't seen her in the streets," the soldier quickly answered. "Aset's temple has been thrown open to take the injured and provide shelter for those accidently caught in the riots. Maybe she's there supervising."

"I think that's very likely," Rasuah said, obviously relieved. "You think the worst really is over?"

"By the gods, I hope so!" the soldier exclaimed. "I've seen nothing like it before—and I can tell you I prefer battle against an army to this kind of duty against people who don't know how to fight, yet fight anyway." He shook his head. "Commander Khakamir drove away those at the palace gates and now we're just trying to make the others go home, but they're behaving queerly."

"I've noticed that," Rasuah said drily.

"If that priest had kept his mouth shut, none of this would have happened. I don't understand how the people got so excited. Most of them seemed to have lost their power to reason. These that we're escorting home hadn't heard the priest, but left their houses to wander around

474

the streets gaping at the rioters. They should have stayed home."

"Are you arresting them?" Rasuah asked.

"Only when we can't calm someone down," he replied. "Even so, there will be a lot of cases for the king to judge when he returns—a lot of wounds to be bandaged and bones to be set."

"I think I'd better go to the temple," Rasuah said.

"And stay there, my lord, or waste no time getting to your house," the soldier advised. "Everyone is going to be ordered off the streets for the night. There will be many patrols to make sure everyone stays off the streets too."

"Maybe it would be a good idea to keep the people in their houses tomorrow as well," Rasuah said grimly.

The soldier nodded. "Heralds are moving through the city instructing the people to remain in their houses or gardens for the next two days and nights, So, be sure you're away from here before the torches are lit. They are the signal to clear the area." He paused a moment, then advised under his breath, "I don't think the soldiers would bother you, my lord, but many of them are in a worse mood than I, and you shouldn't take chances."

Rasuah looked around the now practically deserted lane. "It seems your job is almost done," he observed. "Are the priests of Amen-Ra included in this rule?"

The soldier grinned. "They especially have been ordered to remain within their temple's walls day and night."

"What about Akeset?"

The soldier's grin faded and he shrugged. "If he can be found, he'll be so ordered. Perhaps he's already shut up in his temple."

"I'd shut him in his tomb," Rasuah said with sudden ferocity, and turned away, leaving the startled soldier to stare after him.

When Rasuah entered the courtyard of Aset's temple, he was surprised and refreshed by the orderliness of the crowd within. Unlike the people on the streets, whose eyes were mostly vacant, the eyes he saw here were calm and intelligently focused. The people who awaited attention talked quietly, while others moved purposefully at their various tasks. A woman, whose figure was about Seshena's height and size was standing a short distance away with her back toward him. Rasuah approached her.

"Seshena?" he inquired.

The woman turned quickly. She was a stranger to him. "The high one is in the temple at the shrine of Bast," the woman said quietly. "I'm Amset, one of her assistants." Rasuah frowned, wondering if he should disturb Seshena, but the woman added, "I know you are Lord Rasuah. I think you should go to my high one."

Rasuah nodded his thanks and walked to the temple entrance. Lamps already had been lit and their warm light reflecting from the pale walls gave the vast chamber a cheerful glow. The fragrance of incense, rich and sweet on the air, was pleasantly mingled with the perfume of many recent floral offerings. Rasuah paused halfway across the room, which was filled with worshippers, and again, he was impressed with the purposeful serenity of such a crowd as compared to the people running through the streets. As Rasuah turned toward the shallow room at the side of the temple, where Bast's statue stood, he saw Seshena kneeling at Bast's feet. He hurried to her.

"Beloved?" he whispered.

Seshena turned to look back over her shoulder and stared up at Rasuah with great, dark blue eyes, but she didn't get to her feet. She said nothing in greeting, which alarmed him.

"What's wrong, beloved?" he asked, extending his hands to her.

Seshena shook her head, swallowed as if to rid her throat of something, and took his hands. She got to her feet slowly and Rasuah was further alarmed by the pallor of her face.

"The trouble outside is almost over," he offered.

"That's only the beginning of the pain," she whispered.

476

Rasuah stared down at Seshena and realized her eyes were glazed with tears. "You've received more knowledge from Bast?"

"No," Seshena answered in a soft voice. Her fingers continued to cling tightly to Rasuah's. "The doors of her knowledge have been closed to me. That's how I know the scroll of the divine beings has been opened to a new sheet, which will record even more terrible events soon to come."

Rasuah led her to a small beneh and drew her down to sit beside him. "How can you be certain of that? Maybe you received no answers because this is the end of the matter," he said, wanting to give her hope.

"No," Seshena whispered. "It's the crisis we now are facing. That I may not know what's coming means I'm forbidden to interfere."

"How could you interfere?" he asked.

Seshena sighed. "I'm a winged priestess, beloved. If I could know what's likely to happen and decided to save those involved the pain they must be near to experiencing, I could use my powers to change the coming events by imposing my own will on them. They must be dreadful that Bast refused me even a choice."

"Why should the divine beings stop you from helping someone?" Rasuah asked.

Seshena lifted her eyes to look intently at him for a moment before answering, "Sometimes events, however painful, are necessary for the souls involved to experience, because those souls must learn an essential lesson. I think this is the case now. I cannot tamper with the plans of the One Alone."

"Akeset is soon to be defeated?" Rasuah asked. "Ramessa will punish him for starting this riot?"

Seshena closed her eyes tightly, and murmured, "I think Akeset's starting the riot will mean nothing by the time Ramessa returns. I think even the murders of Reshet and her child will pale before the horror of Akeset's next crime."

Rasuah's fingers lifted her chin and she opened her

eyes. They seemed to glow from a light of their own making. "You do know what will happen!"

"I know nothing more than you," she insisted. "I can only guess."

"What do you guess?" he asked.

"I cannot tell even you, beloved. It's terrible to feel so helpless!" she whispered.

"If you can't stop or alter what will happen, come with me," he said, thinking that his house on the city's edge would be a safer place than the temple.

"Neither I nor my temple is in danger," she said.

He put his arms around her and drew her close. "I want to be sure."

"I'll come to your house, but I'll be a poor companion, because my mind will be haunted by this other thing," she warned.

"I can endure your moodiness and distraction," he said, and held her a moment longer before he rose and drew her to her feet.

As Rasuah and Seshena left the temple, Amset turned to Sena to say, "Our high one is deeply troubled. I'm glad her beloved is with her to comfort her."

Sena nodded and muttered, "I'm troubled too."

Amset's eyes widened. "I didn't know you were a seer."

Sena shook her head. "I'm not, but there's something so menacing in the atmosphere even I can sense it."

Amset sighed. "We all are troubled and try to hide it from each other. How foolish for priestesses to do such a thing. If we're that disturbed, can you imagine how affected our high one, who is far more sensitive, must be?"

"I cannot—nor do I wish to," Sena replied firmly. "I haven't the strength."

Nefertiry and Khakamir had removed their sandals before leaving their little boat. When they had approached the temple's soaring walls, they pulled up the hoods on their cloaks and carefully arranged them around their faces. They knelt at the foot of Asar's statue until time for

478

the temple to be closed for the night. But when they left the main chamber, they worked their way to the fringes of the crowd of worshippers and, reaching a narrow, unlit passageway, slipped into its shadows.

Khakamir was amazed at Nefertiry's ability to recall the temple's plans as she led him down a maze of dark hallways to a small deserted cubicle—usually used by novitiates for study—and there they settled into a heavily shadowed corner to wait.

The moon was just beginning to shine through the narrow slit high in the cubicle's wall and Khakamir had decided that Nefertiry had the patience of a spider spinning its web, when her hand brushed his in signal.

"We must not even whisper once we leave this room," she warned.

Her fingers left his and he heard her robe rustle as she got to her feet even before he did. Quickly, he stood up and sensing she meant to leave the room at once, he reached out to catch her hand, pulling her to him. "One embrace before we go," he whispered. "I know how dangerous what we're going to do is."

Her head lifted and she slid her arms around the tight muscles of his waist. He laid his cheek against hers and inhaled her perfume deeply, the way a man who has dragged himself off the desert drinks water.

"I would yet beg you to forget this, to leave Tamera with me, but I know you won't," he whispered.

"Nothing will happen," she murmured beginning to feel apprehensive herself. "Do you have a premonition?" she asked.

"I'm not inclined to such things," Khakamir whispered. "I merely am the man who loves you. That's what I wanted to say one time more. I love you, Nefertiry. I don't care if you're Ramessa's wife or Seti's daughter. If the priests catch us, they'll have to walk over my body to reach you, I promise."

Nefertiry felt a chill run down her spine. "Don't say such things, Khakamir. You frighten me."

"You should be frightened," he whispered. Then, after holding her tightly against him for a moment more, he released her and walked silently to the door to look out. Seeing no one, he waved her forward.

Again Nefertiry led Khakamir down the maze of narrow, unlit passageways, until they finally approached a large corridor in which lamps hanging from the ceiling at long intervals gave some measure of coppery light. There she stopped and motioned to him that they would next follow this corridor. Khakamir shuddered in anticipation of walking under lamps, however dim. But when she stepped into the corridor, he followed her.

So soundlessly did their bare feet touch the floor Nefertiry felt like a ghost haunting the temple. Although this was one of the main passages of the temple, it was utterly deserted—as she hoped it would remain—but not even a small sound from any of the temple's myriad chambers came drifting down the stone-lined halls. She glanced uneasily around, and Khakamir, too, shifted his eyes in a constant wariness.

The lamps cast streaks of glimmering orange light on the walls, which seemed to animate the painted figures that were carved into the stone. Nefertiry was startled more than once by a hand that appeared to move, a wing to flutter, or an eye that appeared to turn in her direction.

The corridor opened onto a vast room with many other halls and doorways leading from it. Khakamir saw Nefertiry stop and he breathed a silent prayer she wouldn't enter so strategically dangerous a place. But she turned to him and pointed to a series of staggered ledges made by stones protruding from the nearest wall. He nodded, confused by what appeared to him to be merely a decorative effect. Then, she mimed a figure climbing stairs, and he understood. The ledges were stepping-stones, but to where? He frowned as his eyes followed the ledges to what seemed to be a blank wall. Nefertiry gestured that there was a door in the stone above the ledges that could be moved by applying pressure in precisely the right place.

Although Khakamir's scalp prickled as he thought of the noise a moving slab of stone might cause, he nodded. When she began to creep toward the ledges, he followed.

They climbed the ledges slowly, carefully, lest their feet dislodge even a pebble from the stepping stones, and send it clattering below. Khakamir was glad that priests were generally not inclined to athletics and the ledges were close enough together to climb without effort. When they finally reached the top, Khakamir remained to one side, where Nefertiry indicated he should stand; while Nefertiry stooped, her fingertips sensitively moving over the stones near the floor as she searched for the one place that would respond to light pressure. When she finally found it and the panel began to swing inward, she turned to give Khakamir a triumphant look. He was watching the slab, which was greater in thickness at the top than the bottom, swing in and over their heads to form an almost normal-sized doorway. He was relieved at the silence of the panel's motion as well as impressed with the mind that had conceived the idea of so finely balanced and so well-disguised an arrangement.

Nefertiry grasped Khakamir's hand, to direct his attention from the mechanics of the door's design. She gestured that he was to stay outside while she entered the room and searched for the tally scroll she sought.

Khakamir nodded, then turned to touch the head of the small torch he carried to the flame of the nearest lamp and handed it to her. As she moved soundlessly into the chamber to place the torch into a holder set in the wall, he leaned forward to peer curiously at the room.

It was a small chamber—one of many treasure rooms in that temple, he guessed. Its walls, ceiling and floor were lined with undecorated limestone that time had darkened to a smoky gray color. At the far end of the room were great piles of dark-colored sacks, which Khakamir assumed held gold. The nearest wall had shelves that held hundreds of scrolls. He looked at the papyrus cylinders and wondered how long it would take Nefertiry to find the

481

right tally. But she smiled confidently and walked directly to the shelves to begin counting the niches separating the piles of scrolls, first from the floor up, then from the right to the left. He realized she had somehow even learned which niche would be likeliest to contain the tally scroll she wanted.

Khakamir stepped out of the doorway and moved to the side of it, to watch for intruders.

Nefertiry rerolled the papyrus sheet she'd finished studying, replaced it and took another from the niche. She unfastened its case and unrolled it to begin reading it contents, her forehead creasing in her concentration.

A small sound from the doorway penetrated her awareness, and she glanced up, expecting to see Khakamir impatiently motioning her to hurry. Instead, her eyes widened in horror.

Khakamir was standing in the doorway, but he was leaning unsteadily against the stones, the orange fire swiftly fading from his eyes, his mouth soundlessly moving in one word, "beloved." The long, slender shaft of an arrow still quivered in his chest. His sword fell from his numbed fingers to crash on the floor.

"Khakamir!" she gasped and ran toward him, but by the time she reached him, he had sunk to his knees, and she dropped to the floor to kneel beside him.

Once again his lips moved in the word "beloved" and his eyes looked at her with profound regret before they closed and he pitched forward to the floor.

"Khakamir!" she screamed and bent over his body.

"Drag him out of there," came a crisp order.

Still too stunned to think, Nefertiry lifted her eyes to see Akeset, Befen and another priest standing in the doorway. Akeset kicked Khakamir's sword back out of the room, and Befen bent to grasp Khakamir's ankles. He began to pull Khakamir's body out of the room, and Nefertiry leaped to her feet to protest this rough treatment, but she said nothing, because she realized that Khakamir had left his body and no longer felt what was being done to him. She stared at Khakamir being drawn from her presence and tears filled her eyes. When Khakamir's body was outside the doorway, she stepped toward the opening to follow, but Akeset thrust her roughly back into the room.

"How dare you touch me!" she snapped drawing herself to her full height, her tears instantly forgotten.

Akeset stared at her a moment, then smiled. "Look at her!" he exclaimed. "Even now she gives commands expecting us to obey, this little Khatti woman who plays at being our queen."

"Seti's daughter is your queen," Nefertiry said coldly.

"King Seti's daughter!" Befen mocked. Taka, the other priest, chuckled.

"Ramessa knows what I am and he'll have your heads if you touch me again," she warned, putting on her old haughty mask even while her knees shook and her heart froze in terror.

Again Befen and Taka laughed. But Akeset, whose sharp old eyes had known King Seti well, had been staring intently at Nefertiry's face—at the set of her jaw, and especially at her emerald eyes, which held a look he had often seen in Seti's green eyes.

"Silence," Akeset commanded, his hand gesturing the lesser priests back.

"You know me, don't you, Akeset?" Nefertiry said coolly. "You also know the penalty for harming a member of the divine royal house."

Akeset stepped backwards, as if to ward off a threatened blow.

"Release me and I'll make sure only he who killed Commander Khakamir is punished for that. I'll forget all the rest of your plots, Akeset, even the way you had Reshet murdered. I'll give you and the others exile," she promised, keeping her voice firm only by using all her strength.

"Do you want to go into exile, Befen?" Taka asked, laughter in his voice.

"I told you to be silent," Akeset retorted and, pushing Befen behind him, stepped out of the room.

Nefertiry watched while Akeset hastily reached to the top of the doorway and pressed the stone, reversing its delicate balance. She watched silently as the slab swung into place, sealing her in the little room.

"But I am the queen!" she said clearly. The sound of her words echoed from the stone walls, making it seem as if her own voice mocked her. She moved closer to the door, pressed her hands against the unyielding slab, and whispered, "But I am!" More whispers mocked her.

She noticed that the flickering light from the little torch was rapidly dimming, and she realized the flame would momentarily die.

Suddenly she remembered the charm Seshena had made to protect her and she reached for it. She always wore it twined in the ribbon that bound her waist, but her seeking fingers didn't find it. She looked down in surprise. The blue cord tied with magic knots was gone.

"I've lost it, Seshena," she whispered, suddenly chilled with new fear. "It's gone!"

The torch went out and darkness filled the silence. Nefertiry stood motionless a moment, trying to remember where everything was in the little room. Finally, she decided it didn't really matter. The room contained nothing she could use now. She lowered herself to sit on the floor while she tried to think more calmly about her situation.

Akeset gazed at the wall that imprisoned Nefertiry, wondering about what she had said.

"Seti's daughter!" Befen sneered.

"Dispose of this corpse as I instructed," Akeset snapped. He watched Befen swing Khakamir's body over the ledge into the arms of the other priest, who waited below, then again stared at the wall Nefertiry was trapped behind.

Befen straightened and turned to face Akeset. The

expression on Akeset's face made him uneasy. "You don't believe her?" Befen asked doubtfully.

"I've never seen Nefertiry with that look on her face before. It was like seeing Seti risen from the dead," Akeset whispered. "I wonder how—" his voice trailed off.

"You do think she's Seti's daughter!" Befen exclaimed. When Akeset nodded, Befen clutched at Akeset's robe. "If she's of the royal divine blood and we kill her, she'll come back! She'll curse us as only the children of Ra could curse their killers!"

"Don't be foolish. Nefertiry's as mortal as you are. She isn't even a priestess," Akeset said, trying to loosen Befen's grip on his robe. But he recalled the many times Nefertiry had known about his schemes, and he wondered nervously how she had known his unspoken plans. He also wondered how she had been able to close out her thoughts from his probing.

"Children of Ra don't have to be temple-trained!" Befen's voice rose shrilly. "The goddess Wadjet protects the royal head; Sekhmet avenges them! Nefertiry's spirit will return! She'll curse us!"

"Let go of my robe," Akeset snapped. "Although I didn't anticipate this problem, I'll make a spell to deal with it."

"A spell! What spell?" Befen cried, nearly hysterical.

"The spell that destroys the demon Apep should be sufficient to obliterate Nefertiry's soul. Only instead of a wax figure, we have Nefertiry's own body to use, thus ridding ourselves of her physical presence as well as her returning soul," Akeset said, sounding more confident than he felt. "If she does return, she can haunt Tuiah. It was, after all, Tuiah who sent us the warning."

Befen stared at Akeset, and as he recalled what the spell involved, his eyes grew wild with fear. "I couldn't do such a thing!"

"Don't—" Akeset began, but he was too late. Befen had stepped backwards off the ledge and, too surprised

485

to even cry out, fell silently to the floor below, striking the stone with a solid crunch.

Akeset moved closer to the edge and looked down. Befen's skull had been broken like a pomegranate. Akeset whispered, "Fool!" Then, giving one more uneasy glance at the wall of stone that trapped Nefertiry, he shivered before he hurriedly made his way down the ledges.

After Nefertiry settled herself on the floor, her thoughts turned again to Khakamir. A terrible grief tore through her soul. Leaning her head back against the cold stone of the wall, she closed her eyes in an effort to stop her tears, but they wouldn't stop. They welled up like a newly struck spring, running down her cheeks and dripping from her chin to moisten her robe, until she thought she could no longer bear her pain and began to sob aloud. She remembered Khakamir's eyes watching always for her protection and thought of how they had looked when he leaned in the doorway—helpless and filled with sorrow for her, not himself. She remembered the strength of his body, his lithe walk, how he had ridden laughing with her in the sunlight of a long-ago day, the touch of his lips in a happier hour—then the muffled sound of his limp body being dragged away. And she sobbed afresh, for she had done it all to him. He hadn't wanted to love her—she had deliberately lured him, seduced him, knowing from the glow in his slanted eyes how he desired her. She had never told him she loved him, not even in that last moment before he left his body, when he had no voice. His lips had called her his beloved, but she had not once said she loved him.

Aeons later, when her tears were exhausted, she sat drawing ragged breaths, saying, "I wish I had gone away with you when you had life, Khakamir. Twenty crowns can't match the cost of your life. But if your soul is comforted by this, you know I'll soon follow you." As she thought about dying, she felt like screaming in frustration for all the plans she'd made that meant nothing now.

She wondered how Akeset had known she would come to the temple. She'd told no one of her plans but Khakamir. Had all of it been a trap planned toward this end? she wondered. She considered how Akeset had looked when she'd said in desperation that she was Seti's daughter. Akeset had believed her, she was sure, maybe too readily believed her. Had he somehow already known? Only Seshena and Tuiah had known. Seshena never would have told anyone—Tuiah had been afraid even to tell Ramessa.

But Ramessa had known before he'd left for the north. Nefertiry grew cold at the thought. The hairs on her head seemed to lift, and the skin all over her body felt as if it crawled with invisible insects. Ramessa had been so furious with her he'd struggled to restrain himself from killing her in the throne room in front of the court. When she had told him about herself in his chamber, he had said little. She shivered. Had she so misjudged him? Was he capable of murdering her? The sure knowledge that he had killed often and mercilessly in battle and had calmly watched many prisoners being decapitated was like a cold knife in her heart. Perhaps this was why Akeset dared lay hands on his queen. Maybe he was under Ramessa's orders.

Nefertiry once again started to tremble, and she drew her knees to her chest, stiffly clenching her arms around them, curling up in horror like a child. Ramessa had said nothing to her before he'd gone north. Maybe he'd deliberately left the question of her guilt unanswered before the court so no one would grieve too much after her disappearance. Having the priests dispose of her while he was absent would have been a convenient way to rid himself of her. Perhaps he had even laid a trap for Akeset to step into and would later accuse the priest of her murder.

This new wave of horror broke over Nefertiry's head. She felt as if she would drown in it and, like a swimmer relentlessly being sucked by powerful currents to the open sea, she lifted her head and opened her mouth to scream, but no sound came from her lips. The unbending discipline of a long line of kings and queens still flowed in her blood. She shut her mouth, uncurled her body and sat up straight. All the screaming in the world had never frightened away death, she decided.

Suddenly a new thought struck her. That morning almost a month ago Ramessa had led her from the throne room and had made love to her without giving her a chance to prepare herself. How ironic it would be if Ramessa had ordered her death, not knowing she might be pregnant with his child at last, a child doubly royal. She wondered what Seti's spirit thought of his son killing his daughter and possibly his grandchild as well.

A new and even more terrible thought struck Nefertiry. What would Ramessa do with Setnau? She leaped to her feet. No! Surely he wouldn't harm an innocent child! Cold sweat broke over her as she tried to gather her scattered wits. Ramessa had loved Setnau; he'd all but promised him the throne. Nefertiry began to pace the floor. Stumbling over something in the darkness, she fell to her knees and remained there, thinking. If the sight of Setnau offended Ramessa, would he just send the boy to the House of Royal Children and ignore him? She couldn't believe Ramessa would have Setnau killed —the workings of Ramessa's mind couldn't be that alien to her. Again she was wrenched by the destruction of all her careful plans.

"What dreams I had for you, my son," she whispered "How I fought for you every step of the way you'll never know, unless our souls meet soon in Tuat. If you live, I'll become a slowly blurring figure in your memory, and you'll someday forget. And how I fought for you!" Tears again stung her eyes. Finally she thought of Seshena and wiping away the tears that scalded her cheeks, whispered, "Seshena loves you, my little one." Slowly getting to her feet, She screamed into the darkness, "Seshena!

Save him, I beg you! You're the only one I can trust. Please save my child!"

Then, convulsed with sobs she could no longer stop, she stood in the middle of the dark room, her face in her hands, and wept.

Sometime later, long after Nefertiry had stopped crying and sat numbly on the floor with her back against a wall, the stone slab swung open, and Akeset stood in the doorway. She turned her head wearily, blinking at the light, though the lamp he held was small.

"You've come to kill me finally?" she asked calmly, getting slowly to her feet.

Akeset stared at Nefertiry. Even in her plain garments, crumpled and soiled from the floor, even with her lustrous hair snarled, her face smeared with tears and stained with Khakamir's blood, she stood straight, her head lifted as high as if she were in court wearing the double crown. He wondered at this queen's courage and congratulated Seti's ghost on the daughter he had produced.

Akeset said, "Don't speak of death when I've brought you refreshment." He held out a basket with a neatly sliced melon.

Nefertiry gazed at the fruit a moment before she raised her eyes to Akeset's face to say, "Maybe the melon holds death as well as refreshment."

"No," Akeset replied shaking his head. "It holds compassion for one who has been so long without food or water." He extended the basket toward her.

Nefertiry lifted her hands to take the basket and saw Khakamir's blood on her fingers. She looked at Akeset and said clearly, "But I've had a diet of royal tears and a nobleman's blood to sustain me." Then her lips curled with profound scorn for him. "If you persist on this course, you know the penalty your soul will pay even if the hand of man never punishes you."

Akeset stared at Nefertiry's eyes, which glittered like emeralds in the flickering light. They held death. He thrust the basket into her hands and, whirling around, almost ran out of the room. His hands were shaking uncontrollably as he reached for the stone that would close the door. The slab slowly began to lower, and he looked up to stare at Nefertiry, who stood straight and calm. Her eyes fixed him with a hatred so complete he felt as if he looked into the eyes of the avenging goddess herself. When the door had finally closed, he turned to face the priest waiting on the ledge.

"In her eyes was a curse," Taka whispered shakily.

"In her hands is a melon soaked with a powerful drug that will put her into so deep a slumber she'll never speak again to utter curses or anything else," Akeset snapped and turned to hurry down the ledges. "When we come for her in the night, she'll be docile enough."

Inside the stone chamber Nefertiry reflected with some small satisfaction on the look Akeset's face had worn. Her fingers touched the cool, moist fruit, and she wondered if Akeset wanted to poison her. Then, deciding not even the most sophisticated of poisons could be camouflaged by a melon's subtle flavor, she lifted a slice of the fruit to touch it with the tip of her tongue. She tasted it carefully, then put her nose to the fruit and smelled it, discovering nothing. But that small touch of moisture had awakened a thirst so great she trembled. Again she ran her fingertip over the fruit, just to feel its wetness, wondering if she dared eat it. The finger, unbidden, went to her mouth, and she licked it. What did it matter? she decided. If death came in a poisoned melon, perhaps it would be, at least, painless.

Then, Nefertiry lowered herself to the floor so she might eat her melon in comfort, whatever it held.

Several hours later, Akeset again pressed the stone that opened the door and fearfully watched the slab swing away. Hearing no sound from within, he bent forward, holding his lamp high, to peer inside the room. He let out a breath of relief. Nefertiry sat on the floor propped up by the wall, her head on her chest, the
490

melon skins bearing mute evidence that she had eaten the fruit. Akeset stepped back to face the priests that accompanied him. "Taka, carry her out," he ordered.

Taka's eyes widened and he stepped cautiously into the room to gaze at Nefertiry's unmoving form. He looked fearfully at Akeset and asked, "She's dead?" he asked.

"No, no," Akeset hissed. "It's only a sleeping drug—but she'll be unconscious until morning. By that time we'll have accomplished the thing." Akeset glared at the priest, who was obviously not anxious to touch Nefertiry even while she slept. "Pick her up," Akeset ordered. "I want her out on the open desert as quickly as possible. I want to be on my way to Wast before morning."

Taka moved slowly into the room and forced himself to bend and pick up the limp queen.

"Take her down there," Akeset ordered. "Put her in the jar, as I told you before. What's the matter with you?" Akeset snapped. "Do it. She can't hurt you. Look at her! What can she do?"

Taka's eyes dropped to Nefertiry's pale face, but quickly lifted. He turned to hurry down the ledges, wishing her struggle to breathe didn't make her sigh as she did, wishing as he lifted her body to push her into the jar that her arm wouldn't keep falling over his shoulder, wishing as he stuffed the last strand of her hair into the jar and capped it that he had remained at the temple he'd served in Abtu.

The stars shimmered with cold fire in the moonless black of the sky, while on the desert below, three priests of Ra prepared their sacreligious ritual. Beside a small fire that glittered like a dark topaz on the sand, Akeset arranged the articles he'd require for his ritual, while Taka and Anherru pulled Nefertiry's unresisting body from the earthen jar.

"I wish you'd used another jar," Taka said in a hushed tone, wrinkling his nose. "This one was used to store

491

lamp oil and still smells rancid. The jar yet contains enough of the stuff to have soaked these clothes she wears."

Akeset looked up from his preparations and his eyes glittered in the firelight. "I know that."

Taka opened his mouth to ask why Akeset had deliberately chosen this messy jar, then realizing Akeset's purpose, paled and shut his mouth.

"Drag her here," Akeset said softly. Taka and Anherru obeyed, and Akeset knelt beside Nefertiry. As he lifted his eyes, they gleamed with triumph although his hands shook while he wrote Nefertiry's names and all her titles from Khatti as well as Tamera on a piece of new papyrus. "Lift her a little," he muttered.

Taka backed away staring at Nefertiry. "Anherru, it must be you who does it. I cannot," he whispered.

"Consider how your own neck would feel on the royal executioner's table if she lives to speak of what we've done so far," Akeset said venomously.

But Taka shook his head and would come no closer.

Anherru looked at Taka. Aware of the alternative, he bent to lift Nefertiry so Akeset could draw a black cord around her waist. Then, he lowered her body and watched Akeset tie the cord into many little intricate knots, binding the roll of papyrus among them.

Akeset raised the short sword he'd brought, its blade catching orange lights from the fire, and said, "I have brought fetters to thee, Sharula-Nefertiry, enemy of my altar. Thou hast fallen because I have drawn them tight. I have overthrown you, Sharula-Nefertiry, my enemy. Thou shalt never partake of the delights of life; thou shalt never fulfill thy desires. I maketh thee to go back. O, Sharula-Nefertiry, who art hateful, I look upon thee no more." Akeset bent over Nefertiry's legs and picked up one pale foot. "I cut off thy feet and thou wilt be crippled in the next world so thy spirit cannot follow my path," he declared and began to hack at her ankle.

The sudden, sharp pain penetrated even the drug

Nefertiry had been given, and she opened her eyes with a start. Anherru, who had been gazing at her face regretting what they must do to her beauty, stiffened in terror.

"Akeset!" he screamed and scrambled back from her. "She's alive! She's awake!"

Akeset dropped Nefertiry's foot, which was almost severed from her ankle. Afraid she might somehow still utter a curse, he hastily crawled forward to stare down into eyes that glittered darkly green in the fire's flickering light. Her lips parted. Too frightened to realize she could do no more than moan, Akeset raised the sword and screamed, "Get thee back, Nefertiry! I have overthrown thy words. The gods have turned thy face backwards. I cut off thy head to take thy breath and thy life from thee!" And with Nefertiry's eyes still staring up at him, he swung the sword down to her throat. Again and again he swung the sword, chopping her head from her neck, while royal blood sprayed over his arms.

Taka turned away, holding his hands to his ears so he wouldn't hear Akeset continuing to chant as he worked.

"A knife is struck into her head—her name no longer exists on this earth. It is decreed for me to inflict blows upon her."

Even Anherru backed away slowly, as Akeset worked and chanted, "I cut off her hands, that she may not lift them in a curse to me." When Akeset picked up a large rock and lifted it over Nefertiry's lifeless head, Anherru closed his eyes and stopped his ears while Akeset cried, "Thy soul cannot speak or take nourishment; thy spirit's eyes are blinded!"

Akeset finally raised his head to look at Taka, who was still turned away, then at Anherru, who stood trembling uncontrollably. Realizing neither would help him, he put down the sword and got to his feet. With his legs shaking under him, he took a faggot from the little fire and placed it on Nefertiry's oil-soaked robe, which immediately began to blaze.

"She falls into the flame!" Akeset declared. "She is

493

given over to the fire, which obtains mastery over her in the name of Sutekh!" He bent to get another piece of flaming wood and set her hair alight, while his voice carried clearly out over the darkened sands, "Her name no longer exists. She does not exist!" He threw her discarded cloak over her body, and it too was set ablaze while he chanted triumphantly, "Her soul and her body and her spirit and her shadow and her words of power and her bones and her skin will never more exist!"

Nefertiry's body was a fiery mound on the sand. Jackals in the distance, smelling death yet knowing nothing would be left for them, howled mournfully, while the stars shimmered coldly in the moonless black of the sky.

25

The gates of Wast opened and Ramessa and his soldiers entered the city in triumph, finally returning with long lines of Djemeh prisoners after an unexpectedly long and hard struggle. The exultant shouts of the people made Ramessa's victory doubly sweet.

When he had undertaken this venture, Ramessa had expected to be faced with the simple task of driving a few relatively small and poorly armed bands of thieves from Tamera's borders. But King Kapouro of Djemeh had decided to send his son, Prince Meshesher, and a regiment of his army to protect his returning subjects. Ramessa had barely arrived in Sun-Amenti Province before he was advised of the rapid advance of Meshesher's forces. With grief and anger still burning in his soul, Ramessa welcomed battle and led his soldiers into a charge on Meshesher's regiment with a fervor that stunned the Djemeh. Despite the spirit of Ramessa's leadership, it took several days of bitter fighting before

Ramessa's forces were able to push back the Djemeh troops, which were greater in number. Finally, Meshesher, who had found himself facing Ramessa's personal attack just as the horses pulling the prince's chariot dropped and his aide fell out of the vehicle pierced by a spear, called for his depleted forces to surrender.

Now, though he accepted the cheers of his people with his usual outward calm, Ramessa's inner being was bursting with elation. How surprised Nefertiry will be, he thought. He planned to go directly to her chambers as he had done in the past, and, still wearing his dust-coated tunics, take her in his arms. She would, he knew, be suspicious at first; her eyebrows would shoot up. Those brows would quickly lower when he told her that he had decided to forgive her hiring the Shardanans to murder Reshet. Anticipating Nefertiry's welcome, then, caused a smile to break full upon his face, like the sun from behind a cloud.

Riding through the palace gates amid a chorus of trumpets, Ramessa eagerly looked up at Nefertiry's terrace. She wasn't there. His smile faded momentarily before he decided that she was being stubborn or, even more likely, didn't show herself because she didn't know his mind. Again his smile grew in brilliance. Very soon she would know not only his mind.

Ramessa dismounted quickly, and bending to pat Botar's head, wondered why the leopard wasn't with Nefertiry. Botar, he'd been assured, hardly left Nefertiry's side when he was away from the palace. He straightened and studied the group waiting outside the palace doorway. Tuiah's welcoming smile looked as if it had been painted on her face. Nehri's eyes were downcast as were the corners of his mouth, and Rasuah was absolutely grim. Ramessa ran up the steps, feeling very uneasy.

"The peasants looked happier to see me than you, my mother," he said, embracing Tuiah. "And the rest of you greet me as if I'd lost the battle instead of brought victory." He turned to Rasuah. "Why is your face so grim, my friend?" He glanced behind them and asked, "Where's Khakamir?"

"We don't know where Khakamir is," Rasuah said quietly. Seeing Ramessa's confused expression, he explained, "Khakamir disappeared a few days after you'd left the palace—right after he put down a riot Akeset and his priests stirred up."

"A riot!" Ramessa was stunned.

Rasuah took a breath before answering. "Akeset spoke against the queen until a mob gathered by the palace walls. Khakamir drove them away and the royal guards restored order in the town." He paused, then added, "Akeset and his priests have since been confined to their temple's grounds."

Anger flooded Ramessa's eyes with amber. "As well they should be! But Khakamir has disappeared? You mean really disappeared?"

Rasuah nodded. "That's not all," he said. "The queen also has vanished."

Ramessa felt as if he'd been struck. He stepped backwards and his mouth fell open. He couldn't speak.

"Her clothes, her jewels, all her belongings are yet in her apartments as if she would walk in any moment. But she's been gone two decans," Rasuah said. Then, seeing the look that came over Ramessa's face, he added tactfully, "Setnau asks for her daily, and we don't know what to say to him."

"Setnau is still here," Ramessa finally whispered. "What of Chenmet?"

"Chenmet awaits the queen's return as do we all," Tuiah said in an odd tone.

Ramessa looked at his mother, then at Mimut and Nofret, who had moved forward. "Mimut, do you know anything of this?"

"Nothing, my lord," Mimut whispered. "Five days after you left my servant awakened me with this news. The whole harem was stunned." She paused then added, "My lord, I say in all truth none of your wives or concubines knows more than you've just been told. Lord Rasuah has had them questioned—everyone I think in the palace and the royal guards as well have been questioned —and no one knows where she's gone."

Ramessa turned away. Like a man moving in his sleep, he walked into the palace. When he reached the foot of the stairway, he paused. Without looking back at them he snapped, "They'll all be questioned again! I'll do it myself!" Then, he ran up the stairs with Botar at his heels and Nehri struggling to catch up.

As Ramessa came to Nefertiry's rooms, he stopped so abruptly Botar ran into his legs. But he didn't notice it. He flung the door open with such force it struck the wall and bounced back. This time he kicked it and marched inside.

Chenmet, who had been sitting in a chair, leaped up and promptly prostrated herself at Ramessa's feet, crying, "Majesty, did my lady send a message to you that we haven't seen?"

"Get up," Ramessa said brusquely. Noticing that when the servant arose, her face was wet with tears, he said more gently, "Sit down, Chenmet. I've had no message and you must tell me what you know—everything."

Chenmet wiped her eyes and sat down but she stared into her lap as she asked, "The others have told you about the riot?"

"Not in detail, but all I wish to hear of it for now," Ramessa replied. "How did the queen react to it?"

Chenmet's eyes, filled with pride, lifted to meet his. "My lady had me cover the windows so the little prince wouldn't hear what was being said," she declared. "My lady pretended in his presence the day was too hot to let the sun in." She shook her head. "But it angered her, majesty. It hurt her. When the commander came to speak of it with her and she had me take the little prince away so he wouldn't be frightened—but Setnau wouldn't be put off. He questioned me so closely about it and I had to
498

lie many times—may Tehuti forgive me—before my lady came to prepare him for bed."

"What was her mood then?" Ramessa inquired.

"She seemed very cheerful, but I was sure it was for the little one's sake," Chenmet said, shaking her head slowly. "She didn't speak of the riot to me again, I think because the commander had already gone out to put the trouble down. He did so very quickly, I heard later. I never saw the commander after that, although his servant admitted he loaned the commander some old garments of his." Chenmet paused, then added cautiously, "My lady borrowed an old shift and a dark cloak from me. I don't know her purpose."

"Then what happened?" Ramessa urged.

"After my lady ate her evening meal, she dismissed me, saying she had something she must do. She said she would leave the palace for two days and I shouldn't worry—but she wouldn't say where she was going or what she planned to do." Forgetting herself in her anxiety, Chenmet reached out to clasp Ramessa's hand. "My lady didn't run away with the commander!" she exclaimed. "She had something necessary to do with him, but she didn't run away from you, majesty!" Suddenly remembering whose hand she'd caught, she dropped it. "Majesty, I'm sorry!" she stuttered.

"She said nothing—absolutely nothing—more?" Ramessa asked anxiously.

"No, majesty." Chenmet was silent a moment, then lifted pleading eyes to Ramessa and said, "Majesty, she wouldn't have left her jewels, her clothes. She would never have left the prince!"

"I know," Ramessa said brokenly. "Nothing would part her from Setnau." He turned to stare at the door that opened to the terrace, remembering the night Nefertiry had stood there worrying about his going into battle. There was a hardness in his throat which he tried to swallow, but found he couldn't. He walked slowly toward the golden door, that door which had stood so often like a wall between them; pausing before he opened it, he stared at it through his tears. Without turning, he said brokenly, "Keep the queen's apartments in order. I'll find her and bring her back."

"Yes, majesty," came Chenmet's tearful voice behind him.

Ramessa opened the door quietly and walked into his own chamber.

After Ramessa bathed and changed his garments, he started to leave the room. But turning to Nehri, he paused to say, "I don't know how long I'll remain awake tonight, so you may do what you wish this evening."

"I have nothing to do but await you, sire," Nehri whispered, realizing they had spoken no words to each other since Ramessa had gotten down from his horse that afternoon; contrasting his king's exhilarated expression then with his quiet sorrow now, Nehri felt like weeping.

Ramessa descended the stairs slowly, certain that at least Tuiah and Rasuah awaited his company for the evening meal. He hoped fervently no one else was there. He couldn't tolerate anything even resembling a celebration of his military triumph. He wondered how he would be able to ask the painful questions he knew he must.

Entering the dining chamber, he was relieved to see that only Tuiah, Rasuah and Paneb were present. Their eyes lifted anxiously at his appearance. He nodded and walked to his place, saying nothing until a servant approached with a platter of fish. Then he muttered, "Serve the others. I won't eat." Tuiah gave him an apprehensive glance, but said nothing.

Rasuah stared at the food on his plate, he couldn't eat either. Finally, he asked, "Do you want a report about the riot?"

Ramessa watched the lamplight glancing off the ruby liquid being poured into his goblet. "The priests incited
500

the riot. It was put down. That's all I care about it," he said curtly.

"There's a new development on the advance of the island people's army," Rasuah said in a dull tone. "King Hattusil must have withdrawn his support of them." At Ramessa's startled glance, he added, "They attacked Carchemish, which fell after bitter fighting."

"Isn't Carchemish allied with Hattusil?" Ramessa asked.

Rasuah added. "That isn't all. Hattusil apparently gave the invaders permission to camp outside Amor. But instead they moved in close to the city and attacked it."

"If Carchemish fell, I'm sure Amor was defeated," Ramessa concluded.

"There's more," Rasuah warned.

Ramessa picked up his goblet, emptied it, and put it down. "What more?"

"Weshesh has allied itself with the island peoples," Rasuah said quietly.

Ramessa turned to Paneb. "Tell Khakamir to begin gathering all our reserves tomorrow," he ordered. Suddenly remembering that Khakamir was no longer available, Ramessa paled and said, "You must do it, Paneb."

"Sire, I have already begun, anticipating your order," Paneb said.

Ramessa dropped his eyes to stare at the table before him. After an uncomfortably long silence, he asked, "Why wasn't news of Nefertiry's disappearance brought to me?"

"When Chenmet told us Nefertiry said she'd be gone two days, we waited—I waited for another day before I started the investigation," Rasuah said. "I ordered that the news not be sent to you. By then you were fighting the Djemeh and wouldn't have been able to come. You would just have been distracted by worry. In the meanwhile, I hoped we'd find her."

"You haven't found her!" Ramessa said savagely. He lifted his goblet in shaking hands and didn't put it down until he had emptied it. Then, motioning for the servant to refill it, he raised his eyes to regard them one by one. "Has none of you a good word for me?" he asked.

Tuiah studied her son's expression and wished passionately she'd never sent the warning to Akeset. She was certain now that the priest had killed Nefertiry. Although she'd never meant to do more than frustrate Nefertiry's plans, she dared not tell Ramessa of her part in it. Seeing the grief and anger in Ramessa's eyes, she realized again how much he loved Nefertiry, and she was afraid he'd punish even his mother.

"She never confided in me," Tuiah said softly.

"What about you, Paneb? Did Khakamir speak to you of his plans?" Ramessa demanded.

Paneb shook his head slowly. "Commander Khakamir was a man who guarded all his words."

"Don't say 'was' as if he's dead!" Ramessa exclaimed. He fixed his eyes on his goblet. "I won't believe she's dead," he added vehemently.

"Ramessa, I ask you as a friend—not as your first minister—can you think of any reason, however fantastic, for her disappearance?" Rasuah asked softly.

Ramessa looked warily at Paneb. Immediately the captain stood up, saying, "Sire, I've just remembered something I must do. Will you excuse me?" When Ramessa nodded, Paneb bobbed his head and hurried away, grateful for this chance to leave them.

After the door closed behind Paneb, Ramessa said slowly, "I have no idea why she's gone. If she'd wanted to run away from me, she wouldn't have left Setnau behind. Her clothes and jewels, maybe—Setnau, never." He lifted his goblet and took a swallow of wine, then shivered. "I wish I hadn't left her in such a state. You were in court that day. You know what I said. I wish I'd kept silent."

"You didn't speak to her after that?" Rasuah asked incredulously.

"She followed me into my room and told me—" Ramessa hesitated, then continued, "she told me certain
502

things I hadn't been aware of. Although she convinced me then she had nothing to do with Reshet's torture, I said little. I was foolish. I was so upset I wasn't thinking clearly. Later I thought to return home and set things right. I thought that if Nefertiry was uncertain as to my decision for a while, she would be that much more grateful to hear it." Ramessa shook his head slowly. "I thought she would be easier to control." He put his face in his hands and, after a long moment, lifted dry but haunted eyes to say, "Can you imagine my controlling Nefertiry—anyone controlling her? It was what I loved about her most, that I could make anyone in the land bend their knees to me with only my glance, but not Nefertiry." He looked down at the leopard at his feet. "She was—she is—like Botar, unpredictable—fine silk one moment, claws the next, later doing something to make my heart smile. Poor Botar doesn't understand where she has gone. And Ramessa, divine ruler of the land, understands no more than a leopard."

Tuiah wiped her eyes and whispered, "My son, may I go? I cannot endure your sorrow."

Ramessa lifted his eyes to regard his mother quizzically. "Why should you be able to endure it? I cannot." He waved a hand. "Yes, go, go."

Tuiah left, and Ramessa again signaled for his goblet to be refilled. Glancing at Rasuah's expression he said, "Why shouldn't I get drunk tonight? On this of all nights, when I came home to celebrate a triumph against the Djemeh—even worse, to celebrate my triumph against Nefertiry's wiles." He picked up the newly filled goblet, drank its contents and whispered, "I would offer the gods anything they wish if they would let me again contend with Nefertiry's wiles."

"You think she's dead," Rasuah said.

"She wouldn't have left Setnau for so long a time without explanation if she went voluntarily. If she's been captured by someone, I ask you, Rasuah, who could hold her so long without killing her?" Ramessa shook his head.

503

"She would have found a way to escape if only by driving her captors out of their minds with her usual effectiveness."

"Ramessa, Seshena has offered to look into the corridors of hidden knowledge to learn the truth. Shall I bring her to do this for you?" Rasuah asked softly.

"Tell her I would delay for a time the answer I think she'll probably give me," Ramessa murmured.

"She might give the answer of life," Rasuah protested.

"If Nefertiry lives, I'll find her myself. If she's dead, I would cling to the shred of hope I yet possess for a while."

Rasuah was silent a moment before asking, "You wish to question everyone in the palace again?"

"I'll question the nobles, my ministers, the royal guards, the servants, the cooks and the gardeners," Ramessa replied. "I will after that question even the merchants who deliver goods to the door." Ramessa stopped, then added, "I will question the priests and priestesses of every temple in Wast, and especially I will question Akeset."

"When shall I begin gathering them for you?" Rasuah asked.

Ramessa picked up his goblet, then put it down without drinking. He leaned back in his chair and sighed. "I'll begin tomorrow morning—early. I'm too weary to start tonight."

Rasuah returned to his house very late. But he waved Zehzee aside and went to his bedchamber alone. As he opened the door, Seshena got up from a chair and ran to him.

"How did he take the news?" she whispered.

Rasuah slid his arms around her and laid his cheek on the top of her head. "How could he react to such a homecoming? He was shattered, though a lifetime of training kept him calm." Rasuah stepped back from her, but he kept his hands at her waist. "Beloved, he was in agony. I don't think I would have had the kind of discipline he showed."

"Will he let me explore the secrets for him?" Seshena asked. When she looked up at Rasuah's eyes, she knew the answer. "I understand how he feels."

"He's convinced she's dead," Rasuah replied. "He wants to delay knowing it for a certainty." He was silent a moment before he said, "I too think she must be dead."

Seshena said nothing because it was her opinion as well.

After a long moment Rasuah sighed, "I am so weary."

"Sit down for a while," Seshena offered. "When I heard your chariot in the courtyard, I asked Djanah to warm some wine for you."

Rasuah sat in a chair, smiling as Seshena knelt to unfasten his sandals. "Aset's high priestess behaves like a slave," he commented.

Seshena glanced up from her task. "Unlike a slave, who must do her work, I choose to make you comfortable because you're tired and because I love you." Dropping both sandals, she stood up. "I've had a soothing bath prepared."

"You'd best get Zehzee to help me wash," Rasuah said, leaning his head back and closing his eyes. "I think I'll drown if I do it alone."

Seshena smiled and stood up. "I'll be Zehzee tonight."

Rasuah opened his eyes. "Not all night, I hope."

Hearing a soft tap on the door Seshena turned away, saying over her shoulder, "I thought you were tired."

Rasuah was silent, while Seshena took the wine from Djanah, thanked her and closed the door. Then he said, "I'm exhausted, but I've never slept with Zehzee for any reason."

Seshena handed Rasuah the goblet. "Doing so would make me and Djanah very unhappy," she teased. Before he could comment she added, "You know nothing of the arrangements in your own house, I can see. Drink your wine."

Rasuah grinned. "I'd wish them joy only I guess they've been joyful for some years." He sipped his wine slowly.

"You realize I've never favored warmed wine, and drink it only because you went through so much trouble."

"It will loose your tension," she answered calmly and moved around to the back of his chair to begin rubbing his shoulders.

"Ahh," Rasuah sighed and let his chin drop on his chest.

"Don't get too comfortable. I won't carry you to your bath," Seshena warned.

Rasuah's shoulders moved with his soft laugh. "Maybe I won't bathe."

Seshena's hands stopped massaging him. "You'll bathe or sleep with Zehzee after all," she declared. "I'll rub your back later."

Rasuah tilted his head back to finish his wine, then stood up. "You said you'd help me bathe?"

"I'll help you, but from outside the pool. I've already taken my bath. If I take another one so quickly, my skin will wrinkle."

Rasuah put down his goblet. "I don't want your skin to wrinkle, but come with me. You can hold the linen and dry me, or save me in case I begin to drown."

"I surely would save you," she promised and followed him to the bathing chamber.

Later, after he had bathed, he dropped his towel on a table, went promptly to the bed and lay on his stomach. "Aren't you coming?" he asked turning his head to question her. "You promised," he added.

Seshena moved to the bed and sat down, preparing to crawl over his legs and kneel to give him a massage. But Rasuah suddenly twisted his body to grasp her wrists and pull her down so she sprawled at his side.

"I've decided there are better ways than massaging my back to drive the tension from my muscles," he murmured, his face inches from hers.

Seshena's eyebrows lifted, but she asked solemnly, "What ways?"

His lips slowly came closer to possess hers in a lingering
506

caress. Then he withdrew a little to whisper, "Never have I been so grateful that you're here."

Seshena moved closer to rest her cheek against his, feeling the soft dampness of his hair, inhaling the clean scent of his skin. "You're thinking of Ramessa," she murmured.

"I'm thinking of Ramessa who is without his love tonight," Rasuah agreed, pulling her body warmly closer. "The sorrow he endures causes me to want you that much more—I suppose to prove again to myself that you're here, warm and pulsing with life."

Seshena drew her head back and looked at Rasuah, understanding the unspoken fear that had transferred its shadow to him from Ramessa. She kissed him slowly, deliberately arousing him beyond remembrance of fear, pouring into him desire from her own life-essence, making him forget all else. Her fingers caressed him, until the hard muscles of his back seemed to shiver under her hands. He grasped her tightly, almost roughly to him. She opened her eyes and saw his eyes glitter with dark gold fire, while his lips caressed hers, sending a shock through her body and telling her she had achieved her purpose.

A loud rapping at the door caused Rasuah's body to coil like a spring; and for a moment, he looked at Seshena with uncomprehending eyes. Finally, he called, "What is it!"

Through the door, Zehzee answered, "My lord, there's someone here to talk to you!"

Rasuah sat up stiffly. "Have you no compassion?" he snapped.

"He says he has a most urgent message!" Zehzee persisted.

Rasuah got out of bed and turned to Seshena. "Zehzee knows what we're doing, or he'd open the door. It must be important." He pulled on a robe, adding, "It had better be important."

Seshena slid over to sit on the edge of the bed for a moment. Then, she stood up. "If it isn't, if it isn't—" she

507

muttered pulling a shift over her head with trembling fingers.

"Will you see him?" Zehzee called.

"By Heru, give us a moment!" Rasuah snarled. He turned to Seshena. "Are you almost ready? Don't bother with your hair."

Seshena lowered the hand she had lifted to her temple. "I wasn't," she replied. "I was touching my head, where a great aching has suddenly developed."

Rasuah took her hand. "My own ache is located somewhat lower," he said grimly. Then, he led her from the room, distractedly running his fingers through his tangled hair. Facing Zehzee, he snapped, "Where is this messenger?"

"In the hall downstairs," Zehzee replied anxiously. "He appeared not to be the kind of man you'd allow to come very far into your house." At Rasuah's puzzled look Zehzee added, "He looks to be the kind who would leave with anything of value he could carry away."

"For this you've disturbed us?"

Zehzee lowered his voice and said, "He claims he was paid by a certain Shardanan to bring you his message." Zehzee turned and began to walk down the hall muttering, "You'd think I enjoyed leaping from bed in the middle of the night to admit a man who looks as if he could murder us all!"

"Stop grumbling, Zehzee," Rasuah said, hurrying behind the servant.

"My heart is pounding and my head is on fire, and I should smile," Zehzee continued muttering.

"Be silent," Rasuah said.

Seshena smiled, but her smile vanished when she saw the man who had been waiting for them. The stranger looked as treacherous as Zehzee had described; when his eyes fell on her, she felt as if her skin crept several paces around her body.

"Who are you?" Rasuah demanded.

"My name is of the least possible importance in this

matter," the stranger said, "but the significance of my news will depend upon what you do about it."

Rasuah looked closely at the man's gleaming eyes and knew this messenger wouldn't have approached his house unless he anticipated a rich reward and would never have even come near the house in the daylight. "Come into this other room so we may sit down," Rasuah said. When the man's eyes rested questioningly on Seshena, Rasuah added, "She'll hear what you have to say and make sure of its truth."

The man nodded slowly and smiled. "I thought I recognized Aset's high priestess," he replied smoothly and followed Rasuah into a small anteroom off the hall. Rasuah flung himself into a chair and the messenger also sat down. His sharp eyes had quickly taken in their situation.

"Whatever information you have you will reveal before we even mention payment," Rasuah said.

"My lord, I've already been paid," the man answered. "Of course, if you decide to add to my reward, I would be grateful."

"Who paid you?" Rasuah inquired curiously.

"A Shardanan named Shemal, who left Tamera some time ago," the stranger said calmly.

Rasuah lifted his head in wonderment. "You carry out his orders even though he's gone?"

The man's smile faded. "It's wise to carry out Shemal's orders even if he's dead," he replied.

"Why did Shemal pay you to come to me?" Rasuah asked.

"I didn't ask Shemal his purpose. I've just done as he'd ordered me," the man sighed. He ran his grimy fingers appreciatively over the fabric of the cushion he leaned against, then raised his eyes to Rasuah. "The day before Shemal left Tamera, he instructed me to follow the activities of Amen-Ra's high priest and to tell you about anything appearing peculiar."

Seshena's eyes widened as she asked, "Akeset?"

The stranger nodded. "I think Shemal has no love for that priest and wishes him ill even from afar."

Rasuah's eyes narrowed. "You saw something that seemed peculiar?"

"Because of the queen's disappearance, I believe so," the man answered.

Seshena came closer. "What did you learn?"

The man looked up at her for a moment, then sensing Rasuah's frown, turned his eyes to Rasuah. "Although the priest was supposed to be confined to his temple, he traveled to Ahbidew the day before the queen disappeared. The same evening Akeset left for Ahbidew, a man and a woman rented a small boat that also went north. Their faces weren't seen, because they wore cloaks and it was dark. Although they were dressed poorly, the man's speech was refined and he wore a sword of the design used by a high-placed officer in the royal guard."

"Khakamir!" Rasuah breathed.

The man nodded. "That's possible. The man and woman were seen in Ahbidew, by a woman who daily visits the temple." At Rasuah's expression, he said quickly, "She didn't see their faces because they were heavily cloaked even in the temple, but she walked beside them as the temple was being cleared of worshippers. What drew her attention to them was that they silently slipped out of the crowd and into a shadowy passage before everyone else left. The hooded woman dropped this and she picked it up." He extended a hand.

Seshena stared at the blue cord crumpled in the man's palm. Even in its grimy state, she recognized the amulet she had knotted for Nefertiry. "I gave that to Nefer—" she began, but Rasuah silenced her with a warning glance.

"You can say the queen's name within my hearing," the stranger smirked. "I was sure of who the woman was or I wouldn't have come to you. It doesn't matter to me why she was there or what she was doing. I am obeying Shemal's orders." He took a breath and added, "There's something more I've learned that may interest you. I
510

don't know if it's connected with this matter, but I'll tell you anyway."

"What is it?" Rasuah asked.

"I recently followed Akeset to the house of a man who used to be a priest. This ex-priest, Irai was his name, was mad. I wondered why Akeset would visit him. Shortly after Akeset left Irai's house, a great cry went up that Irai was dead. Nothing was reported about this because no one in the house wanted to cause inquiries. I understand there was a large amount of unexplained gold hidden in Irai's bedchamber. In any event, the housekeeper said Irai and Akeset had harsh words—"

"About what?" Rasuah asked tensely.

The man shrugged. "That I don't know." He took a breath and said, "I do know they drank wine together. Hardly had Irai taken a sip when he fell over dead." The man stood up. "If you think my message is of sufficient value, perhaps you'd add to Shemal's payment. I've had to pay many people for the information."

"I don't doubt that, if what you've told me is the truth," Rasuah commented. He looked questioningly at Seshena.

"He has spoken the truth as he knows it," Seshena said promptly. "If you wish to pay him, you won't be paying for lies."

Rasuah went to a cabinet and from one of its compartments, produced a small pouch, which he handed to the stranger. "It's filled with gold."

"I won't even look inside at it, because I believe you to be an honorable and generous man," the stranger replied, stuffing the pouch into his robe. "I thank you, my lord, and wish you good fortune," he said. "My lady, I wish you a pleasant night." Backing away, he bumped into Zehzee, who stood solidly behind him.

"I'll walk with you to the door," Zehzee said and led him away.

"Do you think Irai was killed with poison stolen from Nefertiry?" Seshena finally whispered.

Rasuah nodded agreement. "And I don't care to think

511

of how Akeset got the poison," he said. "What I would like to know is why Nefertiry and Khakamir would go secretly to the temple at Ahbidew."

Seshena considered it for a moment. "I wish Bast would reopen her doors to my sight."

"All I can think of is that Nefertiry wanted to get rid of Akeset. Maybe she sought some kind of evidence against him and took Khakamir to protect her," Rasuah murmured.

"More than protection," Seshena whispered. Rasuah stared at her. At his expression of surprise she whispered, "Khakamir loved Nefertiry." She sighed and added, "You might as well know it now. Setnau is Khakamir's son."

"But how—" Rasuah began.

Zehzee returned then, and Seshena said quickly, "I'll tell you all of it later."

"What do you think of that one's story?" Zehzee asked anxiously. When Seshena turned startled eyes on him, he said, "My lady, Lord Rasuah knows I always listen to such things!"

Seshena looked at Rasuah, who grinned and nodded. "He can be trusted."

"Will you tell the king so he can send soldiers to look for the bodies?" Zehzee asked bluntly.

"No," Rasuah replied. "Long before the army could get to Ahbidew, the bodies—if there are bodies—would have been carried out to the desert and fed to the jackals."

Seshena shivered. "What will you do?"

Rasuah looked speculatively at Zehzee a moment before answering, "Zehzee and I will go to Ahbidew to investigate more discreetly than the army would."

Zehzee paled. "If they would murder a queen, they wouldn't hesitate to kill a servant!"

"Neither would they stop at the first minister, yet I'll go," Rasuah retorted. "If you won't accompany me, I'll have to find someone else, because I can't go alone."

"Who else could you trust as you trust me?" Zehzee

exclaimed, affronted by the idea. Then, it occurred to him that Rasuah had just tricked him. He frowned. "What good would it do for me to accuse you of treachery? What good would it do for me to refuse? You would go anyway with someone less trustworthy. I must go, I can see," he grumbled.

"I'm glad you aren't going to argue with me," Rasuah said. "I've spent enough of the night in conversation. I have in mind a pleasanter use for the remaining hours of darkness."

"When will we leave?" Zehzee asked resignedly.

"Tomorrow after the noon meal, when everyone is resting and we'll be less likely to be noticed," Rasuah replied. "We'll enter the temple at night after everyone has left."

Zehzee turned away muttering, "I'd wager that's what Nefertiry and Khakamir did. I'll probably end up on Akeset's offering table as a sacrifice to Sutekht."

"Let me go with you," Seshena said turning to Rasuah. "I can contend with Akeset."

"Akeset is confined to the temple in Wast. I know, because he's been watched closely," Rasuah said. "I can handle the priests at Ahbidew."

"But they may have killed Khakamir, and he was far from harmless!" Seshena exclaimed.

"Khakamir was trained for battle," Rasuah reminded. "He wasn't used to creeping around in the dark, hunting assassins who have been hired to murder him. I am."

Seshena remembered Rasuah's account of how he had killed the Djemeh assassins Henhenet had hired to murder him. She shuddered and promised, "If you won't let me come with you, I'll spend the whole time in the temple praying for your protection."

"That will be sufficient," Rasuah replied. He slid his arm around her waist and said quietly, "But don't begin your prayers now. I have other plans for what's left of tonight."

Zehzee lifted his head to look at the soaring pylons of the temple, which seemed like black battlements against the dark sky. "How can we get inside now that the doors have been bolted for the night?" he whispered.

"Seshena told me there's a small door at the side of every temple, which is always left unbolted," Rasuah murmured.

"How convenient for us you know Aset's high priestess," Zehzee muttered.

"Yes, it is," Rasuah replied in a hushed tone.

"I suppose she even knows where they'd be likely to keep bodies," Zehzee mumbled.

Rasuah smiled in spite of himself. "She suggested we might investigate the Chamber of the Dead."

"How obliging of her to have an answer even for that problem," Zehzee whispered.

"Doesn't it seem appropriate to put their bodies where mummies await final blessing before burial?"

"I thought bodies were taken care of in Anpu's temple," Zehzee said.

"There is none near Ahbidew," Rasuah replied quietly. He got to his feet and flattened himself against the wall.

"Mummies!" Zehzee muttered.

"Follow me," Rasuah whispered and turned to inch his way along the wall to the gates of the courtyard, which were ajar. "We're fortunate they haven't barred the gates."

"Fortunate," Zehzee mumbled, but Rasuah didn't hear him because he had slipped through the opening. Zehzee rolled his eyes heavenward to beg mercy from the divine beings, then followed Rasuah.

"Let's get inside quickly," Rasuah whispered. "The sky was moonless when Khakamir and Nefertiry came here, but the moon is now at its full and was shining right on you when you stood outside."

"They had the advantage of a dark night, and see what happened to them," Zehzee grumbled.

"That's what I intend to do," Rasuah murmured and turned away to move silently down the dark corridor.

514

"This passageway is so narrow, if we meet anyone, we won't be able to avoid them," Zehzee whispered.

"Then, we'll have to hope we don't meet someone," Rasuah murmured. He paused a moment, looked both ways, then stepped into the dimly lit hall.

"We must go here?" Zehzee whispered.

Rasuah silenced him with an impatient wave and walked soundlessly into the corridor, keeping near the wall, suspicious of even the sighing of the drafts. The corridor brought them to a large chamber, which contained many doorways leading from it. Although Rasuah shivered at having to cross so vulnerable a place, he ran silently over the expanse to slip into another shadowed passageway. When Zehzee joined him, he held up a hand for silence. "I heard a sound," he whispered.

Zehzee's face went pale. "It was the sound of the feet of the sacred bird as he comes for our souls."

Rasuah's hand reached for his dagger. "Does the sacred bird lately wear sandals?"

Zehzee shuddered in reply and flattened himself against the wall behind Rasuah. But no one came.

After waiting for what seemed to be an eternity, Rasuah motioned for Zehzee to continue following him. Zehzee obeyed, though he trembled as he walked.

Rasuah led him down the passageway through one temple chamber after another, until they reached the room where the Sacred Barge was placed. Rasuah paused in the darkness to catch his breath and gaze admiringly at the golden boat, large enough to seat a human being, that gleamed softly in the moonlight. Finally, he traced his way around the room to slip behind a large column and open a small door, revealing a narrow staircase which descended into blackness.

"If ever the night demons gathered in a place, they're waiting down there for us now," Zehzee muttered.

"Close the door behind you and I'll light this little lamp so we can find our way," Rasuah said.

"The demons will only see us better," Zehzee grumbled and closed the door.

Rasuah lit the lamp and began to inch slowly down the stairs, cautiously sliding his feet along each stone step. "Be careful," he warned.

"If I were being careful, I'd be in my bed," Zehzee mumbled, but he too was sliding his feet along the uneven surface of each step. Feeling for a railing, he realized there was none. He moved farther to the opposite side, so his fingers could brush the comfortingly solid wall.

Rasuah reached the bottom and lifted his lamp to look around.

Zehzee turned slowly, staring fearfully at the dark stone walls. Seeing several mummy cases that had been placed on low platforms, he muttered, "I suppose this is our destination."

Rasuah nodded and walked toward the first case to examine its lid. The wooden cover held the carving of a man. He turned away and went to the next case. Its lid was decorated with a woman's likeness. He straightened and gazed at the remaining cases. "Don't bother with the cases that have portraits on the lids. We'll only look inside the plain ones." He explained, "They wouldn't put the bodies in a case meant for someone else."

"Why not?" Zehzee asked. "They've shown less than reverence for them so far."

"It isn't scruples that would stop them, but the relatives who paid for these other cases and expect to see their loved one's bodies in them," Rasuah murmured. He turned to approach another group of mummy cases in a corner. "Help me lift this cover, Zehzee. It has no portrait."

Zehzee's reluctance was in his feet as he moved to the foot of the coffin and resignedly lifted the cover and put it aside. When he straightened, he saw Rasuah frowning at the contents. Although the body was wrapped, it was
516

unquestionably the corpse of a man. Khakamir's sword lay beside it.

"How will we find which body is the queen's?" Zehzee asked with shudder, then added, "I doubt she carried a sword."

Rasuah shook his head. "If Khakamir is here, I think she must also be here. But I have no intention of unwrapping all the unidentified female corpses, however well-embalmed, to find her."

"For that decision I thank Asar," Zehzee fervently whispered. "What will we do?"

"We'll have to take Khakamir's body with us as evidence," Rasuah replied softly. "Later Ramessa can send someone else to search for Nefertiry."

"How can we walk through the temple carrying a mummy case?" Zehzee asked, his eyes wide with horror.

"The same way we came in, I suppose. Replace the lid while I think of how I can light our way up those steps and carry the case up at the same time."

By the time the case was covered, Rasuah had decided all he could do with the lamp was to hold its hanging chain in his teeth. He signaled for Zehzee to take the foot of the case, then stooped to lift the other end.

Progress was slow up the slippery stairway and they paused often to catch their breath. When they finally reached the door at the top, Rasuah exhaled sharply on the little lamp flame, which had been searing his chin all the way, and put it out before he pushed the door open with his foot.

They put down the mummy case behind the sheltering column; and Zehzee leaned his back against the wall to rest, while Rasuah stepped around the column to see if anyone was near. He returned, arching his back as he walked, and whispered, "Are you ready?"

"I'll never be ready to carry a mummy through a temple whose priests want to kill me," Zehzee answered, but he bent to pick up his end of the case.

If the way into the temple had been dangerous, the

threat was tripled by their having to carry the unwieldy case. Rasuah walked as rapidly as he could burdened by the weight. Although Zehzee never asked to stop, Rasuah knew his friend was happy enough to pause each time he did, so they might put down the case, flex their strained muscles and catch their breath. As they crept through the shadowed chambers and down dark passageways, Rasuah thought of Seshena and passionately hoped she was praying for their protection.

After what seemed like three eternities had come and gone, they reached the little door they'd used to enter the temple. Rasuah nodded his head in signal for Zehzee to put down the case and Zehzee gratefully complied. They both leaned against the wall to close their eyes and breathe the sweet cool air of Tamera's night. After they were rested, they picked up the case and stepped into the moonlight to hurry across the courtyard.

But as they approached the gates, they were stopped. A man blocking Rasuah's way demanded, "Who are you? What are you doing here now?"

Mustering all the dignity he could while carrying a mummy case, Rasuah said coldly, "We're guardians for the Chamber of the Dead. Let us pass."

The guard was confused by such activities being carried on at that hour. "By what authority shall I let you pass?" he inquired.

Rasuah nodded to Zehzee to put down the case. "By the authority in my hand." He raised his sword and silenced the guard, then turned to Zehzee. "Now we have two bodies to carry," he whispered.

"But how?" Zehzee murmured. "Can't we leave him here?"

"We don't want the priests to find the guard's body, then think of investigating that chamber below and find Khakamir missing," Rasuah whispered. "It isn't possible to carry them both at once," he conceded. "We'll have to take Khakamir to the boat, then return for the guard."

"If we throw the guard in the river, we won't have to

518

hide him. The crocodiles will dispose of his body," Zehzee suggested.

Rasuah shivered at the idea. But, admitting the complications of carrying an unembalmed body on the boat in the hot sun all the way back to Wast, he nodded agreement.

As Zehzee bent to pick up his end of the mummy case, he whispered, "My back is grateful the river isn't very far away."

Rasuah frowned and murmured, "I'm grateful we're still alive."

"For that my whole body rejoices," Zehzee panted enthusiastically.

Ramessa sat as straight and unmoving as if he were carved from stone, but his mind was streaking from one unanswered question to another. He had already questioned the gardeners, novitiates and most of the priests from Asar's temple at Ahbidew and had learned nothing.

Finally, Ramessa's gaze shifted to the group of priests who hadn't yet been questioned; and when they saw Ramessa's fiery amber eyes turn to them, they huddled close together in fear.

Ramessa lifted one of his scepters and extended it toward the priests, moving it until he indicated one tall, thin man who looked more frightened than the others. "That one," he said.

Captain Paneb went to the hesitating priest, took his arm, and marched with him to the dais. The priest immediately prostrated himself before the step at Ramessa's feet and waited for permission to rise. It didn't come.

Ramessa stood up and stepped off the dais to stand over the priest and silently look down at him for a moment. "What is your name?" he finally asked.

"Anherru, majesty," the priest replied, lifting his head only enough so he looked at the king's golden sandal.

When Ramessa said nothing more, the priest whispered, "May I rise, majesty?"

"Shouldn't a priest's knees be familiar with the surface of floors?" Ramessa asked softly.

Anherru saw the hem of Ramessa's robe shift, and he knew the king had bent slightly to peer down at him. "Yes, majesty," he whispered.

"If your answers are of as little use to me as the others I've heard, I have no need to look at your face," Ramessa said curtly. "You're assigned to the temple at Ahbidew?"

"Yes, majesty," Anherru whispered.

"At last I have found someone who actually admits being assigned to that temple!" Ramessa exclaimed. "Everyone else I've questioned were there on temporary tasks, it would seem. Do you alone carry the responsibility for the temple's many functions? If so, you must be an exemplary priest and surely one who knows everything about the temple's activities."

Anherru shook his head, nodded, then shook his head—all in such rapid succession even he wasn't certain which question he'd answered with which gesture.

"Are you dizzy, Anherru, from all that motion?" Ramessa asked straightening.

"No, majesty," Anherru replied.

"Tell me again how the body of Commander Khakamir came to be stored unidentified in your Chamber of the Dead," Ramessa said softly.

"It is as the others already answered. We found the body by the river," Anherru quickly replied.

"And dressed as he was, you didn't think who he might be and having pity on this stranger's body you quickly dropped him in a vat of natron," Ramessa said sarcastically.

"Majesty, it had to be done before the body began to spoil," Anherru replied.

"Do you enjoy soaking bodies in natron?" Ramessa inquired.

Anherru lifted his head as if shocked. "Of course not,

majesty! I didn't do the embalming myself. I'm not a funerary priest. I'm not even allowed to touch natron!"

Ramessa lifted his foot and lightly kicked the side of Anherru's head. "Would you like to be soaked in it while yet alive?" he asked softly.

Anherru pressed his forehead to the stones, trying to suppress his shudder. "Majesty, surely you joke."

"No. I do not," Ramessa replied. "I will have truthful answers to my questions if I must soak you in natron or—" He paused as if reconsidering. "Did you know Captain Paneb is an excellent man with a beating stick?" Anherru didn't answer, so Ramessa said, "You don't understand me, of course. Let me explain. Whenever I've needed information a man was reluctant to give, I asked Captain Paneb to find a sturdy stick. He has a special skill for applying it to various areas of the body and knows how to cause a maximum of pain, yet preserve the lifespark, so the information can be obtained."

"Sire, I have no information—" Anherru began.

"Many have made the same vow, yet they have related many interesting things later, sometimes only moments later," Ramessa said softly. "How good are you, Anherru, at keeping secrets?"

"Majesty, I'm a priest of Asar's sacred temple!" Anherru exclaimed, raising his head.

"I have lost my patience," Ramessa said quietly. He turned to step up onto the dais and sit on his throne. His eyes were pitiless when he looked at Anherru. "Captain Paneb, have Kharu beat Anherru on the feet until he cannot walk again. If he doesn't speak, continue up his legs, then to whatever other parts you must ruin until he gives the answers I seek."

Anherru had risen to a sitting position and he stared at Ramessa in horror. "Majesty, I'm a priest!" he cried.

"Kharu isn't as skilled with the stick as Paneb, but I can't spare Paneb at the moment," Ramessa said coldly, gesturing to Paneb to have Anherru taken away.

"Majesty, you can't have a priest beaten like a common thief!"

Ramessa turned his eyes to the speaker, who also was a priest. "I have lately seen a strong resemblance between the two. What is your name?"

"Taka," the priest answered.

"Come here, Taka. You're next," Ramessa said quietly.

"Majesty, Taka's right. You can't torture a priest!" Akeset stepped out of the crowd.

Ramessa smiled mirthlessly. "Does a priest's body differ from those of others that he cannot feel pain and thus be induced to answer? I feel pain and I'm the king. My pain at the moment is grief for Commander Khakamir, who was my friend. My agony is the disappearance of my queen. I will know the truth of these matters."

"Majesty, may I speak with you?" Rasuah asked, approaching the dais.

Ramessa nodded. "If this is a matter requiring discretion, you may come to my side," he said clearly. He watched with curiosity as Rasuah stepped upon the dais and bent close.

"Let me call for Seshena while everyone is here," Rasuah whispered. "Maybe she can read the details of these crimes from the brain of those who committed them. Everyone would accept her word."

"I appear to be making no progress this way." He paused, still reluctant to hear what he was sure Seshena would say. He lowered his eyes so the court wouldn't see the emotion that filled them. "It's foolish, I suppose, to be afraid to know the truth when it's a thing that haunts me anyway. Send a messenger for Seshena right away."

"It isn't necessary," came a voice from the back of the court.

Ramessa lifted startled eyes to see Seshena standing in the doorway. "Come forward, Seshena," he directed.

Rasuah watched Seshena walk through the expanse of the glittering room, moving quickly, but with that gliding

522

grace that belied the speed of her steps. He saw that she had worn her temple robe as high priestess in anticipation of all of this. He wondered how much more she already knew as he watched the long pleats of her robe swaying with her steps. When she approached the throne, she sank to the floor in a billow of snowy white folds.

"Rise, Seshena, high priestess of Aset," Ramessa said softly.

Seshena's eyes were like lapis lazuli under the silver head-dress of her station. And when she lifted them to regard her king, it was with the calm, unwavering gaze of a true priestess.

"Your first messenger, whose name is Tehuti, came to me this morning," Seshena said. "A second, mortal messenger was unnecessary." She paused for a moment, then added, "Tehuti told me this is the day to balance the scales of truth."

A murmur ran through the crowd at her words, but she gave no further explanation.

Ramessa lifted his eyes from Seshena's face and looked at the curious throng of ministers, noblemen and priests. "You will wait here while I speak privately with the priestess," he announced.

"You are wise," Seshena whispered, stepping away so Ramessa could descend from the dais.

"I wish not to weep before them," Ramessa murmured, as he led her from the throne room. "I only hope they won't think we're rehearsing a story while we're alone."

"It will be a tale I'll read from the mind of the guilty one," Seshena said, "and I suspect it will be a story unmatched by anything we could devise."

Ramessa turned into a small chamber at the side of the throne room, which was used for such impromptu conferences. A guard closed the door behind them.

"I think you'll wish to sit down," Seshena said softly.

Ramessa gazed at her a moment, dreading to hear the words he knew were coming. "She's dead?" he whispered. When Seshena nodded, he grew pale and sank into a chair. "How?" he asked hoarsely.

"Nefertiry's spirit came to me last night. She would say nothing about how she was murdered. She would only say Akeset killed her," Seshena said quietly. "Khakamir was killed by Anherru, the priest you just sent away to be beaten."

"Anherru will be a smear on the floor when Kharu finishes with him," he said viciously.

"I would ask you to show some mercy, but I think my words would be useless," Seshena commented.

"Mercy? While Nefertiry's blood is yet warm on their hands?" Ramessa asked, a terrible pain slowly rising from his numbness.

"This thing happened according to the plan of the One Alone," Seshena said. "It was the purpose of Nefertiry's living—to stop the corrupt priesthood of Amen-Ra from gaining power. Her death was ordained before her birth. She was born for weeping."

"She would not say how she died?" Ramessa asked quietly, trying to contain the emotions rising in him that threatened an explosion to shatter his sanity.

Seshena shook her head. "She could not bear to speak of it. She came only to accuse her murderer—Akeset."

"Why did she come to you? Why not to me?" Ramessa cried. "How I would have wanted to speak to her once again, to see her again—if only her fleshless soul!"

Seshena dropped her eyes. "She fears you," she whispered. "She thought you arranged for her death. When I denied that, she left me."

Ramessa stared at Seshena. He was momentarily speechless in his agony. That was what he had feared. He put his face in his hands. "By all the divine beings existing in Tuat, why must she have died thinking such a thing?" he groaned. "No, you needn't tell me that answer, Seshena. I already know it. She thought that because I left her without speaking one way or another."

Seshena had no answer to this truth. She waited
524

quietly for Ramessa to pass the first gates in his river of grief.

He sat with his head in his hands, the gold and white striped folds of his headpiece falling over the sides of his face, concealing it, his gleaming scepters forgotten in his lap. She was surprised that, when he finally lifted his head, he had shed no tears. But his amber eyes held green flecks like live sparks burning in them.

"When we go back, what shall I do first?" he asked quietly, his voice like an echo from an empty tomb.

Seshena took a breath so she could answer, "Continue questioning Akeset and Taka."

Without another word, Ramessa picked up his scepters and got to his feet. Then, he opened the door and the guard stepped smartly back. Seshena followed Ramessa as he hurried back into the throne room. When he ascended the dais and sat on his golden seat, he looked at her.

"You have nowhere to sit," Ramessa said quietly. "Would sitting down help with what you must do?"

"If I remain standing and retreat too deeply into my spirit sight, I may lose my balance and fall," Seshena replied.

"If anyone was a friend to Nefertiry, you were that friend," Ramessa said solemnly. "She wouldn't mind if you sat beside me." She looked at him doubtfully, but she obeyed.

When Seshena was seated, Ramessa looked at Rasuah. "We will continue."

Again Taka came forward and Akeset followed slowly. When they knelt before the dais, Ramessa stared down at them for a long time without directing them to rise.

Finally, Akeset raised his head a little and asked, "May we stand up, majesty, while we converse?"

"What can two murderers say that their king will hear?" Ramessa said quietly. The watching crowd gasped

525

and a ripple of shocked whispers ran through the room, that the king accused no less than Amen-Ra's high priest.

Akeset and Taka both lifted their heads from the floor to stare at Ramessa, stunned to silence. Finally Taka, glancing fearfully at Akeset, whispered, "Surely, majesty, you don't mean that!"

Ramessa remained silent for a long moment, a pitiless calm on his face. "Why did you murder Queen Nefertiry?" he asked softly.

"This has gone too far!" Akeset protested, then stopped. The look in his king's eyes silenced him.

"What part did you play in this evil scheme?" Ramessa asked in a lowered tone that held no mercy.

Akeset scrambled to his feet. "Majesty, you were a child in the royal nursery while I was faithfully serving your father!"

"I doubt you served him better than you have me, but at least you didn't murder his wife," Ramessa said quietly. "Where is Nefertiry's body?" he demanded.

"The queen's earth-body has been destroyed. It will never be recovered," a voice answered.

Everyone's eyes shifted to stare at Seshena, who sat rigidly in Nefertiry's place. Her eyes were closed.

"I would lay Nefertiry in the tomb prepared for her, whatever condition her corpse is in," Ramessa said tightly.

"You cannot. The body has been burned and her ashes scattered on the desert." Seshena's words fell on the room like icy stones.

"Tell me how it was done," Ramessa said, his voice breaking.

"The queen went to the temple of Ahbidew with Commander Khakamir to find evidence against Akeset," Seshena said in a strangely expressionless tone. "She thought—and rightly—that Akeset had stolen gold from the treasure room to pay for the torture-murder of Lady Reshet and the infant. She wanted to find the tally scroll and bring it to you. The commander's death was swift. The flight of an arrow drove his soul from his body."

"And the queen?" Ramessa whispered, anguish almost overcoming his control.

"The queen was locked in the treasure room until the next night, when she was given a melon that had been drugged, so she might more easily be carried away," Seshena said. "When she was unconscious, three priests came to take her out—Taka, Anherru, Akeset."

When Taka heard his name fall from Seshena's lips, still staring incredulously at her, he sank back down to the floor as if his legs had melted.

Akeset screamed, "It's a trick! They made up this story!"

At his shrill cry, Seshena opened her eyes, and the court gasped. Even Akeset stepped backwards in fright. Seshena's unfocused eyes were alive with a blue fire, like that of summer lightning.

"The queen was taken to the desert stuffed inside a lamp-oil jar." Seshena continued speaking in an emotionless tone, which made the words she spoke even more bizarre. "While the queen yet lived in her body and could feel the pain of what was done to it, Akeset—terrified that her soul might return to plague him in this life or, even worse, accuse him in the next—performed the ceremony of destroying Apep, using the queen's body as a true priest would have used a wax figure of the demon Apep, using the queen's name for his evil incantation."

Ramessa shivered, then said softly, "No one but high priests and priestesses know what this ceremony involved, because it's a ritual used in the sanctuary. Describe it for us."

"That everyone here may witness the full horror of the crime, I will describe the ritual," Seshena said in the same emotionless tone. "Akeset cut off Queen Nefertiry's feet, so she'd be crippled in the afterlife; he cut off her hands so she couldn't raise them in supplication to the divine beings against him; he cut off her head so she wouldn't be able to control her spirit-body; he smashed her face so her eyes would be blinded, her nose couldn't

527

breathe, her ears couldn't hear, so her voice would be silenced. Then, he set fire to all her parts, so the company of divine beings wouldn't recognize her, so she couldn't return to her body." Seshena paused, then added in the same expressionless tone, "Akeset burned the queen's name and titles so the company of divine beings would forget she had existed."

Ramessa stared into space during this description, too horrified to speak or move. When Seshena's hand touched his elbow, he started, then turned to look at her. Her eyes had returned to normal and he realized she had come out of her trance. "You recount these things with deadly detail," he whispered.

"Truth is not of death and endings, but of life and eternity always," she said softly. "That Nefertiry's soul came to me, whole and unharmed, proves Akeset's ritual failed." She took a deep breath and added, "Most of Amen-Ra's priests have followed Akeset's path to corruption. It was necessary to Tamera's life that they be stopped and Nefertiry was the instrument the One Alone used to make you stop them."

"And I do intend to stop them," Ramessa said clearly and got to his feet. He turned his eyes to Paneb in signal. Paneb approached him with a solemn expression, expecting his king to order him to take Akeset and Taka away.

"What punishment is great enough?" Paneb whispered.

"Give me your sword," Ramessa said softly, laying his scepters on the throne. He put out his hand.

Paneb stared at Ramessa, wondering why he wanted his sword. But he pulled the blade from its scabbard and gave it to his king.

Ramessa stepped down from the dais. Only a few long strides took him to where Taka yet remained on his knees on the floor.

Taka stared up at his king. He watched the sword raise with unbelieving eyes. When it fell in a glittering arc, Taka's separated body fell, spewing scarlet on the hem of Ramessa's robe.

528

Ramessa turned to face Akeset. Akeset backed away slowly. Suddenly taking two swift steps toward Akeset, Ramessa swung the sword at a downward slant to slice through one of Akeset's ankles. Akeset screamed and tumbled to the floor. He continued screaming and writhing helplessly while his king methodically chopped off his other foot—then his hands—and finally, with Akeset moaning weakly for mercy, Ramessa beheaded him.

Ramessa turned away from the mutilated bodies and silently returned the still-dripping sword to Paneb. Then, he turned to face the horrified crowd.

"Their bodies will be burned, not because I fear their curse or return, but because they burned Nefertiry's body," Ramessa said coldly.

He turned away and, with head held high, stalked through the room. The watching crowd never realized that their king's lowered eyes hid the tears he finally felt uncontrollably welling up in him. They only stared at the crimson splashes soiling his white robe.

26

Rasuah came upon his king sitting in the garden in a small glade under a mimosa tree, which rained lavender flowers on his shoulders with every whisper of the breeze. Ramessa's eyes were fixed on Setnau, who played with Botar in the sun under Chenmet's supervision.

"This will be a pleasant setting in which to discuss business," Rasuah commented as he reached Ramessa's side.

Ramessa's eyes left Setnau and lifted to regard Rasuah. "It's a pity the garden's serenity enters neither my nor Setnau's heart," he said, then invited Rasuah: "Sit down, my friend."

When Rasuah had joined Ramessa on the bench, he looked at Setnau a moment before asking, "The boy is troubled?"

"See how his game lacks the normal enthusiasm of a small boy's? It's more as if he does what the watching adults expect of him," Ramessa observed. "Yes, Setnau is very troubled as any child his age would be troubled by the sudden disappearance of his mother."

Rasuah watched Setnau a moment and concluded the boy certainly did seem subdued at his play. "Surely the presence of his father must help."

"Right now this is about as near as I can bear to go to him and it isn't enough," Ramessa whispered. "I cannot make myself go closer, because he'll lift Nefertiry's eyes to me, and that I can't endure just yet." He sighed before observing, "Botar's more comfort to him than I. It's curious that Botar, who never tolerated herself to be handled by any adults other than Nefertiry and myself, much less children, plays so gently with Setnau. She has stayed closer to him than even to me since Nefertiry is gone."

"Maybe she senses something of Nefertiry in Setnau—and surely Setnau's less noisy and rough than other children his age," Rasuah suggested. Ramessa nodded, but said nothing. Rasuah remained uncomfortably silent for a long time, until the question that had been burning him refused to remain unasked. "What will you do about him, Ramessa?"

Ramessa continued to stare at the boy, reluctant to answer. Finally he said softly, "I've already given him all the titles due my son and never will his origin be questioned."

"But if you can't endure going nearer the child than this, if he never knows your embrace, his grief won't be comforted," Rasuah said.

"Chenmet and some others embrace him often, but I cannot," Ramessa said firmly.

"Although you've accorded him the titles, I think he'll never wear the crown," Rasuah said quietly.

"He isn't the child of my body." Ramessa's voice was low, but there was an edge to it.

"His veins yet contain your blood, and for him to wear the crown seemed to be almost all Nefertiry wanted," Rasuah reminded.

532

Ramessa flinched, but said coolly, "Years will pass before I announce which prince will ascend my throne after me."

"During all those years Setnau will never enjoy his father's embrace? Whatever the circumstances of his birth, he knows you as his father," Rasuah reminded Ramessa.

"Most of the royal children have little contact with me," Ramessa murmured. "There are too many of them."

Rasuah let out a heavy sigh, not knowing what else to say. He'd already presumed too far even as a personal friend, but thinking of the lonely years ahead of Setnau pained him.

"You came about some business?" Ramessa asked.

Rasuah nodded. "I've been receiving a steady stream of messages from acquaintances in various countries, all warning the same thing: the island people are getting ready to invade Tamera."

"I'm in the proper mood for a war," Ramessa said softly. He lifted his head and looked at Rasuah. "Which lands have they conquered now?"

"Several of your own foreign provinces have fallen," Rasuah said grimly.

Ramessa frowned. "Which ones?"

"Heteb surrendered Alasa. Pekharu has fled Kode."

"Now Pekharu won't have to worry about my collecting taxes from him."

"Kheta has been invaded and seems ready to fall," Rasuah said.

"Didn't Manefera come from Kheta?" Ramessa asked, narrowing his eyes against the sun's glare.

"Forgive me, Ramessa. Who is Manefera?"

"She was the wife who presented me with a red-haired son. She was the first to feel Nefertiry's teeth," Ramessa said softly. "You were at Akiti then," he recalled.

Rasuah could tell, from Ramessa's tone, that he was rapidly sinking into melancholy. He considered several ways Ramessa might be lifted from this state and decided to provoke him. "From which direction do you think the island people will come?"

"From the sea, of course," Ramessa snapped. "Are they likely to cross the mountains and suffer in the deserts surrounding Tamera? Theyll sail up the outlets of the Nile." Suddenly realizing why Rasuah had asked, Ramessa shook his head and said more calmly. "When the time comes, I'll march north to meet them."

Rasuah inquired, "What of the priests of Amen-Ra?"

"Every temple of Amen-Ra is being guarded by soldiers. As I march north with the main body of my army, I'll stop at the temples and gather up these soldiers." He smiled grimly and added, "When I leave the temples, the soldiers will no longer be needed to guard priests. There will be no false priests left to guard."

"You plan to execute all of them?" Rasuah asked.

Again Ramessa's eyes traveled to rest on Setnau. "There are few who haven't been corrupted, and I have no intention of leaving enemies alive to follow on my shadow."

"What about the priests in the temples to the south?" Rasuah inquired.

"I know the names of the false ones in those places, and I'll send Paneb to clean out their nests. If he goes by ship, he can get to the north in time to join the battle," Ramessa answered.

Rasuah was silent a moment before asking, "What will be my part in this?"

Ramessa regarded Rasuah speculatively for a moment. Then he said, "I would have you temporarily sharpen your old skills as royal envoy and go to Punt. As long as I'm having troubles with so many other lands, it would be an excellent time to strengthen our friendly relations, at least with them."

Rasuah's golden eyes lightened as if in relief. "You would send the two expeditions you mentioned before?" he asked. When Ramessa nodded Rasuah said, "If I must leave Tamera for so long a time, I would marry Seshena and take her with me."

"Then, I must give immediate orders for the celebration!" Ramessa declared. At Rasuah's startled expression, Ramessa insisted. "Did you think you could stand before a priest with two witnesses like a potter's son and a weaver's daughter? The first royal minister and Aset's high priestess must endure a ritual almost the equal of the king's." Ramessa stood up and put his hand on Rasuah's shoulder. "Don't worry about it, my friend. I'll alert the proper people and the thing will be done without your having to expend any effort—except for that fateful moment when you take her hand and pledge whatever it is you two intend to pledge."

Rasuah stood up. "Must it be a public ceremony?" he asked softly.

Ramessa's smile widened. "You will endure it, however reluctant you may be, as I have so many times endured such ceremonies."

"We don't want to share our pledges with a crowd of people who care nothing for us. Neither do we wish to spend hours making a display of ourselves for those same people," Rasuah snapped. After this outburst the golden fire in his eyes diminished, but didn't disappear as he said quietly, "We want to share our joy only with our friends."

Ramessa laid his hand on Rasuah's shoulder and said, "The higher your rank, the more ceremony must accompany whatever you do. Remember that you're above all else intimates of the king and every time someone close to the king so much as gets a stone in his sandal the whole kingdom will ask how he has injured his foot that he limps."

"That may be, but I don't have to pretend to like it," Rasuah replied sullenly.

"Even I, who am the king, too often must pretend," Ramessa said bitterly. "Perhaps thinking of your future happiness will outweigh your annoyance."

"Thought of Seshena seems to be my constant refuge lately," Rasuah replied, then turned and left his king.

Ramessa watched his friend's retreating back and reflected upon those days when he'd been able to lessen his personal frustration during tedious hours by anticipating later being alone with Nefertiry.

As those who were to witness Rasuah and Seshena's wedding entered Amen-Ra's temple, they made their way to the front of the chamber where Ramessa sat and gave obeisance to their king. Ramessa nodded automatically to his subjects, hardly aware of them as individuals. In spite of his determination to fix his mind on the wedding, the rich fragrance of the incense brought poignant memories of the one wedding he'd experienced which had given love to him. The gold and russet flowers banked around the altar, the garlands of white lotuses swaying gently with the air currents were identical to the decorations of the day he'd waited for Nefertiry to enter the temple. He could almost see again her golden figure standing beside him, her liquid green eyes like the darkened Nile raised to look at him when they'd drunk the sacred wine, her trembling hand when he'd pronounced her his queen.

Ramessa took a ragged breath and made a valiant effort to turn his attention to the present day. But his thoughts refused to relinquish his memories, Nefertiry swathed in veils at Kharu, refusing to bow the first time they'd met, Nefertiry walking through the night to meet him under the darkened palms when he'd taken the first kiss from her unwilling lips, Nefertiry blushing when he'd spoken to her of love, Nefertiry waiting for him, her creamy skin made golden by the veiling of his bed.

Echoes of her husky voice, visions of her brows arched above the shifting emerald lights in her eyes, the fragrance of her perfume reaching out to him like a spell from Hat-Hor. The memory of their wedding night came to him; when he'd first looked upon her naked body, she'd anxiously asked if her appearance pleased him. He, almost

536

driven to madness by her body, had restrained himself and been careful with her, for the first time in his life eager to please a woman instead of only himself.

Ramessa clenched his fists. He would not dwell on these things, which could be no more. He must accept that Nefertiry's love was lost to him. But he longed to hear once more even the words she'd spoken that had sometimes been so subtly barbed he'd felt as if he'd been impaled on an invisible spear. Never again would he hear her shouting in anger, using the language of Khatti, so her words wouldn't be understood by anyone passing in the corridor. No more swimming together among the lotuses of their bathing pool. Never again riding in the sun with her hair streaming behind her like a midnight cloud. No more of the sound of her triumphant laughter when she won a game of senit. Never again her quiet wisdom when they sat in audience. No more of Nefertiry but painful memories— because there was nothing left of her, not even a body to lay in her tomb, nothing but echoes that would be heard by him into eternity, the shadows of statues that would haunt his palace until death mercifully closed his eyes. Nothing but memories that ever would twist his heart with grief, and over it all the agony of knowing if he had retracted his public accusation of her, Akeset wouldn't have dared touch her. No one would have risked even whispering of her guilt if they'd known their king had loved her so fiercely he'd have forgiven her anything.

The insistent chiming of many small silver bells finally penetrated Ramessa's consciousness, and he started when his awareness abruptly returned to the present. His blurred eyes focused on Rasuah standing little more than two cubits away, regarding him with quiet sympathy. Realizing that Rasuah had read his thoughts from his face, Ramessa was chagrined. Instantly he raised his head a little higher and, turning his eyes to the temple's entrance, struggled to concentrate his attention on the ritual about to begin.

Ramessa and Nefertiry's tragedy faded from Rasuah's

thoughts as soon as the white-robed figures of Seshena's priestesses filed into the chamber ringing little bells and shaking silver sistrums while their soft chants rose above the music like the joyful murmur of the wind. When the priestesses reached the front of the temple and gathered at the sides of the altar, Rasuah was reminded of the twelve forms of the goddess Hat-Hor and felt eerily as if she personally attended the ceremony. But this thought, too, melted when he turned his eyes to watch the open doorway.

Suddenly Seshena stood on the threshold, silently motionless while her priestesses finished their chant. Then, with only the soft silvery rhythm of the sistrums to accompany her steps, she glided through the clouds of incense like a figure of ivory and lapis lazuli. The sun penetrating through the fragrant haze made shafts of luminous dust between the long shadows cast by the towering columns, revealing glimpses of the pale golden skin under the unpleated sheerness of her dark blue garment, catching fire among the silver lotuses of the filet crowning her hair. And when she reached Rasuah's side, she lifted eyes as darkly blue as that of her robe and fixed him with a gaze that banished all thoughts from his mind but that of her presence. And Rasuah's tilted eyes took on a golden light surpassing even that of Ra's.

Khenti, now the only priest surviving Ramessa's purgation of this temple, prayed for the couple's happy union. When he paused, Rasuah and Seshena recited from memory the pledges they'd previously agreed to share during their marriage. When they finished, Khenti held under their gaze the scroll on which their promises had been recorded; so they could confirm the accuracy of the contract.

As they lifted the cup of consecrated wine to share, their fingers touched, and when Rasuah's mouth touched where Seshena's lips had drunk from the goblet, he felt as if she'd placed a kiss there for his taking. Seshena accepted a bit of consecrated almond cake, and he
538

watched her full lips, remembering only their caresses. They scattered lotus petals on the offering table, and although his hands moved with the same gesture as hers, he was only aware of her long, slender fingers, which had often stroked his temples with caresses as soft as the drift of lotus pollen.

Rasuah wasn't conscious of the passing time. He was unaware of his king watching the radiance on their faces. His own eyes were so filled with the sight of Seshena, his nose saturated with her perfume, her touch so excluding all other sensations, he barely heard the rest of the prayers.

Then, the palace guards, standing stiffly at attention, formed the aisle through which the bridal couple walked as they left the temple. When Seshena and Rasuah stepped into the dusk outside, they were pelted by flowers and sweet-smelling herbs.

Seshena's eyes widened in surprise at the fragrant shower, because she too had forgotten the presence of all others. She looked up at Rasuah and, seeing the golden fire that filled his eyes, sighed. "We must sit through a banquet before we may fulfill what my heart cries out for, beloved."

Rasuah, laughing softly, agreed, but put his arm around her waist and led her through the gathering shadows toward the palace doors.

When Rasuah and Seshena stepped inside, two scarlet-uniformed guards turned to pace ahead of them while two more guards fell into step behind them. At this unexpected escort, Rasuah looked at Seshena, and commented, "I feel like Ramessa going to an audience." Then flinched as a flourish of trumpets greeted their entrance to the banquet room. "Ramessa has overlooked nothing," he murmured, running his glance over the sea of faces awaiting them. Taking Seshena's arm, he followed the guards to their place at the royal table.

Immediately after they were seated, the trumpets sounded again to announce Ramessa's entrance. The guests hurriedly got to their feet amid the noises of goblets being put down and chairs and benches hastily scraping back. Though the rest of the room's occupants made deep bows, those at the royal table remained erect. Rasuah found himself looking at Ramessa in a way he never had before.

Ramessa had been the childhood friend Rasuah had wrestled with, the boy he had learned to hunt with, the young man he had studied combat techniques and had unwisely gotten drunk with. Thus, he had never been greatly impressed with his friend's royalty. But today as Ramessa stood in the doorway to the banquet room, his green and amber eyes had the look of Heru's hawk, his lips were firm and unsmiling, and Rasuah saw his friend almost as if he were a stranger.

Rasuah wondered if Ramessa's eyes had always held that look, if his head had always been that high, if his mouth had before worn this solemn dignity. He tried to remember the many times he'd seen Ramessa in the throne room holding court and found he didn't recognize his friend from previous moments. He wondered if the change was only in his own mind, or if Ramessa had become more kingly in his sorrow. But when Ramessa took his place next to Rasuah and directed the others to rise from their bows and everyone to seat themselves, the moment of unfamiliarity passed, and Rasuah looked again into the eyes of his friend.

"Do the arrangements please you?" Ramessa asked, a glint of humor in his eyes. He looked at Seshena, who sat at Rasuah's other side, then at Rasuah, noting their expressions of impatience, he said, "Nevertheless, you will endure it," and, lifting a hand in signal for the servants to pour the wine, leaned back in his chair to watch the dancing girls.

After the food had finally been cleared away and the tables were bare but for platters of fruit and wine goblets, the guests approached the royal table to present Rasuah and Seshena with gifts. Although the gifts all

540

were beautiful and of great value because of the high places Rasuah and Seshena held in the royal court, the couple grew restless at receiving such a multitude of people. When the last gift had finally been deposited on the glittering pile behind the royal table, more servants came in a long procession, carrying platters of sweet cakes and new wine jars, while slaves stepped behind the royal table with long, gold-handled fans made of scented white ostrich feathers to carefully refresh the air over the king and his honored guests.

Rasuah frequently cast his eyes upward at the small fragments of feathers that broke loose and drifted down on them. Although he appreciated the honor Ramessa had accorded them by arranging so elaborate a celebration, his patience was coming to an end.

"We have entered the last hour of the night, and Ra will soon be sending out his first messengers of morning," Rasuah reminded the king.

"Are you anxious to leave this banquet?" Ramessa asked, feigning surprise.

"We've sat watching the hours drag by as if they were prisoners bound by a rope and straggling reluctantly to the block."

"My arrangements haven't pleased you?" Ramessa asked.

Rasuah recognized the gleam in his friend's eyes and answered, "You have arranged for us the most elaborate and luxurious of traps, but we would escape now."

"My litter has been waiting in the courtyard for you for several hours," Ramessa said, smiling smugly. "I'm surprised you lasted this long."

Rasuah stared at his friend for a moment before commenting, "Your expression reminds me of a crocodile contemplating an unwary goat."

Rasuah stood up immediately and, using the moment it took Seshena to get on her feet, thanked Ramessa for the celebration, then grasped Seshena's hand tightly to lead her around the royal table. As the couple marched

541

swiftly through the room, the surprised wedding guests hastily parted to make way for them. The guards at the door saw the bridal couple approaching, and they looked to Ramessa who signaled them to open the doors, for if he hadn't Rasuah was advancing with so determined an expression, it seemed as if he would walk right over them.

Rasuah's steps didn't slow even as he walked through the corridor to the palace entrance, where at his impatient signal other guards quickly threw open the doors and stepped aside to let him pass.

At the golden litter, Rasuah paused only long enough for one of the attendants to hurriedly pull aside the curtains before he almost pushed Seshena inside. After the attendant had drawn the curtains closed, Seshena regarded Rasuah with a look of reproach while she tried to catch her breath. But a smile broke out on Rasuah's face and she was too surprised to speak.

"He insisted on a wedding equal to his own, an escort of palace guards, dancing girls brought from Abtu, royal wines and an array of rare dishes, a wealth of gifts—all designed to keep us from our bed!" Rasuah exclaimed, laughing. "What a joke to have had this litter here for hours awaiting our retreat! It wouldn't surprise me if he placed wagers as to how long it would take me to lose my patience!"

Seshena smiled at the king's elaborate joke, because she, too, had been taken in. But after a moment, Rasuah's merriment diminished and his laughter faded.

"What's wrong?" Seshena asked anxiously.

"Ramessa played a joke on us. Even now he probably laughs while he recounts it to the others. But it wasn't really a joke," Rasuah said softly.

Seshena stared at Rasuah a moment until she, too, understood. "He tried to divert himself from his own unhappy memories by arranging such a party. Foreseeing that toward the last of it he would be newly pained to watch us go off together while only Nefertiry's memory would accompany him to bed, he made a joke of our leaving."

Rasuah nodded. "He hopes the length of the party and the many goblets of wine he drank will assure his falling quickly to sleep."

Seshena was silent for a long time as she reflected on Ramessa's motives. The soft plodding of the litter bearers' feet had become a monotonous rhythm she no longer heard. Finally, she said, "To give you such a wedding, equal to his own, does you great honor and reveals his affection for you."

"It does that," Rasuah agreed and was silent until the litter bearers stopped and the litter was carefully lowered to the ground.

Remembering Rasuah's forceful entrance into the litter and not knowing what to expect now, an attendant cautiously parted the curtains; but Rasuah didn't seem to notice his presence. He emerged from the litter staring at the space before him as if he was deep in thought.

Finally, Rasuah turned to Seshena and said quietly, "I doubt Ramessa arranged such a celebration so we would leave sadly, reflecting on his loneliness."

"I'm sure he meant us to go happily to your house and put the final seal of love on our marriage contract," Seshena whispered. "Besides, if we enter the house appearing so solemn, Zehzee and Djanah will be alarmed and wonder if we've had harsh words."

But Zehzee and Djanah seemed to have vanished, though a new jar of wine and two silver lotus-shaped goblets stood on a table in Rasuah's bedchamber. Rasuah looked at the goblets and smiled.

"This is either Djanah's doing or Zehzee has a secretly romantic heart," he commented. "These goblets were those my father and mother drank from on the night of their wedding. They've been in my father's family for many generations." He picked up one goblet and lifted his eyes to look at her. "Do you want wine

543

now?" he asked. When she shook her head slowly, he put the goblet down.

Rasuah's arms came silently around her. His soft breath was in her hair as he kissed the back of her head, then bent to touch his lips to the hollow her neck made where it met her shoulder. She leaned back against the warmth of him and covered his hands with her own.

"Your skin is chilled," he observed, stepping a little away and turning her to face him. "Come with me to our bed and sip a little wine. Then, we will share the warmth of our bodies' touching—if you wish nothing else this dawn."

He took her hand to lead her and she followed wordlessly. Like an obedient child she got into bed and accepted the silver goblet he offered. After taking a sip of the sweet, dark wine, she lowered the cup and extended it to him.

"I have obeyed the tradition of your family by drinking from this cup, although I have no taste for wine," she murmured.

Rasuah took the goblet from her and put it on the table next to his own. "And where do your tastes now lie?" he asked, a knowing look in his eyes.

"I would taste you," she whispered.

Rasuah got into bed and, folding her in his arms, felt the chill that yet clung to her skin. "Your body is cold," he said quietly. "Let me warm it with my own." He drew her down to the linens and twined his legs with hers.

Seshena looked up at his eyes and saw the banked fires still glowing in their darkened depths. His lips touched hers briefly and drew a little away, but even that momentary contact flooded her with warmth. She smiled and whispered, "You have more magic than I."

Rasuah's lips curved in a smile and he moved closer to transfer the smile to her mouth in a kiss that lingered, but was no less soft than the first. The warmth that had risen in her increased, showing bright sparks at its edges. At the suddenly insistent movements of his mouth, her

544

sparks caught small, bright flames that raced along her nerves like flashes of summer lightning, igniting her blood to a river of fire flowing through her veins. When he would have drawn away, her hands behind his head clasped him tightly to her. She heard the soft gasp that escaped him, which further enflamed her. Her hands traveled along the firm flesh of his back to his hips and locked his body to hers.

Rasuah felt the levels of his control diminishing like veils, one by one drawn aside and discarded, but he tore his lips from hers to whisper, "If we continue like this, beloved, we well might begin a child. For I have done nothing yet to prevent it." Surprised that his brain still possessed the shred of control necessary to say even that, he gazed down into her eyes and awaited her reply.

"Nor have I," she murmured.

Then he knew her mind was gently entering his awareness, exploring his thoughts to wordlessly learn his opinion. He found himself thinking of what a wonder it was to love a woman who knew his innermost mind and could feel his sensations as easily as her own. When he saw her smile, he knew her decision was the same as his, and he murmured, "Then, let it be as Ptah decides."

Rasuah lowered his body to Seshena's, and, as the waves of the Nile greeted the dawn, did she welcome him. Their kisses became the sparks of the stars in the west, giving one last brightness before they vanished within a greater fire. Her trembling beneath him was the grass's eager shiver in the wind that brought the dawning. He felt as if he drifted like the Nile in a golden light toward the sun.

"Beloved," he began, then stopped—his thought vanished on the morning wind. And like Ra spreading a blaze of gold through the skies, Rasuah's fire ignited the dawn.

27

Rasuah and Seshena stood close together, shivering despite their heavy cloaks, for the sun had only begun to lighten the night skies and the wind from the north carried a sharp chill. The ship on which they stood moved restlessly with the Nile's lapping waves, as if it too were impatient to begin the voyage to Punt—that far-off place where black leopards stalked sleekly beneath fragrant trees and Tamerans traded for gold that had the delicate green tint of almond leaves newly unfurled, and where terraces of myrrh lined the gardens of houses within walled cities.

Rasuah drew Seshena into his arms in an effort to warm her as they waited for Ramessa and listened to the muffled sounds of the crew that had almost finished loading the vessel.

Finally the distant sound of thundering hooves brought a smile to Rasuah's lips. "The king comes," he said. She nodded wordlessly and drew the hood of her cloak closer about her face.

Ramessa's chariot, accompanied by several others, suddenly drew to a stop on the wharf beside the ship.

"We must go down to him," Seshena whispered.

Seeing Ramessa leap lightly from his chariot and turn toward the causeway, Rasuah murmured, "I think not." And he walked slowly toward the causeway to meet the king.

Stepping on deck, Ramessa glanced at the sailors who had finished their work and now huddled together to shiver and wait. "You're almost ready," he said.

Rasuah's eyes traveled over Ramessa's garments. "You also appear ready to go," he observed.

Ramessa nodded. "The army is making final preparations to march."

"You still intend to stop at the temples of Amen-Ra on your way north to punish the priests?" Rasuah asked.

Ramessa's amber eyes filled with live sparks. "Squads of soldiers await my coming at every temple, keeping the priests contained until I arrive. After I've dealt with those traitors, I'll continue north to the battle with the island peoples."

"You're convinced they're coming?" Seshena whispered through chattering teeth.

Ramessa regarded her silently a moment. "You should go into the compartment," he advised. He took a breath. "I've received messages from my spies that the sea people's ships have been launched in our direction. They will, as I'd foreseen, try to enter Tamera by every branch of the Nile that flows into the Great Green Sea." He paused a moment before adding, "I'll stop them."

"Are you sure our ship will be past the river's opening before the invaders come?" Rasuah asked. "I wouldn't care to conduct a battle with Seshena present."

Ramessa shook his head. "You'll have entered the Narrow Sea well before my forces reach the coast. I expect to wait several more days before the enemy ships arrive."

"You'll begin the march immediately?" Rasuah asked.

"I've delayed my departure merely to bid you fair winds," Ramessa replied.

"And what of Setnau while you're gone?" Seshena inquired.

Ramessa glanced over his shoulder. "I have a favor to ask you, Seshena," he said slowly. He saw her eyebrows lift in question, and he said, "Yes, little priestess, you know my mind." He put his hands on her shoulders and regarded her solemnly. "Setnau is still greatly disturbed by his mother's death. I don't know how long it will take to drive the island people back into the sea, but I'm certain the fighting will be bitter. I don't want to leave him alone while I'm gone." He hesitated as his eyes searched Seshena's face. "Nefertiry—" his voice broke over the name, but he continued, "Nefertiry took Setnau to you. She trusted you completely and I know you love him. If you'll take him with you, perhaps seeing a new land will help distract him from his grief. Maybe the sea wind will dry the tears that are always behind his eyes." He paused, continuing to search for her answer in her face. "I would give you Chenmet, who will watch over him closely and lighten your own attendant's chores."

"Say no more, Ramessa," Rasuah interrupted. "We'll take the child. Chenmet or not, watching him won't be too great a task."

Ramessa continued to stare questioningly at Seshena, who nodded in agreement. He squeezed her shoulders in wordless gratitude before he took his hands away. He turned to look down at the wharf and wave in signal.

Chenmet walked slowly up the causeway, struggling under the weight of the child she carried wrapped in blankets. When she stepped upon the deck, she raised her eyes to meet Seshena's.

"Take him into the warmth of the compartment," Seshena whispered. Then, noticing that Setnau's green eyes had opened to gaze up at her, she swallowed and managed to say. "You'll sleep for a while yet, little prince," she murmured. "Then you'll awaken to begin an adventure with us."

Setnau's small mouth curved in a drowsy smile, and he reclosed his eyes, trusting his future to the priestess he knew loved him.

Ramessa came no closer to look at the child, but peered at the small face, blurred by his tears, from a distance. He watched the bundle being carried away to disappear inside the compartment, then he looked at Seshena, but said nothing.

"You won't bid him farewell?" she asked quietly.

Ramessa shook his head. "I've done what I can," he whispered. "I still can't bear to look into his face, much less embrace him. Although I would welcome the visit of Nefertiry's spirit, I cannot endure her face mirrored in his."

"And when we return, do you think you'll be able to bear looking at Setnau? Or will you place him in the House of Royal Children and ignore him?" Seshena demanded. But she realized Ramessa was unable to answer, and said more gently, "If that will be your decision, consider instead another alternative."

Ramessa asked softly, "What alternative?"

"May we keep him and care for him as if he were our own child?" Seshena asked. "I know I give you little time for so momentous a decision, but I would hear your answer before we leave, so I would know how to behave with him in the time we'll have together on this journey."

Seeing Ramessa's hesitance, Rasuah asked softly, "Do you intend to name him your heir?"

Ramessa took a deep, ragged breath and whispered, "Merenptah shows promise."

Rasuah grasped Ramessa's arms and squeezed them. "If you can't treat Setnau like a son while he's an innocent child, if you already know you won't even consider
550

giving him your crown, Ramessa, let us take him. Then he might at least know a measure of happiness."

Ramessa nodded. "Take him, then, as your own," he whispered. "I know in my deepest heart I'll never look at him but think of her and how she died. Since I cannot even lay Nefertiry's body in her tomb, I'll always have the eerie feeling I'll see her again. I'm trying to put down that feeling, but I fear I won't succeed. Having Setnau close by me every day would only add to my torture."

"Perhaps one day you'll forget her and this pain," Seshena offered.

"You don't believe your own words even while you speak them," Ramessa said.

Seshena sighed and nodded in agreement.

"I understand that you've made a visit to Nefertiry's empty tomb," Rasuah said. "You must not do that again if you would ease your pain."

"I went only to supervise its sealing," Ramessa quickly replied.

"It will remain empty?" Seshena asked.

Ramessa lifted eyes of hazy green to look at her. "It was made for my queen. No one but Nefertiry will occupy it." He glanced at Rasuah's hands which still grasped his arms. "I must go," he murmured.

Rasuah again squeezed Ramessa's arms in affection. "May Heru ride with you in your chariot and Montu give you victory."

"I'll win. I always win my wars," Ramessa said curtly. Then in a lighter tone he added, "May Shu bring you fair winds and Tehuti sit on your tongue when you negotiate in Punt." His eyes turned to Seshena and looked at her intently for a moment before he asked, "How can I wish you anything when you're full of Aset's wisdom and contain enough love for all twelve Hat-Hors?"

"You're too generous," Seshena whispered, not knowing what else to say to such lavish praise.

"I'm not," Ramessa replied. He was silent a moment,

then asked, "Will you, as Aset's high priestess, give me peace?"

Seshena nodded and watched Ramessa, her king, lower himself to kneel on one knee before her. Slowly she raised her hands to throw back the hood of her cloak. With one hand uplifted as if she made a pact with heaven and the other hand on Ramessa's forehead she said clearly, "Amen, life of Ra, purifies thee; the rulers of the great city of Tehuti protect thee; Aten, the very face of Ra, makes thee clean; the divine beings of Noph guard thee; Net in Saut purifies thee; the lords of Per-Wadjet watch over thee."

Ramessa got to his feet and looked at her for a moment. "Thank you, Seshena," he said softly. Then he turned away and went down the causeway signaling to the workers on the dock to loosen the lines holding the ship.

Rasuah put his arm around Seshena's waist and led her to the rail, so they might wave to Ramessa, who was standing beside his chariot looking up at them, one hand lifted in farewell, the other hand resting on the head of the leopard that stood at his side.

"Ramessa will decimate the priesthood of Amen-Ra, I have no doubt, spilling their blood in every temple he visits," Rasuah said softly as the ship began to draw away from the wharf. He raised his free hand to salute the king and said tightly, "But I wonder if he looks for his own death in the coming battle with the sea peoples."

As the ship moved farther into the river, Seshena waved to Ramessa's receding figure. "The fighting will be bitter. The invaders will appear on every route—land and water—that goes south from Tamera's coast. But Ramessa looks not for his death. He'll fight like ten demons unloosed. When he returns to Wast, he'll be covered with honors for a victory dearly earned."

"Is this your personal opinon meant to reassure me or a prophecy as high priestess?" Rasuah asked quietly.

"The two are finally incapable of separation," she

552

replied. "He'll return, as I said, and be on the wharf to greet us when we come back."

Rasuah lifted his eyes and looked at Ramessa's figure until it faded into a distant speck, but still he stared in its direction.

Seshena raised her hands, placing them one on each side of Rasuah's face, and turned him toward her. "Look at the eastern heavens," she directed.

Rasuah lifted his eyes to the sky beyond the ship's prow, which was a pale saffron swept with purple clouds silver at their edges.

"This dawn is an empty tapestry awaiting the divine needle of Rennunet, the lady of fortune, to embroider a new pattern on it," Seshena said.

Rasuah glanced down at Seshena and smiled. "And what design do you think Rennunet will choose?" he asked.

Seshena pointed toward the horizon, where the edge of the sun's ascending disc struck a streak of golden fire across the water and extended like a flare into the sky. Seshena smiled and looked up at Rasuah.

"I'm not certain of her final decision," she said, "but she begins with a golden thread."

GLOSSARY

The Egyptian names in this book are authentic translations. Following is a key to their pronounciation as well as some explanations to aid in your enjoyment.

Abtu (Ab-too)—city on the south border of Egypt.

Ahbidew (Ah-bee-doo)—city later called Abydos.

Akeset (Ah-keh-set)—a high priest of Amen-Ra.

Amen-Ra (Ah-men-Rah)—Divine being symbolizing the beneficial qualities of the sun.

Amset (Am-set)—a priestess of Aset.

Amtet (Am-tet)—the royal scribe.

Anherru (An-her-oo)—a priest of Amen-Ra.

Anpu (An-poo)—Divine being symbolizing science, the patron of physicians and guardian of the dead.

Apep (Ah-pep)—demon symbolizing the darkness of ignorance and evil.

Asar (Ah-sar)—Divine being symbolizing the immortality of men.

Aset (Ah-set)—Divine being symbolizing immortal woman, patroness of magic.

Baka (Bah-kah)—the royal stablemaster.

Bast (Bahst)—Divine being symbolizing prophecy.

Befen (Bef-en)—a priest of Amen-Ra.

Chenmet (Shen-met)—Nefertiry's personal servant.

Decan (Dee-can)—ten days.

Djanah (Djah-nah)—Rasuah's servant.

Hapu (Ha-poo)—a royal servant.

Hapy (Hah-pee)—the royal surveyor.

Hat-Hor (Hat-Hor)—Divine being symbolizing all things of sensual pleasure.

Henhenet (Hen-hen-it)—the first royal minister or prime minister.

Heru (Her-oo)—Divine being symbolizing the ruler of the land.

Hesyra (Heh-see-rah)—a nobleman.

Ipuwer (Ee-poo-wer)—a captain in the royal army.
Irai (Ee-rah-ee)—a mad man.
Khakamir (Kha-kah-mer)—the commander of the royal
    army.
Kharu (Kah-roo)—a soldier.
Khenti (Khen-tee)—a priest of Amen-Ra.
Makara (Mah-kah-rah)—a priestess of Aset.
Manefera (Mah-nef-er-ah)—one of the royal wives.
Memnet (Mem-net)—Nefertiry's mother.
Menna (Men-ah)—Ramessa's aide.
Mentemhet (Men-tem-het)—a nobleman.
Merenptah (Mer-en-tah)—a prince.
Metenu (Met-en-oo)—a nobleman.
Mimut (Mee-moot)—one of the royal wives.
Montu (Mon-too)—Divine being symbolizing physical au-
    thority, patron of the army.
Nefertiry (Nef-er-tir-ee)—Queen and first royal wife.
Nehara (Neh-har-rah)—Seshena's servant.
Nehemu (Neh-em-oo)—a priest of Amen-Ra.
Nehri (Neh-ree)—Ramessa's personal servant.
Nofret (Noh-fret)—one of the royal wives.
Noph (Nohf)—city later known as Memphis.
Paneb (Pah-neb)—a captain in the royal army.
Paser (Pah-ser)—a nobleman.
Peheti (Peh-et-ee)—a soldier.
Perabsen (Per-ab-sen)—a nobleman.
Petet (Peh-tet)—a priest of Amen-Ra.
Ptah (Tah)—one of the many names for the Creator or the
    Infinite Intelligence.
Ra (Rah)—the sun.
Ramessa (Rah-mes-sah)—the king.
Raneferu (Rah-nef-er-oo)—one of the royal wives.
Rasuah (Rah-soo-ah)—first royal envoy.
Rehi (Reh-ee)—a frontier official.
Rennunet (Ren-oo-net)—Divine being symbolizing destiny.
Reshet (Reh-shet)—the king's paramour.
Resy (Reh-see)—the royal physician.
Sebeko (Seh-bek-oh)—a nobleman.
Sekhmet (Sekh-met)—Divine being symbolizing justice.
Sena (Se-nah)—a priestess of Aset.
Senti (Sen-tee)—an artist.

Seti (Seh-tee)—Ramessa's father.

Seshena (Seh-shen-ah)—a high priestess of Aset.

Setnau (Set-nah-oo)—a prince.

Susu (Soo-soo)—a soldier.

Sutekh (Soo-tekh)—Divine being symbolizing violence in men.

Suti (Soo-tee)—a caravan leader.

Tamera (Tah-mer-ah)—Egypt.

Tefen (Teh-fen)—a nobleman.

Tehuti (Teh-oo-tee)—Divine being symbolizing intelligence.

Tuiah (Too-ee-ah)—Ramessa's mother.

Wast (Wahst)—city later called Thebes, the capital of Egypt.

Wenamon (Wen-ah-mon)—a nobleman.

Zahte (Zah-tee)—the royal herald.

Zehzee (Zeh-zee)—Rasuah's personal servant.

Sylvia Thorpe

W0109-W

Romantic tales of adventure, intrigue, and gallantry.

☐ BEGGAR ON HORSEBACK	23091-0	$1.50
☐ CAPTAIN GALLANT	23547-5	$1.75
☐ FAIR SHINE THE DAY	23229-8	$1.75
☐ A FLASH OF SCARLET	23533-5	$1.75
☐ THE CHANGING TIDE	23418-5	$1.75
☐ THE GOLDEN PANTHER	23006-6	$1.50
☐ THE RELUCTANT ADVENTURESS	23426-6	$1.50
☐ ROGUES' COVENANT	23041-4	$1.50
☐ ROMANTIC LADY	Q2910	$1.50
☐ THE SCANDALOUS LADY ROBIN	23622-6	$1.75
☐ THE SCAPEGRACE	23478-9	$1.50
☐ THE SCARLET DOMINO	23220-4	$1.50
☐ THE SILVER NIGHTINGALE	23379-9	$1.50
☐ SPRING WILL COME AGAIN	23346-4	$1.50
☐ THE SWORD AND THE SHADOW	22945-9	$1.50
☐ SWORD OF VENGEANCE	23136-4	$1.50
☐ TARRINGTON CHASE	23520-3	$1.75

Buy them at your local bookstores or use this handy coupon for ordering:

FREE
Fawcett Books Listing

There is Romance, Mystery, Suspense, and Adventure waiting for you inside the Fawcett Books Order Form. And it's yours to browse through and use to get all the books you've been wanting... but possibly couldn't find in your bookstore.

This easy-to-use order form is divided into categories and contains over 1500 titles by your favorite authors.

So don't delay—take advantage of this special opportunity to increase your reading pleasure.

Just send us your name and address and 25¢ (to help defray postage and handling costs).

"Luca, what are you doing?"

But the defensive tartness was gone out of Serena's voice.

He pulled her in closer, the darkness wrapping around them but failing to hide that bright blue gaze or the gold of her hair. The slant of her stunning cheekbones.

She wasn't pulling away.

Luca's body was on fire. From somewhere, he found his voice, and it sounded coarse, rough. "What am I doing?"

This...

And then he pulled her right into him and his mouth found hers with unerring precision. Her breasts swelled against his chest—in outrage? He didn't know, because he was falling over the very thin edge of his control.

When he felt her resistance give way after an infinitesimal moment, triumph surged through his body. He couldn't think anymore, because he was swept up in the decadent darkness of a kiss that intoxicated him and reminded him of only one other similar moment...with her...seven years before.

Billionaire Brothers

*One raised in luxury in Brazil,
the other on the streets of Italy...*

Luca Fonseca lives with the shame of his father's unethical dealings and his own mistake of falling for a beautiful face. Now the coldhearted Brazilian is determined to restore his family's reputation—with or without his twin brother's help.

Embittered Max Fonseca Roselli shunned his heritage and his brother, and despite raising himself on the streets of Rome, he has carved out his own successful life. He, too, wants respectability, but he has a very different plan...

Two women will bring these brothers together—but is it enough to restore their brotherly bond?

Find out in:
Fonseca's Fury
January 2015

Don't miss Max's story in:
The Bride Fonseca Needs
June 2015!

Abby Green

Fonseca's Fury

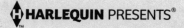
HARLEQUIN PRESENTS®

Recycling programs
for this product may
not exist in your area.

ISBN-13: 978-0-373-137848

Fonseca's Fury

First North American Publication 2015

Copyright © 2015 by Abby Green

Printed in U.S.A.

ABBY GREEN spent her teens reading Harlequin® romances. She then spent many years working in the film and TV industry as an assistant director. One day while standing outside an actor's trailer in the rain, she thought, *There has to be more than this*. So she sent off a partial to Harlequin®. After many rewrites, they accepted her first book, and an author was born. She lives in Dublin, Ireland, and you can find out more here: www.abby-green.com.

Other titles by Abby Green available in ebook:

WHEN DA SILVA BREAKS THE RULES
(Blood Brothers)
WHEN CHRISTAKOS MEETS HIS MATCH
(Blood Brothers)
WHEN FALCONE'S WORLD STOPS TURNING
(Blood Brothers)
FORGIVEN BUT NOT FORGOTTEN?

This is for Helen Kane—thanks for going to Dubai and letting me rent out your house and possibly the most idyllic office space in Dublin. And I do forgive you for leaving me behind in Kathmandu (on my birthday!) while you went off and romanced your own Mills & Boon hero! x

CHAPTER ONE

SERENA DEPIERO SAT in the plush ante-room and looked at the name on the opposite wall, spelled out in matt chrome lettering, and reeled.

Roseca Industries and Philanthropic Foundation.

Renewed horror spread through her. It had only been on the plane to Rio de Janeiro, when she'd been reading the extra information on the charity given to her by her boss, that she'd become aware that it was part of a much bigger organisation. An organisation run and set up by Luca Fonseca. The name Roseca was apparently an amalgamation of his father and mother's surnames. And Serena wasn't operating on a pay grade level high enough to require her to be aware of this knowledge before now.

Except here she was, outside the CEO's office, waiting to be called in to see the one man on the planet who had every reason to hate her guts. Why hadn't he sacked her months ago, as soon as she'd started working for him? Surely he must have known? An insidious suspicion took root: perhaps he'd orchestrated this all along, to lull her into a false sense of security before letting her crash spectacularly to the ground.

That would be breathtakingly cruel, and yet this man owed her nothing but his disdain. She owed *him*. Serena knew that there was a good chance her career in fundraising was about to be over before it had even taken off. And at that thought she felt a spurt of panic mixed with determination. Surely enough time had passed now? Surely, even if this *was* some elaborate revenge cooked up by Luca Fonseca as soon as he'd known she was working for him, she could try to convince him how sorry she was?

But before she could wrap her head around it any further a door opened to her right and a sleek dark-haired woman dressed in a grey suit emerged.

'Senhor Fonseca will see you now, Miss De-Piero.'

Serena's hands clenched tightly around her handbag. She felt like blurting out, *But I don't want to see him!*

But she couldn't. As much as she couldn't just flee. The car that had met her at the airport to deliver her here still had her luggage in its boot.

As she stood up reluctantly a memory assailed her with such force it almost knocked her sideways: Luca Fonseca in a bloodstained shirt, with a black eye and a split lip. Dark stubble shadowing his swollen jaw. He'd been behind the bars of a jail cell, leaning against a wall, brooding and dangerous. But then he'd looked up and narrowed that intensely dark blue gaze on her, and an expression of icy loathing had come over his face.

He'd straightened and moved to the bars, wrapping his fingers around them almost as if he was imagining they were her neck. Serena had stopped dead at the battered sight of him. He'd spat out, *'Damn you, Serena DePiero, I wish I'd never laid eyes on you.'*

'Miss DePiero? Senhor Fonseca is waiting.'

The clipped and accented voice shattered Serena's memory and she forced her feet to move, taking her past the unsmiling woman and into the palatial office beyond.

She hated that her heart was thumping so hard when she heard the door snick softly shut behind her. For the first few seconds she saw

no one, because the entire back wall of the
office was a massive window and it framed
the most amazingly panoramic view of a city
Serena had ever seen.

The Atlantic glinted dark blue in the distance, and inland from that were the two most
iconic shapes of Rio de Janeiro: the Sugar Loaf
and Christ the Redeemer high on Corcovado.
In between were countless other tall buildings,
right up to the coast. To say that the view was
breathtaking was an understatement.

And then suddenly it was eclipsed by the
man who moved into her line of vision. Luca
Fonseca. For a second past and present merged
and Serena was back in that nightclub, seeing
him for the first time.

He'd stood so tall and broad against the
backdrop of that dark and opulent place. Still.
She'd never seen anyone so still, yet with such
a commanding presence. People had skirted
around him. Men suspicious, envious. Women
lustful.

In a dark suit and open-necked shirt he'd
been dressed much the same as other men,
but he'd stood out from them all by dint of that
sheer preternatural stillness and the incredible
forcefield of charismatic magnetism that had
drawn her to him before she could stop herself.

Serena blinked. The dark and decadent club faded. She couldn't breathe. The room was instantly stifling. Luca Fonseca looked different. It took her sluggish brain a second to function enough for her to realise that he looked different because his hair was longer, slightly unruly. And he had a dark beard that hugged his jaw. It made him look even more intensely masculine.

He was wearing a light-coloured open-necked shirt tucked into dark trousers. For all the world the urbane, civilised businessman in his domain, and yet the vibe coming from him was anything but civilised.

He crossed his arms over that massive chest and then he spoke. 'What the hell do you think you're doing here, DePiero?'

Serena moved further into the vast office, even though it was in the opposite direction from where she wanted to go. She couldn't take her eyes off him even if she wanted to.

She forced herself to speak, to act as if seeing him again wasn't as shattering as it was. 'I'm here to start working in the fundraising department for the global communities charity.'

'Not any more, you're not,' Fonseca said tersely.

Serena flushed. 'I didn't know you were…
involved until I was on my way over here.'

Fonseca made a small sound like a snort.
'An unlikely tale.'

'It's true,' Serena blurted out. 'I had no idea
the charity was linked to the Roseca Foundation. Believe me, if I'd had any idea I wouldn't
have agreed to come here.'

Luca Fonseca moved around the table and
Serena's eyes widened. For a big man, he moved
with innate grace, and that incredible quality
of self-containment oozed from every pore. It
was intensely captivating.

He admitted with clear irritation, 'I wasn't
aware that you were working in the Athens office. I don't micro-manage my smaller charities abroad because I hire the best staff to do
that for me—although I'm reconsidering my
policy after this. If I'd known they'd hired you,
of all people, you would have been let go long
before now.'

His mouth twisted with recrimination.

'But I have to admit that I was intrigued
enough to have you brought here instead of
just leaving you at the airport until we could
put you on a return flight.'

So he hadn't even known she was working
for him. Serena's hands curled into fists at her

sides. His dismissive arrogance set her nerves even more on edge.

He glanced at a big platinum watch on his wrist. 'I have a spare fifteen minutes before you are to be delivered back to the airport.'

Like an unwanted package. He was firing her.

He hitched a hip onto the corner of his desk, for all the world as if they were having a normal conversation amidst the waves of tension. 'Well, DePiero? What the hell is Europe's most debauched ex-socialite doing working for minimum wage in a small charity office in Athens?'

Only hours ago Serena had been buoyant at the thought of her new job. A chance to prove to her somewhat over-protective family that she was going to be fine. She'd been ecstatic at the thought of her independence. And now this man was going to ensure that everything she'd fought so hard for was for naught.

For years she had been the *enfant terrible* of the Italian party scene, frequently photographed, with reams of newsprint devoted to her numerous exploits which had been invariably blown out of proportion. Nevertheless, Serena knew well that there was enough truth behind the headlines to make her feel that ever-present prick of shame.

'Look,' she said, hating the way her voice had got husky with repressed emotion and shock at facing this blast from her past, 'I know you must hate me.'

Luca Fonseca smiled. But his expression was hard. 'Hate? Don't flatter yourself, De-Piero, *hate* is a very inadequate description of my feelings where you are concerned.'

Another poisonous memory assailed her: a battered Luca, handcuffed by Italian police, being dragged bodily to an already loaded-up van, snarling, *'You set me up, you bitch!'* at Serena, who had been moments away from being handed into a police car herself, albeit minus the handcuffs.

They'd insisted on everyone being hauled in to the police station. He'd tried to jerk free of the burly police officers and that had earned him a thump to his belly, making him double over. Serena had been stupefied. Transfixed with shock.

He'd rasped out painfully, just before disappearing into the police van, 'She planted the drugs on *me* to save herself.'

Serena tried to force the memories out of her head. 'Mr Fonseca, I didn't plant those drugs in your pockets... I don't know who did, but it wasn't me. I tried to contact you afterwards... but you'd left Italy.'

He made a sound of disgust. 'Afterwards? You mean after you'd returned from your shopping spree in Paris? I saw the pictures. Avoiding being prosecuted for possession of drugs and continuing your hedonistic existence was all in a week's work for you, wasn't it?'

Serena couldn't avoid the truth; no matter how innocent she was, this man *had* suffered because of their brief association. The lurid headlines were still clear in her mind: *DePiero's newest love interest? Brazilian billionaire Fonseca caught with drugs after raid on Florence's most exclusive nightclub, Den of Eden.*

But before Serena could defend herself Luca was standing up and walking closer, making her acutely aware of his height and powerful frame. Her mouth dried.

When he was close enough that she could make out the dark chest hair curling near the open V of his shirt, he sent an icy look from her face to her feet, and then said derisively, 'A far cry from that lame excuse for a dress.'

Serena could feel heat rising at the reminder of how she'd been dressed that night. How she'd dressed most nights. She tried again, even though it was apparent that her attempt to defend herself had fallen on deaf ears. 'I really didn't have anything to do with those drugs. I promise. It was all a huge misunderstanding.'

He looked at her for a long moment, clearly incredulous, before tipping his head back and laughing so abruptly that Serena flinched.

When his eyes met hers again they still sparkled with cold mirth, and that sensual mouth was curved in an equally cold smile.

'I have to hand it to you—you've got some balls to come in here and protest your innocence after all this time.'

Serena's nails scored her palms, but she didn't notice. 'It's true. I know what you must think...'

She stopped, and had to push down the insidious reminder that it was what *everyone* had thought. Erroneously.

'I didn't do those kinds of drugs.'

Any hint of mirth, cold or otherwise, vanished from Luca Fonseca's visage. 'Enough with protesting your innocence. You had Class A drugs in that pretty purse and you conveniently slipped them into my pocket as soon as it became apparent that the club was being raided.'

Feeling sick now, Serena said, 'It must have been someone else in the crush and panic.'

Fonseca moved even closer to Serena then, and she gulped and looked up. She felt hot, clammy.

His voice was low, seductive. 'Do I need to remind you of how close we were that night, Serena? How easy it must have been for you to divest yourself of incriminating evidence?'

Serena could recall all too clearly that his arms had been like steel bands around her, with hers twined around his neck. Her mouth had been sensitive and swollen, her breathing rapid. Someone had rushed over to them on the dance floor—some acquaintance of Serena's who had hissed, *'There's a raid.'*

And Luca Fonseca thought… He thought that during those few seconds before chaos had struck she'd had the presence of mind to somehow slip drugs onto his person?

He said now, 'I'm sure it was a move you'd perfected over the years, which was why I felt nothing.'

He stepped back and Serena could take a breath again. But then he walked around her, and her skin prickled. She was acutely aware of his regard and wanted to adjust her suit, which felt constrictive.

She closed her eyes and then opened them again, turning around to face him. 'Mr Fonseca, I'm just looking for a chance—'

He held up his hand and Serena stopped. His expression was worse than cold now: it was completely indecipherable.

He clicked his fingers, as if something just occurred to him, and his lip curled. 'Of *course*—it's your family, isn't it? They've clipped your wings. Andreas Xenakis and Rocco De Marco would never tolerate a return to your debauched ways, and you're still *persona non grata* in the social circles who fêted you before. You and your sister certainly landed on your feet, in spite of your father's fall from grace.'

Disgust was etched on his hard features.

'Lorenzo DePiero will never be able to show his face again after the things he did.'

Serena felt nauseous. She of all people didn't need to be reminded of her father's corruption and many crimes.

But Luca wasn't finished. 'I think you're doing this under some sort of sufferance, to prove to your new-found family that you've changed… In return for what? An allowance? A palatial home back in Italy, your old stomping ground? Or perhaps you'll stay in Athens, where the stench of your tarnished reputation is a little less…pungent? After all, it's where you'll have the protection of your younger sister who, if I recall correctly, was the one who regularly cleaned up your messes.'

Fire raced up Serena's spine at hearing him mention her family—and especially her sister. A sense of protectiveness overwhelmed her. They were everything to her and she would never, ever let them down. They had saved her. Something this cold, judgmental man would never understand.

Serena was jet-lagged, gritty-eyed, and in shock at seeing this man again, and it was evident in her voice now, as she lashed back heatedly, 'My family have nothing to do with this. And nothing to do with *you*.'

Luca Fonseca looked at Serena incredulously. 'I'm sure your family have everything to do with this. Did you drop a tantalising promise of generous donations from them in return for a move up the career ladder?'

Serena flushed and got out a strangled-sounding, 'No, of course not.'

But the way she avoided his eyes told Luca otherwise. She wouldn't have had to drop anything but the most subtle of hints. The patronage of either her half-brother, Rocco De Marco, or her brother-in-law, Andreas Xenakis, could secure a charity's fortunes for years to come. And, as wealthy as he was in his own right, the foundation would always need to raise money. Disgusted that his own staff might have been so easily manipulated, and suddenly aware of how heated his blood was, Luca stepped back.

He was grim. 'I am not going to be a convenient conduit through which you try to fool everyone into thinking you've changed.'

Serena just looked at him, and he saw her long, graceful throat work, as if she couldn't quite get out what she wanted to say. He felt no pity for her.

She couldn't be more removed from the woman of his memory of seven years ago, when she'd been golden and sinuous and provocative. The woman in front of him now looked pale, and as if she was going for an interview in an insurance office. Her abundantly sexy white-blonde hair had been tamed into a staid chignon. And yet even that, and the sober dark suit, couldn't dim her incredible natural beauty or those piercing bright blue eyes.

Those eyes had hit him right in the solar plexus as soon as she'd walked into his office, when he'd been able to watch her unobserved for a few seconds. And the straight trousers couldn't hide those famously long legs. The generous swell of her breasts pushed against the silk of her shirt.

Disgust curled through him to notice her like this. Had he learnt nothing? She should be prostrating herself at his feet in abject apology for turning his life upside down, but instead she had the temerity to defend herself: *'My family have nothing to do with this.'*

His clear-headed focus was being eroded in this woman's presence. Why was he even wondering anything about her? He didn't care what her nefarious motivations were. He'd satisfied whatever curiosity he'd had.

He clenched his jaw. 'Your time is up. The car will be waiting outside for your return to the airport. And I do sincerely hope to never lay eyes on you again.'

So why was it so hard to rip his gaze *off* her?

Anger and self-recrimination coursed through Luca as he stepped around Serena and stalked back to his desk, expecting to hear the door open and close.

When he didn't, he spun round and spat out tersely, 'We have nothing more to discuss.'

The fact that she had gone paler was something that Luca didn't like to acknowledge that he'd noticed. Or his very bizarre dart of concern. No woman evoked concern in him. He could see her swallow again, that long, graceful throat moving, and then her soft, husky voice, with that slightest hint of an Italian accent, crossed the space between them.

'I'm just asking for a chance. Please.'

Luca's mouth opened and closed. He was stunned. Once he declared what he wanted no one questioned him. Until now. And this woman, of all people? Serena DePiero had a less than zero chance of Luca reconsidering his decision. The fact that she was still in his office set his nerves sizzling just under his skin. Irritating him.

But instead of admitting defeat and turning round, the woman stepped closer. Further away from the door.

Luca had an urge to snarl and stalk over to her, to put her over his shoulder, physically remove her from his presence. But right then, with perfect timing, the memory of her lush body pressed against his, her soft mouth yielding to his forceful kiss, exploded into his consciousness and within a nano-second he was battling a surge of blood to his groin.

Damn her. Witch.

She was at the other side of his desk. Blue eyes huge, her bearing as regal as a queen's, reminding him effortlessly of her impeccable lineage.

Her voice was low and she clasped her hands together in front of her, knuckles white. 'Mr Fonseca, I came here with the best of intentions to do work for your charity, despite what you may believe. I'll do anything to prove to you how committed I am.'

Anger surged at her persistence. At her meek *Mr Fonseca*.

Luca uncrossed his arms and placed his hands on the table in front of him, leaning forward. '*You* are the reason I had to rebuild my reputation and people's trust in my charitable work—not to mention trust in my family's mining consortium. I spent months, *years*, undoing the damage of that one night. Debauchery is all very well and good, as you must know, but the stigma of possessing Class A drugs does tend to last. The truth is that once those pictures of us together in the nightclub surfaced I *had* no defence.'

It almost killed Luca now to recall how he had instinctively shielded Serena from the police and detectives who had stormed the club, which was when she must have taken the opportunity to plant the drugs on him.

He thought of the paparazzi pictures of her

shopping in Paris while he'd been leaving Italy under a cloud of disgrace, and bitterness laced his voice. 'Meanwhile you were oblivious to the fallout, continuing your hedonistic existence. And after all that, you have the temerity to think that I would so much as allow your name to be mentioned in the same sentence as mine?'

If possible, she paled even more, displaying the genes she'd inherited from her half-English mother, a classic English rose beauty.

He straightened up. 'You disgust me.'

Serena was dimly aware that on some level his words were hurting her in a place that she shouldn't be feeling hurt. But something dogged deep inside had pushed her to plead. And she had.

His eyes were like dark, hard sapphires. Impervious to heat or cold or her pleas. He was right. He was the one man on the planet who would never give her a chance. She was delusional to have thought even for a second that he might hear her out.

The atmosphere in the office was positively glacial in comparison to the gloriously sunny day outside. Luca Fonseca was just looking at her. Serena's belly sank. He wasn't even going to say another word. He'd said everything. He'd

just wanted to see her, to torture her. Make her
realise just how much he hated her—as if she
had been in any doubt.

She finally admitted defeat and turned to
the door. There would be no reprieve. Hitch-
ing up her chin in a tiny gesture of dignity,
she didn't glance back at him, not wanting to
see that arctic expression again. As if she was
something distasteful on the end of his shoe.

She opened the door, closed it behind her,
and was met by his cool assistant who was
waiting for her. And who'd undoubtedly been
privy to the plans of her boss well before Serena had been. Silently she was escorted downstairs.

Her humiliation was complete.

Ten minutes later Luca spoke tersely into his
phone. 'Call me as soon as you know she's
boarded and the plane has left.'

When he'd terminated the call Luca swiv-
elled around in his high-backed chair to face
the view. His blood was still boiling with a
mixture of anger and arousal. Why had he in-
dulged in the dubious desire to see her face to
face again? All it had done was show him his
own weakness for her.

He hadn't even known she was on her way

to Rio until his assistant had informed him; the significance of her arrival had only come to light far too late to do anything about it.

Serena DePiero. Just her name brought an acrid taste of poison to his mouth. And yet the image that accompanied her name was anything but poisonous. It was provocative. It was his first image of her in that nightclub in Florence.

He'd known who she was, of course. No one could have gone to Florence and *not* known who the DePiero sisters were—famed for their light-haired, blue-eyed aristocratic beauty and their vast family fortune that stretched back to medieval times. Serena had been the media's darling. Despite her debauched existence, no matter what she did, they'd lapped it up and bayed for more.

Her exploits had been legendary: high-profile weekends in Rome, leaving hotels trashed and staff incandescent with rage. Whirlwind private jet trips to the Middle East on the whim of an equally debauched sheikh who fancied a party with his Eurotrash friends. And always pictured in various states of ine-briation and loucheness that had only seemed to heighten her dazzling appeal.

The night he'd seen her she'd been in the

middle of the dance floor in what could only be described as an excuse for a dress. Strapless gold lamé, with tassels barely covering the top of her toned golden thighs. Long white-blonde hair tousled and falling down her back and over her shoulders, brushing the enticing swell of a voluptuous cleavage. Her peers had jostled around her, vying for her attention, desperately trying to emulate her golden exclusiveness.

With her arms in the air, swaying to the hedonistic beat of music played by some world-class DJ, she had symbolised the very font of youth and allure and beauty. The kind of beauty that made grown men fall to their knees in wonder. A siren's beauty, luring them to their doom.

Luca's mouth twisted. He'd proved to be no better than any other mortal man when she'd lured him to his doom. He took responsibility for being in that club—of course he did. But from the moment she'd sashayed over to stand in front of him everything had grown a little hazy. And Luca was not a person who got hazy. No matter how stunning the woman. His whole life was about being clear and focused, because he had a lot to achieve.

But her huge bright blue eyes had seared him alive, igniting every nerve-ending, blasting aside any concerns. Her skin was flawless, her aquiline nose a testament to her breeding. Her mouth had fascinated him. Perfectly sculpted lips. Not too full, not too thin, effortlessly hinting at a dark and sexy sensuality.

She'd said coquettishly, 'It's rude to stare, you know.'

And instead of turning on his heel in disgust at her reputation and her arrogance, Luca had felt the blood flow through his body, hardening it, and he'd drawled softly, 'I'd have to be blind not to be dazzled. Join me for a drink?'

She'd tossed her head and for a second Luca had thought he glimpsed something curiously vulnerable and weary in those stunning blue eyes, but it had to have been a trick of the strobing lights, because then she'd purred, 'I'd love to.'

The wisps of memory faded from Luca's mind. He hated it that even now, just thinking of her, was having an effect on his body. Seven years had passed, and yet he felt as enflamed by anger and desire as he had that night. A bruising, humiliating mix.

He'd just left Serena DePiero in no doubt as to what he thought of her. She'd effectively been fired from her job. So why wasn't there a feeling of triumph rushing through him? Why

was there an unsettling, prickling feeling of…
unfinished business?

And why was there the tiniest grudging
sliver of admiration for the way she had not
backed down from him and the way that small
chin had tipped up ever so slightly just before
she'd left?

CHAPTER TWO

THE HOTEL WAS a few blocks back from Copacabana beach. To say that it was basic was an understatement, but it was clean—which was the main thing. And cheap—which was good, considering Serena was living off her meagre savings from the last year. She took off her travelling clothes, which were well creased by now, and stepped into the tiny shower, relishing the lukewarm spray.

Her belly clenched minutely when she imagined Luca's reaction to her *not* leaving Rio but she pushed it aside. She'd been standing in line for the check-in when her sister had phoned her. Too heartsore to admit that she was coming home so soon, and suddenly aware that Athens didn't even really feel like home, Serena had made a spur-of-the-moment decision to tell a white lie and pretend everything was okay.

And, even though she'd hated lying—to her

sister, of all people—she didn't regret it now. She was still angry at Luca Fonseca's easy dismissal of her, the way he'd toyed with her before kicking her out of his office.

It had been enough to propel her out of the airport and back into the city. She scrubbed her scalp with unnecessary force, not liking how turbulent her emotions still were after meeting him again, and she certainly didn't like admitting that he'd roused her to a kind of anger she hadn't felt in a long time. Angry enough to rebel…when she'd thought she'd left all that behind her.

When she emerged from the bathroom she had a towel hitched around her body and another one on her head, and was feeling no less disgruntled. She almost jumped out of her skin when a loud, persistent knocking came on her door.

Scrambling around to find something to put on, Serena called out to whoever it was to wait a second as she pulled on some underwear and faded jeans and a T-shirt. The towel fell off her head so her long hair hung damply down her back and over her shoulders.

She opened the door and it was as if someone had punched her in the stomach. She couldn't draw breath because Luca Fonseca was standing there, eyes shooting sparks at her, looking angrier than she'd ever seen him.

'What the hell are you doing here, DePiero?' he snarled.

Serena answered faintly, 'You seem to be asking me that a lot lately.'

And then the fright he'd just given her faded and the anger she'd been harbouring swelled back. Her hand gripped the door.

'Actually, I might ask the same of you— what the hell are *you* doing *here*, Fonseca?' Something occurred to her. 'And how on earth did you even know where I was?'

His mouth was a tight line. 'I told Sancho, my driver, to wait at the airport and make sure you got on the flight.'

The extent of how badly he'd wanted her gone hit her. Her hand gripped the door even tighter. 'This is a free country, Fonseca. I decided to stay and do a little sightseeing, and as I no longer work for you I really don't think you have any jurisdiction here.'

She went to close the door in his face but he easily stopped her and stepped into the room, closing the door behind him and forcing her to take a step back.

His arctic gaze took in her appearance with

derision and Serena crossed her arms over her braless chest, self-conscious.

'Mr Fonseca—'

'Enough with the *Mr Fonseca*. Why are you still here, Serena?'

His use of her name made something swoop inside her. She crossed her arms tighter. It reminded her bizarrely of how it had felt to kiss him in the middle of that dance floor. Dark and hot and intoxicating. No other man's kiss or touch had ever made her feel like that. She'd pulled back from him in shock, as if his kiss had incinerated her, right through to where she was still whole. *Herself.*

'Well?'

The curt question jarred Serena back to the present and she hated it that she'd remembered that feeling of exposure.

'I want to see Rio de Janeiro before going home.' As if she would confide that she also wanted to delay revealing the extent of her failure to her family for as long as possible.

Luca snorted indelicately. 'Do you have *any* idea where you are? Were you planning on taking a stroll along the beach later?'

Serena gritted her jaw. 'I was, actually. I'd invite you to join me, but I'm sure you have better things to be doing.'

His sheer animal magnetism was almost overwhelming in the small space. The beard and his longer hair only added to his intense masculinity. Her skin prickled with awareness. She could feel her nipples tighten and harden against the barrier of her thin T-shirt and hated the unique way this man affected her above any other.

Luca was snarling again. 'Do you realise that you're in one of the most dangerous parts of Rio? You're just minutes from one of the worst *favelas* in the city.'

Serena resisted the urge to point out that that should please him. 'But the beach is just blocks away.'

Now he was grim. 'Yes, and no one goes near this end of the beach at night unless they're out to score some drugs or looking to get mugged. It's one of the most dangerous places in the city after dark.'

He stepped closer and his eyes narrowed on her speculatively.

'But maybe that's it? You're looking for some recreational enhancement? Maybe your family have you under their watch and you're relishing some freedom? Have you even told them you've been fired?'

Serena's arms fell to her sides and she barely

noticed Luca's gaze dropping to her chest before coming up again. All she felt was an incredible surge of anger and hatred for this man
and his perspicacity—even if it wasn't entirely
accurate.

Disgusted at the part of her that wanted to
try and explain herself to him, she spat out,
'What's the point?'

She stalked around Luca and reached for
the door handle, but before she could turn it
and open the door an arm came over her head,
keeping the door shut. She turned and folded
her arms again, glaring up at Luca, conscious
of her bare feet and damp hair, trying desperately not to let his sheer physicality affect her.

'If you don't leave in five seconds I'll start
screaming.'

Luca kept his arm on the door, semi cag-
ing Serena in. 'The manager will just assume
we're having fun. You can't be so naive that
you didn't notice this place rents rooms by the
hour.'

Serena felt hot. First of all at thinking of this
man making her scream with pleasure and then
at her own naivety.

'Of course I didn't,' she snapped, feeling
vulnerable. She scooted out from under Luca's
arm and put some space between them.

Luca crossed his arms. 'No, I can imagine you didn't. After all, it's not what you're used to.'

Serena thought of the Spartan conditions of the rehab facility she'd been in in England for a year, and then of her tiny studio apartment in a very insalubrious part of Athens. She smiled sweetly. 'How would you know?'

Luca scowled then. 'You're determined to stay in Rio?'

Never more so than right now. Even if just to annoy this man. 'Yes.'

Luca looked as though he would cheerfully throttle her. 'The last thing I need right now is some eagle-eyed reporter spotting you out and about, clubbing or shopping.'

Serena bit back a sharp retort. He had no idea what her life was like now. Clubbing? Shopping? She couldn't imagine anything worse.

Her smile got even sweeter. 'I'll wear a Louis Vuitton bag over my head while I go shopping for the latest Chanel suit. Will that help?'

That didn't go down well. Blood throbbed visibly in Luca's temple. 'You leaving Rio would be an even bigger help.'

Serena unconsciously mimicked his wide-legged stance. 'Well, unless you're planning on forcibly removing me, that's not going to happen. And if you even try such a thing I'll call the police and tell them you're harassing me.'

Luca didn't bother to tell her that with far greater problems in the city the police would no doubt just ogle her pale golden beauty before sending her on her way. And that such a stunt would only draw the interest of the paparazzi, who followed him most days.

The very thought of her being spotted, identified and linked to him was enough to make him go cold inside. He'd had enough bad press and innuendo after what had happened in Italy to last him a lifetime.

An audacious idea was being formulated in his head. It wasn't one he particularly relished, but it seemed like the only choice he had right now. It would get Serena DePiero out of Rio more or less immediately, and hopefully out of Brazil entirely within a couple of days.

'You said earlier that you were looking for another chance? That you'd do anything?'

Serena went very still, those huge blue eyes narrowing on him. Irritation made Luca's skin feel tight. The room was too small. All he could see was her. When she'd dropped her arms his eyes had tracked hungrily to her breasts, and he could still recall the jut of those hard nipples against her T-shirt. She was naked underneath.

Blood pooled at his groin, making him hard. *Damn.*

'Do you want a chance or not?' he growled, angry at his unwarranted response. Angry that she was still here.

Serena blinked. 'Yes, of course I do.'

Her voice had become husky and it had a direct effect on Luca's arousal. This was a mistake—he knew it. But he had no choice. Damage limitation.

Tersely, he said, 'I run an ethical mining company. I'm due to visit the Iruwaya mines, and the tribe that lives near there, to check on progress. You can prove your commitment by coming with me, instead of the assistant I'd lined up, to take notes. The village is part of the global communities network, so it's not entirely unrelated.'

'Where is the village?'

'Near Manaus.'

Serena's eyes widened. 'The city in the middle of the Amazon?'

Luca nodded. Perhaps this would be all it would take? Just the thought of doing something vaguely like hard work would have her scrambling back. Giving in. Leaving.

As if to mock his line of thought, Serena looked at him with those huge blue eyes and said determinedly, 'Fine. When do we go?'

Her response surprised Luca—much as the fact that she'd chosen this rundown flea-pit of a hotel had surprised him. He'd expected her to check into one of Rio's five-star resorts. But then he'd figured that perhaps her family had her on a tight leash where funds were concerned.

Whatever. He cursed himself again for wondering about her and said abruptly, 'Tomorrow. My driver will pick you up at five a.m.'

Once again he expected her to balk, but she didn't. He swept his gaze over the minor explosion of clothes from her suitcase and the toiletries spread across the narrow bed. The fact that her scent was clean and sweet, at odds with the sultry, sexy perfume he remembered from before, was not a welcome observation.

He looked back to her. 'I'll have an assistant stop by with supplies for the trip within the hour. You won't be able to bring your case.'

That gaze narrowed again. Suspicious. 'Supplies?'

Luca faced her squarely and said, with only the slightest twinge to his conscience,

'Oh, didn't I mention that we would be trekking through the jungle to get to the village? It takes two days from the farthest outskirts of Manaus.'

Those blue eyes flashed. 'No,' she responded. 'You didn't mention that we would be trekking through the jungle. Is it even safe?'

Luca smiled, enjoying the thought of Serena bailing after half an hour of walking through the earth's largest insect and wildlife-infested hothouse. He figured that after her first brush with one of the Amazon's countless insect or animal species she'd give up the act. But for now he'd go along with it. Because if he didn't she'd be a loose cannon in Rio de Janeiro. A ticking publicity time bomb. At least this way she'd have to admit defeat and go of her own free will.

He made a mental note to have a helicopter standing by to extract her and take her to the airport.

'It's eminently safe, once you have a guide who knows what they're doing and where they're going.'

'And that's you?' she said flatly.

'Yes. I've been visiting this tribe for many years, and exploring the Amazon for a lot longer than that. You couldn't be in safer hands.'

The look Serena shot him told him that she doubted that. His smile grew wider and he arched a brow. 'By all means you can say no, Serena, it's entirely up to you.'

She made a derisive sound. 'And if I say no you'll personally escort me to the airport, no doubt.'

She stopped and bit her lip for a moment, making Luca's awareness of her spike.

'But if I do this, and prove my commitment, will you let me take up the job I came for?'

Luca's smile faded and he regarded her. Once again that tiny grudging admiration reared its head. He ruthlessly crushed it.

'Well, as I'm almost certain you won't last two hours in the jungle it's a moot point. All this is doing is delaying your inevitable return home.'

Her chin lifted and her arms tightened over her chest. 'It'll take more than a trek and some dense vegetation to put me off, Fonseca.'

The early-morning air was sultry, and the dawn hadn't yet broken, so it was dark when Serena got out of the back of the chauffeur-driven car at the private airfield almost twelve hours later. The first person she saw was the tall figure of Luca, carrying bags into a small plane. Instantly her nerves intensified.

He barely glanced at her as she walked over behind the driver, who carried the new backpack she'd been furnished with. And then his dark gaze fell on her and her heart sped up.

'You checked out of the hotel?'

Good morning to you too, Serena said silently, and cursed her helpless physical reaction. 'Yes. And my suitcase is in the car.'

Luca took her small backpack from the driver and exchanged a few words with him in rapid Portuguese. Then, as the driver walked away, Luca said, 'Your things will be left at my headquarters until you get back.'

The obvious implication of *you*—not *we*— was not lost on Serena, and she said coolly, 'I won't be bailing early.'

Luca looked at her assessingly and Serena was conscious of the new clothes and shoes she'd been given. Lightweight trousers and a sleeveless vest under a khaki shirt. Sturdy trekking boots. Much like what Luca was wearing, except his looked well worn, faded with time. Doing little to hide his impressive muscles and physique.

She cursed. Why did he have to be the one

man who seemed to connect with her in a way she'd never felt before?

Luca, who had turned back to the plane, said over his shoulder, 'Come on, we have a flight slot to make.'

'Aye-aye, sir,' Serena muttered under her breath as she hurried after him and up the steps into the small plane. She was glad that she'd pulled her hair up into a knot on top of her head as she could already feel a light sweat breaking out on the back of her neck.

Luca told her to take a seat. He shut the heavy door and secured it.

As Serena was closing her seatbelt she saw him take his seat in the cockpit and gasped out loud, *'You're* the pilot?'

'Evidently,' he said drily.

Serena's throat dried. 'Are you even qualified?'

He was busy flicking switches and turning knobs. He threw back over his shoulder, 'Since I was eighteen. Relax, Serena.'

He put on a headset then, presumably to communicate with the control tower, and then they were taxiing down the runway. Serena wasn't normally a nervous flyer, but her hands gripped the armrests as the full enormity of what was happening hit her. She was on a plane, headed into the world's densest and most potentially dangerous ecosystem, with a man who hated her guts.

She had a vision of a snake, dropping out of a tree in front of her face, and shivered in the dry cabin air just as the small plane left the ground and soared into the dawn-filled sky. Unfortunately her spirits didn't soar with it, but she comforted herself that at least she wasn't arriving back in Athens with her tail between her legs...just yet.

Serena was very aware of Luca's broad-shouldered physique at the front of the plane, but as much as she wanted to couldn't quite drum up the antipathy she wanted to feel for him. After all, he had good reason to believe what he did about her—that she'd framed him.

Anyone else would have believed the same... except for her sister, who had just looked at her with that sad expression that had reminded Serena of how trapped they both were by their circumstances—and by Serena's helpless descent into addiction to block out the pain.

Their father had simply been too powerful. And Siena had been too young for Serena to try anything drastic like running away. By the time Siena had come of age Serena had been in no shape to do anything drastic. Their father had seen to that effectively. And they'd been too well known. Any attempt to run would have been ended within hours, because their father would have sent his goons after them. They'd been bound as effectively as if their father had locked them in a tower.

'*Serena.*'

Serena's attention came back to the small plane and she looked forward, to see Luca staring back to her impatiently. He must have called her a couple of times. She felt raw from her memories.

'What?'

'I was letting you know that the flight will take four hours.' He pointed to a bag on the floor near her and said, 'You'll find some information in there about the tribe and the mines. You should read up on them.'

He turned back to the front and Serena re-strained herself from sticking her tongue out at him. She'd been bullied and controlled by one man for most of her life and she chafed at the thought of giving herself over to that treatment again.

As she dug for the documents she reiterated to herself that this was a means to an end. She'd chosen to come here with Luca, and she was going to get through it in one piece and prove herself to him if it was the last thing she did. She'd become adept in the past few years in focusing on the present, not looking back. And she'd need that skill now more than ever.

Just over four hours later Serena was feeling a little more in control of herself, and her head was bursting with information about where they were going. She was already fascinated and more excited about the trip, which felt like a minor victory in itself.

They'd landed in a private part of the airport and after a light breakfast, which had been laid out for them in a private VIP room, Luca was now loading bags and supplies into the back of a Jeep.

His backpack was about three times the size of hers. And there were walking poles. Nerves fluttered in Serena's belly. Maybe she was being really stupid. How on earth was she going to last in the jungle? She was a city girl… That was the jungle she understood and knew how to navigate.

Luca must have caught her expression and he arched a questioning brow. Instantly fresh resolve filled Serena and she marched forward. 'Is there anything I can do?'

He shut the Jeep's boot door. 'No, we're good. Let's go—we don't have all day.'

A short time later, as Luca navigated the Manaus traffic, which eventually got less crazy as they hit the suburbs, he delivered a veritable lecture to Serena on safety in the jungle.

'And whatever you do obey my commands. The jungle is perceived to be a very hostile environment, but it doesn't have to be—as long as you use your head and you're constantly on guard and aware of what's around you.'

A devil inside Serena prompted her to say, 'Are you always this bossy or is it just with me?'

To her surprise Luca's mouth lifted ever so slightly on one side, causing a reaction of seismic proportions in Serena's belly.

That dark navy glance slid to her for a second and he drawled, 'I instruct and people obey.'

Serena let out a small sound of disdain. That had been her father's philosophy too. 'That must make life very boring.'

The glimmer of a smile vanished. 'I find that people are generally compliant when it's in their interests to gain something…as you yourself are demonstrating right now.'

There was an unmistakably cynical edge

to his voice that had Serena's gaze fixed on his face. Not liking the fact that she'd noticed it, and wondering about where such cynicism stemmed from, she said, 'You offered me a chance to prove my commitment. That's what I'm doing.'

He shrugged one wide shoulder. 'Exactly my point. You have something to gain.'

'Do I, though?' Serena asked quietly, but Luca either didn't hear or didn't think it worth answering. Clearly the answer was *no*.

They were silent for the rest of the journey. Soon they'd left the city behind, and civilisation was slowly swallowed by greenery until they were surrounded by it. It gave Serena a very real sense of how ready the forest seemed to be to encroach upon its concrete rival given half a chance.

Her curiosity overcame her desire to limit her interaction with Luca. 'How did you become interested in these particular mines?'

One of his hands was resting carelessly on the wheel, the other on his thigh. He was a good driver—unhurried, but fast. In control. He looked at her and she felt very conscious of being in a cocoon-like atmosphere with nothing but green around them.

He returned his attention to the road. 'My

grandfather opened them up when prospectors found bauxite. The area was plundered, forest cleared, and the native Indians moved on to allow for a camp to be set up. It was the first of my family's mines...and so the first one that I wanted to focus on to try and undo the damage.'

Serena recalled what she'd read. 'But you're still mining?'

He frowned at her and put both hands on the wheel, as if that reminder had angered him. 'Yes, but on a much smaller scale. The main camp has already been torn down. Miners commute in and out from a nearby town. If I was to shut down the mine completely it would affect the livelihoods of hundreds of people. I'd also be doing the workers out of government grants for miners, education for their children, and so on. As it is, we're using this mine as a pilot project to develop ethical mining so that it becomes the standard.'

He continued. 'The proceeds are all being funnelled into restoring huge swathes of the forest that were cleared—they'll never be restored completely, but they can be used for other ends, and the native Indians who were taken off the land have moved back to farm that land and make a new living from it.'

'It sounds like an ambitious project.' Serena tried not to feel impressed. Her experience with her father had taught her that men could be masters in the art of altruism while hiding a soul so corrupt and black it would make the devil look like Mickey Mouse.

Luca glanced at her and she could see the fire of intent in his eyes—something she'd never seen in her father's eyes unless it was for his own ends. Greedy for more power. Control. Causing pain.

'It is an ambitious project. But it's my responsibility. My grandfather did untold damage to this country's natural habitat and my father continued his reckless destruction. I refuse to keep perpetuating the same mistake. Apart from anything else, to do so is to completely ignore the fact that the planet is intensely vulnerable.'

Serena was taken aback at the passion in his voice. Maybe he *was* genuine.

'Why do you care so much?'

He tensed, and she thought he wouldn't answer, but then he said, 'Because I saw the disgust the native Indians and even the miners had for my father and men like him whenever I went with him to visit his empire. I started to do my own research at a young age. I was horrified to find out the extent of the damage we were doing—not only to our country but on a worldwide scale—and I was determined to put an end to it.'

Serena looked at his stern profile, unable to stem her growing respect. Luca was turning the Jeep into an opening that was almost entirely hidden from view. The track was bumpy and rough, the huge majestic trees of the rainforest within touching distance now.

After about ten minutes of solid driving, deeper and deeper into the undergrowth, they emerged into a large clearing where a two-storey state-of-the-art facility was revealed, almost completely camouflaged to blend with the surroundings.

Luca brought the Jeep to a halt alongside a few other vehicles. 'This is our main Amazon operational research base. We have other smaller ones in different locations.' He looked at her before he got out of the Jeep. 'You should take this opportunity to use the facilities while we still have them.'

Serena wanted to scowl at the very definite glint of mockery in his eyes but she refused to let him see the flicker of trepidation she felt once again, when confronted with the reality of their awe-inspiring surroundings.

She was mesmerised by the dense foliage around them. She had that impression again that the forest was being held back by sheer will alone, as if given the slightest chance it would extend its roots and vines and overtake this place.

'Serena?'

Frowning impatiently, Luca was holding open the main door.

She walked in and he pointed down a corridor.

'The bathroom is down there. I'll meet you back here.'

When Serena found the bathroom and saw her own reflection in dozens of mirrors, she grimaced. She looked flushed and sweaty, and was willing to bet that if she made it to the end of the day she'd look a lot worse.

After throwing some water on her face and tying her hair back into a more practical plait she headed back, nerves jumping around in her belly at the prospect of the battle of wills ahead and her determination not to falter at the first hurdle.

When Serena joined Luca back outside he handed her the backpack. There was a long rubber hose coming from the inside of it to sit over one shoulder. He saw her look at it.

'That's your water supply. Sip little and often; we'll replenish it later.'

She put the pack on and secured it around her waist and over her chest. She was relieved to find that it didn't feel too heavy at all. And then she saw the size of Luca's pack, which obviously held all their main supplies and had a tent rolled up at the bottom.

Her eyes widened when she saw what looked suspiciously like a gun in a holster on his waist. He saw her expression and commented drily, 'It's a tranquilliser gun.' He sent a thorough glance up and down her body and remarked, 'Tuck your trousers into your socks and make sure your shirtsleeves are down and the cuffs closed.'

Feeling more and more nervous, Serena did as he said. When she looked at him again, feeling like a child about to be inspected in her school uniform, he was cocking a dark brow over those stunning eyes.

'Are you sure about this? Now would be a really good time to say no, if that's your intention.'

Serena put her hands on her hips and hid every one of her nerves behind bravado. 'I thought you said we don't have all day?'

CHAPTER THREE

A COUPLE OF hours later Serena was blindingly aware only of stepping where Luca stepped—which was a challenge, when his legs were so much longer. Her breath was wheezing in and out of her straining lungs. Rivers of sweat ran from every pore in her body.

She was soaked through. And it was no consolation to see sweat patches showing on Luca's body too, because they only seemed to enhance his impressive physicality.

She hadn't known what to expect, what the rainforest would be like, but it was more humid than she'd ever imagined it could be. And it was *loud*. Screamingly loud. With about a dozen different animal and bird calls at any time. She'd looked up numerous times to see a glorious flash of colour as some bird she couldn't name flew past, and had once caught sight of monkeys high in the canopy, loping lazily from branch to branch.

It was an onslaught on her senses, and Serena longed to stop for a minute to try and assimilate it all, but she didn't dare say a word to Luca, who hadn't stopped since he strode into the jungle, expecting her to follow him. He'd sent only the most cursory of glances back—presumably to make sure she hadn't been dragged into the dense greenery by one of mythical beasts that were running rampant in her imagination.

Every time the undergrowth rustled near her she sped up a little. Consequently, when Luca stopped suddenly and turned, Serena almost ran into him and skidded to a halt only just in time.

She noticed belatedly that they were on the edge of a clearing. It was almost a relief to get out of the oppressive atmosphere of the forest and suck in some breaths. She put her hands on her hips and hoped she didn't look as if she was about to burst a blood vessel.

Luca extracted something from a pocket in his trousers. It looked like a slightly old-fashioned mobile phone, a little larger than the current models.

'This is a satellite phone. I can call the chopper and it'll be here in fifteen minutes. This is your last chance to walk away.'

On the one hand Serena longed for nothing

more than to see the horizon fill up with a cityscape again. And to feel the blast of clean, cool water on her skin. She was boiling. Sweating. And her muscles were burning. But, perversely, she'd never felt more energised, in spite of the debilitating heat. And, apart from anything else, she had a fierce desire to show no weakness to this man. He was the only thing that stood between her and independence.

'I'm not going anywhere, Luca.'

A glimpse of something distinctly like surprise crossed his face, and a dart of pleasure made Serena stand tall. Even that small indication that she was proving to be not as easy a pushover as he'd clearly expected was enough to keep her rooted to the spot.

He looked down then, his attention taken by something, and then back up at her. A very wicked hint of a smile was playing about his mouth as he said, with a pointed look towards her feet, 'Are you absolutely sure?'

Serena looked down and her whole body froze with fear and terror when she saw a small black scorpion crawling over the toe of her boot with its tail curled high over its arachnid body.

Without any previous experience of anything so potentially dangerous, Serena fought down the fear and took her walking pole and gently nudged the scorpion off her shoe. It scuttled off into the undergrowth. Feeling slightly light-headed at what she'd just done, she looked back at Luca.

'Like I said, I'm not going anywhere.'

Luca couldn't stem a flash of respect. Not many others would have reacted to seeing a scorpion like that with such equanimity. Men included. And any woman he knew would have used it as an excuse to hurl herself into his arms, squeaking with terror.

But Serena was staring him down. Blue eyes massive. Something in his chest clenched for a moment, making him short of breath. In spite of being sweaty and dishevelled, she was still stunningly beautiful. Helen of Troy beautiful. He could appreciate in that moment how men could be driven to war or driven mad because of the beauty of one woman.

But not him.

Not when he knew first-hand just how strong her sense of self-preservation was. Strong enough to let another take the fall for her own misdeeds.

'Fine,' he declared reluctantly. 'Then let's keep going.'

He turned his back on the provocative view

of a flushed-faced Serena and strode back into the jungle.

Serena sucked in a few last deep breaths, relishing the cleared space for the last time, and then followed Luca, unable to stem the surge of triumph that he was letting her stay. And as she followed him she tried not to wince at the way her boots were pinching at her ankles and toes, pushing all thoughts of pain out of her head. Here, she couldn't afford to be weak. Luca would seize on it like a predator wearing its quarry down to exhaustion.

Serena felt as if she was floating above her body slightly. Pain was affecting so many parts of her that it had all coalesced into one throbbing beat of agony. Her backpack, which had been light that morning, now felt as if someone had been adding wet sand to it while she walked.

They'd stopped only briefly and silently for a few minutes while Luca had doled out a protein bar and some figs he'd pulled from a nearby tree—which had incidentally tasted delicious. And then they'd kept going.

Her feet were mercifully numb after going through the pain barrier some time ago. Her throat was parched, no matter how much water she sipped, and her legs were like jelly. But Luca's pace was remorseless. And Serena was loath to call out with so much as a whisper.

And then he stopped, suddenly, and looked around him, holding up a compass. He glanced back at her and said, 'Through here—stick close to me.'

She followed where he led for a couple of minutes, and then cannoned into his backpack and gave a little yelp of surprise when he stopped again abruptly. He turned and steadied her with his big hands. Serena hadn't even realised she was swaying until he did that.

'This is the camp.'

Serena blinked. Luca took his hands away and she didn't like how aware she was of that lack of touch.

Afraid he might see something she didn't want him to, she stepped back.

'Camp?'

She looked around and saw a small but obviously well-used clearing. She also noticed belatedly that the cacophony that had accompanied them all day had silenced now, and it was as if an expectant hush lay over the whole forest. The intense heat was lessening slightly.

'It's so quiet.'

'You won't be saying that in about half an

hour, when the night chorus starts up.' He was unloading his backpack and said over his shoulder, 'Take yours off too.'

Serena let it drop from her aching body and almost cried out with the relief. She felt as though she might lift right out of the forest now that the heavy weight was gone.

Luca was down on his haunches, extracting things from his bag, and the material of his trousers was drawn taut over his powerful thighs. Serena found it hard to drag her gaze away, not liking the spasm of awareness in her lower belly.

He was unrolling the tent, which looked from where Serena was standing alarmingly *small*. Oblivious to her growing horror, Luca efficiently erected the lightweight structure with dextrous speed.

When the full enormity of its intimate size sank in, Serena said in a hoarse voice, 'We're not sleeping in that.'

Luca looked up from where he was driving a stake into the ground with unnecessary force. 'Oh, yes, *we* are, *minha beleza*—that is unless you'd prefer to take your chances sleeping al fresco? Jaguars are prevalent in this area. I'm sure they'd enjoy feasting on your fragrant flesh.'

Tension, fear and panic at the thought of sharing such a confined space with him spiked in Serena as Luca straightened up. She put her hands on her hips. 'You're lying.'

Luca looked at her, impossibly dark and dangerous. 'Do you really want to take that chance?' He swept an arm out. 'By all means be my guest. But if the jaguars don't get you any number of thousands of insects will do the job—not to mention bats. While you're thinking about that I'm going to replenish our water supplies.'

He started to leave and then stopped.

'While I'm gone you could take out some tinned food and set up the camping stove.'

When he walked away Serena had to resist the cowardly urge to call out that she'd go with him. She was sure he was just scaring her. Even so, she looked around nervously and stuck close to the tent as she did as he'd instructed, muttering to herself under her breath about how arrogant he was.

When Luca returned, a short while later, Serena was standing by the tent, clearly waiting for his return with more than a hint of nervousness. He stopped in his tracks, hidden behind a tree. His conscience pricked him for having scared her before. And something else inside him sizzled. *Desire.*

His gaze wandered down and took in the clothes that were all but plastered to her body after a day of trekking through the most humid ecosystem on earth. Her body was clearly defined and she was all woman, with firm, generous breasts, a small waist and curvaceous hips.

The whole aim of bringing her here had been to make her run screaming in the opposite direction, as far away as possible from him, but she'd been with him all the way.

He could still recall the terror tightening her face when she'd seen the scorpion and yet she hadn't allowed it to rise. He'd pursued a punishing pace today, even for him, and yet every time he'd cast a glance back she'd been right there, on his heels, dogged, eyes down, assiduously watching where she stepped as he'd instructed. Sweat had dripped down over her jaw and neck, making him think of it trickling into the lush valley of her breasts, dewing her golden skin with moisture.

Damn her. He hated to admit that up to now he'd been viewing her almost as a temporary irritation—like a tick that would eventually fall off his skin and leave him alone—but she was proving to be annoyingly resilient. He certainly hadn't expected to be sharing his tent with her.

The Serena DePiero he'd pegged as a reckless and wild party girl out only for herself was the woman he'd expected. The one he'd expected to leave Rio de Janeiro as soon as she'd figured she was on a hiding to nothing.

But she hadn't left.

So who the hell was the woman waiting for him now, if she wasn't the spoiled heiress? And why did he even care?

Serena bit her lip. The light was fading fast and there was no sign of Luca returning. She felt intensely vulnerable right then, and never more aware of her puny insignificance in the face of nature's awesome grandeur and power. A grandeur that would sweep her aside in a second if it had half a chance.

And then the snap of a twig alerted her to his presence. He loomed out of the gloom, dark and powerful. Sheer, abject relief that she wasn't alone made her feel momentarily dizzy, before she reminded herself that she really hated him for scaring her earlier.

Luca must have caught something of her relief. 'Worried that I'd got eaten by a jaguar, princess?'

'One can but hope,' Serena said sweetly, and then scowled. 'And don't call me princess.'

Luca brushed past her and took in the camping stove, commenting, 'I see you can follow instructions, at least.'

Serena scowled even more, irritated that she'd done his bidding. Luca was now gathering up wood and placing it in a small clearing not far from the tent. Determined not to let him see how much he rattled her, she said perkily, 'Can I help?'

Luca straightened from dumping some wood. 'You could collect some wood—just make sure it's not alive before you pick it up.'

Serena moved around, carefully kicking pieces of twigs and wood before she picked anything up. One twig turned out to be a camouflaged beetle of some sort that scuttled off and almost made her yelp out loud.

When she looked to see if Luca had noticed, though, he was engrossed in building up an impressive base of large logs for the fire. It was dusk now, and the massive trees loomed like gigantic shadows all around them.

Serena became aware of the rising sound of the forest around them as the night shift of wildlife took over from the day shift. It grew and grew to almost deafening proportions—like a million crickets going off at once right beside her head before settling to a more harmonious hum.

She brought the last of the wood she'd collected over to the pile just as Luca bent down to set light to the fire, which quickly blazed high. Feeling was returning to her feet and they had started to throb painfully.

Luca must have seen something cross her face, because he asked curtly, 'What is it?'

With the utmost reluctance Serena said, 'It's just some blisters.'

Luca stood up. 'Come here—let me see them.'

The flickering flames made golden light dance over his shadowed face. For a second Serena was too transfixed to move. He was the most beautiful man she'd ever seen. With an effort she looked away. 'I'm sure it's nothing. Really.'

'Believe me, I'm not offering because I genuinely care what happens to you. If you have blisters and they burst then they could get infected in this humidity. And then you won't be able to walk, and I really don't plan on carrying you anywhere.'

Fire raced up Serena's spine. 'Well, when

you put it so eloquently, I'd hate to become more of a burden than I already am.'

Luca guided her towards a large log near the fire. Sitting her down, he went down on his knees and pulled his bag towards him.

'Take off your boots.' His voice was gruff.

Serena undid her laces and grimaced as she pulled off the boots. Luca pulled her feet towards him, resting them on his thighs. The feel of rock-hard muscles under her feet made scarlet heat rush up through her body and bloom on her face.

She got out a strangled, 'What are you doing?'

Luca was curt. 'I'm trained as a medic—relax.'

Serena shut her mouth. She felt churlish; was there no end to his talents? She watched as he opened up a complicated-looking medical kit and couldn't help asking, 'Why did you train as a medic?'

He glanced at her swiftly before looking down again. 'I was on a visit to a village near a mine with my father when I was younger and a small boy started choking. No one knew what to do. He died right in front of us.'

Serena let out a breath. 'That's awful.'

A familiar but painful memory intruded be-

fore she could block it out. She'd seen someone die right in front of her too—it was seared
onto her brain like a tattoo. Her defences didn't
seem to be so robust here, in such close proximity to this man. She could empathise with
Luca's helplessness and that shocked her...to
feel an affinity.

Luca was oblivious to the turmoil being
stirred up inside Serena with that horrific
memory of her own. He continued. 'Not as
awful as the fact that my father didn't let it
stop him from moving the tribe on to another
location, barely allowing the parents time to
gather up their son's body. They were nothing
to him—a problem to be got rid of.'

He was pulling down Serena's socks now,
distracting her from his words and the bitterness she could hear in his voice. He sucked in
a breath when he saw the angry raw blisters.

'That's my fault.'

Serena blinked. Had Luca just said that?
And had he sounded ever so slightly apolo-
getic? Together with his obvious concern for
others, it made her uncomfortable.

He looked at her, face unreadable. 'New
boots. They weren't broken in. It's no wonder you've got blisters. You must have been
in agony for hours.'

Serena shrugged minutely and looked away, self-conscious under his searing gaze. 'I'm no martyr, Luca. I just didn't want to delay you.'

'The truth is,' he offered somewhat sheepishly, 'I hadn't expected you to last this far. I would have put money on you opting out well before we'd even left Rio.'

Something light erupted inside Serena and for a moment their eyes met and locked. Her insides clenched hard and all she was aware of was how powerful Luca's muscles felt under her feet. He looked away then, to get something from the medical box, and the moment was broken. But it left Serena shaky.

His hands were big and capable. Masculine. But they were surprisingly gentle as he made sure the blisters were clean and then covered them with thick plasters.

He was pulling her socks back up over the dressings when he said, with an edge to his voice, 'You've said a couple of times that you didn't do drugs… You forget that I was there. I saw you.'

His blue gaze seemed to sear right through her and his question caught Serena somewhere very raw. For a moment she'd almost been feeling *soft* towards him, when he was the one who had marched her into the jungle like some kind of recalcitrant prisoner.

Anger and a sense of claustrophobia made her tense. He'd seen only the veneer of a car crash lifestyle which had hidden so much more.

She was bitter. 'You saw what you wanted to see.'

Serena avoided his eyes and reached for her boots, but Luca got there first. He shook them out and said tersely, 'You should always check to make sure nothing has crawled inside.'

Serena repressed a shudder at the thought of what that might be and stuck her feet back into the boots, but Luca didn't move away.

'What's that supposed to mean? *I saw what I wanted to see.*'

Getting angry at his insistence, she glared at him. The firelight cast his face into shadow, making him seem even more dark and brooding.

He arched a brow. 'I think I have a right to know—you owe me an explanation.'

Serena's chest was tight with some unnamed emotion. The dark forest around them made her feel as if nothing existed outside of this place.

Hesitantly, she finally said, 'I wasn't addicted to Class A drugs...I've never taken a recre-

ational drug in my life.' She tried to block out
the doubtful gleam in Luca's eyes. 'But I *was*
addicted to prescription medication. And to alcohol. And I'll never touch either again.'

Luca finally moved back and frowned.
Serena felt as if she could breathe again. Until
he asked, 'How did you get addicted to medication?'

Serena's insides curdled. This came far too
close to that dark memory and all the residual
guilt and fear that had been a part of her for
so long. At best Luca was mildly curious; at
worst he hated her. She had no desire to seek
his sympathy, but a rogue part of her wanted
to knock his assumptions about her a little.

'I started taking prescribed medication when
I was five.'

Luca's frown deepened. 'Why? You were
a child.'

His clear scepticism made Serena curse herself for being so honest. This man would never
understand if she was to tell him the worst of
it all. So she feigned a lightness she didn't feel
and fell back on the script that her father had
written for her so long ago that she couldn't
remember *normal*.

She gave a small shrug and avoided that
laser-like gaze. 'I was difficult. After my

mother died I became hard to control. By the time I was twelve I had been diagnosed with ADHD and had been on medication for years. I became dependent on it—I liked how it made me feel.'

Luca sounded faintly disgusted. 'And your father...he sanctioned this?'

Pain gripped Serena. He'd not only sanctioned it, he'd made sure of it. She shrugged again, feeling as brittle as glass, and smiled. But it was hard. She forced herself to look at Luca. 'Like I said, I was hard to control. Wilful.'

Disdain oozed from Luca. 'Why are you so certain you're free of the addiction now?'

She tipped her chin up unconsciously. 'When my sister and I left Italy, after my father...' She stalled, familiar shame coursing through her blood along with anger. 'When it all fell apart we went to England. I checked into a rehab facility just outside London. I was there for a year. Not that it's any business of yours,' she added, immediately regretting her impulse to divulge so much.

Luca's expression was indecipherable as he stood up, and he pointed out grimly, 'I think our personal history makes it my business. You need to prove to me you can be trusted—that you will not be a drain on resources and the energy of everyone around you.'

Boots on, Serena stood up in agitation, her jaw tight with hurt and anger. She held up a hand. 'Whoa—judgemental, much? And you base this on your vast knowledge of ex-addicts?'

His narrow-minded view made Serena see red. She put her hands on her hips.

'Well?'

Tension throbbed between them as they glared at each other for long seconds. And then Luca bit out, 'I base it on an alcoholic mother who makes checking in and out of rehab facilities a recreational pastime. That's how I have a unique insight into the addict's mind. And when she's not battling the booze or the pills she's chasing her next rich conquest to fund her lifestyle.'

Serena felt sick for a moment at the derision in his voice. The evidence of just how personal his judgement was appeared entrenched in bitter experience.

Luca stepped back. 'We should eat.'

Serena's anger dissipated as she watched Luca turn away abruptly to light the camping stove near the fire. She reeled with this new knowledge of his own experience. And reeled at how much she'd told him of herself with such little prompting. She felt relieved now that she hadn't spilled her guts entirely.

No wonder he'd come down on her like a ton of bricks and believed the worst. Still…it didn't excuse him. And she told herself fiercely that she *didn't* feel a tug of something treacherous at the thought of him coping with an alcoholic parent. After all, she still bore the guilt of her sister having to deal with *her.*

Suddenly, in light of that conversation, she felt too raw to sit in Luca's company and risk that insightful mind being turned on her again. And fatigue was creeping over her like a relentless wave.

'Don't prepare anything for me. I'm not feeling hungry. I think I'll turn in now.'

Luca looked up at her from over his shoulder. He seemed to bite back whatever he was going to say and shrugged. 'Suit yourself.'

Serena grabbed her backpack and went into the tent, relieved to see that it was more spacious inside than she might have imagined. She could only do a basic toilette, and after taking off her boots and rolling out her sleeping bag carefully on one side of the tent she curled up and dived into the exhausted sleep of oblivion.

Anything to avoid thinking about the man

who had comprehensively turned her world upside down in the last thirty-six hours and come far too close to where she still had so much locked away.

CHAPTER FOUR

THE FOLLOWING MORNING Luca heard movement from the tent and his whole body tensed. When he'd turned in last night Serena had been curled up in a ball inside her sleeping bag, some long hair trailing in tantalising golden strands around her head, her breathing deep and even. And once again he'd felt the sting of his conscience at knowing she'd gone to bed with no food, and her feet rubbed raw from new boots.

What she'd told him the previous evening had shocked him. She'd been taking medication since she was a child. Out of control even then. It was so at odds with the woman she seemed to be now that he almost couldn't believe it.

She'd sounded defiant when she'd told him that she'd been addicted by the age of twelve. Something inside him had recoiled with dis-

gust at the thought. It was one thing to have
a mother who was an addict as an adult. But
a *child*?

Serena had given him the distinct impression that even then she'd known what she was
doing and had revelled in it. But even as he
thought that, something about the way she'd
said it niggled at him. It didn't sit right.

Was she telling the truth?

Why would she lie after all this time? an
inner voice pointed out. And if she hadn't ever
done recreational drugs then maybe she really
hadn't planted them on him that night... He
didn't like the way the knowledge sank like a
stone in his belly.

The crush and chaos of the club that night
came back to him and a flash of a memory
caught him unawares: Serena's hand slipping
into his. He'd looked down at her and she'd
been wide-eyed, her face pale. That had been
just before the Italian police had separated
them roughly and searched them.

The memory mocked him now. He'd always believed that look to have been Serena's
guilt and pseudo-vulnerability, knowing what
she'd just done. But if it hadn't been guilt it had
been something far more ambiguous. It made
him think of her passionate defence when he'd

questioned her trustworthiness. And why on earth did that gnaw at him now? Making him feel almost guilty?

The flaps of the tent moved and the object of his thoughts emerged, blinking in the dawn light. She'd pulled her hair up into a bun on top of her head, and when that blue gaze caught his, Luca's insides tightened. He cursed her silently—and himself for bringing her here and putting questions into his head.

For possibly being innocent of the charges he'd levelled against her.

She straightened up and her gaze was wary. 'Morning.'

Her voice was sleep-rough enough to tug forcibly at Luca's simmering desire. She should look creased and dishevelled and grimy, but she looked gorgeous. Her skin was as dewy and clear as if she'd just emerged from a spa, not a night spent in a rudimentary tent in the middle of the jungle.

He thrust a bowl of protein-rich tinned food towards her. 'Here—eat this.'

There was the most minute flash of something in her eyes as she acknowledged his lack of greeting, but she took the bowl and a spoon and sat down on a nearby log to eat, barely wincing at the less than appetising meal. Yet another blow to Luca's firmly entrenched antipathy.

He looked at her and forced himself to ignore that dart of guilt he'd just felt—to remember that thanks to his mother's stellar example he knew all about the mercurial nature of addicts. How as soon as you thought they truly were intent on making a change they went and did the exact opposite. From a young age Luca had witnessed first-hand just how brutal that lack of regard could be and he'd never forgotten it.

Serena looked up at him. She'd finished her meal, and Luca felt slightly winded at the intensity of her gaze. He reached down and took the bowl and handed her a protein bar. His voice gruff, which irritated him, he said, 'Eat this too.'

'But I'm full now. I—'

Luca held it out and said tersely, 'Eat it, Serena. I can't afford for you to be weak. We have a long walk today.'

Serena's eyes flashed properly at that, and she stood up with smooth grace and took the bar from his outstretched hand. Tension bristled and crackled between them.

Serena cursed herself for thinking, *hoping* that some kind of a truce might have grown between them. And she cursed herself again for revealing what she had last night.

Luca was cleaning up the camp, packing things away, getting ready to move on. When she'd woken a while ago it had taken long seconds for her to realise where she was and with whom. A sense of exultation had rushed through her at knowing they were still in the jungle and that she'd survived the first day, that she hadn't shown Luca any weakness.

Then she'd remembered the gentleness of his hands on her feet and had felt hot. And then she'd got hotter, acknowledging that only extreme exhaustion had knocked her out enough to sleep through sharing such an intimate space with him.

Before Luca might see some of that heat in her expression or in her eyes, Serena busied herself with rolling up the sleeping bags and starting to take down the tent efficiently.

'Where did you learn to do that?' came Luca's voice, its tone incredulous.

Serena barely glanced at him, prickling. 'We used to go on camping trips while we were in rehab. It was part of the programme.'

She tensed, waiting for him to be derisive or to ask her about it, but he didn't. He just went and started unpegging the other side of the tent. Serena hadn't shared her experience of rehab with anyone—not even her sister. Even though her sister had been the one who had sacrificed almost everything to ensure Serena's care, working herself to the bone and putting herself unwittingly at the mercy of a man she'd betrayed years before and who had come looking for revenge.

Against the odds, though, Siena and Andreas had fallen in love and were now blissfully happy, with a toddler and a baby. Sometimes their intense happiness made Serena feel unaccountably alienated, and she hated herself for the weakness. But it was the same with her half-brother Rocco and his wife and children. If she'd never believed in love or genuine happiness theirs mocked her for it every time she saw them.

Without even realising it was done, she saw the camp was cleared and Luca was handing Serena her backpack.

He arched a brow. 'Ready?'

Serena took the pack and nodded swiftly, not wanting Luca to guess at the sudden vulnerability she felt to be thinking of her family and their very natural self-absorption.

She put on the pack and followed Luca for

a few steps until he turned abruptly. 'How are your feet?'

Serena frowned and said, with some surprise, 'They're fine, actually.'

Luca made an indeterminate sound and carried on, and Serena tried not to fool herself that he'd asked out of any genuine concern.

As they walked the heat progressed and intensified to almost suffocating proportions. When they stopped briefly by a small stream in the afternoon Serena almost wept with relief to be able to throw some cool water over her face and head. She soaked a cloth handkerchief and tied it around her neck.

It was only a short reprieve. Luca picked up the punishing pace again, not even looking to see if Serena was behind him. Irritation rose up inside her. Would he even notice if she was suddenly pulled by some animal into the undergrowth? He'd probably just shrug and carry on.

After another hour any feeling of relief from the stream was a distant memory and sweat dripped down her face, neck and back. Her limbs were aching, her feet numb again. Luca strode on, though, like some kind of robot, and suddenly Serena felt an urge to provoke him, needle him. Force him to stop and face her.

Acknowledge that she had done well to last this far. Acknowledge that she might be telling the truth about the drugs.

She called out, 'So, are you prepared to admit that I might be innocent after all?'

She got her wish. Luca stopped dead in his tracks and then, after a long second, slowly turned around. His eyes were so dark they looked black. He covered the space between them so fast and silently that Serena took an involuntary step backwards, hating herself for the reflexive action.

He looked infinitely dangerous, and yet perversely Serena didn't feel scared. She felt something far more ambiguous and hotter, deep in her pelvis.

'To be quite frank, I don't think I even care any more whether or not you did it. The fact is that my involvement with you made things so much worse. *You* were enough to turn the incident into front-page news and put certainty into people's minds about my guilt—because they all believed that *you* did drugs, and that I was either covering for you or dealing to you. So, innocent bystander or not—as you might have been—I still got punished.'

Serena swallowed down a sudden and very unwelcome lump in her throat. She recognised uncomfortably that the need for this man to know she was innocent was futile or worse. 'You'll never forgive me for it, will you?'

His jaw clenched, and just then a huge drop of water landed on her face—so large that it splashed.

Luca looked up and cursed out loud.

'What? What is it?' Serena asked, her tension dissolving to be replaced by a tendril of fear.

Luca looked around them and bit out, 'Rain. *Damn*. I'd hoped to make the village first. We'll have to shelter. Come on.'

Even before he'd begun striding away again the rain was starting in earnest, those huge drops cascading from the sky above the canopy. Serena hurried after him to try and keep up. Within seconds, though, it was almost impossible to see a few feet in front of her nose. Genuine panic spiked. She couldn't see Luca any more. And then he reappeared, taking her hand, keeping her close.

The rain was majestic, awesome. Deafening. But Serena was only aware of her hand in Luca's. He was leading them through the trees, off the path to a small clearing. The ground was slightly higher here. He let her go and she saw him unrolling a tarpaulin. Catching on quickly, she took one end and tied it off to a nearby sapling while Luca did the same on the other side, creating a shelter a few feet off the ground.

He laid out another piece of tarpaulin under the one they'd tied off and shouted over the roar of the rain, 'Get underneath!'

Serena slipped off her pack and did so. Luca joined her seconds later. They were drenched. Steam was rising off their clothes. But they were out of the worst of the downpour. Serena was still taken aback at how quickly it had come down.

They sat like that, their breaths evening out, for long minutes. Eventually she asked, 'How long will it last?'

Luca craned his neck to look out, his arms around his knees. He shrugged one wide shoulder. 'Could be minutes—could be hours. Either way, we'll have to camp out again tonight. The village is only a couple of hours away, but it'll be getting dark soon—too risky.'

At the thought of another night in the tent with Luca, flutters gripped Serena's abdomen. He was pulling something out of a pocket and handed her another protein bar. Serena reached for it with her palm facing up, but before she could take it Luca had grabbed her wrist and was frowning.

She was distracted by his touch for a moment—all she felt was *heat*—and then he was saying, 'What are those marks? Did you get them here?'

He was inspecting her palm and pulling her other hand towards him to look at that, too. Far too belatedly Serena panicked, and tried to pull them back, but he wouldn't let her, clearly concerned that it had happened recently.

She saw what he saw: the tiny criss-cross of old, silvery scars that laced her palms.

As if coming to that realisation, he said, 'They're old.' He looked at her, stern. '*How* old?'

Serena tried to jerk her hands away but he held them fast. Her breath was choppy now, with a surge of emotion. And with anger that he was quizzing her as if she'd done something wrong.

She said reluctantly, 'They're twenty-two years old.'

Luca looked at her, turning towards her. '*Deus*, what *are* they?'

Serena was caught by his eyes. They blazed into hers, seeking out some kind of truth and justice—which she was coming to realise was integral to this man's nature. It made him see the world in black and white, good and bad. And she was firmly in the bad category as far as he was concerned.

But just for once, Serena didn't want to be. She felt tired. Her throat ached with repressed emotions, with all the horrific images she held within her head, known only to her and her father. And he'd done his best to eradicate them.

A very weak and rogue part of her wanted to tell Luca the truth—much like last night—in some bid to make him see that perhaps things weren't so black and white. And even though an inner voice told her to protect herself from his derision, she heard the words spill out.

'They're the marks of a bamboo switch. My father favoured physical punishment.'

Luca's hands tightened around hers and she held back a wince. His voice was low. 'How old were you?'

Serena swallowed. 'Five—nearly six.'

'What the hell….?'

Luca's eyes burned so fiercely for a moment that Serena quivered inwardly. She took advantage of the moment to pull her hands back, clasping them together, hiding the permanent stain of her father's vindictiveness.

Serena could understand Luca's shock. Her therapist had been shocked when she'd told *her*.

She shrugged. 'He was a violent man. If I stepped out of line, or if Siena misbehaved, I'd be punished.'

'You were a *child*.'

Serena looked at Luca and felt acutely exposed, recalling just how her childhood had been so spectacularly snatched away from her, by far worse than a few scars on her palms.

She noticed something then, and seized on it weakly. 'The rain—it's stopped.'

Luca just looked at her for a long moment, as if he hadn't ever seen her before. It made Serena nervous and jittery.

Eventually he said, 'We'll make camp here. Let's set it up.'

Serena scrambled inelegantly out from under their makeshift shelter. The jungle around them was steaming from the onslaught of precipitation. It was unbearably humid…and uncomfortably sultry.

As she watched, Luca uncoiled himself, and for a moment Serena was mesmerised by his sheer masculine grace. He looked at her too quickly for her to look away.

He frowned. 'What is it?'

Serena swallowed as heat climbed up her

chest. She blurted out the first thing she could think of. 'Thirsty—I'm just thirsty.'

Luca glanced around them and then strode to a nearby tree and tested the leaves. 'Come here.'

Not sure what to expect, Serena walked over. Luca put a hand on her arm and it seemed to burn right through the material.

He manoeuvred her under the leaf and said, 'Tip your head back—open your mouth.'

Serena looked at him and something dark lit his eyes, making her belly contract.

'Come on. It won't bite.'

So she did, and Luca tipped the leaf so that a cascade of water fell into her mouth, cold and more refreshing than anything she'd ever tasted in her life. She coughed slightly when it went down the wrong way, but couldn't stop her mouth opening for more. The water trickled over her face, cooling the heat that had nothing to do with the humid temperature.

When there were only a few drops left, she straightened up again. Luca was watching her. They were close—close enough that all Serena would have to do would be to step forward and they'd be touching.

And then, as if reading her mind and rejecting her line of thought, Luca stepped back, letting her arm go. 'We need to change into dry clothes.'

He walked away and Serena felt ridiculously exposed and shaky. What was *wrong* with her?

Luca was taking clothes out of his pack. He straightened up and his hands went to his shirt, undoing the buttons with long fingers. A sliver of dark muscled chest was revealed, the shadow of chest hair. And Serena was welded to the spot. She couldn't breathe.

Finally sense returned. Her face hot with embarrassment, she hurried to her own bag and concentrated on digging out her own change of clothes. The last thing she needed was to let Luca Fonseca into the deepest recesses of her psyche. But, much to her irritation, she couldn't forget the way he'd looked when he'd held her hands out for inspection, or the look in his eyes just now, when she fancied she'd seen something carnal in their depths, only for him to mock her for her fanciful imagination.

Luca was feeling more and more disorientated as he pulled on fresh clothes with rough hands. *Deus.* He'd almost backed Serena into the tree just now and covered her open mouth with his, jealous of the rainwater trickling between those plump lips.

And what about those scars on her hands? The silvery marks criss-crossing the delicate pale skin? He hadn't been prepared for the surge of panic when he'd seen them—afraid she'd been marked by something on the trail— or the feeling of rage when she'd told him so flatly who had done it.

He'd met her father once or twice at social events and had never liked the man. He had cold, dead dark eyes, and the superior air of someone used to having everything he wanted.

He didn't like to admit it, but the knowledge that he'd been violent didn't surprise Luca. He could picture the man being vindictive. Malevolent. But to his own daughters? The blonde, blue-eyed heiresses everyone had envied?

Luca knew Serena was changing behind him. He could hear the soft sounds of clothes being taken off and dropped. And then there was silence for a long moment. Telling himself it was concern, but knowing that it stemmed from a much deeper desire, Luca turned around.

Her back was to him and her legs were revealed in all their long shapely glory as she stripped off her trousers. High-cut pants showed off a toned length of thigh. Firm but curvy buttocks. When she stripped down to her bra he wanted to go over and undo it, slip his hands around her front to cup the generous swells and feel her arch into him.

He was rewarded with a burgeoning erection within seconds—no better than a preteen ogling a woman dressing in a changing room.

The snap of her belt around her hips broke Luca out of his trance and, angry with himself, he turned away and pulled on his own trousers. The light was falling rapidly now, and Luca had been so fixated on Serena that he was risking not having the camp set up in time.

But when he turned around again, about to issue a curt command, the words died on his lips. To his surprise Serena was already unrolling the tent and staking it out, her long ponytail swinging over her shoulder.

He cursed her silently, because he was losing his footing with this woman—fast.

Serena was sitting on a log on the opposite side of the fire to Luca a short time later, after they'd eaten their meagre meal. The tent stood close by, and she couldn't stop a surge of ridiculous pride that she'd put it up herself. He'd expected her to flee back to civilisation at the slightest hint of work or danger, but here she was, day two and surviving—if not thriving. The feeling was heady, and it made her relish her newfound independence even more.

However, none of that could block out the mortification when she thought of earlier and how close she'd come to betraying her desire for him…

She caught Luca's eye across the flickering light of the fire and he asked, 'What's the tattoo on your back?'

She went still. He must have seen the small tattoo that sat just above her left shoulderblade earlier, when she'd been changing. The thought of him looking at her made her feel hot.

The tattoo was so personal to her, she didn't want to tell him. Reluctantly, she finally said, 'It's a swallow. The bird.'

'Any significance?'

Serena almost laughed. As if she'd divulge *that* to him! He'd definitely fall off his log laughing.

She shrugged. 'It's my favourite bird. I got it done a few years ago.' *The day she'd walked out of the rehab clinic, to be precise.*

She avoided Luca's gaze. Swallows represented resurrection and rebirth… Luca would hardly look that deeply into its significance, but still... She had the uncanny sense that he might and she didn't like it.

She really wanted to avoid any more probing into her life or her head. She stood up abruptly, making Luca look up, his dark gaze narrowing on her. 'I'm going to turn in now.' She sounded too husky. Even now her body trembled with awareness, just from looking at his large rangy form relaxed.

Luca stirred the fire, oblivious to her heated imaginings. 'I'll let you get settled.'

Serena turned away and crawled into the tent, pulling off her boots, but leaving her clothes on. Then she felt silly. Luca hadn't given her the slightest hint that he felt any desire for her whatsoever, and she longed to feel cooler. She took off her shirt and stripped down to her panties, and pulled the sleeping bag around her.

She prayed that sleep would come as it had last night, like a dark blanket of oblivion, so she wouldn't have to hear Luca come in and deal with the reality that he slept just inches away from her and probably resented every moment.

Luca willed his body to cool down. He didn't like how off-centre Serena was pushing him.

Making him desire her; wonder about her. Wanting to know more. She was surprising him.

He'd been exposed to the inherent selfishness of his mother and women in general from a very early age, so it was not a welcome sensation thinking that he might have misjudged her.

Lovers provided him with physical relief and an escort when he needed it. But his life was not about women, or settling down. He had too much to do to undo all the harm his father and grandfather had caused. He had set himself a mammoth task when his father had died ten years ago: to reverse the negative impact of the name Fonseca in Brazil, which up till then had been synonymous with corruption, greed and destruction.

The allegations of his drug-taking had come at the worst possible time for Luca—just when people had been beginning to sit up and trust that perhaps he *was* different and genuine about making a change. It was only now that he was back in that place.

And the person who could reverse all his good work was only feet away from him. He had to remember that. Remember who she was and what she had the power to do to him. Even if she *was* innocent, any association with her would incite all that speculation again.

Only when Luca felt sure that Serena must be asleep did he turn in himself, doing his best to ignore the curled-up shape inside the sleeping bag that was far too close to his for comfort. He'd really *not* expected to have to share this tent with anyone, and certainly not with Serena DePiero for a second night in a row.

But as he lay down beside her he had to acknowledge uncomfortably that there was no evidence of the spoilt ex-wild-child. There wasn't one other woman he could think of, apart from those whose life's work it was to study the Amazon, who would have fared better than her over the past couple of days. And even some of those would have run screaming long before now, back to the safety of a research lab, or similar.

He thought of her putting up the tent, her tongue caught between her teeth as she exerted herself, sweat dripping down her neck and disappearing into the tantalising vee of her shirt. Gritting his jaw tightly, Luca sighed and closed his eyes. He'd accused her of not lasting in the jungle, but it was he who craved the order of civilisation again—anything to dilute this fire in his blood and put an end to the questions Serena kept throwing up.

A couple of hours later Luca woke, instantly alert and tensed, waiting to hear a sound outside. But it came from inside the tent. *Serena.* Moaning in her sleep in Italian.

'Papa...no, per favore, non che... Siena, aiutami.'

Luca translated the last word: *help me.* There was something gutturally raw about her words, and they were full of pain and emotion. Her voice cracked then, and Luca's chest squeezed when he heard her crying.

Acting on instinct, Luca reached over and touched her shoulder.

Almost instantly she woke up and turned her head. *'Ché cosa?'*

Something about the fact that she was still speaking Italian made his chest tighten more. 'You were dreaming.' He felt as if he'd invaded her privacy.

Serena went as tense as a board. He could see the bright glitter of those blue eyes in the gloom.

'Sorry for waking you.'

Her voice was thick, her accent stronger. He felt her pull abruptly away from his hand as she curled up again. Her hair was a bright sliver of white-gold and his body grew hot as he thought of it trailing over his naked chest as she sat astride him and took him deep into her body.

Anger at the wanton direction of his thoughts, at how easily she got under his skin and how she'd pulled away just now, almost as if he'd done something wrong, made him say curtly, 'Serena?'

She said nothing, and that wound him up more. A moment ago he'd been feeling sorry for her, disturbed by the gut-wrenching sound of those sobs. But now memories of his mother and how she'd use her emotions to manipulate the people around her made Luca curse himself for being so weak.

It made his voice harsh. 'What the hell was *that* about?'

Her voice sounded muffled. 'I said I was sorry for waking you. It was nothing.'

'It didn't sound like nothing to me.'

Serena turned then, those eyes flashing, her hair bright against the dark backdrop of the tent. She said tautly, 'It was a dream, okay? Just a bad dream and I've already forgotten it. Can we go to sleep now, please?'

Luca reacted viscerally to the fact that Serena was all but spitting at him, clearly in no need of comfort whatsoever. She pressed his buttons like no one else, and all he could think about right then was how much he wanted her to submit to him—anything to drown out all the contradictions she was putting in his head.

He reached out and found her arms, pulled her into him, hearing her shocked little gasp.

'Luca, what are you doing?'

But the defensive tartness was gone out of her voice.

He pulled her in closer, the darkness wrapping around them but failing to hide that bright blue gaze or the gold of her hair. The slant of her stunning cheekbones.

She wasn't pulling away.

Luca's body was on fire. From somewhere he found his voice and it sounded coarse, rough. 'What am I doing?'

'This…'

And then he pulled her right into him and his mouth found hers with unerring precision. Her breasts swelled against his chest—in outrage? He didn't know, because he was falling over the very thin edge of his control.

When he felt her resistance give way after an infinitesimal moment, triumph surged through his body. He couldn't think any more, because he was swept up in the decadent darkness of a kiss that intoxicated him and reminded him of only one other similar moment...with her... seven years before.

CHAPTER FIVE

SERENA WAS STILL in shock at finding herself in Luca's arms with his mouth on hers. When he'd woken her at first, she'd had an almost overwhelming instinctive need to burrow close to him, the tentacles of that horrible nightmare clinging like slimy vines to her hot skin.

And then she'd realised just who she was with—just who was precipitating such weak feelings of wanting to seek strength and comfort. Luca Fonseca, of all people? And that dream... She hadn't had it for a long time—not since she'd been in rehab. And to be having it again, *here*, was galling. As if she was going backwards. Not forwards. And it was all his fault, for getting under her skin.

Fresh anger made her struggle futilely against Luca's superior strength even after she'd let the hot tide of desire take her over, revealing how much she wanted him. She pulled back, ripping her mouth from his, mortified to find herself breathing harshly, her breasts moving rapidly against the steel wall of his chest, nipples tight and stinging.

Her body and her mind seemed to be inhabiting two different people. Her body was saying *Please don't stop* and her head was screaming *Stop now!*

'What is it, *minha beleza?*'

The gravelly tone of Luca's voice rubbed along her nerve-endings, setting them alight. Traitors.

'Do you really think this is a good idea?'

Dammit. She sounded as if she wanted him to convince her that it was, her voice all breathy.

His eyes were like black pits in his face and Serena was glad she couldn't make out their expression. She half expected Luca to come to his senses and recoil, but instead he seemed to move even closer. His hands slipped down her arms and came around her back, making her feel quivery at how light his touch was— and yet it burned.

'Luca...?'

'Hmm...?'

His mouth came close again and his lips feathered a kiss to her neck. Liquid fire spread through Serena's pelvis. *Damn him.*

She swallowed, her body taking over her mind, making her move treacherously closer to that huge hard body.

'I don't think this is a good idea. We'll regret it.'

Luca pulled back for a moment and said throatily, 'You think too much.'

And then he was covering her mouth with his again, and any last sliver of defence or righteous anger at how vulnerable he made her feel drained away. She was drowning in his strength. Mouth clinging to his, skin tightening all over as he coaxed her lips apart to explore deeper with his tongue. His kiss seven years ago had seared itself onto her memory like a brand. This was like being woken from a deep sleep. She'd never really enjoyed kissing or being touched by men...until him. And now this.

Barely aware of the fact that Luca was pulling down the zips of their sleeping bags, she only knew that there was nothing between them now, and that he was pulling her on top of him so her breasts were crushed against his broad chest.

Both hands were on her head, fingers thrust deep into her hair, and Luca positioned her so that he could plunder her mouth with devastating skill. Serena could feel herself getting damp between her legs.

Luca drew back for a moment and Serena opened her eyes, breathing heavily. With a smooth move he manoeuvred them so that Serena was on her back and loomed over her. He looked wild, feral. Exactly the way she imagined the marauding Portuguese *conquistadores* must have looked when they'd first walked on this land.

He smoothed some hair behind her ear and Serena's breath grew choppier. Her fingers itched to touch him, to feel that chest, so when his head lowered to hers again her hands went to the buttons of his shirt and undid them, sliding in to feel the dense musculature of his chest.

She was unable to hold back a deep sound of satisfaction as her hands explored, revelling in his strength. She dragged her fingers over his chest, sliding over the ridges of his muscles, a nail grazing a flat hard nipple. Her mouth watered. She wanted to taste it.

His beard tickled her slightly, but that was soon forgotten as his tongue thrust deep, making her arch up against him. He was pulling down the strap of her vest, taking with it her bra strap, exposing the slope of her breast.

When Luca pulled back again she was gasping for breath. She looked up, but everything was blurry for a moment. She could feel Luca's fingers reach inside the lace cup of her bra, brushing enticingly close to where her nipple was so hard it ached. He pulled it down and Serena felt her breast pop free of the confinement. Luca's gaze was so hot she could feel it on her bare skin.

He breathed out. *'Perfeito…'*

His head came down, and with exquisite finesse he flicked his tongue against that tip, making Serena's breath catch and her hips move of their own volition. He flicked it again, and then slowly expored the hard flesh, before placing his whole mouth around it and suckling roughly.

Serena cried out. Her hands were on his head, in his hair. She'd never felt anything like this in her life. Sex had been something to block out, to endure, an ineffective form of escape…not something to revel in like this.

His hand was on her trousers now, undoing her button, lowering the zip. There was no hesitation. She wanted this with an all-consuming need she'd never experienced before. His hand delved under her panties as his mouth still tortured her breast.

When his fingers found the evidence of her desire he tore his mouth away. She could see his eyes glitter almost feverishly as he stroked her intimately, releasing her damp heat. Serena whimpered softly, almost mindless, her hips jerking with reaction.

'You want me.'

His words sliced through the fever in her brain.

Serena bit her lip. She was afraid to speak, afraid of what might spill out. Luca was a master torturer. With his hand he forced her legs apart as much as they could go, and then he thrust a finger deep inside, where she was slick and hot. She gasped.

'Say it, Serena.'

He sounded fierce now, his finger moving intimately against her. *Oh, God…* She was going to come. Like this. In a tent in the middle of nowhere. Just from this man touching her…

Feeling vulnerable far too late, Serena tried to bring her legs together—but Luca wouldn't let her. She could see the determination on his face. The lines stark with desire and hunger. One finger became two, stretching her, filling her. She gasped, her hands going to his shoulders.

The heel of his hand put exquisite pressure

on her clitoris. She was unable to stop her hips from moving, rolling, seeking to assuage the incredible ache that was building. And then his fingers moved faster, deeper, making Serena's muscles tighten against him.

'Admit you want me...*dammit*. You're almost coming. *Say it.*'

Serena was wild now, hands clutching at him. He was looking down at her. She knew what was stopping the words being wrenched from her: the fact that Luca seemed so intent on pushing her over the edge when *he* appeared to be remarkably in control. The fact that she suspected he just wanted to prove his domination over her.

But she couldn't fight it. She needed it—*him*—too badly.

'I do...' she gasped out, the words torn from her as her body reached its crescendo against the relentless rhythm of Luca's wicked hand and fingers. 'I do...want you...*damn you.*'

And with those last guttural words she went as taut as a bowstring as the most indescribably pleasurable explosion racked her entire body and broke it apart into a million pieces before letting it float back together again.

Serena had orgasmed before. But never like this. With such intensity...losing herself in the process.

* * *

Luca's brain had melted into a pool of lust and heat. Serena's body was still clamping around his fingers and he ached to be embedded within her, so that the inferno in his body might be assuaged.

But something held him back—had held him back from replacing his hand with his erection. At some point he'd become aware that he needed this woman on a level that surpassed anything he'd ever known before.

And, worse, he needed to know that she felt it too. So making her admit it, making her *come*, had become some kind of battle of wills. She'd confounded him since she'd turned up in his office, just days ago, and this felt like the first time he'd been able to claw back some control. By making her lose hers.

But now, as he extricated his hand and her body jerked in reaction, it felt like an empty triumph. Luca pulled back and gritted his jaw at the way his body rejected letting Serena go. He pulled on his shirt, feeling wild. Undone.

Serena was moving, pulling her clothes together. He saw her hands shaking and wanted to snarl. Where was the insouciant, confident woman he remembered meeting that night in

Florence? She bore no resemblance to this woman, who was almost *impossibly* shy.

Luca lay back, willing down the throbbing heat in his blood. Cursing the moment he'd ever laid eyes on Serena DePiero. She went still beside him, and even that set his nerves on edge. Sizzling.

Eventually she said hesitantly, 'You didn't...'

She trailed off. But he knew what she'd meant to say, and suddenly her unbelievable hesitance pushed him over another edge. He'd cursed this woman for a long time for sending his life into turmoil, and yet again she was throwing up another facet of her suddenly chameleon-like personality. The most in control he'd felt around her since she'd come back into his life had been just now—when she'd been surrendering to him even though she'd obviously hated it.

He would have her—completely. In his bed. On his terms. Would reveal this hesitant shyness to be the sham that it was.

And then, when he'd had her, sated himself, he would be able to walk away and leave her behind for good. One thing was certain: he'd wanted her since the moment he'd laid eyes on her, and not even his antipathy for her had put a dent in that need. If he didn't have her he'd be haunted for ever. And no woman, however alluring, retained any hold over him once he'd had her.

He came up on one elbow and looked down, saw her eyes flash blue as she looked at him. Her mouth was swollen.

Luca forced down the animalistic urge to take her there and then. He was civilised. He'd spent years convincing people that he wasn't his lush of a mother or his corrupt father.

'No, I didn't.'

He saw her frown slightly. 'Why didn't you...?'

He finished for her, 'Make love to you?'

Serena nodded her head, pulling the sleeping bag back up over her body. Luca resisted the urge to yank it back down. *Control.*

His jaw was hard. 'I didn't make love to you, Serena, because I have no protection with me. And when we do make love it will be in more comfortable surroundings.'

He sensed her tensing.

'Don't be so sure I want to make love to you, Luca.'

He smiled and felt ruthless. '*Minha beleza*, don't even *try* to pretend that you would have objected to making love here and now. I felt your body's response and it didn't lie. Even if you don't like it.'

She opened her mouth and he reached out and put a finger to her lips, stopping her words.

'Don't even waste your breath. After that little performance you're mine as surely as if I'd stamped a brand on your body.'

She smacked his hand away, hard enough to sting. 'Go to hell, Luca.'

Luca curbed the desire to show Serena in a more subtle way that what he said was true, but it was true that he didn't have protection, and he knew that if he touched her again he wouldn't be able to stop himself.

So he lay down and closed his eyes, just saying darkly, 'Not before I take you with me, *princesa*.'

The fact that he could sense Serena fuming beside him only made him more determined to shatter her control again.

She would be his.

The following day Serena was galvanised on her walk—largely by the depth of her humiliation and her hatred for Luca. She glared at his back as he strode ahead of her and mentally envisaged a jaguar springing from the jungle to swallow him whole.

She couldn't get the lurid images out of her head—the way she'd so completely and without hesitation capitulated to Luca's love-making. The way he'd played her body like a virtuoso played a violin. The way he'd controlled her reactions while maintaining his own control.

His words mocked her: *'After that little performance you're mine.'* She felt like screaming. Unfortunately it had been no performance—which was galling, considering that for most of her life she'd perfected the performance of a spoilt, reckless heiress.

But on a deeper level what had happened last night with Luca terrified her.

For as long as she could remember there had been a layer between her and the world around her and she was still getting used to that layer being gone. She'd first tasted freedom when her father had disappeared and they'd been left with nothing. It had been too much to deal with, sending her spiralling into a hedonistic frenzy, saved only by her sister taking her to England and to rehab.

Since then she'd learnt to deal with being free; not bearing the constant weight of her father's presence. Her job, becoming independent, was all part of that process. Even if she still harboured deep secrets and a sense of guilt.

But when Luca had been touching her last night—watching her, making her respond to his touch—her sense of freedom had felt very flimsy. Because he'd also been touching a part of her that she hadn't yet given room to really breathe. Her emotions. Her yearning for what her sister had: a life and happiness.

And the fact that Luca had brought that to the surface made her nervous and angry. All she was to him was a conquest. A woman he believed had betrayed him. A woman he wanted to slake his desire with.

A woman he didn't like, even if he ever conceded that she might be innocent.

She'd known that the night they'd met first. He'd had a gleam of disdain in his eyes that he'd barely concealed even as she saw the burn of desire.

And yet, damn him, since she'd walked into his office the other day it was as if everything was brighter, sharper. More intense. *Bastard*.

Serena crashed into Luca's back before she'd even realised she'd been so preoccupied she hadn't noticed he'd stopped. She sprang back, scowling, and then noticed that they were on a kind of bluff, overlooking a huge cleared part of the forest.

To be out from under the slightly oppressive canopy was heady for a moment. Ignoring Luca, Serena studied the view. She could see that far away in the distance the land had been eviscerated. Literally. Huge chunks cut out. No trees. And what looked like huge machines were moving back and forth, sun glinting off steel.

Forgetting that she hated Luca for a moment, because unexpected emotion surged at seeing the forest plundered like this, she asked, a little redundantly, 'That's the mine?'

Luca nodded, his face stern when she sneaked an illicit glance.

'Yes, that's my family's legacy.'

And then he pointed to a dark smudge much closer.

'That's the Iruwaya tribe's village there.'

Serena shaded her eyes until she could make out what looked like a collection of dusty huts and a clearing. Just then something else caught her eye: a road leading into the village and a bus trundling along merrily, with bags and crates hanging precariously from its roof along with a few live chickens.

It took a few seconds for the scene to compute and for Serena's brain to make sense of it. Slowly she said, 'The village isn't isolated.'

'I never said it was totally isolated.'

The coolness of Luca's tone made Serena step back and look up at him, her blood rapidly rising again. 'So why the hell have we been trekking through a rainforest to get to it?' She added, before he could answer, 'You never said anything about it being optional.'

Luca crossed his arms. 'I didn't offer an option.'

'My God,' Serena breathed. 'You really did do this in a bid to scare me off... I mean, I know you did, but I stupidly thought...'

She trailed off and backed away as the full significance sank in. Her stupid feeling of triumph for putting up the tent last night without help mocked her now. She'd known Luca hated her, that he wanted to punish her...but she hadn't believed for a second that there had been any other way of getting to this village.

All this time he must have been alternating between laughing his head off at her and cursing her for being so determined to stick it out. And then amusing himself by demonstrating how badly she wanted him.

Luca sighed deeply and ran a hand through his hair. 'Serena, this *is* how I'd planned to come to the village, but I'll admit that I thought you would have given up and gone home long before now.'

His words fell on deaf ears. Serena felt exposed, humiliated. She shook her head. 'You're a bastard, Luca Fonseca.'

Terrified of the emotion rising in her chest, she turned and blindly walked away, not taking care to look where she was going.

She'd landed on her hands and knees, the breath knocked out of her, before she realised she'd tripped over something. It also took a moment for her to register that the black ground under her hands was moving.

She sprang back with a small scared yelp just as Luca reached her and hauled her up, turning her to face him.

'Are you okay?'

Still angry with him, Serena broke free. And then she registered a stinging sensation on her arm, and on her thigh. She looked down stupidly, to see her trousers ripped apart from her fall, and vaguely heard Luca curse out loud.

He was pulling her away from where she'd tripped and ripping off her shirt, but Serena was still trying to figure out what had happened—and that was when the pain hit in two places: her arm and her leg.

She cried out in surprise at the shock of how excruciating it was.

Luca was asking urgently, 'Where is it? Where's the pain?'

Struggling, because it was more intense than anything she'd ever experienced, Serena got out thickly, 'My arm...my leg.'

She was barely aware of Luca inspecting her arm, her hands, and then undoing her trousers to pull them down roughly, inspecting her thigh where it was burning. He was brushing something off her and cursing again.

She struggled to recall what she'd seen. Ants. They'd just been ants. It wasn't a snake or a spider.

Luca was doing a thorough inspection of both legs and then moving back up to her arms. In spite of the pain she struggled to get out, 'I'm fine—it's nothing, really.'

But she was feeling nauseous now, with a white-hot sensation blooming outwards from both limbs. She was also starting to shake. Luca pulled her trousers back up. She wasn't even registering embarrassment that he'd all but stripped her.

She tried to take a step, but the pain when she moved almost blinded her. And suddenly she was being lifted into the air against a hard surface. She wanted to tell Luca to put her down but she couldn't seem to formulate the words.

And then the pain took over. There was a sense of time being suspended, loud voices. And then it all went black.

'Serena?'

The voice penetrated the thick warm blanket of darkness that surrounded her. And there was something about the voice that irritated her. She tried to burrow away from it.

'*Serena.*'

'What?' She struggled to open her eyes and winced at the light. Her surroundings registered slowly. A rudimentary hut of some kind. She was lying down on something deliciously soft. And one other thing registered: mercifully...the awful, excruciating pain was gone.

'Welcome back.'

That voice. Deep and infinitely memorable. And not in a good way.

It all came back.

She turned her head to see Luca looking at her with a small smile on his face. *A smile.* He was sitting down near the bed she lay on.

She croaked out, 'What happened?'

His smile faded, and it must have been a trick of the light but she could have sworn he paled slightly. 'You got stung. Badly.'

Serena recalled the ground moving under her hands and shuddered delicately. 'But they were just ants. How could ants do that?'

Luca's mouth twisted. 'They were bullet ants.'

Serena frowned. 'Should that mean anything to me?'

He shook his head. 'Not really, but they deliver a sting that is widely believed to be the most painful on record of any biting insect—like the pain of a bullet. I've been bitten once or twice; I know exactly what it's like.'

Serena felt embarrassed. 'But I passed out like some kind of wimp.'

Luca had a funny look on his face.

'The fact that you were semi-conscious till we reached the village and kept fighting to walk was a testament to your obviously high pain threshold.'

She lifted her arm and looked at it. There was only a very faint redness where she'd been bitten. All that pain and not even a scratch left behind? She almost felt cheated. And then she thought of what he'd said and her arm dropped.

'Wait a second—you carried me all the way here?'

He nodded. There was a scuffling sound from nearby and thankfully Luca's intense focus moved off her. She looked past him to see some small curious faces peeping around the door. He said something to them and they disappeared, giggling and chattering.

Luca turned back. 'They're fascinated by the golden-haired *gringa* who arrived unconscious into their village a few hours ago.'

Serena was very disorientated by this far less antagonistic Luca. Feeling self-conscious, she struggled to sit up, moving back the covers on the bed.

But Luca rapped out, 'Stay there! You're weak and dehydrated. You're not going anywhere today, or this evening. The women have prepared some food and you need to drink lots of water.'

Luca stood up, and his sheer size made Serena feel dizzy enough to lie down again. As if by magic some smiling women appeared in the doorway, holding various things. Luca ushered them in and said to Serena over their heads, 'I have to go to the mines. I'll be back later. You'll be looked after.'

Weakly, Serena protested, 'But I'm supposed to be taking notes...'

Something flashed in Luca's eyes but he just said, 'Don't worry about that. There'll be time tomorrow, before we have to leave.'

'Before we have to leave.' She felt a lurch in her belly and an awful betraying tingle of anticipation as to what might happen once they did leave this place.

The following morning, early, Luca was trying not to keep staring at Serena, who sat at the end of a long table in the communal eating hut. She was wearing a traditional smock dress, presumably given to her by one of the women to replace her own clothes, and the simple design might have been haute couture, the way she wore it with such effortless grace.

A small toddler, a girl, was sitting on Serena's lap and staring up at her with huge, besotted brown eyes. She'd been crying minutes before, and Serena had bent down to her level and cajoled her to stop crying, lifting her up and settling her as easily as if she was her mother.

Now she was eating her breakfast—a manioc-based broth—for all the world acting as if it was the finest caviar, giving the little girl morsels in between her own mouthfuls. She couldn't have looked more innocent and pure if she'd tried, tugging remorselessly on his conscience.

A mixture of rage and sexual frustration made Luca's whole body tight. The remnants of the panic he'd felt the previous day when she'd been so limp in his arms after being stung still clung to him. She'd been brave. Even though he knew he was being completely irrational, he couldn't stop lambasting her inwardly for not behaving as he expected her to.

Their eyes met and caught at that moment and he saw her cheeks flush. With desire? Or anger? Or a mixture of both like him? Suddenly her significance wasn't important any more—who she was, what she'd done. Or not done. He wanted her, and she would pay for throwing his life out of whack not once but twice.

Resolve filling his body, he stood up and said curtly, 'We're leaving for the mines in ten minutes.'

He didn't like the way he noticed how her arm tightened around the small girl almost protectively, or how seeing a child on her lap made him feel. All sorts of things he'd never imagined feeling in his life—ever.

Her chin tipped up. 'I'll be ready.'

Luca left before he did something stupid, like take up his phone and ask for the helicopter to come early so that he could haul her back to Rio and douse this fire in his blood as soon as possible.

CHAPTER SIX

A FEW HOURS later Serena was back in her own clothes, now clean, and sitting cross-legged beside Luca in the hut of the tribal elders. She was still smarting from the intensity of his regard that morning at breakfast. As if he'd been accusing her of something. Her suspicions had been reinforced when he'd said, with a definitely accusatory tone, on their journey to the mines, 'You were good with that little girl earlier.'

Serena had swallowed back the tart urge to apologise and explained, 'I have a nephew just a little bit older. We're very close.'

She hadn't liked being reminded of that vulnerability—that from the moment she'd held Siena's son, Spiro, he and Serena had forged an indelible bond and her biological clock had started ticking loudly.

For someone who had never seen the remotest possibility of such a domestic idyll in her life, she was still surprised at how much she craved it.

And she hated it that she'd barely slept a wink in the hut because she'd missed knowing Luca's solid bulk was just inches away. She dragged her attention back to what she was meant to be focusing on: writing notes as fast as Luca translated what he wanted taken down.

They'd spent the morning at the mines and she'd seen how diplomatic he had to be, trying to assuage the fears of the miners about losing their jobs, while attempting to drag the mine and its administration into the twenty-first century and minimise further damage to the land. It was a very fine balancing act.

When he was being diplomatic and charming he was truly devastating. It gave Serena a very strong sense of just how seductive he could be if…if he actually liked her. The thought of that made her belly swoop alarmingly.

He turned to her now. 'Did you get that?'

She looked at the notes quickly. 'About coming up with ideas to actively promote and nurture growth in the local economy?'

He nodded. But before he turned back to the tribal leader Serena followed an impulse and touched his arm. He frowned at her, and she smiled hesitantly at the man Luca was talking to before saying, 'Could I make a suggestion?'

He drew back a few inches and looked at her. His entire stance was saying, *You?*

Serena fought off the urge to hit him and gritted her teeth. 'Those smock dresses that the women make—I haven't seen them anywhere else. Also, the little carvings that the children have been doing... I know that this village is twinned with another one, and they have monthly fair days when they barter goods and crops and utilise their skills and learn from each other...but what about opening it up a bit—say, having a space in Rio, or Manaus, a charity shop that sells the things they make here. And in the other village. A niche market, with the money coming back directly to the people.'

'That's hardly a novel idea,' Luca said coolly.

Serena refused to be intimidated or feel silly. 'Well, if it's not a new concept why hasn't one of these shops been mentioned anywhere in your literature about the charity? I'm not talking about some rustic charity shop. I'm talking about a high-end finish that'll draw in discerning tourists and buyers. Something that'll inspire them to help conserve the rainforest.'

Luca said nothing for a long moment, and then he turned back to the chief and spoke to him rapidly. The man's old, lined face lit up and he smiled broadly, nodding effusively.

Luca looked back to Serena, a conciliatory gleam in his eyes. 'I'll look into it back in Rio.'

The breath she hadn't even been aware of holding left her chest and she had to concentrate when the conversation started again. Finally, when Luca and the chief had spoken for an hour or so, they got up to leave. The old man darted forward with surprising agility to take Serena's hand in his and pump it up and down vigorously. She smiled at his effervescence.

Following Luca out into the slightly less intense late-afternoon heat, she could see a Jeep approach in the distance.

Luca looked at his watch. 'That'll be our lift to the airfield. We need to pack our stuff up.'

He looked at her and must have seen something that Serena had failed to disguise in time.

His eyes glinted with something indefinable. 'I thought you'd welcome the prospect of civilisation again?'

'I do,' Serena said quickly, avoiding his look. But the truth was that she didn't…exactly. Their couple of days in the rainforest… the otherworldly pace of life in the village…

it had soothed something inside her. And she realised that she would miss it.

Afraid Luca might see that, she folded her arms and said, 'Are you going to give me a chance?' And then quickly, before he could interject, 'I think I deserve it. I don't want to go home yet.'

Luca looked at her. She could see the Jeep coming closer, stopping. She held her breath. His gaze narrowed on her and became...*hot*. Instantly Serena felt something spike. Anticipation.

He came closer, blocking out the Jeep arriving, the village behind him.

'I've no intention of letting you go home.'

Serena's arms clenched tighter. She didn't like the way her body reacted to that implacable statement and what it might mean. 'You're giving me a trial period?'

Luca smiled, and it made Serena's brain fuzzy.

'Something like that. I told you I wanted you, Serena. And I do. In my bed.'

Anger spiked at his arrogant tone, even as her pulse leapt treacherously. 'I'm not interested in becoming your next mistress, Fonseca. I'm interested in working.'

Luca's eyes flashed at her use of 'Fonseca'.

'I'll give you a two-week trial. Two weeks of working in the charity by day and two weeks in my bed by night.'

Serena unclenched her arms, her hands in fists by her sides, hating the betraying sizzle in her blood. Had she no self-respect?

'That's blackmail.'

Luca shrugged, supremely unconcerned. 'Call it what you want. That's the only way you'll get your trial.'

Serena swallowed a caustic rush of tangled emotions along with the betraying hum of desire. 'And what about your precious reputation? If people see us together? What then?'

Luca moved closer. Serena's words struck him somewhere deep inside. What *was* he doing? he asked himself. All he knew was that the things that had been of supreme importance to him for a long time no longer seemed as important. There was only here and now and this woman. And *heat*. And need.

Yet he wasn't losing sight of what had driven him for all these years completely. He was cynical enough to recognise an opportunity when it arose. Having Serena on his arm would mean news, and news would mean focus on the things close to his heart. Like his foundation.

He said now, 'I have every intention of people seeing us together. You see, I've realised that seven years is like seven lifetimes in the media world. You're old news. And if anyone does make something of it I'm quite happy for you to be seen by my side as someone intent on making up for her debauched past by doing charity work. Everyone loves a redemption story, after all. And in the meantime I get what I want—which is *you*. You owe me, Serena. You don't think I'm going to give you a two-week trial without recompense, do you?'

Serena just looked at him. She was too stunned to say anything. What Luca had said was so…*cold*. And yet all she could feel was *hot*. She should be slapping him across the face and taking a bus back to Manaus and the next flight home. Maybe that was what he was doing? Calling her bluff. Goading her. She couldn't imagine that he didn't have a string of willing mistresses back in Rio.

But that only made something very dark rise up: jealousy.

'We leave in fifteen minutes.'

With that he turned and strode away, as if he hadn't just detonated a bomb between them. She watched him incredulously, and then stalked to the small hut.

As she packed up her small backpack a few minutes later she alternated between the longing to to find Luca and deliver that slap to his face which he so deserved and pausing to remember how it had felt when he'd kissed her and touched her the other night.

She'd never really enjoyed sex; it had been another route to oblivion which had invariably ended in disappointment and an excoriating sense of self-disgust.

But Luca... It was as if he was able to see right through to her deepest self, to the part of her that was still innocent, untainted by what she'd seen and experienced as a child...

'Ms DePiero?'

Serena whirled around to see a young man in the doorway of the hut.

'Senhor Fonseca is waiting for you at the Jeep.'

Serena muttered something about coming and watched the man walk away. Something inside her solidified. She could leave and go home, lose any chance of a job with the charity and start all over again. Concede defeat. Or...if she was going to admit to herself that she wanted Luca too...she could be as strategic as him.

But if she was going to stay and submit to

his arrogant demands then it would be on *her* terms, and she would gain from it too.

Luca sent a wary glance to Serena, who was sitting on the other side of the plane. She was looking out of the window, so he couldn't see her expression, but he would guess that it was as stony as it had been when she'd got into the Jeep and on the silent journey to the private airfield near the airport.

He wasn't flying the plane this time. Ostensibly so he could catch up on work, but for possibly the first time in his life he couldn't focus on it.

All he could focus on was Serena, and the tense lines of her slim body, and wonder what that stony silence meant. He knew he deserved it. He was surprised she hadn't slapped him back at the village. He'd seen the moment in her expression when she'd wanted to.

He'd never behaved so autocratically with a woman in his life. If he wanted a woman he seduced her and took her to bed, and they were never under the impression that he was in the market for more than that.

But this was Serena DePiero. From the first moment he'd ever seen her he'd been tangled up into knots. The last few days had shown him a vastly different woman from the one he'd met before…and yet hadn't he seen something of this woman in her eyes that night in the club? He didn't like to admit that he *had* seen that moment of vulnerability.

His conscience pricked him. *He'd all but blackmailed her.* He wasn't so deluded that he couldn't acknowledge uncomfortably that it had been a crass attempt on his behalf to get her where he wanted her without having to let her know how badly he needed to sate this hunger inside him.

He opened his mouth to speak to her just as she turned her head to look at him and those searing blue eyes robbed him of speech. She looked determined.

'I've been thinking about your…proposal.'

Luca's conscience hit him again. He winced inwardly. Never had he imagined that she would be so diplomatic when he'd been such a bastard. 'Serena—'

She held up a hand. 'No, let me speak.'

He closed his mouth and didn't like the flutter of panic at the thought that he might just have completely mismanaged this. She could leave now and he'd never see her again.

'If I agree to stay and do this trial for two weeks… If I do well—prove that I'm

capable...and...' She stopped, a dark flush
staining her cheeks before she continued. 'If I
agree to what you said...then I want you to assure me that you'll give me a job—whether it's
here or back in Athens. A proper contracted,
paying job for the charity.'

The relief that flowed through Luca was
unsettling and heady. His conscience still
struck him, but he was too distracted to deal
with it.

He held out a hand towards Serena and
growled, 'Come here.'

The flush on her cheeks got pinker. 'Luca—'

'Come here and I'll tell you.'

He saw her bite her lip, the dart of her pink
tongue. After a few seconds her hands went
to her belt and she undid it and pushed herself up and out of her seat. As soon as she was
within touching distance Luca had closed a
hand around her wrist and tugged her so that
she fell onto his lap with a soft *ooph*.

'Luca, what are you—?'

He couldn't help himself. He covered her
mouth with his and stopped her words. A very
dangerous kind of relief flowed through him.
She would be his. She wasn't leaving. Her
arms crept around his neck after a moment
of resistance. Her mouth softened under his.

And when he swept his tongue along hers, and she sighed, he could have howled with triumph.

Before he lost it completely he drew back, his breathing laboured. He touched a hand to her jaw, cupping it, running a finger along its delicate line. He looked into her eyes and said, 'Yes, I'll give you a job.'

He could feel Serena's breath making her chest shudder against him. The pressure in his groin intensified.

'I want a signed agreement, Luca, that you'll keep your word.'

Indignation made anger flare. 'You don't trust me?' It had all been about him not trusting *her*. Luca had never considered her not trusting *him*, and it didn't sit well.

Serena's lush mouth compressed. She didn't answer directly, she said, 'A promise on paper, Luca, or I'll leave as soon as we touch down.'

Any feeling of triumph or any sense of control slipped out of Luca's grasp. His hands were around Serena's hips, holding her to him, and as much as he wanted to push her back, tell her that no woman dictated to him...he couldn't. The taste of her was on his tongue and, dammit, it wasn't enough. Not yet.

So he finally bit out, 'Fine.'

* * *

Serena took in the frankly mind-boggling three-hundred-and-sixty-degree view of Rio de Janeiro outside the glass walls of the penthouse apartment. It was at the top of the building she'd come to that first day.

She turned to face Luca. 'This is your apartment?'

He was watching her intently and inclined his head. 'Yes, but I only use it if I'm working late, or for entertaining clients after meetings.'

Or for entertaining mistresses?

Suddenly she didn't feel half as sure as she had on the plane, when Luca had pulled her into his lap to kiss her. Now her doubts and insecurities were back. Luca affected her... too much.

She crossed her arms. 'I can't stay here. It's inappropriate.'

Luca stifled an inelegant snort. 'This from the woman who was photographed at her debs in an exclusive Paris hotel in a bathtub full of champagne while dressed in a priceless gown?'

Serena flushed, recalling her father's malevolent smile and even more malevolent tone of voice: *'Good girl. We wouldn't want people to think you're becoming boring, now, would we?'*

Serena chose to ignore Luca's comment.

'What about the apartment I was meant to stay in? The one for staff?'

'It's no longer available; someone else took your place there.'

'Well, that's hardly my fault, is it?' she retorted hotly.

Luca's jaw firmed. 'It's either here, Serena, or if you insist, the charity will be put to the expense of finding you somewhere else.'

'No!' she shot out, aghast. 'But it's just—'

He cut in coolly. 'You're staying here. I'm sure you can put up with it for two weeks.'

This was what she was afraid of. He made her emotions and blood pressure see-saw out of control.

Luca looked at Serena and narrowed his gaze. She was skittish, nervy. A million miles from the woman who had melted in his arms just a short time before.

'Serena, what is it?'

She was angry, her cheeks growing pink. 'I've agreed to sleep with you to get a job— how do you think that makes me feel?'

Luca's conscience pricked but he pointed out, 'You're not sleeping with me yet.'

She went redder.

Luca felt something give inside him and ran a hand through his hair impatiently. 'Look, I behaved like a boor earlier. The very least you deserve is a trial period. I would have given it to you anyway.'

She looked at him, surprised, and it affected him more than he'd like to admit.

'You would? And what about a job?'

Luca schooled his features. 'That depends on your trial period—as it would for anyone else.'

He moved closer then, and put his hands on her upper arms. 'And you are *not* sleeping with me to get a job. You're sleeping with me because it's what you want. What we *both* want.'

She just looked at him, and something desperate rose inside Luca. He ground out, 'The door is behind me, Serena. You can walk out right now if that's what you want and you'll still get your trial.'

For an infinitesimal moment she said nothing, and he was reminded of telling her where the door was before, willing her to use it. Now he'd launch an army if she tried to leave. He had to consciously stop his hands from gripping her arms tight, as if he could restrain her from walking out. He could see her throat work as she swallowed. Her eyes were wide, pupils as black as night.

She opened her mouth and he kept his eyes

off the seductive temptation of those soft lips. He needed to hear this too badly. Needed her to stay.

'Serena...'

Her tongue moistened those lips. Luca's pulse jumped.

Her voice was husky. 'I just want a chance.'

The tension in Luca's body spiked. *Damn her.* 'And? What else?'

She turned her head away and bitterness laced her voice. 'You know I want you. In the tent...you made me show you. You humiliated me.'

Luca's chest was tight enough to hurt. An alien sensation. He cursed softly and felt as if some layer of himself was being stripped away when he admitted, 'Do you know how hard it was for me to stop myself from taking you that night?'

Those blue eyes locked with his. She whispered, 'You made me feel as if you just wanted to prove your dominance over me.'

Luca tipped her chin up with a finger and felt her jaw clench. He smiled, and it was wry. 'You credit me with far too much forethought. I needed to hear you say it...that you wanted me. You made *me* feel that much out of control.'

Instantly something flashed in those piercing eyes—something that made some of Luca's tightness ease.

'You're so in control. It's almost scary.'

Now Luca was the one to grit his jaw as he recognised that no one had ever said that to him before—certainly not a woman. Serena's gaze seemed to see right through him to where he stood as a small boy, witnessing the awesome power parents had to rip your life apart. He knew his desire for control and respectability stemmed from that chaotic, messy, tumultuous moment. And here he was, skating far too close to the edges of losing it all again. And yet...he couldn't walk away.

He said, with quiet conviction, 'If I was to kiss you right now you'd see how thin the veneer of my control is, believe me.'

Something hot flared in the bright blue depths and he stifled a groan of pure need. But he would not take her now, like this, after trekking in a jungle for days, when they were both dizzy with fatigue.

It was the hardest thing in the world, but he let her go and stepped back. 'I have work to catch up on—some conference calls to make. And I'm sure you'll appreciate a night in a real bed again. My assistant will be here in the morning to take you down to the charity offices where you'll be working. And tomorrow evening I'm taking you to a charity function.'

Serena's heart palpitated with a mixture of relief and disappointment. So he wasn't staying tonight? And then shame lanced her that she hadn't been strong enough just to walk away. That a part of her wanted to explore what this man was offering, almost more than she wanted to prove herself or ensure her independence.

The last three and a half years had been all about finding and nurturing an inner strength she'd never known she had. But Luca made her feel weak, and it scared her. But not enough to turn away from him. Damn him.

'Okay.'

Luca said nothing for a long moment and then he said quietly, *'Boa noite,* Serena. *Até amanha.'*

Till tomorrow.

He turned and walked away and the slick, modern apartment was immediately cavernous without him. They'd only spent four days together but it felt like a lifetime. Serena battled the urge to flee, once again questioning her rationale... But her decision to stay had nothing to do with being rational. That had fled out of the window as soon as Luca had pulled her onto his lap on the plane and kissed her witless.

Doubts and fears melted away. She wasn't going anywhere. She couldn't.

As soon as that registered in her body fatigue and exhaustion hit her like a freight train. Along with the realisation that she had hot water at her disposal and could finally wash.

Pushing all thoughts of Luca and what the immediate future held out of her head, she unpacked, took the longest and most delicious shower she'd ever had in her life, fell facedown onto an indescribably soft bed, and sank into oblivion.

Luca stood at the window of his office a floor below the apartment. Rio was a carpet of twinkling golden lights as far as the eye could see. He spoke into the mobile he held to his ear.

His voice was tight. 'Let's just say that I have my doubts about whether she did it or not, and I'd appreciate your help in finding out.' There was a pause, and then Luca said curtly, 'Look, Max, if it's too much trouble—' He sighed. 'Okay, yes. And, thanks, I appreciate it.'

Luca cut the connection and threw his phone down on the table behind him. It bounced off and hit the carpeted floor. He ignored it and turned back to the view. Any conversation with his brother drove his blood pressure skywards. He knew that Max didn't blame Luca specifically for the fact that they'd been split up the way they had between their parents... but guilt festered inside Luca even now. He was the elder twin and he'd always felt that responsibility keenly.

Pushing thoughts of his brother aside, Luca hated to admit it, but he felt altered in some way. As if some alchemy had taken place in his head and body since he'd stood looking at this view the last time—just before Serena had arrived almost a week ago.

He scowled at his fanciful thoughts. There was no alchemy. It was physical attraction, pure and simple. It had been between them from the moment their eyes had first locked. And now he was going to sate it. That was all.

The fact that he was prepared to allow Serena DePiero to sign an agreement which would potentially offer her employment with his company for the foreseeable future, *and* to be seen with her in public, were things that he pushed to the deepest recesses of his mind.

He focused instead on the increasing anticipation in his blood and his body at the knowledge that soon this ever-present hunger would be assuaged.

CHAPTER SEVEN

THE FOLLOWING EVENING Serena waited on the outdoor terrace that wrapped around the entire apartment, a ball of nerves in her gut. The fact that Luca had said he was taking her to a charity function had been conveniently forgotten when she'd succumbed to exhaustion the previous evening—and in the whirlwind of the day she'd just had.

She'd woken early and had some breakfast just before his sleek assistant Laura had arrived, cracking a minute smile for once. She'd handed Serena a sheaf of papers and hot embarrassment had risen up when she'd seen it was the contract assuring her of work if she completed her trial period successfully. The contract she'd demanded.

To her relief there was no mention of the more personal side of their agreement. Luca's cool efficiency was scary.

After she'd signed, Laura had taken her

down to the first floor, where the offices for the charity were based, and introduced her to the staff. Serena had spent such a pleasant day with the friendly Brazilians, who had been so nice and patient with her rudimentary Portuguese that she'd almost fooled herself into forgetting what else awaited her.

But she couldn't ignore it any longer. Not when she'd returned to the apartment to find a stylist and a troupe of hair and make-up people waiting to transform her for Luca's pleasure. Or *delectation* might be a better word. She felt like something that should be on display.

An entire wardrobe of designer clothes seemed to have materialised by magic during the day, and this whole process brought back so many memories of her old life—when her father had insisted on making sure his daughters had the most desirable clothes...for the maximum effect.

The thought of the evening ahead made her go clammy. Right now, weakly, she'd take a jungle full of scorpions, snakes, bullet ants and even an angry Luca Fonseca over the social jungle she was about to walk into.

And then she drew herself up tall. She was better than this. Was she forgetting what she'd survived in the past few years? The intense personal scrutiny and soul-searching? The constant invasion of her privacy as she'd faced her demons in front of strangers? And not only that—she'd survived the jungle with Luca, who'd been waiting for her to falter at every step.

Although right now that didn't feel so much of a triumph as a test of endurance that she was still undergoing. They'd exchanged the wild jungle for the so-called civilised jungle. And this time the stakes were so much higher.

At that moment the little hairs all over her body stood up a nano-second before she heard a noise behind her. She had no time to keep obsessing over whether or not she'd picked out the right dress. Squaring her shoulders, and drawing on the kind of reserves that she hadn't had to call on in years, Serena turned around.

For a second she could only blink to make sure she wasn't dreaming. Her ability to breathe was severely compromised. Memories of Luca seven years ago slammed into her like a punch to the gut. Except this Luca was infinitely harder, more gorgeous.

'You've shaved...' Serena commented faintly. But those words couldn't do justice to the man in front of her, dressed in a classic tuxedo, his hard jaw revealed in all its obduracy, the sensual lines of his mouth even more defined.

His thick dark hair was shorter too, and Serena felt an irrational spurt of jealousy for whoever had had his or her hands on his head.

She was too enflamed and stunned by this vision of Luca to notice that his gaze had narrowed on her and a flush had made his cheeks darken.

'You look…incredible.'

Luca's eyes felt seared, right through to the back. She was a sleek, beautiful goddess. All he could see at first was bare skin, arms and shoulders. And acres of red silk and gold, sparkling with inlaid jewels. A deep V drew his eye effortlessly to luscious curves. There was some embellishment on the shoulders and then the dress fell in a swathe of silk and lace from her waist to the floor. He could see the hint of one pale thigh peeping out from the luxurious folds and had to grit his jaw to stop his body from exploding.

She'd pinned her hair back into a low bun at the base of her neck. It should have made the outfit look more demure than if her hair had been around her shoulders in a silken white-golden tumble, but it didn't. It seemed to heighten the provocation of the dress.

Luca registered then that she looked uncomfortable. Shifting minutely, those long fingers were fluttering near the V of the dress, as if to try and cover it up. The woman Luca had seen in Florence had been wearing a fraction of this much material and revelling in it.

She was avoiding his eye, and that made Luca move closer. She looked up and his pulse fired. He came close enough to smell her clean, fresh scent. Suddenly it felt as if he hadn't seen her in a month, when it had been just a day. A day in which he'd had to restrain himself from going down to the charity offices.

Danger.

He ignored it.

He might have expected her scent to be overpowering, overtly sensual, but it was infinitely more subtle.

Familiar irritation that she was proving to be more difficult to grasp than quicksilver made him say brusquely, 'What's wrong? The dress? You don't like it?'

She looked up at him and need gripped Luca so fiercely that his whole body tensed. But something very cynical followed. He'd had an entire wardrobe of clothes delivered to the apartment—and she wasn't happy?

Her eyes flashed. 'No, it's not the dress.' Her voice turned husky. 'The dress is beautiful. But what were you thinking, sending all those clothes? I'm not your mistress, and I don't want to be treated like one.'

Surprise lanced him, but he recovered quickly. 'I thought you'd appreciate being prepared for a public event.'

Serena looked down and muttered, 'You mean public humiliation.'

Something shifted in Luca's chest. He tipped up her chin, more concerned than he liked to admit by her uneasiness. Colour stained her pale cheeks and Luca almost gave in to the beast inside him. *Almost*. With a supreme effort he willed it down. 'What I said before… about exposing you to public scrutiny…that won't happen, Serena. I won't let it.'

Her eyes were wide. *Wounded*? Her mouth thinned. 'Isn't that part of the plan, though? A little revenge?'

Luca winced inwardly. What did this woman do to him? She called to his most base instincts and he could be as cruel as his father ever had been. Shame washed through him.

He shook his head, something fierce erupting inside him. 'I'm taking you out because I want to be seen with you, Serena.'

As he said it he realised it was true. He genuinely wanted this. To have her on his arm. And it had very little to do with wanting to punish her. At the thought of adverse public reaction a protective instinct nearly bowled him over with its force.

Before he could lose his footing completely, he took her by the hand and said gruffly, 'We should leave or we'll be late.'

In the lift something caught his eye, and he looked down to see Serena's other hand clutching a small bag which matched her dress. Her knuckles were white, and when his gaze travelled up he could see the tension in her body and jaw.

The lift jerked softly to a halt and almost against his will Luca found his hand going to the small of Serena's back to touch her. The minute his hand came into contact with the bare, warm, silky skin left exposed by the backless design she tensed more.

He frowned as something had dawned on him. 'Are you...*nervous*?'

Serena's eyes flashed with some indefinable emotion and she quickly stepped out of the open doors of the elevator, away from his touch, avoiding his narrowed gaze.

'Don't be ridiculous. It's just been a while since I've gone to anything like this, that's all.'

Luca sensed that there was a lot more to it than that, but he gestured for her to precede him out of the building, realising too late what awaited them outside when a veritable explosion of light seemed to go off in their faces. Without even realising what he was doing he put his arm around Serena and curved her into his body, one hand up to cover her face, as they walked quickly to his car, where a security guard held the passenger door open.

In the car, Serena's heart was pumping so hard she felt light-headed. The shock of that wall of paparazzi when she hadn't seen it in so long was overwhelming. And she couldn't help the fierce pain of betrayal. Everything Luca had just said was lies...and she hated that she wouldn't have expected it of him.

She was a sap. Of *course* he was intent on—

Her hand was taken in a firm grip. She clenched her jaw and looked at Luca in the driver's seat. His face was dark...*with anger*?

'Serena, I had nothing to do with that. They must have been tipped off.'

He looked so grim and affronted that Serena

felt something melt inside her. Felt a wish to believe him.

'It won't happen again.'

She took her hand from Luca's and forced a smile. 'Don't worry about it.'

The imprint of Luca's body where he'd held her so close was still making her treacherous skin tingle all over. The way he'd drawn her into him so protectively had unsettled her. She'd felt unprotected for so long that it was an alien sensation. Maybe he *hadn't* planned it. She recalled him biting off a curse now, as if he'd been as surprised as her...

Once they'd left the paparazzi behind she pushed a button to lower her window, relishing the warm evening Rio breeze and the tang of the sea.

'Are you okay?'

Serena nodded. 'Fine—just needed some air.'

The setting sun was bathing the sky in a pink glow, and from somewhere distant Serena could hear cheers and clapping.

She looked at Luca. 'What's that?'

Luca's mouth twitched. 'Every evening sunset-worshippers applaud another stunning sunset from the beaches.'

Serena couldn't take her eyes off the curve of

Luca's mouth. 'I love that idea,' she breathed. 'I'd like to see the sunset.'

She quickly looked away again, in case that dark navy gaze met hers when she felt far too exposed. Her cheeks were still hot from that moment when she'd been captivated by the way he filled out his suit so effortlessly. The obviously bespoke material did little to disguise his sheer power, flowing lovingly over defined muscles.

'Where do you live when you don't stay at the apartment?' Serena blurted out the first thing she could think of to try and take her mind off Luca's physicality.

He glanced at her, his hands strong on the wheel of the car.

'I have a house in Alto Gavea—it's a district in the Tijuca Forest, north of the lake…'

She sneaked a look. 'Is it your family home? Where you grew up?'

He shook his head abruptly, and when he answered his voice was tight. 'No, we lived out in the suburbs. My parents wouldn't have approved of living so near to the beaches and *favelas*.'

Serena thought of what he'd told her about his parents so far and asked, 'You weren't close to them?'

His mouth twisted. 'No. They split up when we were six, and my mother moved back to her native Italy.'

Serena had forgotten about that Italian connection. 'You said *we*... Do you have brothers and sisters?'

She could sense his reluctance to answer, but they weren't going anywhere fast in the evening traffic. Luca sighed. 'Yes, I have a twin brother.'

Serena's eyes widened. 'Wow—a twin? That's pretty amazing.' Her mind boggled slightly at the thought of *two* Lucas.

He slid her a mocking look and said, 'We're non-identical. He lives in Italy; he moved there with our mother after the divorce.'

Serena processed this and turned in her seat to face him. 'Wait...you mean you were split up?'

The thought of anyone splitting her and Siena up at that young age made her go cold. Siena had been the only anchor in her crazy world.

Luca faced forward, his voice emotionless. 'Yes, my parents decided that each would take one of us. My mother chose me to go to Italy with her, but when my brother got upset she swapped us and took him instead.'

Serena gasped as that scenario sank in. 'But that's…horrific. And your father just let her?'

Luca looked at her, face hard. 'He didn't care which son he got as long as he got one of us to be his heir.'

Serena knew what it was to grow up under a cruel tyrant, but this shocked even her. 'And are you close now? You and your brother?'

Luca shrugged minutely. 'Not particularly. But he was the one who bailed me out of jail, and he was the one who arranged for the best legal defence to get me out of Florence and back to Rio, avoiding a lengthy trial and jail time.'

His expression hardened to something infinitely cynical.

'A hefty donation towards "the preservation of Florence" was all it took to get the trial mysteriously dismissed. That money undoubtedly went to corrupt officials—one of whom was probably your father—but I was damned if I was going to hang for a crime I wasn't even responsible for. But they wouldn't clear me completely, so every time I fly to Europe now I come under the radar of Europe's law enforcement agencies.'

Serena felt cold. She turned back to the front, staring unseeingly out of the window, knowing it was futile to say anything. She'd protested her innocence till she was blue in the face, but Luca was right—his association with her *had* made things worse for him.

They were turning into a vast tree-lined driveway now, which led up to a glittering colonial-style building. When Luca pulled up, and a valet parker waited for him to get out, Serena took several deep breaths to calm her frayed nerves.

Luca surprised her by not getting out straight away.

He turned to her. 'I'm not interested in the past any more, Serena. I'm interested in the here and now.'

Serena swallowed. Something fragile seemed to shimmer between them...tantalising. And then he got out of the car and she sucked in another shaky breath.

He came around and opened her door, extended a hand to help her out. She took it, and when his gaze tracked down her body and lingered on her breasts a pulse throbbed between her legs.

He tucked her arm into his as they moved forward and joined similarly dressed couples entering a glittering doorway lit by hundreds of small lights. It was a scene Serena had seen a million times before, but never heightened like this. Never *romantic*.

She asked herself as Luca led her inside, greeting someone in Portuguese, if they really could let the past go. Or was that just what Luca was willing to say so that he could bed her and then walk away, with all that resentment still simmering under the surface?

'Do you think you could crack a smile and not look as if you're about to be subjected to torture?'

Serena glanced at Luca, who had a fixed social smile on his face. She sent up silent thanks that he couldn't read her thoughts and said sweetly. 'But this *is* torture.'

Something flared in his eyes—surprise?—and then he said, 'Torture it may well be, but a few hours of social torture is worth it if it means that a *favela* gets a new free school staffed by qualified teachers.'

Serena felt immediately chastened. 'Is that what this evening's ball is in aid of?'

Luca looked at her assessingly. 'Among some other causes. The global communities charity too.'

Serena thought of that sweet little girl in the village—a million miles away from here...and yet *not*.

'I'm sorry,' she said huskily. 'You're right—it *is* worth it.'

Serena missed Luca's speculative look because a waiter was interrupting them with a tray of champagne. Luca took a glass and looked at her when she didn't.

She shook her head quickly and said to the waiter, 'Do you have some sparkling water, please?'

The waiter rushed off and Luca frowned slightly. 'You really don't drink any more?'

Serena's belly clenched. 'No, I really don't.' She made a face. 'I never liked the taste of alcohol anyway. It was more for the effect it had on me.'

'What was that?'

She looked at him. 'Numbing.'

The moment stretched between them...taut. And then the attentive waiter returned with a glass of water on a tray for Serena. She took it gratefully. Luca was getting too close to that dark place inside her.

To her relief someone came up then, and took his attention, but just as Serena felt hopeful that he might forget about her she felt her heart sink and jump in equal measure when she felt him reach for her hand and tug her with him, introducing her to the man.

* * *

Luca was finding it hard to concentrate on the conversation around him when he usually had no problem. Even if he *was* with a woman. He was aware of every tiny movement Serena made in that dress, and acutely aware of the attention she was attracting.

He was also aware that she seemed ill at ease. He'd expected her to come back into this kind of environment and take to it like the proverbial duck to water, but when they'd first come in she'd looked *pained*. It was just like in the jungle, when she'd proved him resoundingly wrong in his expectations of her.

Now her head was bent towards one of the executive team who managed his charities abroad, and they were engaged in an earnest conversation when Luca would have fully expected Serena to look bored out of her brains.

At that moment her head tipped back and she laughed at something the other woman had said. Luca couldn't breathe, and the conversation stopped around them as she unwittingly drew everyone's eye. She literally…*sparkled*, her face transformed by her wide smile. She was undeniably beautiful…and Luca realised he'd never seen true beauty till that moment.

His chest felt tight as he had a vision of what

he'd subjected her to: dragging her into the jungle on a forced trek. She'd endured one of the most painful insect bites in the world. She'd stayed in a rustic village in the depths of the Amazon without blinking. She'd endeared herself to the tribespeople without even trying. It had taken him *years* to be accepted and respected.

And the miners—some of the hardest men in Brazil—weathered and rough as they came—they'd practically been doffing their caps when Serena had appeared with him, as if she was royalty.

Luca could see the crowd moving towards the ballroom and took Serena's hand in his. She looked at him with that smile still playing about her mouth and a sense of yearning stronger than anything he'd ever felt kicked him in the solar plexus. A yearning to be the cause of such a smile.

As if she was reading his mind her smile faded on cue.

'Come on—let's dance,' Luca growled, feeling unconstructed. Raw.

He tugged Serena in his wake before he remembered that he didn't even *like* dancing, but right now he needed to feel her body pressed against his or he might go crazy.

When they reached the edge of the dimly lit dance floor Luca turned and pulled her with him, facing her. The light highlighted her stunning bone structure. That effortlessly classic beauty.

Unbidden, he heard himself articulate the question resounding in his head. 'Who *are* you?'

She swallowed. 'You know who I am.'

'Do I really?' he asked, almost angry now. 'Or is this all some grand charade for the benefit of your family, so you can go back to doing what you love best—being a wild society princess?'

Serena went pale and pulled free of Luca's embrace, saying angrily, 'I've told you about me but you still don't have the first clue, Luca. And as for what I love best? You'll never know.'

She turned and was walking away, disappearing into the vast lobby, before Luca realised that he was struck dumb and immobile because no woman had ever walked away from him before.

Cursing under his breath, he followed her, but when he got to the lobby there was no sign of a distinctive red dress or a white-blonde head. The way she'd stood out in the crowd mocked him now. His gut clenched with panic.

He got to the open doors, where people were still arriving. He spotted the valet who had taken his car and accosted him, asking curtly, 'The woman I came with—have you seen her?'

The valet gulped, visibly intimidated by Luca. 'Yes. Sir. I just saw her into a taxi that had dropped off some guests.'

Luca swore so volubly that the valet's ears went red. He stammered, 'Do—do you want your car?'

Luca just looked at him expressively and the young man scurried off.

They were on a hill overlooking the city. Luca looked out onto the benignly twinkling lights of Rio and the panic intensified. He recalled Serena saying she wanted to see the sunset... Would she have gone to the beach? At this time of night?

Panic turned to fear. He took out his phone and made a call to Serena's mobile but it was switched off. Rio was a majestic city, but at night certain areas were some of the most dangerous on earth. Where the *hell* had she gone?

Serena stalked into the apartment and the door slammed behind her with a gratifyingly loud bang. She was still shaking with anger, and her emotions were bubbling far too close to the surface for comfort.

She kicked off her shoes and made her way out to the terrace, taking deep breaths. Damn Luca Fonseca. It shouldn't matter what he thought of her...but after everything they'd been through she'd foolishly assumed that he'd come to see that she *was* different.

This was the real her. A woman who wanted to work and do something worthwhile, and never, ever insulate herself against life again. The girl and the young woman she'd been had been born out of the twisted machinations of her father.

Her hands wrapped around the railing. Self-disgust rose up inside her. To think that she was willing to go to bed with a man who thought so little of her. Where was the precious self-esteem she'd painstakingly built up again?

She knew where... It had all dissolved in a puddle of heat as soon as Luca came within feet of her. And yet she knew that wasn't entirely fair—he'd treated her as his exact equal in the jungle, and earlier, in the charity offices, she'd been surprised to find that he'd already put in motion discussions on her idea for a high-end tourist shop showcasing products from the villages and credited her with the plan.

She heard a sound behind her and tensed. Panic washed through her. She wasn't ready to deal with Luca yet. But reluctantly she turned around to see him advancing on her, his face like thunder, as long fingers pulled at his bow-tie.

She still got a jolt of sensation to see him clean-shaven. It should have made him look more urbane. It didn't.

CHAPTER EIGHT

LUCA THREW ASIDE his bow-tie just before he came onto the terrace and bit out, 'Where the hell were you? I've been all over the beach-fronts looking for you.'

His anger escalated when he saw Serena put her hands on her hips and say defiantly, 'What was it? Did you think I'd hit some nightclub? Or that I'd gone to find some late-night pharmacy so I could score some meds?'

Luca stopped. He had to acknowledge the relief that was coursing through his veins. She was here. She was safe. But the rawness he felt because she'd walked out on him and looked so upset when he'd suggested she was acting out a charade was still there.

An uncomfortable truth slid into his gut like a knife. Perhaps this *was* her. No charade. No subterfuge.

And just like that, Luca was thrown off-centre all over again.

He breathed deeply. 'I'm sorry.'

Serena was surprised. She blinked. 'Sorry for what?'

Honesty compelled Luca to admit, 'For what I said at the function. I just... *You...*'

He looked away and put his hands on his hips. Suddenly it wasn't so hard to say what he wanted to say—as if something inside him had given way.

He dropped his hands, came closer and shook his head. 'You confound me, Serena De-Piero. Everything I thought I knew about you is wrong. The woman who came to Rio, the woman who survived the jungle, the woman who gave those villagers the kind of courtesy not many people ever give them...she's someone I wasn't expecting.'

Serena's ability to think straight was becoming compromised. Emotion was rising at hearing this admission and knowing what it must be costing him.

Huskily she said, 'But this *is* me, Luca. This has always been me. It was just...buried before.' Then she blurted out, 'I'm sorry for running off. I came straight here. I wouldn't have gone near the beaches—not after what you said. I do have *some* street-smarts, you know.'

Luca moved closer. 'I panicked. I thought of you being oblivious to the dangers.'

Now Serena noticed how pale Luca was. *He'd been worried about her.* He hadn't assumed she'd gone off the rails. The anger and hurt drained away, and something shifted inside her. A kind of tenderness welled up. *Dangerous.*

She had to physically resist the urge to go to him and touch his jaw. Instead she said, 'I'm here…safe.'

His hands landed on her hips and he tugged her into him. She was shorter without her heels. He made her feel delicate. Her skin was tingling now, coming up in goosebumps in spite of the warm air. Emboldened by his proximity, and what he'd just said, she lifted her own hands and pushed Luca's jacket apart and down his arms.

He let go of her so that it could fall to the ground.

Without saying anything, Luca took her by the hand and led her into the apartment, stepping over his coat.

Serena let herself be led. She'd never felt this connection with anyone else, and a deep-rooted surge of desire to reclaim part of her sexuality beat like a drum in her blood.

Yet when Luca led her into what she assumed was his bedroom, because of its stark, masculine furnishings, trepidation gripped her. Perhaps she was being a fool? Reading too much into what he'd said? Didn't men say *anything* to get women into bed? There was so much in her past that she was ashamed of, that she hadn't made peace with, and Luca seemed to have an unerring ability to bring all of those vulnerabilities to the fore. What would happen when he possessed her completely?

Her hand tightened around Luca's and he stopped by the bed and turned to face her. Serena blurted out the first thing she could think of, as if to try and put some space between them again. 'I lost my virginity when I was sixteen…does that shock you?'

He shrugged, his expression carefully veiled, 'Should it? I lost mine at sixteen too —when one of my father's ex-mistresses seduced me.'

Serena's desperation rose, in spite of her shock at what he'd just revealed so flatly. 'It's what men expect, though, isn't it? For their lovers to be somehow…innocent?'

Luca made a face. 'I like my lovers to be experienced. I've no desire to be some wide-eyed virgin's first time.'

A wide-eyed virgin she certainly was *not*. Innocence had been ripped from her too early.

Luca pulled her closer and heat pulsed into Serena's lower body. She could feel his arousal between them, thick and hard. It scattered painful thoughts and she welcomed it like a coward.

'I want you, Serena, more than I've ever wanted anyone. I've wanted you from the first moment I laid eyes on you...'

For a heady moment Serena felt an overwhelming sense of power. She reassured herself that the emotions rising inside her were transitory; sex had never touched her emotionally before, so why should it now?

When he reached for her Serena curled into him without even thinking about it. It felt like the most necessary thing. The world dropped away and it was just them in this tight embrace, hearts thudding, skin hot.

His fingers spread out over her back, making her nipples harden almost painfully against the material of the dress. And then he lowered his head and his mouth was on hers, fitting like the missing piece of a jigsaw puzzle. Serena's lips opened to his on a sigh, tongues touching and tasting, stroking intimately. Her hands wound up around his neck, fingers tugging the short strands of hair, exploring, learning the shape of his skull.

Luca's wicked mouth and tongue made her strain to get even closer. After long, drugging moments he drew back, breathing harshly. Serena had to struggle to open her eyes.

'I want to see you,' he muttered thickly. 'Take down your hair.'

Serena felt as if she was in a dream. Had she, in fact, had this dream more often than once in the past seven years? She lifted her hand to the back of her head, feeling incredibly languid, and removed the discreet pin. Her hair tumbled around her shoulders, making her nerve-ends tingle even more.

Luca reached out and ran his fingers through it, then fisted it in one hand as the other reached around her to draw her into him again, kissing her with ruthless passion, tongue thrusting deep.

Serena's legs were starting to wobble. Luca's mouth was remorseless, sending her brain into a tailspin.

His hands came to the shoulders of her dress and pulled with gentle force, so the material slipped down her arms, loosening around her chest. She broke away from his mouth and looked up into dark pools of blue, feeling insecure.

Her arms came up against her breasts. Luca drew back and gently tugged them away, pulling the front of the dress down, leaving her bared to him.

She wore no bra, and Luca's gaze was so hot her skin sizzled. He reached out a hand and cupped the weight of one breast, a thumb moving over one puckered nipple. She bit her lip to stop from moaning out loud.

And then Luca put his hands on her hips and pulled her into him, hard enough to make her gasp, and replaced his thumb with his mouth, suckling on that hard peak roughly, making her back arch.

His erection was insistent against her and Serena's hips moved of their own volition.

Luca lifted his head. *'Feiticeira.'*

Her tongue felt heavy in her mouth, 'What does that mean?'

'Witch,' Luca replied succinctly.

And he kissed her again before her mind could catch up with the fact that his hands were now pushing her dress down over her hips so that it fell to the floor in a silken swish.

He put one hand between their bodies and Serena held her breath when he explored down over her belly and lower, until he was gently pushing her legs apart so that he could feel for himself how ready she was.

Serena felt gauche, but wanton, as Luca moved his hand between her legs, over her panties. She lowered her head to his shoulder when her face got hot, and her breathing grew harsher when his wicked fingers moved against her insistently.

He slipped a finger under the gusset of her panties and touched her, flesh to flesh. Serena bit her lip hard enough to make tears spring into her eyes. She wanted to clamp her thighs together—the sensation was too much—but Luca's hand was too strong.

Her legs finally gave way and she collapsed back onto the bed, heart thumping erratically.

Luca started to undo his shirt, revealing that broad and exquisitely muscled chest. A smattering of dark hair covered his pectorals, leading down in a silky line under his trousers to where she could see the bulge of his arousal.

Serena's brain melted and she welcomed it. She didn't want to think or analyse—only feel.

His hands moved to his trousers and he undid them and pushed them down, taking his underwear with them. His erection was awe-inspiring. Long and thick and hard, a bead of moisture at the tip.

'Seven years, Serena,' he said throatily, 'For seven years I've wanted you above any other woman. No one came close to how I imagined this.'

She looked up at him, taken aback. She watched as he reached for something in a drawer in the side table. He rolled protection over his length. There was something unashamedly masculine about the action.

'Lie back,' he instructed gruffly.

Serena did, glad he was giving instructions because she couldn't seem to formulate a single coherent thought.

Luca curled his fingers under the sides of her panties and gently took them off. Now she was naked. And even though she'd been naked in front of men before it had never felt like this. As if she was being reborn.

Luca came down over her on strong arms, their bodies barely touching. He kissed her, and those broad shoulders blocked everything out. Serena reached up, desperate for contact again, her hands touching his chest and moving down the sides of his body, reaching around to his back, sliding over taut, sleek muscles.

Luca broke away. 'You're killing me. I need you...*now*. Spread your legs for me.'

Serena's entire body seemed to spasm at

that husky entreaty. She moved her legs apart and Luca came down over her, his body pressing against hers. She could feel the thick blunt head of him pushing against her, seeking entrance.

She opened her legs wider, every cell in her body straining towards this union. Aching for it. She looked up at him, her whole body on the edge of some unknown precipice.

As if some lingering tension shimmering between them had just dissolved, Luca thrust in, hard and deep, and Serena cried out at the exquisite invasion.

It was sore…he was so big…but even as she had that thought the pain was already dissipating to be replaced by a heady sensation of fullness.

'Serena?'

She opened her eyes. Luca was frowning. She hadn't realised that she was biting her lip.

He started to withdraw. 'I've hurt you.'

There was a quality to his voice Serena had never heard before. She gripped him tight with her thighs, trapping him. 'No,' she said huskily. 'You're not hurting me… It's…been a while.'

He stopped, and for an infinitesimal moment Serena thought he was going to withdraw completely. But then he slowly thrust in again and relief rushed through her.

Luca reached under her back, arching her up into him more as he kept up a steady rhythm that made it hard to breathe. She could feel her inner muscles tight around him, saw his gritted jaw, the intense look of concentration on his face.

Luca pressed a searing kiss to her mouth before trailing his lips down, closing them over one nipple and then the other, forcing Serena's back to arch again as spasm after spasm of tiny pleasures rushed through her core.

She locked her feet around the back of Luca's body and he went deeper, but she couldn't break free of that sliver of control that kept her bound, kept her from soaring to the stars. A blinding flash of insight hit her like a smack in the face: she recognised now why she couldn't let go in this moment of intense intimacy— the reason why she'd never let herself feel this deeply before—it was because she'd always been too afraid of losing control.

Which was ironic. But being out of control on drink and medication had been—perversely—*within* her control. This wasn't. This was threatening to wrench her out of herself in a way that was frankly terrifying.

A small sob of need escaped Serena's mouth
as that elusive pinnacle seemed to fade into the
distance. The turmoil in her chest and body
was burning her. But she couldn't let go—even
as she heard a guttural sound coming from
Luca's mouth and felt his body tense within
her before deep tremors shook his big frame
and his body thrust against her with the unconscious rhythm of his own release.

She felt hollowed out, unsatisfied.

Luca withdrew from her body, breathing
harshly, and Serena winced minutely as her
muscles relaxed their tight grip. As soon as
Luca released her from the prison of his arms
she felt the need to escape and left the bed.

She barely heard him call her name as she
shut the bathroom door behind her, locking it.
Her legs were shaking and tears burned the
back of her eyes as the magnitude of what had
just happened sank in. There was something
fundamentally flawed, deep inside her. She'd
been broken so long ago that she couldn't function normally now. And Luca had to be the
one to demonstrate this to her. The ignominy
was crushing.

Serena blindly reached into the shower and
turned the spray to hot, stepping underneath
and lifting her face up to the rush of water.

Her tears slid and fell, silent heaves making her body spasm as she let it all out.

She heard banging on the door, her name. She called out hoarsely, 'Leave me alone, Luca!'

And then, mercifully, silence.

Serena sank down onto the floor of the shower as the water beat relentlessly down over her body. She drew her knees up to her chest and dropped her head onto them and tried to tell herself that what had just happened *wasn't* as cataclysmic as she thought it was.

Luca looked at the locked door. He wasn't used to feeling powerless, but right now he did. He cursed volubly, knowing it wouldn't be heard because he could hear the spray of the shower and something that sounded suspiciously like a sob.

His chest hurt. Was she crying? Had he hurt her?

Luca cursed again and paced. He went to his wardrobe and took out some worn jeans, pulled them on, paced again.

Dammit. No woman had ever reacted like that after making love with him. Running to the bathroom. *Crying.* And yet...

Had he really made love to Serena? Luca

asked himself derisively. Or had he been so overcome with lust that he'd not taken any notice of the fact that she clearly hadn't been enjoying herself?

He winced now when he thought of how tight she'd been. And her husky words... *It's... been a while.* To be so tight he'd guess a lot longer than 'a while'. Which meant what? That her reputation for promiscuity was severely flawed, for a start. And she'd been awkward, slightly gauche. Not remotely like the practised seductress he might have expected.

He'd seen how her face had tightened, become inscrutable. She'd shut her eyes, turned her head away... But Luca had been caught in the grip of a pleasure so intense that he'd been unable to hold himself back, releasing himself into her with a force unlike anything he'd known before.

For the first time in his memory Luca was facing the very unpalatable fact that he'd behaved with all the finesse of a rutting bull.

The spray of the shower was turned off and Luca became tense. He felt a very real urge to flee at the prospect of facing Serena now. But that urge stemmed from some deep place he wouldn't acknowledge. She hadn't reached him there. No one had.

* * *

When Serena emerged from the bathroom, dressed in a voluminous terrycloth robe, she still felt raw. The bedroom was empty, and a lurch of something awfully like disappointment went through her belly to think that Luca had left.

And then she cursed herself. Hadn't she told him to *'leave me alone'*? Why on earth would he want to have anything to do with a physically and emotionally wounded woman when there had to be any number of willing women who would give him all the satisfaction he might crave without the post-coital angst?

Still…it hurt in a way that it shouldn't.

Serena belted the robe tightly around her waist and, feeling restless, went out to the living area. Her hair lay in a damp tangle down her back.

But when she looked out through the glass doors she saw him. He hadn't left. Her heart stopped as something very warm and treacherous filled her chest.

As she came closer to the open doors she could see that he'd pulled on soft faded jeans. His back was broad and smooth, his hair ruffled. From her hands or the breeze? Serena hovered at the door, on the threshold.

And then Luca said over his shoulder, 'You should come and see the view—it's pretty spectacular.'

Serena came out and stood not far from Luca, putting her hands on the railing. The view was indeed exquisite. Rio was lit up with a thousand lights, the Sugar Loaf in the distance, and the beaches just out of sight. It was magical. Other-worldly.

'I've never seen anything like this,' she breathed, curiously soothed by Luca's muted reaction to her reappearance.

He said lightly now, 'I find that hard to believe.'

Serena's hands tightened on the railing. 'It's true. Before...I wouldn't have noticed.'

She could sense him turning towards her and her skin warmed. Just like that. From his attention. She glanced at him and his face looked stark in the moonlight.

'Did I hurt you? You were with me all the way and then...you weren't.'

'*No!*' Serena blurted out, horrified that he would think that. 'No,' she said again, quieter, and looked back at the view. 'Nothing like that.'

'Then...what?'

Why wouldn't he let it go? Serena wasn't used to men who gave any consideration to how much she'd enjoyed sex—they'd usually been happy just to say they'd *had* her. The wild child.

Luca's voice broke in again. 'You've already come in my arms, so I know what it feels like, but you shut down.'

Serena got hot, recalling the strength of her orgasm when he'd been touching her in the jungle… But that had been different… He hadn't been *inside her*.

And she hadn't been falling for him.

The realisation hit her now, as if she'd been blocking it out. She *was* falling for him—tumbling, in fact. No wonder her body had shut down. It had known before she did. She'd been right to fear his total possession.

She looked at him, shocked, terrified it might be written over her head in neon lights. But he was just raising a brow, waiting for an answer. Oblivious.

Her mind whirling with this new and fragile knowledge, she whispered, 'I told you…it's been a while.'

'What's "a while"?'

Serena stared at him, wanting him to let it go. 'Years—okay? A long time.'

Something in his eyes flashed. 'You haven't had any lovers since you left Italy?'

She shook her head, avoiding his eye again, and said tightly, 'No—and not for a while before that.'

God, this was excruciating!

'The truth is I've never really enjoyed sex. My reputation for promiscuity and sexual prowess was largely based on the stories of men who'd been turned down. I'm afraid I'm not half as debauched as you might think…a lot of talk and not a lot of action.'

Luca was quiet for a long time, and then he said, 'I could tell you weren't that experienced. But you were touted as one of Europe's most licentious socialites and you didn't do much to defend yourself.'

She sent him a dark glance. 'As if anyone would have believed me.' She looked out over the view and felt somehow removed, suspended in space. 'Do you know how I learned to French kiss?'

She could sense Luca going still. 'How?'

Serena smiled but it was bitter, hard. 'One of my father's friends. At a party. He came into my room.'

She let out a shocked gasp when Luca grabbed her shoulders and pulled her around to face him. His face was stark, pale. His reaction took her aback.

'Did he touch you? Did he—?'

Serena shook her head quickly. '*No*. No. My sister Siena was there…we shared a room. She woke up and got into bed beside me and the man left. After that we made sure to lock our door every night.'

Luca's hands were still gripping her shoulders. '*Deus*…Serena.'

He let her go and ran a hand through his hair, looking at her as if she was a stranger. On some deep level Serena welcomed it. The other thing was too scary. Luca looking at her with something approximating gentleness…

She saw a lounger nearby and went over and sat down, pulling her knees up to her chest. Luca stood with his back to the railing, hands in his pockets. Tense.

As if the words were being wrung out of him, he finally said, 'It's not adding up. *You're* not adding up.'

'What's not adding up?' Serena asked quietly, her heart palpitating at Luca's intent look.

'You've had nothing but opportunities to be difficult since you got here and you haven't been. No one can act that well. A child who is medicated for being difficult, wilful…who grows into a wild teenager hell-bent on caus-

ing controversy wherever she goes…that's
not you.'

Serena's heart beat fast. She felt light-headed.
Faintly she said, 'It *was* me.'

Luca was grim. '*Was?* No one changes that
easily, or that swiftly.'

He came over and pulled a chair close, sat
down. Serena knew her eyes had gone wide.
She felt as if she were standing on the edge of
a precipice, teetering, about to fall.

'I want to know, Serena… Why were you
put on medication so young?'

'I told you…after my mother died—'

Luca shook his head. 'There has to be more
to it than that.'

Serena just looked at him. No one had ever
been interested in knowing her secrets before.
In rehab the professionals had been paid to
delve deep, and she'd let them in the interests
of getting better.

Luca was pushing her and pushing her—
and for what? As if he'd welcome her darkest
secrets…

The desire to be vulnerable and allow herself
to confide in him in a way she'd never done before made her scared. It was too much, coming
on the heels of what had just happened. Realising she was falling in love with him when

he was only interested in bedding her. She'd been at pains to let Luca know that this was the real her, and yet she knew well it wasn't. There was a lot more to her. And she couldn't let it out. She felt too fragile.

Acting on a blind instinct to protect herself, Serena stood up abruptly, making Luca tip his head back.

Coldly she said, 'There's nothing more to it—and I thought men didn't like post-coital post-mortems. If we're done here for the evening I'd like to go to bed. I'm tired.'

She went to walk around Luca, her heart hammering, but he grabbed her wrist, stopping her in her tracks. He stood up slowly, eyes narrowed on her.

'What the hell…? *If we're done here for the evening?* What's *that* supposed to mean?'

Serena shrugged and tried to affect as bored a demeanour as possible. 'We've been to the function, we've slept together…' She forced herself to look at him and mocked, 'What more do you want? For me to tuck you in and read you a story?'

Luca's face flushed. He let her wrist go as if it burnt him. He seemed to increase in size in front of her, but instead of intimidating her it only made her more aware of him. He bristled.

'No, sweetheart, I don't want you to tuck me in and read me a story. I want you in my bed at my convenience for as long as I want you.'

He was hard and cruel. And more remote than she could remember ever seeing him. Something inside her curled up tight. But still that instinct to drive him away from seeing too much made her say nonchalantly, 'Well, if it's all the same to you, I'd appreciate spending the rest of the night on my own.'

Liar, her body whispered. Even now between her legs she was getting damp with the desire to feel him surge deep inside her.

So that she could shut down all over again? More humiliation? No, she was doing the right thing.

He came close...close enough to make sweat break out over Serena's skin... If he touched her he'd know how false she was being.

But he stopped just inches away and said, 'We both know that I could have you flat on your back and begging me for release in minutes...a release that you *will* give me next time, Serena.'

He stepped back and Serena felt disorientated. He thought she'd *wilfully* kept herself from being pleasured just to thwart him in some way?

He swept her up and down with a scathing glance. 'But right now I find that my desire has waned.'

He turned and strode back into the apartment and Serena started to shake in reaction. Everything in her wanted to call out to him.

But wasn't this what she wanted? To push him back? The shackles of her past had never felt so burdensome as they did right then. She recognised that they were protecting her, but also imprisoning her.

She could imagine Luca getting changed, walking out through the door, and her gut seized in rejection. Luca was the only person she'd come close to telling everything. She could remember the look on his face just before she'd turned cold. He'd been *concerned*. Until she'd convinced him that she had nothing to say except that she wanted him to leave.

And why wouldn't he leave? He was proud enough to take her at face value. She knew how quickly he damned people—after all he'd damned her for long enough... But that had been changing.

A sense of urgency gripped her—so what if he *did* just want her in his bed? Suddenly Serena knew that in spite of how terrified it made her feel, she desperately wanted to lean on Luca's inherent strength and face these last demons that haunted her still. She was sick of letting her past define her, of being afraid to get too close to anyone in case they saw inside her.

After all, what was the worst that could happen? Luca couldn't look at her any more coldly than he just had. And if he didn't believe her...? Then at least she would have been totally honest.

She heard a movement and saw Luca stride towards the front door, dressed now in black trousers and a black top.

He looked utterly intimidating, but Serena gathered all of her courage, stepped into the apartment again and said, 'Wait, Luca, please. Don't go.'

CHAPTER NINE

LUCA STOPPED AT the door, his hand on the knob. Had he even heard that? Or was it his imagination conjuring up what he wanted to hear from a siren who had him so twisted inside out that he barely knew which way was up any more?

He didn't turn around and forced out a drawl. 'What is it, *minha beleza*? You're ready to come this time?'

He felt dark inside, constricted. He'd really thought he'd seen something incredibly vulnerable in Serena—he'd finally believed that she truly was exactly as she seemed—and then... *wham!* She couldn't have made more of a fool of him if she'd professed undying love and he'd believed her.

There was no sound behind him and he whirled around, anger like a molten surge within him. When he saw the pallor of Serena's cheeks and how huge and bruised her eyes looked he pushed down the concern that rose up to mock him and said scathingly, 'Nice try, *namorada*, but I'm not falling for whatever part you want to play now. Frankly, I prefer a little consistency in my lovers.'

Luca went to turn and leave again, but Serena moved forward jerkily. 'Please, just wait—hear me out.'

He sighed deeply, hating the ball of darkness in his gut. The darkness that whispered to him to run fast and far away from this woman.

He turned around and crossed his arms, arching a brow. 'Well?'

Serena swallowed. Her hair was like a white-gold curtain over her shoulders, touching the swells of her breasts under the robe. Breasts that Luca could taste on his tongue even now.

Incensed that she was catching him like this, and yet still he couldn't walk away, he strode past her over to his drinks cabinet and delivered curtly, 'Spit it out, will you?'

He poured himself a glass of whisky and downed it in one. Hating that she'd even made him feel he needed the sustenance. His hand gripped the glass. He wouldn't look at her again.

'Serena, so help me—'

'You were pushing me to talk...and I didn't

want to. So I pretended just now…pretended that I wanted to be alone. I didn't mean what I said, Luca.'

Luca went very still. An inner voice mocked him. *She's still playing you.* But he recalled the way she'd looked so hunted…just before something had come over her expression and she'd morphed into the ice queen in front of his eyes.

Slowly he put the glass down and turned around. Serena looked shaken. Pale. Yet determined.

'I'm sorry.'

Her voice was husky and it touched on his skin like a caress he wanted to rail against.

He folded his arms. 'Sorry for what?'

She bit her lip. 'I wanted you to think that I'd had enough so you'd leave, but that's not true.'

'Tell me something I *don't* know,' Luca drawled, and saw how she went even paler.

He cursed out loud and went over to her, taking her by the arm and leading her to a couch to sit down.

'Serena, so help me God, if this is just some elaborate—'

'It's not!' she cried, her hands gripped together in her lap. 'It's not,' she said again. 'You were just asking me all these things and I felt threatened… I've never told anyone what happened. I've always been too ashamed and guilty that I didn't do something to stop it. And for a long time I doubted that it had even happened...'

Luca knew now that this was no act. Serena was retreating, her mind far away. Instinctively he reached out and took her hands, wrapping them in his. She looked at him and his chest got tight. *Damn her.*

'What happened?'

Her hands were cold in his and her eyes had never looked bigger or bluer.

'I saw my father kill my mother when I was five years old.'

Luca's mouth opened and closed. 'You *what*?'

Serena couldn't seem to take her eyes off Luca, as if he was anchoring her to something. Her throat felt dry.

'When I was five I heard my parents arguing...nothing new...they argued all the time. I sneaked downstairs to the study. When I looked in through the crack of the door I could see my mother crying. I couldn't understand what they were arguing about, although in hindsight I know it was most likely to do with my father's affairs.'

Luca was grim. 'What happened?' he asked again.

'My father backhanded my mother across the face and she fell... She hit her head on the corner of his desk.'

Serena went inward.

'All I can remember is the pool of blood growing around her head on the rug and how dark it was. And how white she was. I must have made a sound, or something. The next thing I remember is my father dragging me back upstairs. I was crying for my mother... hysterical. My father hit me across the face...I remember one of my baby teeth was loose and it fell out... A doctor arrived. He gave me an injection. I can still remember the pain in my arm... The funeral...everything after that... was blurry. Siena was only three. But I can remember the doctor coming a lot. And once the police came. But I couldn't speak to them. I wanted to tell them what I'd seen but I'd been given something that made me sleepy. It didn't seem important any more.'

Her voice turned bitter.

'He got it covered up, of course, and no one ever accused him of her death. That's when it started. By the time I was twelve my father and his doctor were feeding my medication habit.

They said I had ADHD—that I was difficult to control. Wilful. That it was for my own good. Then my father started saying things like *bipolar*. He was constantly perpetuating a myth of mental uncertainty around me—even to my sister, who always believed that I tried to take my own life.'

'Did you?' Luca's voice was sharp.

Serena shook her head. 'No. But even though I denied it my sister was programmed by then to believe in my instability just like everyone else. My father even made a pretence of not allowing me to take drugs for the condition— while he was maintaining a steady supply to me through the doctor on his payroll.'

Luca shook his head. 'But why didn't you leave when you could?'

Serena pushed down the guilt. She had to start forgiving herself.

'I couldn't see a way out. By the time I was sixteen I was living the script my father had written for me years before.'

She reeled off the headlines of the time.

'I was a *wild child. Impossible to tame. Out of control.* And I was addicted to prescription drugs… Siena was innocent. The good girl. Even now Siena still retains an innocence I never had. My father played us off against each other. If Siena stepped out of line I got the punishment...never her. She was being groomed as the perfect heiress. I was being groomed as the car crash happening in slow motion.'

Luca's hands had tightened over hers and it was only then that Serena realised how icy she'd gone.

'Why haven't you ever gone to the police about your mother's death?'

Shame pricked Serena. 'Who would have believed disgraceful, unstable Serena De-Piero? It felt hopeless. *I* felt hopeless. And in a way I had begun to doubt myself too...had it really happened? Maybe I was dreaming it up? Maybe I *was* just some vacuous socialite hooked on meds?'

Luca was shaking his head and Serena instantly went colder. She'd been a fool to divulge so much. She pulled her hands back.

'You don't believe me.'

Luca's gaze narrowed and his mouth thinned. 'Oh, I believe you, all right. It just about makes sense. And I met your father—he was a cold bastard.' He shook his head. 'He turned you into an addict, Serena.'

Something fragile and treacherous unfurled inside Serena. *Acceptance.*

She said huskily, 'I'm sorry about before. I didn't want to tell you everything.'

'So what changed?'

Serena felt as if she was being backed into a corner again, but this time she fought the urge to escape or to push him away. 'You deserved to know the truth, and I was being less than honest.'

'Less than honest about what?'

He was going to make her say it.

Serena was captivated by Luca's gaze. Time seemed to have slowed to a throbbing heart-beat between them. In the same moment she was aware of a giddy rush through her body— a sense of weightlessness. She'd told someone her innermost secrets and the world hadn't crashed around her.

Serena's belly swooped and she took a leap into the void. 'I didn't want to spend the rest of the night alone. It was just an excuse.'

Luca looked at her and something in his eyes darkened. *Desire*. He cupped her face in his hands and slanted his mouth over hers in a kiss so light that it broke Serena apart more than the most passionate kisses they'd exchanged.

When he pulled back she kept him close and whispered shakily, 'Will you stay, Luca?'

She suddenly needed him desperately—

needed a way to feel rooted when she might float off altogether and lose touch with the earth.

Luca kissed her mouth again and said throatily, 'Yes.'

He stood and pulled Serena up with him, and then he bent and scooped her into his arms as if she weighed no more than a feather. Her arms moved around his neck but she couldn't resist trailing her fingers along his jaw, and then reaching up to press a kiss against the pulse she could see beating under his bronzed skin.

His chest swelled against her breasts and her whole body pulsed with heat and awareness.

He put her down gently by the rumpled bed, where the scent of their bodies lingered in the air, sultry... Even though they'd already made love Serena was trembling as if they hadn't even touched for the first time.

They came together in a kiss of mutual combustion.

There was no time for Serena to worry about her body letting her down again because she was too feverish for Luca—hands spreading out over his bare chest, nails grazing his nipples, causing him to curse softly. Her hands moved to his trousers, and she unzipped them, freeing his erection. She took him in her hand, relishing the steely strength.

Luca's hands were busy too, opening the belt of the robe and sliding it over her shoulders. Serena looked up at him and took her hands away from his body so that the robe could fall to the floor.

His gaze devoured her...hot. Dark colour slashed his cheeks as he tugged his trousers down and off completely, kicking them aside.

He pushed her gently onto the bed. Serena was shocked at how fast her heart was racing, how ragged her breath was.

Gutturally he said, 'I want to take this slow—not like before.'

But Serena was desperate to feel him again. She was ready. She shook her head and whispered, 'I don't want slow. I want *you*.'

He caught her look and said rawly, 'Are you sure?'

She nodded again, and saw his jaw clench as if he was giving up some thin shred of control. He reached for protection and she watched him smooth it onto his erection, an almost feral look on his face.

Serena's sex pulsed with need. She lifted her arms and beckoned him, spreading her legs in a mute appeal.

His eyes flashed and he muttered something indistinct. He leant down to place his hand on her sex, cupping its heat. Serena found his wide shoulders and gripped him, biting her lip.

He spread his fingers and explored her secret folds, releasing the slick heat of her arousal.

His voice was rough. 'You're so ready for me.'

'Please...' said Serena huskily. 'I want you, Luca.'

Every cell in her body felt engorged with blood as he came down over her, pressing her into the bed, his body hard next to her softness. Crushing it deliciously.

He bent his head and took one pebbled nipple into his mouth, his teeth capturing it for a stinging second before letting go to soothe it with his tongue. This teasing was almost unbearable.

Serena was about to sob out another plea when he pushed his thick length inside her. Her eyes widened and she sucked in a breath as he pushed in, relentless, until he was buried inside her.

'You're so tight...like a vice.' He pressed a kiss to her mouth, hot and musky. 'Relax, *preciosa*...'

The endearment did something to Serena.

She felt her body softening around him. He slid even deeper and a look of deep carnal satisfaction crossed his face, making something exult inside her. A sense of her own innately feminine power.

Her nipples scraped against his hair-roughened chest with a delicious friction as Luca started to move in and out, each powerful glide of his body reaching deeper inside Serena to a place she'd locked away long ago. She couldn't take her eyes off him. It was as if he was holding her within his gaze, keeping her rooted in the inexorable building of pleasure.

He reached around to her thigh and brought it up over his hip, his hand smoothing her flesh, then gripping it as his movements became harder, more powerful. That hand crept up and cupped her bottom, kneading, angling her hips, so that he touched some part of her that made her gasp out loud as a tremor of pleasure rocked through her pelvis.

Unconsciously Serena tilted her hips more and Luca moaned deeply. His thrusts became faster and Serena could feel the tight coil of tension inside her, tightening and tightening unbearably, to a point of almost pain.

She was incoherent, only able to stay anchored by looking into Luca's eyes. When she closed hers briefly he commanded roughly, 'Look at me, Serena.'

She did. And something broke apart deep inside her.

Her whole body tautened against his, nerves stretched to screaming point. Luca moved his hand between them, his fingers finding the engorged centre of her desire, and he touched her with a precision that left her nowhere to hide or hang on to. She imploded. Her control was shattered—the control she'd clung to all her life. Since her world had fallen apart as a child, when being *out* of control had become her control.

In one instant it was decimated, and Serena soared high on a wave of bliss that was spectacular. The definition of an orgasm being a *petit mort*, a small death, had never felt so apt. She knew that a part of her had just died and something else incredibly fragile and nebulous was taking its place.

She floated back down to reality, aware of her body milking Luca's own release as he shuddered and buried his head in her shoulder, his body embedded deep within hers. Her legs wrapped around him, and the pulsations of their mutual climaxes took long minutes to die away.

* * *

Luca was in the kitchen the following morning, making breakfast, before he realised that he'd never in his life made breakfast for a lover. In general he liked being in a situation where he could extricate himself rather than have to deal with the aftermath and unwelcome romantic projections.

But here he was, cooking breakfast for Serena without half a second's hesitation or any desire to put as much space between them as possible. His head was still fuzzy from an overload of sensual pleasure and the revelations she'd made.

He couldn't help thinking of her: a little girl, traumatised by the violent death of her mother, with a sadistic and mercurial father who tried to discredit her as soon as he could. Somehow it wasn't that fantastical to believe her father capable of such things.

He thought back to that night when he'd watched Siena come to bail Serena out of jail. The way she had tended to Serena like a mother to her cub...the way Serena had leant on her as if it was a familiar pattern. Both had been manipulated by their father's machinations. Both had been acting out their parts. The good girl and the bad girl.

It all made a sick kind of sense now, because Luca knew he hadn't imagined the vulnerability he'd sensed about her that night he'd first met her...

A sound from behind him made him tense and he turned around to see Serena, tousle-haired and dressed in the robe, standing in the doorway. She looked hesitant, shy, and Luca was falling, losing his grip. Everything he thought he'd known about her...*wasn't*.

His hands gripped the bowl he was using to whisk eggs. 'Hungry?'

'Starving.'

Serena's voice was husky, and it fired up Luca's blood, reminding him of how she'd shouted out his name in the throes of passion just short hours before. How she'd begged and pleaded with him. How she'd felt around him. *Deus*.

Serena came into the kitchen feeling ridiculously shy. Luca looked stern, intense.

'I didn't know you cooked.'

Luca grimaced in a half-smile, some of the intensity in his expression diminishing slightly as he continued whisking. 'I don't...I have a very limited repertoire and scrambled eggs is about as haute cuisine as it gets.'

Serena sat up on a stool by the island and tried not to let herself melt too much at seeing Luca in such a domestic setting in worn jeans and a T-shirt, his hair mussed up and a dark growth of stubble on his jaw.

'Where did you learn?'

He was taking thin strips of bacon now, and placing them under a hot grill. He didn't look at her. 'When my mother left, my father let the housekeeper go; he always felt it was an unnecessary expense.'

Serena felt indignation rise. 'But how did you cope? Did your father cook?'

Luca shook his head. 'I was at boarding school outside Rio for most of the time, so it was only the holidays when I had to fend for myself.' His mouth twisted. 'One of my father's many mistresses took pity on me when she found me eating dry cereal. She taught me some basics. I liked her—she was one of the nicer ones—but she left.'

More sharply than she'd intended, Serena said, 'She wasn't the one who seduced you?'

Luca looked at her, a small smile playing around his hard mouth. 'No.'

Embarrassed by the surge of jealousy, Serena said, 'Your father never married again?'

'No.'

Luca poured some delicious-smelling coffee out of a pot into big mugs, handing her one. Serena bent her head to smell deeply.

'He learnt his lesson after my mother walked away with a small fortune. She'd come from money in Italy, but by then it was almost all gone.'

Serena thought of his parents not even caring which boy went with who and felt sad. She remarked almost to herself, 'I can't imagine how I would have coped if Siena and I had been separated.'

Luca put a plate full of fluffy scrambled eggs and crispy bacon in front of Serena. He looked at her as he settled on his own stool. 'You're close, aren't you?'

Serena nodded, emotional for a second at the thought of her sister and her family. 'Yes, she saved me.'

Luca's gaze sharpened. 'It sounds to me like you saved yourself, as soon as you could.'

Serena shrugged minutely, embarrassed again under Luca's regard. 'I guess I did.' She swallowed some of the delicious food and asked curiously, 'Is your twin brother like you? Determined to right the wrongs of the world?'

Luca sighed heavily. 'Max is...complicated.

He resented me for a long time because my
father insisted on leaving everything to me—
even though I tried to give him half when our
father died. He was too proud to take it.'

Serena shook her head in disbelief, and was
more than touched to know that Luca had been
generous enough to do that.

'He had a tougher time than me—our mother
was completely unstable, lurching from rich
man to rich man in a bid to feather her nest,
and in and out of rehab. Max went from being
enrolled in an exclusive Swiss boarding school
to living on the streets in Rome...'

Serena's eyes widened.

'He pulled himself out of the gutter with
little or no help; he wouldn't accept any from
me and he certainly wouldn't take it from my
father. It was only years later, when he'd made
his first million, that we could meet on common ground.'

Serena put down her knife and fork. Luca
had shown signs of such intransigence and an
inability to forgive when she'd first come to
Rio, but now she was seeing far deeper into
the man and realising he'd had just as much of
a complicated background as she had in many
respects. And yet he'd emerged without being
tainted by the corruption of his father, or by

the vagaries of his mother—vagaries that she understood far too well.

For the first time Serena had to concede that perhaps she hadn't done too badly, considering how easy it would have been to insist on living in a fog, not dealing with reality.

Luca was looking at her with an eyebrow raised. He was waiting for an answer to a question she hadn't heard. She blushed. 'Sorry. I was a million miles away.'

'You said when you first got here that you wanted to see Rio?'

Serena nodded, not sure where this was going or what might happen after last night.

'Well…'

Luca was exhibiting a tiny glimmer of a lack of his usual arrogance and it set Serena's heart beating fast.

'It's the weekend. I'd like to show you Rio.'

The bottom seemed to drop out of Serena's stomach. She felt ridiculously shy again. Something bubbled up inside her—lightness. *Happiness*. It was alien enough to take her by surprise.

'Okay, I'd like that.'

CHAPTER TEN

'HAD ENOUGH YET?'

Serena mumbled something indistinct. This was paradise. Lying on Ipanema Beach as the fading rays of the sun baked her skin and body in delicious heat. There was a low hum of conversation from nearby, the beautiful sing-song cadence of Portuguese, people were laughing, sighing, talking. The surf of the sea was crashing against the shore.

And then she felt Luca's mouth on hers and her whole body orientated itself towards his. She opened her eyes with an effort to find him looking down at her. Her heart flip-flopped. She smiled.

'Can we stay for the sunset?'

Luca was trying to hang on to some semblance of normality when the day that had just passed had veered out of *normal* for him on so many levels it was scary.

'Sure,' he said, with an easiness belying his trepidation. Serena's open smile was doing little to restore any sense of equilibrium.

One day spent walking around Rio and then a couple of hours on the beach was all it had taken to touch her skin with a luminous golden glow. Her hair looked blonder, almost white, her blue eyes were standing out even more starkly.

That morning they had taken the train up through the forest to the Cristo Redentor on Corcovado and Serena had been captivated by every tiny thing. Standing at the railing, looking down over the breathtaking panorama of Rio, she'd turned to him and asked, with a look of gleaming excitement that had reminded him of a child, 'Can we go to the beach later?'

Luca's insides had tightened ominously. She didn't want to go shopping. She wanted to see Rio. Genuinely.

Before they'd hit the beach they'd eaten lunch at a favourite café of Luca's. At one point he'd sat back and asked, with an increasing sense of defeat, 'Your family really aren't funding you...are they?'

Immediate affront had lit up those piercing eyes. Luca wouldn't have believed it before.

But he did now, and it had made something feel dark and heavy inside him.

'Of course not.' She'd flushed then, guiltily, and admitted with clear reluctance, 'My sister and her husband paid for an apartment for me in Athens...when I was ready to move on. But I'm going to pay them back as soon as I've made enough money.'

Darkness had twisted inside Luca. People got hand-outs all the time from family, yet she clearly hated to admit it. And this was a woman who had had everything...a vast fortune to inherit...only to lose it all.

She'd flushed self-consciously when she'd caught him looking at her cleared plate of *feijoãda*, a famous Brazilian stew made with black beans and pork. 'My sister is the same. It's a reaction to the tiny portions of food we were allowed to eat by our father, growing up.'

Her revelation had hit him hard again. The sheer abuse her father had subjected her to. Anger still simmered in his belly. Luca had felt compelled to reach out and take her hand, entwining his fingers with hers—something that had felt far too easy and necessary.

'Believe me, it's refreshing to see a woman enjoy her food.'

Her hand had tensed in his and she'd said,

far too lightly, while avoiding his eyes, 'I'm sure the women you know are far more restrained.'

Was she jealous? The suspicion had caught at Luca somewhere deeply masculine. And that deeply masculine part of him had been triggered again when he'd insisted on buying her a bikini so she could swim at the beach, as they hadn't been prepared.

He took her in now, as she lay beside him, the three tiny black triangles doing little to help keep his libido in check. He was just glad that the board shorts he'd bought to swim in were roomy enough to disguise his rampant response.

As if aware of his scrutiny Serena fidgeted, trying to pull the bikini over her breasts more—which only made some of the voluptuous flesh swell out at the other side.

Luca bit back a groan.

She'd hissed at him in the shop, 'I'm not wearing that—it's indecent!'

Luca had drawled wryly, 'Believe me, when you see what most women wear on the beaches here you'll feel overdressed.'

And when they'd hit the sand Serena's reaction had been priceless. Mouth open, eyes popping out of her head, she'd watched the undeniably sensual parade of beautiful bodies up and down the beach.

Luca hadn't been unaware of the blatant interest her pale blonde beauty had attracted, and had stared down numerous men.

The sun was setting now, and people were starting to cheer and clap as it spread out in a red ball of fire over the horizon, just to the left of one of Rio's craggy peaks.

Serena sat up and drew her legs to her chest, wrapping her arms around them. She smiled at Luca, before taking in the stunning sunset and clapping herself. 'I love how they do that.'

Her pleasure in something so simple mocked his deeply rooted cynicism. And then Luca realised then that he was enjoying this too, but it had been a long time since he'd taken the time to appreciate it. Even when he'd been younger he'd been so driven to try and counteract his father's corrupt legacy that he'd rarely taken any time out for himself. He'd fallen into a pattern of choosing willing women who were happy with no-strings-attached sex to alleviate any frustration.

He'd never relaxed like this in a typical *arioca* way, with a beautiful woman.

The sun had set and she looked at him now, and all he could see was the damp golden hair trailing over her shoulders, close to the full thrust of her breasts. Her mouth, like a crushed rose petal, was begging to be tasted. And those wide eyes were looking at him with a wariness that only fired his libido even more.

He said roughly, 'Let's get out of here.'

Serena couldn't mistake the carnal intent in Luca's eyes. He'd been looking at her all day as if he'd never seen her before. And today… today had been like a dream.

Her skin felt tight from the sun and sea, and she didn't know if it was just Luca's unique effect on her, or the result of watching the Rio natives embrace their sensuality and sexuality all afternoon, but right now she trembled with the sexual need that pulsed through her very core and blood.

'Yes,' she said.

She stood up, and Luca stood too, handing her the sundress she'd put on that morning.

They walked the short distance back to Luca's car and when he took her hand in his, Serena's fingers tightened around his reflexively. He wore an open shirt over his chest, still in his shorts, and her heart clenched because he looked so much younger and more carefree than the stern, intimidating man she'd met again the day she'd arrived in Rio.

When they began winding up through the hills, away from the beaches, Serena asked, 'Where is this?'

Luca glanced at her. 'We're going to my home in Alto Gavea. It's closer.'

Serena's heart beat fast. *His home.*

The rest of the drive was in silence, as if words were superfluous and might not even penetrate the thick sensual tension between them.

This part of Rio was encased in forest, reminding Serena of the rainforest with a sharp poignancy. And Luca's home took her breath away when he turned in to a long secluded drive behind fortified gates.

It was an old colonial house, two-storey, white, with terracotta slates on the roof, and it was set, literally, in the middle of the lush Tijuca Forest.

He pulled the car to a stop and looked at her for a long moment. They were suspended in time, with no sounds except for the calls of some birds.

Then he broke the spell and got out of the car, helping Serena out of the low-slung seat. She let out a small squeal of surprise when he scooped her up into his arms and navigated opening the front door with commendable dexterity.

He took the stairs two at a time and strode into a massive bedroom. Serena only had time to take in an impression of a house that was cool and understated. In his room, the open shutters framed a view showcasing the illuminated Christ the Redeemer statue in the far distance on its hill overlooking Rio.

Everything became a little dream-like after that, and Serena knew that on some level she was shying away from analysing the significance of the day that had passed.

Luca put her down, only to disappear into a bathroom, where she heard the sound of a shower running. When he emerged he was taking off his clothes until he stood before her naked, unashamedly masculine and proud.

'Come here.'

She obeyed without question. When she stood before him he reached down for the hem of her dress and pulled it up and off. Then he turned her around and undid her flimsy bikini top so that it fell to the floor.

He turned her back and hooked his fingers into the bottoms, and pulled them down until she could step out of them at her feet. In that moment, naked, she'd never felt more womanly or more whole. Or more free of the shadows that had dogged her for as long as she could remember. They weren't gone completely, but it was enough for now.

He took her hand and led her into the bathroom, which was fogged with steam that curled over their sticky, sandy bodies. Standing under the hot spray, Serena lifted her face and Luca covered her mouth with his, his huge body making the space tiny.

When he took his mouth off hers she opened her eyes to see his hot gaze devouring her. And just like that she was ready, her body ripening and moistening for him, ravenous at the sight of Luca's gleaming wet and aroused body. He lifted her and instructed her to put her legs around him—then groaned and stopped.

She looked at him, breathless with anticipation. 'What's wrong?'

'No protection, *preciosa*. We need to move.'

Serena was dazed as he carried her out of the shower, her legs still wrapped around his waist. She could see the pain on his face at the interruption but she was glad... She'd been too far gone to think about protection herself.

He put her down on the bed and reached for a condom from his cabinet, ripping the foil and sheathing himself with big, capable hands. Serena felt completely wanton as she watched this display of masculine virility.

And then he was coming back down over her, pushing her legs apart, settling between them, asking huskily, 'Okay?'

She nodded, her chest tightening ominously, and then Luca was thrusting in so deep her back arched and her legs went around his waist. It was fast and furious, his gaze holding hers, not letting her look away.

Bliss broke over her after mere minutes. She was so primed—as if now it was the easiest thing in the world and not something that had been torturously elusive when they'd first made love.

Serena bit into Luca's shoulder as powerful spasms racked her body just as he reached his own climax, his body thrusting rhythmically against hers until he was spent. He collapsed over her and she tightened her arms and legs around him, loving the feel of him pressing her into the bed, his body still big inside hers.

Eventually he withdrew, and Serena winced as her muscles protested. Luca collapsed on his back beside her, his breathing as uneven as hers. She looked at him to find him watching her with a small enigmatic smile playing around her mouth.

He came up on one arm and touched his fingers to her jaw. 'You make me lose my mind every time...' he admitted gruffly.

Serena looked at him. Somehow his confession wasn't as comforting as she'd thought it might be. It left her with a definite sense that Luca did not welcome such a revelation.

And then he was kissing her again, wiping everything from her mind, and she welcomed it weakly. She was far too afraid to face the suspicion that she had fallen in love with this man and there was no going back.

Three days later

'Miss DePiero? Senhor Fonseca said to let you know that he's been unavoidably detained and you should eat without him.'

'Okay, thank you.' Serena put down the kitchen phone extension and looked at the chicken stew she'd made, bubbling on the state-of-the-art cooker. *Unavoidably detained.* What was that code for?

Crazy to feel so disappointed, but she did. She'd spent her lunch hour buying ingredients, and as soon as she'd finished work at the charity office she'd rushed back to start cooking.

And now she felt ridiculous—because wasn't this such a cliché? The little woman at home, cooking dinner for her man and getting all bent out of shape because it was spoiled?

Mortified at the thought of what Luca's reaction would have been to see this attempt at creating some kind of domestic idyll, and losing any appetite herself, Serena took the chicken stew off the cooker. When it had cooled sufficiently she resisted the urge to throw it away and put it into a bowl to store in the fridge.

Feeling antsy, she headed outside to the terrace. The stunning view soothed her in a way that Athens had never done, even though she now called it home.

'*Maledire*,' she cursed softly in Italian. And then she cursed Luca, for making her fall for him.

The weekend had been...*amazing*. She remembered Luca kissing the tattoo on her shoulder. He'd murmured to her, 'You know the swallow represents resurrection?'

Serena had nodded her head, feeling absurdly emotional that he *got it*.

When they'd woken late on Sunday Luca had told her that he had to visit a local *favela* and she'd asked to go with him. She had seen first-hand his commitment to his own city. The amazing Fonseca Community Centre that provided literacy classes, language classes, business classes and a crèche so that everyone in the community could learn.

When she'd gone wandering, left alone briefly, she'd found Luca in the middle of a ring of men, doing *capoeira*, a Brazilian form of martial arts. He'd been stripped to the waist, his torso gleaming with exertion, making graceful and unbelievably agile movements to the beat of a drum played by a young boy.

She hadn't been the only woman ogling his spectacular form. By the time he'd finished, a gaggle of women and girls had been giggling and blushing. But a trickle of foreboding had skated over her skin… That had been the moment when he'd caught her eye and she'd seen something indecipherable cross his face. By the time he'd caught up with her again there had been something different about him. He'd shut down.

He'd brought her back here, to this apartment, and even though he'd stayed the night and made love to her, something had been off. When she'd woken he'd been gone, and she hadn't seen him again until late that evening, when he'd arrived and, with an almost feral look on his face, had kissed her so passionately that all tendrils of concern had fled, to be replaced with heat, distracting her from the fact that he clearly hadn't been interested in anything else.

The truth was that every moment she spent with Luca was ripping her apart internally. Especially when he looked at her as if she were some kind of unexploded device, yet kissed her as if his life depended on it. Clearly he was conflicted about her. He'd admitted that it was hard for him to come to terms with the fact that she wasn't what he'd believed her to be. And Serena had the gut-wrenching feeling that Luca would have almost preferred it if she *had* been the debauched, spoilt princess he'd expected.

She had to face the fact that her confession, while liberating for her, had not proved to be so cataclysmic for Luca.

And of *course* it wouldn't have been, Serena chided herself. For Luca this was just…an affair. A slaking of desire. The fact that it had brought about her own personal epiphany was all Serena would have to comfort her when it was over, and that would have to be enough.

When Luca walked into the apartment it was after midnight. He felt guilty. He knew Serena had been making dinner because she'd told him earlier, when he'd seen her on a visit to the charity offices. It was a visit that had had his employees looking at him in surprise, because he usually conducted meetings in his own office and had little cause to visit them.

The apartment was silent, but he could smell the faint scent of something delicious in the air. When he went into the kitchen it was pristine, but he opened the fridge and saw the earthenware bowl containing dinner. The thought that perhaps she hadn't eaten because he hadn't been there made him feel guiltier. He hadn't even known that Serena could cook until she'd told him she'd taken lessons in Athens.

And he hadn't known how deeply enmeshed he was becoming with her until he'd looked at her in the *favela* and the enormity of it all had hit him. It had taken seeing her against that dusty backdrop—Serena DePiero, ex-socialite and wild child, looking as comfortable in the incongruous surroundings as if she'd been born into them like a native. In spite of the white-blonde beauty that had set her apart. He'd certainly been aware of the men looking at her, and the same black emotion that had gripped him at the beach had caught him again.

Jealousy. For the first time.

It was in that moment that a very belated

sense of exposure had come over him and made him pull back from a dangerous brink. Luca knew better than anyone how fickle people were—how you couldn't trust that they wouldn't just pull your world out from under your feet within seconds.

His own parents had done it to him and his brother—setting them on different paths of fate almost as idly as if they were Greek gods, playing with hapless mortals. For years he'd had nightmares about his parents pulling them limb from limb, until their body parts were so mixed up that they didn't even know who was who any more.

Serena was getting too close—under his skin. Everything kept coming back to how badly he'd misjudged her—and never more so than now. He'd just had a conversation with his brother, who was in Rio on business.

And yet as he stood in the doorway of her bedroom now and saw the shape of her under the covers, the bright splash of white-blonde hair, he was taking off his clothes before he even realised what he was doing, sliding in behind her, wrapping himself around her and trying desperately to ignore the way his soul felt inexplicably soothed.

Even as she woke and turned towards him,

her seeking sleepy mouth finding his, Luca was steeling himself inside—because this would all be over as soon as she knew what his brother had just told him. Because then everything that had bound them from the past would be gone.

But just…not yet.

When Serena woke in the dawn light, the bed was empty. But the hum in her body and the pleasurable ache between her legs told her she hadn't dreamt that Luca had come into her bed last night. Or dreamt the mindless passion he'd driven her to, taking her over the edge again and again, until she'd been spent, exhausted, begging for mercy.

It was as if Luca had been driven by something desperate.

She blinked, slowly coming awake. And even though her body was sated and lethargic from passion, her heart was heavy. She loved Luca, and she knew with cold certainty that he didn't love her. But he wanted her.

His love was his commitment to the environment, to making the world a better place in whatever small way he could, born from his zeal not to be like his predecessors—a zeal she could empathise with.

And Serena knew that she wouldn't be able to continue falling deeper and deeper without recognising that the heartbreak would be so much worse when she walked away.

It was only when she sighed deeply and moved her head that she felt something, and looked to see a note on the pillow beside her. She reached for the thick paper and opened it to read:

Please meet me in my office when you wake. L.

A definite shiver of foreboding tightened Serena's skin. No wonder there had been something desperate in Luca's lovemaking last night. This was it. He was going to tell her it was over. The signs had been there for the last few days, since the *favela*.

Anger lanced her. To think that he would just send her away so summarily after sating his desire, which was obviously on the wane, and after she'd enjoyed working in the charity office so much. But, as much as she'd come to love Rio de Janeiro, she didn't relish the thought of being in such close proximity to him in the future—seeing him get on with his life, take another lover.

She wasn't going to let him discard her completely, though; no matter what had happened between them personally he owed her a job. In any event, she knew now that she had to go home. So, while Luca might be preparing to let her go, Serena told herself stoutly that she was ready.

It was only when she noticed her hands trembling in the shower that she had to admit her anger was stemming from a place of deep fear that she was about to feel pain such as she'd never felt before—not even when she'd been at her lowest ebb, trapped by her addictions. Before, she'd anaesthetised herself against the pain. Now she would have nothing to cling on to, and she wasn't sure how ready she was to cope with that.

CHAPTER ELEVEN

WHEN SERENA KNOCKED on Luca's office door about an hour later she felt composed, dressed in plain trousers and a silk shirt. Hair tied back. It had been a mere two weeks since she'd come here for the first time, but she was a different person.

Damn him.

His assistant opened the door and ushered her in, and it took a second after the girl had left for Serena to realise that there was another man in the room. He was standing on the other side of Luca's desk, and Luca stood up now from his high-backed chair.

'Serena—come in.'

Her heart lurched. So formal. For a crazy moment Serena wondered if the other man was a solicitor, so that Luca could get out of the contract?

When she came closer, though, she saw a resemblance between the two men, even though

this man had tawny eyes and dark blond messy
hair. They were almost identical in size and
build. The stranger was as arrestingly gorgeous as Luca, but in a more traditional way—
in spite of the scar she could see running from
his temple to his jaw. He oozed danger, even
though he looked as if he might have stepped
from the pages of Italian *Vogue* in an immac-
ulate dark suit.

She sensed a subtle tension in the air, and
had just realised herself who he was when
Luca said, 'This is my brother—Max Fonseca Roselli.'

She came forward and took the hand offered
to her, suffering none of the physical reaction Luca caused within her with only a look.
Even so, she saw the unmistakably apprecia-
tive gleam in his unusual golden-green eyes
and could well imagine that he must leave a
trail of bleeding hearts wherever he went. He
had that same indomitable arrogance that Luca
wore so well.

'Nice to meet you.'

His hand squeezed hers. 'You too.'

Serena pulled away, getting hot, sensing
Luca's intense focus on them and Max's de-
sire to needle his brother. When she looked at
Luca, though, he gave nothing away and she

cursed herself. Of *course* he wouldn't be pro-prietorial or jealous.

Luca indicated for them to sit down and said heavily, 'Max has some news for you...and me. I thought I owed it to you to let him tell you face to face.'

Now Serena was nervous, and she looked from him to Max and back. 'What is it?'

Luca explained. 'I asked Max to look into what happened at the club that night—to do some digging.'

Before she could properly assimilate that information, Max drawled in a deep voice, 'My brother knows I have some...less than legitimate connections.'

Serena looked at him and her heart went out to both of them for what they'd been through as children. The way their parents had all but rolled the dice to decide their fate.

Huskily she admitted, 'I... Luca told me what happened.'

Max's eyes flared and he shot his brother a scowl.

Luca said warningly, 'This isn't about *us*.'

For a second Serena could have laughed. They might not be identical, but right then she could see how similar they were—and they probably didn't even know it themselves.

Max looked back to her. 'I did some digging and discovered who did plant the drugs on Luca that night. He was a small-time dealer and in the crush he spotted you together. He knew that if he could plant the drugs on you or Luca no one would ever dispute that you had been involved.'

Shame lanced Serena to be reminded that everyone knew of her exploits and how tarnished her reputation was, even as her heart beat fast and she wondered why Luca had asked his brother to do this.

Max continued. 'He's actually in jail at the moment on another charge, and he's been bragging to anyone who will listen about how he set you and Luca up—it would appear that he couldn't bear to keep such a coup to himself. He's been charged with the offence and hasn't a leg to stand on because he's confessed to so many witnesses.'

For a moment the relief was so enormous that Serena felt dizzy, even though she was sitting down. She looked at Luca, whose face was stern. 'You can clear your name.'

He nodded, but he didn't look happy about it. He looked grim.

Max stood up, rising with athletic grace. 'My flight leaves in a couple of hours. I have to go.'

Serena stood up too. 'Thank you so much. This means…a lot.'

Max inclined his head before sending an enigmatic look to his brother. 'I'll be in touch.'

Luca nodded. They didn't embrace or shake hands before Max left, striding out with that same confident grace as his brother.

When he was gone, Serena sank down onto the chair, her head in a spin. She looked at Luca, barely taking in that he looked a little pale, his face all lean lines. 'How…? Why did you ask him to do this?'

He sighed heavily. 'Because I owed it to you to find out the truth. After all, you've been nothing but honest with me. The fact is that I think I suspected you were innocent in the jungle. This just proves that you were as much a victim as I was. You deserve to have your life back, Serena. And you deserve to have the slate cleared too. My lawyers and my PR team will make sure this is in all the papers.'

Serena felt an almost overwhelming surge of emotion to think that Luca was going out of his way to clear her name too. Perhaps now people wouldn't always associate her with feckless debauchery.

Treacherously, this made her hope for too much, even when *The End* was written into

every tense line of Luca's body. Clearly he just
wanted to move on now.

It made her want to push him away again,
for making her feel too much. For making her
fall in love. *Damn him.*

'And if Max hadn't found the culprit so easily? Would you have believed me anyway?'

Luca stood up and paced behind his desk,
his white shirt pulled across his chest, trousers
hugging slim hips. Just like that, heat flared in
Serena's solar plexus.

He stopped and looked at her. 'Yes.'

Serena cursed herself for pushing him. She
hated herself for the doubt, for thinking that
he was lying. And then she had to concede
that Luca *didn't* lie. He was too moral. Too
damn good.

She stood up again, her legs wobbly. 'Well,
thank you for finding out.'

Luca looked at her for a long moment, and
then he said, 'Serena—'

She put up her hand, because she couldn't
bear for him to say it. 'Wait. I have something
I need to tell you first.'

His mouth closed and he folded his arms
across his chest. Serena knew she couldn't be
anything else other than completely honest.
She had been through too much soul-search-

ing to ever want to hide away from pain again. She might never see him again. The urge to tell him how she felt was rising like an unstoppable wave.

'I've fallen in love with you, Luca.'

He looked at her, and as she watched, the colour leached from his face. She broke apart inside, but was determined not to show it.

'I know it's the last thing you want to hear. We were only ever about...' she stalled '...not *that*...and I know it's over.'

She gestured with a hand to where Max had been sitting.

'After this...we owe each other nothing. And I'm sorry again that your association with me made things bad for you.'

Luca unfolded his arms and slashed a hand in the air, looking angry. 'You don't have to apologise—if I hadn't been so caught up in blaming you, I would have ensured a proper investigation was carried out years ago. You had to suffer the stigma of those accusations too.'

Serena smiled bitterly. 'I was used to it, though. I had no reputation to defend.'

'No—your father took care of that.'

Responsibility weighed heavily on her shoulders. 'I have to go home... I have to tell people about my father—see that he's brought to justice finally.'

'If there's anything you need help with, please let me know.'

Her heart twisted. So polite. So courteous. A million miles from their first meeting in this office. And even though she knew her own family would be there to back her up, she felt an awful quiver of vulnerability—because, really, the only person she wanted by her side the day she faced her father again was Luca.

But that scenario was not to be part of her future.

She hitched up her chin and tried to block out the fact that she'd told Luca she loved him and had received no similar declaration in return. That fantasy belonged deep where she harboured dreams of the kind of fulfilment and happiness she saw her sister experiencing with her family. But at least she could take one good thing with her.

'Are you still going to give me a job?'

'Of course—wherever you want,' Luca said quickly, making another piece of Serena's heart shatter. He was obviously *that* eager to see her go.

'I'd like to go back to Athens today.'

Luca said tightly, 'Laura will arrange it for you.'

'Thank you.'

So clipped, so polite.

Before anger could rise at Luca's non-reaction to her baring her soul to him, she turned to leave.

She was at the door before she heard a broken-sounding, 'Serena...'

Heart thumping, hope spiralling, Serena turned around. Luca looked tortured.

But he said only two words. 'I'm sorry.'

Her heart sank like a stone. She knew he didn't love her, but she marvelled that the human spirit was such an irrepressibly optimistic thing even in the face of certain disappointment.

She forced a smile. 'Don't be. You've given me the gift of discovering how strong I am.'

You've given me the gift of discovering how strong I am.

Luca was stuck in a state of paralysis for so long after Serena left that he had to blink and focus to realise that Laura was in his office and speaking to him, looking worried.

'Senhor Fonseca? Are you all right?'

And as if he'd been holding something at

bay, it ripped through him then, stunning and painful in its intensity, like warmth seeping into frozen limbs. Burning.

'No,' he issued curtly, going over to his drinks cabinet and helping himself to a shot of whisky.

When he turned around, Laura's eyes were huge and she was pale. And Luca knew he was coming apart at the seams.

He forced himself not to snarl at the girl, but the pain inside him was almost crippling. 'What is it?'

Laura stuttered, making him feel even worse. 'It's—it's Miss DePiero. I just thought you'd want to know she's on her way to the airport. She's booked first class on a flight to Athens this afternoon.'

'Thank you,' Luca bit out. 'I'm going to be unavailable for the rest of the day. Please cancel all my appointments. Go home early if you want.'

Laura blinked and said faintly, 'Yes, sir.' And then backed away as if he might explode.

He waited until Laura had left and then left himself, knowing nothing more than that he needed to get out—get away. Because he felt like a wounded animal that might lash out and cause serious harm.

He was aware of one or two people approaching him as he walked out of the building, but they quickly diverted when they saw his face. He walked and walked without even knowing where he was going until he realised he was at Ipanema Beach. Where he'd taken Serena just a few days ago.

The scene was the same, even during the week. The beautiful bodies. The amorous couples. The crashing waves. But it mocked him now, for feeling so carefree that day. For believing for a moment that he could be like those people. That he could *feel* like them.

Anger rose up as he ripped off his tie and jacket, dropping them on a bench and sitting down. That was the problem. He knew he couldn't feel. The ability had been cut out of him the day he and his brother had been torn apart.

As young boys they'd been close enough to have a special language that only they understood. It had used to drive their father crazy. And Luca could remember that they'd sensed something was happening that day when their parents had brought them into their father's study.

Luca's mother had bent down to his level and said, with the scent of alcohol on her breath,

'Luca, darling, I love you so much I want to take you to Italy with me. Will you come?'

He'd looked at Max, standing near his father. Luca had known that Max loved their mother—he had too—but he didn't like it when she came home drunk and falling down. He and Max would fight about it—Max hating it if Luca said anything critical, which he was more liable to do.

He'd looked back at his mother, confused. 'But what about Max? Don't you love him too?'

She'd been impatient. 'Of course I do. But Max will stay here with your father.'

Panic had clutched at his insides, making him feel for a moment as if his bowels might drop out of his body. 'For ever?'

She'd nodded and said, slurring slightly, 'Yes, *caro,* for ever. We don't need them, do we?'

Luca had heard a noise and looked to see Max, ashen, eyes glimmering with tears. 'Mamma…?'

She'd made an irritated sound and said something in rapid Italian, taking Luca by the hand forcibly, as if to drag him out. Luca had felt as if he was in some kind of nightmare. Max had started crying in earnest and had run to their mother, clutching at her waist. That was when Luca had felt some kind of icy calm come over him—as if Max was acting out how he felt deep inside, but he couldn't let it out. It was too huge.

His mother had issued another stream of Italian and let Luca go, shoving him towards his father, prising Max off her and saying angrily, '*Bastante!* Stop snivelling. I'll take you with me instead. After all,' she'd said snidely over Max's hiccups, 'your father doesn't care *who* he gets...'

The black memory faded. His mother had told him she loved him and then minutes later she'd demonstrated how empty her words were. Swapping one brother for the other as if choosing objects in a shop.

Serena had told him she loved him.

As soon as she'd said the words, Luca had been transported back to that room, closing in on himself, waiting for the moment when she'd turn around and show him that she didn't mean it. Not really. She was only saying it because that was what women did, wasn't it? They had no idea of the devastation they could cause when the emptiness of their words was revealed.

But she hadn't looked blasé. Nor as if she

hadn't meant it. She'd been pale. Her blue eyes had looked wounded when he'd said, 'I'm sorry.'

He thought of her words: *You've made me see how strong I am.*

Luca felt disgusted. And how strong was *he*? Had he ever gone toe-to-toe with his own demons? No, because he'd told himself building up trust in the Fonseca name again was more important.

He heard a sound and looked up to see a plane lifting into the sky from the airport. He knew it couldn't be her plane, but he had a sudden image of her on it, leaving, and panic gripped him so acutely that he almost called out.

It was as clear as day to him now—what lay between him and his brother. He should have ranted and railed that day when their parents had so cruelly split them up. He should have let it out—not buried it so deep that he'd behaved like a robot since then, afraid to feel anything. Afraid to face the guilt of knowing that he could have done more to protect them both.

If he'd let out the depth of his anger and pain, as Max had, then maybe they wouldn't have been split apart. Two halves of a whole, torn asunder. Maybe their parents would have been forced to acknowledge the shallow depths of their actions, their intent of scoring points off each other.

It all bubbled up now—and also the sick realisation that he was letting it happen all over again. That while he'd had an excuse of sorts before, because he'd only been a child, he was an adult now—and if he couldn't shout and scream for what he wanted then he and Max had been pawns for nothing.

And, worse, he'd face a life devoid of any meaning or any prospect of happiness. Happiness had never concerned him before now. He'd been content to focus on loftier concerns, telling himself it was enough. And it wasn't. Not any more.

Serena stood in line for the gate in the first-class lounge. She was grateful for it, because there was enough space there for her to feel numb and not to have to deal with a crush of people around her.

She couldn't let herself think of Luca, even though her circling thoughts kept coming back to him and that stark look on his face. *I'm sorry.*

She was sorry too. Now she knew how he'd

felt when he'd told her that he wished he'd never set eyes on her.

She wanted to feel that way too—she actively encouraged it to come up. But it wouldn't. Because she couldn't regret knowing him. Or loving him. Even if he couldn't love her back.

For a wild moment Serena thought of turning around and going back, telling him she'd settle for whatever he could give her... And then she saw herself in a few years...months...? Her soul shrivelled up from not being loved in return.

The man ahead of her moved forward and the airline steward was reaching for her boarding pass.

She was about to take it back and go through when she heard a sort of commotion, and then a familiar voice shouting, 'I need to see her!'

She whirled around to see Luca being restrained by two staff members a few feet away, dishevelled and wild-looking in shirt and trousers.

'What are you *doing*?' she gasped in shock, stepping out of the way so that people could continue boarding.

She wouldn't let her heart beat fast. She couldn't. It didn't mean anything.

His eyes were fierce. 'Please don't go. I need you to stay.'

A feeling of euphoria mixed with pain surged through her. 'Why do you want me to stay, Luca?'

The men holding him kept a tight grip. Luca didn't even seem to notice, though. He looked feverish, as if he was burning up.

His voice was rough with emotion. 'When you told me you loved me...I couldn't believe it. I was too afraid to believe. My mother said that to me right before she swapped me for my brother...as if we were nothing.'

Serena's belly clenched. 'Oh, Luca...' She looked at the security men, beseeching, 'Please let him go.'

They finally did, but stayed close by, ready to move in again. Serena didn't care. She was oblivious.

He took her hand and held it to his chest, dragging her closer. She could feel his heart thudding against his chest.

'You say you love me...but a part of me can't trust it...can't believe it. I'm terrified that you'll turn around one day and walk away— confirm all my twisted suspicions that when people say they love you, they'll annihilate you anyway.'

Serena felt an incredible welling of love and reached out her other hand to touch Luca's face. She knew he was scared.

'Do you love me?'

After a long moment—long enough for her to see how hard this was for him to admit—he said, 'The thought of you leaving, of life without you...is more than I can bear. If that's love then, yes, I love you more than I've loved anyone else.'

Serena's heart overflowed. 'Are you willing to let me prove how much I love you?'

Luca nodded. 'The pain of letting you go is worse than the pain of facing my own pathetic fears. You've humbled me with your strength and grace.'

She shook her head, tears making her vision blurry. 'They're not pathetic fears, Luca. I'm just as scared as you are.'

He smiled, and it was shaky, all that arrogant bravado replaced by raw emotion. He joked, 'You? Scared? Not possible. You're the bravest person I know. And I have no intention of ever letting you out of my sight again.'

Serena smiled and fought back tears as Luca pulled her in to him and covered her mouth with his, kissing her with unrestrained passion.

When they separated, the crowd around

them clapped and cheered. Giddy, Serena blushed and ducked her head against Luca's neck.

He looked at her. 'Will you come home with me?'

Home. Her own place—with him.

The ferocity and speed with which they'd found each other terrified her for a moment. *Could she trust it?* But she saw everything she felt mirrored in Luca's eyes, and she reached out and snatched the dream before it could disappear.

'Yes.'

The next day when Serena woke up she pulled on a big T-shirt and went looking for Luca in his house in Alto Gavea. She still felt a little dizzy from everything that had happened. She and Luca had come back here from the airport, and after making love they'd talked until dawn had broken. He'd promised to go to Athens with her to start the lengthy process of telling her family everything and pursuing her father.

She heard a noise as she passed his study and went in to see him sitting behind his desk in only jeans. Stubbled jaw. He looked up and smiled, and Serena couldn't help smiling back goofily.

He held out a hand. 'Come here.'

She went over and let him catch her, pulling her onto his lap. After some breathless kisses she moved back. 'What are you doing?'

A glint of something came into his eyes and he said, 'Catching up on local news.'

He indicated with his head to the computer and Serena turned to look. When she realised what she was seeing, she tensed in his arms. The internet was filled with photos of them kissing passionately in the airport—obviously taken by people's mobile phones. One headline screamed: *Has Fonseca tamed wild-child DePiero at last?* Another one: *Fonseca and DePiero rekindle their scandalous romance!*

She felt sick and turned to Luca, who was watching her carefully. 'I'm sorry. This is exactly what you were afraid of.'

But he just shrugged, eyes bright and clear. No shadows. 'I couldn't care less what they say. And they have it wrong—you tamed *me*.'

Serena let the past fall away and caressed Luca's jaw, love rising to make her throat tight. 'I love you just as you are.'

Luca said gruffly, 'I want to take you to every beach in South America to watch the sunset—starting with the ones here in Rio.'

Serena felt breathless. 'That could take some time.'

Luca kissed her and said, 'At least a lifetime, I'm hoping.'

He deliberately lifted up her left hand then, and pressed a kiss to her ring finger, a question in his eyes and a new tension in his body. Serena's heart ached that he might still doubt her love.

She nodded her head and said simply, 'Yes. The answer will always be yes, my love.'

Three years later.

The wide-eyed American reporter was standing in front of Rome's supreme court and saying breathlessly, 'This is the trial of the decade— if not the century. Lorenzo DePiero has finally been judged and condemned for his brutality and corruption, but no one could have foreseen the extent to which his own children and his wife suffered. His landmark sentencing will almost certainly guarantee that he lives out the rest of his days in jail.'

The press were still stunned to have discovered that the privileged life they'd assumed the DePiero heiresses to have lived had all been a lie.

Behind the reporter there was a flurry of activity as people streamed out of the majestic building. First was Rocco De Marco, the illegitimate son of Lorenzo DePiero, with his petite red-haired wife Gracie. Quickly on their heels were Siena Xenakis and her husband Andreas.

But the press waited with hushed reverence for the person they wanted to see most: Serena Fonseca. She had taken the stand for four long days in a row and had listed a litany of charges against her father. Not least of which had been the manslaughter of his wife, their mother, witnessed by her when she was just five years old.

If anyone had been in doubt about the reliability of a witness who had been only five at the time, the further evidence of her father's systematic bullying and collusion with a corrupt doctor to get her hooked on medication had killed those doubts.

Her composed beauty had been all the more poignant for the fact that she hadn't let her very advanced pregnancy stop her from taking on such an arduous task: facing down her father every day. But then, everyone agreed that the constant presence by her side of her husband, Luca Fonseca, had undoubtedly given her strength.

They finally emerged now—a striking couple. Luca Fonseca had an arm curved protectively around his wife and the press captured their visible smiles of relief.

Lawyers for the respective parties gave statements as the family got into their various vehicles and were whisked away with a police escort to a secret location, where they were all due to celebrate and unwind after the previous taxing months.

Luca looked at Serena in the back of the Land Rover, their hands entwined. He lifted them up and pressed a kiss to her knuckles. 'Okay?'

Serena smiled. She felt as if a weight had finally been lifted off her shoulders for the first time in her life. She nodded. 'Tired...but happy it's finally done and over.'

Luca pressed a long, lingering kiss to her mouth, but when he pulled back, Serena frowned and looked down. Immediately concerned, Luca said, 'What is it?'

Serena looked at him, a dawning expression of shock and wonder on her face. 'My waters have just broken...all over the back seat.'

The driver's eyes widened in the rearview mirror and he discreetly took out a mobile phone to make a call.

Serena giggled at the comic look of shock and pure fear on Luca's face. He'd been on high alert for weeks now, overreacting to every twinge Serena felt. And then it hit her—along with a very definite cramping of pain.

Her hand tightened on his. 'Oh, my God, we're in labour.'

Luca went into overdrive, instructing the driver to go to the nearest hospital.

Their police escort was already peeling away from the rest of the convoy and the driver reassured him in Italian, 'I'm on it—we'll be there in ten minutes.'

Luca sat back, heart pumping with adrenalin, a huge ball of love and emotion making his chest full. He drank in his beloved wife, her beautiful face, and those eyes that never failed to suck him in and make him feel as if he were drowning.

'I love you,' he whispered huskily, the words flowing easily from his heart.

'I love you too.'

Serena smiled, but it was wobbly. He could see the emotion in her eyes mirrored his own. He spread his hand over her distended belly, hard with their child who was now starting the journey to meet them.

His wife, his family...*his life*. He was enriched beyond anything he might have believed possible.

And eight hours later, when he held his newborn baby daughter in his arms, her tiny face scrunched up and more beautiful than anything he'd ever seen in his life—after his wife—Luca knew that trusting in love was the most amazing revelation of all.

* * * * *

LARGER-PRINT BOOKS!

GET 2 FREE LARGER-PRINT NOVELS PLUS
2 FREE GIFTS!

HARLEQUIN®

Romance

From the Heart, For the Heart

LARGER-PRINT BOOKS!
GET 2 FREE LARGER-PRINT NOVELS PLUS
2 FREE GIFTS!

HARLEQUIN

super romance

More Story...More Romance

YES! Please send me 2 FREE LARGER-PRINT Harlequin® Superromance® novels and my 2 FREE gifts (gifts are worth about $10). After receiving them, if I don't wish to receive any more books, I can return the shipping statement marked "cancel." If I don't cancel, I will receive 6 brand-new novels every month and be billed just $5.69 per book in the U.S. or $5.99 per book in Canada. That's a savings of at least 16% off the cover price! It's quite a bargain! Shipping and handling is just 50¢ per book in the U.S. or 75¢ per book in Canada.* I understand that accepting the 2 free books and gifts places me under no obligation to buy anything. I can always return a shipment and cancel at any time. Even if I never buy another book, the two free books and gifts are mine to keep forever.

139/339 HDN F46Y

Name _____ (PLEASE PRINT)

Address _____ Apt. #

City _____ State/Prov. _____ Zip/Postal Code

Signature (if under 18, a parent or guardian must sign)

Mail to the **Harlequin® Reader Service:**
IN U.S.A.: P.O. Box 1867, Buffalo, NY 14240-1867
IN CANADA: P.O. Box 609, Fort Erie, Ontario L2A 5X3

Are you a current subscriber to Harlequin Superromance books and want to receive the larger-print edition?
Call 1-800-873-8635 today or visit www.ReaderService.com.

* Terms and prices subject to change without notice. Prices do not include applicable taxes. Sales tax applicable in N.Y. Canadian residents will be charged applicable taxes. Offer not valid in Quebec. This offer is limited to one order per household. Not valid for current subscribers to Harlequin Superromance Larger-Print books. All orders subject to credit approval. Credit or debit balances in a customer's account(s) may be offset by any other outstanding balance owed by or to the customer. Please allow 4 to 6 weeks for delivery. Offer available while quantities last.

Your Privacy—The Harlequin® Reader Service is committed to protecting your privacy. Our Privacy Policy is available online at www.ReaderService.com or upon request from the Harlequin Reader Service.

We make a portion of our mailing list available to reputable third parties that offer products we believe may interest you. If you prefer that we not exchange your name with third parties, or if you wish to clarify or modify your communication preferences, please visit us at www.ReaderService.com/consumerchoice or write to us at Harlequin Reader Service Preference Service, P.O. Box 9062, Buffalo, NY 14269. Include your complete name and address.

HSRLP13R